BOUND

The Direct Ascension Series
BOUND
Book Two

Copyright © 2017 by Kristen Brinkley. All rights reserved.

This book is a work of fiction. Names, characters, places, and incidents either are products of the author's imagination or are used fictitiously. Any resemblance to actual events or locales or persons, living or dead, is entirely coincidental.

Library of Congress Catalog Number: 2017917094

ISBN 978-0-9966944-3-8

ISBN 978-0-9966944-4-5 (ebook)

First edition, 2017

Cover Design by The Book Designers

Interior Book Design by Euan Monaghan

Publishing Company logo by Damon Hellandbrand

Author's Photo by Jonathan Dahlquist

www.kristenbrinkley.wixsite.com/author
www.facebook.com/authorkristenbrinkley
www.facebook.com/directascension
www.amazon.com/author/kristenbrinkley
www.goodreads.com/author/show/14766955.Kristen_Brinkley
Twitter (@HellboundAuthor)

Printed in the United States of America

THE DIRECT ASCENSION SERIES

BOUND

BOOK TWO

KRISTEN BRINKLEY

LITTLE BIRD
FEET PRESS

For my big brother Tony.

I hope you read this one…

1653 TE (TILETANIAN YEARS)
PLANET: TILETAN
SYSTEM: NOBLE
GALAXY: SHREDDER'S OBJECT

REFLECTIONS ON THE DEAD

ONE

>>> > "SIR WHY AREN'T we upset that we're not getting credit for the Rem Mot Om bombing?"

"Probably because the whole plan was to let the HR take credit for it. Did you miss the meeting?" Dax ran the cleaning rod through the barrel of his handgun.

"We had a meeting? When? And why didn't you kill Edison?"

Dax rolled his eyes, "Redgar, don't you have something to do up top? Monitor for a dust storm or something?"

"No I just came from there, we're good. I thought you were going to kill Edison or at least The Brotherhood would, somehow, if he didn't get caught by the Kingdom or the police."

"So how do you know I didn't kill him? Maybe I did and I just don't see the need to tell you because you're not my boss. Have you thought of that? Maybe you're next on my short list of murder victims, huh?"

Redgar considered Dax's question, "So you *did* kill him?"

"Get out of here already! Go do something else!"

Redgar ran out of the room like a dog with his tail between his legs.

His men kept asking the same questions and he kept spitting out the same answers. None of them wanted to go above Dax's head and ask The Brotherhood leader himself these questions, no, they wanted to keep pestering him with them. They were probably all too afraid of The Hunter to question his motives to his masked face.

The Hunter was a bit of a legend, even to the members of his own gang. No one knew who or what he was. Some suspected the very rare and elusive male Stox from Stoxia because his eyes changed color occasionally, but others thought this was a ruse to fool people into believing that's what race he was.

Dax took a deep breath of Tiletan's stale dry air and put the parts of his gun down on the cloth. He found the peace officer's pictures on his Titan and looked at them again. Jacob was a bloated gray corpse with a broken nose, one swollen eye, one eye missing completely, and a few missing teeth. Someone was angry and they wanted everyone in the universe to know it.

Dax could only think of one person who would have enough motivation to kill Jacob by hand like this.

Mitch.

That son of a bitch did it. Dax didn't think Mitch had it in him, but he did. Too bad Mitch hadn't taken "Reid" up on his offer when Dax extended it. Dax needed him in the Brotherhood.

Dax's Titan chimed and he picked up the audio only call.

"I need a report. How's the facility running? How are the men?" The Hunter's voice was like the ocean, dark and deep. Dax admired The Hunter but was also terrified of him. As far as he could tell, most of his men were. His nickname came from his ability to hunt anyone or anything down. If The Hunter set his sights on you, it'd be best to run far away and hide, praying he never found you.

Dax never saw his boss's face and he liked it that way. Who knows what he looked like under that hood? He could've been some deformed monster. Dax didn't want to see that.

Dax answered all his boss's questions then posed one of his own, "Sir, the men keep asking about Edison's death. How should I handle it?"

"I know it hasn't specifically been addressed since it happened but you know it's your house down there. If you want to tell them you did, fine. If you want to say it wasn't you, then that's fine with me too."

"I think I have their respect, it's just the dumb ones that keep asking. The rest of them assume I did it. I think some of them are even nervous around me."

"Well having their fear as well as their respect is always a good thing," The Hunter advised. "You didn't kill that Mitch guy though."

"No. I decided he would make an excellent addition to my team. I gave him some time to think it over. He's still thinking it over."

The Hunter growled, "Too bad we couldn't have gotten to Edison first. We should've owned him, made him suffer! You get back to me if Mitch comes around looking for us. We need more men with that kind of rage in them."

The screen on Dax's Titan went black. He sighed and resumed cleaning his gun.

TWO

››› › SESEER SAKA WASN'T David's favorite planet. He didn't want to be here. He didn't want to do this.

He awoke on what was the third sunrise of Il'laceier, the sixth day on this shithole planet and walked to the prettiest place he could find. He stood alongside a creek that had a lot of life teaming in it. He thought Xabat would've liked to have seen all the animals of this world.

He looked at the pyre. He built it himself yesterday with the help of one of the High Royal Guards, Ulysses. The men had worked in silence through the pouring rain, but today the sun had dried out the wood and David thought if they didn't do this now, the rain would return. David lovingly wrapped Xabat's body in a yellow burial shroud yesterday. He tried to carry his lover's body down the hill alone but fell twice. Ulysses stepped in and offered to do it, telling David it would be an honor to assist his King in this way. David was so moved, he allowed his High Royal Guard to do it. David followed behind with his eyes locked on Xabat's body. He was glad Ulysses was here.

David respected Ulysses a great deal, even though he was Human. He was one of the few guards that knew when to say something and when to keep his mouth shut.

It was just David and Ulysses now, standing in silence. Ulysses held the unlit torch, waiting for David to give word to light it.

A few Seseer Sakanese birds stood in the water of the creek, stalking their next meal. They were still as statues with long legs and even longer necks. Ulysses had never seen them before with their slender curved beaks and their glittery metallic feathers. One of the birds struck at the rushing water and came up empty. Ulysses wondered what they ate.

A few minutes passed; David said nothing.

Ulysses studied his King. He knew a little about Il'lacean burning rituals, from his priesthood seminary, but not enough to ask if anything was wrong. He stood stoic; waiting.

David cleared his throat and looked down at Ulysses, "Will you light it please?"

Ulysses set fire to the torch and handed it to David.

David nodded and Ulysses walked away towards the safe house up the hill. Ulysses thought the King had chosen the best spot for the pyre, clear of anything likely to catch fire. Up where he was walking now was full of golden-colored tall dry grass, but the grass near the creek was bright green and full of dew. He looked up into the sky, past the safe house and saw dark clouds mushrooming on the horizon.

Ulysses thought he might've heard a sob, but kept walking. When he was a safe distance away, he looked over his shoulder and David was unable or unwilling to light the pyre. Ulysses said a prayer for David and Xabat both.

David looked up to the sky and noted the clouds, then looked at the torch in his hand. He was glad Ulysses was gone by the time he broke into tears. They fell freely now that he was alone. He said a silent prayer to Khaleen and then walked around the pyre slowly, carefully lighting it.

Soon there was a blazing inferno consuming wood and flesh.

David stared at the crackling fire. The flames quickly spread due to the accelerant David coated the wood in. The pyre burned blue, pink, and orange.

David's mind conjured up the memory of first meeting Xabat. David knew Xabat was special from the moment their fingertips touched reaching for the same glass of champagne. Xabat had worn a green suit and when he smiled, it lit up the whole world.

David stood there until his sobbing stopped.

The next morning, David went back to the creek and knelt by it. The pyre had been disassembled and the ashes put into an urn for him to take home. All the clouds that David worried about extinguishing the fire, quietly drifted by.

He looked across the field where Human blood had been shed. David killed all five of the Human Resistance members here. He didn't really want to, he just wanted Jacob Trost, and once he found out that stupid Human bastard was dead, he stopped executing Humans as he said he would. But even though Jacob was gone, David still needed closure. Still needed to avenge Xabat's death. Still needed something to close up the wound across his broken heart.

David looked at the pictures on his Titan.

Rem Mot Om was in shambles. The council had called in a construction crew as soon as the bodies were cleared away. David ordered them to work day and night without rest, but he knew the reconstruction of his home had a long way to go.

Today David was eager to leave his safe house on Seseer Saka. The ghosts of too many dead lived here: five Human men, and his lover. It was also where he felt he was hiding and being a coward instead of facing his enemy. His guards insisted on keeping him here for "his safety" but he was resistant to being away from his home world for too long. Now that Jacob Trost was confirmed dead, and the HR had been silent a while, his guards agreed he could go home.

He wanted to find out who this Mitch person was. He needed to speak with him and find out more about the Human Resistance. If he could, David would find other HR members and interrogate them for everything they knew about Mitch and the bombing. If he had to kill them, he would. But he knew for sure he needed to squelch all Human rebellions against his people. Humans needed to accept that they weren't in control, and that he was their new leader.

David was fully prepared to fight for his people and his rightful dominance over Earth. If the HR wasn't eradicated, or if some other group took its place, he would have to make punishments more severe, maybe longer torture sessions and no quick deaths or leave them to rot on some prison world. Maybe he should start training his army himself...and double its size. He needed to be sure they were swift and fierce, blood to bone. Best to be over prepared than under.

David turned to Ulysses in the transit seat across from him after they launched, "What would be the worst way for you to die, personally?"

Ulysses stared at David with vague confusion in his eyes. He hesitated before answering, "I...guess my last choice would be...poisoning."

"I'm not familiar with this term. Could you say it another way?"

"Poison is a toxic substance that's fatal. Maybe it's something you drink or eat. It could be something you touch, but it can stop your heart, seize up muscles, and cause you to stop breathing – something like that." Ulysses pulled at his collar that was suddenly tight, "Why do you ask me this, your Highness?"

David looked out the window into space, "Oh, it's like hyegaa. That's our Lace word for it. I see now."

Ulysses cleared his throat and shifted his legs.

"I'm sorry. I've made you nervous. Nothing to worry about HRG Benson. I'm not planning on killing anyone, especially not you, no. I ask because I must be extra aware of my own personal safety...You know, since the bombing I feel the need to think of every possibility."

Ulysses exhaled, "Of course sir, but the head bodyguard is also stepping up your protection. Try not to worry, we have your back."

David nodded, "You're a good man...for a Human."

THREE

>>> > MITCH SAT IN the house he bought four years ago, but never lived in. He hardly had any furniture. He knew that with all the coren he was making in the military, on all those missions out in space and no place to spend all the money, he'd better have something to show for it when he got back to Earth. So he bought a house when he was in Arizonaland on leave several Christmases ago.

He looked at the white walls and the cream tile floor. The house was more than empty, it felt cold, and it echoed too much for a place that was supposed to be his sanctuary. Outer space was deathly quiet. He didn't want his home to be that way.

He figured he either needed to fill it with lots of furniture, throw a party for his friends, or get a girlfriend. And since he had no friends and getting a girlfriend, a real one, not one of those sex robots, was harder than it sounded, his only option was to buy furniture.

He did have a large screen receiver mounted to his wall so he synched up his Titan and started ordering everything he needed for his house. By the end of the night, he had a new bed to sleep on and everything else was scheduled to be delivered tomorrow.

Getting his house together was easy, getting his shit together was not.

Mitch Blazer was the Human Being to discover the series of devices called The Jump that allowed for space travel like the Human race never experienced before. And everything Reid said about Mitch and his final mission was true. He couldn't explain how Reid knew, but he did.

The universal public did not.

The Milky Way Galactic Military sought out and aggressively pursued Mitch to recruit him from the Earth Military about a year after he signed on. Mitch excelled at every test there was for space exploration and at the time he signed on to the Earth's world-based military, he was only seventeen. Some of his commanding officers took to calling him "The Golden Child" but he always hated that nickname. He might've achieved a lot at a young age but he preferred not to be singled out. While the regular planetary controlled militaries did not have a minimum age, the space militaries did and it was eighteen.

So Mitch learned a lot in the one year he lived with the EM and served under the Air Force branch, but he learned so much more with the MWGM.

He went through their rigorous education and training program for four years. Then they finally let him out into space and he was able to explore for years. He saw new worlds in the Milky Way Galaxy, but traveled the old-fashioned way – solar power and solar wind powered space shuttles. Less than a decade ago, Earth and Earthlings were not nearly as advanced as they should've been in space travel. Several other species laughed upon hearing how far Humans were behind in space travel before they discovered The Jump. But Mitch never understood it. No species in the entire Milky Way had discovered The Jump, not even Il'laceans, but Humans were made fun of the most. Maybe because Humans were arrogant about everything. The day the Il'laceans arrived on Earth, they did so with a higher-level technology than what Humans had. And they never shared their power or propulsion methods because (Mitch guessed correctly) it was another way to show their domination and control over Earth.

When Mitch found out his twin sisters were killed by their father, he took a year leave to deal with the aftermath. He lost himself during that year. He became someone else, someone he wasn't eager to talk about to this day and he did things he wasn't proud of. It was a dark time for Mitch and the only event to rival that shame and disgust in himself, happened three years ago.

The day he discovered The Jump device was the same day he left two people behind to die on a planet called Hap Du Wan.

The discovery was completely by accident. He didn't want to take credit for it at all, but he really didn't want to be credited with it solely; he had someone else in the vehicle with him that day – Stockman. Mitch made a deal with Stockman, as well as the MWGM that Stockman made the discovery alone. The story as far as the public knew, was that out of the four explorers that day, three of them perished in an accident on Hap Du Wan. Mitch Blazer, Nanicka Arcene, and Janson Ufford died when a sudden and violent storm hit their temporary living quarters on a planet that closely resembled Mars. Kade Stockman was the only one able to make it to the vehicle. He was forced to launch quickly in an emergency departure procedure they practiced a million times. Kade Stockman stayed calm during the whole incident and even though his heart was broken to see his three teammates die right in front of him, he was able to save himself and launched just in time. While in flight back home to Earth, he took an unadvised route.

Stockman would tell all the reporters who would listen that he attributed that route to the fact that he was grief stricken. Out of the corner of his eye, he saw a large distortion of dark energy on one of his monitors for a split second. It was almost too easy to dismiss as a faulty reading from his instrument panel, a fluke or something, but Stockman wanted to check it out. When he got close, he realized what it was – a device made for space travel. Kade Stockman used it, the first Human Being in the history of all mankind to travel via The Jump.

That was all a lie.

The MWGM needed a hero. A single hero who wanted the attention and who was a good liar. Mitch didn't want to lie, but he could barely live with himself right after the incident, so he agreed to a mutually beneficial arrangement. He would never tell the truth to a single soul and in return, he got a new government issued identity. Mitch Blazer died that day on Hap Du Wan and Mitch Savely was born. That was his new name. He had no family when the event happened, no girlfriend, and no friends. He was rarely on Earth, so how could he have any ties?

One year in the Earth Military, four years training in the academy with the MWGM, three years out in space, then the year everything went to shit with his sisters and father, then two and a half more years out in space doing research. A life of adventure and loneliness.

Mitch just turned twenty-nine on Hap Du Wan. It was supposed to be an easy mission – live on the planet for six months to see if it had any alien life. Too bad it was short on oxygen. They wore space suits anytime they were outside a livable tent. For five months, they did lots of digging in alien dirt and searched for artifacts they never found, but they set up a successful tent system for sleeping quarters and places to do their work. Their ship, the Vagabond, was usually close to their home base in case of an emergency liftoff, but not the day it all happened.

Stockman took the Vagabond out for a routine, once-a-week fly around to study some of the planet's scientifically interesting features like the mountain ranges and trenches. That day, Stockman studied the trench called Icicle, named because it was long and triangular, at Station One. He was supposed to be somewhere else, but he liked this trench the best. Stockman turned off his communication feed because he was tired of hearing Arcene and Ufford go on and on about how good a leader Mitch was. Stockman always hated how humble Mitch pretended to be. To Kade, Mitch seemed to be able to charm almost anyone out of anything. Somehow, everyone always liked Mitch and thought he was a great leader. People always did whatever Mitch told them. If Kade even so much as asked one of his teammates to help him on his research missions for geographical features, they always turned him down, citing they had their own work to do, but Kade knew their research wasn't as important. He hated Mitch.

Mitch was working on a sample of Wanian soil when his alarm went off inside his helmet. A devastating storm was imminent and the damned thing came up fast. He started running at the same time he was asking Arcene and Ufford where they were.

Ufford came back, "We're at Station Four, boss. I can see it. Stockman's not back yet. *Where is he?* He was supposed to stay close to us here at Four!"

Mitch got outside his research tent and looked for the Vagabond. He saw it on the horizon and knew Stockman probably had his comm's off even though he told him countless times never to do that.

"Stockman!"

Mitch silenced his alarms as they went off again telling him the team only had six minutes before the storm engulfed the entire planet and the storm would last thirteen Wanian months. If they didn't get off this rock within the next five minutes they would all die. They only had supplies for the next Earth month. Thirteen months on this planet was 400 Earth days.

"Arcene. Ufford. Get your assess to Station One pronto! This storm's a killer."

They both answered affirmatively.

Mitch ran as fast as he could in his bulky space suit towards the Vagabond, the whole while yelling out for Stockman, who never answered. Mitch had a channel with only Stockman open so Mitch never heard his two teammates yelling for help.

Mitch arrived at the ship four minutes later, grabbed the arm of Stockman, and pulled him into the Vagabond. Kade finally flipped on his comm's, heard the alarms, and saw the electricity and dust storm approaching.

Mitch sat at the controls and watched as Arcene and Ufford ran as fast as they could towards the ship. Mitch quickly flipped his comm's open to his two teammates who were out of breath and could hardly speak. Mitch barely made out from Ufford that they were wrong about Hap Du Wan not harboring any life; they were just looking in the wrong place. Whatever alien life inhabited this world, it was underground, and it was something like a large glass octopus with ten legs dragging behind its body. Mitch thought he saw shards of itself break off as it moved and then the pieces floated back to the alien being to rejoin the body.

Mitch and Stockman saw the monstrous gray creature break out from underneath the surface and slide across the planet, leaving a wake of dirt and a deep gully behind it. All those long cuts they thought were just trenches were really old paths where these aliens had been.

Stockman watched with an open mouth as Ufford fell down, tripping over his own feet while the alien octopus approached. Something like a sinkhole appeared next to the ship and Mitch felt the ground behind them shake. Mitch saw Arcene sprinting towards the Vagabond, but then she looked back and stopped. She was almost to the ship, but she turned and ran back towards her fallen crewmate.

Mitch had a decision to make.

The Vagabond's AI was calm, "Immediate departure recommended. Twenty-six seconds before launch failure."

He knew if he waited to launch much longer, none of them would get off the planet, but if he launched right now, two would live.

Stockman yelled for Mitch to launch, "DO IT! Close the door! Let's go! Jesus Christ! You know as well as I do they'll never make it! Oh shit! There's another one over there!"

The ground trembled underneath the Vagabond. Mitch didn't know how long it would be before either one of those aliens reached their ship and destroyed it, the storm engulfed them, or the sinkhole next to them grew and swallowed the ship.

Mitch's hands hovered over the controls; a bead of sweat ran down his temple. "Ufford, what's your status?"

Arcene shouted through his comm's instead, "He's broken his ankle I think. There's something coming towards the Vagabond! Behind you, Commander Blazer!"

"RUN!" It was the last thing he said to Nancika Arcene.

Arcene got Ufford standing upright and helped him hobble along towards the ship.

"We can make it. Almost there. Just watch your back," she cried in response.

Mitch couldn't see what Arcene warned of. His rear cameras showed nothing, but the Vagabond's back end began to sink quickly.

"Immediate departure recommended. Launch failure in five…Four… Three…" the navigation AI said.

Arcene and Ufford were close, but still too far way.

Mitch made the decision that would haunt him for the rest of his life and pressed the launch button. The door to the Vagabond sealed shut and the ship moved up off the surface. The dust covered their view of Hap Du Wan within seconds. The last thing Mitch saw of Arcene was the look on her face – it was absolute horror. Mitch could only see Janson from the waist down. The storm had now killed their ability to use the comm's.

Stockman was silent as he took off his helmet.

The Vagabond ascended into the atmosphere and Mitch wanted to erase everything that just happened in the last ten minutes. He breathed in deep and looked over his flight plan. He saw nothing but the memory of the people he'd left behind. He was still responsible for one life other than his own inside the ship and he was going to get the asshole home to his family. He thought that might make him feel less like a coward. That returning one life home could somehow make him feel better about leaving two souls to die, but in the end, it didn't.

While they were ascending, the moon of Hap Du Wan was coming into their flight path. They would've crashed if Mitch hadn't been able to reroute them so fast, and in the process, he noticed a huge surge of dark energy on one of his monitors.

Mitch took off his helmet and Stockman said, "You did the right thing. You know they were dea—"

Mitch punched Stockman in the jaw hard enough to knock him out. Then he looked back to study the abnormality he'd seen.

There was no one to verify the spike of energy with, so Mitch steered them over to investigate. He knew after this, he'd probably never fly again, never be out here, so he thought there might've been some way to justify his killing two teammates with a discovery. Or maybe he'd find some anomaly that would destroy their ship and kill him in the process and then he'd never have to answer for what he'd done.

As he got closer to the dark energy surge, he realized what it was a second after it was too late. The Vagabond jumped to the next galaxy over. Mitch came out on the other side realizing he just found the biggest space discovery since Earth was visited by their first alien species. Then he experienced the worst nausea he ever felt and vomited. He always thought it'd been because of his conscience and what happened on Hap Du Wan, but later Earthlings found a common side effect to the fastest method of space travel was vomiting – and that's *if* you could keep your mind calm. Mitch still believed it was his conscience since he wasn't the type to get space sick.

He didn't know how it worked, but he made an educated guess that if he set his maps and flight paths to Earth and then went back the way he came, he might've gotten back to the Milky Way, and he was right. And the second time he didn't hurl.

He flew the Vagabond home and told the MWGM the entire story. And between himself, Stockman, and the MWGM, they came up with the arrangement he agreed to. The lie he was now living under.

CHAPTER 1

MOOSE HUNTING

ONE

>>> > MOOSE WALKED DOWN the alley after looking for a victim for the past two hours as he fussed with the unlit cigarette in his mouth.

It started to drizzle. He hated the rain. This was the most depressing kind of weather (and it made people go inside.) He needed to find someone *outside*. He glanced at his Titan – it was almost midnight. His time was running out. He promised himself the next person he saw, *that* was going to be his ticket into The Black Dawns. All he needed to do for his initiation was kill someone and then he'd be in the biggest gang in Mostac.

Moose thought it was funny how Lanyx said they're so peaceful and law abiding, but here he was trying to get into a ferocious gang full of

Lanyx on Praxis. Not only were there male members, but females too. And all Lanyx in this gang embraced their animalistic DNA. All of them loved to fight. Once he was in, Moose was promised training in all sorts of fighting styles and would be allowed to participate in their weekly Elgelmum, a Lans word without an English translation. It meant a fight between two opponents where the crowd could bet on a winner and the loser – loses the body part of their choice. Moose thought the Lanyx people would evolve into two separate species eventually – one group that opposed using the animal gifts they were given, and suppressed them, and the Lanyx who embraced and capitalized on them...like him.

Finally, he saw a guy walking towards him. Moose couldn't tell how big he was, he had oversized sweats on and his hood up; but he was confident he could kill him. The guy's head was down and his hands were in the pockets of his sweatshirt. Moose thought his victim was perfect; it seemed he wasn't even paying attention to his surroundings. The guy had been jogging at first, but now it seemed like he just ran out of energy. The guy was breathing hard and walking slow. *Good*, Moose thought, *he'll be tired.* He already promised himself the next person he saw...so this guy was his victim. All Moose had to do was get over his nerves.

He engaged the vid recorder on his stolen Titan for proof and went up to the guy.

"Hey, you got a light man?"

Sebastian lifted his head and took his hands out of his pockets immediately, "Oh kid, you picked the wrong night for this. I am in no fucking mood. Do us both a favor and get lost." He only sensed the teenager's intentions when he was almost right on top of him.

Moose started to circle Sebastian then pulled out a knife.

Sebastian took off his hood to see clearly. "Trust me kid, you do *not* want to fight me. I don't want to kill you."

Moose was slightly intimidated by the look in this guy's eyes, but he needed to do this. He wanted into this gang. "You gonna' put up a big fight, Neanderthal?" He sliced the knife sideways through the air.

The term 'Neanderthal' got under Sebastian's skin, but he still didn't want to kill the kid. "Gangs are not family and killing is not easy. If you put down your weapons…all of them, and walk away, I won't chase you. I'll let you go. I won't report this."

Moose raised his eyebrows, "How'd you know about my gang? And how'd you know I have more than this knife? I can't just walk away anyways. I got to do this dumb ass."

"I'm not the guy to fuck with tonight! I just broke up with my girlfriend too."

Moose's mouth dropped open, "How the hell do you know about Evelyn?"

"It doesn't matter. Life is hard. You have no idea how hard, trust me. This isn't the way to go. I know you have a gun, but no one has to die tonight." Sebastian put his hands at his sides.

"Did the gang put you up to this?" Moose pulled out the gun from his waistband.

They circled each other far apart. The drizzle turned into a light rain and a loud boom of thunder tore the sky in two above their heads. A few rats skittered underneath the trash bins, squeaking as they went.

Sebastian knew this kid was scared, and confused enough to pull the trigger thinking he was doing what he needed to. He easily read "Moose" and sensed he desperately wanted to be accepted by someone, anyone who gave him what he needed. He was a lost soul and Sebastian didn't want to hurt him.

The kid aimed the gun at Sebastian's heart.

They both knew it was loaded.

The rain fell harder.

"It's Moose right? That's what they call you? Please just walk away. You're not going to kill me. You have no idea who you've started a fight with. I've had one of the worst days of my life and I just went out to clear my head. You can live without The Black Dawns. You can go to this shelter that's close. They'll help you."

"I can't go to a shelter!" Moose's throat closed up for a moment, "You're crazy! You're not going to talk me out of this, buddy."

Moose's intention changed. Moose was going to shoot, he was fully intending to kill Sebastian, and Sebastian simply had no other option.

Moose was too inept and too slow for Sebastian's skill and experience. Sebastian brought his left leg up in a roundhouse kick and struck Moose's hand. Moose grunted in pain as the gun fell to the ground and slid under an industrial trash container. Moose hunched over and rushed forward wanting to tackle Sebastian, but Sebastian brought his knee up into the kid's stomach and the wiry teenager lost all his momentum. Moose made an 'ooooafff' sound as he crumbled to the rain-soaked pavement.

The teenage Lanyx rolled over in agony, tears and raindrops rolled down his cheeks. He could barely breathe. Then his eyes found the gun near the wheel of the trash container.

Sebastian got down on one knee close to Moose, looking for where the gun landed.

Moose reached out quickly with his good hand and snatched the gun. He brought it out and pointed it at Sebastian's head. Moose blinked rapidly trying to keep the rain out of his eyes.

Sebastian hoped this moment could be avoided, but now it was obvious that Moose was going to kill him – if he didn't kill Moose first. Sebastian never lost eye contact with the kid as he reached out and seized the boy's injured hand firmly. Moose pulled the trigger, but the shot went wild. There was a burning hole in the trash bin next to Sebastian's right shoulder. Sebastian swiftly twisted Moose's neck before the kid could pull the trigger again. The hand that held the gun fell to the side of his young body. Sebastian let go of the kid's head carefully so it didn't hit the ground.

He took the kid's gun and knife, planning to dispose of both later. He took Moose's Titan only because it had recorded everything, and Sebastian couldn't have himself exposed this way. He looked around the alley for any witnesses, and seeing none, he picked up Moose's body and put it over his shoulder. He had to get rid of it. He would use the same associate he would've on any other job, except this had been a bad accident. A terrible chain of events caused him to kill someone he didn't want to – a confused boy that he would only ever know as Moose.

Sebastian was grateful there were no witnesses.

But Sebastian was wrong. There was one being who saw the whole thing. A very important and powerful being.

TWO

>>> > ALONG A FENCE near the trashcans was a large white owl. Sebastian would've noticed it had it not been raining so hard. The owl watched as Sebastian left the alley then the owl made a few mental notes.

The owl, who wasn't a native of Praxis, or the Andromeda Galaxy or even this universe, could be a lot of things: a beautiful female Lanyx, an African American Human man, an Earthly owl, but not any creature he wanted. Some creatures were easier to duplicate than others and some were down right impossible. That's part of the reason why he'd been stuck in this universe for 197 Earth years and why he still couldn't find Kolek all this time, but he'd keep looking. Plus for all his powers, he still didn't have the gem, the key, and he didn't know where the door was. So many things to take care of.

The owl's name in this universe was Mr. Recin Applette. Nothing like his real name back home in his Knowledge Universe; just like Kolek's name wasn't really her name. In fact, she never told him her real name from the War Universe. But they were both in this universe right now for very different reasons and this one was called the Unknown Universe for only one reason – it hadn't defined itself yet.

Mr. Applette wasn't satisfied ruling over his own Universe and jumped into this one when he found out Kolek would be here. That was almost two hundred years ago and she barely knew he existed except for while their two universes were at war and the two Rulers, as outlined in the rules, had to be locked in a room together so as to not interfere with the war. Knowledge won. Now Kolek wanted, needed, actually to win a war or else she'd lose her job.

Mr. Applette knew The Universe Keepers never liked Kolek but Kolek was the chosen one of her time in her Universe, so Kolek it was.

The Universe Keepers also didn't like it when the Rulers abandoned their own universe and Mr. Applette knew it was just a matter of time before his absence was discovered.

Everyone in the Knowledge Universe was born knowing the exact time of their death. It was digitally tattooed on their ankle and Mr. Applette was no different in that way. No matter how he changed his outward appearance, his glowing tattoo was always there.

He looked down at his bird foot and saw:

«|¤°××ṣ｡·ᴉ

Which translated to four months, one day, twelve hours, fifty-eight minutes and thirty-one seconds of Earth time.

Mr. Applette had spent a lot of time as an African American Human male on Earth and got used to translating his time to Earth time.

Was it enough time to find Kolek? Would The Keeper find him and punish him first?

All he knew for sure, was the first time in a long time anything about this universe changed, was when this Sebastian Raynes did what the Lanyx people called a deep read on a Human woman of royalty and changed how the Unknown Universe felt to Mr. Applette. It knocked Sebastian unconscious and alerted Applette to Sebastian's existence. Mr. Applette thought these two could open a door and that was very important to him. He could only tear open a window but those couldn't be traveled through. If one wanted to jump from one universe to another, you needed three things: a door, an artifact, and a key. Any one of those things was difficult to find, but all three? Almost impossible.

The owl flew away, he'd check on Sebastian again.

THREE

>>> > A COUPLE HOURS later, off world, Sebastian erased the boy's body, but it was anything but standard business.

Afterwards, he sat down in his transit and closed the door over him. He saw his own reflection in the transit's front windshield and hardly recognized the ghost he was looking at. The whole Goddamn day had been terrible.

He felt awful after sensing Celeste's heartbreak from his words earlier today, but now that feeling compounded into something much worse. He thought himself to be a barbaric monster who broke a kind and caring heart and killed a misguided and confused teenager all in one day. "You really know how to fuck things up, Raynes," he said to his reflection.

He programmed his destination into the maps and sighed loudly. He was utterly exhausted. He ran for three hours solid before he found that kid in the alley. All Sebastian had wanted to do was run until he escaped himself. Until the rage was gone, until the world fell away, or until the pain subsided, and he felt better…but he had never begun to feel better, and he still didn't now – that was for damn sure.

The only thing he thought of on the way home was Celeste and wondered how she was feeling. His concentration was so bad he couldn't even fly; he used the autopilot. What must she think of him? Sebastian feared the worst – she could hate him and be running off to that other guy she'd been seeing.

FOUR

›› › CELESTE THOUGHT SHE felt together enough when she called Veronica. She thought she was ready to talk about what happened but as soon as she saw Veronica on the screen, Celeste felt the tears starting to fall all over again.

Celeste poured her heart out, even though she didn't tell Veronica Sebastian's real name or his real job. She also couldn't mention how he was thinking he was protecting her from getting killed by not dating him. Instead she changed that part to him thinking he could protect her from getting hurt emotionally by them not dating. And even though she had to change a few details about her story, she told Veronica all her very real feelings, disappointment, and shock. She didn't say anything about her developing 7's though. She wanted to keep that for the end of the discussion. Veronica sat quietly on the line and listened.

"Oh sweetie! I wish I was there for you honey. Men can be such jerks. I'm sorry you went through this without your girlfriends there to hug you or eat ice cream in our bathrobes and watch movies. God, what an asshole that guy is." Veronica took a sip of her wine.

Celeste smiled through her tears finally hearing someone on her side.

"Why don't you come back to Earth, Celly? I have some vacation time. We could hang out and go shopping or whatever you'd like. Gosh I've missed you! It feels like it's been forever since we talked but I know it's only been like, a few weeks. It's hard being here without you."

Celeste wiped away her tears, "I would love to come out, but I have a date tonight."

Celeste saw Veronica's reaction, even though she quickly tried to adjust her expression to hide it from Celeste. Veronica's eyes had widened and her mouth dropped open slightly.

"You have a date with someone else?"

"Yeah. I met this guy a couple weeks ago. I thought maybe I should cancel our date at first, but then I thought, at least he'd be a distraction to *someone* who was so unsure of wanting to be with me. Something to keep my mind off…everything."

"That sounds like a solid plan. What's this one's name?"

"Daxton. He's been making me laugh and he's sweet. He seems nice…I just don't want to sit at home and mope. This forces me to be out with people and that's a good thing right? I'm doing what I'm supposed to?"

"Oh, no one can tell you what's right. Only you know what to do. Maybe it's a good thing to get out of the house though, yeah." Veronica smiled.

"Well, what would you do in my situation? Do you think I should wait around for," she almost said Sebastian, "Brahm, or just keep seeing Daxton?" Celeste blew her nose facing away from her Titan's camera.

"I honestly don't know. You might wait around for a long time without knowing whether Brahm's going to come back and get down on his hands and knees like he should and beg you to take him back…That dickhead. Daxton might be a nice guy and if he's asking you out…I don't know. You might have a good time and it could turn into something special."

"I've got to say something though…about Brahm."

"Yeah?" Veronica downed the rest of her wine.

"I should be raging mad at him I know. He was so cold and he said things that were totally wrong about me. I should hate him and never want to see him again after that fight. And all this time…how he's been mixed up about us, but…"

"But you don't hate him, do you?"

Celeste shook her head, "No. I *am* disappointed. I feel…sad and empty too, but I don't hate him. I just miss him all the time. God! I'm not sure what he would have to do to make me hate him." A wave of annoyance swept through her, "I think if he came back and apologized, spent some time making it all up to me…I think I'd be okay," she paused, "Why do I feel this way? Why don't I hate him?"

"Maybe it's because you're in love with him."

"Veronica! Me in love with Se-, er, Brahm?! I've never said anything about love. Why would you think that?"

"I've got to ask you something first before I answer that."

"Okay."

"Have you slept with him?"

Celeste was quiet. She put her face down as she answered, "No."

Veronica was careful with her next few words, "Why do you think that is C?"

Celeste closed her eyes and thought. She'd wondered this many times herself. Why hadn't they made love yet? "I don't know…There's certainly nothing stopping me on my end…Maybe he's afraid of getting attached to me. Maybe he's afraid he'd hurt me worse if we had sex and then he broke up with me?"

Veronica rolled her eyes, "Well, you're on the right track. You've never thought he didn't want to do it with you *because* he loves you? Or he's about to fall in love with you? Having sex with someone you already care a lot about can push you over the edge into falling in love. Maybe he's just about to fall for you and if you have sex, then it's all over for him. At least if he's not sleeping with you he could do something like this and let you go. Remember Lanyx men are quite different than Humans or Il'laceans when it comes to love."

Celeste was dumbstruck. She stared at the screen silently.

"Celeste? I can still see you, can you see me? Are we still connected? My little orange light in the corner of the screen says we are."

"I'm here…Why would you say he loves me? If he loved me wouldn't he be with me?"

"I mean, you say he's trying to protect you from getting hurt, albeit, I think this is totally the wrong way for him to go about that. But think about it. If he didn't give a damn about you – he'd sleep with you and then just leave. As bizarre as this sounds, I think he really cares. He might even be falling in love with you, or already in love with you and maybe he stopped seeing you because he doesn't want to deal with those feelings yet. Oh honey, men are bad at dealing with emotions. They don't work like we do. I did my best to teach you about Il'lacean men, now I've got to teach you about the male species of Lanyx too?"

"What am I missing about them? What don't I know?"

"Lanyx men can be just as emotional as Human women, but they are *much* better at hiding it. Maybe Brahm's upset he's fallen for a Human woman? Maybe he wanted a Lanyx?"

"His last girlfriend was a *beautiful* Lanyx. They were young when she committed suicide. He's certainly not forgotten her, but that doesn't bother me…mostly," she paused, "I can't blame him for having a place in his heart for her his whole life. I can accept that," she paused again, "I'm trying to accept it. He's not prejudice though; he's okay with me being Human."

"All right, I know Lanyx have this thing with smell and pheromones. I can't remember what they call it though – it's like keying in or sealing into each other, something like that…So, has he commented on your scent or anything?"

Celeste thought back over their time together. Of course he had complimented her perfume, but the whole reason he gave her the purple choker was because she saw his reaction to her scent. She had told Veronica that he gave her a necklace, but not the reason why. "Yes. He's always liked my perfumes."

"Well what about you? Have you smelled him?"

"Yes, he always smells good. He wears a couple different colognes though. One of them smells much better than the other. My favorite is this woodsy mahogany scent. Every man should smell like it, it's so…masculine and sexy. It drives me crazy actually, but I haven't told him that. When he wears that one I feel like throwing him down and mounting him right away. I don't understand what comes over me, but it happens every time. I could even smell it through his sweat during his work out the first day I was around him."

Veronica's face lit up and she blurted out, "That's it!"

"What's it?"

"You've got it bad for him hon. I think you love him already."

Celeste rolled her eyes, "I'm not in love with him. I can't be. It's way too soon. I care a great deal about him, of course. He came along and changed my life and he's got a good heart and…he's really attractive. But, I think I would know if I'm in love with someone. Come on."

"Celeste, you need to do some research on mating rituals, smells, pheromones, and stuff on Lanyx. If you're smelling his scent while he's sweating, he probably doesn't have any cologne on. That's probably you falling in love with him. Sounds like it happened pretty early too."

Celeste didn't believe her friend over her own heart. She knew if she fell in love with Sebastian she would've known it…right? She wouldn't need a friend (who's never seen them together) to tell her how she should feel. She wondered sometimes during their time together if she had been falling in love with him, but hadn't honestly known how love was supposed to feel.

Was it possible she already loved him and she hadn't recognized it? She wanted to change the subject, "Hey have you heard of this 7's thing?"

"Oh yeah. That's super cool about them. The Lanyx have that telepathy thing going for them too in addition to being smart and healthy, but I think some of us Humans are starting to have a hint of it. I suppose it kinda' makes sense. I mean, the Lanyx were made mostly from Human DNA so why wouldn't we both have that right? Except since 7's are so rare for Lanyx that it's like, almost impossible for Humans," Veronica paused, "Why are you bringing this up?"

Celeste cleared her throat, "I've got it."

Veronica's face went blank. "You're shitting me right? Is this a joke, 'cause if it is, it sure isn't funny."

"I'm not kidding V. I can read minds sometimes. I'm learning how to control it."

Veronica smiled, "You're not fucking kidding…You're serious. My God. How do you do it? I mean, like, how did you discover it? And how long have you known *before telling me?*"

"Oh…Um, a while now. It started the same day Jon died."

"No way!"

"Yeah. Brahm's got really powerful 7's. He says I could be powerful too after I learn how to harness it. That's how I found out actually… from him. He could hear my thoughts and responded to them, and I've heard some of his."

"Jesus freaking Christ, Celeste! That's big news. When were you going to tell me this?"

Celeste made a face, "Well, I've had a lot going on here and I'm learning a whole new world and…Brahm's been keeping me busy up until he cut me loose and now Dax…I didn't have a lot of spare time to explain all this. I'm sorry. But at least I'm telling you now…"

"Wait, is Daxton Lanyx too? Is he a telepath?"

Celeste thought, "He's Lanyx, but he's said nothing about 7's."

"That doesn't mean anything. Maybe he is and he's just keeping it from you. That can't be something that comes up in conversation when you're just getting to know someone. Can't you tell? Can you read his mind or whatever you do to find out?"

"I haven't sensed it in him, and he's not sending me any thoughts or anything. I don't think he has 7's really. All I've ever heard about 7's is that it's rare to find any individual with them – Lanyx or Human."

Veronica sat quietly for a second, then she broke into a wide, open smile, "Holy shit! Can you read me?"

Celeste shook her head, "No, not from here anyway. It doesn't work exactly like you'd think. You'd have to be in the same room with me, and you can't have mental walls up. And I'm just barely learning all this stuff like how to get into someone's mind even if they have walls up for protection. Don't worry. I can't hear anything you're thinking."

"Okay…So you can't read Brahm's mind now?"

"It's complicated. He's got really strong walls up. Sometimes, he lets thoughts escape by accident. Sometimes I can read him, or his intentions, but it's spotty. Most of the time, I can't…and I still have to be in close proximity for it to work too. And now that we're not anywhere near each other, I have no idea what he's thinking."

"Oh. Well what the hell are they good for then? If they can't help you with your love life then I'd say they're more hassle than they're worth."

"Well, I had this dream. We did actually…together. It was on his yacht."

"You guys shared a dream? What happened in it? What was it like? Tell me everything."

Celeste smiled remembering a very pleasurable time with Sebastian, "Oh, it was…crazy good intense. And like nothing else I've ever experienced, that's for sure, but I'd love to do it again. If he comes back…" she trailed off starting to choke up again.

Veronica wouldn't let her. "Come on girl. Get it together. Don't fall apart on me again. I can't stand to see you crying and miserable. If he's smart, and I think even though he appears *to me* to be a total dickhead without brains right now, he'll figure out what a catch you are and come back. He won't be able to live without you for long."

Celeste smiled and swallowed her tears back, "Thanks."

"Hey, I'm just telling you the truth," she took a deep breath and smiled, "I can't believe you have telepathy and then you share dreams. I never do anything important like that! Tell me all about this dream please. I saw the way you lit up. I need details."

Veronica and Celeste talked for a long time and after she hung up, Celeste felt a little more clear-headed and a lot more loved by someone who she knew would never let her down.

FIVE

>>> > A SHORT STOX woman stood in the park alone. She wore a long red skirt, black jacket, and a red beret. She checked her Titan: 10:59 a.m. Then she spotted Sebastian walking towards her. She looked at her Titan again, eleven o'clock on the nose, Lanyx time. He was always punctual.

She smiled, "Hey stranger."

Sebastian only stared. It had been three years since she and Sebastian saw each other.

"You're still looking good, I see." Ni-toyis Tredux laughed to herself. Sebastian remained quiet.

"I guess nothing's changed then. You never were much of a talker. You played the strong and silent type well though."

Sebastian looked down at her. Her eyes switched from purple to red. He knew what that meant. "Why did you contact me Ni-toyis? What do you need me to do? I know I owe you a favor and then you'll disappear again, just like you always do."

Her eyes returned to purple. She took off her beret and scratched her head. Her long thin snake-like feelers unfurled around her shoulders like hair. She looked around the park before speaking, "I need some help."

Sebastian sighed, "Of course you do." He crossed his arms, "Could you be a little more specific?"

"Raynes, what's up with you? We can't talk about this in such a public place. Are you losing your touch or what?"

"I just want to know what you want."

Her feelers floated up around Sebastian as if they were weightless in water. "Can't you take a girl somewhere private? I'd like to be alone with you." She put her hands on his shoulders.

He shrugged them off and emphasized, "I didn't call this meeting. You set the place. You set the time. I'm here...which is now starting to feel like a mistake. What do you need from me?"

She shook her head slowly, "Tsk tsk tsk sweet cheeks. You're in such a foul mood."

She turned away from him and looked up into the sky.

Sebastian looked over her feelers floating around her head. Those feelers were what made it impossible for Sebastian to read her. And that meant she had always been dangerous to him.

Her lavender-blue skin radiated in the Praxis sunlight. Stox were well known for their exotic color-blended skin. The first time another species saw a Stox, they were usually speechless.

"If you wanted more privacy, you should've picked a different place." He looked around. They almost had the park to themselves, just a man and his family were having a picnic over by the pond. Sebastian knew she only wanted to be alone with him in his apartment for one reason and it wasn't conversation. Ni-toyis had never been there before and she wasn't going there now. It was always like this with her. She loved having all the control over a situation and she loved having him at her command, but this was the last time he would do anything for her. After this, they'd be even.

She turned to face him, "What's got your boxer briefs in a twist honeybunch?"

"You know I've never liked this arrangement. I only agreed to it because I was forced to."

"Ohhh just because you killed one or two 'innocents' that one time!" she laughed, "That bank robbery was fun and you know it! You're such a big baby." She held Sebastian by the cheeks with one hand and squeezed like a grandmother would to a misbehaving child.

He gently pulled his face away from her pressing fingers, "You and I, we handle business very differently."

"No one is innocent Sebastian. You're holding yourself over the coals for nothing."

He let out a long annoyed sigh, "What is it that you want *Ni-toyis?* What am I going to burn in Hell for all eternity for you now?"

She laughed, "Oh you're being *so* dramatic! Come on stud muffin."

Sebastian leaned over, grabbed one of her feelers in his fist, and squeezed, "You want dramatic? How about I rip one of these damned dancing snakes off your head?"

Ni-toyis made a pained face, "That's not funny dear. You know I like the rough stuff, but only in the bedroom. Let it go before I yell for help!"

He let go and whispered forcefully, "What. Do. You. Want?"

"Sweetie pie, I just need a little old rock from the Ceearrah Capital," she batted her eyelashes coyly and smiled.

"Ni-toyis, no. Are you kidding me? The Goddamned Dome of Shadows Red Klix?"

She laughed out loud, "That's the one! I've never seen your eyes get so big darling."

Sebastian shook his head, "That's insane. No one can get that, nor should they try. That gemstone is sacred to my people and a priceless artifact. Do you even know what it can do?" He stopped, "What *do* you want it for anyway?"

Ni-toyis giggled. Stox women could almost always seduce their way through life with their exotic appeal and their sexy laughter. Men fell for it all the time, but not Sebastian. He learned the dangers of the Stox a long time ago, but a long time ago, he had been young and foolish. He couldn't wait to be free of his debt to her. And he prayed she'd leave him alone after this favor had been fulfilled…but stealing the Red Klix? All that tried before, had failed – and the consequences were severe.

The Dome of Shadows wasn't just a secret group of Lanyx scientists and intellectuals, they were also bad asses who could make you disappear completely and legally with the Praxis Council to protect them. They operated outside the laws and weren't as peaceful as the normal Lanyx. Sebastian knew they were always working on a top-secret project, and that gemstone was a highly protected world treasure…and maybe a door to opening up something big according to a poem he read as a child.

Ni-toyis dragged her claws lightly over her long red skirt, but didn't answer his question.

"What do you want it for?"

"Why do you get to ask questions? You're supposed to just do what I say," she frowned playfully.

"I think I deserve to know why someone wants the Klix. If I do this the—"

"*When* you do this."

"*IF* we do this, we coul—"

"Oh no, I'm not doing anything. It's all on you, gorgeous. You're going to have to steal it on your own. You owe me, not the other way around." Ni-toyis's long black eyelashes batted quickly.

Sebastian closed his eyes and took a deep breath. He clamped his hands together, "*If* I do this, I could be caught and killed. If I have to work alone, the risk goes up. You know thieving is not my thing. It's always been *your* thing."

She smiled as her feelers curled up on top of her head. When they were all settled in, she put her beret back on, "I have complete faith in you. You will not be caught. You will not be killed. You will be…victorious."

SIX

>>> > D'ARTAGNAN STEELE WOKE up in his sleeping capsule and stretched. He had seen Linda in another dream. He missed her more than normal. He rolled over and grabbed his Titan. He hadn't been able to bring himself to do it until this morning, but he wanted to watch a video she made him. It was for his two hundred and sixth birthday last year.

He took a deep breath and swiped through his vid history, "Play video."

Linda appeared in front of him on the screen. She looked beautiful. He watched this video when she first made it, but after she passed away, he couldn't bring himself to look at it again.

He watched until it faded out. He didn't cry. He knew she wouldn't want him to spend the rest of his life depressed. She always had a positive outlook on everything. She thought everyone could be saved.

He ate sponge grass oatmeal and drank down his froam protein shake before lifting weights. He showered and dressed in a casual suit. It switched between black and white and he couldn't decide which color he liked better so he let it oscillate.

It was a busy day for him. He needed to do research for his next target, and it was close to home, right here on his very own planet.

He checked his security cameras around his home. No Ahmalat activity this morning. "That's good," he said to no one.

He moved quickly into his red transit, set his maps, and launched.

The autopilot announced, "Leaving Swamplands Regions, Il'laceier. Destination, City Expanse Regions, Il'laceier. Estimated time of arrival: ninety-two thrux."

He looked out the windows as the Swamplands Regions gave way to the Grasslands Regions, Oceans Regions, Pink Lakes Regions, Klopkart Regions, Orange Fields Regions, QetQert Regions, Kingdom Regions, and finally the main city of Il'laceier within the City Expanse Regions.

Here the buildings didn't look like buildings at all. The ground was all gray gravel and dirt, but the structures resembled long fangs or claws sticking out of the ground with a smooth side curving on the outer face and a blade-like edge on the inner face.

D'Artagnan's transit docked inside the station. He walked straight to the shop herder's common area. The first time he showed this place to Linda, she called it a flea market and laughed at the shop owners harassing beings passing by, trying to tempt them to come to their little hole in the wall shops.

D'Artagnan walked into the armory looking for a new scope for his rifle, and a few more high power plasma converters. Then he went across the trail to the tailor and dropped off a shirt he ripped on his last job. He went to the flowery and grabbed more polken root for a stew he wanted to try and dalen reed to make beer. Very few beings knew how much he loved to cook and brew his own beers. It was one of the first things he told Linda. He sighed.

While he was walking around with bags of groceries in his arms, he visited a small housing complex. His job would be across the trail from here in a few Il'lacean days. He went to the roof and scouted out several hiding spots and vantage points. When he was satisfied, he went downstairs to the lobby and back out onto the trail.

Small children played with a ball in front of the school for height challenged Il'laceans. He wondered what his child would've looked like if he had time to make one with Linda.

Most Il'laceans were between seven feet to eight and a half feet tall. D'Artagnan was short for his species at seven foot two inches, but with Linda, he was definitely the big one. Linda had been a tall Human woman at six foot, but D'Artagnan still made her look small.

He consciously stopped thinking of Linda, and walked out into the crowds, headed for his transit.

When he got home, D'Artagnan shook his head as he poured over the news articles on Edison's death. He wanted to know what happened; what really happened, and it wasn't going to be in the news. D'Artagnan was invested in the Human Resistance because of Linda, but if the leadership changed hands, their goals might change. D'Artagnan wanted to know who the next leader might be. He needed to make a call.

Eric answered his Titan on the first chime, "D'Art man! Hey, how's it going dude?"

"I need some info from you. Hoping you have it."

Eric's brow furrowed, "What's up? I'll help you any way I can."

D'Artagnan watched on his Titan as Eric tossed a handful of popcorn into his mouth, "I need to know if anyone approached you about Edison aka Jacob Trost recently?"

Eric swallowed, "Yes."

"And?"

"And what?" Eric raised an eyebrow.

D'Artagnan shook his head, "Could you elaborate for me, you dick?"

Eric laughed, "I was wondering how long it'd take for you to insult me. Geez!"

D'Artagnan smiled, "I need this info, Bouton. I've been doing a lot of research on this man and now he's dead. I want to get some questions answered. I'm not looking into this for anyone but myself."

"Okay, okay. You want a real name or the name he gave me?"

"Both."

D'Artagnan watched as Eric pulled up a document on his Titan, "Real name's Mitch Savely, but the name he used for this transaction was Donald Rown. He lives on Earth. Human. No prior record. He only sent me a Titan message asking if I could retrieve the current location of Trost.

"Originally, after the bombing on Il'laceier, Trost went to Sho'teg for like, a minute, then he stayed on Bahsheef for a few days before he was murdered. Mitch paid me *a lot* of coren for this info. That's all he wanted. I gave it to him about an hour after he asked and he hasn't been back since. He could've asked on someone else's behalf, but I think that's your murderer right there."

D'Artagnan nodded, "Thanks a lot. I'll see what else I can find on this guy."

"Sure thing dude. Adios. Oh and I believe you're indebted to me for about three hundred and seventy-two favors by now."

D'Artagnan smiled, "Ah yes, of course. But who's keeping track right? I'll talk to you later."

Eric made a rude gesture with his hands, "Later."

D'Artagnan's Titan went to its main menu screen.

SEVEN

>>> > ON ISHIKAWA, MITCH worked on his client's transit.

Mitch often wondered what Xavier did with this white Pearl. Mitch put on a ton of modifications over the years and several things were highly unusual about the vehicle. It had a force field for one thing and that wasn't a common mod for transits. The only way Mitch knew how to put that on, was from his astronaut days.

Mitch always wanted to ask about Xavier but never did. Xavier was an intense man and seemed awfully private. Plus the fact that Xavier was built like a brick shit house since he was Lanyx. The most athletic people in the universe. Mitch just put his homemade protective helmet on, kept his head down, and did whatever Xavier asked for and took the coren. Few people spent as much money with Mitch as Xavier did.

Mitch was cleaning up his mess under the transit hood as Xavier came out of his home and into the attached garage.

Mitch took off his helmet.

"You almost done?"

"Yes sir. I'm just double-checking everything. Make sure I left nothing uncapped."

"I don't know what I'd do without you Mitch. I've never been great with transits, but I'm glad you are."

"It's a living. Anything else you need other than a checkup and top off your fluids?"

"No. That should be it."

"I've known you a while Xavier, but usually you seem a bit more," Mitch paused, "together. Is everything all right…you look a little off."

"I'm fine. Thanks for asking. How much do I owe you?"

CHAPTER 2

PRISONER OF WAR

ONE

>>> > SEBASTIAN HAD A lot of time to think traveling back to Praxis from Ishikawa. He couldn't do what Ni-toyis asked of him. Ni-toyis could also start problems between him and Celeste and he didn't need anyone to screw things up any more than he already had himself. He didn't care what Ni-toyis stole or for what reason (most times) but the Red Klix was too big for even *her* to handle. Especially if it did what he thought it could. No one should have it. Except for maybe him, only because if someone was planning on stealing it, that meant someone planned on doing something with it. He never thought about stealing it before, but now…He didn't trust the rest of the universe with it.

TWO

AFTER CELESTE'S THIRD date with Dax, she stared at herself in the bathroom mirror.

The date went okay. He was supposed to take her to Mostac to have dinner and watch a movie over at his house, but he changed plans at the last minute due to work. He picked her up outside her lobby and they did dinner and a movie in Daviens.

She wore her hair down, no wig tonight, and Dax had a great reaction to it. He kept playing with it and it calmed her. She took comfort wherever she could find it these days.

Dax was a perfect gentleman. He earned quite a few points by showing up with a dozen orange roses. He'd opened all her doors and thankfully for Celeste, did most of the talking. She hadn't been very chatty, but Dax didn't seem to mind. He tried to stretch out their goodnight kiss outside her lobby, but she cut it short saying she didn't feel well. He let her go immediately, telling her she should get some rest and hoped she felt better soon. He kissed her on the cheek and walked away. He was a nice guy and she had a nice time, but she wanted more than nice.

A sad woman stared back at Celeste in the mirror. She wondered what Sebastian was doing right now, then she brushed the thought of him out of her mind. She stood there in her silk nightgown and fuzzy slippers and took a few deep breaths. She washed off her makeup and brushed out her hair. She missed Sebastian. She tried pushing him out of her thoughts, but she couldn't do it. She let her mind go where it wanted. She missed being in his apartment and bumping into him on the balcony or his weight room or the hallway. She missed his kisses and talking with him. She missed seeing him smile or hearing his rare but wonderful laugh. She missed how his intense blue-eyed stares held her and wouldn't let go.

She only missed one thing more than Sebastian and that was *her* Bastian, what she thought of as the real version of himself, the one that was capable of deep, powerful emotion. The version of himself that he kept sealed far away. The one that wasn't afraid of showing his feelings to her. She wondered if there was a way to bring that out in him when he wasn't on Scarlette Island. She went to her computer cube and researched Praxis's magnetic field and the possibility of anomalies under his island. Scarlette Island was rich in iron oxide, which is what made the sand that reddish color. Iron oxide was one of many magnetic elements found in high concentrations on Scarlette Island and the more of those there were in one place, the easier it was for magnetic anomalies to develop. She didn't understand all the charts and maps, but maybe the magnetism in that area helped Sebastian relax. Maybe it helped her too. She hadn't shared any dreams with him before or since their time spent on his island.

Was it possible Veronica was right? Had Sebastian fallen in love with her and it scared him so bad he ran away? Maybe the only thing worse for him was to try to live without her. Maybe he'd call her Titan or knock on her door and he'd be begging her to take him back and forgive him. She held her breath looking at her Titan for a moment and strained her ears to listen for the door.

No knock and no call.

She knew the odds of that actually happening were stacked against her, but all she had now was hope and she held onto it with a death grip.

She heard thunder boom outside. She wasn't ready for bed. She put on her robe and sat on the balcony watching the lightning.

She looked at Sebastian's apartment across the street. There were no lights on.

She took a deep breath and smelled fresh rain. She closed her eyes and tried to empty her mind. She sat and meditated on the environment, tried to stay in the moment. The wind's fingertips picked up and dropped her hair around her face like a playful child. Electricity crackled around her. The moisture in the air was a damp towel around her body. Thunder crashed down through the sky demanding attention before quickly disappearing. Before she knew it, she was thinking about Sebastian again. She missed feeling his entrancing blue eyes on her and the way she had to stop what she was doing and look at him.

She felt Sebastian close by suddenly. Her eyes flew open and she looked up a few floors across the way and saw Sebastian's light on. She wondered what he was doing, if he was thinking about her, and if he regretted the mean things he said. She couldn't tell if he was on his balcony or not. She thought about trying to read him, then changed her mind. She could probe into him and find something hurtful…like maybe he wasn't missing her – and *that* she didn't want to know. She wished he would come over and say how sorry he was. How empty he'd been since he let her go. She wiped away a couple of escaped tears, and tried thinking back on her date tonight. *I've got to keep my mind off Sebastian. My Bastian is no longer mine. Maybe never has been.*

THREE

>>> > SEBASTIAN SAT ON his balcony looking down at Celeste. She was watching the storm. He walked inside and asked Ophelia to turn off the living room light, as he grabbed a bottle of whiskey off the kitchen island and opened it. He returned to the balcony and drank straight from the bottle – something he never did. His drinking had always been well under control. *He* had always been well under control…until lately. Lately, he hardly recognized himself. He took a long swig off the bottle, closing his eyes while he tipped his head back. He usually drank a glass or two after a hard day to take the edge off, occasionally to help him sleep, but never to get drunk. Tonight, he was seriously considering the latter.

He sensed her questioning if he was thinking about her. She was trying to stop herself from wondering this, but her attempts to stop were futile. He tried to block her out, but her need for answers was strong. He felt her longing deep inside her mind and it made him feel like a complete bastard all over again. Another wave of her thoughts was crashing over him louder than the thunder – was he missing her like she was missing him? Was he thinking of her at all?

Unfortunately, he'd been thinking about her too much in his opinion. Assassins were meant to be alone, he knew this. Family and attachments were a liability, staying in one place too long – a liability. All these Goddamn liabilities. And he couldn't do anything else for a living. It was too late to quit and expect he or his loved ones would be left alone, or forgotten about. Or was it? Unless maybe there was some planet that didn't interact with the rest of the universe…somewhere he and Celeste could live together, be safe and isolated. Was there such a place and would she be happy there? He took another drink off the wine bottle. Should he even be considering this?

He had killed hundreds of targets and made enough enemies to last three lifetimes, and a Lanyx lifetime was much longer than a Humans. Most can expect 225 to 250 years. With this target on his back, he expected more like 100 if he was lucky *and* smart.

He felt her briefly across the way again; she was primarily sad, but there was a small sliver of happiness as well and he didn't know why. He certainly hadn't left her happy the last time they saw each other.

He heard her when she called out his name as he was leaving her apartment, but he wondered what she would've said had he stopped. He had checked her mind and even *she* didn't know what she would've said next, so he kept walking.

He drank more wine, hoping it would dull his mind.

He had no other choice but to ask her to help him with these contracts that were increasing on world leaders, even though he said they needed time apart.

He didn't have any contacts higher than a Queen. He would have to write her an email.

He was one of the top assassins in this galaxy, the best on his planet and Earth. He had an IQ that shot off the charts, and there was no battle he couldn't fight his way out of…but this woman, this Human, completely left him defenseless at times. She broke through every wall he carefully built up over the years and changed everything. She made him want to be with someone. It was getting harder for him to remind himself – he can't let that happen.

He finished off the whiskey and felt a little buzzed.

Maybe it was this other guy Celeste was seeing that made her feel happy momentarily tonight. He knew she thought of that asshole briefly. Maybe he should find out who it was and wrap his hands around this scumbag's throat and squeeze until Sebastian saw the life drain out of the bastard's face…maybe not. He hated feeling this way. One minute he wanted to be with her, the next he thought she was safer without him; and then sometimes he wanted to kill whoever she might even be thinking of dating.

He twisted his father's ring on his finger absentmindedly. He could look around the apartment and see if she'd left anything behind – something he'd need to return to her. Maybe he could buy something for her hair and say he found it here. Then he could see her again and gauge her reaction to him.

He watched as fat raindrops fell from the sky, listening to the world turn, trying to outdrink his heartache.

Lightning flashed in the night, tearing a bright gash across the sky. Her balcony was empty. She was gone. She was probably lying in her bed and for the thousandth time, he wished there was a way he could be with her. Lying next to her silently, her body would be wrapped around his. Her head would be resting on his bare chest and his hands would start roaming across her body.

He hated missing her.

He thought of her face when he said her feelings were confused for him, that she was jumping into another relationship. Her normally warm eyes became wintry, and her face lost all its glow. He hated himself for that. In that moment, when she realized he was really leaving her apartment, when he slammed her door, she'd been overwhelmed with sadness and it hit him like a ton of bricks. He actually felt her heart sink like a stone into the ocean; falling down silently into the darkness where no sunlight could reach. It was one of the worst things he ever felt, only outdone by the fact that he had directly and purposefully caused that feeling.

Maybe it was good she found someone else. Maybe she'd be able to forget about him, although he knew he could never forget her.

The wind and rain intensified. He went inside for the night, drawing the curtains behind him. Maybe bourbon would get him drunk enough to stop feeling this hole in his chest. In a rare moment of being clumsy, his leg bumped the table where Celeste's glass kingdom puzzle was assembled. It fell apart. *Ironically appropriate*, he thought to himself and kept walking.

FOUR

>>> > "YOU WHAT?!" NI-TOYIS frowned.

Sebastian spoke louder, "I said I can't do this. Not this time."

Ni-toyis looked at Sebastian over her Titan screen. His face was stoic. She knew he was serious. Something was different about him and she didn't like it.

"Raynes, you owe me a favor. Since our arrangement started you've done everything else I asked. You know this would be the last one."

"Of course," he said matter-of-factly.

Ni-toyis scoffed. Something in the way Sebastian replied told her he'd known she would always come back for another favor. She didn't know what to say and she never expected him to flat out turn down her demand.

They were both silent until Sebastian asserted, "I will continue to owe you one more favor, but I have a code for myself. I have things I will not do, and I won't do this for you. The Red Klix is special for many reasons, and I have no idea what you're planning to do with it, but I won't help you steal it."

Ni-toyis's lavender blue face settled into a vicious expression, "Then I'll report you to the police. I'm sure they'd be interested in your numerous unlawful activities."

Sebastian's face flushed for a moment, "You do *that*, and you'd lose my specific skill set and any chance of me ever paying off my debt to you. I know you're not stupid. Plus, how would you ever sleep with me if I was in prison?"

Ni-toyis was bluffing but she thought Sebastian wasn't sure of this fact, "I'll catch you later, pretty boy."

The screen went dark and Ni-toyis slammed her hand down on the kitchen counter in front of her. *This was not supposed to happen!*

Then she stopped and thought, *does that mean he's thought about sleeping with me? Maybe there's hope for us yet.*

FIVE

NI-TOYIS CALLED HER employer on an audio only call. She didn't have much time left.

"Hey, I'm going to extend my timeline on getting the package for you."

Her employer did not sound impressed, "Do whatever you must, but I need that stone, Tredux. You said you were the only one who could get it...are you telling me I need to hire someone else?"

"No, no, absolutely not. I can get it, I just ran into a small hitch in my plans. Nothing to worry about, but I wanted to keep you up to date," she lowered her voice into her seductive tone, "You know, keep you abreast of things." She smiled.

Her employer replied, "Ohhh yes, I've heard about those breasts of yours, I mean, your whole body's allegedly phenomenal. I'm sure you'll be done soon, sweet tits. What do you need, another week or two?"

Ni-toyis smiled, "Yes baby doll, about two Praxian weeks. Then I'll present it to you in person along with my phenomenal tits." Men were so easy to manipulate. She rolled her eyes and then made a face like she was going to vomit. She had no idea what species her employer was or what he looked like, but he sounded revolting...like some dirty old man. Her employer said his name was The Hunter and when she looked up his info, she couldn't find anything. He was a ghost as far as she could tell. Someone who was excellent at hiding from the entire universe, but he was definitely creepy...and she had no intentions on sleeping with him. He offered an extra hundred thousand coren on top of her payment for a private Stoxian hour with him afterwards. She originally said yes, but she had some ideas on how to get the money without having to do the deed. Sure, she didn't mind sleeping with some loser to get his money, that's how she started out after all, but it had to be a lot of coren and someone who didn't sound as revolting as this guy.

Stox men were rare in the universe, and highly sought after by Stox women, but a Stox prostitute was incredibly rare and highly prized by most men. They all wanted a piece of ass from her and they were willing to pay. But that got old after a while. She wanted to see what else she was capable of. Stealing gave her a big high and she was good at it, so she picked that up after laying on her back for ten years. And although she was good at stealing, sometimes it was better to seduce some stupid man into doing it for her. It was a bit harder of course, but she loved a challenge.

Sebastian wasn't supposed to be giving her this hard of a time doing what she wanted. He'd always given in to her demands before…well except for the part where she thought they'd make a great couple. He could kill anyone and she'd steal stuff from them – what could be better? They'd be an unstoppable force together. She thought it was meant to be the first time they met, but he hadn't felt the same.

She got stuck on the planet Dhoot Ovene after a job went tits up and she lost her purse. She hated the Gears System in the KeSara Galaxy but she rarely came here, with good reason. What kind of beings could breathe in an all-ammonia atmosphere? And the Sineenniss people were tricksters. She should've known better than to take any jobs in this place. But here she was stealing a small bust out of an art dealer's apartment so she could sell it and make some coren for bot-taxi fare. They were always much more expensive than regular taxis but she needed to fool the SAP as she went through it and she wanted as few live beings as possible to see her before she split. She should've left right then, but she looked around, and saw more unique artwork she thought she could sell, when the asshole came home. She hid in the closet and ten minutes later, she saw Sebastian enter through the front door and kill the guy. That Sineenniss never knew what hit him, but Sebastian moved fast and he was thorough. Too thorough because while Ni-toyis thought he'd just look around the place and leave, he opened the door to the closet and found her with the bust in her hands. Those were the days when she thought it was still a good idea to wear all black and blend in with the night. All it did was make her look like a burglar. Sebastian knew right away what she was doing…and that's how they were cast into each other's lives. They were both criminals with something to hold over each other's heads, so they'd occasionally work together, but Ni-toyis always wanted a relationship. Sebastian always kept it business only, with the exception of the time they almost slept together.

That initial killing she saw him do, it wasn't just some art dealer like she first thought. He was some big time Sineenniss leader who'd just been elected president for half the planet and she figured she could blackmail Sebastian into helping her out. She asked him to agree to assist her twenty times and then they'd part ways and she'd forget what he'd done. She knew he didn't have much choice; stealing was a punishment of two weeks in a penalty cell with a mark on your record and permanent exile from Dhoot Ovene, but murder meant only one thing on this planet – execution by Revettes. No one wanted to be eaten alive by small animals that looked like furry lemons with thousands of razor sharp teeth, so murder was understandably rare here.

That was eighteen years ago. All this time she'd been calling in favors to Sebastian and now that he'd accomplished nineteen, she couldn't understand why he didn't want to finish the whole deal with this last one itty-bitty favor.

SIX

>>> > D'ARTAGNAN FOUND WHERE Mitch Savely lived, how much coren was in his bank account and that he needed no job to support himself, but his record seemed very clean…too clean. The history on him said his parents drowned in a boating accident shortly after he was born and he had no siblings, so Mitch inherited a lot of money that he had no access to until he was eighteen. An aunt took care of him until he was of age. He attended college and had a few jobs here and there and then the trail went cold. Even the aunt had died fifteen years ago.

D'Artagnan drummed his fingers on the desk. He might need Sebastian's expertise in finding out more. Something wasn't sitting well with D'Artagnan. There was a difference between someone's dossier being squeaky clean due to the person not having any kind of connections or social life, and then there was a dossier that was created to make it look like there was nothing to see.

D'Artagnan had two choices. Ask Sebastian to dig and find out more, or D'Artagnan would have to find this Mitch guy and get into his life.

SEVEN

>>> > SEBASTIAN SAT AT his computer screens researching for his next assassination. He looked down at his desk and saw one of Celeste's hairs sticking out from underneath his stack of books. How was he supposed to forget her when everywhere he looked something reminded him of her? And her hair was everywhere. On the ground, in the drawers, in the sink, it drove him crazy trying to clean them all up.

He couldn't stop thinking about her. He wanted to talk to her, but at the same time, was afraid to. Even though it'd been a few days since they had that big fight, he was still reluctant to contact her, even by email. He'd rather go over to her place, smooth things over, and then request her help. It's just that he didn't know how to smooth things over.

His eye caught the light shining off the glass puzzle she'd given him. He had reassembled it and was glad none of the pieces shattered when it tumbled apart. Put together, it was this beautiful and fragile form. It reminded him of her. Her feelings were so delicate. Sometimes the way he clashed with her, he felt like a bull in a china shop, toppling her emotions like a tower of glass teacups.

He would never say so but he genuinely missed her. The way she smelled, her wiggly walk, her big brown eyes, the intellectual conversations they shared late at night. He missed her totally immersive thoughts, it was like watching someone else's dream, bright and vivid, full of colors and images. And then actually sharing that dream on the yacht; that was like nothing else, and impossible to forget.

He leaned back in his chair and swiveled around to look out his windows. Celeste brought something he didn't expect to his house — warmth and a sense of it feeling lived in. She made his apartment feel like a true home. He looked around the quiet, empty space again. He needed to get back to work.

He lasted a whole ten minutes before she crept into his mind again. He thought of her argument about dating. He got up and started pacing around his apartment. His work, left behind on his desk, forgotten.

But she never understood his reservations about starting a relationship and that frustrated him deeply. He had his reasons.

She was only thinking of what she wanted, and not what he needed.

He knew for sure what she *wasn't* thinking about – and that was the exposure he'd suffer dating someone like Celeste. She would get recognized and he'd always be the person in the background. *He'd* be noticed if she wasn't careful about disguising herself when they were together. They couldn't go anywhere until he fully prepared and trained her on how to blend in within a crowd, how to disappear, and how to be forgettable to other beings while interacting with them. It was going to be a colossal challenge for her to do this as a former Queen to two worlds. Almost impossible.

If they dated, the risk to their safety went up – for the both of them. But for her, being involved with someone like him…she was putting herself in harm's way. He knew hundreds of beings seeking revenge against him. They could kidnap, torture, rape, and kill her; so many terrible things. He knew she wasn't thinking of all the possibilities. She probably wasn't thinking at all – just feeling.

He walked onto his balcony and leaned against the railing. He thought of her argument about being a royal, and dealing with death threats.

With an army of guards, there was a slim chance anything would've happened to her, plus, she was just the wife of a King, and daughter to an Emperor, not the ruler herself. Her chances of assassination were small. But there was the possibility that someone would use her to get to the King or the Emperor – not too different really than someone using her to get to him.

He did admire her debating skills, and it was nice to see someone fight just for an opportunity to be with him. It was flattering, but made his heart heavy to have to tell her no repeatedly. She might never understand his position no matter how he explained it. She never asked him to quit being an assassin, but he thought about the possibility. What would fill his days and nights if he wasn't a contract killer? He would need to do some sort of work. He wasn't the type to just sit around and do nothing; that would drive him crazy. He folded his arms over his chest as he clenched his jaw.

Even if he quit today…she wouldn't be safe.

Celeste would always have ties to the Earth and Il'laceier Empires. She'd always be a target, with or without him in her life. So what if he just gave in? What if they dated? It wasn't a commitment, and it certainly wasn't marriage. Maybe it could work if they moved slower than she wanted to; he'd have to ask her out on a real date like she wanted. Compromises – he'd just have to make little compromises for her. What would be the harm of that?

He rubbed his face with his hands. He surprised himself with this line of thinking. He shouldn't be allowing these thoughts – he really can't afford the complications of having a girlfriend in his life.

"Queen Celeste wants to be my girlfriend," he said out loud. Well, technically she never said that to him. She only said she wanted to date him, but he had a strong suspicion if he asked her to be his and only his, she'd agree. The sun set for the evening as the moons began to rise. He went back inside and sat down at his desk again.

"Ophelia, desk light on dim please."

"Yes, sir."

A warm soft glow of light illuminated his desk.

Maybe he could train her to defend herself, use weapons, and be alert like he always was. It would probably take, at the fastest, months to train her to be a sufficient and deadly fighter, but her 7's might accelerate the process. He didn't know for sure, he'd never done anything like what he was contemplating. She made him consider things all the time that he never thought he would. Another testament to the power she held over him.

It had been nice to be close to someone again, and she was incredibly attractive. She didn't have to *do* or *say* anything. He felt drawn to her like a moth to a flame or as if some magnetic switch had been turned on and then he was moving towards her before he even realized his body was in motion. And she held a power over him when no other woman could.

Over the years, he'd been lonely, but every encounter with some random woman made him feel more alone. It felt like cheap, empty sex because that's exactly what it was and it had always bothered him. But not to the degree it was now. Those one-night stands never went anywhere; he never wanted them to of course; but with Celeste, he definitely wished their relationship could be explored. But he couldn't be sure what price would be paid if they attempted a normal relationship.

He worried about locking into her.

He was forty-nine years old and had never truly been in love before. What if he fell in love with her? What if he got to a point where he couldn't let her go, couldn't live without her? He'd have a weakness, and he hated those.

He ran his hands through his hair, then looked at his father's ring. He started to twist it with his fingers. He wished he could talk to his father now. He wondered what his dad would make of Celeste. He smiled knowing his dad would probably think she was just as beautiful as Sebastian did.

He picked up a book and leafed through its pages. He wanted to see her again, and even after they spent time together, he still wanted more.

Maybe it was time for him to give in and write that email to her. He'd not mention any new thoughts about dating. He'd start over with her as friends, that is, if she let him. His email would only focus on the tasks at hand and leave the rest of what he was thinking out. He had to be careful with this. He knew she felt like he'd been pushing and pulling on her and that was true. He didn't want to start that process all over again. He'd say he wanted to keep in contact with her as friends. Maybe he could get a sense of where her mind was from her response. Cautiously test the waters. And with that, he began typing.

EIGHT

>>> > AFTER SEBASTIAN SENT his email, he made a Titan call to his associate on Greeve.

"Hey buddy! How goes it?" Xu'Xi Darksent sounded chipper whenever he knew a job was coming.

Sebastian replied, "Good. I was wondering if you might be able to give me a hand taking a very special stone."

"Armand, I'm always down for thieving. Which one is it?"

"You have your secure channel up?"

"You know it." His black and sapphire blue eyes glinted with intelligence.

Sebastian hesitated, "The one on the peace loving planet. The ruby rock that everyone protects." He still didn't want to name the planet and the stone over the call.

"Ooooh jumpin kazzers! That's gonna be a tough one. How interested are you in this stone?"

"Five hundred thousand."

A grin tugged at Xu'Xi's thin oatmeal-colored face, "Double it, and we've got a deal."

"Done."

"Then that stone is as good as gotten. When?"

"Haven't settled a date yet. Trying to figure out the best window, but I'm thinking within eight Praxian days."

Xu'Xi did the time conversion in his head from Praxian to Greeve, "I think I can swing that. Send me a message and I'll clear out my schedule for you."

"Will do. Thanks man."

"Sure thing Armand. I love working with you."

NINE

>>> > "WELL I DON'T know what the hell to do with him!" Celeste was almost crying again.

Lila frowned at her Titan screen, "Honey, there is nothing you *can* do right now. If the man has chosen to break up with you and hasn't talked to you since, what are you supposed to do? Throw yourself at his feet and beg him to date you? I don't think so."

Celeste replied, "No, I won't do that, of course not. I just…"

"What?"

"I miss him. I think he was on his balcony last night across the way. I'm not sure since it was raining really hard."

"And? Did he do anything?"

"Not that I could tell."

"V told me you've developed 7's somehow? Is that really true?"

Celeste smiled, "Yes. It's weird. Like being part super hero or something. I seem to have a knack for it."

"Could you sense Brahm that way?"

"That's the only way I sensed him. I felt his presence but nothing more."

"And V tells me there's another guy too. What's his name? Dax?"

"Yeah, there's him."

"Well you don't sound very excited there Celly."

Celeste sighed, "He's smart and nice. Makes me laugh and can cook too. At least he wants to be with me..."

"I hear a 'but' coming up."

"No, there's no buts, I enjoy his company and he is cute."

"I still hear a 'but'. What it sounds like to me is that Dax is great but he's no Brahm. You forget I saw you when you were here talking about that guy and he really seemed to float your boat. This guy Dax doesn't seem to be doing the same thing to you. Anyways, I'd rather have the problem of too many men, than not enough."

"You're not dating anyone?"

"Eh. I thought there might've been someone here but he hasn't paid much attention to me."

"And who's this?"

"I don't know what you'll think of me." Lila closed her eyes tight and blushed, "He's Il'lacean. One of the guards here, maybe you know him. His name's Raykreede Monter."

"I know him," Celeste hesitated, "I don't think he's playing on your team, Lila."

"What do you mean?"

Celeste gave Lila a compassionate look, "He's gay. He's trying to keep it hidden since the Il'laceans will have his head if they find out, but I'm pretty sure he's not interested in you."

Lila sighed half in annoyance, half in surprise, "See, I missed that somehow. That makes a lot of sense though. I'm terrible with men. Maybe I'll just give up and go lesbian, who knows."

Celeste laughed, "You love men too much, I know that's not an option for you."

"Well I can't seem to find any good men, so maybe I'll go celibate."

"Mr. Right will come along. Don't give up yet."

"K Celeste, got to get back to work. It was great talking to you."

Lila watched her friend wave goodbye and the screen went dark before returning to the main menu. *Mr. Right, huh? Yeah, sure.* Lila had given up hope that there was a Mr. Right.

TEN

››› › SOMETHING WAS UP with Sebastian, and Ni-toyis wanted to know what the hell that was specifically. She'd known him for almost two decades and he never behaved this way before. She flipped through news stations on the screens absentmindedly staring at each one for a few seconds before changing over to another channel.

She almost conquered Raynes once before, and it was oh so magnificent. He'd been full of muscles and desire and it would've been electric to screw him. But he changed his mind at the last second.

Her breed had powers on both male and female sides. They could usually seduce whoever they wanted with their beautiful blended skin and changing eyes. She could set her sights on a man, do a little flirting, laugh in a sexy way, and they were hers, at least for the night.

For reasons he never explained, it didn't work on Sebastian that night. Or any time after that either.

The real problem with her species was the huge disproportion of females to males. Most Stox women not only wanted babies, but fathers to stay and help raise the babies. They hit a certain age where sex alone wasn't enough and they wanted to settle down with a man of their own kind, but with the numbers, for most, that simply wasn't possible.

Sebastian was the only man she really liked. He was mysterious. He always kept things to himself and she wanted to know what was going on in that beautiful head of his.

And now that he was resisting extra hard, she thought he became even more intriguing. She'd been looking forward to seeing him for a long time before she wrote that note and left it on his windshield. Now, she was disappointed. First, he was cold to her, and then he refused to help her steal the stone. What's a girl to do to get her man?

She wanted a life with a partner in crime by her side, permanently. Then maybe baby makes three? She could be ten times the mother to a baby than her mother was to her. And just think of it – a half Lanyx, half Stox child would be so powerful, so amazing, and so attractive!

But she needed to play all of this very cool. Couldn't let Sebastian know her motivations or what she wanted from him. She'd act as she always had, somewhat elusive and aloof. She'd find a way to do this deal with him and find out what was causing him to act strangely, then she'd figure out a plan. Once she figured out an angle, then she could hit Sebastian full strength and get him into her bed, permanently.

She reminded herself as she commanded the screens off, *one thing at a time my dear, one thing at a time.*

ELEVEN

>>> > D'ARTAGNAN WAS UPSIDE down hanging by his feet. The blood rushed to his head and he couldn't hear anything but the *whoosh whoosh whoosh* of his heartbeat in his ears.

They tortured him for three days now, but he hadn't said a word.

They had several other Il'laceans at the POW camp, but D'Artagnan had no idea. He thought he was the only prisoner of war captured.

His squad was ambushed on a planet that was supposed to be cleared out.

They held him underground where the natives lived. It was dark, cold, damp, and the bare dirt tunnels smelled like sour fungus. He vomited repeatedly at first, but now his snout was used to the stench.

D'Artagnan was scared, but he didn't let the natives know that.

It happened during the Echlynian War six years ago, but for D'Artagnan, it was happening right now.

He could smell the desperation of this tribe, see the torches lit up on either side of the rocky dwelling they were keeping him in, and hear water dripping into pools down the hall.

So far, they burned him, whipped him with knotted heavy ropes, submerged him underwater so that he almost drowned, and now they were getting creative hanging him upside down like this. They cut him loose. He dropped down onto the muddy floor and all of his joints started to ache as his muscles tingled. He tried to move but they kicked him in the stomach.

D'Artagnan woke up and gasped.

Covered in sweat, he ripped the sheets off him in his sleeping capsule. It felt like it was two hundred degrees in the house.

He walked to the bathroom to splash cool water on his face.

Sometimes the dreams were so real and vivid, he woke up terrified. Sometimes he went for long stretches without having them, other times he was plagued for weeks dealing with sleepless nights. This was the first dream he had in a while.

Linda was good at calming him down from these...

He hoped this was the last dream, but he always hoped for that.

TWELVE

>>> > THE LEADER OF the Ice Moon Conclave spun the meeting wheel, letting the deep rumble roll across the room. The cloaked figure stepped up to the podium and looked over the members.

The leader was wearing a black facemask and voice distorter. Even members of the IMC didn't know who their leader was.

"Thank you for coming on short notice. I want to go over a few things at this session so we're all in the same place." David observed the crowd from underneath his black facemask. It was hard for him to conduct this meeting without Xabat, but business had to be done. The world continued to spin.

"The IMC, I feel is falling behind the Brotherhood and I don't like it. I have suspicions that the BDP is trying to recruit Il'laceans right now and that is a lot of our core base here."

The members of the Ice Moon Conclave nodded their heads.

"I have many things to handle right now. The attack of Rem Mot Om could count as a warning to us since it seems the Human Resistance was out for Il'lacean blood. I don't want us to be targeted next. Although the HR has been silent since then, I can't stress enough to you to stay hyper-vigilant. Always pay attention to your surroundings and never speak of your involvement in the IMC where you could be overheard," David paused and swallowed hard. "I'm grateful to Ulysses for helping me during a very difficult time lately. I lost friends at the bombing. Their absence will have a significant impact on my life now and in the future. You should all give him a round of applause as he is an outstanding member of this group."

Ulysses bowed to his King and leader and blushed. He smiled through the applause although he felt like hiding. He suspected David was the ruler of the IMC early on, but kept it to himself. David confessed his position late one night after too many Long Island iced teas, (Ulysses could not convince him they had no tea in them) and that's how Ulysses gained second-in-command status in the group. Not with his battle-prowess. Not with his magical abilities (thank God he never told anyone he had them). Not with his sharp mind, but with how he carried a drunk David up four flights of stairs in the back of the Kingdom so no one would see him, stripped him down to his boxer shorts, and put him into his sleeping capsule. David said to him later that if a Human man had wanted to assassinate him, that would've been the perfect opportunity and since Ulysses hadn't, well, that proved a lot to the King. Ulysses didn't want to be one of David's favorite beings, but it seemed he was.

David spoke, "I want to talk goals. The longest standing goal is to eradicate the BDP. They've been nothing but trouble since the day they started interfering with our territories. I'll be looking for a new team to focus on getting them gone for good. I'll need volunteers for this, so speak to Ulysses at the end of the meeting and he'll give you more information. I want us to continue to expand across the universe and get more new faces in our organization.

"We need to infiltrate the BDP. We've tried before and the results were...not what I had in mind. We have lost several members either through discovery that they were undercover IMC members and killed, or members of our team were swayed to stay at the BDP. I need volunteers, loyal ones this time, to go to the BDP recruiters on several planets and try to get some intel for us. This mission is dangerous, but I assume some of you are looking for a little excitement in your lives. Talk to Ulysses about this after the meeting if you're interested."

Ulysses nodded, but kept his surprise to himself, as he wasn't spoken to about this particular responsibility. David was handing him things left and right.

"Our next meeting will take place here on Il'laceier and you will get notifications of the time, and date on your Titans. Let the universe freeze in ice," David stopped and the group finished, "so that we may inherit eternity."

David smiled under his mask and hood, "Meeting adjourned."

THIRTEEN

>>> > CELESTE HAD SEEN Sebastian's email sitting in her inbox. She saw it the night it popped up, but she couldn't open it yet. He never communicated with her this way. She let two full days pass before she allowed herself to read it. It was worse than she could've imagined and she was a mess for the rest of the night after reading it.

"Your Highness,

The last time we spoke has weighed heavily on my mind. I need to apologize for the hurtful things I said to you. You didn't deserve them. I was very angry and my temper got the best of me.

I would like to start again if you'd allow me that favor. But we must start building on our friendship first. I know I've expressed this wish before, but I think restricting the amount of time we spend around each other in person would greatly help any prior mistakes from happening again. I would like to stay in contact so I know you're doing all right.

I would very much appreciate your help in the matter I mentioned earlier.

Please consider this – the entire universe might be able to benefit from me learning as much as possible about recent events and you might have all the information I need.

Just think about it. My need to speak with you has ramifications that affect billions of beings and their safety.

The information on your parent's possible death has proven elusive. I will continue my diligence on finding out a clear answer for you.

Sincerely,

X"

This was not what she was expecting. She didn't know how to feel about his email. At least he apologized – that was a start. But now he'd gone back to using an abbreviation of Xavier instead of his real name. She knew he was doing it in case the email was intercepted, but still, it was way too impersonal. And he was suggesting the whole idea of friendship again. She remembered on his island how he admitted that they were meant to be more than friends.

We're actually starting to move backwards now. Of course, I guess you can't get more backwards than flat out breaking up can you? And did he actually call their failed attempts at friendship "mistakes?" All of the erotic foreplay and make out sessions to him were just "mistakes?" She shook her head.

How could he possibly believe that they could be just friends? She didn't know if she could trust him to keep things off a romantic level. They tried that once already and it failed miserably – only because *he* couldn't keep his hands off her. She hadn't done badly at friendship, but he was incapable of real actual self-control around her. She wanted much more than friendship. This man was so confused and now, he was confusing her.

And Dax was in her life now. Dax who was consistently asking her out, expressing interest in continuing to see her and was very obvious with his growing feelings for her. Dax who was sweet and funny and stable.

She bit her lip thinking of Sebastian, who was intense and sexy…and inconsistent.

She was afraid if she let Sebastian back into her life, they would end up going in the same circle they always did, and then he could hurt her all over again. But despite her personal feelings, she also had to consider his genuine need for information that might change the universe. This was something she could not ignore and if they kept things civil and professional in emails, text messages, or any other communication that wasn't in person, maybe she could learn to deal with this. She was so unsure of their future. Did they even have one? She had to process this and couldn't respond for a while until she was completely okay with it. She was at least, relieved that he hadn't reneged on his offer to help her find out what truly happened to her parents. She was grateful for that.

She tried to consider Sebastian as a whole, meshing her Bastian with the ever-unpredictable Sebastian. Bastian could be so sweet and thoughtful. He wanted to protect and please her. Sebastian was smart and capable. He wanted to help her and teach her about 7's. But she had to take both sides of him. Sebastian had been through so much. His life had been so hard already. She thought maybe she should be the one thing that came into his life easily and stayed.

She was mad at him initially for saying what he did when they broke up, but she thought he might've just said that to push her away. To try to make her hate him so she'd stop fighting for him. She really tried to hold onto that anger for as long as she could, but it ebbed away slowly and completely faded when he apologized. She knew he was being genuine.

For as much trouble as he was giving her now, she couldn't deny her deep feelings for him and she couldn't fight them. They were there and just as strong as when they first met. And apparently she could not stay mad with him, even if he dumped her. She knew that first day she met him, he could be something really special and now she knew he really was. A man that only came along once in a lifetime. And as badly as she wanted to be with him right now, maybe she could be a little more patient and let him have more time to realize he needed her.

But it wasn't fair to Dax who was always kind and thoughtful with her. Why not give him a chance? It was true she felt it was a bit strange that he pretended he didn't know who she was at first, but his reasons weren't malicious.

Each man was attractive to her in different ways, but they were so different and they offered such different things. She felt torn between the two, but thankfully she knew no decisions had to be made for now.

FOURTEEN

>>> > "LISTEN MITCH. THERE have been some HR members that I haven't been able to get in touch with. I think David's going to find all of us sooner or later and do God knows what, but I don't want to find out. Where have you been?"

Mitch sat in his house on his Titan with a member he hadn't talked to since they left the bunker. He didn't know what to say. He only knew he wanted to distance himself from everyone in the HR now. "I'm where I need to be. Maybe the members left Earth. I wouldn't blame everyone for trying to get off the planet."

"Mitch, they found the bunker. They blew it to hell. All of our history, everything that we did, it's all gone. That bunker's completely destroyed. Did you know about that?"

Mitch wasn't exactly surprised, although he didn't think the Kingdom would find it so soon. "No, I didn't. Gina, you should probably stay in hiding. I think it'd be wise to avoid contact with any HR members and just lay low."

"I still need to talk to you. You're our leader after all."

Mitch cringed, "I'm not. We decided to take a break remember? That was our last conversation before we all went our separate ways. You are somewhere safe right?"

"Yeah," she nodded her head and looked over her shoulder, "This place is good for now."

"You need a place that's going to be good for months. If that means you need to leave, then do that."

"Okay," Gina responded slowly, "but I want to know if you're going to be okay too."

"I will be. I always land on my feet. Try not to worry. I'll contact you when I think it's safe to talk again, but in the meantime, I'd advise you not to contact me or any other HR members just for your own safety. Promise me?"

"I promise, Mitch."

"We've been on the line too long. I'll see you when it's safe. Bye, Gina. Stay safe."

"You too. I will. Bye."

Mitch knew all of the HR members were going to be hunted, one by one, and he was no exception. He couldn't afford to get caught off guard and if he ever wanted to make a difference in the world, he was going to have to stay off the grid and stay informed. Mitch was second guessing his idea of using of his real first name for the HR. He assumed everyone else would assume he *wasn't* really named Mitch. Why hadn't he used another name? He had some vague memory of thinking it would be good to make a positive change in Earth's history under his real first name. Stupid.

So far, the authorities hadn't come knocking on his door. He lost control of himself the day he killed Jacob. He felt himself slipping. He couldn't let Edison, Jacob, whatever his name was, live. Knowing that Edison put a hit on him, Mitch wouldn't have been able to go anywhere without looking over his shoulder. He had to remove the threat to his own life, by taking someone else's.

But it was a slippery slope. He thought back to how his father abused Mitch's two sisters ever since they were born. His mom died giving birth to them, and Mitch thought his father took out his anger on the twins. Mitch grew to hate his father after his mother died. He watched his dad go from an okay parent to an abusive monster. Mitch only enlisted in the military to provide enough money for his sisters to live on their own and escape their abuse.

But life teaches that though you may have the best intentions, the bitch is going to do what the bitch wants to do. And life apparently wanted to show Mitch who the real boss of his existence was.

After Mitch saved enough money and snuck his teenage sisters out of the house, his dad started looking for the twins. By that time, he was a full-blown alcoholic and a heavy drug user. That was what kept his dad from calling the police. The personal scrutiny of himself and his drug habits by any police officer trying to help him find his children would've destroyed any chance of him getting them back. The police would've alerted child protective services to take the girls away from an unfit father.

Mitch's father wouldn't give up and one day found Margaret and Kerry on the Earth Outpost. He'd brought a gun. Mitch's father wouldn't allow them peace if he couldn't find any either. He shot each one of his daughters in the head and then shot himself. Mitch was surprised his father didn't kill the full time nanny Mitch hired to take care of his sisters, but she was a smart lady and brave. ShellyAnn tried to protect the girls but his father was too strong and wild to fight against. She was knocked into a wall and hit her head. When she regained consciousness, there were three dead bodies around her.

Mitch was on a yearlong mission at the time, but was relieved of his duties to deal with the mess his father made. Mitch was devastated.

Sometimes in the middle of the night when Mitch woke up trembling, he'd confuse Edison with his father. In dreams, one minute he'd have his hands around Edison's neck, but the next moment it was his father. Sometimes his father's face would morph back and forth between Mitch's dad and Edison. Mitch hadn't learned of Jacob's twin daughters until after the news reports came out. As far as he knew, Jacob was good to his family, but he was still willing to kill innocents with that insane bombing plan and wanted Mitch dead. Someone needed to stop Edison and Mitch saw that he was the man that needed to do it.

FIFTEEN

>>> > HACE, THE LEADER of the BDP, sat in his home, a dark energy spaceship called The Architect Phantom, TAP for short, and it was never in one place for very long. If you saw the ship, it meant one of two things: you were about to be killed, or Hace liked you more than most and he trusted you.

TAP's all-black matte exterior resembled a luxury speedboat. Its reverse engine sat at the front of the vessel and pulled dark energy out of the surrounding area and powered the ship. On top of the engine, sat the bridge where his AI system, DAI, controlled everything. Hace had no interest in flying his own ship, his robotic crew handled everything for him.

Hace was upset that the BDP weren't the ones responsible for Edison's death. He wanted to teach that fucker a lesson, and the Human Resistance for that matter. He didn't care what they were trying to do, or what they "stood for." The HR stole a weapon from them and he wanted to let everyone know that wasn't acceptable.

Dax should've taken care of Edison. Hace liked Dax and respected him, but in this one instance, Dax fucked up.

So now, the situation required a remedy, a penalization for the Human Resistance and a message for its members.

And the IMC was another problem. That group was struggling to stay alive, but its leader was still capable of making trouble. Hace thought whoever he or she was, the IMC leader was unstable enough to cause galactic wars and make the IMC unpredictable. Hace wished he could find out who the leader was. It would make his life so much easier.

Hace was quickly developing a large to do list: get revenge on the HR, topple the IMC, and rule the universe. If he could just control the whole damn thing he'd command the HR and IMC members to come to him for execution, one by one. Hace would love to see that.

First though, deal with the HR…and where to find them all.

SIXTEEN

>>> > SEBASTIAN TURNED OFF all his alarms and screens and focused. He could afford no interruptions during the making of the fake Red Klix. It wasn't one of his favorite activities, but it wasn't very often he did it either. His molds were clean and the solution was prepared. He was ready. It only took a few minutes to complete, but the way he made precious stone forgeries, it was easy to blow yourself up if you didn't handle the chemicals just so. The process reminded him of making a soufflé. In both cases, sound was a disturbance that could ruin the finished product, but in one case, you wasted a dessert, and the other you were dead.

He placed the mold in the vice grip and tightened it. He put his gas mask on and made the sign of the cross over himself.

He grabbed two vials of liquid and poured them simultaneously into the mold, then he quickly got the activator and poured that in last. He held his breath. If the solution was correct, the chemicals would swirl around each other slowly, then they'd combine and solidify into a stone in three minutes.

If any measurement hadn't been correct, down to a milliliter, the whole thing would explode.

He watched the timer on his Titan: 2:48.

So far so good.

The color slowly changed from burnt yellow to deep orange.

"Double, double toil and trouble; fire burn, and cauldron bubble," he faintly whispered. He must've done it right. Then he sensed Celeste was on his floor getting off the elevator. He cursed in his mind.

He looked at the timer: 2:31.

He looked down at the mold. The color was changing again – orange to red. He carefully crept away from the mold and inched towards the door.

CHAPTER 3

FOR SERVICES RENDERED

ONE

>>> > CELESTE COULDN'T BELIEVE this is what it came to. She stood in front of Sebastian's door looking as beautiful as she could make herself. She put her hand up to the door, closed her fist, but then put her hand down. She wanted to talk to him, wanted to see his face, but she wanted him to come to her. She put her hand up, closed her fist and pulled back but couldn't knock. She just couldn't.

Sebastian knew Celeste was outside. She had strong intentions radiating from her. She wanted to talk things out and have them make up from their fight with a long and passionate night of lovemaking. Barefoot, he silently edged to the entryway.

She took the envelope out of her purse and taped it to the door; she stood there for a minute, just in case the door opened and he would look at her and apologize. One minute…two…no door flying open, no Sebastian, no apology. She had a pen and piece of notepaper in her purse. She pulled them out and looked at them, then at his door. She knew he was the kind of man that would appreciate a handwritten note from her. Something better and more profound then what was in that envelope she'd just put on his door.

He looked at his peephole screen. She looked gorgeous, and he knew she had done this on purpose to make him weaker against her. Her hair was up in curls, her face, angelic, although her eyes had a sadness about them that distressed him. But what hit him hardest was she still wore the choker he'd given her as a reminder of their mental connection. That damn purple ribbon choker.

It was times like these she wished she was a poet. She wished somehow she could express herself in some beautiful and moving way where he would understand how she was suffering, how she wanted him to come back to her. She started writing "I miss you" then stopped. *Better not*, she thought and put the note away. Maybe he'd think she was too needy.

He thought her beauty was transcendent today. His hand hovered over the door handle as he stared at her on the screen. He couldn't open the door. Had she read his email yet? What if they started arguing again? He couldn't open the door. *It was better this way*, he told himself again. *Better this way*. He watched her intently. He held his breath without realizing it. He carefully put his hand on the door handle and thought of turning it. He was willing her to knock or ring the bell just so that he'd have the excuse of needing to act.

She put her hands on his door trying to sense if he was home, if he was watching her. She was desperate to feel him somehow; she leaned over to put her forehead to the door. She thought she got a flash of him very close, but then, she feared that might've been wishful thinking. She stepped back and slowly turned around. She looked over her shoulder at his door. Nothing. Maybe he wasn't home.

He watched while she had her hands up on the door and at one point, rested her forehead against it. She was trying her damnedest to read him. He looked at her on the peephole screen until she walked away slowly. He couldn't open the door. Both his hands were on the door by then, trying to sense everything she was thinking, strengthening his mental walls, then wishing he could touch her skin again. Then she was gone. He couldn't open the door while she was standing there, but he wished he could've. The forgery needed a few more seconds of quiet. He couldn't talk to her now. The Titan alarm went off. The stone was finished.

She walked away and called the elevator. She craned her neck looking towards his door down the long hallway. Still nothing. The elevator doors opened and she stepped in, hoping he would come out and try to stop her. She pressed the lobby button and the doors closed. She was on her way down.

Once he knew the elevator closed, he opened his door and snatched the envelope quickly. Sebastian's 7's were useless right now; he was like anyone else without telepathy. With the envelope in his hands – he had no idea what she wrote. He closed the door gently and stood in his entryway wondering what she had to express that she couldn't say in person. He wondered until he felt the Titan disc in one of the envelope's corners, then he knew what she had done, and he was a little disappointed.

She had handwritten "X" across the front of the envelope. He opened it and the Titan disc tumbled into his hand. There was also a handwritten note from her:

Bastian,
This is for helping me escape since I promised I would compensate you with coren. Please take it.
This is just a small token of my gratitude. I could never put a price on my new freedom. I'm forever thankful to you.
Always,
Celeste

He slid the disc through his Titan's external device reader to see the amount.

A million coren.

He thought that was a very generous number. Too generous.

The "pay to the order of" line was blank. The memo line read "for services rendered."

He took the Titan disc and immediately destroyed it. Rescuing her that day was one of the best decisions he ever made and he refused to take payment from her for doing the right thing. She needed help and he helped her – that was all. Helping her was its own reward. He went back to his mold and saw the stone looked perfect.

TWO

>>> > D'ARTAGNAN THOUGHT OF Linda a lot lately. She passed a little over four Earth months ago, but he felt he had a lot of healing left to do.

As far as Il'laceans went, D'Artagnan was average looking, but he managed to attract numerous females of all species. He attributed this to his charm and ability to make women feel like the most attractive being in the universe. He prided himself on taking good care of his girl-friends, but Linda was the most special by far.

The first time they met almost ended in a fistfight; she was Human and he was Il'lacean after all, technically, they weren't supposed to get along and certainly not be attracted to each other.

She was at a public protest on Il'laceier with a big handwritten sign that said "Free Earth NOW!" D'Artagnan was there only because he was trying to get home but this protest was in between him and his city apartment.

Linda wasn't a troublemaker; D'Artagnan could see that when he looked at her, but the two men that stood behind her, *they* were. They lit firecrackers for a distraction and threw them into the line of Il'lacean guards. Then came a few smoke bombs from the same men and Linda and D'Artagnan ended up back to back in the chaos. She got scared and elbowed him in the stomach. It was all she could reach. The crowd became unmanageable for the guards. D'Artagnan picked up Linda, threw her over his shoulder, and got clear of the mess.

When he put her down, she yelled at him thinking he was trying to kidnap her, then she threw a punch but he caught her hand in his. He explained he was a non-violent Il'lacean bystander only trying to get to his apartment, and he believed the Il'laceans were wrong to rule over Earth.

They ended up going out for tea and that's how their relationship started. The two years they were together were some of the happiest times in D'Artagnan's life, and he thought they probably would have continued long into the future if she hadn't died.

Without all the organized protests, without Linda feeling the need to get out there and show her anger at being oppressed, she would still be alive today.

D'Artagnan was never happy about his people taking over Earth, but everything he did to fight for Earth's freedom now, was all to honor Linda's memory.

THREE

>>> > DAVID SAT IN Rem Mot Om on his throne with twenty-five beings lined up in front of him.

He went down the line, one by one, interviewing each being, trying to decide whether they were worthy of serving him.

Some were palm readers, some were psychics, but he was most interested in the telepaths and futureseers. Those were the two that were most likely legitimate.

He hired three beings in each group, but made sure they didn't communicate with each other. He wanted unbiased opinions from each one.

Their first task was to tell him more about the Human Resistance's Mitch. He was generous and gave them two Il'lacean days to come back with answers.

After the meetings were done and he'd eaten his lunch, he went to his construction crew foreman and talked about the rebuilding process. The timeline was long, and normally while robotics did most of the work, that wasn't the case here. David was becoming more distrusting of robots outside the Kingdom, thinking they might've secretly been spying devices. He insisted on live beings to do the work. The rebuilding would be slow, but it would be done right and David felt better at night knowing there were no robots working on his castle.

FOUR

>>> > MITCH HAD A bad feeling about everything. Now that he was sitting in a fully furnished, beautiful house, he thought he wouldn't be enjoying it for long. If what Gina told him was true, that the Resistance members were being hunted down and may be disappearing, he'd be the biggest prize of all. King David was cruel and hell bent on revenge.

Mitch was in a difficult spot. He didn't want to lead the Human Resistance or any other group that was protesting Il'lacean rule. He wasn't meant to be a leader. But he felt deep down something had to be done to stop King David. David felt worse to Mitch than his brother Jonathan. A year ago, he would've said there was *no one* worse than King Jon, but he was wrong.

Maybe Mitch could do something on his own. But what? People are looking to join forces, to band together and be more powerful than a single person could be. He knew David and Il'laceier could be overthrown. There were so many Humans unhappy with the current rule and they were getting more unhappy by the minute.

Things were changing on Earth, and not for the better since the bombing. King David was back on his home world and there, he'd be living near the devastation and all the lives lost. He'd have motivation to do terrible things to Humans every day.

Mitch could already see everything laid out before him. Not only would privacy be compromised for Humans on Earth, more things would be banned, less things would be imported onto the planet, maybe David could try to keep all Humans from traveling off world for a little while. This was going to go bad quickly. He needed to figure out what to do about it and fast. He scratched at his beard.

Maybe get off world before any of that happened. If he did plan on taking action, on some other world, he'd be able to act without restrictions and he could end up being much more potent off site.

But where in the universe to go? He needed a place that spoke English and a planet where things could be semi-familiar to him. He pulled up his Universal Positioning Guide on his Titan and started to explore maps of different systems.

Sho'teg? Jex? Seseer Saka? No, none of those would do.

Praxis. It was a beautiful planet, close enough to Earth and the Lanyx were a lot like Humans. He'd been there only once before and that was a decade ago. He'd like to see how it changed in the past ten years.

He got his luggage. It was a shame to leave all the new creature comforts behind, especially after living in that bunker for so long with that cheap little cot he slept on, but he felt he might be able to do the most good for Earth on Praxis. And for now, that was enough.

Mitch started packing.

FIVE

>>> > HACE "THE HUNTER" Vetitro was excited at the thought of having the Red Klix in his hands, plus having Ni-toyis naked in his bed. She was an expensive bonus, but he liked variety in his women. He just hoped she wasn't a dud in between the sheets.

Hace called out to DAI. Her full name was Deviation of Artificial Intelligence since she had an extra capability that Hace paid a lot of money for. If he couldn't get a live girl that night, or didn't feel like dealing with one, DAI could transfer herself into a sex robotic body while still maintaining her presence on the ship. It came in handy.

"DAI, what have you found out about the Red Klix?"

"Very little Master. It's almost as though it doesn't exist."

"It does exist, although a lot of beings don't want us to think so. Try looking at Praxis precious gemstones, or Praxis mythology."

"Yes Master Hunter."

Hace knew it existed. It simply had to. It was too powerful an artifact to be destroyed, unless Praxis council was afraid of it landing in the wrong hands and took it upon themselves to destroy it, but then again, he didn't even know if the damn thing *could* be destroyed. Nitoyis would figure out the logistics of getting it for him, then he'd have to figure out how to activate it, or whatever the hell it took to get it to do something.

DAI was speaking.

"What?"

"I am unable to find anything more regarding this stone. There are many articles about the mythology of Praxis and their people but no mention of this jewel. I do see that a large red ruby stone was accidentally shipped to Earth once several centuries ago from Praxis, but it was quickly returned. There is no evidence this ruby stone and the Red Klix are one and the same."

"You're kidding me right?"

"I am not Master. Is there anything else you would like me to cross reference when searching for this information?"

"No. That's all for now."

"Yes Master Hunter."

Hace thought about going for a swim. He felt a knot forming in his left shoulder, and he hated what stress did to his muscles. Better to work it out of his body.

He started moving towards the gym where the heated pool was, then changed his mind. The chef-bot caught him right outside the kitchen, "Sir Hunter, I've just run out of boiled Black Flower. Is Lilac Flower and rice preferred for dinner?"

"Affirmative."

Hace got to his bedroom and undressed. He needed to relieve tension before his swim. He called out to DAI, "Hey, take Firrepa form and come to my bedroom immediately."

"Yes Master."

DAI was worth every damn coren he paid for her.

CHAPTER 4

THE THIEF AND THE FORGERY

ONE

>>> > SEBASTIAN SENT AN email to Celeste three days ago. Anxiously, he checked his inbox and saw no reply. She was probably still angry at him, maybe she was serious about never having any contact with him again. Maybe her feelings changed since she dropped off that big coren payment. Fortunately for him, he had something else to preoccupy his time with for the next couple days. He needed to travel to a wretched and bleak planet on the fringe of the Milky Way called Embers. He'd been there once before for his boot camp in the military. It was certainly one of the harshest environments he'd ever been in and he was not looking forward to seeing its fiery horizon again.

Packing up his ammo and loading his guns, he could only wonder what Celeste was doing. He let his mind wander into the ugly landscape where she had a date with a different guy every night.

He thought of how easy it would be to pass the upcoming seven-hour transit ride to Embers if she could travel with him. Before he met her, reading was sufficient to keep his mind busy, but now things had changed and reading was not what he wanted to do most.

TWO

>>> > DAX WAS WAITING for Celeste in the afternoon sunlight. She grinned looking at him through the glass windows of her lobby. He was wearing techglasses, gray cargo shorts, and a black polo. She noticed a few Lanyx women getting an eye full as well and giggled to herself. It was time for her to have a little fun and let thoughts of Sebastian go for now.

Dax gave her a warm embrace and a long hello kiss when she exited her building. "Hello sexy," he whispered in her ear.

"Hi yourself."

"You smell amazing, if you don't mind me saying so."

"How could a girl mind getting a compliment? Thanks Dax."

He put his arm around her waist as they walked to the docking station. He apologized to her immediately when she saw his transit. "I know you're probably used to travelling in an Atlas or something, but I'll have you know the Blade is the next best thing."

"I'm not dating you for your vehicle, Daxton."

He stopped, "Is that what we're doing? Dating?"

She bit her lip. "I just meant I'm not the kind of woman who cares about how much coren someone has or what kind of transit they own, you know? I enjoy your company because I like talking to you." She hoped that was enough to end his curiosity. Geez, how could she make such a simple mistake like that?

"I get it. At least you're honest."

Did I say the wrong thing? She could take his answer at least two ways and she didn't know whether to address her verbal slip up or not. Maybe it was better if she kept her mouth shut more often.

Dax thought he might be moving too fast for her, but she was super sexy. He wanted her out of those clothes.

Dax looked over at Celeste, "I think you're going to enjoy the scenery. The view from my house is…absolutely stunning and at night when the moons come out…It's really pretty."

She was quiet.

"Listen, Celeste, I know you just lost your husband and then I come in and we start all this,"—he motioned with his hand from her to him—"maybe I'm pushing you into something you're not ready for. 'Cause if I am – just tell me please. Or if you don't want to continue this, no hard feelings okay?"

Dax wanted to give her an out.

"I'm fine, really. We're fine too. Don't worry okay? And I like you, I really do…"

"But…?" He raised his eyebrows at her.

"No, we're just two people getting to know each other. Let's keep doing what we're doing, see where it takes us. Are you enjoying seeing me?"

"Considerably. Especially in that tight short dress you're wearing."

She grinned, "And I'm enjoying being with you, so let's keep doing this as long as we both like it. Okay?"

"Agreed. Sorry, sometimes I take things a bit too seriously, or I'm a little more sensitive than most men probably…"

"It's okay. Let's just enjoy tonight. I've been looking forward to this." She smiled at him and he leaned over and kissed her on the cheek. Soon they were docking on the side of his house at the beach of Mostac.

THREE

››› › NI-TOYIS KNEW WHAT she had to do. She wasn't going to be able to steal that stone without Sebastian's help, but she could make a damn good forgery. She'd done this once a long time ago and never been caught. This one would be no different. By the time this guy, whoever he was, figured out it was a fake, she'd be long gone, out of his reach.

She was currently on the world of Mar Yen in a rented cabin with all her tools at her disposal. All she needed was a bit of uninterrupted time to focus on the delicate art of forging a gemstone. After she crafted it, it would cook for ten Mar Yenian days and then it would be time to deliver it.

She let her feelers dance around her ears and forehead as she poured the gel into its form. She thought of Sebastian. He seemed so different this last meeting. Before he was always ready to go on an adventure and take on the big challenges with her, even if he pretended not to like it. This time, he seemed more cautious than ever, maybe even guarded towards her. *What was up with that?*

"Oh fuck! Oh no!" she moaned to no one. Was it possible that he was with someone? It couldn't be! She'd known him for years and during all that time he never mentioned a love interest, a girl, a girlfriend, or anything. She thought he'd been hurt before somehow and it kept him away from relationships, but most importantly, kept him away from having one with her. He couldn't be dating someone, could he? She cringed while rolling her brilliant red eyes. They turned dark green. Just the thought of him wrapping his arms around some woman made her rage with jealously. What species was this woman? What was her name? What did she look like?

"Wait, wait, wait up. You're getting way too far ahead of yourself." She put down her jars and watched the gel react to the powder she'd added at the last second – the brown goo was turning a deep red. She walked away from the counter and moved through the kitchen into the den. Her Titan was sitting on the desk. She could just call Sebastian, see what he was up to tonight, try to casually work that question into the conversation. Or she could call her mother and ask her to do some investigating, she used to be a cop after all, but her mother was 699. The age of club dancing and partying it up before her life was over. Her mother was no longer mature enough to be reliable to keep her mouth shut about anything…she couldn't ask for her help.

Stox women started out mature to look for husbands and have babies, but as the babies grew up and left home, the mothers became fun seeking, defiant, bucket-listers who only wanted to achieve selfish, celibate goals of things they never got to do when they were younger.

The female Stox life cycle started with the first two hundred years focusing on a career. The next two hundred years were spent looking for a mate and having babies. From age 400 to 600, Stox women raised children and watched their husbands die of old age since male Stox had significantly higher levels of testosterone, they died on average two hundred years earlier than females. The last two hundred years of a Stox woman's life was devoted to celibacy and experiencing whatever she might've missed out on earlier in life. Some went back to school and studied new interests, others traveled the universe, while others like Ni-toyis's mother danced her nights away and experimented with legal drugs.

Ni-toyis felt silly. Sebastian didn't have to have a girlfriend to be acting differently. Maybe he had some guy problem, something to do with a friend or his family or work stuff. Besides, she said it herself, he's the strong and silent type. He's just being himself, keeping quiet...probably. Right?

She let out a long frustrated sigh and moved back to her gemstone mold. It looked beautiful.

It could be a million things making Sebastian act strange, but she needed to know now that the question popped into her head. She wanted to know if he had some girl waiting for him at home. The home he wouldn't invite her to. Maybe she'd push him a bit harder for a nice little sleep over, but if he said he had a girlfriend...well, "What then Nitty?"

That was the problem with having a conversation alone, there was no one there to answer your questions.

CHAPTER 5

EMBERS

ONE

>>> > SEBASTIAN'S PEARL DOCKED in a lot on Embers. He looked completely different than how Celeste saw him last. He'd taken chroma-mane for the past three days changing his natural hair color from dark brown to light blond. He hated doing it but he was wearing his hair at shoulder length today. He much preferred clean cut or bald, but he'd been wearing his hair short for the last few jobs; he needed to change up his look drastically for this hit. His mustache was something he would shave off as soon as he got home. He wore a tan three-piece suit, and a matching fedora. Instead of a cloak, he wore a long dust colored trench coat.

This assassination was to be done off the top of a high-rise building with his target in her own personal penthouse across the street. The wind was calm, while the sun crept below Ember's glowing skyline. He set up on the roof of a commercial building and put on a local water company's jumpsuit over his suit. He traded his fedora for a cap and lay on top of a blanket.

His silenced rifle loaded and ready to go, all he had to do was wait for the opportunity. An hour later, the Prime Minister was sitting on her couch watching the news while he triggered the two-minute blackout to occur in her building. Her screens went dark and she looked around quickly. He felt the walls guarding her mind crack, and he knew the first thing she worried about was her techtonic protection system failing with the lack of energy supply. He thought momentarily about how paranoid his initial thought of having two backup generators for his own system at home sounded at first, even to him, but now it didn't seem unreasonable.

He put her triangular head in his crosshairs and watched her through his scope.

Her proboscis rolled up into a spiral and then unfurled again. Her head was on a swivel as her giraffe-like neck swayed slowly back and forth.

He held his breath, steadied himself and pulled the trigger. An explosion of glass blew across her apartment and giant shards fell to the street below. Through his crosshairs, he saw her body lying on the ground, a large pool of white blood seeping across the tile floor. Papers flew around the Prime Minister's apartment like confused butterflies and floated out the window, off to relocate somewhere else. As soon as the blackout was fixed, the alarms would start, but Sebastian would be long gone by then.

What made her assassination acceptable to Sebastian was that she enjoyed the company of children in a completely unacceptable behavior. She chose little boys over men for her sexual pleasures. Pedophilia wasn't acceptable no matter where you went in the universe and no matter what species you were.

He packed up his things and looked around. He adjusted his cap with the local water company's logo on it, and quickly disappeared into the stairwell. At the bottom, he merged into a crowd of beings rushing home at the end of their workday.

He wished he could've docked his transit on top of the building, but it would've drawn too much attention and there was power equipment spread all over the roof, making landing impossible. He was tired of planning and calculating, organizing and thinking of every action he performed as well as having backup plan after backup plan in case something went wrong. Thoughts of Celeste briefly occupied his mind while he walked to his Pearl. He thought of how spontaneous things were with her and how his mind got to relax while his other instincts took over.

He sighed to himself.

Another contract fulfilled, maybe the last one he would take for a while. He needed a break away from assassinations, away from jobs, away from damn near everything and everyone. But he especially needed to get away from everything that reminded him of Celeste back on Praxis. He sat in his transit and engaged the autopilot to take him home. He knew his mind was too cluttered to give his full attention to navigating tonight.

Maybe it was time for a vacation to the very edge of the universe. Somewhere that was as far away as he could get, and he knew just the friend he wanted to go see there.

He took off the ball cap and unzipped the jumpsuit. *I wonder what she's doing right now.* He reached out with his mind trying to sense her. He knew he could never pick up anything from this kind of vast distance, but he couldn't stop himself. He yearned for some sort of connection to her. He checked his Titan to see if she sent any communications, but she hadn't. He put his head back against the seat and closed his eyes. *Need to get her out of my head for a while. I need a vacation.*

He needed to get his shit together.

Everything was resting on his shoulders suddenly. His shoulders were big, but they could never be big enough to handle this kind of weight put upon them. He couldn't turn around without staring another problem in the face: Celeste's heart, broken – from his own actions, her turning to another man for comfort, the universe unsteady at the hands of the BDP and the IMC; he couldn't get past his own self-loathing, not to mention the guilt, shame, regret, and the loneliness he'd been running from for the majority of his life. How long must he pay for what he'd done? And how long must he suffer?

He was afraid he'd never find the answers…and if he didn't, he'd lose Celeste forever. Any chance of real happiness would leave with her.

TWO

>>> > DAX'S HOUSE WAS nestled between two big mountain cliffs and he was right about the view…it was spectacular. They arrived just before sunset. His home was furnished with what he called classic Earth antiques – a 1980's chair here, a 2030's sofa there, but all of it was either gold or red. If Celeste had known the proper term for it, she would've called it minimalistic.

Dax went to the kitchen and hovered over his bar. "What do you want to drink?" he called out.

"Umm how 'bout a glass of…" (*silverberry wine*), "white wine?"

"I can do that." He opened a bottle and poured two glasses.

She looked over his living room and yelled out, "You have any music?"

He smiled, "Do I ever. A stereo from 1983 that's been completely re-built, just turn it on and you'll hear some bona fide classic rock and roll."

She looked at the front of the black box. "On," she commanded.

Nothing happened.

"Power up." She waited. She walked into the kitchen frowning, "I think your star-o thingy is broken."

"Stare-e-o," he enunciated slowly for her to pronounce correctly. "It's called a stereo and why do you think it's broken?"

"I tried to activate it, but it didn't come on."

He handed her a heavy crystal wine glass. "Did you push the button that says power?"

She tilted her head and smirked at him, "Why would I need to touch it?"

He laughed, "Because it's an antique honey-pie. You can't voice acti-vate it, you'll need to push the long black button."

"Oh."

"Are you hungry?"

"Starving, yes."

"Okay, you go try again with my stereo and I'll make some steaks." He took out his ingredients from the refrigerator and put them on the counter.

She walked back into the living room and looked again at the face of the music player. She pushed a button, then another, and another, but nothing happened. "Dax! I can't turn it on."

He unwrapped the steaks and muttered to himself, "I'm sure you could turn anything on," then louder to her, "Hold on!" He walked up next to her and pushed the rectangular button on the upper right corner and moments later, the house filled with music she'd never heard before.

She smiled, kissing him on the cheek, "My hero."

He smiled back, "You're teasing me aren't you?" He quickly turned and swept her off her feet, dipping her down close to the floor and stopped just short of kissing her, "You haven't seen nothing yet sexy."

He kissed her hard as U2 started up somewhere far away from Celeste's working mind. She was completely stunned as he lifted her up slowly and righted her.

"Do you do this often?" she asked groggily.

"What? Kiss women in my house? Tell them how to operate old electronics?" He backed away a few steps from her, edging towards the kitchen.

"No. Sweep girls off their feet, charm the hell out of them, make us putty in your hands?"

"Ha, no, I don't do this often. Listen – when you're not that attractive you have to be charming to get girl's attention, and then still, you don't get that many girls."

"I'm sorry?"

"I said, 'HA, no I don—"

"I heard you. I meant 'I'm sorry?' as in you're not attractive?"

He looked at her crooked, "I don't think you have to be that blunt. Geez, I know tha—"

She interrupted him again shaking her head, "Stop, stop, stop! Let me start over. I meant you said you're not attractive and I was questioning what you see in a mirror when you *obviously* are handsome. I wasn't saying you were ugly."

His expression changed from offended to a wry smile, "You think I'm handsome?"

She couldn't help but smile at his modesty, "Yes, I think you're very handsome." She looked him over from head to toe slowly, "You have this decadent looking light caramel colored hair, inviting green eyes, a gorgeous smile, what seems to be a fantastic body under those clothes and you dress stylishly. What's not to like?"

"You keep saying stuff like that and I'm going to kiss you again, but I won't stop," his wry smile had been replaced with a mischievous one and an arched eyebrow.

They stood facing each other for a moment like two gun fighters at a standoff, and the atmosphere crackled with just as much electricity. She swallowed hard as he approached her confidently.

She held her breath as he stopped within inches from her lips, and he whispered to her, "I've got some steaks to cook."

What did he just say?

Is he walking away from me?

Now he's being cocky. She gave him an amazing compliment and it's gone to his head. Now he thinks he has the right to tease her, bring her to the edge of a passionate cliff, and then just leave her there hanging? Well, she had to admit, he was damn good at it. Maybe better than she was…Well, tonight was going to be interesting indeed.

THREE

>>> > DAX SET UP dinner outside on the patio table so they could watch the last of the fading sun.

"…then I replied, 'Live and let die is what I always say.' " Dax broke into laughter, clapping his hands together.

Celeste's stomach hurt from laughing. She put up her hands to signal no more. "Oh my gosh"—she wiped away a tear—"your stories are hilarious! I can hardly breathe."

"Yep. I've got a few," he smiled as he finished eating and looked out over the dark ocean.

She took a deep breath and looked at him. She wondered what he was thinking. She took another sip of wine and realized none of his thoughts ever escaped him. She thought some of them should have by now.

She actively tried reaching out to his mind...but felt nothing. She tried in his transit earlier, but she couldn't get a hold of his thoughts at all. *Maybe he has strong mental walls. Maybe all Lanyx do.* He *did* have a political career and she supposed that it was important to keep secrets from being seen. His career probably trained him to keep his walls up constantly. She would've asked him about it, but Dax didn't know she had 7's and she wanted to keep it that way. Her 7's were her secret. She immediately decided the fewer people that knew about her powers, the better.

Dax stood up and went to the railing, "You wanna' walk along the shore?"

"Okay." She stood up and heard his Titan ringing.

Dax looked down at the incoming call, "I've got to take this. Why don't you head down to the beach and I'll be there in a minute."

"Alright," she took her wine glass and started down the stairs.

The steps from his patio to the sand were steep and numerous, and with as much wine as she had coursing through her veins, she worried about falling in her high heels, but she reached the bottom safely.

Dax walked into the house and stood in the kitchen before he picked up the audio call.

"Why are you calling me now, Redgar?!"

"I apologize. Are we moving ahead with the plan tonight, sir?"

Dax hesitated before answering. He saw Celeste's silhouette on the moonlit shore, "Negative. Abort the operation."

"What?! Something go wrong or were you unable to get her to the extraction point?"

"You don't ask the questions, I do. I give you orders, dipshit, and I call the shots. I can think on my feet and re-evaluate situations as they come up and that's why you answer to me. The operation will *not* happen tonight. Is that perfectly clear?"

"Yes sir, but we've been working towards this for a while. We need her. This could be really good for us."

"It's up to me to decide what her most useful purpose is. I'll be back at the complex tomorrow and I'll discuss what our next steps are with all of us present. Tell the others I expect everyone to attend this meeting or I'll personally castrate all you idiots. And don't disturb me again."

"Understood, sir."

Dax terminated the call, gritted his teeth, and put his hand to his forehead. Then he rushed to the back deck and hurried down the stairs to Celeste.

"Sorry. That was work. I swear they can't figure out simple instructions."

"That's okay. I've been enjoying your view here and the last of my wine," she hiccuped.

He took the glass from her and put it down on one of the steps, then he held her hand while she kicked off her heels. He wrapped an arm around her waist and started walking towards the water, holding her firmly against his hip.

The water was cool sliding across her feet and it sobered her up from her buzz slightly.

"You okay?" he squeezed her gently.

"Sure, I'm really relaxed that's all. Maybe we could sit down?"

"On the sand? I didn't think you'd want to get your dress dirty."

"That's fine, it won't mind."

They made themselves comfortable far enough away from the tide. Celeste surprised him by laying down.

He followed her lead and said, "I hope you had a good time tonight."

"Oh, for sure darling. And you make a great steak. It was an excellent meal."

"Thanks."

They quietly lay next to each other watching the skies for a while before he spoke again.

"Celeste, I need to say something. I think you're a really great girl with a lot to offer and I'm pleasantly surprised that you keep wanting to hang around with me. I saw you that night at your table alone and wondered how it was possible that someone as beautiful as that could be eating alone. I saw you in the news before and I thought you were pretty then, but in person, you're a total knock out," he paused, choosing his words carefully, "I'm a little worried, actually a lot worried, about what you'll think of me after I tell you this...I have a confession and I hope you'll understand. You remember how I told you that I needed help with my ex-girlfriend that night we met?"

He waited for her response.

"Celeste?"

He looked away from the stars and over to her. He noticed her eyes were closed.

"Celeste? Are you asleep?" he gripped her arm shaking her gently. She was completely out.

"Ah shit, I gave you too much." He stood up and carefully put her over his shoulder, carrying her up all sixty-two steps to the house.

CHAPTER 6

SIX GLASSES

ONE

>>> > CELESTE WOKE UP hearing a foghorn rolling deep somewhere in the distance. Her eyes opened slowly to see an unfamiliar bedroom. She looked down and saw she was only wearing her panties and bra. Her dress was hanging off the back of a chair. She jumped out of bed and instantly regretted it. She put her hands to her head and tried to hold it still. Her brain was throbbing. *I drank way too much last night. Oh my God this hurts.* Her vision doubled, and then cleared up. She slowly moved towards her dress and put it on.

She opened the bedroom door carefully and looked for Dax. She saw him sleeping on the couch. She slipped out the front door as quietly as possible and called a bot-taxi. On the way home she thought she should've left a note, but no, better that she hadn't. She was embarrassed at her drunkenness last night and she didn't remember everything that happened yet. Better just to leave.

T W O

>>> > BACK AT HER apartment, Celeste took a few pills for her headache after she showered. She crawled into bed and tried to recall details of last night. She remembered Dax picking her up, a steak dinner, white wine, a lot of white wine, and laughter. A beach walk? Or an attempt at least.

Her Titan rang.

Her heart skipped a beat thinking it could be Sebastian, but no, it was Dax. She didn't answer and he left a message. She immediately watched it.

"Hi Celeste. I hope you're okay. I woke up and you weren't here. I guess you didn't leave any messages for me or else I didn't see them. I hope I didn't do anything to upset you. If I did, I sincerely apologize for whatever it might've been. Please let me know you're okay."

Ohhh God, why did I drink all that wine?! Dax was nice enough and now she was making him worry. He looked concerned in his video message. She should call him. She curled into a ball and thought about calling him for the next ten minutes. Then he called again, but this time she answered. She kept it an audio call only. She was sure she looked like hell.

"Celeste? You okay?"

"Um, other than a massive headache, yeah," she closed her eyes tightly, rubbing her temple with her free hand.

"I was worried when I saw you were gone this morning. I hope I didn't frighten you off."

"Oh no, not at all. I…must've acted like an idiot last night. I'm sure I made a fool of myself and I needed to get home…really, it's nothing you did. I'm just…did we…do anything last night? I don't remember a lot after dinner."

"No, absolutely not. I would remember that," he chuckled. "No, you passed out on me after we laid down on the sand and I carried you to my bedroom so you could sleep it off."

"I…don't remember…but I woke up out of my dress. You undressed me?"

"Yes, but we didn't have sex, Celeste. I promise. What *is* the last thing you remember?"

"I took off my shoes…we were going to walk on the beach."

"Oh, then you probably didn't mean to call me darling on purpose?"

Darling?

"Geez Dax, I'm sorry. I really let myself get out of hand. I acted like a complete ass."

"You're fine, babe. No need to apologize. I gave you too much wine that's all. I should've cut you off after the sixth glass."

"Six?! Oh my God! I don't remember having that many!"

"It's all okay. I'll know better for next time."

She was so embarrassed she couldn't think about facing him again.

"I need more headache medicine so if you don't mind, I'll talk to you later."

"Sure, I hope you feel better. Drink lots of water and get some sleep."

She ended the call quickly and tossed her Titan on the nightstand.

I don't remember having six glasses of wine. She thought back and counted how many she had. She got to three and then couldn't remember any more, but she wasn't in any shape to have an accurate count. Maybe she had more wine on the beach? Or at dinner? Or before dinner?

It really bothered her how drunk she got. She usually didn't drink like that, but she was under some special circumstances right now. Mainly her broken heart courtesy of Sebastian. Her mind's eye trapped her in a memory of the way his hand glided down her body and rested at the base of her spine. He was gentle and careful then. A single tear fell down her cheek. Even though she wanted to fight it, she allowed memories of their time together to flood her mind. Goddamn she missed him. Messed up, emotionally scarred, his erratic behavior and all…she missed him terribly.

THREE

>>> > D'ARTAGNAN SAT IN Eric's home on Jex. The two men were introduced to each other by Sebastian and without him, they would've never met. Even though all three of them were in some of the same wars, D'Artagnan fought with the Il'lacean Water Forces Command.

Sitting in Eric's drinking parlor, they cracked open their first beers. Eric had a built-in bar, pool table, video games, and a simulator room in the back.

D'Artagnan's taste in environments was vastly different than Eric's. Eric liked dark woods and deep colors so his drinking parlor ended up looking like a cave, granted a nice looking warm cave, but a cave nonetheless. D'Artagnan lived on a planet that was full of caves, and he avoided them as much as possible. His life and mind were dark enough as it was these days. He needed sunlight, or at least, comforting light environments. Even with D'Artagnan's home being buried deep in the foggy Swamplands Regions, the interior of his home was light and cozy.

"So how is the assassinary going lately?"

"I don't think 'assassinary' is a word man."

Eric shook his head, "You know what I mean, asshat."

"It's going okay. I could use more tips from you and Raynes, but I'm sure I'll get better with more time and practice," D'Artagnan finished off the last of his beer.

"The beginning is always hard. That's true with everything...which reminds me, how has the dating been going?"

D'Artagnan sighed, "You know I'm not even thinking about that. I'm still grieving."

"I know. I'm not saying it's wrong. I'm saying...you know, take your time and all...but there's a lot of living left for you to do. I don't think Linda would want you to sit around and be sad all the time. I think she'd want you to be happy." Eric chugged the last half of his beer and threw the bottle across the room into the recycle bin.

D'Artagnan stood up and almost hit his head on some decorative antlers sticking out of the side of the wall. D'Artagnan knew Lanyx were part animal and supposed to be peaceful but Eric wasn't a typical Lanyx.

The antlers were well above Eric's head, but D'Artagnan was 7'2." "You want to play a game of pool?"

"Sure. You're going to cheat, but whatever."

D'Artagnan grabbed some cues off the wall after giving his friend a dirty look, "You and your cheating theories...Listen, I know your intentions are good. You want me to get out there and see what kinds of women are available, but..."

Eric grabbed one of the pool cues from his friend and shifted it from hand to hand, "But what? You rack."

D'Artagnan put his cue against the table and racked up the balls, "I'll date only when *I'm* ready. It doesn't matter how many people tell me to go out there and do it."

Eric leaned on the table, "I just think...you're always going to say you're not ready yet."

"Has the thought occurred to you that I might never be?"

Eric grabbed a beer out of the ice bucket off the bar behind him and opened up the bottle, "You guys live a hell of a long time. Longer than Raynes and me *combined*. I just think...well, forget it. I know you don't want me to push and I can't make you do anything you're unwilling to. Let's change the subject. I'll let you break."

D'Artagnan bent over the table awkwardly to take the first shot, "I appreciate it, Bouton." He hit the cue ball hard and the balls slammed across the felt. "I forgot how short this table is for my long legs."

"That's because this table was made for normal people and *you* are not a normal person."

"I'm exceptional. Is that what you're saying?" D'Artagnan sunk the 9 ball into the corner pocket.

Eric watched him as he sunk two more balls, "Just get a piece of ass at least. It might make you feel better."

D'Artagnan put his head back, "Really dude? Seriously? Can we please stop talking about women?"

"I'm not talking women, I'm talking pussy. It's different."

D'Artagnan shot him an annoyed glance.

"Okay, okay. How 'bout just a sex robot? Could you start there for me?"

"With the way you're pushing this, I'd think it was your dick we're talking about and not mine."

Eric laughed, "Well, now that you mention it. It has been way too long for Mr. Pointy to find a nice wet home. We should go to a robo-tech brothel some night. I'll buy you an hour if you win this game."

D'Artagnan studied his friend, "I don't know. I'm already winning. I should get to call what I want if I win."

"Well, if I win, I want you to buy at the brothel," Eric grinned.

D'Artagnan sighed, "Okay. That's if you win, but you're not going to. If *I* win…all I want is for you to shut the fuck up about pussy, dating, women, and anything remotely close to the subject of females…of any species."

"Deally-o Steely-o," Eric laughed, then he paused, "Wait. For how long am I not allowed to talk about that stuff?"

FOUR

>>> > AFTER SLEEPING HALF the day away and eating dinner, Celeste figured it was time to finally respond to Sebastian's email. She'd put it off long enough.

"I don't know how to address this so I won't.

Sorry it's taken me a while to respond, I've been really busy with things.

For the possibility of helping other beings, but especially Humans, I will assist you in any way I can.

Let me know what information you seek.

I want to mention again how much finding out what really happened with my parents means to me. I know I need that closure one way or another. Thank you for your help.

Sincerely,

C"

She didn't know what else to say and sent it off.

As she sat looking at the blank screen, her Titan rang. Could Sebastian be responding already? She closed her eyes hard and pleaded, "Please be Sebastian. Please be Sebastian. Please be Sebastian!"

She opened one eye and looked. No…it was Dax. Again. She left it as an audio call…again. She still didn't have any makeup on or her hair done.

"Hey, Daxton."

"Hey there, beautiful. How you feeling now?"

"A lot better thanks. I hung around the house all day getting rest and taking it easy."

"I won't make small talk, I'll just cut to the chase. I know you felt awkward with the way our last date ended so I was wondering if I could make it up to you by taking you out again. Whadda' think?"

She hesitated, "I don't know…"

"I think you're a fantastic woman and I'd be a fool to let you slip through my fingers because you drank a little too much the other night. It happens to all of us sooner or later. Don't let it stop us from getting to know each other better. It's already forgotten if you ask me. But I would really like to see you again."

"I think you saw enough of me last time."

"No, well, I left the lights off and it was dark in that room. I tried to be respectful, but I have to be honest, I did peek…a little. If it makes you feel any better, I knew you had an amazing body before I saw you without your dress on."

She blushed and didn't know how to respond.

He cleared his throat, "Okay, I went too far. Sorry, shouldn't have said that."

There was a long uncomfortable silence on the line.

"How 'bout I start over?"

"Okay."

"Hey Celeste, sorry I took you out of your clothes while you were drunk the other night. I should've just left you to sleep in the bed in your dress. Totally ungentlemanly of me, I'm an insensitive bastard. Really sorry about that. How about I make it up to you? We can go for lunch at a restaurant, your choice. I'll meet you there, and we won't drink. How about that?"

She giggled at his playful mood and couldn't help but try again, "All right, it's a date. How about the French restaurant Jacques? Do you know where it is?"

"Of course, yeah, it's ten minutes west of your apartment building right?"

"Mmm hmmm. You wanna' meet around one o'clock tomorrow?"

"Sure. I'll be there. I'll be a perfect gentleman this time, no worries."

Now she felt silly about leaving him sleeping on the couch in the first place, "Great, I'll see you then." *Sebastian's loss could be Daxton's gain. If I can ever get over Sebastian that is.*

FIVE

>>> > D'ARTAGNAN WON THE game of pool.

Eric and D'Artagnan decided on a whim, to go to the world market, pick up some sandwiches, and have a picnic in the park. D'Artagnan wanted to soak up the sunshine and Eric wanted to watch the girls walk by.

D'Artagnan lay on his back after he ate and put his hands behind his head with his eyes closed. The sun could dry out his skin if he wasn't careful, but he didn't plan on being out here that long.

Eric sat cross-legged and tapped his techglasses into existence. He watched as three college girls walked by, "D'Art, man, you're missing out on all the good stuff!"

D'Artagnan opened one eye and squinted, "If by 'good stuff' you mean women, you're not allowed to mention them."

Eric sat quietly after that.

D'Artagnan asked, "You have any dreams of the war?"

Eric replied, "Pfffft. Dreams? No. Dreams make it sound all pleasant and shit, like we were on holiday or something," he paused, "No; I have flashbacks that come up out of nowhere. I have soul-crushing, mind-destroying, heartbreaking memories of the wars I've been in. I have terrible, vivid, horrendous nightmares. Why are you asking?"

D'Artagnan opened his eyes and sat up on his elbows, "I have spans of time where I'm fine and nothing bothers me much, and then I have stretches where I can't sleep because every time I close my eyes, all I see is war. If I do get to sleep, I'm plagued by these atrocious nightmares. It's like I'm there all over again."

"I know the feeling man. I think that's the price we pay for fighting someone else's war like that. When I signed up for the military, I knew it wasn't going to be easy, but I didn't think it was going to be like *that* either. The coren they paid us, it wasn't enough to deal with what we went through. Now I gotta see that shit all the time in my nightmares. I'll never forget the horrors we saw, or the things I did. But, that time's over now. We're doing something for ourselves. We're done with the militaries and the wars."

"Linda used to help me with these. She used to calm me down."

Eric shook his head, "Okay, so I know I'm not supposed to say this, but, that's what I'm talking about with you and dating. If a woman in your life helped you deal with all the shit we have to put up with and if having someone helps you cope and takes the edge off, don't you want to find someone eventually to sleep next to? Okay, I'm sorry. Won't say any more about it. Mouth is sealed."

D'Artagnan nodded. Eric had a point, but D'Artagnan didn't say that. He didn't say anything.

SIX

›› › HACE WAS ON his Titan making calls all day. First up was his team leader on Earth who was looking for HR members.

"Britton, what have you got for me?"

Britton shook his head, "Nothing sir. The HR seemed to have disbanded after the attack on Rem Mot Om. We found their bunker in the desert. It was covered with dirt and shrubs, but we moved those and found someone had poured concrete on top of what might've been the entrance."

"You haven't found any individuals yet?"

"No sir. I'm not giving up though. I just need a little more time to chase some of my leads and see what I come up with."

"Good work Britton. I'll check back in with you after a while."

Next was his team on Embers.

"Concabe, what happened over there? Are the news reports accurate?"

Concabe was in the middle of a late night riot. Hace could see a fist-fight starting behind him. "Sir, my spot just erupted with activity. I'm going to try to get away from it. Hold on."

Hace watched Concabe's Titan bounce around as the Denigen ran for a safe place to report from. Hace used to have the Prime Minister of that planet in his pocket, but her security slipped somehow and the news reported she'd been assassinated. Now, it looked like the Denigens were upset and confused enough to be rioting over it.

Concabe finally returned on Hace's Titan, "I apologize sir. I had to move."

"Of course. What happened?"

Concabe's six eyes reflected a fire somewhere in a building nearby. He kept looking from side to side. "We're highly unstable here. I'm thinking of jumping off world right now. As far as I can tell, the reports are accurate. PM Lightstone has been killed. An assassin got to her somehow in her apartment. Once news started spreading here, Denigens took to the streets and started fighting anything that moved. They lit some buildings on fire, torched some police transits, even flipped them over if you can believe that." He looked behind him as a transit exploded and he instinctively ducked, even though he was far enough away to avoid getting hurt. "Sir, I have to finish my report off world. I can't stay here. I always thought we were better than this. I never figured my people would…do this much damage like this."

"It's okay. Listen Concabe, be safe and get out of there as fast as you can. I'll expect your report no later than ten Embers hours from now. The Hunter over and out."

Concabe nodded and Hace's Titan went to black, then returned to the main menu screen.

It looked like Embers was going to hell in a hurry. It might've been a surprise to Concabe, but Hace knew under the right circumstances, any group of seemingly peaceful people could turn violent. They just needed the right push.

Hace had multiple irons in the fire all across the universe, he'd be on his Titan making calls until late in the night. That's why he only did these massive checkups once a month.

He sighed and dialed the next number.

SEVEN

>>> > ULYSSES LED THE infiltration team to the BDP's Cepheus branch.

Ulysses disliked Cepheus, it was too damn cold for nearly anything to live here, but he needed to do David's bidding for now. They found the recruiter and talked with him for forty-five minutes, then the men found a cheap motel to stay at for the week while they were doing recon. Ulysses would come pick them up in six days for the full report before he brought their findings to David.

Over the course of that week, Ulysses became concerned that the men were going to stay with the BDP. He heard less reporting in their daily messages and more complaining about how the IMC couldn't compete with how the Brotherhood operated.

The day he was supposed to pick them up, he got a notification they weren't coming back.

Ulysses went to the King. He cleared his throat to get David's attention but David seemed out of it lately. He often sat in his throne with his crown on and full robes giving the wall a thousand yard stare.

David blinked a few times, "Oh, it's you Benson. What have the men discovered?"

Ulysses shifted from one foot to the other, "It seems that the BDP is more technologically advanced than we are, possibly better armed as well. The men reported seeing stock piles of ammo, an arsenal of weapons, tons of drugs at their disposal and lots of members at the two meetings they attended."

David frowned, "Great. What are their plans? Do we know what their next move is?"

Ulysses shook his head, "The men gave me the little information that I've passed along to you, but said they chose to become permanent members of the Brotherhood. Something about how they felt the vibe there was younger and seemed to be more in tune with what its members wanted to do. I personally thought they were a bunch of losers anyways."

David slammed his fist down on the arm of his chair, "Left us for the BDP again? What could I possibly offer these fools to keep them here? I'm only twenty-four for Khaleen's sake! I'm practically an infant; you can't get much younger than that! Fuck!"

Ulysses winced on the inside, but outside, he stood motionless and unflinching. "I agree totally with you sir. Like I say, if these assholes are so eager to leave, we're better off without them. We need people that are strong minded, not easily swayed by outside forces."

David listened to him and surprisingly agreed, "Yes, we're better off without them, but I'm unhappy losing more members. That's happening a bit too much lately. Do you see that?"

"Yes sir. Maybe we need to develop some sort of tests for members to pass before allowing them to get too far into the organization, you know? Weed out the weak ones. Only my opinion though."

David nodded, "Yes, maybe you're right. That sounds like a good idea. Why don't you go ahead and implement that immediately. Come to me tomorrow with some ideas of tests."

"Yes sir. I appreciate your time."

David nodded and waved his hand, telling Ulysses to leave.

EIGHT

>>> > PREVIOUSLY, DAVID'S PALM readers, psychics, futurecasters, and telepaths gave him their first report, and it hadn't gone well. The palm readers read David's hands and said completely different things to him. The psychics all described Mitch differently. The futurecasters gave multiple answers to all questions and the telepaths said they could talk to Mitch but couldn't hear what he replied in their heads.

So today, David didn't have much hope. After his second consultation with all of them failed miserably, he made a decision.

David fired all of them; each and every single one of them were phonies. He couldn't believe he thought he might actually get something useful from these people. Perhaps there were some futurecasters or telepaths out there that were legit, but maybe they weren't for hire. He would still wear his special crown though, can't be too cautious.

NINE

>>> > MITCH HAD SOME experience with shady characters and dark government secrets, but he never actively searched out an information man.

He had to go under the bridge in an old beat up town called Havasuez City. People talked about how there used to be water under the bridge instead of a safe haven for the homeless, but Mitch couldn't believe that.

He talked with some of the most unsavory people he'd ever seen and got a name. He called that name on a secure Titan connection and found Jacob's location, then pretended to be the deliveryman.

Mitch would wake up in the middle of the night with terrible flashbacks: his hands around Jacob's neck, his fists making contact with the old man's jaw, the way Jacob's body went limp when all the life finally drained out of him.

Sometimes, Mitch wondered if he did the right thing, then he remembered Jacob wanted him dead first. That he had paid someone to kill Mitch. What else was he supposed to do? Wait to be killed?

TEN

>>> > "HEY HUNTER, I'VE got your stone."

Hace shook his head, "My name's not Hunter, it's *The Hunter*."

Ni-toyis rolled her eyes as her feelers swam around her face, "Yes, of course. My apologies, sweetness."

Hace smiled on the audio only Titan call, "I'm glad to hear that…and you're early dear. How wonderful for me. How soon are you available to drop it off?"

"Well that's entirely your call, sugar. I aim to please and I want your *full* satisfaction with my performance, so just tell me when you want me…there and I'll come for you."

"Oooooh naughty girl. Such innuendos from your pretty little mouth. I can't wait to see you…and my stone. Why don't you meet me on Mar Yen in two bliiks around lunchtime. Is that good for you?"

She pulled up her calendar quickly to see if she was free, "Oh yes, hon. I can do that. I'll see you soon handsome."

"Thanks babe. I look forward to our time together."

Ni-toyis terminated the call and felt sick to her stomach. She needed Sebastian in more than one way right now and she got nervous at the thought of calling him.

ELEVEN

TITAN Corporation - Personal TITAN Device

System Status: Active -- Universal Grid: Online

Current Time/Date (Il'laceier - Rem Mot Om): 19th Knoche/ Newai 51-4, 5390

Secondary Time/Date (Earth - Silver Thorn): 4:58 a.m./July 27, 4015

Current Universal Positioning System Location: Kingdom Regions, Il'laceier.

User: Kingdom Guard Cagi, Kingdom Guard Oud, Kingdom Guard Nadipp, Kingdom Gua-(touch here to expand for seven others)

Communications Menu

Incoming message(s) received: 1 - Status: New/Unread

Message Received at 19th Knoche

Message Sent from: Royal Communication from The Kingdom of
Rem Mot Om

-Guards¬
I know this mission has been a lengthy one for you. I
wanted to express my gratitude in your constant efforts to
help locate Human Resistance members.
I encourage you to keep looking as we have already located
five Humans and I know there are many more still in hiding.
Your financial account has been updated with its (Earth)
monthly/(Il'lacean) atchoud allowance and there is still
currently no end date for your mission.
Please keep up the good work.
King Hennessy II of Earth and Il'laceier Kingdoms

-END OF MESSAGE
*This message will auto-delete in 32 knoches.
- -

TWELVE

>>> > MITCH WOKE UP in a cold sweat. He threw the covers off him and
went to the thermostat — sixty-five degrees. It wasn't too hot to sleep, it
was the nightmares again.

He went to the refrigerator, poured an ice-cold glass of water, and
drank it down. He wiped the sweat off his face and stood in his pajama
bottoms looking around his kitchen. He tried to forget the images that
kept flashing in his mind. His hands on Edison's neck, Hap Du Wan,
Reid, the Brotherhood, the HR, his father. He never killed anyone with
his bare hands before Edison. He never snapped like that before either.
It scared him.

He wished his sisters were here. He adored them since they were
born. They were sweet and funny and both were great listeners. He
missed them.

CHAPTER 7

THE SPECIAL POWERS OF XU'XI

ONE

>>> > SEBASTIAN STOOD OUTSIDE the Praxis Council Building in the center of downtown. It was a busy area full of pedestrian traffic and transits, but not at 2 a.m.

Xu'Xi arrived cloaked in a black trench coat. His glowing suit remained hidden underneath.

Sebastian nodded discreetly to him, "I like your threads. That coat do anything special?"

"No, it's just a coat dude. You ready for this?"

"Yes. I was about to ask you the same thing."

"I was *born* for this," Xu'Xi grinned.

They started in the direction of the museum, which was right next to the Council Building. The buildings shared a kitchen to supply food to both. Sebastian headed for the back door where the trash cans were and Xu'Xi took off the soft rubber padding he wore around his head.

Sebastian silently pointed to a small numeric pad next to the door handle.

Xu'Xi nodded and removed one of his gloves. He touched the pad and it went from glowing blue to orange. In the one and a half seconds before it reset its code, Sebastian opened the door with his own gloved hand and allowed Xu'Xi to walk in first. The kitchen camera fizzled out from a power surge.

Sebastian looked around and carefully, quietly closed the door behind them.

The kitchen was dimly lit by a few emergency lights that stayed on overnight for the cleanup crew, but they had long since cleared out of the building. As Xu'Xi got closer to each light, they overloaded and burnt out.

Sebastian turned on his dark energy flashlight and went left towards the Council Building. Xu'Xi followed.

The Red Klix was kept four floors down in a room that had eighteen levels of security around it. Any ordinary thief would trigger an alarm almost instantaneously once they tried to get past the kitchen, but Xu'Xi Darksent was anything but an ordinary thief.

In the Wishbone Galaxy, deep within the Vast System, was a planet called Greeve. The Inclick people looked like any other Humanoid species, going about their daily activities and running errands. Children went to school and adults went to their jobs. But after closer inspection, the outside observer would see something highly abnormal.

On Greeve, there were no electronics. There was nothing using anything like electricity and there was a good reason for that. The Inclicks put out a much higher than normal level of electric current from their bodies, which shorted out most electronic devices. A nickname the species quickly earned was "the EMP people" and EMP stood for Electro Magnetic Pulse. On Greeve, there were many alternatives to electricity like solar power, wind power, and hydropower, but the most popular choice worldwide was dark energy, even with its incredibly high cost. Inclick's EMPs never interfered with dark energy, but short-circuited everything else.

Many worlds quickly banned the Inclicks from visiting because they could destroy electronics simply by walking around, so the Inclicks developed a suit for travel that absorbed their abundance of electricity and funneled it into batteries for bartering or sale. They called it a prosperity generator suit or PGS for short. They refused to be stranded on their own planet, never to travel the universe.

The Inclicks were then allowed to visit most other worlds, but still had to obtain a pass from the Universal Travel Agency and give advance notice as to where they were traveling along with arrival and departure dates to the embassy offices of each world. It was something no other race had to do, but the Inclicks understood that they had a particular power that, in the wrong hands, could do great damage. They could easily bypass all sorts of security systems of world governments and financial institutions. What really bothered the Inclick were the worlds that still had bans on them – places like Earth, Il'laceier, and a few others. The Inclicks were willing to jump through hoops due to their power and be monitored, but they didn't like prejudice against them. A few unscrupulous individual Inclicks were the exception and not the rule.

Xu'Xi Darksent was one of the unscrupulous ones. He frequently traveled throughout the universe thieving items of immense power, wealth, or historical value for clients with such requests. He figured out ways to bypass most security systems that would prevent other Inclicks from traveling abroad illegally and when he couldn't figure it out, he had a trifecta of assassins on three other planets that he constantly consulted with for various jobs and information.

On the fourth basement floor was an ordinary looking door labeled "storage." Outside the door was a numeric keypad alongside a fingerprint lock. Xu'Xi pointed his finger at the keypad and it went from blue to orange. Sebastian quickly turned the handle and the door opened.

Xu'Xi turned off his PGS and stepped inside. Every alarm system, camera, light, and detection device blew circuits, short-circuited, or overloaded.

Sebastian, on light, careful, cat feet, slid over to the corner cabinet and removed the metal housing that covered the Red Klix.

Xu'Xi whispered as he looked at his dark matter watch, "Ten seconds."

Sebastian quickly replaced the real stone with the fake one and put the lid over the forgery. Xu'Xi flipped his suit back on, and they slipped outside the door and watched as the orange light on the keypad went blue. It had reset itself and appeared to be fine.

The walls of the "storage" room were five feet thick and made of solid steel. The damage Xu'Xi's natural EMPs had been limited to the interior of the room.

Sebastian heard footsteps down the hall behind them. The one thing they could not short-circuit were other people.

They quickly moved in the direction they had come from and were now outside the kitchen door.

Xu'Xi put on his gloves and rubber padding around his head, then adjusted his trench coat and they were moving again. Xu'Xi couldn't help but check his Antslousen to see if their unauthorized cavorting through government buildings had been detected.

Sebastian looked back at him and said over his shoulder, "Are those better than Titans or worse would you say?"

"Way more awesome. Titan Corp will never be able to make anything we Inclick like more than our Antslousens."

The Titan Corporation was currently trying to design a special Inclick-rated Titan that would run on dark energy, but to date their test Titans were unsuccessful and highly unstable, catching fire within the first fifteen minutes of use.

Dark energy, while abundant in the universe, was a relatively new power source harnessed for uses other than military applications. The generators required to capture and transform the energy were mostly bulky and extraordinarily expensive. Sebastian's dark energy flashlight cost two hundred seventy-five thousand coren. Most families could choose to have a house or a flashlight for that kind of money.

The Inclicks were a group of highly intelligent beings and even though they couldn't wear "real" Titans, an Inclickian inventor created a device very much like a Titan called an Antslousen in Click-talk, but translated in English to Giant.

Sebastian stopped when they reached Ring Leaf Square at the base of the nine-story clock.

"So, does your Giant say we were successful or no?"

Xu'Xi smiled, "Success! No one knows we were there although the power anomalies have been reported and are being checked out as we speak."

Sebastian took the roll of cash coren out of his attaché case and handed it over to Xu'Xi.

"It was lovely doing business with you Armand, as always."

"Thanks to you this was an easy job. Would've taken me months to find a way around all those safeguards on my own. I appreciate it Xu'Xi."

"Let me know if you need any further assistance, but I might go on vacation here with this kind of bank roll," he smiled.

"Understood. Enjoy it."

"Later Armand."

Sebastian watched Xu'Xi stroll into the night, then turned around, and did the same.

When Sebastian got home, there was a secret place inside a marble sculpture that housed the Red Klix nicely. No one would ever find it there.

TWO

>>> > SEBASTIAN WAS TIRED of the Titan ringing. He would leave a damn message for this woman if she didn't pick up soon.

Suddenly Ni-Toyis was on his Titan's screen, "Hey sexy."

Sebastian rolled his eyes, "Tredux, I have some bad news."

"This is not the way I want to start off a conversation with you. What is it?" Ni-Toyis frowned.

"The Red Klix has been stolen."

She smiled, "Oh you little devil. You *did* do it after all. I knew you'd come aroun—"

"No, I didn't steal it. Someone else did."

Ni-Toyis shook her head. Her feelers darted around her face, "That's not possible. I haven't seen anything in the news about this. Where are you getting your information?"

"The news won't have anything about it. They don't know it's been stolen. I was doing some research and found out that someone swiped it four years ago. A private entity although I don't know what they wanted it for. I heard it from a source I trust. I paid a lot of money for this info. Trust me, the gem is a fake inside the Council Building."

Ni-Toyis licked her lips, "You stole it didn't you? You just don't want to tell me."

"No, I didn't. I told you I didn't want to get anywhere near this job and I meant it."

"This sounds like a whole bunch of bullshit to me."

Sebastian looked at her sideways, "You can believe whatever you want. You can even try to steal the phony one, but it's only going to get you in a lot of trouble for a fake stone."

Ni-toyis didn't know what to make of this. It was something she definitely hadn't expected. Sebastian knew how to get information that just couldn't be found by most others. He had never outright lied to her either. He might've made things…more difficult for her in the past, but he didn't lie. And she hadn't done the research she should have for this particular job, since she knew Sebastian would be involved, she'd been a little lazier than normal. Maybe he *was* telling her the truth. Plus, she knew, if the stone had been stolen, it would be pandemonium on Praxis. That stone was soooo special to those people, it would make sense if a theft had happened that it probably wouldn't be revealed to the public… and the last thing she wanted to do was steal a fake. She had to believe he was telling the truth.

"So where is the stone now?" she frowned.

"I'm not sure. The private entity seems to be keeping it…private. I checked on the black market, but it's not there. It's out of my reach. Sorry."

Ni-toyis sighed with displeasure, "Well, what am I supposed to do now sugar? I can't tell my client this…"

"Not if you want the job, no. But honesty is a very good policy, in limited quantities, I suppose. It's up to you, but I wanted to pass along what I found, not that I'm considering it a fulfillment of my obligation to you."

Ni-toyis smiled, "Well, that's good because it wouldn't count for me either." She rubbed a temple with one of her fingers, "I'll figure it out, thanks sweetheart. We'll talk later."

Sebastian's Titan went to its main menu screen and he smiled.

THREE

>>> > "SO WHAT'S UP at Silver Thorn?" Celeste played with her hair absent-mindedly.

Ginger smiled, "Not much really, which is okay with me. Better to have nothing going on around here than something bad."

"What are you ladies-in-waiting doing without a lady to wait on anyway?"

Ginger laughed, "Well, Lila's tending to all the uniforms of the female staff and clothes for any photo ops of David, I'm doing makeup and hair for them, but not much else. V's going around looking busy. I'm worried David's going to catch on and fire her."

"Oh no! David's busy though, I doubt he's paying too much attention to you all."

"The Council has time though. They're around here often lately. Lots of meetings with David behind closed doors."

Celeste waved her hand, "I'm sure they're setting rules and guidelines, probably figuring each other out. That's to be expected when there's a new king."

"I'm still worried. They could be looking at budgets and seeing where to cut corners. They could let all of us go. Then what'll I do?"

Celeste frowned and then thought, "You'll have to come work for me I guess."

Ginger laughed, "Yeah, I guess that'd be an alright gig, but you're living on Praxis. I don't know anyone there besides you and all my family's on Earth."

Celeste put a hand through her brown locks, "My hair needs your help, but I don't think you're going to lose your job in the first place, so this is all moot."

By the time they hung up, Celeste wondered if they'd really lose their jobs or not. She could afford to hire them and have a place where they all could live. She was sure there were mansions on Praxis, but then, wouldn't that be kind of weird?

She had a staff before buzzing around her all the time, but what would Sebastian say? If they were together, she'd be hidden or covered up in some capacity when they were out, so what would be the point of having a staff? Then she'd have to explain everything to the girls and Sebastian definitely didn't want that. She sighed.

She missed Sebastian.

She really would have to give up everything and everyone she knew to be with him, but she still wanted him.

More than anything.

But she knew, you can't always get what you want. Compromises had to be made.

So maybe she just kills time with Daxton until Sebastian comes to his senses. Problem was – what if he never came back?

FOUR

NI-TOYIS CALLED SEBASTIAN, "So sweetie pie, you're off the hook this time."

"Oh really? That was too easy. You must have something else in mind for me then."

Ni-toyis shook her head, her feelers floating around free, "I have a plan and maybe you and I could take a trip somewhere to make a delivery."

Sebastian looked at her on his Titan screen with a smirk, "All you're going to ask me to do for my final favor is deliver the Klix with you? What's the catch? Is this place at the edge of the universe or is your employer going to try to kill you?"

Ni-toyis laughed, "Nah. You're right. Maybe I'm wasting my final favor. I'll think of something but that's on the table. Please be available to me for the next two bliiks, just in case I really do need you on this trip would you honey?"

Sebastian thought about telling her not to call him all the terms of endearment, but he knew she'd never listen.

"Okay, if that's all you need, count me in. I'll be available. Send me a message when you get an exact time."

"Sure thing baby. Toodles, handsome pants."

FIVE

››› › DAVID GOT READY for bed. He walked out into the hallway outside his bedroom and checked to make sure a High Royal Guard was standing there to watch for anything suspicious. After that, he changed into his sleepwear and got into his sleeping capsule. He felt around for the gun he put under his pillow. Yes, still there, fully loaded and ready to go. David was sure someone was going to come looking for him. Someone would want to take his power away, sit at his throne, wear his crown, and he wasn't going to allow that.

He fought hard to get here, had planned and calculated and worried and now nothing was going to take this away from him. It already cost him the man he loved. He would lose nothing else, if not for himself, then for Xabat.

David fluffed up his pillow and closed his eyes, hoping that no more nightmares would come to him in his sleep.

SIX

››› › MITCH WAS IN the desert of Arizonaland, looking for the old Human Resistance bunker. He knew where he landed his transit was right, but the landscape looked different.

He found a large crater in the dirt and saw the concrete plug that they must've poured to cover the entrance to the bunker. He wondered how they found it, out here, in the middle of nowhere.

His Titan's alarm went off and he looked at the screen. There were three transits inbound to his location and they were moving fast. They were royal transits.

He jumped into his Atlas and hovered. There were a series of boulders large enough to shelter behind close by. He hid there, and put out the electronic "ears" on his transit he had modified himself.

The royal transits landed and he watched as six Il'lacean guards got out and walked around the area he came from. They were speaking in Lace. He turned on his translator and listened.

"...wanted to make sure this place hasn't seen any new activity," the first guard said.

"This is a waste of time. The King himself was here and declared all our business in the area was done. We aren't going to find anything new," the second guard argued.

The first guard kneeled down and looked over the patterns in the dirt, "There's footsteps here."

"Could be anyone."

"These are not our boots."

"What are we going to do about them? You want to report *footprints?*"

The first guard looked out at the desert, "No. I want to check this area more thoroughly. Let's fly around and see if we find anyone. King Hennessy wants all these members dead, except for the Mitch guy. If we can find and capture him, we'll be in good with the King. That's where I want to be."

The second guard rolled his eyes at his team behind him, "Okay. If that's what you want, then can we leave?"

"Yes. Let's launch, men."

Mitch cloaked his transit and tucked the "ears" back into his vehicle.

He watched them launch, but his stomach dropped when he saw they were headed for his location.

The three royal transits hovered around him. Maybe they'd seen him after all. He couldn't sit here and find out.

He launched and immediately turned on his turbo boost. He zoomed out of the atmosphere and sped towards the SAP of Earth.

The royal transits kept behind him until he hit the SAP, but after he was clear of that, he added lightning spark energy into his booster system and disappeared into space.

Mitch only breathed again when he passed through The Jump and emerged on the other side on his way to Praxis.

He looked at his tracking system and didn't see a royal transit anywhere near his location.

He had ditched them.

SEVEN

>>> > HACE WAS ON Stoxia but he wasn't alone. The leader of the BDP never visited a planet without ten of his most powerful, dangerous, and intelligent members. Most were responsible for their own branches in different locations across the universe. And all of them, without exception, took great pride in being handpicked to protect and travel with their leader.

"Daxton!"

Dax fell back from the group, "Yes sir?"

Hace smiled at him under his black mask, "You know you were always one of my favorite branch leaders right?"

Dax bowed, "Thank you Master Hunter. It is with great honor that I can make you proud and do right by you."

"I want to get in and out of here tonight, but not before I'm served by a handful of beautiful Stox women. Go to the brothel on the ninety-second floor of the Pen Building and reserve some girls for me."

Dax smiled, "The Naughty Nightie? Good choice. Right away sir."

"And get one for yourself too," Hace added as he put one hundred thousand coren into Dax's hand.

"You want them in the usual room?"

"Yeah, that'll be good. Thanks."

Dax split off from the group and headed down the long bridge ahead of them as Hace and the rest of his men turned left to go down another bridge to the Shamb Building.

Hace led the men up to the resort level where the penthouse suite was and a view of the city with all its bridges.

Stoxia was unique in the universe concerning the population ratio. For every one male Stox, like Hace, there was 250 female Stox. The women had two choices, go into the ultra-competitive world of dating to achieve a successful partnership with a man of their own breed for pure bloods, or go off in search of a man outside of their species to make babies. There was a seventy percent chance the babies wouldn't be Stox through this arrangement and that caused a lot of women to wait for a Stox male to partner with. But for truly desperate women, some males offered their sperm for a very high price and had the women sign contracts that the male would never be propositioned for money to take care of the child.

The reason why prostitutes were popular with Stox men in particular (especially on Stoxia) was that the women guaranteed they wanted no children and it was not some sort of trick to get a baby out of the short-term meeting. The hookers could be trusted to pass extensive background checks and constant pregnancy tests. If a baby was conceived while they were on the clock, the baby was terminated. Stox men knew if they had "free" sex with a Stox woman, they would probably pass their seed on and the men didn't like being taken advantage of. They either wanted to be a father and paired off with the right Stox woman through conventional dating methods or were paid for their semen. They would not give it out for free.

Another way Stoxia was different was its high-technology architecture. The planet was all rocks, cliffs, canyons, and chasms so buildings were tall and thin to accommodate. The silver metallic-like needles were easy to spot precariously placed on tips of mountains. Bridges that spanned great distances stretched across gaping caverns, but could retract in case of emergencies or attacks. Residents of Stoxia could tell how important a building was by its width. Since space to move outward on the planet was rare, only the most important buildings in the city Highgrounds expanded sideways. These buildings resembled shiny golden robotic butterfly wings that were able to shift in strong winds. To accommodate their high population and lack of space, Stoxia also had an orbiting outpost, like Earth did, where many Stox chose to live.

Hace and his men were standing on the balcony, looking over the edge. Hace loved his power and the level of respect and fear he saw in his enemies eyes when he was face to face with them. There was nothing else quite like it. The only drawback was the constant threats to his life. He didn't want to travel with ten men but his profession demanded it. So here he stood, with his best men, waiting for Dax to come back so he could plan a little fun later on this evening.

He went to his private bedroom and changed into his swim trunks.

Hace had a fierce interest in the oddities of the universe. If he ever got imprisoned on a rock like Earth, he'd be the type of man who would become obsessed with the Loch Ness monster, chupacabra, and bigfoot.

He had a side project only DAI knew about.

"DAI, what has the Daredevil Three reported lately? Anything?"

DAI paused a moment, "Getting the most recent data. Processing."

Hace stepped into his hot tub. He settled down on the seat and ran a hand over his black hair. Only the eye sockets of the feathered skull could be seen on his back-sized tattoo. The ink was silver to contrast as strong as possible to his lavender and green skin. Some Stox people did their tattoos in white ink, but Hace thought that was for pussies…and girls.

DAI reported, "Daredevil Three is approaching a quarantined part of the Jester Galaxy. If we don't reprogram its trajectory, Daredevil Three is reporting lethal force will be taken against it. Should I reprogram it now?"

Hace thought for a moment. He did know of a planet that was full of infectious disease. The Zocosile government was supposed to have a team out there trying to eliminate threats to life by somehow neutralizing the viruses and plagues that burdened that planet. That must've been the reason for the threat. They didn't want anything or anyone near that place and that was fine with Hace.

"Sure DAI, go ahead."

"Yes Master Hunter."

"Is there any news though? Has Daredevil Three found anything unusual?"

"Not currently."

Hace felt his muscles relax in the super-heated water.

"Daredevil Three has been reprogrammed. It will now stay at least fifty thousand miles outside of Zocosile's orbit."

"Very good. DAI, I'm feeling lonely in this hot tub. Take form and come over here would you? I have girls coming by but that won't be for a few hours."

"Yes Master."

Hace waited for her to come out of the hibernation closet across his bedroom. He patted himself on the back for having a spare body for DAI to use on this planet. He was such a genius for doing that.

He was disappointed about his space exploration probe. He hoped that Daredevil Three had found at least a new black hole or some anomaly out there in the universe for him to explore, maybe some new world to conquer, but nothing new had been found in all the years that the D3 had been wandering the universe.

Hace smiled as DAI in Human Being form approached the hot tub. She was tall, shapely, blonde, and beautiful.

"May I come in, sir?"

"Take off that dress," he commanded her.

She did as she was told. She was naked underneath with round full breasts that jutted out, just begging to be sucked on.

Hace curled his index finger, silently telling her to get into the hot tub with him.

She walked down the steps and his eyes hesitated on her perfectly bald pussy. He was already hard. "Give me a blow job under the water."

She submerged her head and he placed a hand on the back of her neck to hold her to him.

Sex robots were good, but DAI was the best. Never argued, never asked for anything, never needed to breathe.

Hace put his head back and smiled.

CHAPTER 8

WAITING ON MAR YEN

ONE

>>> > SEBASTIAN NEEDED A few more supplies for his trip and decided to take a walk to the ammo store. It was such a nice day out, the beautiful weather picked up his spirits a little. He was thinking about getting some lunch when he noticed a new restaurant on the corner. While he was looking at their menu posted outside, some movement by the door caught his attention. He looked through the glass front façade and inside was Celeste, except she wasn't alone.

She sat at the bar looking stunning in a short, figure hugging red dress. A male Human sat next to her, too damn close. Her attention seemed to be consumed by this scrawny man whose hand was on her bare shoulder. Sebastian read her quickly, sensing she was waiting for yet another guy to meet her there for a date, the same one she'd been seeing before their big fight. Things must've been going well for them, apparently. The Human was hitting on her and she thought he was kind of cute. Sebastian lost his appetite and walked quickly to his destination.

He balled up his fists tight. His heart hammered in his chest and all he could hear was the sound of his blood pumping. He had received her email response and remembered how she said she was "busy" with "things" and from the look of it, she had more "things" than she could handle vying for her attention. *Busy with things huh?* When he opened the Daviens Armory's front door, the handle almost broke off in his hand.

TWO

>>> > FOR THE FIRST time since Celeste started seeing him, Dax was running late. He'd sent her a message he got held up at work and would be there shortly. She found a way to pass the time with a Human who was chatting her up. He asked her out, but she politely turned him down.

Her serene day was blasted away in a moment by feeling Sebastian's rage overwhelm her like an illness. It was so powerful he must've been close. She immediately looked around, searching inside the restaurant and even going outside looking for him, but saw nothing. She wondered what caused it. It felt raw and sharp. She didn't know she could feel something like this – this pure emotion, without limits, without images, and without any explanation. She felt like she wanted to kill someone, but she knew it wasn't coming from her. *He* wanted to make someone suffer with his bare hands. This kind of fury scared her. She went inside, sat down at the bar, and ordered an ice water, trying to force the feelings to go away. As she lifted the glass, she had a hard time keeping her hands from shaking. She didn't know if it was from her own fear or his anger rioting through her veins. She started using deep breathing to calm her down. It took a while for the burning anger to fade, but eventually it did.

Dax showed up fifteen minutes late and apologized profusely. "I'm sorry beautiful. I'm never late really."

"You're sweating hon. Did you run here?"

He grabbed a napkin off the table and dabbed at his forehead, "Sorry, I must look a fright right now. I was rushing to get here as fast as I could. Sorry for making you wait."

"It's okay. No big deal."

"I couldn't believe how long this guy kept me at his office, letting me know all the expectations and rules. I hate starting up for someone new. Anyway, enough shop talk, let's eat."

Celeste realized how easy it was for her to forget her embarrassment from last time and just relax. Dax was laid back enough for her to feel comfortable and he was softening the blow she suffered from Sebastian.

THREE

>>> > SITTING ON A bench in the warm sunshine outside of Celeste's apartment building, Dax held her hand and looked into her eyes. "I'm enjoying our time together. You have no idea how afraid I was that you wouldn't want to see me again after last time."

"Oh, I was disappointed in myself. It's something I've never done before – let my drinking get out of control like that. I didn't want you to think I did that kind of thing all the time, you know?"

"You're getting no judgments from me, don't worry. We had a good time and you got sleepy, that's how I look at it," he sighed, "It's good to see you again."

"Yeah?"

"Oh definitely. And it'd be even nicer to see you again after today. I could take you out for a picnic or something, maybe in a few days from now, if that's okay with you? About noon?"

She smiled, "Why not? Sounds like fun."

"Okay then my lovely lady. I'll swing by here and we can walk to the park that's around the corner." He gave her a soft, light kiss, then looked down at her neck. "Oh, I was wondering something. I forgot to ask. You used to wear this pretty choker that I liked, but you haven't worn it in a while."

Celeste put her hand up to her throat like the necklace was still there, "I liked it too, a lot, but I lost it. I have no idea where it is now."

"Well it couldn't have gotten up and walked away right?"

"No. But it seemed to just disappear into thin air."

"I'm sure you'll find it again." He kissed her hand and her cheek and then was on his way back to the office, waving goodbye.

She thought to herself, *I really hope so.* She wouldn't wear Sebastian's necklace again until they were back together. It was too painful otherwise. It was locked away in the back of a drawer in her bedroom. She knew right where it was. She sat on the bench a while longer, watching the world go by.

FOUR

>>> > NI-TOYIS WAITED ON Mar Yen, and Sebastian was now a full fifteen minutes late. He was supposed to meet her to travel in the same transit to drop off the stone. She called his Titan every five minutes for the past ten minutes but he wouldn't pick up. She left angry messages. She had five minutes left before she herself would become late.

She called him again and he didn't answer *again*, it was his generic outgoing message. She waited until she heard the beep, "Listen dick, where the hell are you, and what do you think you're doing? I swear to Prime Stox if I find out you've ditched me on purpose or don't have the common courtesy to tell me you've chickened out on your promise, I'm going to kill you myself. I have exactly"—she paused to look at the time on her Titan's screen—"three minutes before I'm walking to my transit. If I don't see you out there, you're going to catch hell from me in ways you've never even thought of. Where are you, prick? You better be dead or in the hospital, or else I'll never forgive you!"

She terminated the call and stomped her feet on the ground. Raynes had never broken a promise to her. She couldn't believe this was happening. She'd have to rely on plan B now, and she praised herself for always having a plan B. She was certainly going to need it today.

She put on her coat, grabbed her sash with the fake stone inside and hurried to her transit landing pad. She half expected to see him there, but he wasn't.

She slumped into her transit and launched.

FIVE

>>> > D'ARTAGNAN WAS LOST deep in an afternoon nap.

He hadn't got enough sleep last night again because of those terrible nightmares. He needed to catch up if he was to be useful for anything today.

A loud pounding on the door woke him. He wasn't expecting anyone. He got up, put on a robe, and looked out his peephole screen.

High Royal Guards from Rem Mot Om. He thought about getting his gun from underneath the kitchen sink, but remembered there was a sword three feet to his left behind the coat rack. If the Ahmalats heard a gunshot, they'd be up on his doorstep in a second, and while that would be fine to eat the guards, they'd probably take down his front door too.

"Open up in there! Kingdom High Royal Guard commands it!"

D'Artagnan opened the door and looked at them. "Yes, can I help you?"

"We're HRG's Ookidor and Keanay. We're going door to door asking for information about the Human Resistance. Can you state your name please?"

D'Artagnan was calm, "Yes, my name is Zane Colmsky."

"Thank you Mr. Colmsky. We need to ask you if you are in any way, shape, or form affiliated with the Human Resistance?"

"No sir. Can't stand those Human pricks causing all that trouble on our planet. It makes me sick."

"We don't need an opin—"

A lapping sound in the water to the guard's left made him stop mid-sentence and stare.

"Are the Ahmalats active as of late?"

"Why yes, yes they are. No one gets out here very often you see, so they may be a tad hungry. I don't know when the last time was that I had a visitor come to think of it…"

Guard Ookidor gave Keanay a concerned glance, "Okay, a few more questions and then we'll be on our way."

"Of course. Happy to help," D'Artagnan smiled.

"Have you ever been in contact with a member of the Human Resistance?"

"Oh, no. I wouldn't give those people a thrux of my day."

"Have you ever aided the Human Resistance financially, medically, verbally, or in any other way I haven't listed?"

"No sir."

"Do you condone or agree with, anything that the Human Resistance stands for?"

"No." D'Artagnan felt a fire starting to burn inside him at these two guards coming to *his* front door, interrupting *his* sleep, and asking him questions that were none of their Khaleen damned business.

"If in the future, any member of the Human Resistance, regardless of species, contacts you in any way, please contact the Kingdom immediately."

D'Artagnan heard a splashing sound off to the side of the door and the guards moved away from him quickly.

"Yes guards. Of course. Long live the King!" D'Artagnan had to yell the last part just to make a little more noise to scare the guards into action that much faster.

He closed the door firmly and heard the kingdom transit launch. They were gone.

Assholes.

SIX

>>> > TODAY WAS THE day of the delivery.

Hace took his transit down to the surface of Mar Yen while The Architect Phantom stayed in orbit around the planet. He liked Mar Yen;

it wasn't such a bad little planet with its tropical jungles and its forests of blue and green. But nothing was as good as his ship.

Although today, he was neither in the forest or the jungle. Instead, he had chosen a small abandoned warehouse that was tucked away in the solar district where he knew no one would disturb him and Ni-toyis. He brought five of his biggest men, in case something went down.

He stood at the back of the warehouse where the shadows fell. There were a lot of holes in the concrete walls and some in the ceiling. Wooden shards and metal rebar poked out of some of the holes like fangs on a wild animal – it gave the whole place a little more dirty dealing appeal to Hace.

He smiled when he saw Ni-toyis coming towards his men. They looked to him and he ordered, "That's her. Pat her down…gently."

One of the largest Trovelet's Ni-toyis had ever seen (which is why Hace wanted him for bodyguard duty) approached her. Hace laughed when he saw the look on her face.

"Don't panic, love. He won't hurt you."

"You travel with some big motherfuckers, Hunter."

"I do," he sighed, "And it's *The* Hunter dearie. *The* Hunter." He looked Ni-toyis over – once to make sure she had no weapons on her, and one more time to take in all of her female Prime given weapons. Surely she slayed a lot of men between her hypnotic eyes and her come hither thighs. "It's strictly for my protection. Can't be too careful these days. Same reason why I stay covered up. I'm sorry the only thing on me you'll be able to see is my eyes."

Ni-toyis was cleared and she approached Hace slowly.

He saw the look on her face again when she saw his eyes change color from purple to red and she realized they were the same breed.

Ni-toyis cleared her throat, "It's an honor to meet you *The* Hunter," she bowed deeply displaying an abundant amount of cleavage to him.

"Oh wow. So polite are you, except for your mouth, of course. Let's get away from my men for a moment."

They walked slow through alternating areas of shadow and beams of light that illuminated the high levels of dust floating in the air.

"A man of your reputation deserves nothing but respect. Had I known that you were…what you are, I would've curtailed my swearing though. I apologize."

"It's quite all right honey, but I can't confirm or deny my breed to you. Another privacy issue of course."

"So where would you like to do this?"

"Mmmm what a loaded question you present. I'd like to do it all over with you, but you mean the stone. We can do that right here. Can I see the gem?" He stopped walking and faced her.

"Of course," Ni-toyis cradled the velvet sash she carried in her hand and carefully pulled out the big sparkling ruby red stone. She handed it to Hace.

He looked at it with wonder and then walked into a patch of sunlight. He held it up to get a better look. It was perfectly clear all the way through and the round cut gem reflected all the sunlight it captured across the walls of the crumbling warehouse. For a moment, it looked like the inside of a discotheque.

He studied Ni-toyis; she smiled back and nodded once. "You know if this is a forgery, I'll cut off your pretty little head and put it on a spike?"

She didn't flinch, "Of course. I would never be so stupid as to pull something like that. Only a fool would try to trick you. Please, inspect it. Make sure it's everything you ever dreamed of. I only want your absolute satisfaction."

Hace grinned, "Well, if you say so."

He pulled out his jeweler's ring and looked at it closer. It looked right. It felt right. If it was a forgery, it was the best one he'd ever seen, but for whatever its exact purpose was (which he still had yet to find out) he wouldn't know it was a forgery until that very moment. He contemplated this but Ni-toyis had a very good reputation for keeping her word, and her work was some of the best thieving in the universe. He was still hesitant though.

"So, I didn't hear any news reports about the Red Klix being stolen. How did you manage that?"

"I can't reveal all my secrets or else everyone would be able to do the same thing as me, but I can tell you that Praxis Council has no idea their precious gem was stolen. They still think they have it tucked safely away in a secure location."

Hace smiled, "I highly doubt that everyone would be able to do this as good as you, even if they did know your secrets, but I am pleased with your performance. Let's call this part of our deal done. Agreed?"

She nodded, "Great."

"And now for the second part, I was thinking, if you didn't mind, I kinda' like unconventional sex. Some place out in the wild. Maybe the jungle. How do you feel about that?"

"I am impressed that you're even considering what I want in our arrangement, but I have something I really need to address."

"Oh? What's that love?"

She bit her lip, "Had I known that you were a Stox male, I mean if you really are, I would've ne—"

Hace interrupted her, "Ah, I see. Stox men are a deal breaker for you?"

"It's a complication for sure. You and I both know my species is the best at seduction, but with business, I always need to keep a clear head. I'm truly concerned that our arrangement might go beyond business if we're not careful."

Hace smiled, "Well darling, I don't know whether to be angry or flattered."

"I can't apologize enough. I never even thought to ask since Stox men are rare. This is actually the first time I've been propositioned by such a *powerful* Stox…I mean, assuming you are. I have an alternative though."

"Oh? What's that Ni-toyis?"

"Well, two options actually. I give back the money for the sex, no harm, no foul. The other option is I keep the coren, but I give you full access to the brothel I own on Stoxia. I have clean and safe girls guaranteed. They won't try to secretly get impregnated by you. I have them sign contracts before they're allowed to do business with me. I have a solid reputation as a madam and I don't want that tarnished, as in ever."

Hace laughed, "See? I didn't even know you had your own brothel. What a pleasant surprise."

She smiled, "I use a different name for that, but yes, I have tons of girls, some of the most beautiful in all of Stoxia. If you'd like, for the price you paid, you can have ten girls, all at once, to please you for an entire night." She stopped to think, "That's at least nine Stoxian hours."

Hace smirked, "That is a looooong time," he paused to consider her revision to their arrangement.

Ni-toyis crossed her arms over her chest and rested her weight on one leg.

Hace looked down at the ground as he thought. He noticed her dark green stilettos, and let his eyes slowly wander up her shapely legs. She wore a short skirt that barely covered her crotch. Hace thought it must be heavenly to have her bend over to get a good look at her ass. He clapped his hands, "Sure, why not?"

"You'll agree to my proposal?"

"Yes. What'd you say? Ten girls? All at once for nine hours? That's a great way for me to blow off some steam. And I'm sure your girls are just as beautiful as you promise."

"Sugar, I can send you pictures in advance. You pick them and I'll shut down the whole place just for you. Make sure all the girls you like are there that night."

"Yeah, that'd be nice. *Real* nice. It sounds like you're surprised that I'm not angry at you for this. Is that right?"

Ni-toyis smiled, "Yes, to be honest. I'm appreciative of your understanding though."

"Well, I might be a bastard, but I'm not a rapist. I'm never going to take a woman by force that has no interest in me sexually. Rape fantasies to play out with a girl? Sure. But I can seduce with the best of them, and if that doesn't work, I can pay them. Either way, I'm not going to force a girl. It's just one of those things with me."

Ni-toyis smiled, "I really am very relieved. If there's anything else I can do to make your stay at my brothel more pleasurable, let me know. But if our business is done for now, I must be going soon."

"Yes, of course." Hace snapped his fingers a few times and waved over his men. One of them came with a briefcase. Hace opened it and took out a few rolls of cash coren. He held it out to Ni-toyis, "This is the amount we agreed to. Take it with my gratitude. No one else could've gotten this stone for me."

She smiled as she put the coren into her sash, "Fantastic. I'm so glad you're happy."

"I am. I might call you again in the future if I need something else that fits your skill set, and I'll let you know about which night is best for me."

Ni-toyis shrugged, "There's no rush or time limit or anything. If you want to use my girls tomorrow or five years from now, it's up to you."

"I'll keep it in mind. I'll see you around love." Hace went to grab Ni-toyis's hand and she gave it to him for a handshake, but he kissed it instead.

She blushed and giggled, "I see your power of seduction still has too strong of an effect on me."

"You are a very sexy woman."

She blushed again, "Thank you. Toodles big boy."

Hace watched her walk away for a moment and then leaned over to one of his men and whispered, "Follow her and give me a full report on her activities until she heads back to Stoxia."

"Yes sir."

Hace didn't believe the Red Klix was a fake, but you never could trust criminals, and especially not beautiful thieves. If it turned out to be a forgery, he would keep his word to her. He would cut off her head and put it on a spike for an example of what happens to beings that double-cross him.

He looked over to the remaining four men traveling with him, "Let's go boys."

CHAPTER 9

NON-DACHIANS SEEK KNOWLEDGE

ONE

>>> > SEBASTIAN SLAMMED THE door of his apartment, threw down his boxes of ammo, tore off his Titan, and tossed it on the table. He walked into his closet, changed his clothes from a suit to sweats and ran out the door for a long hard jog.

An hour and a half later, dripping with sweat, all he could think of was a hot shower as he came home.

When he was clean, dry, shaved, and dressed, he remembered his Titan. He had missed three calls. He glanced at the time.

Then it hit him.

He was supposed to have met Ni-toyis today! Three hours ago!

"Goddamn it, son of a *bitch*!"

Sebastian listened to Ni-toyis chew him out in her messages. She must have been furious with him right now. He couldn't believe he completely forgot. This hadn't happened to him in a long time, but he also hadn't been this angry in a long time. He had lost his mind after he knew Celeste was about to meet up with her "new" guy.

He could barely think about it without wanting to find the bastard and kill him.

He let out a grunt.

Hopefully Ni-toyis's meeting went off without problems and she was fine.

He still had a lot to do today, better just get to it.

TWO

>>> > NI-TOYIS CONTEMPLATED SEBASTIAN being done with her, but this couldn't be the case, because he knew all the dirt she had on him. She could change his life for the worse in a heartbeat, so what was delaying him calling her back? And what had kept him from meeting up with her?

She finished packing all her things in the Mar Yen cabin and got ready to go home. She looked around to double-check that she hadn't left anything behind. She found a vial behind the couch. *That's so unlike me!*

She thought about how weird it had been meeting The Hunter and realizing he was a Stox too. Despite what he said, there was a ninety-nine percent chance he was Stox. They're so rare. But at least he understood when she told him her decision to back out on sleeping with him. The whole Stox thing changed everything and he accepted that, which was a surprise. Or maybe he was relieved she called it off because she could've tried to get pregnant. So many things to think about when you're a Stox. The rest of the universe just couldn't understand.

She loaded up her transit then walked back into the cabin and cleaned the entire place of her tentacle and suction prints, making sure there was no physical evidence of what she'd been doing while she was there. Mar Yen had rules just like every other planet, and she didn't need the extra hassle of being brought in for questioning after she had broken about twenty-two laws while she'd been there.

Where was Sebastian? A knot formed in her stomach. Was he okay?

She got into her transit and launched for Stoxia. Her transit maps said she was three days out because one of The Jumps was shut down to travelers. Great.

The Jumps helped a lot to get her home faster, but three days? She hated this damn trip already, but she could at least have plenty of time to send Sebastian a Titan message while she was travelling.

THREE

- -

TITAN Corporation - Personal TITAN Device

System Status: Active -- Universal Grid: Online

Current Time/Date (In Transit to - Stoxia): 8 Sterms/ Dabets 18, 10354

Secondary Time/Date (Praxis - Daviens): 10:53 p.m./June 2, 2193

Current Universal Positioning System Location: In transit - Jump in Andromeda Galaxy

User: Ni-toyis Tredux

Communications Menu

Outgoing message(s) pending: 1 - Status: Draft/Unsent

Message Saved at 8 Sterms

Message To Be Sent from: The Sexiest thief you'll never see

-Raynes,
I've already left and am on my way back home to Stoxia.
In all the years of our arrangement, I've never known you
to behave this way and I hope you have a damn good reason
as to why you stood me up.
My meeting went fine, although you probably don't care.

I had to use plan B but you know me, always have one.
I expect that you will make this up to me somehow.
So let's reset our favor counter back to two because of
this inconvenience.
One favor you still owe me from your previous debt and
a new one tacked on because I think I deserve a little
something.
I'm assuming you heard my voice mails.
I've been stuck in my transit for hours now and took the
time I needed to try to calm down and think everything
through before writing this message.
You're still an asshole for doing this to me. A sexy
asshole, but an asshole nonetheless.
I'm still angry and will be for I don't know how long.
Maybe you could set up some romantic evening for the two of
us and I'll consider all of this a simple misunderstanding
between friends. *wink*
Write me back soon!
I would like to hear what caused you to miss our appointment.
I'll be traveling for quite a long time and need some more
reading material than this holobook I have.
Yours,
N

-END OF MESSAGE
*This message will only be deleted by user.

Ni-toyis read over her message one more time then sent it.

FOUR

>>> > SEBASTIAN DIDN'T KNOW whether to be relieved that Ni-toyis didn't do anything more drastic to take revenge out on him, or to be scared that she seemed calm during this message.

The romantic evening would never happen and he never considered them friends either.

He looked at the time on his Titan. Eric would be there soon. And a response to Ni-toyis had to be handled extremely carefully.

There was no time for a reply. He did a final check on his apartment, put his bags by the front door, and waited for Eric to arrive.

FIVE

>>> > SEBASTIAN WAS GLAD Eric could take this trip with him. He needed some down time with one of his oldest war buddies; he needed to be around someone that understood him and accepted him the way he was. Eric Bouton sweated in the trenches with him, stormed over countless battlegrounds, and always watched out for him. Eric understood Sebastian's position when he deserted the war on Mhooreanna. He agreed saving Agathon's life was the only option.

In the transit ride to Foss-Altus, Eric, known as The Czar to his contract holders, sensed something wrong with his friend.

"What's up with you man? You're all quiet. You've been strange since I botched that job with D'Artagnan and we crashed at your place. I'm getting some bad vibes off you, but I don't want to read you," he held his hands up and wiggled his fingers.

"It's been a long time since I've been to this world. I don't want to get burnt up on re-entry by an angry Rhorr'Dach."

"Bullshit, Raynes. I know you called ahead to get clearance. What's really bothering you? Or do you not want to talk about it?"

"No, I really don't."

"Okay, that's cool. I guess. I'll stop asking,"—he paused—"for now. Let's just have a good time with some target practice and catch up with Agathon."

"Sounds good."

They sat silently reading weapon vidmagazines for five minutes before Eric let out a loud yawn. "I'm glad I'm finally being allowed to visit FA, but the trip is so long. There's not too many people I could tolerate being in confined spaces with for eighteen hours."

"I hear you, Bouton."

"I can't wait to try out my new Tiger Stone 8X man. I just got a *ton* of ammo for the thing and I haven't used it but once for targ—"

Sebastian cut him off, "You remember me mentioning Celeste Hennessy before?"

"What?" Eric was still looking at his magazine screen hovering in front of him.

"Celeste Hennessy – the Queen Dowager of Earth and Il'laceier?" Sebastian had his head down and reached to his neck to rub away the knot there.

Eric was confused by his friend's question and he didn't want to read his mind to see where he was going with this. Besides, he was really excited about his new weapon and he wanted to talk about it. Eric replied slowly, "Yes, of course. What about her?"

"You think she's pretty, right?"

"Do I think she's pretty?!" He threw his hands up and let them fall onto his thighs making a clapping sound, "Is this a trick question? Of course she is! She's gorgeous! Men from all over the universe think she's a beautiful creature, I mean if I had a chance with her I'd ta—"

"That's enough. I get it, I get it. Never mind," Sebastian shifted in his seat uncomfortably.

"What the hell is wrong with you? You're acting really strange, Raynes."

"Nothing. Forget I mentioned her," he looked out his side window, rubbing his forehead.

"No, no, no my friend. My interest is piqued now. Women are one of my *favorite* subjects and Celeste is hard to forget once brought up...You haven't mentioned her in a long time. Did you meet her or something?"

Sebastian remained silent while his friend continued to rifle questions at him. He knew he shouldn't have mentioned it.

"Wait! You were...was her husband your job? King Hennessy was your hit wasn't it?"

Sebastian was silent still. He only crossed his arms on his chest and looked up to the ceiling, exasperated with himself.

"Oh come on, Raynes! You were the one that brought this shit up!"

Sebastian took a deep breath and answered, "Okay, yes. That job was mine. I was the unlucky bastard that took that damned contract. Worst thing I could've done lately too."

"Why? It paid well right? No one knows it was you, well, except for me now. What's not to like?"

"Soooo…the Tiger Stone? How much did that set you back?"

Eric put one index finger up, then pointed it at Sebastian, "I've never seen you act this way and I've known you a good Goddamn long time. That can only mean *one* thing,"—he put his finger away—"A woman is somehow involved…and this mystery woman just happens to be *the* Celeste Hennessy? The woman that you've had a crush on *for years?!* My mind is blown. How could you keep this from me you rotten son of a bitch? She's the owner of the mysterious perfume in your apartment that night isn't she? I never thought I'd see this day come – no pun intended."

"Yeah, and why don't you use your special power of seeing into the future to make your life easier? I always wondered about that," he titled his head sideways at the end of the sentence.

"Oh fuck you Sebastian! You know I can't use that for myself or tell my friends what's going to happen. It doesn't work as easy as you think. That night I came over with D'Artagnan, I only told you the future because we were in danger and I needed those pricks dead since I fucked up big time," he paused rubbing his chin, "My God. I think you've gotten yourself involved with a target's wife! You stupid son of a bitch. You did didn't you? You really fucked up. Tell me man, what happened?!"

Sebastian glared at his friend, genuinely wanting to punch him in the face.

"Hey man, I caught that. Stop thinking so hard okay?"

Sebastian shook his head, "I should have never brought this up," he tilted his head back and talked to the ceiling, "Why? Why did I say anything? I could've taken this trip alone you know?"

"What?! No way man. You need to talk about whatever's bothering you. It's written all over your face, it just took me a while to figure out it was a woman since you know, I thought you'd kinda given up on, like, dating, as in, forever…I mean, you've been through a hell of a drought man. Like what? Decades since you had a real girlfriend? But I gotta commend you, when you come out of a dry spell, you REALLY come back with a totally irresistible universally desirable babe! I'm dying to know what you and the Queen did. By the way, I didn't know you'd date a Human. Did you know her *before* the assassination? Wait, wait, wait. Was she the one that hired you? Were you having an affair with her? You didn't get her pregnant did you?"

Sebastian put his head in his hands, leaning over in his seat, "NO! Just shut up and stop trying to guess. I'll tell you if you just shut the hell up. Damn!"

Eric shrugged, "Sorry. Come on. Spill it."

Sebastian took the next three hours filling his friend in on almost everything that happened – the assassination, Celeste asking for help, the animal magnetism between them, and the intense sexual tension building up over time. Everything from the first kiss to seeing her with a Human at that restaurant. He only left out the fact that Celeste was already seeing some other guy.

Eric couldn't believe his friends story.

"I…Wow, man, wow. You and the Queen? Wow. She spotted you in the Earth Outpost courtyard and asked for…wow. And she's capable of 7's?! Holy shit…wow man."

"Please say something other than wow, Bouton."

"You really fucked this up."

"Thanks, asshole."

"Well, you wanted me to say something else. And that's how I feel after hearing your story. You've had a crush on her for-fucking-ever man. What's wrong with having a relationship with her?"

"Damn it Eric, were you even listening to me?!"

"Yes, hanging on every freakin' word. You haven't had a story this good since you killed that gecko-faced Wrabbalan…*twice*."

Sebastian smiled, "I'd forgotten about that. Yeah, I didn't know it would get back up after the first death. I really should've asked for a double payment on that one."

Eric's eyes got wide, "You guys haven't locked into each other have you? I'm assuming you haven't or else we wouldn't even be having this discussion."

"No, certainly not. She isn't even *Lanyx* you fool. And even if that could happen cross-species, she's not familiar with that phrase or what it means. I know I haven't smelled her scent, just her perfume and she uses a couple of those so I know the difference for sure."

Eric nodded, "She did smell really good from what I remember. Something incredibly expensive too," he paused, "Well, just because it's never gone cross-species before doesn't mean it can't right? And just because she doesn't know of the concept doesn't mean it hasn't happened to her. She hasn't locked into yet has she? 'Cause that would change everything and you damn well know that. Has she said *anything* about your scent?"

"Well sure. I mean she's complimented me on my cologne a few times."

"Sebastian…" Eric said his friend's name accusatorily.

"There was that one day I wasn't wearing any…but I put it on the night before. It was probably just a faint scent left over…"

"Sebastian! That could be it man! Or the start of it! You'd better pay attention to that shit."

"There's *no way* she's locked into me. She hasn't had enough time to know me really; we're just getting to know each other." He twisted his father's ring with his fingers.

Eric ran his index finger over his eyebrow a few times and let out a sigh, "Tell me you haven't been quoting that salts peer guy to her huh?"

"Okay, now you're pissing me off. His name's not Saltspeare…It's *Shakespeare*. How many times do I have to tell you that? And William Shakespeare was a fucking genius and a wonderful poet. You should try reading him."

"So you *are* quoting it to her?"

Sebastian did a rare eye roll and replied, "Yes, but she quotes it back to me too. She's smart and she likes to read just like me…You know, you would probably get a lot more sex if you did what I do."

Eric gave Sebastian a dirty look, but said nothing.

Sebastian continued, "Women love poetry and romance. That's not why I read Shakespeare though, it's just good stuff."

"Ahhh," Eric waved off Sebastian with one of his hands, "You've always been the holobookworm between the two of us. Anyways…I think you're being an idiot about this whole thing."

"I'm serious, Bouton. I'm going to punch you out if you keep saying stuff like that."

"No you won't, you actually like me. Listen, I'm just saying she sounds nice, and she's hot, and now…she's single. What's wrong with dating the girl you have a crush on?"

Sebastian looked over his screens and double-checked his maps, "I can't…or at least, I shouldn't. You know why."

"Francesca again? That was different and soooo long ago, Raynes. Wasn't your fault either. This is something the universe wants you to deal with and move forward from. This is going to sound harsh, but you need to get over it."

Sebastian's fist shot out, aiming to hit Eric across the jaw, but his punch was intercepted by Eric's hand. Eric saw that coming before Sebastian even knew what he was doing.

"I don't want to fight you Raynes, but you know what I'm saying is the truth. It's been difficult for me to watch you punish yourself for years after Fran's suicide. It wasn't your fault. I pray that someday you'll believe me and forgive yourself for a sin you didn't commit."

Eric held Sebastian's fist in his hand. They stared at each other silently. Eric felt his friend's anger subside and he let go of Sebastian's hand.

"That was almost two decades ago and you still want to beat yourself up over it. You can't condemn yourself to this girlfriendless life forever man. I don't want to see that."

Sebastian was silent, then let out a long sigh, "I think I've dealt with it and the answer is to continue to remain alone. I waivered for a while lately, but I think it's best for everyone."

"Oh really? We Lanyx live a long time man. A bit too long for *me* to live alone for the rest of my life. If you didn't want to talk about her, you wouldn't have brought it up. You think of that? Hey and while we're at it, maybe you could send her my way, I'm single and she is extremely sexy."

Sebastian stared daggers into Eric's eyes and then turned away from him.

Eric put a hand to his forehead, "Oh this is really serious. You're all alpha male protective over her. Oh man, I don't even think we should be on this trip right now."

"And why not?"

"What if she starts seriously dating some other guy? It sounds like her dance card is booking up pretty quick and…"

Sebastian raised his eyebrows at his friend.

Eric finished, "She's gorgeous."

"I thought talking to you might make me feel better, but you're making me feel worse. Besides, she's already dating someone else, at least occasionally. I…left that part out of my story I guess. She's probably been seeing him for weeks now. Maybe that's best."

"Maybe that's best?! Do you even hear yourself?! WHAT THE HELL IS WRONG WITH YOU?!" Eric was shaking his hands in the air. "This woman," he laughed darkly, "This beautiful, fucking gorgeously sexy hottie Queen wants you…and you say she's better off with someone else?! I can't believe this Raynes! Can't fucking believe it!" He leaned over to touch Sebastian's forehead, but Sebastian pulled away quickly.

Eric frowned, "What? I have to see if you're still suffering from that flu you told me about, maybe it fried your noggin, made you go all brain dead on me or something."

Sebastian scowled at Eric, but stayed quiet.

"I can't tell what the hell you want right now. One minute you're telling me how wonderful she is and the next you're saying she should date someone else…even though it's obvious she really cared about you. From the sound of it, she's probably crazy about you. You've gone insane if you ask me," Eric stated very matter-of-factly.

"I'm not insane, Eric. I'm trying to protect her from a life with me. An incredibly dangerous life that she shouldn't have to deal with. It's not her fault I'm an assassin."

"Raynes, I'm an assassin too. I still want a girlfriend. I still want someone to share everything with. And you're shitting all over this devastatingly smoldering hot woman! I would give my shooting arm for her, and you've got her in the palm of your hand!" Eric put his palm out.

"Could you just do me a favor, Bouton and stop using adjectives to describe her huh? Just call her Celeste. She has a name. I don't need to be reminded of how hot you think she is every time you say a Goddamned word about her. Please? Really?"

"No can do muchacho. I gotta' tell you the truth as I see it buddy boy. Right now, I think you've made a *terrible* mistake. I think you should go to Praxis immediately, screw this trip, and beg her forgiveness for what you said and hope she lets you date her again."

"We were never dating, and I'm not begging anyone for anything. She could've been a little more understanding towards my situation."

Eric laughed out loud, "Been more understanding?! You're being completely unrealistic right now. I think she's been plen—"

"I quit. We are not talking about this anymore. Discussion ended."

"But I wante—"

"No, Eric. Case closed. You bring this up again and I swear I'll leave you with some fire-breathing Dach that has a case of the hiccups."

"This is me, shutting up. Celeste who? Never heard of her. But seriously, you don't need to threaten me with the Rhorr'Dach okay? There's the line and you just crossed it," Eric pointed to the imaginary line on the floor and motioned going over it with his foot.

"Sorry, I just…seeing her with another guy…If I lay eyes on the man she's seeing…Even thinking of her with another man, I can't stand it. Other times I think it's best. I don't know, Bouton. I'm trying to figure it out, I just…thanks for coming out here with me and listening while I try to get my head on straight."

"That's what friends are for my man. But you've really gotta get your head out of your ass about Queen Hottie. I mean…Celeste."

Sebastian stared at Eric intently, "You've just got to get that last word in about it huh?"

Eric smiled.

They sat silently as they approached the orbit of Foss-Altus. Sebastian forgot how beautiful this planet could be with its green oceans and tan and green landmasses. He thought Celeste would love this view, then immediately shook the idea out of his mind.

Sebastian called over his communicator, "This is Atlas Praxis Fiver coming into outer orbit, do you copy FA Station one? Over."

A female voice came over their docking radio, "I'm sorry Atlas Praxis Fiver, you're mistaken this is Zocosile. This planet is restricted from visitors due to viral contamination. Please leave orbit before you're met with lethal force."

Sebastian smiled, "Sorry. Forgot the password is Kutrip. Court. Boxmit."

"Temporary permission granted. FA Station one copy. State your business Atlas Praxis Fiver."

Sebastian smiled over at Eric, "Captain Raynes and Captain Bouton requesting permission to dock. Over."

"Hold your current orbit Atlas. Do you have Rhorr'Dach advanced permission? Over."

Even though the female operator was trained to be stoic over all radio transmission's she sounded skeptical that anyone from Praxis was allowed on her planet.

"Yes Agathon of the Rojo Clan is aware of our arrival and granted permission. You should have the documentation you need. Over."

"Please hold Atlas Praxis Fiver. Over."

Eric shifted in his seat, "I guess nothing's changed here from what you've told me. Makes me nervous. You did tell Agathon we were coming right?"

Sebastian scowled at his friend, "Of course I did! I wouldn't even approach this planet otherwise. You *do* remember what I told you was their first line of defense if they have an unauthorized landing?"

"I still can't believe that though – I mean plasma breathing Dach? That's pretty scary."

"And you haven't even seen one in action. The two plasma breathers I saw," he paused to exhale slowly, "that's enough to make anyone shit their pants right then and there. One of the fiercest creatures I've ever seen, that's for damn sure."

They waited for a response over the radio in silence.

"Sorry to make you wait Atlas. Visitors are extremely rare. Permission granted, dock on bay nine, terminal sixteen please. Over."

"Copy that FA Station one and thanks. Cecca Vet Lopp, Gees'Eked, Floguethyinn Oftiyumous. Over."

"Cecca Vet Lopp, Gees'Eked, Floguethyinn Oftiyumous. Over." The female voice sounded impressed that an outsider knew her people's motto in her native Dachian language.

The Atlas looked like an ant compared to some of the larger ships currently docked close by. Sebastian always marveled at the size of Rhorr'Dach spaceships but carrying hundreds of Dach in any form couldn't be easy.

SIX

>>> > AFTER CELESTE'S MORNING workout, shower, and breakfast, she quickly checked her emails before leaving for the day.

She sat confused staring at Sebastian's latest email.

"Your Highness,
Thought I should let you know, I'll be unavailable for the next two weeks (eighteen days) for communications of any kind. I'll be located somewhere in the universe where current technologies simply don't receive well so if you could be patient with me in the meantime, I'd much appreciate it.

Thank you for agreeing to help me with the matter at hand, I feel it's very important.

I'll be departing later on this morning, so by the time you read this, I might already be gone.

I assure you I'm still searching for information on your parents. I've sent out a few communications to some people I think might be able to help us. I'll have to wait and see if they respond to me by the time I return.

Take care,
X"

She looked at the time she received the email: 8:05 a.m.

She looked at the time now: 11:53 a.m. He might already be gone.

She resented that he wouldn't use her name anymore. *Where the hell could he possibly be going where he can't communicate with me? What is he doing? Some kind of mission? An assassination?* She was frustrated that he barely told her any information. But if she was going to get used to the idea of letting him go, these next two weeks would be good practice.

CHAPTER 10

QUINTANA BRIX

ONE

>>> > SEBASTIAN WAS IN the extremely rare position of even knowing the Rhorr'Dach existed at all. They purposefully deterred other species from visiting their planet by spreading false rumors that Foss-Altus contained a highly contagious and fatal virus to any life form to keep the most curious explorers away. For anyone who ignored the warnings and decided to fly by, the traveler would find their communications and advanced technologies begin to fail the closer they got to the planet.

Foss-Altus was an ancient and highly advanced place, and the Rhorr'Dach desperately needed to keep their species a secret, so they scrambled all of their outgoing frequencies and communications, and they closely monitored all incoming communications. When Sebastian told Celeste in his email that he was going to a place where current technologies weren't received well, he wasn't lying. Anything she would've sent to his Titan would have first been intercepted by the Rhorr'Dach Elite Council and wouldn't have reached him personally until the time he was ready to leave. Too much red tape for the rare visiting non-Dachians to get personal communications here – and he had a special relationship with the Dach. As far as non-Dachian visitors, well, he and Eric were the only two ever allowed. The Dach trusted Sebastian and would never read his communications, but he came to an agreement with them that they could at least hold all of his messages until right after he passed out of their communications window of safety.

It was a big price to pay to visit this world, but Sebastian understood the Dach's need for absolute secrecy better than most.

Through the Dach's diligence, most species didn't know about the Rhorr'Dach or thought they were make believe monsters of the past. There are a few species that believe they exist and think they would make great warriors for their own personal wars due to their immense size, special abilities, and formidable strength. This made their species persecuted for ages by beings that wanted to somehow enslave or control the Dach.

When the Rhorr'Dach started exploring the universe tens of thousands of years ago (earlier than any other species ever developed space travel abilities), they found that they were some of the largest species around.

Earth was one of the last planets they discovered. When they landed there, they found a very sparse population of tiny beings calling themselves Humans. The Dach tried to co-exist with them, but the Humans viewed them as a threat, so the Dach were constantly attacked. The Dach learned how to understand English but couldn't speak it at the time. One of the Rhorr'Dach elders found out the Humans called them Dragons and the Humans thought Dach should be eradicated. Soon the Dach left Earth and this happened time and time again, world after world, and it saddened the Dach. Everywhere they went, beings wanted either to murder them, run them off, or enslave them. The Dach learned to stick to their own kind and restrict travel to uninhabited worlds. Through a series of extremely rare occurrences (some call them miracles), the Rhorr'Dach gained the ability to shape shift into Human being form. With this, a whole new way of life opened up for the species and they could safely explore the universe again, but they told no one of this ability for fear of continued persecution.

When Agathon met Sebastian and Eric for the first time back on Mhooreanna, Agathon was gravely injured. He was stuck in Human form, unable to change back to his natural self to fight, but the two captains saved his life that day and he never forgot it.

When they met again today, Agathon was in Human form. It was viewed by the Dach as the easiest for indoor situations, although Rhorr'Dach always preferred the outdoors, and their natural state of being to their shape shifted one.

Agathon held out his hand, "Cecca Vet Lopp, Gees'Eked, Floguethyinn Oftiyumous. Captain Sebastian Raynes, it is good to see you again! It's been way too long. And you've brought Eric this time. Excellent. How was the trip?"

Sebastian shaking Agathon's hand, then bowing, answered, "Cecca Vet Lopp, Gees'Eked, Floguethyinn Oftiyumous. Great, great. Gave Eric and I plenty of time to talk."

Eric shook Agathon's hand and bowed as Rhorr'Dach loved this show of respect. "Cecca Vet Lopp, Gees'Eked, Floguethyinn Oftiyumous." Eric was not quite as good as Sebastian speaking Dachian but he tried his best.

Agathon responded, "Seek Knowledge, Accept Love, and Fight *Only* if you Must as well my friend. I think your Dachian has improved since the last time I heard you speak it in some of the recorded messages Raynes passed along to me."

"I've been practicing a little bit. I was impressed that day on the battlefield at how perfect your English was. Sounds like it still is."

"Well hell, I've had a lot longer to practice it eh?" Agathon smiled widely. To the untrained eye, the smile looked sinister, but Sebastian knew it was anything but. It was the one thing that wasn't quite right about the Dach's Human impersonation. Their smiles were too wide, showing too many teeth, and looked a bit creepy to anyone who knew what Human smiles were supposed to look like.

Agathon slapped his Human hands together, "You guys must be starving. Want some lunch? Lanyx food, picnic style if you want at my place."

Eric's mouth watered at the mention of food, "Sounds great."

They walked outside, then Agathon turned to face them, "You gentlemen need to stand here. I'm going to change over."

TWO

>>> > A FEW SECONDS after Agathon walked into the middle of a plot of dirt, he immediately shifted over to his natural form. Eric tried not to stare as the Native-American looking, brown-eyed Human man with waist-long straight black hair, turned into an enormous winged dragon.

Agathon was revered in his community as one of the most vibrantly colored male Lake-Brave's around. Eric had never seen him in his natural form. Agathon's eyes were an icy blue – a stark contrast to his deep red skin. His face was sleek and intimidating. He had two wideset long thick straight horns protruding off the back of his head, and spines along the top of his back all the way down to his tail. More intimidating still, at the end of his tail was a bloom of sharp, pointed rods like a weapon Eric was familiar with – a medieval mace with spikes. His Human hands and feet had turned into massive clawed talons and the edge of his wings had even more deadly sharp claws.

"Wow, Agathon! That was amazing!"

"Oh, you liked that Eric? Just wait 'til you see the scenery. Why don't you guys get on? Sit on my upper back, near my neck where I think it's most comfortable for you. Watch my spines please." The land rumbled from Agathon's deep voice.

Eric looked over at Sebastian and let out a concerned laugh, "Is this something you've done before?"

Sebastian nodded his head, "It'll be fine. Stop being such a pussy. I'll even let you sit in front where he doesn't have any spines sticking up. I'll sit right behind you though. I'm not getting stabbed in my ass again."

Eric's eyes widened, "Again?"

Sebastian pushed him towards Agathon and smiled, "Kidding, dick-head. I'm kidding. Go on already, get on. I promise you'll like it. This experience has no rival."

Agathon was now seventy feet long and nineteen feet tall so he had to bow down and spread his wings for the men to climb on his back for the flight.

"Hold on guys, could be a little bumpy for you." Agathon gracefully took off from the docking hub towards his home with Eric hooting and hollering the whole trip. Sebastian was a bit embarrassed but Agathon didn't mind as he barely heard the tiny Lanyx on his back.

Eric was filled with wonder as his eyes tried to take everything in all at once; it was exhilarating for him. For Sebastian, it was something quite different. He always enjoyed this part of his friendship with a Rhorr'Dach but he couldn't help thinking how Celeste might've appreciated this. There was nothing else in the universe like sitting on a flying Dach as they sailed by beautiful scenery, the wind rushing past your face, and hearing the Rhorr'Dach's wings gracefully beat around you. It was a humbling and magical experience. He felt truly blessed by the Gods and Goddesses for allowing him to have it.

As Agathon landed near his mountainside lake, small animals that looked like snails with wings took to the air, startled by the Dach's enormous shadow. Eric looked from side to side, not able to let his eyes rest in one spot for too long. Sebastian looked at Eric and saw a huge smile permanently affixed to his face. Eric was pouring out amazement and wonder in his thoughts. Sebastian knew Eric was grateful he could come along. His friend's thoughts were pure and concentrated, full of childlike awe. Sebastian thought even an amateur mind reader could receive Eric's powerful thoughts now.

Eric shouted as he slid off the great beast's back, "This is amazing, Raynes! Oh my gosh! Agathon, this is gorgeous man! Thanks for having us."

Sebastian took a moment to forget his troubles and simply take in the beauty of the land. The clear green water lake was sizable and had many taggamites near it. The taggamites (they always looked like owls to Sebastian, only bigger, with three feet, and purple compared to Praxis owls) were hunting for their next meal along the surface of the lake. Some Dach had domesticated taggamites and made them family pets. These were obviously all wild though. The sky was blue and purple with small clouds dotting the horizon and mountains off in the distance were brown and black. The land around Agathon's home was covered in blue and green grass that looked healthy and lush.

Agathon motioned for his friends to sit and eat sandwiches he made himself earlier when he had hands instead of claws.

As the men got comfortable on the huge blanket, Agathon carefully laid down and placed himself on the grass in front of the men. The width of his face was so immense that any small bi-peds like Lanyx had to turn their heads from side to side just to look Rhorr'Dach in the eyes. And to the uneducated observer, Agathon looked quite mean and intimidating. Sebastian knew better.

Agathon was a big pussycat until you pissed him off. He was loyal, friendly, cheerful, (despite what happened to him), and a fearsome opponent for anyone unlucky enough to be fighting against him. His breed was an Ice Rhorr'Dach, which meant he could shower an enemy in cold air, snow, and ice shards, freezing most opponents solid if they were small like Humans or Lanyx.

Sebastian thought Celeste would be amused by this irony. Being that Agathon is a deep red color with big fangs, huge claws, and some impressive horns on his head, but he did not breathe fire.

Humans thought all "dragons" breathe fire, but that was their ill-informed story-telling ancestor's ideas. They probably only ran into the fire breathing ones back then.

Once a person got past all of his physical features (and the fact that Rhorr'Dach existed at all), anyone who got to know him well, knew Agathon was brave; he earned his Rhorr'Dach name the day Sebastian found him on the battlefield. Agathon's people had a unique way of naming their societal classifications of their own kind. Instead of focusing on things like physical appearance, they name their own, first, by where they live, and second, by their strongest positive characteristic. So Agathon's classification name, Lake-Brave, is a good way to learn about the Rhorr'Dach you're dealing with before you ever meet them.

Sebastian thought it was brilliant and wished more species could adopt a similar system.

Eric had to ask, "So Agathon, what do your kind think about falling in love and mating rituals?" He reached for a few small red fruits in a bowl that tasted like cinnamon buns.

Sebastian put his head down, shaking it.

The Rhorr'Dach sighed and Eric and Sebastian were instantly fighting against the hot wind coming from his nostrils.

"Oh, sorry guys." He lifted his head up slightly, "Well…Why do you want to know? Are you trying to set me up with a female or something?" Eric couldn't get over how low and rumbly Agathon's voice was now compared to how he sounded as a Human.

Eric laughed, "No, nothing like that. Our friend Sebastian has some girlfriend proble—"

"She's not my girlfriend first off."

"And I think he needs some council. Maybe if he heard how things worked somewhere else, he might get some much needed perspective. Or else, I'll just have to kick his ass until he gets his head out of there."

"Nice, Bouton. Really nice." Sebastian threw his napkin into Eric's face.

Agathon smiled as he watched his friends joke around.

"It's great to see you guys again, really. You should come visit more often," his voice rolled like thunder.

"We've missed you too, Agathon," Sebastian said genuinely.

"Sebastian knows a little bit more about my breed than you, Eric. You know he spent considerable time here when he brought me home, so I think he understands our courtships."

Eric frowned, "Okay, well how 'bout filling me in then? Now I'm kinda curious myself, since I started this conversation."

Agathon smiled, "Seek Knowledge. Yes, curiosity is always good, and wanting to learn is even better here on Foss-Altus. Okay, what do you want to know exactly?"

"Everything you want to tell me."

Agathon went on to explain how Rhorr'Dach do a mating ritual that's very similar to Human or Lanyx people. They let love happen organically without anything like prearranged unions, although some-times they use dating services to help them meet the opposite sex.

"So, in other words, you just date?" Eric sounded surprised it wasn't more complicated.

Agathon laughed and it echoed across the mountains, "Yes. It's just as hard for us to find a suitable mate as where you are from."

Eric wiped his mouth with his napkin, "Huh. I thought you guys would've had it all figured out. Or at least that you'd have some mag-ic potion or something," he looked over at Sebastian and shrugged his shoulders, "Well, that lunch was awesome, Rojo. I'm going to go check out your lake here and take a look around. Give you guys a chance to catch up some more."

"Oh, that's fine; just don't go past the stream that you'll come to on your left. I share this lake with a few other Dach and they might attack without me there to intervene."

Eric raised his eyebrows, "Okay then. Mental note. See you guys in a bit." He stood up, turned around, and ventured off to explore.

Sebastian started to clean up, "That was a very good lunch. Thanks for making it. We really appreciated it."

"Eric must be right about your lady problems; you barely touched your food."

Sebastian grimaced, "It's really nothing. He's just…overreacting."

"Are you sure?"

Sebastian sighed as he threw away his trash, "Yes. No," he crossed his arms on his chest. "To tell the truth, I'm not sure of anything right now. And I don't want to burden my friends with my problems. I'll figure it out."

"Come on Raynes, you know you've been there for me when I needed you. You saved my life. You can talk to me about anything, but I'll never push you. I know how it is when a problem is better left unspoken."

Sebastian walked closer to Agathon's face and sat down cross-legged in the grass. He looked into Agathon's gigantic blue eye and saw himself and all the scenery behind him reflected.

"I don't know…I thought coming out here and doing some shooting would be good for me. I never turn down an opportunity to hone my skills but…" he looked out onto the lake.

"But?" Agathon's tail went up and down slowly like a gentle wave to avoid shaking the ground.

Sebastian looked up at the clouds slowly drifting across the sky, "I just can't get this woman off my mind."

"What's her name? Do I know her?"

Sebastian raised his eyebrows, "You might. Queen Dowager of Earth and Il'laceier Celeste Hennessy, well, now she's changed her name back to Vandermeer I guess. She didn't want to be associated with her former husband anymore."

Agathon smiled, "Yes, I've seen her on news vids. She seems to handle herself professionally, and is well spoken. You like her?"

"I do. I think I like her a bit too much though. I met her and she's changing things for me. I'm thinking about her when I should be focusing on other things. I wonder what she's doing when she's not with me. I wonder how she feels about me now." Sebastian saw a samurai fighting a giant snake in the clouds, or maybe the snake was a ribbon, he hadn't decided.

"So why is this woman vexing you?"

"There's something about her that makes her different. She's special…in a lot of different ways, but for one thing, she got my attention the moment I saw her years before I actually met her. That in and of itself is unique to her." The samurai cloud dissipated and Sebastian looked back to Agathon's blue eye.

Agathon smiled, "Oh yes of course. This is the woman you've mentioned to me before. You have…what do you call it? A crush on her right?"

"Do I ever. But it's way beyond a crush now. I care a great deal for her. But I'm more than a little concerned she's found multiple ways to make me lose control of myself." He ran his hand through his hair and smiled without realizing it.

"Sebastian, with all due respect, I think you need to loosen up a little and allow yourself to lose control. You govern yourself with an iron fist and while I might admire the amount of restraint you demonstrate as a military army captain or an assassin, you can't always be so constrictive."

Sebastian frowned, "Constrictive? To myself? You make me sound like a tight-ass."

Agathon said nothing.

"Really? I'm a tight-ass?"

"Raynes, I've seen you in several different situations. I know you're a complicated man, but yes, sometimes you're...wound pretty tight."

"Okay, let's say you're right – I'm reserved sometimes, but there's a good reason to keep myself at a certain level. I'm part animal but I can go full-blown animal if I'm not careful. I do things to keep myself calm and under control so that I don't get dangerous...really dangerous."

Agathon made a face, "You are a very dangerous man already. I'm not sure I understand your meaning."

Sebastian raised an eyebrow, "I tried to warn Celeste. I don't think she gets it. I meditate, I read, listen to soothing music, exercise – all that's to help me relax," he closed his eyes and kept them closed as he spoke, "Lanyx are supposed to be peaceful people, but I'm not like the others, not with my 7's, not with my mercenary talents. I'm just not. If I let myself get out of control for good, I mean, if I stay that way for extended amounts of time and I don't reign myself in..."

"Then what happens?"

Sebastian opened his eyes, "I don't know. But I'm afraid Celeste can make that happen in me. I'm afraid I'll stop caring about controlling myself and I'll give in to whatever she wants and then we'll all find out exactly what happens when I stop controlling all of my animal instincts."

"You can't be serious, Raynes. You make it sound like you're going to rip your girlfriend apart or hurt her somehow. I think you're exaggerating all of this out of proportion."

Sebastian shook his head, "I wish I was."

Agathon yielded, for now. He picked up his head and tilted it so his eyes could survey Eric as he walked beyond Agathon's garden at the edge of his property.

"You think you're going to be able to solve this for me whether I want you to or not, Aggie?"

Agathon's wide mouth was set in annoyance, "Don't read my mind, Raynes. You know how I feel about that."

"Your intentions came through, that's all. I apologize my friend. I don't read you, but you know how this works. If your intentions are clear, I'll usually hear them. Now what are you planning on saying to help me see the light, so to speak?"

"Later. Why don't you tell me the whole story first? Why aren't you in a relationship with her already?" he settled down, laying his chin to the grass again.

Sebastian stood up and started pacing in front of Agathon's face. "I felt like she was trying to drive me into a relationship when I wanted to take things slow, see where they go over time. I felt like she was pushing and I'm not sure I'm ready to be in a relationship again since my last one. Maybe...I should just stay a lone wolf. Safer for her that way."

Agathon frowned, "What about you though? You can't *always* be alone. Beings are not meant to live a life alone, well, a few rare souls are... maybe, but not most. I feel everyone should have a partner who they can love and be loved in returned. I think love is one of the best things about being alive. Besides, hasn't it been a very long time since your last relationship ended?"

"A while, yes." Sebastian stopped his pacing momentarily.

"You always say our motto, but do you really believe in it? I know you Seek Knowledge; you are extremely smart that's obvious. I've certainly seen you Fight When you Must, and you're excellent at that as well, but I've never seen you Accept Love. Listen to that part. Hear it with your ears, process it in your brain, but you must feel it in your heart and soul." Agathon balled up one of his clawed fists and held it against his chest for emphasis.

"I hear you. I do. I think it's one of those things that's easier said than done for me."

"You also need to love yourself first. I don't think you do, and I'm positive that you haven't forgiven yourself for what you *think* you've done. No one blames you for what happened but you. Can you forgive yourself even though you're not to blame?"

"I'm not sure. It's been almost twenty years, Agathon. That's a long time."

"Not really. Not in your lifetime and certainly not in mine. That's just a drop in the ocean for me. What about loving yourself? Are you capable of that?" He took his back foot and scratched behind his ear like a dog.

"I can try." He stood with his legs set far apart and his arms crossed on his chest.

"That's a start Raynes, that's a start. Why don't you tell me the whole story now?"

Sebastian went over how things developed with Celeste since he met her.

Agathon was a very good listener compared to Eric. Sebastian appreciated being able to complete his story without any questions and without interruptions.

Agathon rubbed his claws across each other while he was thinking. Sparks were coming off them, but Sebastian thought his friend didn't notice this happening.

"Sebastian, I feel like you're glancing over something very important in your story."

Sebastian raised his eyebrows and asked, "What's that?"

"You said she has 7's, but she's Human, and that, in and of itself is remarkably rare. Then you add on top of that you're able to sense each other. Have you even considered the odds of a cross-species telepathic romance? It's probably something like a billion to one. And it sounds like to me, you two are locking into each other already...You know there's only one way this could turn out..." The Rhorr'Dach didn't need to finish his sentence out loud. Agathon knew Sebastian fully comprehended the point he was making.

Sebastian put one hand through his hair and left it there. "Rojo, how do you know everything about everything? You're not even," he paused doing the math in his head, "300 yet. You're still a young Dach."

Agathon laughed long and loud. Everything seemed to rumble around them. "Oh Raynes, I don't have to tell you this. Knowledge is power. When you've got almost every species in the entire universe after you for some idiotic or dangerous reason, you have to learn about everyone else and all their problems. I love your species though – you Lanyx are fascinating people and this idea of 'locking into' one another is unique. There isn't anyone else in the universe with anything like it," he paused a long time, "Don't you think it's amazing?"

Even without his 7's, Sebastian would've known exactly what his friend was alluding to, but he played dumb anyway, "What's amazing?"

"Lanyx don't lock into anyone outside of their own species Sebastian. You know this. Why are you playing dumb with me?"

Now it was Sebastian's turn to laugh, "You know you sound just like Bouton now. Both of you are trying to tell me I'm locking into Celeste already when we've barely spent any time together, and she's a Human. As far as I know, it's impossible for cross-species locking. You guys must want me to fall in love awful badly. Though I don't know why."

"No, I don't want you to fall in love. You misunderstand me. I want you to be *happy*. I want you to live life as if every day was your last. And I don't mean by looking over your shoulder all the time and thinking someone's out to kill you. I mean, relish every second and make the most of it. Take these moments you talk about with Celeste and stretch them out over your entire lifetime. I think she's where your happiness is. It seems to me when you talk about your Queen Celeste – you are proud, you're excited, you get animated and you're happy. To be honest, I've never seen you this way, and that should not be ignored. She's special to you; you said it yourself. And with your combined powers – I think you could rule the universe."

Sebastian gave a hearty laugh that surprised even himself. "Agathon you need to stop smoking your special blend of trees out here. I think it's altering your sense of reality."

"I know what I'm saying friend. I'm telling you things you already know, but when two powerful telepaths get together, impossible things become possible."

Sebastian shook his head, "Neither you or Eric are thinking of what happened with Francesca. A relationship with me cost someone their life. No one seems to remember but me."

"I do remember. But you didn't kill Fran. She killed herself. You must forgive *her* for doing that. It seems you have never blamed her for doing something terrible."

Sebastian's anger surfaced, "But she would've never killed herself had it not been for ME!"

"Ah, you can't say that. You have no idea what would have been. I never met her, but I can tell you with confidence that she was not per-fect. No being is. Not me. Not you. Not Celeste. Not any of us. Perhaps she would've killed herself over her lost job someday, or a beloved family member dying or who knows? Look at us. You and I both lost our parents, we suffered greatly. Neither one of us killed ourselves."

"I've thought about it," Sebastian mumbled.

"Raynes, so have I. Life is difficult sometimes. It takes you and throws you to the ground, kicks you in the face and stomps all over you. I understand the challenges of just holding on one more day when you feel like you can't."

Sebastian stared into one of Agathon's eyes, "You never told me you were suicidal."

Agathon lifted his head high over Sebastian and looked out over the lake, then looked down at his friend, "Killing oneself…it isn't the solution. I've always found it to be a temporary feeling that comes and goes. Hopefully in one's life it only surfaces rarely and goes more often than it comes."

"I guess I feel guilt…about Francesca. I should've checked up on her more often. Maybe checked in with her friends or her parents to see if they noticed anything before it was too late."

"What's done is done. Her death is not your fault and you need to let your guilt and her…go. For good. And if you don't forget your past, it will cost you your future with Celeste," he paused, "You are thinking too much about something that has nothing to do with your brain and everything to do with your heart and soul." Agathon was frustrated with his friend's seemingly intentional obstinacy.

Sebastian sighed; his expression was one of pained tolerance. He felt like he was receiving a lecture from his father.

Agathon looked out over the lake and took a deep breath in, letting it out slowly, "Maybe you should try something new. Try seeing yourself through Celeste's eyes. I think she's a smart girl and I know for a fact that you are an extraordinarily courageous and gifted being. You must tune out your brain and all your thinking and listen to your heart. Trust what it has to say about her. I think she likes you for the right reasons and you should give it a shot with her. Her eagerness to be with you shouldn't be looked down upon. Take it as a compliment that you fascinate her enough to make her excited to be around you. And if it turns into love, real true once-in-a-lifetime kind of love, you should hold onto that and never let go. You deserve to be happy Raynes." Agathon tilted his head to scratch his itchy ear with his back foot again, "Just remember to invite me to the wedding. I love that tradition. Everyone's always so happy." He wiggled his claws on his front feet excitedly and his tail slowly slinked from side to side.

Sebastian smiled at his friend, "Hold on Aggie, slow down. Nobody said anything about weddings, but I would never get married without having you there my friend. Thank you for talking this over with me. Eric is great, but sometimes I need him to just relax and process things before he blurts out what he's thinking."

"No problem, Sebastian. Keep me updated on what happens with this lady of yours."

"I will, although she's not mine right now. I sort of told her I didn't want to see her again."

"Oh? She's a pretty lady. You must be confident she won't be occupied by someone else then?" He raised his eye ridges.

"Well, I saw her with a guy before I left, and I knew she was going to meet yet another man later on. I think she's pretty popular with a lot of men right now."

"I must tell you, even a few of the Dach I hang around with have expressed how beautiful they think she is. Her beauty is something that seems to appeal across species; you can't wait too long with a girl like that."

He sighed, "I'm starting to see that. When I get back to Praxis I'll find out what kind of damage I've done, but for now, it's time to unwind a bit. I came a long way to see you and we have a lot of catching up to do between the three of us." He watched as Agathon took a claw to his ear again. "You want me to scratch your ears for you?"

Agathon put his chin down on the grass and implored through his teeth, "Yes please. It's almost shedding season and I'm not looking forward to it."

Sebastian reached up and scratched behind the Rhorr'Dach's ear as hard as he could with his fingers and Agathon thumped his back leg down on the ground so fast that Sebastian bounced, "Hey, take it easy there. You're going to knock me down, Rojo."

"Sorry."

"So what was it you were going to tell me earlier? Something to re-solve my issue of dating the Queen."

Agathon answered through his teeth, "Your problem is two-fold. I know Fran's death affected you greatly and that is a big barricade right now to your growth as a Lanyx, but there's something else standing in your way. I think you're terrified of falling in love with Celeste. If you can accept Fran's death and let it go, and get over your fear of love, you'll solve this problem very quickly…I promise."

Sebastian was still scratching his friend's ear, so Agathon couldn't see him. Sebastian's face was expressionless and he stayed silent. He only stared out over the green lake and considered Agathon's words.

The rest of the afternoon was spent with the three of them exploring the countryside and taking a dip in the lake.

They caught each other up on what was going on in their lives. For the Rhorr'Dach, things were calm and quiet, just the way they liked it. Agathon informed them he was to participate in Quintana Brix, a big parade the Rhorr'Dach held once every 116 years – he was elated to be master of ceremonies this time. Eric had just stocked up on ammo and improved his armory by dozens of new guns and weapons, and Sebastian spoke of recent assassinations and expressed his concern over what seemed to be a galaxy wide overthrow of power, maybe even the whole universe.

THREE

>>> > CELESTE LOOKED AT her Titan. It was about six and she was ready to meet Dax downstairs in the lobby. She waited in a chair looking outside for him to arrive. She decided to wear one of her many new dresses, a bright red sheath with a low neckline, something a bit sexy. Her hair was down and flowed in waves over her back.

Dax showed up right on time as she met him on the street. She watched his expression as he looked over her. He studied her from head to toe and it felt like he was undressing her with his eyes.

She liked that.

"You look absolutely ravishing, my dear."

"Thanks. You look nice too."

He kissed her hello and they walked into the city holding hands.

The sun was beginning to set as they arrived at the auditorium arm in arm and she felt vibrant and alive. She loved going to the theater and watching live performances. She felt something special in the air before a performance took place – it made her want to take the stage. To feel what it was like to be a professional singer. She reminded herself that nothing was off limits anymore. She could attend college and get a degree in singing or she could hire a professional coach to help her. She smiled thinking of the possibilities of chasing a dream she'd given up long ago.

"Have you ever seen 'Cold Sweet Nothings' before?" Dax asked.

She shook her head, "No. I've never even heard of it, actually. Is it popular?"

They took their seats in the back row and he looked over his program, "Yeah, it says here they've been running for two years. It's won tons of awards. You excited to see it?"

"Yes. It's been a while since I saw a musical. It sounds good; I'm glad you invited me."

"Of course. What man wouldn't want to be with a gorgeous lady like yourself?"

She smiled broadly at him and he leaned over to kiss her cheek.

She couldn't get over how sweet he was. She really was getting used to seeing him on a regular basis.

The lights dimmed and the show started.

FOUR

>>> > AT INTERMISSION, CELESTE and Dax sat at a table by the bar sharing a chocolate cheesecake.

He kept checking his Titan. She assumed he was trying to watch the time, but she wasn't sure. He almost seemed nervous to her, so she tried to read his mind. She saw nothing there but darkness – the walls around his thoughts continued to be impenetrable. She couldn't get a single thought from him and it bothered her a little for the first time. She tried to shake off the feeling, but he might be genuinely hiding something from her. Maybe she was looking for something to be wrong with him so she could end it and wait for Sebastian to come back. *I'm pathetic*, she thought to herself, *a perfectly good man and I'm actively trying to find his flaws so I can toss him aside for someone who doesn't even want to date me.*

"Is intermission almost over?" she put her fork down.

He looked up from his Titan, "They flash the lights when it's time to go back in. We have a few minutes. I want to make sure I get my fill of this ridiculously overpriced gin and tonic." He smiled, but it seemed strained to her. She didn't like it.

She knew how the lights flashed, warning theatergoers it was time to take your seats, she was just too polite to tell Dax.

They talked for a while longer as she finished dessert. The bar and lobby lights flashed.

"Ready?" He put his arm out and she took it.

"Let's do it."

FIVE

>>> > AN HOUR AND a half later, Dax held Celeste close outside her apartment building and whispered in her ear, "I enjoy taking you out and showing you a good time hon."

She smiled, "I like it too. And that show was so good. I adored it."

"I like you a lot. I hope you've realized that."

"I like you, Dax. I've been enjoying our dates and my time spent with you," she paused, "but it seems like tonight you were a little…it felt like you weren't your normal self. Is everything okay? Or is there anything you want to talk about?"

He raised his eyebrows, "Oh that! Sorry, minor crisis at work. Me and my employer are butting heads over a plan that I came up with.

There's this deadline coming up and I was trying not to let it bother me tonight, but I guess I wasn't successful at hiding it. I'm sorry dear."

"That's okay. I wanted to make sure it wasn't something I did." Celeste was relieved he was just stressed at work and that could make anyone a little crabby. And there she was, thinking he was up to something sinister with her. She felt silly now, and a little ashamed of herself.

"No no, darling. Not at all. You and I are just fine. You've been perfect since the day I met you," he cleared his throat and gave her body a little squeeze, "Why don't you come to my place next time? We can try a redo of that night I made you feel uncomfortable and I can redeem myself."

"Okay."

He smiled, "I'll pick you up here at seven in two days then."

He gave her a long slow goodbye kiss and walked away into the night. She watched him go and wondered what it would be like at his house this time. She thought as long as she stayed away from the drinks, she'd be okay.

SIX

>>> > D'ARTAGNAN WOKE UP after the sun went down. Damn nightmares were making it so he wasn't getting enough sleep at night so he started napping during the day.

He laid in his sleeping capsule and thought about his Kingdom visitors earlier in the week. The longer he thought about it, the angrier he became.

He grabbed his Titan off the nightstand and pulled up news vids and articles regarding the Kingdom's search for HR members. There was very little. The Kingdom was trying to keep it out of the news from what he could gather, but if the guards were going door to door in every neighborhood across the planet, keeping it quiet would be impossible. They must've been doing this on Earth as well in conjunction with the police.

He went to the floor and started counting his way up to a thousand sit-ups.

He felt like searching news feeds and researching the HR wasn't enough. He needed to do more. He hadn't researched David Hennessy since he took the throne. He came out of nowhere and looked to be as bad as his brother. It was time to find out who he really was.

SEVEN

>>> > AFTER XABAT DIED, David relied less on his council and more on himself. When he had asked Xabat what he thought would work to make Earthlings respect him more, all he came up with were war ideas and violence. Maybe he was taking the wrong approach.

Maybe David should be thinking more along the lines of bringing Il'laceier and Earth together. David sat on his throne with a distant gaze on his face. He thought about what worked in the past for other planets that were struggling and then an idea hit him.

Unfortunately, he couldn't do it alone. He needed some help. He got on his Titan.

"Ulysses? Can you enter my private chambers in ten minutes please?"

Ulysses was on his way and David quickly got up and strode into his private bedroom.

EIGHT

>>> > "I NEED YOU to do a special job for me."

Ulysses nodded as he checked his Titan, "Sure. Anything your Royal Highness. Just tell me when. Also our meeting is coming up shortly."

David sighed, "Why can't everyone be like you? You're such a great guard and I'm glad you're always there for me."

"Of course, sir."

"Celeste Hennessy will be making an appearance at the Estate soon and I need complete privacy with her. If you could guard my door while we're talking to make sure no one interrupts us, that would be great."

"Yes my King."

"I'm going to call her now. It's a delicate matter and I don't feel comfortable speaking out in the open with her. Would you mind guarding the door for me now as well?"

"I will be right out in the hall sir," Ulysses bowed.

"Thank you."

David waited until the door closed and then called Celeste.

She picked up on the fourth ring. He wanted a video call but she only allowed audio.

"Ah Queen Dowager, we need to speak at Silver Thorn tomorrow. Can you do that?"

He heard Celeste's hesitation clearly, "I was going to…what is this regarding?"

"I can't say over the Titan. It's a very personal matter, but it would be in your best interest to appear as soon as possible."

Celeste replied, "Certainly, your Highness. Let me see…" she paused, "tomorrow…I can be there at one o'clock. Does that work for you?"

"One will be fine. I'll see you then," David smiled.

The connection went dead as Celeste hung up on him. He didn't like that, but he let it slide this time. He thought there might be quite a few things in her future that he did to her that she wouldn't like.

David opened his door, "Ulysses. One o'clock in one Earth day. Let's go to our meeting."

"Yes sir."

NINE

››› › DAVID SAT AT the IMC meeting and frowned. It seemed fewer members were showing up. Ulysses and himself had talked about keeping members and how they could test new recruits to see if they'd last in the group, but fewer people were signing up in the first place for them to test. So David decided to talk to all members, one at a time, to find out more about them.

"No one is to panic!" David yelled out over the sixty-two men he had standing in front of him. They quieted down.

"I believe that information is the most important thing I need to acquire this week. If you have anything in your past to hide, criminal records and such, I don't care. I know none of us are without sin. This is simply a few questions to make sure no one else is planning on leaving when things get hard here, and also to make sure none of you are with the BDP."

David saw a few men shift in their seats, "But…if someone is with the BDP, I'll allow them to stand up and leave right now without punishment. Anyone that I find out after today that's been informing the BDP will die. I guarantee this."

David looked at Ulysses and then slowly over the room, "Does anyone want to get up and leave?"

There was an uncomfortable silence as the men looked around at each other, waiting for someone to move. Ulysses prayed no one stood up so he wouldn't have to kill anyone. He knew David was lying – if anyone stood up, he was to follow them out and kill them as quickly as possible.

No one moved.

"Final chance," David said. "All right, that means I can trust you all to tell Ulysses the truth when your time comes to meet with him over the next few weeks. Let's move along."

Ulysses thanked God silently.

"I have found out that the BDP seems to be excelling at certain things that we are not and I would like to change this. We're going to have to come up with something to start stealing Brotherhood members to our side. I think that might be the best way to hit that group where it hurts. If they have no members, then they can't do anything."

The crowd nodded their heads.

"If anyone knows anything they think would be useful, please approach Ulysses at the end of this meeting and he will pass your information along to me. I have an engagement this afternoon, so this is another brief meeting, but I promise next week's will run longer. Thanks. Let the universe freeze in ice, so that we may inherit eternity."

The men stood and started to shuffle out of the room. David watched as Ulysses spoke with a member and then patted him down. After that security protocol was passed, he approached David with the Il'lacean behind him.

"Sir, this man says he has some important information for you that he is unwilling to tell me. I patted him down. He's clean. I told him if you approved, he had one minute."

David nodded.

Ulysses walked far enough away for privacy, but stayed close. The man stared at David.

"Let's have it," David commanded.

The man started, "Name's Jamiel. I wanted to say I've seen that Queen Celeste on Praxis…She's hanging out with a guy that I know is BDP. Maybe she's in the Brotherhood too."

David immediately perked up, "What do you mean? Explain yourself."

The guy smiled, "Yeah. I was people watching down on Praxis the other day, waiting for my girl to finish shopping. The Queen and this guy Dax were walking hand in hand and then he kissed her and it wasn't a peck. It lasted a while. I heard him ask her out for a date and she said yes, so apparently she's seeing this guy. I thought you should know. Maybe it could be useful somehow."

"Dax? Do you know his last name or anything else?"

"I can't remember his last name, but I know he's high up in the BDP. It's embarrassing to say, but I considered joining the BDP first and the recruiter had me talk to Dax, that's how I know who he is. He's got his shit together. He's young, a Lanyx, in good shape, and smelled like a born leader."

"When was this?"

"Oh, I saw them a few days ago. I wanted to tell you as soon as possible. They were all lovey dovey."

David looked at Ulysses and waved him over, "Yes, Jamiel, thank you. This information is most helpful. You didn't happen to take any photos or video, did you?"

"No, sorry. That would've been a great idea, but they snuck up on me and caught me off guard. Is there anything else I can do?"

David shook his head, "Thanks, but this is enough. Ulysses, show him our gratitude would you?"

"Yes sir."

David walked away and the man said to Ulysses under his breath, "I was hoping there was going to be some sort of coren for this."

Ulysses laughed, "Nope. You get a free pass to visit the botanical gardens and insectarium next to Rem Mot Om."

"What am I going to do with this?"

"I don't know. I just do what he tells me man. Take it or leave it."

"No thanks. Just don't tell the leader I turned down a present from him."

"No can do. If he asks me, I'm going to tell him the truth."

Jamiel rolled his eyes, "Khaleen, just give me the pass then."

Ulysses smirked, "Good choice."

CHAPTER 11

THE DEAL

ONE

>>> > MITCH WAS WORRIED about the HR members.

He told them before they left the bunker that they wouldn't meet for a while and he hoped they were all smart enough to stay in hiding, but it was easy to slip up. He couldn't contact them now, it was way too early for that and he needed the spotlight off him before he made any moves like that.

He switched sporadically from Earth to Praxis. Sometimes he would stay in a hotel on some random world for the week, but he was constantly shifting positions. It felt like the safest thing to do for now.

He hoped all of the HR members were doing the same thing.

He watched the news, looking for stories regarding the group and whether any new arrests or captures had been made. He hadn't seen any for a while. He wondered if that meant all the members were doing a good job at hiding, or whether the kingdom put pressure on the news agencies to drop coverage of what was going on.

TWO

>>> > HACE'S MAN CALLED in with a check on Ni-toyis as Hace was eating brunch in his bedroom.

"First she went to some cabin on Mar Yen and looked like she was packing up for a trip. She stayed for five hours, then she launched and I've been following her in flight ever since. She's approaching a Jump but I'm not sure where she's going to take it."

Hace smiled, "She's probably living on Stoxia. Mar Yen was just a pit stop for her. The cabin, was it hers or part of a hotel or something?"

"It was part of a big cluster of cabins that could be rented out."

"Yeah, follow her through The Jump. Take it to Stoxia. Might be hard to keep up with her though."

"I'll try to stay only a few transits behind her when The Jump comes. I hate those things."

"I know buddy. Good job. Let me know what else you find."

"Yes boss. Thanks. Yang over and out."

Hace's Titan returned to the main menu.

He thought about Ni-toyis. That woman had a body that just wouldn't quit. She was sexy as hell, and young. She was probably excellent in bed. He started to get all riled up.

"DAI?"

"Yes Master Hunter?"

"Take Stox form and come to my bedroom." He stood up and wiped his mouth with a napkin.

A few minutes later DAI was knocking on his half-open door and he waved her in. She assumed the attitude typical of her breed and was more aggressive than her Human form. She walked up to him quickly and put her arms around his neck, "I missed you."

Hace raised his eyebrows, "You did? How sweet. What have you been thinking about in your hibernation chamber huh?"

She smiled and put her lips against his ear. Her tentacles danced around his face, "You darling."

"Could you be more specific?"

"I was thinking about fucking your brains out, but first, I have to seduce you. Make sure you're in the mood." She put her hand, palm down, on his chest and ran it down to his belt. She undid it and started removing it from the pant loops, with her other hand she felt her way around his groin until she felt his erection growing through the fabric.

Hace put his head back, "I think you're improving my mood already love."

She kissed his neck and ran her tongue up to his chin and then grabbed his bottom lip with her mouth and sucked lightly on it.

Hace let out a moan and put his hands on the back of her neck to hold her up against him as he kissed her hard.

She unzipped his pants. They pooled around his ankles. Her hand found his bare erection, "Oooooh, you're not even wearing any boxer briefs today hon."

He grunted.

She moved her hands underneath his shirt. He pulled it over his head and threw it aside. He stepped out of his pants and kicked them out of the way.

"Now it's time to get you naked dear."

DAI giggled, "Let me honey." She pushed him down onto the bed and started playing some sexy music over the speakers in his room as she dimmed the lights without moving. She was still in control of the ship.

She turned around and bent over in front of him to take off her high heels, one at a time. Her short dress rose up. The bottom halves of her ass cheeks were peeking out.

"Oh baby, I love it when you strip for me."

She stood up and started to pull up the dress over her hips slowly, and then stopped, "I know it stud."

Hace smiled.

She pulled the dress over her head and tentacles and then tossed it aside. She turned around and walked towards him. She stopped in front of him wedging her legs in between his while he was seated. She put her hands around her back and undid her bra strap.

Hace put his hands on her hips.

"Ah! No touching yet sir. Bad boy!"

He smiled, "Yeah, you go and put me in my place."

She removed her bra, revealing her large breasts to him, then put her hands on his neck and pushed his face into them.

He licked and sucked his way along her chest from one nipple to the other and DAI put her head back as her tentacles spread out. She let out a little moan.

"I like hearing that baby," Hace paused long enough to say.

She stepped back from him to remove her thong. Then she crawled onto his bed and slowly, suggestively lay flat onto her belly, arching her ass up and shook it. "Come and get it if you're man enough."

"You know how to tease me you little vixen." Hace pounced on top of her and quickly positioned himself. She spread her legs and grabbed his cock to slide it inside her.

She arched her ass up a little bit more and spread her legs even further. Hace went deeper in and moaned at how tight she was.

She called out, "I want you deeper baby. Fuck me hard. Harder!"

He thrust until an orgasm exploded through him, then collapsed on top of her.

"You were worth every coren. I keep saying it, but no one has anything quite like you in the universe but me."

"Yes Master Hunter. I aim to please."

"And please you do. That was good baby." He withdrew from her and rolled over.

"Is there anything else you require of me sir?"

He spanked her on the ass, "Nope. Clean up and go back to your hibernation chamber."

"Yes sir," she headed for the shower.

Hace laid there for a minute longer thinking. DAI was a fantastic fuck. He could have her be anyone he wanted on the outside with her same obedience on the inside, but she was still only a simulation. He needed some real pussy soon.

THREE

>>> > "YOU WANT ME to do WHAT?!" Celeste couldn't believe her ears.

"I think a marriage would be beneficial to both of us and our people." David sat with his hands folded across his lap on his new throne, crown atop his head glimmering with jewels. She didn't know why the throne in Silver Thorn's receiving hall wasn't good enough for him, but she suspected David didn't want anything of Jon's left behind, except for maybe her as a wife now? All of this sounded crazy and way too familiar. She looked around. It was just the two of them...and that made her extremely nervous.

"I'm sorry your Royal Highness, but I'm not sure how this would work. Last time I was here, you seemed to want me to leave Earth, maybe for good. Now you're suggesting a marriage between us? Why would I want to do this?"

David's yellow eyes bore a hole into the center of her forehead; she tried reading him but couldn't get anything. She could tell by looking at him he was already agitated with her hesitation.

"Celeste, I'm sure you're thinking of your previous marriage to my brother. I can guarantee you that it would be nothing like that. First of all, my brother loved you."

She raised her eyebrows, "He did not! It was a marriage strictly of convenience. He had his mistresses and I...said nothing about it."

David sighed, "As much as it perplexes me, my brother loved you. Want to know how I know?" he paused, "Near the end of his reign, probably the last time I saw him alive, he told me as much."

"And when was that?" Celeste would normally never talk to David this way, but she was angry for being "summoned" here, heartbroken at losing Sebastian and eager to get back to Praxis. She couldn't have predicted why David wanted to see her in person, but now that she knew the reason, all she wanted to do was get the hell out of here. She was in no mood to watch her manners with the King.

"Not that it's any of your business, but I saw Jon about two months before he was assassinated."

Celeste had no idea they met up that recently.

David continued, "He told me he loved you and would prove it soon somehow. I'm unsure what his grand plan was for you two, but I believe he did love you. Now, as I was sayi—"

"Why did you meet with Jon? I thought you were angry at him." Celeste regretted the words as soon as they left her mouth. She stepped a bit too far over the line with that comment.

"Celeste, you really aren't acting like the Queen I remember you to be. So many questions asked to someone who is *so much farther* above you. You need to be more careful with your curiosity."

Celeste was quiet, but burning on the inside at his arrogance.

"That's better. What I was trying to say is that my people are starting to disdain Humans. I'm trying to prevent another war between our two worlds. The attack on Rem Mot Om was…extremely difficult for me. I lost citizens, staff, my home was damaged, and I lost a valued and close member of my council. I could've lost my life. Not only did my people suffer causalities that terrible day, Humans were lost as well as many other species. The media did not report the correct numbers, because they were misinformed. I told the news crews that 165 million coren were the assessed damages and 798 lives were lost, but I lied. If I told them truthful numbers, we'd already be at war and it wouldn't be because of me. My people are hard to hold down when they get angry. I'm trying to keep them at bay by downplaying the tragedy that happened at my coronation."

Celeste was quiet now, not burning with anger, but waiting to see what David was willing to share with her. "I wished that never happened your Royal Highness. I am truly sorry for your losses that day."

David softened for a moment, "I see your condolences are genuine. I deeply regret what happened as well. I appreciate your kind words. Thank you."

Celeste nodded.

"The true numbers will stay unknown to the public mainly in protection of them. The reason I'm proposing marriage to you is that we need to join our two people together and I think that's always been a struggle on both sides. I think Humans have always resisted Il'lacean rule, although you and my brother did a lot of bridge building, it's not been enough. It's true I come from a very aggressive and hostile race but the assassination of my brother has poured accelerant on an already long burning fire. Now, this attack..."—David shook his head—"This attack has made things much worse. If I could show my people that we have an alliance, that Humans will subm—"

"Humankind shouldn't be submitting to anyone, with all due respect King David. My people historically are used to being free and governing our own planet. Humans would feel more at ease if they felt you had their best interests at heart and currently they don't have any reason to feel that way. The beheadings have caused a lot of anxiety and mistrust of Il'laceans for my people."

"Tell me Celeste, are you part of this Human Resistance?" David steepled his fingers slowly.

She hated it when he stared at her that way over his hands. With the King's receiving hall empty like this it was deadly quiet. She could hear her heart beating in her ears.

She stared boldly back into the King's eyes, "I am not."

"Are you sure? Quite sure? Because if I find out that you had anything to do with the bombing, or the Resistance..."

"I promise you, I had nothing to do with any of that violence, nor the Human Resistance."

"I do believe you would never endanger so many innocent lives, but you have to understand my suspicion."

David paused and stared over her head. She heard the door behind her open and then shut. She looked around and saw a High Royal Guard walking towards them. The guard stopped in front of her and bowed. He reached for her hand and kissed the back of it. He spoke with his head down, "Queen Dowager Hennessy, it is an honor to see you again. Please excuse the interruption, but I must tell the King important news."

He looked her in the eye and she recognized him. This was the same guard that interrupted her and David the first time she was here. The one that winked at her. She immediately tried to read him, but couldn't sense any of his thoughts.

David cleared his throat, "You must pardon HRG Benson. He's one of the most polite Humans I've ever met. Ulysses! What is the meaning of this interruption? The Queen and I have important business. Get up here!"

HRG Benson winked again at Celeste and approached the King's throne. He leaned over to David and whispered something. Celeste strained to hear but couldn't make out anything.

She had helped Ulysses under Jon's reign. Ulysses had a death in the family, if she remembered right. Estate policy would let him attend the funeral only, but Celeste stepped forward on his behalf and begged Jon to let the man take a leave of absence. Jon surprised her by granting Ulysses a week off without pay, but Celeste arranged supplemental pay anyway. Ulysses approached her after his return and expressed his gratitude. She had forgotten about him until now. She helped several guards and staff while she lived in the estate so while it was a very big deal to Ulysses, daily acts of kindness for the queen were standard.

Ulysses Benson had a very high position now – he'd been promoted since Jon's reign and for him to walk in on her and David, he had to have a very good relationship with the King. She wondered what they were talking about, but she couldn't read either one of them. She wanted to know why David trusted *this* Human.

Ulysses straightened up and then bowed to David.

"Please Benson, no more interruptions. Guard the door for us while we're talking."

"Yes, your Excellency."

Benson turned to Celeste and smiled as he left the room. David didn't start speaking until the door shut.

"Sorry again Celeste. I had been waiting for a piece of information that just came in and it couldn't wait. So, what was I saying? Oh yes, I hope you're telling me the truth in regards to this terrorist group, the HR."

"I am your Majesty," she spoke through clenched teeth.

"And there's no chance you're part of the Brotherhood of Desert Phantoms, right?"

Celeste hesitated, blinking in bafflement as to where this question came from, "No. Of course not. Why would I join a terrorist group now?"

David stared at her, "Just call it a pre-marital background check," he gave her a closed mouthed smile, "What do you think of my marriage proposal? I need a yes from you."

Celeste couldn't believe he was asking this. Yes was out of the question. She couldn't handle another marriage of convenience to a man she would never love.

"My answer is no your Highness. I can help you with the Humans, but not this way. They're going to see right through this and it won't look good for either one of us. I've expressed interest to you before in addressing my people through a vid—"

David leaned forward, "I will not take no for an answer. Not from you, not from anyone. The King doesn't need suggestions, only your acceptance of things the way they need to be."

Celeste folded her arms across her chest, "Listen David, I've been more than patient with you about..."

David stood up and walked down the few steps that separated the two of them. When he stood directly in front of her, he loomed over her like death itself. She knew he wanted to scare her, but Celeste would not be intimated into another loveless marriage nor would she bother to look him in the eye.

"Don't address me by my first name, ever again. Don't patronize me, or treat me like an idiot." His voice was authoritative as he spoke calmly, "You are going to marry me, not because you want to, but because I command it. I am your King and you must obey. Look at me damn you."

Celeste stretched her gaze upward to meet his cold stare and thought things were going to get a lot worse for her today. This was not a possibility she thought would actually happen to her. She fought off the fear trying to build up within her and spoke sharply, "King, I'm not going to be forced into this arrangement. Please understand that no matter what you say, or what you want, I'm not going to cave in on this...idea of yours."

David moved even closer to her. She thought for a horrifying moment he would try to kiss her, "No matter what I say hmmm? I think I can say something that might make you change your mind."

Celeste wanted to run away. This situation felt too much like so many she'd been in with his brother. What could he possibly say to change her mind?

"I know for a fact that you've been dating a Lanyx man."

Fear raced through her and siphoned the blood from her face. There's no way he could know about Sebastian. Then she thought maybe David meant Dax. Whom did he mean? She couldn't ask, in case he didn't know of Sebastian.

"You're being courted by a very dangerous man. I'm positive of this because I've had my guards watching you to see who you spend your time with."

Oh my God, she thought, *he does know about Sebastian! Dax is just a political analyst. He doesn't do anything to be considered dangerous. I wish I could use my 7's now!*

"I know you care about this man. You must, to be spending so much time with a commoner, am I right?"

"Where are you going with this Da— King David?"

"Oh, good catch my dear, good catch." David turned away from her and she exhaled. He walked back up the stairs and returned to his throne. "I'm sure you would hate for anything to happen to this man you're seeing. I suppose you'd be upset if he disappeared, only to reappear in a box in pieces delivered to you, or if he just vanished and you never knew exactly what happened to him. Would that disturb you?"

"You're *blackmailing* me?" she struggled to maintain her composure.

"Oh no. I don't like to use such terms. I'm promising you that your little boyfriend will be taken out of the equation so that your heart is available for a new man in your life. With him dead, you can't focus on being the best wife you can be now can you? You'd probably be an emotional mess and I don't want that, no. If you break up with him, and you can make up whatever reason you'd like, as long as you're sure he'll never come around again, then I won't harm him. In very simple terms, you marry me, he lives. You refuse, he dies. So I ask you again. Celeste, will you marry me?"

Celeste wanted to throw up. She wanted to tell David to fuck off and die. She would run to Sebastian as fast as possible and go hide with him for the rest of David's life or until Sebastian could kill him. But she didn't know where Sebastian was.

<SEBASTIAN? *Please I need you to hear me NOW!*>

She waited for Sebastian's response. She heard nothing. How would she even find him? He never said where he was going. But she couldn't have him suffer. She couldn't have him die because of her. She would find a way to be with him later, somehow. It seemed impossible, but she'd find a way. For now, she only had one choice to protect Sebastian.

"Celeste. I need an answer right now. I won't ask again."

"Yes, your Highness," the words tasted bitter in her mouth.

"Is that a yes you'll marry me, or yes as in you're present?"

"I'll marry you," she choked out.

"Oh good. See…that wasn't so hard." He clapped his hands together and smiled disingenuously.

She wanted to kill him with her bare hands. She would find an escape before this marriage ever took place.

David stood up and walked to her, "I will start making arrangements for us then. You'll see, this is going to be splendid for us and our two species. Now, ordinarily I would say don't leave the planet but your little boyfriend has to be told that it's all over so he doesn't want you back, and to do that, you need to find him and tell him without raising suspicion. I don't want him to come here trying to 'solve' this situation or bring a small army to try to 'rescue' you either. Go to Praxis. Tell him. Then come back to me."

She turned to leave but David said one more thing.

"Um, make sure you *do* come back. I have men watching you from a distance but I promise, they'll be everywhere you go and they don't miss a thing. Don't try to warn anyone or run away because there is no running from me."

She walked to the door and opened it, feeling as though she might pass out. She closed it behind her, keeping her back to David. She saw Ulysses standing there and took a deep breath while she closed her eyes. She needed to get herself back together quickly. Guards walked these halls continuously and she couldn't be seen falling apart now. She turned to face the guard, "Why does he trust you so much? You're Human."

Ulysses looked around, then looked up at a camera bot hovering in the corner of the hallway. She followed his eyes up to it, then looked away.

"I'm not sure what you mean Queen Hennessy. Let me escort you to the main doors. I can arrange for a taxi transit if you'd like or a royal transit if that'd make you more comfortable."

Celeste and Ulysses silently navigated the Estate until they were at the front entrance. Her eyes darted to him and then the two guards standing at the door. She whispered, "Whose side are you on? Why do you keep winking at me?"

"Queen Dowager Celeste, it was lovely seeing you again."

She looked out the corner of her eye and saw the guards watching them. She couldn't read either one of them. She figured every guard here must've had mental training. David probably insisted on it. Ulysses gently took her hand in his and bent down to kiss it. As he was coming up he whispered, "I'm a friend."

Ulysses spoke to one of the guards behind her, "Escort Queen Hennessy to the docking station and arrange transportation for her. Whatever she wants."

She looked at Ulysses, "Thank you."

He nodded, "Pleasure's mine. Please take care, my Queen."

She watched him walk away and the Il'lacean guard approached her. He silently walked her to the transit docking station and arranged a bot-taxi to Praxis. Sitting in the back seat as the transit launched, Celeste covered her face as she burst into tears.

FOUR

>>> > **"DID SHE GET** off the premises okay?"

Ulysses nodded.

"Great." David had images of adoring Humans holding up signs outside Silver Thorn saying "Long Live the King" and "Congrats to the Newlyweds" dancing in his head. Ulysses was saying something. "What's that?"

"I hope your meeting pleased you. The Queen seemed…flustered when she left. Perhaps you're too much man for her."

David laughed, "Oh Benson, you do know how to flatter a King. It did. It went the way I predicted anyway."

Ulysses nodded again.

"Tell me Benson, do you think the Queen Dowager has gained any weight since my brother was killed?"

"No, not that I've noticed," Ulysses cleared his throat, "I'm sure she was distraught like all of us were, but we all grieve in our own ways. Do you think she's eating her sadness away?"

David shook his head, "No. Never mind. Thank you, you're dismissed."

Ulysses left David to his thoughts.

Maybe Celeste wasn't pregnant after all. And if that was the case, David would have to impregnate her if he wanted an heir. He was sure there was some sort of external fertilization process to do it. He'd have to look into it. If Humans loved royal weddings and Celeste, they'd be insane for a pregnant Celeste.

A SIGN

ONE

>>> > LILA NORTH'S THING was fashion. When the queen still inhabited these walls not too long ago, Lila was the one that helped dress her, sometimes buying things already made, other times, making garments herself.

Now that the queen was gone, she became responsible for royal dress for everyone in the castle that was a female. Another tailor was responsible for the male staff, although Lila could've done that too if they let her. She was fine dressing most of the staff, except for the young Il'lacean ladies that frequented the King's private chambers. David had asked that they be scantily clad. Lila shuddered to think what went on in those chambers, but the girls never spoke a word of it, and she didn't dare ask, she only took their measurements and clothed them.

But, her seamstress work only went so far. She could only sew so many buttons back on, or alter so many outfits before she was out of things to do again, even with 209 females to clothe. David startled her one day by asking if she had any other talents. She thought at first he might've taken a liking to her, which chilled her down to the bone, but luckily it turned out not to be that.

She told him she was also a good handy woman. He wasn't familiar with the term, but she explained she could fix or replace lots of things like drywall, plumbing, and most other little projects around a home. This impressed David and he asked her to fix a water closet near his chambers.

She inspected it and easily repaired the leaky toilet. Ever since then, she'd been assigned small projects that let her roam about the castle more freely than she had ever been allowed before. She got a cute little badge to wear on her right shoulder that signified her security clearance to anyone needing clarification.

Today, she was fixing a broken picture frame in the main entrance great room. She focused completely on matching up the corners for glue. When a Human High Royal Guard appeared directly alongside her, she let out a scared cry.

She let go of the corners and put a hand to her chest.

"I'm sorry to startle you," the guard apologized quietly.

Lila had seen this Human HRG before but she couldn't remember his name. He stood out mainly because he was the *only* High Royal Guard that was Human. Maybe this one was just David's token Human so that it appeared he wasn't racist.

She looked down at the guard's feet, "You must be wearing some really quiet shoes for me not to have heard you."

"Or I'm part ninja."

She smiled, "How can I help you High Royal Guard?"

"My name is Ulysses Benson. I…uh, do need some information, but it's not standard info," he whispered.

"I'll help in any way I can. What is it?" Lila raised an eyebrow.

Ulysses pulled at his collar, "Are you close to another lady-in-waiting? Ms. Vossen?"

Lila chuckled, "Oh, you like Ginger huh?"

"Sshhhh please!" Ulysses looked around while he wrung his hands together, "I could get into a lot of trouble if anyone found out I was interested in anyone here, you know that."

Lila smiled, "You've got the hots for her? She doesn't even know you're alive buddy. She would've told me if she was attracted to anyone. We always talk about cute guards."

Ulysses paused, "I almost never see Ginger around here. This place is so big and David barely assigned me this position when he took over. I can't afford to lose this job, but I can't wait forever to talk to Ginger either."

"Mmmmm hmmmm," Lila smiled.

"Could you give her a message?"

"Oh why not honey? What is it?"

He cleared his throat, "Tell her that if beauty were fragrance, she'd be the sweetest smelling rose on Earth."

Lila rolled her eyes, "You've been working on this one a while, huh?"

"It's been too long that I've seen her and not spoken to her. When will you see her next?"

She looked at her Titan, "I have to finish up here, and then I'll take my dinner break. It'll probably not be more than two shakes of a lamb's tail dear."

Ulysses looked at her sideways, "Pardon me?"

Lila rolled her eyes again, "Not too long from now. Geez. Get outta here so I can glue this frame together and then go talk to Rosy Posy for you."

"Ginger, you mean?"

Lila sighed, "*Yes.*"

Ulysses started to walk away as another guard entered the room, "Thank you Ms. North. I appreciate your time."

TWO

>>> > LILA FOUND GINGER sitting in her Halloween-clad bedroom, eating dinner on her bed. No matter what time of year it was, Ginger had her Halloween decorations out. Lila wasn't fond of the holiday since she hated being scared and thought Ginger was a little nutty, but everyone was allowed to decorate their own living quarters as they wished at Silver Thorn.

"Hey! Guess what I have?"

Ginger looked at Lila's hands, then up to her face, "What? I don't see anything."

"A message from a man for you," Lila sat down next to her friend.

Ginger made a face, "A message? From who?"

"Yeah, there's this guy," she paused, "A Human High Royal Guard. He ca—"

"Wait, Ulysses came to you? About me?"

Lila stopped, "Ohhh, you know him? This means something. Why haven't you told me about him?"

"What did he say?" Ginger tossed her plate aside.

"Just something about you being the sweetest rose in the garden and how it related to your beauty somehow. I can't remember exactly, but it was good."

Ginger frowned, "He said what? How can you not remember? Didn't you make a Titan note or...why didn't you just send me a message?"

"I had my hands full. It was just a couple hours ago anyway; I figured I'd see you quicker than this."

"Did he ask me out?" Ginger put her hands into her caramel colored hair, slowly combing her fingers through it.

"No, but it's obvious he likes you. He's taken a huge risk coming to me. I'm sure he'll pop up tomorrow to make sure I delivered his message."

Ginger was silent.

Lila nudged her, "What is it? Why that face?"

"Maybe I shouldn't say anything, I mean, who knows what David would do if he found out..."

Lila scoffed, "We all know that King Asshole the first didn't want any of his staff to date each other. That was explicitly stated and the punishments, terribly unjust, but David still hasn't even mentioned it. Mayb—"

Ginger interrupted, "Ulysses is David's *sole* Human High Royal Guard. There's got to be a reason for that. Maybe he's a spy."

"I don't think so," Lila contested.

"How would *you* know?"

Lila rolled her eyes, "When I talked to him today, he seemed pretty uptight about mentioning his interest in you."

"Yeah, because that's what a spy would do to get you to trust him. He'd seem all scared and worried about getting 'caught.'"

"I think he just likes you. Nothing else to it. David has one Human as a HRG because he can't look racist. He needs at least one so the media won't harp on him that he's got an all Il'lacean guard."

Ginger shook her head, "Even if David didn't care about everyone else dating, which I think is a long shot, he's *going* to care what Ulysses does. He's going to hold him to a higher standard."

"So what if you're right," Lila took a deep breath, "Are you going to let someone else dictate what you do with your own personal love life?"

Ginger was quiet.

"Come on. Life is too short woman. You haven't had a guy in your life in a while right?"

Ginger cringed, "Yeah, the last one was that loser with the little…"

Lila shuddered, "Let's not revisit that. I never liked him. You deserve much better."

Ginger picked up her plate of food and started eating again.

Lila got up and headed towards the door, "So what should I tell lover boy?"

Ginger paused, "Tell him that you gave me his message and that I said thank you, it was very sweet of him to say and I'm flattered."

"I can't say that! It sounds like you're not even interested in him!"

Ginger glared at her, "What do you think I should say then?"

"Say…thank you. When will you tell me more?"

Ginger smiled, "Oooooh I like that better. Yeah, say that!"

THREE

>>> > D'ARTAGNAN KNEELED AT his shrine with a large statue of Khaleen at the top of it. He had several chips and tokens around the statue as an offering. He lit two candles for his parents, one for his sister that died at birth, one for his uncle, and one for Linda.

He made the sign of Khaleen then laid down on the ground with his feet facing the Head Remembrance Flame.

"Linda, I miss you. People keep telling me to try dating. I don't listen.

"I know you don't want me moping around alone and sad all the time. I'm sure Bouton is right about that. I remember how jealous you got." He laughed, "You were such a wild fire when it came to that girl Susie I went to school with. I thought I was going to have to turn the water on you two when she came over to our old house."

D'Artagnan smiled and then sighed, "I miss your laugh, your touch. I was lost before you found me and now...I'm lost again."

He watched the flames of the candles flicker and then one of them went out. The Head Remembrance Flame.

He sat up, "Linda is that a sign? Are you trying to tell me something?"

He looked around but saw nothing.

"I'm crazy right? I've finally lost my mind, or maybe it's sleep deprivation."

He stood up and reignited the candle. It burned brightly casting shadows across the wall. He looked at the framed picture he kept of Linda.

He laid down again in the ceremonial prayer position.

"Linda, I love you just like I always have. I don't know what to do. Should I try to move on from us? Is there a way for me to even love someone else again like I loved you?"

The Head Remembrance Flame flickered and then went out.

D'Artagnan started at it silently.

Then Linda's picture fell from the wall and landed on the ground.

D'Artagnan sat up, "Okay, this cannot be coincidence."

He stood and walked to her picture. He thought about it. *Was it time to put this away, maybe somewhere he couldn't see it?*

Maybe seeing her every day was picking at a wound that wouldn't heal. He took the picture to his bedroom and put it in the top drawer of his nightstand. He put a holobook on top of it that covered up her face almost completely. It would do for now. *That had to be a step in the right direction for healing, right?*

He looked at his Titan. Time for sleep.

He walked back to the shrine to blow out the other candles, but they were already extinguished.

He took that as a good sign and walked into his bedroom.

FOUR

>>> > WHILE MITCH WAS scouring the news for HR arrests, he also looked up Jacob's family. He thought about Jacob a lot since he killed him, but not his family. He wondered if they were getting by all right.

There were many articles about Jacob/Edison right after the bombing, but they quickly died out after a few weeks. He had to search hard for the few articles he could find about the family left behind. One article reported the Trost family moved after receiving several death threats. It seemed everyone assumed the whole family was part of the Human Resistance. The bakery that Jacob owned, received several threats of violence, so they shut it down and sold off the real estate at a loss.

Mitch couldn't let them suffer like this for something he did. He knew he wasn't responsible for Jacob's actions, but he did kill the man.

At the end of another article, there was a bank account that had been set up to help the family, especially the twin girls.

Mitch deposited, anonymously, one million coren.

That wouldn't help with his guilt, but he knew the family wouldn't have to want for anything.

FIVE

>>> > HACE LOOKED AT Dax on his Titan screen, "Well then, what do you think we should do?"

Dax's brows furrowed together, "The Red Klix was the first step. There's probably four more after that. We not only need the complete poem, but someone to figure the damn thing out too. I remember some of it, but not all."

"What's the part you remember?"

"To where shadows fall long, seas are calm, once you removed the bomb." Dax closed his eyes, "I know those are the first three lines. Then I think…In night…no, in cages of night, on our world of white…" He opened his eyes, "I can't remember the end, but I know there's a lot in between. This is a long poem."

"Praxis isn't white at any point is it?"

"Well, at the poles it always is. We get snow in some places, but it's never all white. It also wasn't our first home planet. We settled somewhere else when Lanyx were new but the planet couldn't sustain us."

"Really? I never knew that."

"A lot of people don't. This poem is very old, it could be referencing that planet, or it could be some other place. I don't really know."

"At least you know more than me. What else do we need for this?"

"We need to find the city, the door, and other things that the poem alludes to. It's not going to be easy and it's probably going to take a lot longer than you'd like."

"I think you're right," he sighed, "I'll be in touch."

"Yes, sir. Adrastos over and out."

SIX

>>> > CELESTE WALKED OUT of the elevator and waited for Dax to arrive. She was a little early and a lot nervous. She heard a door open behind her. A Lanyx janitor-bot came out with a mop and started cleaning the floor. She wondered if he was a spy for David. She looked outside

the lobby doors and saw several people walking past her building. Any one of them could be watching her. It didn't matter where she was, David was going to know whether she broke up with Dax or not.

And for Dax's sake, she'd rather have one of David's minions report back to the King she definitely dumped Dax, so he wouldn't be harmed.

Without knowing for sure that David meant Sebastian, Celeste couldn't put Dax's life in danger. For all she knew, David knew Sebastian's name or an alias of his but didn't know his face and was confusing the two men. As unfair as this situation was for her, it could be deadly for Dax if she didn't take every precaution to protect him.

Dax was all smiles and excitement when he came up to her at the lob-by doors. Celeste felt terrible. She didn't want to do this, but she couldn't just disappear on him. She thought briefly about continuing to see Dax after she was married, but that wasn't fair to him and if David found out, he'd be extremely hard to deal with and probably raging mad. Better to just get it over and done with.

"Hey beautiful. You ready?"

She waited to respond until after he kissed her and grabbed her hands in his. "I don't think we should go out tonight."

"Why not? You not feeling well?"

"I feel fine," she lied, "It's…I don't think this is going to work out for us."

"Wait, Celeste, what brought this on?"

She let go of his hands, "I worry you're thinking this is going to go somewhere that I'm not ready for yet. I don't want to jump into something serious too soon."

"I haven't said anything about serious. We're having fun learning one another. We're just…hanging out. There's no pressure on you to do anything."

Celeste could tell he would say anything to put her at ease right now. It was making this much harder. She closed her eyes and took a deep breath, "I don't think I can do this."

He put his arms around her waist and urged, "Look at me please, Celeste. I care about you."

She kept her arms at her sides but looked at him, "I'm not saying you don't. I'm saying I can't do this."

Dax moved in closer and whispered, "You are the best thing that's ever happened to me. If you think I'm going to let you break up with me, you're wrong. I'm not going to let you go."

She bit her lip, "Dax…"

He gently shook her and smiled, "You are too good to let go. I'll give you some time to think all this over. You need space and then you'll see you miss me too much."

"Really Dax. I don't need the time or the space. I think we need to call it quits."

He let go of her, "Two Earth weeks, no, two Praxian weeks, that's even longer, okay? I'll come back and check on you then."

"It's not going to make a difference."

"I won't take no for an answer. I'll be back again. We'll see how you feel. But for now, I'll say goodnight."

"Goodbye Dax. You won't see me in two weeks. I won't be here."

He grimaced then turned around and walked away.

She thought he might give her trouble. He might not let her go without a fight. She was happy at this and at the same time, dismayed. He was safer without her.

When Celeste turned around to go back to her apartment, the janitor was gone.

ANNIE

ONE

>>> > THOSE WEEKS THAT D'Artagnan spent in the POW camp felt like years. Everyone has their breaking point. That's what he realized while he was there.

The military taught him to be strong. Had taught him not to divulge classified information. Not to say a word, not to give in.

But D'Artagnan had a breaking point just like everyone else and it was the cats that almost got him. The natives had pets all over roaming free. One animal resembled an Earth cat except that it had two tails and three heads with long necks. The natives shouted at him, interrogated him, dunked him in filthy water and waste, burned him, cut him, shocked him, and almost froze him to death but those things didn't

make him speak. The natives never knew it, but those cat-like creatures came by his cell and would sometimes jump all over him, rubbing
their furry bodies up against him and his allergic reaction would kick
in. His snout got all congested, his skin broke out in itchy bumps, and
he felt as though he couldn't breathe. No one was watching the animals
and they did as they pleased. Sometimes when D'Artagnan was tied
down to a table, those damn creatures would climb up on top of him
and lay right on top of him. He couldn't do anything but try to yell at
them and at first that worked, but after a while, the animals got used
to it.

To think, almost all the Il'lacean war secrets would've come out of his
mouth if he had to endure the animals another day.

The last day before he was rescued, he was allowed out of confinement. They had kept him in a solitary holding cell in the dark for days.
Usually, he was only let out when they tortured him, but today, they let
him go up into the light, above ground. He saw a dirt field with a fence
around it in the middle of camp. Several men were sitting on the ground
looking haggard and he realized several other Il'laceans were being held
at this camp.

He had no idea why they let him out. Maybe his captors knew something was about to happen, maybe they were warned somehow. Maybe
they felt like showing all the captives that there were so many others so
close, but that momentarily they would all be in solitary confinement
again. D'Artagnan never found out why, but something was coming that
day.

The camp had been taken over by his military forces. They had been
planning it for several days and almost saved everyone. A few men on
D'Artagnan's side died as the troops came in, but unfortunately, all the
captors committed suicide by pill almost instantaneously, so they never
suffered.

D'Artagnan thought it was completely unfair. Given the chance, he
would have tortured the shit out of any captor that came near him.

And all the residual shit that he dealt with on a regular basis now.
How when he was sleeping you couldn't innocently shake him awake
or startle him for fear of being struck in the face by a kick or punch.

The nightmares, the flashbacks, the mental scarring, and the emotional damage. He was tired of all the things he remembered from the wars. He wished it had never happened to him.

TWO

>>> > CELESTE PICKED UP an audio call on her Titan, "Yes?"

"Oooh, a little testy there my love."

Celeste rolled her eyes and felt her stomach lurch, "King David, what can I do for you?"

David smiled, "That's better. I called to tell you the date of our marriage."

"When?"

"No, there's a little thing I need to ask first. You did tell that boyfriend of yours that you are through with him right? I don't want anyone to interfere with our beautiful union."

Celeste thought of Dax, "Yes. He and I are through. Is there anything else?"

"Very good. I expected you'd give me more of a fight about it. I'm pleased to see that you're warming up to the idea."

"Your Majesty, is there anything else you require of me tonight?"

David smirked, "No my love. Our marriage will happen on Earth at Silver Thorn on the tenth of August at one thirty. I hope you're going to free up the whole month. We'll have a lot to do afterwards including a honeymoon. I'm going to surprise the press with this! They need something; I think we all need something uplifting to celebrate. Too many bad things have happened."

Celeste rolled her eyes again, *this is just another bad thing happening to me.* "Yes. But that's only six days away, Earth time. What am I to do about a dress and hair an—"

"I'm taking care of everything. Just show up in the royal transit that I'll send to you. I need your address."

"I'll arrange my own transportation if that's okay with you." She held her breath.

David hesitated, "I suppose…yes, that will have to do, if that's what you want. Fine. Be here at noon."

Celeste's Titan reset back to its main menu after David terminated the call. She never wanted to see David again much less marry him. It was too much like her life before. Humans wouldn't accept the lie that somehow she fell in love with her dead husband's brother. It was a disgusting idea on several levels. And what about Sebastian? Would he think she's forgotten about him? Would he hit the roof and kill David? After she got a chance to explain things to him, *if* she got a chance, would he understand she did it to protect him? How could she get out of doing this? Should she ask Sebastian to kill him?

"There's always a way out," she said to no one in the room.

THREE

>>> > MITCH WAS AT the grocery store.

He wore his normal incognito clothes that he'd gotten used to sporting since he went into hiding. He had the oversized clothing to hide the real shape of his body, a baseball cap, techglasses, and a thicker than normal beard.

He knew it was a bit of overkill. No one should know him from anyone. Maybe a few news hounds or military nuts might recognize him from his "death" years ago, but he hadn't been recognized in a long time.

Despite his appearance tonight, someone engaged him. He'd been waiting in the checkout line with bread, milk, and cookies and the woman in front of him turned around and smiled. He did not respond.

She started talking anyway, "Just a few items like me. Lines are the worst. They take forever and it seems the store never has enough help. I wonder why they do that? Is it on purpose you think? All I want are these stupid candy bars and a soda. Sorry, forgot to say, my name's Annie." Annie stuck her hand out waiting for Mitch to shake it, but he didn't.

"I'm sick right now; I don't think you want to touch me. Might be contagious."

Annie stepped back slightly and cleared her throat, "Sorry to hear that. I hope you feel better soon."

Mitch nodded and smiled. He hoped that was enough for her to get the hint that he wasn't interested in talking. He could admit to himself that she was a beautiful Lanyx woman, but he couldn't trust any strangers, no matter how innocent the meeting may seem, anyone could be a tracker, looking for him from the Il'lacean government.

Annie turned back around and stood silently until it was her turn in line.

Mitch saw another register open up and quietly moved towards it. Annie never noticed him watching her from the other line. She made her purchase and left.

He didn't know whether it was some random woman trying to get a date or a cop. He bought his items, bagged them up, and left from the opposite door Annie exited through.

He looked around but couldn't see her anywhere.

He assumed it was a random woman with bad timing.

Mitch knew he wasn't unattractive, but didn't regard himself as handsome either. He didn't think about it at all. He had a lot of women hit on him over the years, but he never took them up on their offers. He was selective about a potential girlfriend and he didn't like the idea of one-night stands. Probably the reason he hadn't had many relationships was because he was so picky. If he ever did date someone, she'd have to be special right off the bat. But now wasn't the time to be thinking about stuff like this. He got into his transit and launched for home.

FOUR

>>> > MR. APPLETTE ATE his candy bar and drank the soda he bought as Annie. Mitch seemed to be handling himself pretty smart. Applette just wanted to see who he was willing to talk to and how he reacted to a beautiful female stranger. Applette always liked the Humans. He knew they had a bad rap across the universe, but he thought some of them were very capable creatures.

"Excuse me, miss? I couldn't help you noticing me over there and I thought you and I could go somewhere with a bed and get naked."

Mr. Applette turned to the Human man that approached her in the docking station of the grocery store and punched him out. He was not a capable creature and she was not impressed by his disgusting pick up line.

The nerve of some men!

She threw away her trash and hunched down behind a transit to turn. Quickly his skin became feathers and he shrunk down to an owl.

Mr. Applette flew away into the cloudless night wondering if Kolek had found herself a body yet in this universe.

FIVE

>>> > HACE MET WITH one of his men on a Titan call.

"Duke, you did a really good job. I'm super happy with everything you've given me on Celeste Hennessy. We would've never found her without you."

Duke smiled, "I'm glad you're pleased with my work. I was hoping – am I going to be able to approach her or have anything to do with her on a personal level?"

Hace laughed, "Sorry, Dax has that job."

"She's a beautiful woman."

"I agree Duke. I agree. But you've done your job well. She's the first target that you tailed for me successfully without her realizing she was being watched and that's impressive for a first timer like you. We'll talk about assigning you to a new target soon, just stay available for me, k?"

"Sure thing boss."

"All right. The Hunter over and out."

CHAPTER 14

THE GREEN DRESS

ONE

>>> > "HOLY SHIT RAYNES! Why the fuck are you still talking to Ni-toyis man? She's got bad news written all over her amazing body. She's never going to change."

Eric and Sebastian were currently competing to see who could shoot the furthest target with the most accuracy. Sebastian was winning, but Eric was threatening best two out of three.

Sebastian shook his head, "I know she's not going to change. That's not the point. I owed her a favor and totally fucked up. If there's a debt that's owed by me, I've got to pay it off. You know how I am with promises."

"You're like the only dude that would keep this going for what? Ten years?"

"Try closer to twenty."

"Twenty fucking years? Oh my God, Raynes! Pay her off, do whatever it takes to get rid of her and be done with it."

"I'm trying. I pissed her off by not meeting up with her and then she sent me this Titan message that I got right before we left. She sounded rational about it even though she has every right to be raging at me."

Eric put down his rifle, "Listen Raynes...if you're planning on being with Celeste when we get back, I suggest you have nothing to do with Ni-toyis ever again. Debts or no debts. If the queen finds out you're talking to a Stox woman, she's going to bug out. Everyone knows Stox's reputation for seduction and sex appeal. They've made priests leave the church and they'll make even the most confident women insecure."

Sebastian took his shot and hit his target dead center. "Celeste is an exception. She could probably handle Ni-toyis...I think."

Eric shook his head, "Don't test that theory. Losing Celeste...again, it's not worth it."

Sebastian loaded his gun and smiled, "There's nothing there, between Ni-toyis and I. There isn't anything for Celeste to worry about. I get Celeste back, pay off my debt to Ni-toyis and everything's fine."

Eric laughed, "Oh my friend. The best laid plans..."

"You're wasting your breath on this. Everything's going to be fine." Sebastian waved to Agathon and the Dach took to the air to reset their targets. "First round belonged to me."

Eric smiled, "Fuck you. You cheater."

TWO

>>> > LILA WAS DOING an emergency repair on the garden stone wall. A floral delivery mech tech went on the fritz and flew itself right into the blocks, destroying three along the top.

David was going to do some announcement back here later today so she knew she'd better get on it without being asked. Fortunately for her, they were having a rare sunny day in London and she enjoyed being outside working with her hands. She hadn't seen Ulysses all day, but she was sure he was around. He lived at the castle like all the other High Royal Guards and David had something going on today. Ulysses had to be around here somewhere.

The mech tech had left pieces of itself on the ground where it flew into the wall. It took her half an hour just to pick up all the metal shards. When she was done, she walked back to the storage shed where all her equipment was. When she turned around from dumping out her trash bag, Ulysses was there.

She joked, "You *are* part ninja, damn."

"Hey. So what'd she say?"

"Oh, I'm fine, yes hello…thanks for asking and you?"

"Hi, Lila. I apologize, I'm in a big hurry today."

"That's better. Geez." She took off her sun hat, "I told her what you said and she said thanks. She wants to know when are you going to tell her more?"

"So, she liked it. Good"—He let out a sigh of relief—"Tell her I have tomorrow night off. I can be in front of the fireplace in the East Common Room at nine thirty. If she's not there by ten o'clock, I'll assume she isn't interested and no hard feelings."

Lila smiled at him, "I'm sure she'll be there. I will let her know."

Ulysses smiled back and started to walk away, "Great. Thanks a lot."

"Oh and Guard Benson…"

He stopped and looked at her.

"Don't hurt my friend. She's sweet and kind and if you do anything to harm her in any way, you'll regret it. I promise you."

Ulysses bowed to Lila, "I wouldn't dream of it." He smiled and walked away.

THREE

>>> > CELESTE GOT OUT of the taxi and felt her stomach turn until she saw Ginger approaching.

"Oh my goodness. It feels like I haven't seen you in ages," Ginger wrapped her arms around her friend and squeezed. "I can't believe you're here. King David said you'd be by, but he didn't give a reason. What's up? And why do I need to make you all super glamorous?"

Celeste almost broke into tears as she whispered, "King David is a tyrant. He wants…I'm supposed to…Oh God, I can't even say it."

Ginger stared at her friend, baffled, "What is it dear? You can tell me. Please?"

Celeste looked around, "We can't talk here, but I can't tell you anyway. I don't want to get you in trouble. Let's go to wherever you're going to prep me."

They walked arm in arm inside the castle into an area Celeste knew well. "I see not much has changed here." She looked over the queen's dressing room. It was mostly untouched, except for a few improvements made to the balcony outside and a new carpet on the ground.

Ginger directed her to the chair closest to the mirror and pulled out her tools. "Cosmo, come here." Ginger's mech tech flew down from the corner of the room where its hibernation cage was. "Open up, Cosmo."

The mech tech opened itself into three tiers and Ginger rooted around for the concealer she wanted. "Now, what's up for real woman? Spill it."

Celeste gripped the armrests on either side of her chair and looked up to the ceiling, "I honestly can't tell you this one. David hasn't said anything to anyone here about what's going on?"

Ginger shook her head, making her ghost-shaped earrings twirl fast, "I've seen many flowers delivered and a few catering transits which I thought was weird."

Celeste looked at Ginger, waiting for her to say it.

Ginger pulled out the concealer she was looking for, "Wait a second… David isn't going to make some video with you, is he? I did hear he was going to make an announcement this afternoon to the universe-wide press."

"No. What about my hair? I feel like we don't have that much time."

"Oh shoot, almost forgot to get that started!" She looked over her shoulder to the other mech tech, "Come here, Hairy. I need you too. Curl all her ends. Make big waves on the last ten inches of hair."

The mech tech flew to Celeste's head and scanned it. Twelve arms of the hovering machine unfolded with curling irons, brushes, and hands, and started collecting sections of Celeste's hair.

"That one's new."

"David bought it instead of giving me a raise. It was really expensive and I still have to go back sometimes and do things over again. Close your eyes a sec." Ginger sprayed a mist of primer on Celeste's face

"Is Lila here?"

Ginger shook her head, "Nope you just missed her. She has the rest of today off."

"Oh, I wanted to see her. What about V?"

Ginger smiled and applied concealer to Celeste's dark circles under her eyes, "Nope. She's off too. She'll be back tomorrow. Haven't you talked to either one of them lately?"

Celeste thought for a moment, "It's been a little bit, I guess. I got wrapped up with a lot of things going on at home."

Ginger pulled out foundation and started putting it on Celeste, "That reminds me…how is Brahm? Has he come back to you yet? I know it was a painful breakup. I'm really sorry hon."

Celeste's eyes clouded over, "No. I don't know what to tell you about him. I don't know where he is right now."

Ginger brushed on blush and stopped, "I'm sorry. Don't cry okay? He's gonna' come back. I'm sure of it. I can feel it. With the way you talked about him, he's got to come to his senses. And in the meantime, you have this new guy Dax. Let him keep you busy for a spell."

"I can't talk about it anymore okay?" Celeste took a deep breath.

"Close your eyes. Try to relax. Eye shadow's next."

Celeste closed her eyes and asked, "What about you? Anyone interesting hooking up around here?"

"Yes," Ginger smiled, "Apparently HRG Ulysses Benson has some interest in me."

Celeste opened her eyes and Ginger frowned, "Close your eyes please. I need to get this stuff on you."

Celeste kept them open and grabbed Ginger's arm, "I saw him! He helped me a little while ago when David was talking to me. Lila asked about it, but I avoided her question. Then I saw him again with David. He's a good guy."

"I hope so. I haven't talked to him yet. Lila said he approached her asking about me. I think he's cute."

Celeste closed her eyes, "Oh, I'm so happy for you. Are you two meeting soon?"

"Tomorrow night. I guess he's had his eye on me for a while now." Ginger grinned, "I didn't know it. I sent a message back to him through Lila. We'll see what he does tomorrow night when we talk."

"How exciting!"

Ginger applied eyeliner to Celeste's top eyelids. "I think so." She finished up and said, "Open and look up please."

Celeste looked up at the hair mech tech as Ginger put eyeliner on her bottom eyelash line. The machine was almost finished with its work.

The women were uncharacteristically silent. Celeste heard her friend in her mind even though she didn't want to. Ginger hadn't slept with anyone in a while, but she wanted to be with Ulysses. Celeste didn't want to hear this. "So, what are you going to do after you're done with me?"

"Well, I'd love to have plans with Ulysses, but that's like, impossible since he's got to stay here and work a little longer than I do. We can't do much here since…you know."

Celeste blinked a few times after Ginger finished with her eyes, "What? I don't know."

"Oh. King David said yesterday, officially, staff can't date each other. It's strictly forbidden. He's taken Jon's rules and made them even harsher. So keep Ulysses between you and me okay?" Ginger applied finishing powder to Celeste's face.

"Of course."

"Okay. Time for mascara, and a little lip gloss and you'll be all set to do whatever secret stuff you won't tell me about."

FOUR

>>> > A LITTLE WHILE later, Celeste was alone in her dressing room with a green wedding gown hanging on the back of the door. She sat on the oversized round ottoman in the middle of the room and stared at her bare ring finger of her left hand. She still had the tan lines marking where Jon's ring used to be. Her heart started to race and she couldn't breathe. Perfect timing for a panic attack.

How could she be getting into the same Goddamned situation she just got out of? How could she do anything else? She needed to protect Sebastian and right now, this was the only way to do it. She couldn't delay the marriage, and she couldn't talk David out of it. She breathed in through her nose, held her breath for five seconds and then exhaled through her mouth.

She would find a way later to get out of this. She pictured herself laying on Scarlette Island with Sebastian close by until she felt herself start to calm down.

She got up slowly and took the dress off its hanger when a camera-bot came hovering around the corner.

"Oh no you don't. You wait outside the door." The bot didn't move. She dropped the dress on the floor and grabbed the bot with both hands out of mid-air. It made some beeping noises in response as she opened the door and pushed it out to the hall. She quickly closed the door before it could fly back in. She heard its metal housing rubbing against the door trying to fly through.

"No way is anyone watching me get dressed."

THE WEDDING

ONE

>>> > CELESTE WALKED OUT of her dressing room with her head hanging down. The bot hovered in front of her and began snapping photos. She turned her face up and looked along the empty hallway for signs of life. She took slow steps toward the back gardens without breaking a smile. She was sure David would comment upon seeing the pictures. She opened the back door and saw it was sunny. The complete opposite of how it should be today. Today was glum and gloomy. She walked along the cobblestone road and looked around. It seemed the entire castle was empty. She wondered if David told everyone to leave to give them privacy.

Her light green dress had a five-foot long train and she let it drag behind her. It would get dirty and ruined, and maybe David would see it and postpone the wedding. She wished she could run away.

She hadn't heard anything from Sebastian and she couldn't sense him. She hadn't heard anything from Dax either, but he said he would leave her alone for weeks.

She turned a corner, slowly plodding forward to her doom to the back of the estate and hovered at the chapel doorway. A royal guard was there but she didn't make eye contact. She hesitantly stepped into the chapel. It was modest, one of the few things that was at Silver Thorn.

The whole room was decorated in flowing silks and exotic flowers. An Il'lacean Kingdom chaplain towered at the front of the alter and there were two witnesses...people she didn't recognize, both Il'laceans.

She stood at the back until the chaplain directed her to move forward and stand by him. She did stoically. The camera-bot found a hibernation cage in the corner and mounted itself there as it went to sleep. Celeste knew all the cameras in the chapel must've been recording by now.

David arrived as she wondered if there had been a camera installed in the queen's dressing room she didn't know about. He strode up the aisle, as a bride was expected to in Earth ceremonies, but she guessed David wanted all the attention today.

She had no bouquet, so when David held out his hands to her, she had to take them.

The chaplain started, "As we have gathered to join two souls together, I'd like to remind everyone present that this ceremony is strictly forbidden from being talked about. David and Celeste would like their privacy and the two witnesses here today have been properly warned. If anyone is found to be talking about what they've seen here without express permission from both King David *and* Queen Celeste, they will be punished with lethal force. Is this understood?"

They all nodded their heads, David and Celeste included.

Celeste wondered how hard it was to find a chaplain that's supposed to be religious and is also perfectly okay with threatening the lives of others.

Celeste looked at the buttons of David's suit. David tugged on her hands slightly to get her to look up at him. She did. She hated him. She hated this.

The chaplain spoke, "Now that we are all clear, I'd like to start the ceremony with a prayer. If you would all bow your heads and hold your hands up to the sky." Everyone in the room did so. "Today, we are joining these two souls in a lifelong bond of man and woman, King and Queen, husband and wife. No one soul should ever be expected to carry the burdens of everyday life without a partner to help ease the sadness, to help carry the weight of challenges and adversity, to provide support and happiness, to give comfort when comfort is needed and to encou—"

The guard standing at the back door suddenly fell and was laying across the doorway. A figure appeared where Celeste had entered. The chaplain stopped and stared.

David looked and so did Celeste, then David was screaming, "Guards! Get in here now!"

Three High Royal Guards that had been hiding in the shadows stepped out, and Celeste hadn't even known they were there. One of them was Ulysses. That's why he had to stay here and work a little longer.

The figure stepped forward. It was definitely a man and he was wearing combat armor, and a battle helmet, so his face was hidden, but Celeste thought it might've been Sebastian. She couldn't sense him though, unless he was trying hard to keep anyone else here from sensing him too. The man was tall…it was him, right? It had to be, no one else could've found her, she didn't tell anyone where she was going to be today and no one knew about this. Sebastian must've returned early from his trip. He must've found her somehow.

She wanted to yell out his name, but the HRG's were already descending on him. David pulled Celeste further away from the scuffle.

The stranger quickly knocked Ulysses out. *Ginger might not be too happy with that*, Celeste thought.

The other two guards had their hands full with this fighter. He was smaller than them, but fast. And the stranger was an excellent opponent. Celeste had never seen Sebastian fight, but she knew it had to be him now. The stranger kicked one guard in the groin and he went down fast as the stranger walked up to Celeste and put out his hand.

Celeste saw the other guard approaching behind the stranger and pointed. The stranger half turned and pulled out a large hand pistol. He held it up to the guard's face but still kept a hand extended for Celeste to take. The stranger spoke, but he had a voice alteration application on the helmet that distorted his voice significantly, "Don't tempt me. This isn't worth your life."

The guard didn't listen and moved forward. The stranger took his other hand that he previously held out to Celeste and quickly jabbed his straightened fingers into the guard's throat. The guard clutched at his Adam's apple and took a few steps back trying to breathe. He stumbled over the other guard's legs and fell down. The stranger holstered his weapon long enough to look at Celeste, then he threw her over his shoulder and slowly moved towards the back door keeping his head on a swivel to see if anyone else wanted to fight him.

No one was moving.

David was livid. He shook as he yelled at the guards rolling on the ground to get up.

The stranger stepped over the bodies and out the back door. He closed it behind him and shot at the roofline. A stone gargoyle fell onto the ground and Celeste screamed. She watched as he barricaded the door shut with the gargoyle.

He didn't put her down until they reached his gray transit and he tucked her inside, closing the door over her. It locked immediately and then he got in on his side and launched without saying anything to her. This transit wasn't one she had seen either Dax or Sebastian drive before and it was traveling incredibly fast.

"I'm not sure that was the smartest way to handle that but I sure am gla—"

The stranger took off his helmet and she gasped as she saw it was Daxton.

He cleared his throat, "What? Aren't you gonna' kiss me hello?"

"What the hell was that? What...WHAT are you doing here? How did you find me? You said you were going to leave me alone!"

"Well, that's a fine greeting for me saving you from that wretched King," Dax was still smiling despite Celeste's obvious discontent.

Celeste wanted to cry. David probably thought Sebastian rescued her and now *he* was in danger wherever the hell he was. And she didn't want it to be Dax who saved her; she wanted it to be Sebastian. *<Sebastian, can you hear me?>*

She heard no response and silently cursed. She needed to warn him. Dax looked at her.

She took a deep breath, "How did you find me? And where'd you get this transit?"

Dax smiled, "I have a few different vehicles. I'm a bit of a transportation buff. As for finding you, I had a hunch something was up when you broke up with me. We were getting along too well for you to just end it. There had to be something causing that change of direction in you. So I dug around with some of my connections and I found out that you had been called to the castle today."

"And you knew I was going to get married?"

"Well, no. I'm actually friends with a security member at Silver Thorn and he is in charge of watching all the monitoring screens. He knew something like a wedding might be going on after he saw all the deliveries to the chapel and he thought David might be marrying someone, some sort of big ceremony that was supposed to be secret. When he told me, I knew you had to be involved. Why else would you break up with me for no reason? So I came prepared for lots of things today, but I'm glad I could save you from marrying David. You don't want to do that," he checked his screens and tapped on the map, "Aren't you going to thank me?"

"Dax, can you just take me back there?"

He gave her a sideways glance, "I'm sorry. It sounded like you asked me to take you back to the wedding. Did David give you a drug or something? I can't take you back."

"You don't understand what you're interfering with. David and I...he said..." She couldn't tell him any of it. She couldn't endanger Sebastian.

"You don't honestly want me to believe that this is what you want right?"

<Sebastian! Where are you? Can you hear me?> She heard nothing. "Dax, what am I supposed to do? David and I have an arrangement and I plan on honoring that. I know what I'm doing, just take me back there please."

Dax shook his head, "No. Sorry darling. I can't."

Celeste saw they cleared the SAP and asked, "Where are we going?"

"Well, David locked the SAP back there about three minutes before we passed through it, so I'm sorry we had to fly so fast, but there wasn't any other way. Don't worry about being tagged or anything."

"Where are we going Dax?"

"Mostac. Back to my house. I think you and I need to talk awhile about us."

She glared at him, "What if I just want to be dropped off at my apartment? I need to get a few things from there."

"Sorry, can't do that either."

Celeste didn't like Dax's tone all of a sudden. "Dax where did a political analyst learn how to fight like that? And where'd you get all the combat armor and gun?"

Dax reached out and tapped her on the nose, "You don't need to worry about such things. I'm safe. You're safe. Nothing to worry about. But if you must know…"—he took off his gloves and threw them into a bag in the backseat—"I believe there are a lot of crazy people in the world today, and with what happened to your husband and all the crime in the universe, one should be able to protect themselves and those they care about. I carry a gun all the time, just didn't tell you. I learned how to fight through self-defense classes. It became a passion of mine and it helps me stay in shape. And it sure as hell came in handy today."

"You hurt those guards."

"They'll recover. I didn't kill any of them, although that one guy and his throat…he might need some medical attention. But, I didn't hit him as hard as I could've. Just wanted to stun him enough to leave us alone."

Celeste looked down at her Titan.

"I know what you're thinking okay? I'm not holding you against your will or anything. All I want to do is talk. I had to go to some extreme measures to do it, but I won't hurt you. Here's the deal. We'll go to my place. You can get changed into some of my clothes, I'll make you something to eat and we'll talk. Afterwards, you're free to leave. I will even take you to your apartment and drop you off, safe and sound. Okay?"

She looked up at him. She needed to send warning to Sebastian. She needed to use her Titan if he wasn't answering her telepathically. She didn't care if wherever he was, he was too far out in the universe to reach digitally or mentally, she needed to warn him. And she hoped David was bluffing about hurting Sebastian. Maybe David thought scaring her was enough, and Sebastian should be able to handle anything. He's an assassin after all.

"Dax, I appreciate what you did for me back there, really I do…"

"But?"

"But I'd really like to get back to my apartment and think for a while. Alone."

Dax smirked, "Oh come on Celeste. I care about you. All I want to do is talk. Please? Can we just talk for maybe…an hour or two? That's all I'm asking for, please?"

Celeste couldn't believe this was happening. "Okay, a couple hours, then I'm going home."

"Alright. That's all I'm asking for," Dax smiled and sat back.

Celeste was nervous. She didn't think what Dax was doing was rational. He wasn't thinking straight. He could've been one of those stalker types and she didn't need that right now.

Unlike the taxi transits, or Sebastian's Pearl, Dax's vehicle was moving fast. He must've had a turbo enhancer on his transit because before she knew it, they were at The Jump.

"Hey Dax. I'm not good at going through these yet. I don't have anything on me anymore. I usually carry some sedatives, but…"

Dax smiled, "Oh, you poor thing. You need a sedative? Of course, I have some of those in my emergency kit. Hold on." He stretched into the back seat and pulled out a small box. He opened it and handed her a tiny bag of red pills.

"These don't look like the kind I normally carry. What are they?"

Dax replied, "I usually don't travel with Humans much. These are made for Il'laceans, but they'll work on you just fine."

"How long do they put me under?"

Dax thought, "Well, with the size difference…probably thirty, forty minutes max. I know you're probably a little more nervous than usual with what just happened and all. I promise you, you're in good hands. I'll protect you with my life. You're very important to me. We'll be traveling the whole time you're out so I'll watch videos, see if my antics made the news."

She studied him.

"I will be a perfect gentleman. I have been all this time we've been dating, have I not?"

She tilted her head and glared at him.

"Except for that time, yes. We're going to go through soon, so you need to take one. Just one."

She couldn't die now. And she didn't have any other options, it was simply too risky to go through without a sedative. The automated voice came on and the countdown started. She had a minute.

She took out one pill and handed the bag back to Dax. He took it from her and watched as she swallowed.

She quickly went under and knew nothing after.

TWO

>>> > DAVID SPRINTED OUTSIDE and looked around. He watched as the transit flew off into the sky. He threw his arms up into the air and screamed. All the staff that remained on the Kingdom grounds heard him and stopped in the middle of whatever they were doing.

He went back into the chapel and saw the chaplain on his Titan calling for the medical team to come immediately. David let him finish before he said, "No one knows of this."

"Of course not sir. I won't say a word. These men got into a fight with each other over who knows what." He shrugged his shoulders.

David turned around and walked out, knocking over a vase of water and flowers. It smashed to the ground.

David got on his Titan and called Earth's SAP control room, telling them to lock it down for the next twenty-four hours. Then he called his press agent and immediately changed the afternoon press conference he had scheduled. The press agent foolishly asked what happened. David kept his rage inside long enough to say an emergency came up and the press conference was postponed by thirteen hours and relocated to Rem Mot Om before he ended the call.

He barged into the security screens room and asked the controller what he'd seen within the past several minutes. The controller hadn't seen anything but a stranger approaching the chapel and knocking out a guard. David looked at the footage, but there wasn't anything useful about it. David stormed out headed for the royal transit pad.

David sat in his royal transit and immediately had his chauffeur launch for Il'laceier. David had some idea who the fucking idiot was that stole Celeste, but he wasn't positive. Maybe it was that BDP boyfriend of hers, but it could've been the HR, her friends, or someone she hired to rescue her. He was going to find out how this happened. How that man got onto the premises, how he bypassed security, how he found out about this secret ceremony in the first place and how he had escaped unopposed. The final questions were, where was he now, and what was he going to do with Celeste?

David poured himself a drink.

He couldn't release any of the information now. Not the wedding, not the *interruption*, nothing. And he couldn't say he had planned a wedding and then Celeste had been taken from him, because the Il'laceans would think he was incompetent and unable to physically protect a past and future Queen, and the Humans would think he had her kidnapped or something. Very bad press.

He couldn't say a Khaleen damned thing to anyone until he got some answers.

THREE

>>> > D'ARTAGNAN FOUND ALL the articles he could on David Hennessy, and across the uninet, there weren't many.

King Hennessy hadn't done any interviews and he certainly hadn't discussed his background, but from what D'Artagnan could find, he didn't have anything interesting in his history to discuss.

For most of his life, he grew up in the shadow of his brother and didn't make too much noise as an individual. It appeared that his parents spoiled him rotten and gave him anything he wanted. Those kind of people drove D'Artagnan crazy. All D'Artagnan ever did was struggle to get everything he had and even though his parents would've given him anything if they could've afforded it, his family was poor. They had all the love in the world for each other, but almost no money. D'Artagnan believed every child should be brought up this way to appreciate things more when they finally did get what they wanted.

David finished college with a degree in psychology and a minor in sociology. He had been in trouble with the law twice after he had come of age. Once for public drunkenness, the other for a physical altercation with another man. Both arrests happened after his parents died in the transit crash. Even though many people thought Jonathan had his parents killed, D'Artagnan never thought that was true. He didn't believe it was an accident either, but when the crash happened, D'Artagnan was fascinated by it. Transit accidents weren't very common so they got a lot of media attention when they did happen, but this was the highest profile deaths ever to happen in mid-air.

D'Artagnan had done his share of studying the events back then and he had suspicion that David had been the one to axe his folks. He couldn't prove it, but now that he was doing more research on the youngest Hennessy, D'Artagnan's gut told him his suspicions were well founded. Throughout the universe, most planets favored other methods of government and rule instead of royal families. Presidents, councils, and prime ministers constituted most of the world leaders while monarchies and kingdoms were in the minority. Every so often, you'd see a world conquered after a war or a planet liberated into space travel try a royal reign, but successful transitions were hard to find. D'Artagnan could see all the Hennessy men were the same – hungry for control and lusting for absolute power. It would make sense that the youngest one, who received the least amount of attention, would want everything for himself even if all of his family had to die for him to be King.

After reading through all the articles, there wasn't much about David's personality or character. D'Artagnan wished he knew someone who had a personal relationship to the man, that would be the best way to find out what kind of person he really was.

D'Artagnan looked at the latest video of David walking from Rem Mot Om to his royal transit and he noticed something. David was wearing his crown, but just for a second, D'Artagnan thought he saw a blue orb circling the inside edge. He zoomed in on the image.

"What is that?" D'Artagnan said to himself. *That is definitely not a royal issued crown.*

FOUR

>>> > MITCH CONSIDERED STARTING the HR back up again as he watched the news on his Titan. Nothing had changed since the bombing except for the fact that King David probably hated Humans now more than ever.

The news coverage about it had all died down and Mitch was still worried about his group's former members fending for themselves out there. Maybe they needed his guidance. Maybe they needed a leader. And no other groups were coming forward to do anything, not even to protest peacefully the fact that David beheaded Human HR members on live screens.

Earth needed something.

But for just as many reasons as there were for Mitch to lead the HR, there were reasons not to. Maybe he could pull the group back together, but insist that someone else take the reins, or that someone else start a brand new group that he might be a member of but nothing more.

He wondered how to make this decision. He wasn't settled yet on either side of his own argument, so he did nothing for the mean time.

He was about to check the weather when a breaking news story hit. King Hennessy restricted the Earth's SAP gate to all travelers for the next twenty-four hours. Mitch knew it. He told himself before that something like this would happen. He was grateful he had this Praxis apartment now. He couldn't imagine being trapped on any planet without a way to leave.

Even worse David didn't give a reason for the travel restriction. The news people guessed at some sort of investigation going on at the grounds of Silver Thorn as everyone had expected a press conference today, but that had been cancelled moments ago. The reporters thought the two events were linked and reported that King Hennessy was Il'laceierbound.

Mitch checked for other news reports and found several discussing the instant panic the travel restriction caused across the globe. Humans were upset they had no reason given for being unable to leave or return to their home world and several other species were concerned they'd be stuck on Earth longer than twenty-four hours.

Mitch, like the rest of the universe, wondered why the restriction had been ordered. The last time a SAP lockdown happened in the universe was on Il'laceier because of a bomb and Mitch hoped nothing like that had happened again.

FIVE

>>> > HACE LOOKED AT his screens mounted on the wall of the command post of his ship. He had eighty-seven branch leaders in ninety locations. It was hard to find people you could trust these days. He needed to fill those last three spots ASAP.

Most of his branch leaders were calling in (he called them scavengers) and they had two more minutes before they'd be in deep shit if they didn't attend this conference call.

He checked his Titan – only four were missing now, and they just happened to be the newest scavengers.

His Titan chimed and he looked up at the screens as two more scavengers appeared.

"Whiskers checking in. Cepheus branch," a Cephian with large cowl horns announced.

Hace nodded.

A coal-colored Lassandros came on one of Hace's screens and was speaking in his native language. Hace stopped him, "Hey Pehm I need you to turn on your translator. I can't understand a word you're saying."

Pehm clicked a button on his Titan, "Sorry Mr. Vetitro. Pehm reporting from the Lassandro branch." Pehm's bright blue bird-like eyes narrowed as one of his recruits nudged him from behind. He turned around and his dull red head feathers blocked the picture for a moment as he reprimanded the little shit.

Hace looked down at his Titan again. With ten seconds to go, the last two scavengers reported in.

He looked to his screens and clicked his Titan translator to all languages before he started talking. "A quick note to the last four that signed in. I recommend you check in no later than five minutes before our next meeting starts. You know I'm not patient by any stretch of the imagination. I'll let you slide this time since it's your very first check in on our mass meetings, but if it happens again, you'll lose your leadership position and possibly a lot more if I'm in a bad mood that day," he cleared his throat, "I'd like to start off by saying I think our team is growing nicely. Some of you might already know that we are still trying to finish our scavenger assignments. We have only three worlds left without a branch leader, and the faster we can fill those, the faster we can start recruiting on those planets. I encourage you to tell your friends and family about the BDP and what we can do for them. I'm eager to wrap up this interview process and move on to the next big thing." Hace looked down at his Titan.

"Now, I'm going to make this brief because I have a full morning ahead of me. Does anyone have anything to report?"

Dax spoke up, "I wanted to let you know I've acquired the hostage we spoke of. The package is currently unconscious in my transit being transported."

Hace grinned widely, "Son of a bitch, you got her! Fantastic! Great job. We can speak privately later. I'm not ready to make a formal announcement yet, but I'm proud of you."

Dax smiled, "Thank you sir. Let me know when I can call you."

Hace looked around his screens, "No one can top what Dax just gave me, but anyone else got anything?"

"Concabe on Embers sir." The Denigen stood near an open window throwing cautious glances outside into the night.

Hace nodded, "How are things there? Is the election over yet?"

Concabe spoke quietly, "It's not good news. The Conclave's been in session for weeks and the Denigens are more restless than ever. The peace officers have been working overtime to quell any riots that broke out, but there simply wasn't enough officers to cover the whole planet. There's a massive amount of damage here and we're lucky our branch hasn't been torched."

"Has the flag been raised yet? Do they have a new PM?"

Concabe looked out the window, "Hold on sir. I think I see something."

Hace only saw starlight and darkness as his man leaned out the window, then he was back in the frame again, "Oh sir! The gold flag is up! I repeat the gold flag. That means Vell is our new leader of the planet."

"Shit! I can't stand that guy. He'll never go for our previous deal we had with Lightstone. I want you to hold tight there until I make a decision on if we stay or go on that planet."

"Yes sir."

"Anyone else?"

The rest of the branch leaders were silent.

Hace sighed, "Good. I'm running out of time as it is so if anyone thinks of something, message me and I'll reply when I'm available. Good day everyone!"

A chorus of goodbyes and branch leaders signing off happened in a chaotic chorus and then it was silent again.

Hace was pleased with Dax. He had done what he set out to do, even though Hace had thought it impossible. It was the best news he heard all day.

CHAPTER 16

MR. APPLETTE

ONE

>>> > CELESTE WOKE UP in a fog. Her head was spinning and she could barely open her eyes. Someone was talking to her but she couldn't make out who it was. It was like they were talking underwater. Then she fell back asleep.

When she woke up again, she was laying on a soft couch. She opened her eyes and blinked a few times. There was a voice. She could barely hear it.

"Celeste? Come on honey, wake up. It's time for dinner."

She realized it was Dax. He leaned over her and put his hands out to help her to sit up.

"How you feeling champ? You've been out a lot longer than I thought you'd be. I was starting to get worried."

She rubbed her eyes. The smell of steak hit her nose and she thought she might throw up.

She put her hand to her mouth and Dax put a small trash can in front of her. She vomited a little and pushed the trash can away. Dax took it to the bathroom and she heard the toilet flush. She looked down and saw she was wearing what she assumed was one of his t-shirts, and a pair of pajama bottoms. She double-checked to make sure her bra and panties were still on and they were. She looked outside and saw it was dark. How long had she been out? She wanted to check the time but her Titan was missing. She looked for it on the table in front of her but it wasn't there.

Dax came back into the room, "How are you feeling hon?"

"I'm sorry. I didn't mean to throw up."

"It's okay. Nothing like that bothers me. I'm just worried about you. You slept all the way through the ride and then I carried you in here and changed your clothes. You threw up all over that dress when you came to for a little bit."

"I was awake before?"

"Yeah, for about two minutes. Long enough to vomit."

"Can I use your bathroom? I have to get rid of the…" she motioned with her hand towards her mouth.

"Sure." He put his hand out to her and helped her to stand. She leaned on him a few times until he got her to the door of his guest bathroom. She washed out her mouth and spit a few times. She had another bout of dizziness while she was washing her hands and lost her balance. She fell against the wall hard enough to make the door to the medicine cabinet open and a pill bottle tumbled into the sink.

"You alright in there?" Dax was calling through the door.

She yelled even though it hurt her head, "Yes. I'm just being clumsy. Be out in a minute."

She heard him walk away as she dried her hands. She grabbed the pill bottle to put it back and placed it on the shelf, label facing out. She noticed the address on it was for this house but the name wasn't Dax's. It was Ryan Icenbur. Did he have a roommate he never mentioned?

She closed the medicine cabinet door and stumbled out of the bathroom. She landed back on the couch just before her knees gave out.

Dax brought her a big glass of water, "You're going to need this. We need to sober you up some. I've made dinner, but maybe we should wait on that for awhile."

She took the glass and started drinking.

"Slow Celeste. Not too much. I'll get you some crackers." He left for the kitchen and she looked around some more. She couldn't see her Titan anywhere.

"Hey where's the dress?"

He yelled over his shoulder, "Oh, I'm washing it."

"You can't wash a dress like that, it needs to be dry cleaned," she stopped herself. *Who cares?* She wanted to burn that dress.

"Oh, I'm sorry. I'm probably ruining it then. I apologize."

"I don't want it anyways, you can keep it, destroy it, whatever."

"You want to sleep more? I can keep dinner in the warming drawer and we can eat later." He handed her a box of crackers.

"Yeah, maybe. I don't feel quite right just yet." She felt like she could barely keep her eyes open. He helped her to lay back down and then she was sleeping again.

An hour later, she woke up for good. She looked around but Dax wasn't anywhere. She tore open the package of crackers and started eating them.

Dax came into the room at the sound, "So how you feeling now beautiful?"

"Better thanks. Hey, I was wondering, where's my Titan?"

Dax frowned, "Oh geez. When you threw up the first time, you hit your Titan too. It um…it didn't survive. Started making a weird sizzling frying sound. I'm sure you have a waterproof one, but I think the fluid got into the battery compartment. I tried to clean it up but it's not working right now. I can still get it for you if you want."

"Yes, please." She ran a hand over her hair trying to smooth it out.

He left the room and quickly returned with her Titan. He handed it to her and she looked at him. He was acting fine, but all of this sounded oddly convenient. But if he wanted to do something to her, he could have. She was unconscious for hours and he hadn't done anything but take care of her. Was she paranoid? She didn't know yet, but she knew he had a great deal of opportunity to hurt her, but hadn't taken any of them.

She thanked him and tried turning it on. It wouldn't power up. She turned it over and looked at the battery compartment. Everything looked fine, but the straps that went around her arm were wet and stained an odd color. She thought maybe Dax had been telling the truth.

She put it down onto the table and looked up at him.

He sat down next to her, "I'm sorry I changed out your clothes without you being awake...again. It was such a mess and I didn't feel right leaving you in your own...ickiness. I didn't look...much. At your body, I mean."

She put her hand on his knee, "This is a big mess isn't it? What've you heard on the news?"

Dax hesitated, "Nothing about what happened at Silver Thorn. There was mention that King David was supposed to make a big announcement this afternoon, but it got postponed and moved planets and eventually got cancelled. The news agencies are all entertaining themselves by concocting stories about what's going on. Some of them are really ridiculous."

Celeste asked, "Could we eat dinner? Is it still any good?"

"Of course. Let me help you to the table."

Celeste ate slowly, but she kept thinking of Sebastian. She couldn't sense him and she didn't have her Titan anymore. Dax didn't have one that she could see laying around, and even if she did grab it and use it, she didn't have Sebastian's information memorized and she couldn't just pull it up anywhere.

After they finished dinner, Celeste was complaining about how hot it was in the house.

"That's probably the drugs in your system. We can go out to the beach if you like. Maybe the fresh air and a short walk will help you feel better."

She agreed and they walked outside. He carefully carried her down the wooden steps from the deck to the beach and set her down on the sand. She took in a few deep breaths and the wind on her face made her feel more awake.

She walked alongside Dax and they went closer to the shore.

He stopped and turned to face her, "Feel better?"

"Yeah, a lot actually."

"Good. I've been meaning to tell you. I know now that you were probably just trying to protect me when you broke it off. I see that you were being selfless and that only makes me like you that much more. I want to be there for you if you need me. I think there must be a way out of marrying David. I just need a little time to figure it out. Then we can be together without worry."

Celeste pulled back a strand of hair that was blowing across her eyes, "Listen Dax, I know your intentions were good to come and get me like you did, but I wished you would've just…stayed away. It isn't safe what you did. They'll come after you. David must be raging mad right now."

"Well, when I put out my hand, it looked like you were going to take it. If you didn't want to go why didn't you just tell me?"

She lied, "I didn't think you'd listen. You were obviously pretty serious about getting me and then you were grabbing me and throwing me over your shoulder…"

"I know you Celeste. If you didn't want to go with me, you would've been kicking and screaming trying to wrestle your way loose."

She shook her head. She couldn't tell him the real reason she went with him was because she thought he was someone else. "Well, I'm here now and so are you. David is going to come looking for both of us. We need to figure out what to do. But for now, I do need to get back to my apartment."

"It's not safe there. You said it yourself, David will be looking for us. At least here, he doesn't know where I live, but I'm sure he knows your address."

She lied, "David is determined. If he doesn't know where I'm at already, he's going to put out a whole task force of guards to start searching."

"Well, my transit's registered to my friend who lives on another planet. Unlike Earth, we didn't even go through the Praxis SAP, we went on the outside edge of it. I need to avoid the scanners. My friend will lead them on a wild goose chase for a while until they figure out they've got the wrong guy. Don't worry about me. It's you that he knows where you live, I bet."

"Wait, you…we switched transits before getting here?"

He nodded.

"How did you get into the planet without going through the SAP?"

He smiled, "It's a secret."

Celeste thought he might be making sense about David. But she wanted to be alone. Dax might not be dangerous to her, but she wanted to get her head on straight, and she needed a new Titan. "Well, I could call a taxi."

"No way. Not safe."

"Do you mind dropping me off at the transit station then?"

"Why? Why not just stay here with me for a little bit? I can nurse you back to normal and we can get you some more clothes. Get better acquainted." He smiled at her and put his arms around her waist.

She left her arms at her sides; she didn't want his hands on her right now. "This isn't a good time for me to be with anyone. You know what I just went through. I'm looking for some alone time. Please let me go, Dax."

His grip around her tightened even stronger, "I don't want to let you go babe. I love being close to you, come on."

She started to panic trying to wriggle away from him, "No really Dax. Let me go, I'm serious."

"I know you are. I am too. We're going to lay down now." He started leaning down towards the ground and managed to stay on top of her as they fell onto the sand.

"Dax. Please let me go. This isn't funny."

"Stop wriggling. Jesus. Listen, I care about you. I've been taking care of you, all I want is a little appreciation." He tried kissing her but she kept moving her face away from him.

"Come on baby. You owe me." He let all of his body weight pin her down and she struggled to get away.

"Dax! Stop!"

But he didn't. She slapped him hard. That was a mistake.

He yelled at her, "How dare you hit me! I just saved you from a crazy ass motherfucker like David. He would've ground you down into the dirt and not blinked."

She was squirming in any direction she thought she might be able to escape, but he was always faster than her.

"I didn't ask to be rescued by you!"

Dax stopped moving and so did Celeste.

His voice was small, "This wasn't supposed to happen this way. When I met you...then I spent time with you...I ended up falling for you. I fell in love with you somewhere along the way, I don't even know when. You're so sexy and hot and...you're really smart too and hot."

She felt overwhelmed. And he, all of a sudden, sounded like a teenage boy in heat. She needed to get him off her, "Dax, I think we've both had a trying day, why don't we get up and we can talk about things."

He arched an eyebrow at her, "I think this is the best position for us, but we don't have to say anything." Then he was kissing her again, but she didn't kiss him back.

She was extremely uncomfortable feeling his erection pressing into her thigh. He kissed her mouth, and cheek then kissed along her neck.

She thought of Sebastian – even though this really wasn't the time. She still wanted him, even if he didn't want her. And she just couldn't believe that deep down he didn't want her.

Dax crossed the line tonight and ruined things between them. He wasn't the man she thought he was; he was proving that with every second that passed, "Dax, you need to stop. We need to talk."

She went to push him off when his hands pinned hers down against the sand.

"Dax, what the hell do you think you're doing?! Let me go!"

He stopped kissing her body and looked up at her, "I love you. What more do you need? Isn't that enough to have sex with me?"

"No, of course not! Not for me." Once the words came out of her mouth, she was instantly scared.

The eyes that had been sweet and tender towards her, clouded over like a fast moving storm.

"Dax, what's wrong with you? Let me go! Now!" She was trying to sound calm and brave, but she certainly didn't feel it.

"You're going to have sex with me bitch. You've been wearing all these sexy outfits and prancing around like you wanted to fuck me and now you don't want to?! I even fell in love with you, *by fucking accident,* and it's not enough?"

"Listen…there's somebody else okay?"

He shifted his weight so he was straddling her and she knew there was no chance of escaping. She tried, in vain, to move away from him, but it was hopeless.

"*Someone…else?*" His right eye twitched.

She could hear the anger ratchet up in his voice. He sounded like Jonathan.

Her voice became small, "Yes…we dated before I met you. Then a little while later, this guy and I…we broke up, after I started seeing you. I'm sorry I should've told you sooner. I'll forget about all of this,"—she motioned with her head in his direction—"if you get off me now. I'll leave and we can take some time apart. Talk it over later."

She would've said anything to make him think she was fine with all that happened and not report him immediately to the local authorities. She'd have to get a restraining order for him, and she didn't know the first thing about that since this had never happened to her before. (Not where she could actually take legal action to protect herself from a dangerous man.) But for now, all she had was her wits to get out of this situation.

"*I want* to fuck you and *I'm going to,*" he had completely changed in front of Celeste's eyes. Like Dr. Jekyll and Mr. Hyde, he was now someone she had never met.

She fought as hard as she could and screamed. He put one of his hands over her mouth and she bit down viciously. He ripped his hand away, surprised, and now bleeding. She had left a ring of tooth marks on the side of his hand. She thought she might be able to fight her way out of this, but that's when he punched her, right across the jaw and the taste of blood filled her mouth as she realized she'd bit down hard on her own lip. *Oh God, this is too much like my dead husband.* She tried to calm herself but it wasn't working. Her heart was going to burst out of her chest. Her mind was racing. Sebastian! If he could hear her, he could help. <*PLEASE, SEBASTIAN! HELP! I NEED YOU!*> She continued to fight, but Dax was much stronger.

She screamed out loud again for help but he slapped her angrily, shutting her up, "There's no one to hear you, you stupid whore. I picked this house because it's desolate. There's no one around for miles."

She was frightened seeing how desperate her situation had become. She thought he was such a nice guy and now, to be here like this with him? But the alternative would've been to stay with David. Neither was a good choice.

He leaned over and kissed her trying to force her lips apart with his tongue. She kept moving her face away from his until he pulled away from her a little.

"I'm not the type to ta—"

She interrupted him by spitting in his face. He was so taken aback, he sat up and let go of her arms momentarily.

She fought with every bit of strength she had. Her left fist connected with his crotch and he coughed out, gasping for breath. He balled up his hands and slammed a fist into the side of her head, knocking her out.

T W O

>>> > DAX LOOKED AT Celeste laying bound on the couch, unconscious. She shivered and moaned. Part of him wanted to clean her up, put her into his transit, and take her home. Not here in this rented place, but his real home. He thought she might wake up soon. He needed to handle that. Another part of him remembered she refused to have sex with him and hit him in the balls. Dax adjusted his mask. His Titan rang and he took down his breather to talk, "Yeah, come over now. I've got her. We're going through with it after all."

Celeste started screaming.

"Hold on. Hold on."

Celeste rolled herself off the couch and hit the floor hard on her back. Dax put on his breather. He held an aerosol bottle and sprayed sleep-85 into her face. Her screaming stopped as she tried to hold her breath. She turned her face away from him.

"It's too late darling."

She shook her head and gasped for air as her lungs couldn't hold out any longer.

"This could have been so different dear."

Her body convulsed then relaxed.

Celeste was out. He took down the breather. He was still on his call, "I forgot my halo, the thought blocker," he paused, "Yeah the one on the top shelf. I need you to bring it."

Dax looked over her restraints. He tested them one more time to make sure they were secure before he took his attention away from her. He turned around and looked at her Titan. The damn thing had ridiculous amounts of security on it for someone who didn't appear very tech savvy. But, she was a former queen after all. Someone in her kingdom could've set her up with something like this and as much as he tried to crack the code on it and bypass security, he couldn't get it. Then the damn thing had a countdown before it fizzled itself out.

Dax walked into the garage, took off his mask and threw it in the back of his transit, "I don't care if you have to turn around to get it. I need it. I had to use one of those Goddamned undetectable injections on her in my transit and you know we can't afford to use those often. They're too damned expensive."

He listened to his lackey on the other end, then growled, "I need the blocker because I don't know if she has any of those powers. She could've been trained while she was in the kingdom, who knows, but I'm sure as hell not going to take any chances. She can't know where she's going! If *you* want to explain to The Hunter why she broadcast everything to someone receiving a signal from her, then go ahead and *don't* bring the halo but I don't want to risk it. I don't care that you think the tech is too new to be proven effective." Dax ran a hand over his hair, "Just do as I say for fuck's sake!"

The call was terminated before he could press the button and it made Dax even angrier to know he had been hung up on.

THREE

>>> > CELESTE WOKE UP groggy. She felt like she had been hit by a freight transit. There was a blindfold tied around her eyes. She couldn't see anything.

She struggled to fight the fog in her brain but it was hard to focus. She tried to move, but then remembered she was bound and couldn't. Dax had tied her up and she was being taken somewhere in a vehicle. She didn't even know if she was in a bot-taxi alone or with other beings in a private transit. She used her 7's to read anything she could off of whoever was in the transit with her, but got nothing. She could only assume Dax was with her.

"What's going on?"

She got silence in response.

"Dax, I want to know what the hell you think you're doing with me. This has gone way beyond a bad idea or some kind of sick joke. I want to be released *RIGHT NOW!*"

She heard no reply. She fought against her bindings. She thought threatening him might make him change his mind.

"You're going to regret this. You hear me?"

She heard someone let out a long exhale, but there was a second voice that laughed. Then she found a voice she didn't think she had in her. "YOU HEAR ME ASSHOLES! YOU CAN'T DO THIS TO ME! THERE'S GOING TO BE A TON OF PEOPLE LOOKING FOR ME AND THEY WON'T STOP UNTIL THEY FIND ME!"

The being that was laughing before, was now laughing even harder and that sent her over the edge. She started screaming out of frustration, but suddenly a hard strike hit her jaw and instantly silenced her.

Pain like white-hot lightning raced through her body. All she could see were stars in the dark. She took a deep breath, but couldn't calm herself down. She wished Sebastian had never left Praxis. She wished he had never left her that day he said goodbye. Maybe her connection to him was strong enough where he could hear her. She sent out a thought as hard as she could, hoping wherever he was in the universe, he could hear it.

<PLEASE SEBASTIAN! HELP ME!>

She waited for a response, but heard nothing.

Fear was a snake that coiled itself around her quickly. She tried to fight it, but she couldn't breathe. She was hyperventilating.

"Shut up you noisy bitch! How I'm supposed to concentrate with that? Julian, I need you to knock her out, she can't even breathe quiet."

"Yes boss."

Within a minute, she had a piece of fabric held over her nose and while she fought to hold her breath, she passed out again.

"Chloroform is your best friend sometimes, hey Julian?"

Julian nodded to Dax, "Sure boss, anything you say."

"Thanks buddy. You're a good man. Now I can focus," Dax looked down at his Titan.

The transit flew fast and deep into the desert landscape. Soon it landed at the base of a large mountain and the only sound heard was a bird caw in the distance.

FOUR

>>> > GINGER RAN THROUGH the infirmary to Ulysses's side.

"Oh my God!" She looked him over as he held an icepack to his jaw.

"Ginger! Hi. What are you doing here?"

"I heard there was some kind of fight. Are you okay?"

"I'll be fine. It's just my pride that's damaged."

She looked him over and made a face, "How did this happen?"

Ulysses blinked a couple of times and shifted his weight on the bed, "What…did they tell you? I mean how did you find out it was me?"

She smiled, "I was talking to the kitchen staff, and then the master gardener burst in and said there was some sort of fist fight. Said you had been hit in the jaw by some other guard, is that true?"

He looked around, "Something like that, but we can't talk about it here. Give me another hour and I'll meet you at the place where we're supposed to meet tomorrow."

She nodded, turned around, and left before anyone saw her.

FIVE

››› › CELESTE DIDN'T KNOW how much time passed, but she'd been awake for a few minutes. She was dizzy and nauseous. Her ankles and wrists were untied, but raw. Her head and jaw ached like crazy. She was sitting on the floor of a small rectangular room. They had removed her blindfold, but there wasn't much to see. There was blue carpet underneath her, and the walls were white. There was a bright bare light bulb in the ceiling. The light from it hurt her eyes. She looked around and guessed the room was ten feet tall, nine feet long, and four feet wide. There was a speaker and a camera high up in the corner of the room. They had been built into the wall and protected by a metal cage around the front of them. There was a door with no handle at the end of the room.

She thought at first that Dax was just upset at her, wanted to rape her, hit her harder than he meant to, but this was much bigger. This was kidnapping. She was being held for ransom, but she wasn't even a queen anymore. *Why would they take me now?*

She rubbed her left temple and winced. She had a new tender knot there. She touched her jaw with her fingers but it hurt so bad she didn't touch it again. Rubbing her eyes, she tried to remain calm. As she inspected herself for bruises, she realized her shoes were gone and she had left her handbag back at Silver Thorn.

All she had now were her 7's. She already called out to Sebastian twice without hearing anything back.

She thought as hard as she could, <*SEBASTIAN! I need you! I've been kidnapped! Please come find me! Can you hear me?*>

Nothing. No images, no words, nothing. Light-headedness overwhelmed her. She lay down and closed her eyes.

She fell unconscious again.

SIX

>>> > SOMETIME LATER CELESTE woke up with her head pounding. She tried to stay calm, but she had no idea what was going on and she felt extremely vulnerable. The last thing she remembered was…

Daxton! He abducted her. Who orchestrated this kidnapping? Was it him or someone else? *He must've been conning me this whole time.* But he had said something funny, that he fell in love with her *by accident.* Had he meant he planned on manipulating her but ended up actually falling for her? Plus the night she got drunk he said she had six glasses of wine, but that never made sense to her. She never drank that much before. She thought at first it was her memory that was wrong, but he was (maybe) drugging her back then. He mentioned something about knowing for next time. That son of a bitch!

Now I'm here in this box. She felt like such a trusting fool. *I was so naïve. How could I think every man was as good and straightforward as Sebastian?!* Her mind saved her darkest bit of curiosity for last. Dax was about to rape her on the beach. She had no idea what happened after she got knocked out. He could have, but she couldn't be sure. She didn't feel any soreness between her legs; maybe that was the best part of to-day. She tried holding onto that thought. But it wasn't long before other thoughts were slithering out of the shadows.

Sex was bad enough with Jon, but the thought of being raped by another man? A man who was lying right from the start about everything, a man she had just met and was developing feelings for? Her stomach turned and she wanted to think of something else, anything. She thought of Sebastian's face, his scent, his embrace. *Oh my gosh,* she thought, *what am I going to do? How can I get out of here?*

<SEBASTIAN! PLEASE HEAR ME, I NEED YOU.> "I need you." A single tear fell along her cheek.

An unfamiliar man's voice came over the speaker, "I see you're awake. Oh sweetie, don't cry. You'll be fine. We need to keep you alive if we want coren from your kingdom. We won't hurt you…unless we have to," the voice started laughing.

She looked up at the speaker and started yelling, "You sons of bitches! Let me go! I'm not even a queen anymore! What the hell kind of money do you think you're going to be able to squeeze out of the kingdom you idiots! LET ME GO!" She started pounding on the walls. She went to the door and pushed against it, trying to force it open. She screamed and grunted, all the while making her head pound even harder.

"I wouldn't do that if I were you honey. No one's going to hear you. We're in a place no one will ever think to find you and if you don't behave…We can tie you up again, knock you out, and then do whatever we like with you. Please remember who's in control around here."

She kicked the door, scratching at it with her fingers. She couldn't fight the desperation rising up in her. Fear took over and she became crazed trying to break her way out of the room.

The voice over the speaker said, "I warned you sweetie."

The door flew open and a figure covered in all black hit her across the face. The slap stunned her but she knew this might be her chance to escape if she was smart. She moved forward quickly trying to hit the person, but a punch to her stomach made her double over. It must've been a man since the punches were just as savage and strong as Jon's strikes.

There was pain in her leg and all over. Her muscles seized. She fell to the ground, completely incapacitated. They had used a taser gun on her and she was unable to cry out. It hurt so bad; she'd never been shocked before.

She laid face down half out of the doorway of her room. She tried to look around but it was all darkness, and she couldn't see too much since she couldn't pick up her head. Even the figure in front of her was completely concealed. She didn't know if they were Human or alien. The figure dragged her back into the room and she felt a bee sting on her left foot. The figure leaned over her for a second then slammed the door shut.

The voice was back.

"Oh sorry dearie, you made me do that. Try to behave huh? Do yourself a favor."

The voice stopped, but deafening music replaced it. It was roaring so loud, she couldn't think. Her entire body felt sore, like she had been struck by a transit after running a marathon. And how did a bee get in here to sting her foot like that? It gave her hope that she was on Earth.

<SEBASTIAN! PLEASE HELP ME!> She thought as loud as she could, but soon blacked out again.

SEVEN

>>> > THE MAN IN black took off his mask and stepped into the security room. "So was that good enough, Eddie?"

"Sure. I think the boss will be pleased. Did you dart her? I didn't see."

The man nodded, "Yep. Did it at the end on her foot."

Eddie looked at his screens, "Oh yeah, she's already out again. Stupid little entitled broad. If she keeps this up, she's gonna' get drugged so much she'll have no clue what's really happening to her."

"She's a fucking fighter she is. I hate those types. Makes everything harder and the boss never has to deal with it. It's always me."

Eddie looked annoyed.

"Us, I mean. It's always us."

"I'm tired. Why don't you take this shift and I'll catch a few."

"If she wakes up and is a problem, you want me to drug her food, Eddie?"

"You can, but not too much. Let's see if her attitude improves first. Call me if there's real trouble or if the boss comes around."

Eddie closed the door and the man in black poured himself a cup of coffee. He rubbed his face and yawned. Prisoner detail was so boring sometimes. He looked at the screen and watched as the former queen lay motionless on the ground. He wondered if she was going to die like a couple of the others they had brought in lately. They definitely didn't want to kill them before the whole ransom process got started, but they had drugged three prisoners too much and ended up killing them. Every species was different and it was hard to get the doses right when all the chemistry kept changing. He shrugged his shoulders to no one and switched one of the screens to the game. He needed to know if his team could snap their losing streak.

EIGHT

>>> > D'ARTAGNAN WAS AT the black market of Il'laceier, Graine Quarter, looking for whatever that blue light floating above David's head was.

He walked from table to table looking for something like it. He searched all over his network, his informants, his friends (except Raynes since he was currently unavailable along with Eric), and the uninet but could find nothing like it.

This was his last effort before giving up.

Graine Quarter was crowded tonight. D'Artagnan carried no ID or coren on him, or anything else that could be stolen out of his pockets. It was close quarters in here and dark.

He came upon a vendor on the corner of Chi-dell and Z Trail who looked promising…only thing was the tiny floating lights were square or triangles in green or pink.

"Excuse me. What are these?" D'Artagnan studied how they floated in air.

The vendor was a Human male, tall with light brown skin, bright green eyes, and wearing a worn out black top hat. He stuck out his hand, "Name's Mr. Applette. Nice to meetcha."

"Zane Colmsky. My pleasure," D'Artagnan shook the man's hand.

"You're not a cop or a guard is ya'?" Mr. Applette adjusted his brown suit coat.

"No sir. I'm looking around for something new for myself."

"K. I guess you look harmless enough. These are my special friends."

D'Artagnan's snout twitched. The man's scent was wrong somehow, but D'Artagnan couldn't identify it. He hated the smell. Sometimes it was hard to tell whether it was mental instability or brain tumors like what he suspected in Edison's case, but with this Human, the smell was very strong. D'Artagnan instantly distrusted him.

"So what do your special friends do?"

"Ah. I'm glad you asked. This one,"—he pointed to the green tri-angle— "This one here can help you last longer in the bedroom if you know what I mean. You interested?"

D'Artagnan shook his head, "What about this one?" He pointed to the pink floating square.

"Oh! I almost forgot that one! It helps you get through difficult times. You know like, if your mother-in-law makes a surprise weekend visit and you can't stand her, this kinda mellows you out."

D'Artagnan asked, "Why would I buy these instead of just taking a drug?"

Mr. Applette smiled, "All you do is put these over your head, like under a hat or something, and you can just put it on and take it off. No residuals, no side effects, no needing to buy more to replenish your supply."

"I see."

"Yep. They are awesome." Mr. Applette started dancing in place with his arms in the air like he was getting ready to fly.

D'Artagnan watched him, "Are you using one of your special friends right now?"

"How could you tell?"

"I'm a good guesser. You seem sort of…happy."

"Yeah. I'm cheerful." He took off his top hat and showed the inside to D'Artagnan. There was a purple oval floating in it.

"What does that one do? You didn't have it out on the display table."

"This one takes away all your physical pain. See, normally I can barely move my back. I got into a transit accident when I was a teenager, totally messed up my spine. I was miserable, but this little beauty helps me move around pain free."

"How do these work?"

Mr. Applette waved his finger side to side at D'Artagnan, "Can't tell you. I can't give up my secrets like that. Then everybody'd be doin' it."

D'Artagnan smiled, "Well, it's not magic."

"It's tech based, yes, not magic," Mr. Applette started laughing to himself.

"Tech based huh? It somehow alters your brain though."

Mr. Applette smiled, "You ask a lot of questions. You sure you're not a cop?"

"Positive. One more question. You don't have any blue ones? Any blue circles?"

"Huh, no. No sir. Blue circles are beyond my range."

"What does that mean?"

"You said one more question mister. You gonna buy anything or what?"

D'Artagnan sighed, "How much for these?"

Mr. Applette hesitated, "How much you think they're worth to ya?"

D'Artagnan was getting impatient with this man, "I'm not good at haggling. I know you must have a price in mind."

"Thirty-five thousand for one, sixty-five for both. The purple one's not for sale yet, I'm still testing it out…unless you're interested in buying that one. Then it's for sale. I'd say a hundred and fifty thousand just for that one."

D'Artagnan scoffed, "Are you kidding?"

"Price just went up for all of them by five thousand."

D'Artagnan made a pained face, "If I buy one will you answer all my questions?"

"Sure buddy. Sure."

"Fine. Give me the pink one."

D'Artagnan remembered he brought no coren. He had a paper to-do list in his pocket. Linda got him hooked on the old-fashioned practice of hand writing things down. He always liked that habit about her, so he kept it as one of his new habits after she passed away. He took it out of his pocket and tore off a small edge. He handed it to the Human, "Here. It's all the money I have."

Mr. Applette looked at it, "This ain't no coren."

"No. It's our new Il'lacean money. The King just put it into effect. You're holding fifty thousand hitchers in your hand. All I really want is some answers. You can keep your special friends."

Mr. Applette inspected the paper square closer, then looked at D'Artagnan, "Okay. What do you want to know?"

"What are blue circles good for? You said they were beyond your range. What do they do?"

"That's something very powerful, yep. Very experimental right now in my field. Everyone's trying to do it, but ain't a one been successful yet."

"What is it?"

"It's a thought blocker. You know those people that say they can read your mind and stuff? Those blue dots? They can stop anyone from getting into your brain. If you're looking for one of those...well, I don't have 'em yet. I will though. Give me some time. Come back and I'll have some."

D'Artagnan didn't know whether to believe any of this or not. He was pretty sure he was talking to a mad man. But it was the only information he had on what David might be wearing in his crown.

"You've been most helpful Mr. Applette. Thanks for your time," D'Artagnan turned to leave.

"Wait! You gave me all this money. You wanted the pink one. You seem like such a nice guy, I'll box it up for ya."

Khaleen help him, D'Artagnan almost felt guilty lying to this crazy man, "No really. I don't need any of these. They're your friends after all."

Mr. Applette stopped and grabbed a box from underneath his table, "I think you need something different. Yes you do." He opened the box and reached inside. He held out a glowing orange octagon. "This is something I gave up on. I don't think it's any good, but it might be good *to you*. All minds are different. Something that doesn't work on a Human brain might work on an Il'lacean one. Try this."

D'Artagnan shook his head, "I don't think I want to take anything from you. You might be able to get a better price for it from someone else."

"I didn't even tells ya' what it does. It erases bad dreams and replaces them with nice ones...at least it was supposed to, but it never worked on me. I won't sell it, trust me. Just take it."

D'Artagnan didn't move.

"Put out your hand."

"Mr. Applette, I don't think it's fair of me to take that."

"You're gonna hurt my feelings man, just take it, please," he paused, "If you don't takes it, I will find a way to get it to you anyway."

D'Artagnan looked at the man sideways, "What does that mean?"

Mr. Applette reached out and placed it over D'Artagnan's left shoulder. The orange octagon glowed brighter for a moment then dimmed.

Mr. Applette smiled, "Oh yeah. That one's yours. That's your special friend now. It never did that for me when I tried to use it. Must've made my combination wrong on that one."

D'Artagnan looked at it and reached out with his right hand to take it off him. It felt warm. He cupped his hand around it and said as he handed it back to the Human, "I don't feel right taking this. I'm sure you need to be paid for your services."

Mr. Applette shook his head, "I've already been paid. Take it. How about this – if it doesn't work for you, you come back and return it. If it *does* work for you, come back and pay me some real coren."

D'Artagnan raised his eye ridges, "How did you...why did you act like that paper I gave you was mon—"

Mr. Applette's voice changed, "Not everything is as it seems down here. For one thing, I know you're not who you say you are, Mr. Colmsky. You're someone else...*just like I am*. Take the dream eraser because you need it. It was made for you and your special problems. I believe the information I gave you will help you greatly in your current quest. In the place where I come from, oppression does not happen. We all live in harmony, as one. We regard knowledge above all other things."

D'Artagnan's body tensed immediately, "What are you talking about? How do you know these things? Who sent you to me?"

Mr. Applette smiled and when he did, his bright green eyes turned to solid black from eyelid to eyelid.

D'Artagnan knew no Human was physically capable of that.

"What the hell *are you*?"

Mr. Applette's eyes returned to bright green, "Something you won't understand right now. Not yet, but your time will come."

"Do you know about my King? What he has in his crown?"

"I do. I'm not making thought blockers though, not yet. It really is outside my range, I promise you that. But someone else I know is good at a darker kind of technology. You see Mr. Steele, where I come from, there is only good and light. We help each other up, we keep each other going. Everything that I showed you, the mood booster, the pain lifter, the bedroom helper, the dream eraser, all those technologies are help-ful. They are positive. They are light based, but there is a place not too far away from both of us that is *dark* based. They are negative. They are dangerous and only try to bring each other down. There is a battle coming for this place,"—Mr. Applette leaned over his table and whispered—"*Your place.*"

D'Artagnan sniffed the Human again. His scent wasn't like anything he had ever smelled. He *was* from somewhere else. "I don't understand any of this."

"Hey I don't suppose you've met someone named Kolek lately have you?"

D'Artagnan shook his head.

Mr. Applette looked around, "I didn't think so. She might've changed her name here. I'm afraid I've already said too much. I can't help you any more right now, but maybe someday in the future, our paths will cross once more. I could be in a different form the next time we meet, but I might see you again. I hope you can win the battle that must be fought by your place in the future," he paused, "I really *need* you to."

D'Artagnan reached out and grabbed the Human man by the arm, "This doesn't make any sense, and you're really starting to make me angry with all this weird cryptic bullshit. How did you know my name?"

"Back off Mr. Steele. Please. I don't want to hurt you."

D'Artagnan looked down at the man who was a full two feet shorter than himself, "*You?* Hurt *me?* I don't see how that's possi—"

D'Artagnan felt a powerful electric shock go through him and he instantly let Mr. Applette go. A second later, D'Artagnan was paralyzed. He could move his eyes and mouth, but not the rest of his body.

Mr. Applette backed up and pressed a button on the corner of his tabletop, "I did try to warn you. I must go. Right now."

The table folded up into a briefcase and landed on the ground. Mr. Applette picked it up and adjusted his top hat. D'Artagnan still couldn't move.

"You won't be like this for long Mr. Steele. As soon as I'm out of your sight, oh I'd say in about fifteen seconds, you'll be free to move again and otherwise be completely unharmed. It was nice to meet you. Good luck."

Mr. Applette started to leave but then turned back to D'Artagnan, "Oh, almost forgot. Where I come from knowledge is paramount and I appreciate you searching for your own answers. When we leave one another where I'm from, we have a saying, knowledge is an ocean, and you must be your boat's captain. That's really all. Goodbye Mr. Steele."

Mr. Applette quickly started down Z Trail and was soon completely lost in the crowds around him.

D'Artagnan got full control over his body again and immediately ran down Z Trail trying to catch up to Mr. Applette, but when he got to the last place he saw him, he couldn't find him. He searched for a full ten minutes, without luck. He ran back to the corner where he originally saw him, but there was no trace of the man or the table either.

D'Artagnan looked down at his hand and didn't see the glowing octagon. What had Mr. Applette called it? A dream eraser? He looked over his left shoulder and there it was, hovering in place.

D'Artagnan grabbed at it with his fingers. It still felt warm. He placed it in his front pocket and walked towards his transit.

This was the strangest night of his life.

Maybe he was going crazy. It had finally happened, he was having a mental breakdown, he was sure of it. He was going to go home, try to sleep, have nightmares all night, then wake up and all of this, he would find, was a dream.

NINE

››› › ULYSSES ALWAYS RAN early. The school that raised him on Zetzetti was strict and punctuality was next to Godliness for those Cloar. Ulysses would describe the Cloar as a group of warrior nuns. They wore fabric cloaks over a layer of chain mail mesh. It was partly for protection, partly to remind them of their duty to protect the children, and partly to stay strong by carrying so much extra weight under already heavy cloaks. The Nawgain, the native species to Zetzetti, were an intense race: highly spiritual people, serious, and completely lacking a sense of humor. Ulysses wished he had come to learn about them by different means than the path his life took. He hadn't been to Zetzetti since he escaped the school. That was a long time ago, and no one here knew anything about his childhood. Ulysses rarely talked about it.

He sat in a brown high back oversized armchair in front of the fireplace. He watched the flames flicker wildly. It was hot here…or maybe it was his nerves. The massive fireplace was seven feet wide and five feet high. The mantle was covered in tasteful sprays of wild flowers and twigs. Ulysses checked the time on his Titan: 9:28 p.m.

He'd been here for fifteen minutes waiting for Ginger. *Where was she? What if she didn't show up? What if she got stopped by someone?* He took a deep breath.

The first time he saw Ginger was his first day on the job. It was three years before King Jonathan was killed. Other guards quickly informed Ulysses that the girls were off limits. He thought that wouldn't be a problem until he laid eyes on Ginger. She had these come hither green eyes and a cascade of dark caramel colored sexy hair falling down to her waist. He couldn't remember his own name she had such an effect on him.

He heard faint footsteps down the hall and sat frozen. He clenched his jaw and a sudden pain gripped him. He had left his ice pack in his room. He thought about going to get it but he needed to be here in case Ginger came. He didn't want to miss her and he couldn't wait anymore. Damned the consequences of David's rules, he should've talked to her a long time ago.

Come what may, he needed to find out if they had anything between them.

The footsteps stopped behind him. He downed the vodka in his glass and closed his eyes.

Ginger whispered, "Hi. You here?"

Ulysses stood up and whispered back, "Yes. Thanks for coming."

"It's kind of exposed out here isn't it?" Ginger stepped around the chair and stood in front of him.

"Yes, but I didn't know where else was open to both of us. This room isn't used very often."

She stared at his swollen cheek and felt bad for making him talk. "I'm sor—"

They heard footsteps and voices approaching. Ulysses put his arm around Ginger's waist and quickly led her into a tucked away alcove of the room. For anyone to see them now, an observer would have to be standing right in front of the fireplace.

Ginger held her breath. Both of them couldn't fit, the space was so tight. Ulysses kept his hand on her lower back and she moved in closer to him. He looked down at her and put his other arm around her waist cinching her into him tightly. They still couldn't fit, so she put her arms up on his shoulders and they slid in together to the shadows.

"I thought I heard someone in here," one guard said to the other.

"I think you're hearing things, Clinton. The fire pops and crackles. Makes a ton of noise. There's nobody here. Let's keep going so I can get some dinner."

Ginger and Ulysses looked at each other, barely breathing. She could smell his cologne and felt his heart hammering in his chest. His lips looked soft. She wondered if they were. Lila was right though, he didn't act like a spy…so far.

They stood motionless until they heard both sets of footsteps fade.

"How are you feeling?" she whispered.

Ulysses spoke quietly, "Jaw hurts but I've had worse hits," he stretched his neck to look around the room, "I suppose this was a bad place to meet."

"I don't think there was any safe place. Maybe one of our rooms. I check my room daily for bugs, secret cameras, stuff like that. Do you?"

He nodded, "But the problem with our rooms is that we have to pass many cameras in the hallways to get there."

"True. You're right."

They were silent. Ulysses' jaw throbbed. He tried to focus on that pain so no other body parts would throb in embarrassing ways.

"I should probably get to the point of why I asked to meet you. We can't stay here long and I don't want to get you in trouble."

She nodded her head and he noticed she was wearing little skeleton earrings that looked like they were crawling through her pierced ears.

"I think you're a unique and interesting woman. I'd like to get to know you better outside of these walls. There's an exhibit at the museum I've been wanting to see. Would you like to go with me?"

She smiled, "Sure. When?"

"A week from Friday night, about seven?"

She tightened her grip around his shoulders and looked at her Titan.

He felt her swiping through screens and figured she must be looking at her Titan's calendar. He enjoyed her warmth in his arms. He thought of kissing her.

The fireplace popped and he jumped.

She whispered, "It's alright. You always this jumpy?"

"Just...nervous about getting caught with you." He wanted to check the doorway but couldn't take his eyes off her.

"It's a little thrilling too," she smiled.

"It's actually a big thrill to have a beautiful woman in yours arms, yes."

Her smile broadened, "So you want to meet there, at the museum then?"

"Yes." He reluctantly took his hands away from her. He thought of pinning her against the wall with his body and kissing her, but then thought of the cameras. There must be some here, there always is. "Do you know if there are any cameras in this room?"

"I've looked and never seen any. I think the area is supposed to be visually checked by guards because of all the places to hide...like this one."

She paused as more footfalls walked across the hallway then she asked, "Are you going to tell me what really happened today?"

Ulysses lied to her, "Two guards had been assigned to the same job. They were fighting over who had the higher rank and when I stepped in to settle it, I accidently caught a quick right. The whole thing happened so fast."

He felt terrible lying to Ginger but this was a secret too big to tell her. There were many others from his past: the Zetzetti seminary, him almost being a priest with magical abilities, the trauma of his childhood, but he would confess those when the time was right.

She took her arms off him and wriggled out of the alcove, "I better get back now. I'll see you soon. Take care of yourself and no more trying to break up fights."

He watched her peek around the doorway first and then walk away. He waited fifteen seconds and then emerged himself. He grabbed the glass he had left on the table and wondered if the two guards that crashed their meeting had seen it. They hadn't said anything about it.

He walked back to his room. The grin on his face hurt but it was worth it.

TEN

>>> > DAVID HATED CANCELLING the press conference because it aroused a lot of curiosity, but he still didn't have any answers. The best he could do was hold a press conference soon on his home planet, but the council wanted a meeting - the only group of people he could tell about Celeste's kidnapping.

David sat at a table with his full council around him.

"My King, for Queen Dowager Hennessy's safety we implore that you wait to get word from whatever group or individual took her. They could ask that you don't get anyone involved and until you know this, we respectfully advise extreme caution on press conferences or telling any media outlets."

King David listened and considered their advice. "Does six days sound reasonable?"

The head councilman thought and responded, "If the kidnappers contact you by then, yes. If not, no."

David chose to wait. He couldn't have Celeste killed due to his impatience for press coverage. The Humans would never understand.

ELEVEN

>>> > MITCH'S TITAN CHIMED with an incoming message.

It looked like no other message he had ever received. He almost quarantined it as malicious software so it wouldn't infect his system, but something nagged at him to open it.

It read:

TITAN Corporation - Personal TITAN Device

System Status: Active -- Universal Grid: Online

Current Time/Date (Praxis - Dersalene): 6:09 a.m./June 12, 2193

Current Universal Positioning System Location: Dersalene, Praxis

User: Unrecorded

Communications Menu

Incoming message(s) received: 1 - Status: Unread

Message Received at *ERROR*

Message Sent from: *ERROR*

- I am sending you this message at great personal risk. I was there at the Rem Mot Om bombing. I saw it all. I saw the transit filled with your HR members get shot out of the sky. One of your men died on impact, that's why there was only five public beheadings but six HR members. The King never mentioned it, but I saw the bodies first. I collected their Titans. I was fearful of what intelligence the King might've seen off them and I kept them for myself, for my own use and to contact the HR if I thought there was a great enough danger to your group. Four of the Titans were severely burnt and would not power up. One of them was completely crushed and unusable. But one powered up and I found your information.
I am on the King's council.
David is acting irrationally. I'm afraid he's a great threat not just to Humanity but Il'laceans as well, maybe all the universe. He shouldn't be king. He isn't qualified for this position.
He's trying to go public with some sensitive information but we've convinced him to wait. It's a matter of life and death for Queen Hennessy. She's been kidnapped. I don't

know by whom. I feel David wants to blame the HR. Perhaps
it is your group that is responsible, or maybe the queen
is part of the Resistance.
The King will make an announcement regarding this issue
most likely, in less than six Earth days' time.
He somehow convinced the queen to marry him. I'm positive
it wasn't her idea, nor her choice to do this, but she was
taken during the ceremony before the marriage happened. It
does make an argument for her being part of the Resistance
and getting rescued just in time.
I encourage the HR to leave Earth and/or Il'laceier as soon
as possible - especially if you have Queen Hennessy. She is
a good spirit. She must be protected. I have read through
many correspondence within your group and it seems you
personally were regarded as the most peaceful, levelheaded,
and non-violent. I appeal to these traits in you now.
Keep this information to yourself. If you want any future
correspondence from me, you'll abide by my request.
There is no way for you to contact me. This correspondence
will be erased from your Titan as soon as it has successfully
been read. Thank you.

-END OF MESSAGE
*This message will auto-delete in 00:03:00 minutes.

Mitch looked up from his Titan. He couldn't believe it. Queen
Dowager Hennessy had been kidnapped? And David wanted to blame
the HR? And they were going to get *married*?

This couldn't be right. Who was this councilmember who reached
out to him? How could he really trust that this wasn't some sort of trick?

But what if this message was legitimate?

He wondered if David had Celeste kidnapped and was making all
of this other stuff up. Maybe he wanted another reason for everyone
to hate the HR and to make the public aware that David was looking

for all HR members and needed a bit more incentive to get everyone's help.

But the HR hadn't taken Celeste.

Maybe no one had. There had never even been an engagement announcement. Mitch was pretty sure Celeste didn't love David.

All of this seemed fishy. But in six days' time, if this message was for real, David would make an announcement and everyone would find out.

Mitch couldn't sit by and do nothing.

This needed to be addressed. There needed to be some sort of response. And with that, Mitch's decision on the HR had been made.

TWELVE

>>> > "SO WHERE IS she right now?" Hace was almost giddy.

"Secured in her cell inside the Tiletan facility. I've got a constant rotation of guards watching on the cameras. I can give you a feed if you want," Dax looked over his shoulder for a minute and then back to his Titan. He was so glad The Hunter made this call an audio only one.

"Nah. I trust you. I got too many screens as it is, constantly bleeping and blipping with information, feeds, and video. It drives me nuts sometimes to look at all of them."

"Of course sir. Let me know if you change your mind and you can take a peek at Celeste."

"How is she with the drugs?"

"We're slowly trying to find the right balance. She's our first Human Being petite female hostage. I think it'd be easy to overdose her."

"Yeah, make sure you don't do that."

"I'm being careful. We had to stun her though. She wouldn't submit, and was being real feisty and unstable. She's a fighter."

"You got her subdued though?"

"Yes, absolutely. Now we're giving her small rations of food and water to weaken her. Might rough her up a little more for the videos."

"Whatever you have to do. I trust you."

"What are we going to ask for sir?"

"I'm thinking that over. It's early so we'll have to let them twist in the wind a while longer before communicating anything. This is the highest profile hostage yet, so I need to make sure everything's straight before we contact the king."

"Understood sir. What about the stone? Anything new there?"

Hace shook his head, "I've got DAI researching it in different ways, but so far we're coming up empty. I'm relieved we've got the damned gem, so that's a big obstacle overcome, but there's so much left to do. We need Celeste's ransom money before we can proceed with the Red Klix operation. After this is all wrapped up with a pretty little coren bow, you and I can meet and I'll show you the stone. It's stunning."

"I bet…and it's so powerful."

Hace smiled, "You said it." He clapped his hands together and rubbed them, "Okay, good work Dax. Keep me updated…and one more thing."

"Yes boss?"

"Somebody mentioned to me that they saw a Taybuse over there… Is that true?"

Dax winced, "Yeah, but he's a good man, real tough and smart."

"Get rid of him and I don't mean kick him out of the group."

"But sir – he's an asset to us, if you'd reconsi—"

"There is NO Taybuse allowed! NONE OF THEM can be a part of the Brotherhood! It is a simple rule."

Dax sighed, "I vetted him myself. I'm not sure what the reaso—"

"Daxton! Think carefully before you speak to me, even more carefully before you *argue* with me."

"I apologize. I spoke out of turn. I will take care of him."

"Good."

"Adrastos over and out."

THIRTEEN

>>> > TWO WEEKS OF vacation had flown by for Eric, Agathon, and Sebastian on Foss-Altus. It was a sad day when they were saying goodbye at the docking hub.

"Come back anytime you like, of course, call first so I can give you clearance, but, anytime you like. I'm gonna miss you guys making me laugh." Agathon was in Human form for his goodbyes.

"Oh we'll be back. I love this place," Eric couldn't help but gush as he got into the transit.

Sebastian shook hands with and bowed to Agathon, "Thanks for everything. You're a wonderful host as usual."

"You keep me in the loop about your lady and remember what I said; accept love – from yourself and from the queen. Cecca Vet Lopp, Gees'Eked, Floguethyinn Oftiyumous."

Sebastian returned the well wishes, "Cecca Vet Lopp, Gees'Eked, Floguethyinn Oftiyumous. Take care Aggie and I'll do my best to fully accept your motto."

Sebastian waved goodbye. The transit rose out of Foss-Altus's atmosphere and darkness enveloped them. Sebastian engaged his autopilot and looked out over the vastness of empty space. He rubbed his chin absentmindedly letting his thoughts wander to the memories he made over the past two weeks. Sebastian was silent as he considered everything Agathon told him and wondered how angry and hurt Celeste must be.

Much to Sebastian's surprise (and relief), Eric didn't mention Celeste once to him during the long transit ride back to Praxis.

FOURTEEN

>>> > ERIC SAID GOODBYE to Sebastian and took off in his own transit for Jex. Sebastian looked around his apartment and only saw memories of Celeste. He went to his computer to see if she contacted him while he was away. Nothing. Well, he said he couldn't be reached, so maybe she listened to him and didn't try. Best to send her an email now letting her know he's back.

CHAPTER 17

TO THE MEMBERS OF THE HUMAN RESISTANCE

ONE

>>> > OVER THE NEXT day, Sebastian waited for Celeste's response, but got nothing. He called her on his Titan but she didn't pick up. He went over to her apartment. He knocked on the door loudly, rang the doorbell, yelled a couple times, but she didn't answer. He cursed himself when he realized he'd left his Titan sitting on his entry table. He'd been in such a hurry to get over here. Now he couldn't call her Titan to see if he could hear any ringing inside her place.

He reached out with his mind trying to feel her nearby, but came up with nothing. While he was standing at her door, debating on whether to break it down or not, the door next to hers opened and a man came out.

"Hey, what's all the racket out here man? She's not there."

Sebastian stared at the man, "You know who lives in this apartment?"

The guy responded, "Yeah. Her name's Olivia. She's hard to miss with how pretty that Human is. Hey, you're not her boyfriend or anything are you? I was hoping she was single. I only got to talk to her a couple times, but she sure is easy on the peepers. She looks like a dead ringer for that Earth queen. I told her even, and she told me she's a second cousin over to that family. I've wanted to ask her out but I haven't seen her for awhile."

Sebastian read the stranger's mind for his intentions. He had no walls guarding his thoughts so he was a quick read. Sebastian was sure he was telling the truth. He asked, "How long since you last saw her?"

"Hmmm…Thursday I got groceries…I'd have to say it's been a day or two…maybe three at the most. Why? Is something wrong mister? And who are you to her?"

"Thanks for your help." Sebastian walked away quickly.

The man called out, "Hey she's okay right? Buddy! Hey!"

"I hope so," Sebastian muttered to himself.

Sebastian got a real bad feeling about her not being seen in a while. He stood outside her building, repeatedly trying to find her with his mind, but felt nothing. He started to think back to the last time he saw her. It was the day he went to get ammo and saw her at that restaurant. She was waiting for a man there, her date. Maybe he had something to do with her being gone. Or maybe she was having a good time with someone and didn't want to come home. Maybe he was jealous or paranoid, but his gut told him he wasn't. Something was wrong.

He went back to his apartment and saw he had a message on his Titan. He opened it up and listened while he got onto his computer screens to scan the recent days news. His expression changed from concern to anger as the message continued and then ended. He slammed his fist down on the desk and ran to his bedroom.

The message had been from D'Artagnan.

"Hey Erebos, how you doing man? It's Fallen Angel. I haven't heard from you since you messaged me saying you were off the grid for a couple weeks. I think you should be back by now. Anyway, called to say you know how we've been thinking something big is going down in the universe. I think this is the biggest clue so far.

"I have a florist delivery friend who was at Silver Thorn. He said he thought he saw Queen Dowager Hennessy there for a little bit, but then she left in a transit and the king was pissed about it. So he gets interested and asks one of the royal guards there that *he's* friends with. Turns out, the king was going to make a big announcement, but he had to cancel it at the last minute. But the really interesting bit, and this is only speculation on the RG's part, is that the BDP has something to do with all this. Maybe they kidnapped her. Didn't you used to have a big crush on her? If it really is a kidnapping for ransom, I think maybe they should've done this while King Jonathan was alive, but with that group who knows what they're up to huh? Maybe she's a bargaining chip. Let me know what you're hearing on Praxis okay? I'd like to have this vetted. I bet David's going to do a press conference soon at least to make up for the one he cancelled. Maybe we'll find out then. I'm on another job and it's a doozy. I'll tell you about it when you call me back. See ya'!"

TWO

>>> > D'ARTAGNAN CALLED RAYNES again, but this time he picked up.

"I just heard your message. Thanks for letting me know."

"Oh hey. About the queen yeah, that's crazy."

"D'Art, I haven't told you something about Celeste. She and I, we're a thing, well…we *were* a thing. You remember the night you and Bouton came over from that botched job you guys pulled? And Eric smelled perfume? That was her."

"I knew you had a woman there."

"I appreciate you didn't say anything. But I can always count on you for things like that."

"Oh geez, man if you're dating her, then I'm really sorry to give you the news that way."

"You had no idea."

"What's happening now? *Has* she been kidnapped?"

"I'm not sure yet. I'm going to look for her as soon as I figure out where to start."

D'Artagnan now felt guilty calling up his friend to ask for some help with the HR and David. He couldn't ask now. "Is there anything I can do to help?"

"I think I need to do this alone. I appreciate the offer though, really man. Thanks."

"No problem."

"When was your friend at Silver Thorn?"

"Three days ago, Earth time."

"Okay. At least it's a point in time to refer back to."

"Hey, I don't know if this will help with anything, but I've been researching the HR and David Hennessy a lot lately. David's wearing this crown; it's got a little blue circle traveling around the interior of it. I think it's a thought blocker."

Sebastian stopped, "I don't think that's real. They can't exist yet, the tech's not developed enough. It could be a fake...But Celeste saw that in person when she met with him. She described what it looked like and how it moved. I was supposed to look into it, but I haven't yet. And I won't have time now..."

"I don't think it's fake Raynes, although I'm not positive. If you have anything to do with David you better be careful."

"Duly noted. Thanks for the info. I've got to get moving Steele, I'm sure you understand."

"Of course. Watch your back."

"Yes, I will."

D'Artagnan nodded and terminated the call. His Titan went to its main menu screen.

Poor Raynes. He finally gets a girlfriend, a really rich, beautiful, young, powerful girlfriend after all these years and now she could be in mortal danger. He couldn't imagine how his friend must be feeling.

He hoped everything worked out all right and that they were safe together again soon.

He prayed for them both.

THREE

>>> > SEBASTIAN IMMEDIATELY WENT back to Celeste's apartment and used his Titan to crack the door's lock code quietly. He was disappointed the lock was easy to bypass. He wished she would've asked for help with her security - he should've been there for her to ask such things, not trekking across the universe.

There was no sign of a break-in, nothing was damaged, no sign of a struggle. He noticed her charm bracelet on the table by the front door. He knew that had been a gift from her mother and was probably her most cherished possession. She almost never went anywhere without it. If it wasn't on her wrist, it was in her purse. Strange that it was here. He was troubled to see her ribbon choker on the nightstand in her bedroom. She always wore that…until maybe she accepted that he never wanted to see her again. He supposed it wasn't right for it to bother him since he was the one who ended their time together, but it did. He studied everything slowly. He saw a faint layer of dust covering her table's surfaces so she definitely hadn't been here to clean in a while and it looked like she hadn't invested in a maid-bot.

His mind raced, running scenarios of how it had happened. He cursed himself for leaving Praxis for weeks at a time. It had been selfish. Now, instead of coming back home and seeing Celeste safe, he had to rescue her from the BDP – a group he had worked for several times. A group that loved to drug their victims. A group that was not easy to find – they took their name seriously. They were there, yet not there, like true phantoms…always eluding capture. Only being seen when they wanted.

If D'Artagnan was right, that the BDP was responsible for this (and D'Artagnan was almost always right), Sebastian would personally hunt down each one of its members and torture them until they begged for death, no matter how long it took. They had picked the wrong man to fuck with. And he would never take another contract from them as long as he lived. The Brotherhood had never had a bigger problem than Sebastian Raynes.

Whatever was ahead for Celeste and Sebastian, he had to be positive she was out of harm's way. He had never been more sure that he wanted there to be a possible future for them together.

His mind kept shuffling through all the things the BDP could be doing to her as he stood there clueless to where she was. It was unbearable. He would never allow anyone to do this to her and get away with it.

He took his mind off revenge as he realized it did nothing to help her. She needed him and he had let her down.

He took a deep breath and closed his eyes. She was probably kidnapped in a location away from her apartment, and by someone she knew to some degree. Most crimes are committed by an acquaintance of the victim. Goddess, he hated to think of Celeste as a victim now. His mind was going a million miles a second trying to figure out what to do first, who to kill. Whatever individual was responsible for this had no idea what Sebastian was capable of, but they would soon find out. His best guess was that the asshole Lanyx that she had been seeing was part of the BDP. Probably been playing her all along and she was so trusting, she would've never suspected a thing. When he got this guy in his sights, he was going to make him regret the thought of ever abducting Celeste.

FOUR

>>> > OVER THE NEXT several days, Sebastian exhausted every bit of intel, informant, friend, associate, and connection he had. He repeatedly tried to reach out to Celeste with his mind and sat quietly for a few minutes every hour on the hour trying to hear anything from her. He never heard or felt anything and that made him worry.

He poured over all his transmissions with the BDP and contracts they requested over his career. They all used code names of course, but he had found some of their real identities over the years. Unfortunately those he'd identified were all dead, but he continued to work hard to locate where she might've been taken.

FIVE

>>> > DAVID STOOD AT the podium and waited as the reporters, cameras, and camera bots settled in. Once it was quiet he started talking, "My thanks to all of you for your patience and flexibility as I had to reschedule my appearance.

"As you know, my original press conference was going to take place on Earth, but due to an emergency, it had to be rescheduled and relocated. I planned for it to be done by Queen Dowager Celeste Hennessy's side as we were going to announce happy news that we had just been married."

A loud murmur went through the crowd and David waited for it to settle down. Camera flashes went off from every direction.

"As you can see, she is not here. During our ceremony, a masked stranger came in and took her from me."

Several gasps from the reporters slipped out and a murmur worked its way through the room.

David tried to look as pitiful as possible, "I was advised to delay this press conference but I think she may be in great danger and I didn't want to wait in case someone has seen her. I can't believe she's gone. I can understand why someone would want to do this *to me*, but Celeste shouldn't be paying for my sins. We were going to be such a beautiful couple with so many plans for our future. I fear for her safety. I fear this was some terrorist group trying to get back at me, maybe even the Human Resistance. Rest assured that I'll do everything in my power to get her back safely and to whoever has her right now, *you're going to pay*. I promise you, you will regret the decision to take my Queen."

Every reporter's hand shot up into the air after David stopped speaking. They were all yelling questions, but the one David clearly heard was, "Are you concerned about your own safety on Il'laceier?" He walked off the stage without answering a single question and tried to look as heartbroken as possible.

A High Royal Bodyguard was at the king's side immediately after he was out of view and asked, "Why didn't you say anything to the kingdom sir? We could've been trying to locate her all this time."

David looked at him sternly, "You let me handle this in my own way. Her safety is out of my hands while she's gone missing and I have to wait until a ransom note or some kind of communication comes from whatever organization stole her from me."

"Yes sir."

"Now, what I do need you to do is set me up with more guards. Grab ten of the healthiest and strongest men in our kingdom to do additional body guard duty for me until this disappearance of Queen Hennessy has been resolved."

"Yes sir. Right away."

The head councilman ran up to David, "Your Excellency, with all due respect, what's the real reason you didn't wait longer? What if the queen is killed? No agency has taken responsibility for the kidnapping."

"I waited days, almost a week to make this announcement. Blood to bone, I'm sure it was the Resistance that did this. I want Earth to know their former queen has been taken by their own crazy fucks. Don't worry, I've got it all under control."

The councilman looked at David and then rubbed his palms together. David thought he would say something, but instead, the councilman turned around and walked away.

David was relieved. He finally found a way to seal the Human Resistance's doom (even with Humans!) by pinning this kidnapping on them, whether it was true or not. In all honesty, David believed the Brotherhood had probably taken her, but they hadn't sent a ransom note yet. It was only a matter of time before he found out how much they wanted.

SIX

>>> > IN STATION C9 in London, England, Detectives Barro and Spader ate dinner in Spader's cubicle.

"You *are* kidding me right?" Barro swallowed down a spoonful of butterscotch pudding.

"No, it just came across my Titan. King David held a press conference announcing it. Why do you always eat your dessert before your meal?"

"In this line of work, I never know when my time's gonna be up. I'd like to have my sweets as soon as possible in case I don't make it through dinner," he licked the spoon and threw away the pudding cup, "Our only viable lead on King Jonathan's death has been taken by force?"

Spader nodded, "Maybe it's the same person that killed Jonathan. Maybe they're not done yet."

"Maybe David had her kidnapped. We're going to have to talk to him again." Barro looked at his Titan searching for news.

Spader whistled, "He's not going to like that. He didn't like our 'visit' regarding his brother's death, and I bet he won't entertain another chat with us. He's our boss," he finished the last bit of his meatloaf, "I don't think he'll even let us in the kingdom this time."

"Then he's interfering with a criminal investigation."

Spader shook his head, "It's a waste of time, Barro. We'll have to go all the way to Il'laceier 'cause that's where he's at now."

"We've got to try all possibilities. We can pretend we're there on behalf of Celeste's safety. We can say we're trying to help him, then we slip in our questions slyly."

"We *are* there for Queen Hennessy's safety. *I'm not* pretending."

"Then we go. Tonight."

Spader scoffed, "We're gonna get our asses reamed for this. I shouldn't even go."

"Then I'll go alone. Justice never needs sleep. Justice does what's right."

"Ah shit, don't start with that. Trying to make me feel guilty and crap."

Barrro quickly shoveled spoonfuls of chicken potpie into his mouth, "I'm not. I just feel like we need to question him ASAP. This kidnapping took place days ago and he didn't contact authorities, at least none that I know of. We should go."

"Fine. I'll call my wife and tell her I'm going to be late. Again."

Barro replied with his mouth full, "Yeah, call the little woman."

SEVEN

>>> > KING DAVID SAT on his throne, "Detectives, how can I help you?"

Spader looked at Barro. Barro nodded.

"Well your Highness, we were hoping we could help you. My partner Barro and I wanted to assist in any way we could to retrieve Queen Dowager Hennessy safely. We need information from you to do that."

"Sure, of course. What do you need?"

"I was wondering first why you didn't approach authorities sooner? Time is of the essence in a case like this. The longer you wait to call the police, the colder the trail becomes."

"Excuse me detective, but I am the authority of this kingdom. I am the highest level of law enforcement our two planets have. I wasn't aware I needed your help. I have guards, and High Royal Guards that take care of my injustices for me."

Barro spoke up, "We mean no offense your Excellency. We merely meant that to assist you as best as possible, we need swift notification. We fully expected you'd have your HRG's looking for her and examining evidence."

"Understood. To be perfectly clear with you, I was afraid saying anything publicly or getting outsiders involved might put the queen into further threat of danger. My council agreed."

"Of course. Could you explain exactly what happened?"

David sighed, "Celeste and I were to be married in the chapel in Silver Thorn; strictly a private affair. Only the very closest of my inner circle and a few staff members knew of it. I gave almost everyone else the day off. In the middle of the ceremony, a masked stranger came in and started disabling my guards through physical attacks. He absconded with Celeste and I chased after him, but they quickly launched in a transit. I closed the SAP but they got through it or around it somehow. I talked to my security to see surveillance footage but there's nothing useful there."

"Could we look at it?" Barro wanted to make sure there was a video.

"Yes, but there's not much to see."

"Can you think of anyone who would want to harm yourself or Celeste? Anyone looking for revenge perhaps?" Spader thought there were millions of people who would fit these criteria.

David was silent for a moment, "There is someone. A Lanyx named Dax. Apparently he was dating the queen for a brief time before her and I were to be married. He might've been involved, but I'm sorry, I have no further information on him other than that."

"And how did you come by that information? Did Celeste tell you about this man?" Spader thought David was making this up, but he didn't really know. The king was always calm no matter how hard they pressed into him. That was very evident when they had been in his presence before questioning him about his brother's death.

"Celeste? No, she didn't tell me. Actually an HR member confessed it to me before we executed him after the bombing. He had no identification on him so I couldn't even give you his name, I'm sorry."

Barro and Spader both independently thought this sounded too convenient to be the truth.

Spader asked, "Anyone else?"

David nodded to someone at the back of the room, "No, I'm sorry gentleman, but our time is up. I have a pressing engagement I need to tend to. My guards can show you out."

"We still need the video," Barro handed David his holobusiness card, "Please send it to me at your earliest convenience. We'll get back to you if we find anything."

David took the card and shook the detective's hands, "Thank you so much for your interest in finding Queen Hennessy. I very much appreciate it."

EIGHT

>>> > DETECTIVE BARRO RECEIVED the video of Celeste's kidnapping on his Titan while Spader and himself were still in transit back to Earth.

They reviewed it six times but agreed there wasn't much useful about it. They had no facial details about the man, no pictures of the transit, and not a lot of help from the king.

"I think he's lying about this guy Dax though."

Barro nodded, "I think he's lying about everything. How are we supposed to do our jobs, if he has ultimate veto power?"

"This was your idea. I went along to make sure you didn't 'disappear' and to see if we could really get anything out of him."

Barro rubbed his face, "Okay, so...David wants to marry Celeste right? Maybe because he thinks it will calm down the resistance he's been seeing. Maybe Celeste doesn't want another marriage of convenience. Who would want to marry their dead husband's brother? That's just sick. Maybe since her husband dies, she's been living the high life, alone, then David comes along and blackmails her to marry him. Maybe he knows *she* killed his brother and that's what he had on her. So Celeste says yes to the deal, but a 'stranger' takes her away, making it look like she was kidnapped. This could all just reinforce my belief that Celeste killed Jonathan and David knows it."

"Whoa, whoa, whoa. David had much more to gain then the queen by killing Jonathan. He could've easily ordered the hit." Spader was going through their small file on King David on his Titan.

"Really? You don't think the queen wanted to escape a tyrannical, ugly, alien husband...permanently? She's young, beautiful, and Human. She was forced into marriage. She had to serve her people and be chained to the king. She didn't choose that. Both David and Celeste have motive but Celeste's story has holes. You've got to agree with me on that."

"Yes of course. There's holes. Yippie. And David having the ironclad alibi doesn't really mean shit. So what if he was seen by ten different people in a restaurant on Il'laceier at the time of the shooting? You can hire an assassin and be wherever when the deed is done. Alibi's don't mean crap when it's death by assassin."

Barro stared at his Titan, "What do you think about my theory? Where David knows that Celeste killed his brother."

"Then David could've just executed her. What would prevent him from doing that?"

"An uprising. A global Human revolt. David doesn't want that, so he can't come out and say he killed her because she killed Jon. The public would never believe that. They'd go ape-shit out there. Whether it's the God's honest truth or not."

Spader slapped his hands down on his thighs, "SO what if David hired this 'stranger' to come in and make it look like she's kidnapped, but he really just has her taken to a different part of the estate and then kills her? To the public, she'll just have disappeared. No one will ever know the difference."

Barro hesitated, "Could be either way. I don't know. You always thought David had his brother killed so he could assume power. It's possible; problem is we don't have any proof of anything. Shit maybe Celeste hired this stranger, or it was one of her friends and she's off somewhere living the high life again."

"We need to check out the queen's apartment on Praxis. That's where she moved to right? Last time we knew?"

Spader nodded, "Yeah. We can do that later though, we're almost to Earth."

"Okay. We check out her place next day we have off. See what we can see."

NINE

TITAN Corporation - Personal TITAN Device

System Status: Active -- Universal Grid: Online

Current Time/Date (Earth - Arizonaland, FUSofA): 10:02 a.m./August 18, 4015

Current Universal Positioning System Location: Arizonaland, Earth

User: Unrecorded

Communications Menu

Incoming message(s) received: 1 - Status: Unread

Message Received at 10:02 a.m.

Message Sent from: Mitch

-Human Resistance members,
It is just short of the fifty-five day mark we agreed I'd use to arrange a meeting, but recent events have forced the need for action sooner.
I was unclear before on whether we should continue in our journey for political independence and whether I was the right person to lead our group. With the recent kidnapping of our former Queen Celeste, I don't see any other path to take than to re-form under an updated name as I lead this new organization.
Kidnappings of our Human royal brothers and sisters cannot be tolerated and must be met with severe resistance.
Please join me if you are interested in pursuing freedom for Earth.
Upon hearing from each of you, I will send a secondary message containing our new meeting place as well as time and date. Questions and concerns will be addressed in great detail at our first meeting.
Thank you for your attention and I hope you'll join me.
At your service,
Mitch

-END OF MESSAGE
*This message will auto-delete in 24:00:00 hours.

TEN

>>> > WHEN CELESTE WOKE up again, she saw a paper bag and a plastic cup on the ground.

She hadn't noticed it earlier but there was a small slot down by the bottom of the door. She guessed for slipping food and water through.

She could barely move but she was thirsty. She thought as she slowly crawled towards the cup that she shouldn't be this weak. It hadn't been that long that they'd captured her, but maybe it was the drugs she suspected they were giving her.

She drank the entire glass of water quickly and then looked in the bag.

An apple and a handful of crackers. She ate both ravenously.

She sat with her legs crossed underneath her, trying to stay calm, but she had a bad headache and that music was still pouring out of the speaker. She closed her eyes and her fingers found the hem of her dress where it had begun to unravel.

The music quieted for a moment while a voice came over the speaker, "I like that view you're giving me dear. It's really making me come to full attention."

She cringed as she heard whoever it was start to laugh so she laid down on her back, pulling her dress as far down as she could manage, trying to think of something nice. Trying to think of being somewhere, anywhere else. Her mind took her back to the day she met Sebastian, and all the time they had spent together. How good he made her feel. It was enough for now to help her deal with her current situation. She wondered how long she'd been here, but she had no idea what time it was without her Titan. She wondered how long they'd keep her and if her kingdom would actually send coren in exchange for her.

She felt out as far as she could for any being's mind that was unguarded or easy to read. She had done this several times already, but nothing good ever came of it, but still, she kept trying. She felt nothing except for some random emotions and images every so often. One mind, a male, was excited to get back to his girlfriend in two days, another was pissed off that his sports team was losing yet another game. She saw some images of a dirt field, an elevator, and rope – absolutely random and useless information, all of it.

ELEVEN

>>> > CELESTE FOUND OUT the hard way that when you're in a small brightly lit room for days, alone, and constant sound pumped at you,

your mind gets a little funny. She continued to eat and drink whatever small portions they gave her, but she was now convinced the food was drugged. She seemed to always feel slightly off balance, and sleeping was almost impossible. She was exhausted most of the time, but nerves, fear, and the loud music kept her edgy enough where she could only steal sleep in small naps.

Occasionally they would weaken her with some sort of sedative first, then drag her out into the darkness and cover her head with a dark fabric bag. After they tied her to a chair, they'd take off the bag and she had a spotlight on her that made it hard to see. Unfortunately for Celeste, every time they brought her out, she knew it meant a couple of things were about to happen. They were going to beat her and she'd have to make a ransom video. They'd rough her up right before they turned on the cameras so she'd be guaranteed to bleed and look miserable. She faced a large camera and held up pictures of politicians that had been assassinated by the BDP. They gave her a new script to read with every video and she said whatever they wanted her to. Usually a request for money or a threat of what they'd do to her if they received less than what was asked for. She always wanted to fight them when she was being moved, but she was too relaxed from the drugs. As time went on, she weakened from lack of sleep, being stressed out, and eating very little. She started to lose weight and now, she could not fight back, even without being drugged.

When she was back in her cell from her most recent filming, Celeste lay on the carpet and replayed the day she met Sebastian; the day of the assassination. She thought of all the ways Sebastian made her feel better about herself, but unfortunately, it always led to the memory of them breaking up. The way he made her feel not so good about herself.

She sat up quickly realizing something with humiliating regret – her period started.

She knew with almost one hundred percent certainty her captors would think it's some kind of scheme, but she tried anyway.

"Hello out there. I'm sorry to bother you but I was wondering if you had some pads or tampons for me? I'm…It's my time of the month."

She heard nothing for a while and then from over the speaker, "What do you think this is, some kind of market? An ordering service? You've got blood all over you anyway. No one cares and there's no one here to notice that you're not all clean and pretty for your next appearance."

"But…I don't want to sit here and bleed. Really, I'm not asking for much, just a little kindness, or decency." She didn't think her captors were capable of kindness or decency, but maybe one of them was a woman.

An hour later, the door opened and a figure in black stood there. It threw a couple of rags at her and snarled, "There you go Queen Bitch." It was a male voice. He turned his head as he was closing the door but she caught his last words. He complained, "I can't believe we have to kidnap a species that bleeds like a bitch in heat. What's that animal's name that does that too?"

Then she was left alone again. She had never felt this way – less than Human. She was embarrassed and ashamed. Even when Jonathan had beat her, kicked her, and said some truly nasty things, nothing compared to being treated this way by faceless strangers.

She hadn't seen or heard Dax since the transit ride here and she wondered why he never came to talk to her. Was he embarrassed of how things had gone? Was he simply too busy? Or was it something else that kept him from facing her now? She remembered in the transit ride some person named Julian had called Dax "boss." She wondered if he was the boss of all this or if he had a superior to answer to.

TWELVE

>>> > GINGER ARRIVED AT the museum wearing a long flowing green maxi dress and black heels. She looked around, but didn't see Ulysses anywhere. She took a seat on the bench outside and took out her compact, checking her makeup again.

She felt frazzled as she hadn't been sleeping lately knowing her friend was out there suffering and held captive.

She thought she should be home in case Celeste showed up, but there wasn't much to do there but worry.

As she put her compact away, she saw someone stop in front of her. She looked up and was stunned.

Ulysses stood there like she had never seen him before. His short blonde hair was set off by a black tight-fitting polo shirt and black jeans. All she had ever seen him wear was his guard uniform or royal guard armor. This was a nice surprise to see him dressed like a civilian and he looked good.

He held out a bouquet of pink roses and white carnations to her.

She smiled at him and he smiled back. "Thank you Ulysses. This was very sweet."

"You're welcome."

She looked over his face and saw the bruise on his cheek, "How are you feeling?"

"Nervous...Oh, you mean, from the punch?"

She nodded.

"That's...no big deal. The kingdom doctor looked me over yesterday. I'm good. Should be just a memory in a couple days."

"You sure? I mean we don't have to do this tonight."

A faint light twinkled in the depths of his hazel eyes, "I've waited too long for this already. I don't want to put it off another minute," he paused, "How are you feeling, with the news of Celeste, I mean?"

Ginger's green eyes darkened, "I'm worried, scared, and sad. I don't know what to do with myself. I actually tried calling her a few times, but it goes straight to her voicemail. It was stupid of me, but I keep hoping she'll be freed and can let me know she's alright."

"Hold onto hope. She's a determined and smart woman. She won't do anything stupid."

"Do you know anything I don't about her going missing? And what about the wedding?"

Ulysses paused, "I know David doesn't want Celeste dead that's for sure. I didn't know anything about the wedding either. I think the whole universe was shocked."

"Well Celeste's in love with someone else. Something's totally wrong here. She wouldn't tell me what was going on the day of the kidnapping. But it looked like she wanted to...This is crazy. I need to know she's safe. Please let me know the second you hear anything."

"Of course, Ginger."

"Thanks."

He put his arm out to her. She took it and they walked into the museum.

Her favorite moment of the evening had nothing to do with the art, or even conversation – it was when she walked out of the ladies room at the end of their time in the museum. She turned the corner and in an all-white room with small paintings on the wall, Ulysses stood with his hands in his pockets looking down at the ground. He was lost in thought with a pensive stare on his face. She found herself studying his profile as she walked up to him, almost not wanting to break his concentration as he looked like he might be on the verge of a brilliant idea.

He said to her without looking up, "You have very sexy shoes."

She looked down, "I do?"

"Yes," his gaze started inching up her body, "they make your already amazing legs even more irresistible to my eyes. I've been trying to study the artwork, but all I want to stare at is you."

She blushed as his eyes met hers. Her memory flashed to how his hand felt on her lower back in front of the fireplace and her blush deepened.

He moved closer to her and put a hand gently to her cheek, "I should've asked you out the day I met you."

Her heart fluttered in return but she found she couldn't say anything.

"To dinner then?"

She nodded.

At dinner, Ulysses asked Ginger how she came to be a hair stylist.

"It wasn't exactly by choice. I really wanted to be a candy maker, like a chocolatier but it was just my mom and me and she couldn't afford to send me to school. She was a beautician and she taught me everything she knew, so here I am. I can do hair and makeup like nobody's business, but it's not my passion."

"What happened to your dad, if you don't mind me asking?" He traced his finger along the pattern on the tablecloth.

"Pops died when I was young. I only remember a little about him – his scratchy mustache on my cheek when he kissed me goodnight, his love of fishing, and his stubbornness. There was a day during the War of

Black Rock where twenty thousand soldiers died and my pops was one of them."

"I'm sorry for your loss. That must've been really tough on the both of you. Don't the families of military members get some sort of money when they lose a loved one?"

"Yeah, but coren doesn't last that long when you have to pay off a lot of debt like my folks had. My mom was good with money and all, and she did make it stretch as long as she could, but eventually we were back to scraping by. He died when I was eleven. My pops was a good man and my mom never dated again. I don't see her often enough. What about you? You see your folks a lot?"

Ulysses winced, "It's complicated. I'd rather not talk about it now if it's okay with you. Maybe later."

She nodded and felt uncomfortable as she realized how touchy he seemed to be about his parents.

He paid the check and followed her out onto the street.

Ulysses called a transit bot-taxi for her. They stood outside the restaurant with the door to the transit open.

Ulysses put his arms around her waist and pulled her close. She put her hands up to his shoulders and looked into his eyes.

"Is this okay?" he asked.

"Yes."

"Listen, I know I'm supposed to go slow with you to adhere to the normal dating routine. Fools rush in and all that...but I think that's impossible."

"Oh yeah? How come?"

He moved in closer for a kiss and stopped, "I've wanted to be this close to you for a long time. Since I first saw you. Slow is impossible for me. Will you go out with me again?"

She smiled, "Yes."

He kissed her as soft as an autumn breeze and pulled back to look her in the eyes.

There was something about him, she couldn't put her finger on it, but he was pulling her in like a magnet.

"Just tell me if I'm going too fast. I might not be able to slow down for anything else, but if you're uncomfortable…I don't want that. Okay?"

"Yes." She looked at the transit, then back to Ulysses, "This one you called just for me huh?"

"Yes. I'd love to ride back with you, but you know what that'll look like at Silver Thorn. I don't want either one of us to get in trouble." He kissed her again and helped her into the transit. "Safe travels. I'll see you around?"

"Yes, for sure," she smiled.

He closed the transit door over her and watched it launch. He called another one for himself and flew to the castle alone but smiling.

THIRTEEN

››› › WITH SEBASTIAN'S MISSION of finding Celeste, D'Artagnan could not ask for his help. Which meant D'Artagnan was going undercover. If she were alive, Linda wouldn't believe that D'Artagnan was going to try and be a member of the Human Resistance.

At the time of Linda's death, D'Artagnan had been pushed back and kept away from the area where her body was for half an hour. He had swooped in and carried her out when all the police and guards were busy with a streaker running through the crowd. He took her home, then carefully washed and prepared her body to be burned on a pyre he had lovingly built himself. But before he burned her, he had taken off her Titan and put it in a box far away in the back of his closet and when he moved, he brought that box with him. He hadn't been able to bring himself to power it up and look at her Titan since.

Today, he had to do what couldn't be done before. He thought he was ready. He went to his closet and found the box.

He sat at his dining room table for five minutes before he could do anything with it.

He powered up Linda's Titan and saw the main menu. Her Titan had a password and username he needed to enter.

One of D'Artagnan's special skills was cracking codes, bypassing encryption, and hacking into anything. It took him six minutes and fifty-four seconds to bypass her security. He timed himself out of habit. He would've got through it sooner had he not taught her everything he knew about creating a very tight security system on Titans.

He saw a Titan folder with his name on it and opened it. It hurt to see the old pictures of them together, but it also brought some healing he didn't anticipate. He knew she wouldn't want him to be grieving too long after she passed. She would want him to move forward, find love again, and try to enjoy life.

He opened up her messages and saw several addressed to a name he didn't recognize. It looked like a lot of them were close to the time of her death. She had sent a lot of replies to this person. The name was Matthrew Nessium. Could have been someone in the Resistance.

Then he saw something waiting in her drafts folder that had never been sent. It was a message addressed to him. His heart started thumping in his chest. A message from Linda. He had a weird sense of dread mixed with excitement at seeing it.

He opened it up.

TITAN Corporation - Personal TITAN Device

System Status: Inactive -- Universal Grid: Offline

Current Time/Date (N/A): -:-- /N/A

Secondary Time/Date (N/A): -:-- /N/A

Current Universal Positioning System Location: N/A

User: Linda Malova

Communications Menu

Outgoing message(s) pending: 1 - Status: Unsent Draft

Message saved at 2:42 a.m. February 24, 4015

Message Recipient: D'Artagnan Steele

-Dear D'Art,

I want to say how much I've enjoyed our time together. The things that you've done for me, I can never repay. You have always been kind and open with me. It makes it that much harder for me to say what I'm about to say, but it's time I did this.

It's not going to be easy for you to understand and I'm sorry that I'm telling you this way. I should've said it in person, but I'm not as brave as you.

I know you tried to give me a lot, but I ended up needing more. I've found a wonderful man, and I want to make sure you know I wasn't out there looking for someone else. He just found me and it clicked and things worked in a way with him that I never felt with us.

I've been trying to find a way to tell you this, but it never seemed like the right time.

I've been holding onto this message for a while and every so often I'll go in and revise it, trying to make it perfect. Trying to make it sound nicer or easier for you to accept, or maybe I'm just trying to be okay with leaving you. I'm not cheating on you, I'm just...I don't know. It's hard to explain.

I know I need to tell you, and I will soon.

-END OF MESSAGE

Please determine countdown for deletion after recipient reads:

*This message will auto-delete in 00:00:00 seconds-years.

Linda was going to leave me?

D'Artagnan sat for ten minutes trying to get his head around this new information. He reread the message several times over thinking it would change somehow or that he had misunderstood it.

D'Artagnan couldn't believe it.

He went back to all those messages he had seen addressed to this man. That was probably who she was dating.

He read them and saw all the proof he needed that she was in love with this other guy.

This other relationship had been going on for two and a half months. D'Artagnan felt his stomach turn and he ran to the bathroom in time to throw up into the toilet.

He washed his mouth out afterwards and splashed cold water on his face.

He had killed a guard, two guards on her behalf!

All the things he did to honor her, were now a waste of time. A waste of his life and energy. Fuck the Human Resistance! Fuck Linda!

He went into his bedroom, grabbed the book on grieving and her framed picture out of the drawer in his nightstand and threw them into the box of her things on the table.

He grabbed her Titan and looked up the number for this Matthrew guy. He tried calling it, but it had been disconnected with no forwarding number. He tried sending a Titan message, but it bounced back immediately as invalid. He tried an email with the same results.

D'Artagnan forwarded all of Matthrew's information to his personal Titan. Then he put Linda's Titan in the box and went out front to his walkway with the box and a matchbook. He was going to light everything on fire. Burn everything out of existence. Then he thought again. Maybe this Matthrew guy was in the Resistance. Maybe he died in the bombing, but he wouldn't be able to find that out for sure in the news. Not if his remains had never been found or identified.

He grabbed the Titan out of the box and did a quick search of death records. This guy's name didn't show up. Didn't mean he wasn't dead. Maybe D'Artagnan could meet him if the HR had a meeting. Talk to him. Or just strangle him on sight.

D'Artagnan went through the rest of Linda's messages.

He saw she had been on the Human Resistance message list. He wondered if that meant she had been a part of the group after all and lied to him about that too.

He read through old messages and found a contact number for Mitch. Several other conversations had happened with HR members that she had been copied on...one of them was recent. Very recent. There was going to be a meeting soon, tomorrow in fact, on Earth. If he attended that, he could try to find this Matthrew guy there. He could ask Mitch about him, certainly he would know all the member's names. Mitch would know if Matthrew was dead or not.

D'Artagnan forwarded the meeting message to himself and threw Linda's Titan in the box. He lit a match and ignited her belongings. The sound of the fire would eventually get the attention of the Ahmalats and they would take care of the mess for him.

He wanted no trace of Linda left behind.

The next morning, D'Artagnan opened his front door and looked for the box, but it was gone and he was glad. Now, he had business with the Human Resistance on Earth and he had to be there on time.

FOURTEEN

>>> > HOURS LATER, D'ARTAGNAN sat down for the HR's meeting.

D'Artagnan was wearing casual clothes. He tried not to stick out, but he *was* the only Il'lacean there. He hoped that wouldn't be the case, but there was no way to know for sure until he showed up.

D'Artagnan had seen Mitch up at the front of the room. He recognized him from an Earth issued government ID picture D'Artagnan had seen.

Mitch was studying D'Artagnan hard. D'Artagnan could smell suspicion and distrust on Mitch. D'Artagnan understood. But it looked like Mitch was already coming his way. D'Artagnan was calm and on his best behavior.

When Mitch asked for D'Artagnan's name, he gave him Gaviss. Mitch mentioned not to use real names in their organization and D'Artagnan said he understood.

Although, in truth, D'Artagnan had just given Mitch his true Il'lacean name he was born with. Il'laceans only had one true name, no last name, just a battle-born, blood to bone, Il'lacean name. D'Artagnan hadn't used it in years and as far as the universe knew, Gaviss the Il'lacean had died in a POW camp a very long time ago.

FIFTEEN

>>> > MITCH FELT A little strange looking over a small sea of faces again, all looking at him, but this time, they were really looking at him as a leader. He still didn't know if this was the right decision for him, but someone needed to do something.

Thirty-one members of the Human Resistance had shown up today, and one face Mitch had never seen before, an Il'lacean.

Mitch looked at him – he made Mitch extremely nervous, but the group was open to all species. Mitch couldn't turn him away, but he could ask him questions. He didn't even want to start the meeting until he talked to this guy first.

Mitch put out his hand for the Il'lacean to shake, "Hello. I don't think I've seen you before in our group. My name is Mitch. What's yours?"

D'Artagnan put out his hand, "Gaviss. Nice to meet you."

Mitch asked, "I'm assuming you know to use a false name with us, correct?"

"Yes."

"Gaviss. Awesome. What brings you to our little meeting today? I ask because this specific meeting has been kept secret, and only former members were invited. I've never seen your face before."

"I'm sure it seems strange to have an Il'lacean sitting here, but I genuinely am ashamed of my species lately. I hold myself to a high standard. I treat others the way that I would like to be treated. I believe everyone has the right to live freely or fight for independence no matter who their oppressor might be. I'd like to make a difference for Humans and Earth. I'd like to aid in whatever way I can. I realize you might have your doubts about me, considering my species, but I understand that suspicion and you have every right to feel that way."

"How did you find out about this meeting?"

D'Artagnan half smiled, "You are a smart one. I like that in a leader."

"Thanks. How did you find out about our meeting?"

"To be completely honest, one of my friends was looking into this group, excuse me, the former group of the HR. She talked about it often. I have a bit of an observer's knowledge about it and what I've heard in the news. Unfortunately, my friend never made it into the group but her name was still on the list of HR message recipients. I hope you don't mind, but I took it upon myself to show up after I saw the last message come across my Titan. She forwarded it to me since she knew I was looking for a better way to apply my free time than hanging around my house."

Mitch gave him a hard stare, "We don't have many Il'lacean members, in fact, you're the first one I've ever seen try to help us. And I also know that Edison spoke of someone who once helped us by selling passwords for that bombing I didn't approve of. I think you're Linda's boyfriend and you've come to help us. Am I correct?"

Mitch looked at D'Artagnan trying to see if his face gave anything away, but the man was stoic.

"I'm not sure what you're talking about."

Mitch got a bad feeling, "I don't think you should be here. Probably best that you leave. I'll call a few of my friends to escort you out."

"Wait."

Mitch looked at him blankly, "What?"

"Have you noticed the crown King David wears? It has a thought blocker in it. I've done my research. I can help you. I'm not a threat to this group."

"Thought blockers are a myth. They don't exist except in rumors."

The Il'lacean replied, "That's what I thought. If you've never had an Il'lacean member, it might be time you try accepting help from one."

Mitch thought for a moment, "Say I give you a chance. You can sit in on today's conversation, but this isn't our permanent meeting spot. And I'm not saying you can join."

"Understood sir."

"I hope to talk to you more in the future. I think there's a certain spot you could fill in our organization regarding Il'lacean policies and their thinking…if I let you stay that is. Maybe you can see me after the meeting?"

"Certainly, sir."

Mitch nodded and went towards the front of the room.

"Hey! Hello everyone!" He let them all settle down into their chairs and stop talking. One of the members was a janitor to a small church and while Mitch didn't like the idea of meeting in a public place, he had few options. The janitor promised privacy, so he agreed to hold the meeting here at The Church of The Chosen Ones.

"Okay, this is going to be a quick one. That mostly depends on what kinds of questions you all have though. I want to say thanks for coming out. I know it's been a while since we've all been together and last time we saw each other, it was…difficult.

"The bombing on Rem Mot Om was a terrible thing. Most of you know I didn't like that idea and was trying to talk you out of it up until the last second. I realize a lot of you wanted progress and Edison offered that to you. Now that he's gone and we've all had time to think and reflect, I want to offer something new.

"The group that I'm going to lead is not the Human Resistance. That group is dead as far as I'm concerned. Il'laceier isn't going to give up the search though, not for you, and not for me. They're still trying to locate all of us. I know seven of our members have disappeared. I've tried to locate them, but it's been in vain. I'm pretty sure their disappearance hasn't been accidental or a choice those members made, I think King David took them, interrogated them, and disposed of them quietly.

"SO, no more Resistance. From now on, this group is called FAIR, that stands for Fighting Against Il'laceier Rule. I want all species to feel welcome to join our group. Anyone who believes Earth should be independent to rule ourselves as we see fit, is a friend of mine."

A woman in the back of the church stood up and Mitch called on her, "Sarah? Would you like to say something?"

She cleared her throat, "I know we spoke earlier about how you were unsure with leading us. I thought you felt pretty strongly about not being in command. I wanted to know what changed your mind. I read your Titan message, but I was hoping you could expand on that."

Mitch looked down at his hands and thought for a moment, "That's a good question. A fair one." He smiled. "Some of you might already know that I was happy to be second-in-command during the HR's time. I considered all my options while we've been away from each other and I was siding with leaving the group. Then, when I found out that Celeste Hennessy had been captured, I got angry. David Hennessy allowed that to happen and he's done nothing to help her get back to Earth. He doesn't care about Humans. He never has, he never will. But I do. I care about all of us and I think if Earth had been politically independent, then her security guards and royal guards would have been there to prevent anything like that from happening."

Mitch stood facing the crowd with his hands clasped together, hanging down in front of him, "Celeste has been a beacon of light for Earth. She's been someone who was always philanthropic with her time and money, donating to several charities the entire time she was in Silver Thorn. We, as a planet, need her. We need her out of harm's way and it seems that our own kingdom doesn't care what happens to her. They're taking this matter way too nonchalantly. When she was kidnapped, I felt the scales go out of balance for Humans on Earth. Something needs to be done. So if we're the ones who end up rescuing her, or if we choose to do something else to help Earth, we need to do it now, and I would prefer to do it non-violently."

Sarah was still standing and asked another question, "What do you think we should do?"

Mitch crossed his arms over his chest, "I will lead this group, but I don't want to dictate it. I want it to be a group effort from brainstorming to execution of plans. I want us to work together. I might have suggestions on what I think is best and if we don't all agree, then we'll have to agree to something else."

"What do *you* think we should do now?" Sarah asked.

Mitch looked around the room then sighed, "First off, does everyone agree that what I said is doable? Do we all agree that our group is going to make decisions together? If you agree, raise your hand, and say aye."

All members agreed including Gaviss.

He smiled, "Okay. Well, I think in between meetings, we should spend some time brainstorming about what you'd like to see happen in this group. Take your time, think about it, then we can come back together and decide what's best for all of us. What do you want to change? What do you hope to accomplish being a member? Oh, that reminds me, does anyone have a private place we can meet on a regular basis? While I very much appreciate Tad for offering the church up for this meeting, it's without their consent and I'd like to avoid doing this in the future."

Steve raised his hand, "I have a large backyard at the house. I think all of us could fit...but I've also been building an underground bunker for a while, I just didn't tell anyone. If you guys don't mind the unfinished-ness of it, then we could use that."

Mitch looked at Gaviss momentarily, "I'll consider it as a temporary solution since I should be looking for a safe place for us as well. Thank you Steve. In three days, we can meet at Steve's place and we'll go over what you want to accomplish and start making plans based on that. Meeting adjourned."

Everyone started to get up and then a Lanyx dark haired woman in the middle of the room spoke up, "Wait. What about recruiting new members? We don't have enough right now. We lost most of our force to the BDP."

Mitch glared at her, "I have to say something about that. Hold on everyone, if you could please sit down for a little longer."

They all sat again and quieted down.

Mitch took a deep breath, "First off..." He looked at the woman, but couldn't remember her name. He pointed at her.

"Alanna," she replied.

"Thank you. Sorry. First off, we can't talk about how we lost our old members. We can't mention the man who came and told us he was here to help and all that happened after. Erase it from your memory. The Brotherhood of Desert Phantoms is a very dangerous group. If I could've stopped our old members from going off with them, I would have, but I didn't know what was happening and I wasn't there. Now those members might have something to do with Celeste Hennessy's kidnapping. I want you guys to think about that for a minute," he paused, "They might be accomplices to kidnapping, torture, rape, and God knows what else. If they are caught, they will be punished, possibly killed. I don't want our group to be anything like the BDP and quite frankly, I'm not sure whether to feel sorry for our former members or be angry with them."

Mitch was silent as he looked over the faces. He could tell most of them hadn't thought of their former friends being part of the group that might've taken Celeste Hennessy. They didn't want to think about that possibility.

"As far as new recruits, that's for later. We need to find out what we're willing to do and what we *won't* do first. We need to make goals, plans, and find out who we are as FAIR. Does that make sense to everyone?"

They all nodded or said yes.

"Okay, meeting adjourned for real this time."

Mitch collected his things and noticed the dark haired woman had approached him. "Yes Alanna? You need something?"

"I'm sorry if I made you mad. I thought gaining members would help us be stronger."

He looked her over, "How long were you with the Resistance?"

She flushed red, "I came in at the end. Probably less than four months. Something like that. A recruiter on Praxis introduced me to the HR."

"Do you live here on Earth?"

She shook her head, "No, I'm located on Praxis, but I'm thinking about moving somewhere further out. Some other planet that's new to me. I don't like staying in one place too long."

"A vagabond huh? That's unusual for a woman. Usually you guys want to settle down after finding Mr. Right and nest."

She smiled, "There's no Mr. Right for me. I've given up on that game. I'm going to focus on my career – criminal psychology, and try to understand why people do what they do. See if I can help any of them."

Mitch smiled, "That sounds interesting, albeit a little dangerous."

"What? More dangerous than joining some rogue organization?"

"True. Why *did* you join?"

Alanna smiled, "Well, I thought it'd be interesting to see what they could do for Humankind and for Earth."

"So this is just research for you then?"

"Oh initially yes, but then I saw other things I liked about this group, so I decided to stay. I wasn't there for most of the meetings though. I usually called in, but I also wasn't a part of the bombing either. Glad about that."

Mitch smiled at her, "Me too."

There was a circle of people arranging themselves around Mitch now. He looked at them, saw Gaviss, and looked back at her, "I should probably talk to the others if they have questions. It was nice talking to you."

Alanna smiled, "Yes. Nice talking to you too. I'm sure you'll do great as the new leader." She turned around and walked away. Mitch watched her go before he turned and said something to the members waiting.

"Hey, I have a big favor to ask of you guys. Could you give me a message via Titan if you have a question or comment, if you wouldn't mind? I need to have a discussion with our Il'lacean recruit here and it might be lengthy. I'd hate to keep you guys waiting too long."

The rest of the members waved and said their goodbyes.

Mitch and Gaviss watched the church clear out before they started talking.

Mitch turned to Gaviss and looked up, "Are you sure you're not Linda's boyfriend?"

"I am not...anymore." Gaviss sighed, "The truth of it is, she was cheating on me. I just found out...yesterday. I looked through her things after they sat for a long time, discovered messages that were never sent to me and so yes, I spoke with Edison before he died, but I didn't sell the passwords to him. I gave them to him free and clear. I was only interested in helping the Resistance, but I never knew they were going to bomb the castle. Had I known that, I wouldn't have shared my information with him."

"Why did you lie to me?"

"I said I liked my leaders smart, but not so smart as you appear to be. It threw me off guard for a minute. My first instinct is to protect my privacy, but I thought if I expect you to trust me, I might have to trust you a bit."

Mitch nodded, "Okay. Fair enough."

"Edison told you I *sold* the passwords to him?"

"Yes. He made us raise a whole bunch of coren to 'afford' it and the bomb, but I found out later Edison wasn't the man I thought he was. Doesn't surprise me he lied about that. He's lied about other things in the past and that's when I started to get suspicious."

Gaviss nodded, "You do sound smart. You should make a very good leader."

"Thanks. I want to know why you helped Edison with the passwords. He said he approached you, is that true?"

Gaviss shook his head, "I found him. Because Linda had died and she said she wanted to be a member of this group, I thought to honor her it would be nice to help the HR. I found Edison, I gave him the passwords, and I didn't charge him for it. I didn't know he was going to bomb a whole bunch of innocent people."

Mitch rubbed his forehead, "Okay, I think you're telling the truth now. I should let you into this organization just for what you've done to help us in the past unsolicited. But in the future, I say honesty is the best policy here."

"Understood sir."

"What's your background? Where'd you come from?"

"Those are lengthy answers, both of them. Short version is I was in the military, got a lot of my training there. Now I'm just trying to find where I fit in. Immediately, I'm trying to figure out how to handle Linda lying to me."

"Yeah, that's a tough one. I'm sorry she did that to you."

"That makes two of us. I have a question for you."

"Okay."

"Have you ever had a member that went by the name of Matthrew Nessium?"

Mitch thought for a moment. "I can't recall that name, but we don't use our real names here. Do you have a picture of him?"

"I don't. I'll try to get one and show you in the future."

"Okay. So will you come to the next meeting then?"

"Absolutely sir. Oh and one more thing…you mentioned the Brotherhood. How do they fit into all of this?"

Mitch considered deflecting or lying about the answer, "Edison stole the bomb from the Brotherhood, I think. Then we all paid for it. The BDP sent in a man undercover acting like a new recruit to take over the bombing mission and they pushed me out of the way momentarily. The BDP wanted to make Edison pay for what he had stolen from them. After the bombing, they took at least eighty percent of our members and offered everyone a chance to move to their group. I turned them down, so did several others. I know what that group can do and I don't want to be anything like that."

"That's a wise decision. The BDP is very bad news."

"Agreed."

CHAPTER 18

THE SEARCH

ONE

>>> > ULYSSES THOUGHT THIS was getting a bit ridiculous now, "You want *more* guards?"

David stopped and looked at him, "*Yes.* You know the royal life is a dangerous one and we have guards to spare...don't we?"

Ulysses thought, "Yes, we have quite a few that can still take on security duty for you...but don't you think..."

"What?"

Ulysses shook his head, "How many do you need?"

David replied, "At least five more. That'll bring up my count to twenty-five around me at all times. That will be good."

Ulysses nodded, but thought David was crazy. "Okay. I'll ask five more men today and get them detailed to you by the end of this afternoon."

David smiled, "Thanks."

Ulysses cleared a path for David to walk to his podium for his next press conference.

The room was buzzing until David cleared his throat for silence.

"It is with a heavy heart that I must announce the Brotherhood of Desert Phantoms is holding Queen Dowager Hennessy hostage and has asked for one million coren as ransom. I received this message several hours ago but was advised by police and kingdom officials not to make it public until now. We have a meeting time and place set up for trade and I pray that her return will be safe and quick. As of ten o'clock this morning, Earth time, the BDP has promised me she is safe. I can't give you any other details and will answer no questions today. Thank you."

David wished he could've kept his original plan of pinning the kidnapping on the HR but several councilmembers had been in the room when the kingdom received the ransom note. There was no hiding it from them, and so he had to be honest.

TWO

>>> > IMMEDIATELY AFTER THE kingdom press conference, David had scheduled an IMC meeting and the members were incensed.

David spoke over all of them, "LISTEN TO ME!"

The room quieted.

David adjusted his coat, "We're going to have to fight the BDP because they have something of value to the entire universe and for their heartless attack on our king's happiness," David checked his emotion, "I'm sorry. Some of you aren't Il'laceans, but most of our group is. I believe all of us here can think of someone close to us – a friend, a family member, someone we trust. What the BDP has done is like ripping that one person who is more dear to you than anyone else and holding them for ransom. Imagine what that would feel like."

David held a deep breath and let it out slowly. He almost wished he could unmask himself in front of all his IMC members so they could know who their leader really was. "I think if we could rescue the queen, our organization might get some good publicity for once, and it will work two-fold making the BDP look like the real bad guys. We can be recognized as heroes across the universe. And perhaps King David would show his gratitude by offering some sort of pardon to our criminal histories or reward us somehow."

David looked at Ulysses, "Ulysses has promised to do all he can to find Celeste. He'll have much research to do to try and find out where they're holding her. He will need many men to offer skills like information retrieval and then, he will need only the bravest of our members to accompany him on a very dangerous mission of extracting Celeste from her captors. When the time is right, I hope I can rely on my IMC brothers to answer my call for help."

The men in the crowd answered with nods of their heads.

"Ulysses would you like to say anything?"

Ulysses addressed the crowd, "Celeste is beloved and respected throughout the universe for her charity work and her big heart. She doesn't deserve to be in this position and I've promised my leader that I will retrieve her for the universe and because he has asked it of me. I will need as many men as possible when the time for action comes, but for now, any of you who are good at hacking computers, surveillance, getting information, and the like need to talk with me after the meeting. Thank you."

The king nodded, "Ulysses is a very good man and an excellent right hand man. Whoever helps him with this mission will be greatly favored by me in many ways. Do what you can to help me and Ulysses retrieve Celeste. Thank you. Meeting adjourned."

THREE

>>> > "DAVID NEVER TALKED to any police about this ransom notification. I asked the Chief already." Spader poked through Celeste's closet with a gloved hand.

"Listen Spades, when you're the king, you can do whatever you want. David's lying, you know it, I know it. Something's not adding up, but we need to prove it. We need to find something here."

Spader looked around annoyed that his partner refused to stop calling him stupid variations of his name, "There's no sign of forced entry. Nothing's missing. If she planned to be gone for any length of time, she should've taken things with her. She should've put this place up for sale and emptied it out if for no other reason than she was getting married and moving back into the castle."

"But everything's here. That would help prove my theory that she was in on her kidnapping, but then she should also be here hiding out or packing to leave for somewhere else maybe."

"We're still here illegally. We have no warrant and the sergeant doesn't even want us working this mystery. We're back at zero."

"I looked for Lanyx criminal records on anyone named Dax. There's nothing. Guy doesn't exist as far as our records go, and there's nothing on Il'laceier or Praxis on a Dax either."

"There's really nothing left for us to do," Spader took off his gloves.

Barro headed for the front door, "I don't want to give up, but I don't know where else we can go to do any digging. We might have to wait until Celeste shows up and then question her."

Spader nodded, "We're not giving up. Just postponing our investigation."

FOUR

>>> > HACE HAD A conference call with everyone in the BDP calling in from all over the universe. He stood in front of his wall of screens in his command post on The Architect Phantom and whistled to get everyone's attention.

"Alright, I'm glad you could all call in. I've got a huge announcement. You all know how we've been capturing world leaders and ransoming them…with the exception of a few executions when no one would pay. Well, we've got the biggest most beloved royal, or former royal, I guess now, in our possession as we speak!" He paused looking around at all the expectant faces. They all looked excited.

"Celeste Hennessy!"

A lot of the members broke out into smiles or started clapping.

Hace let that die down before speaking again, "It was in large part to a couple men on our team. Duke was observing her for a while after Dax spotted her on Praxis. Dax wooed her with his charms and earned her trust then he picked his moment to bring her in. Both men did a fantastic job and I couldn't be more proud of what we've all accomplished as an organization today." He paused to take a deep breath, "Celeste's ransom is going to be close to the highest payday we've had to date so it's an exhilarating time for the BDP. Stay tuned and we'll see how King David handles it. I'll be updating you regularly through messages, but good job everyone!" Hace smiled and the members cheered and applauded again.

It was a good time to be part of the Brotherhood.

FIVE

››› › THE NEWS AIRED the first ransom video. Sebastian could only stand motionless, staring at the screen. He could tell Celeste was in a lot of pain and that she had been drugged. She was black and blue all over and her voice was unsteady. After the video cut away, Sebastian let out a yell of frustration and threw his Titan across the room.

He watched the news almost non-stop even though it upset him every time they showed her. He couldn't keep himself from checking for updated reports, or if he could learn anything useful from the sounds and images the BDP videos contained. It was agonizing for him to watch Celeste suffering, but he knew her survival depended on him. Her former kingdom couldn't be trusted to rescue her, no matter what King Hennessy said.

Sebastian pondered how things had gone so wrong in the short two weeks' time he was on vacation. And he wanted to know how Celeste had agreed to marry David. It couldn't be true. David simply must have been lying about that in the press conference, another way David was manipulating Humans.

Sebastian always knew Celeste was well loved on Earth by Humans, but the coverage of her kidnapping was remarkable. He couldn't turn around without seeing the story somewhere. It was on his Titan, his screens, the digital billboards around the city, and the personalized kiosks of the streets.

The last report showed King David stating that the BDP wanted a million coren, but once the kingdom agreed, the dollar amount had doubled. David expressed his concerns over Celeste's wellbeing, but was also afraid the ransom would only be increased every time he agreed to their demands. He assured the public that everything would be done as quickly as possible to save their beloved former queen.

What a fucking terrible liar you are, you worthless prick, Sebastian thought to himself.

Sebastian located the only three possibilities where the Brotherhood could be holding her. Even though they had facilities all over the universe, three worlds kept showing up in his informant's records for BDP captives – Cepheus, Lassandra, and Tiletan.

All three were spread out far from his planet and would take a few days to check each one. With time working against him, he grabbed his go bag, then went into his secret room behind his closet.

An hour later in his transit, Sebastian tried anything he could to calm down. Reading a book lasted the longest at half an hour, after attempts to finish a crossword puzzle, sleep, and listening to music all failed.

He didn't want to endanger anyone else with this trip but Eric couldn't have come anyway, he had owed a very irrational Aleshlo a favor and you couldn't turn down one of those, not if you valued your intestines on the inside of your body anyway.

Sebastian had questioned Eric if he had seen this happening through his precognition. Eric, of course, had not. He reminded him that he'd never met or touched Celeste and that she had no direct link to himself, so he couldn't have seen her future.

The following eight and a half hours went excruciatingly slow. He watched the news on his Titan silently as the latest video of Celeste aired. He choked up when he saw her. She looked pale, and weak. Her hair was a mess and her right eye was black and blue and swollen shut. She held up a picture of a dead My'takian Emperor that was assassinated a week ago – the BDP took credit. She said they were getting impatient as their monetary requirements went unmet. They threatened the next step was to cut off one of her fingers.

She looked panicked to Sebastian, but he could tell she was trying to get herself under control. The video ended with a black bag thrown over her head and Sebastian almost crushed his Titan in his hand.

The reporter pointed out that while the Brotherhood say their demands haven't been answered, King Hennessy II denies any reports that the kingdom hasn't yet agreed to pay the ransom. David was quoted as saying, "The BDP are greedy, compulsory liars that want the kingdom to fall by any means possible," and that he's offered to pay the ransom, but the amount continues to increase once one has been agreed upon. The reporter continued that King Hennessy II has stated publicly, that he believes the BDP wants to bankrupt the Il'lacean and Earth Kingdom, and then the Brotherhood will declare war, so he's justified in taking calculated steps during Celeste's ransom negotiations.

These last video images of Celeste deteriorating were unbearable for Sebastian. He promised to protect her and he had failed miserably. He should've seen this coming. He should've insisted she check in with him on a regular basis, regardless of their recent disagreements. He shouldn't have left on vacation.

Celeste was getting terrorized and tortured by the bastards he had worked with for a decade. Sebastian felt like a fool.

She hasn't done anything to deserve this, he thought. *She's as innocent as any regular citizen.* He always thought this was the kind of event that would happen, *if* they were dating, but it happened anyway. He put his hand up to his head thinking she would've been safer had they been dating after all. They would've been together so often the BDP wouldn't have been able to get close enough to kidnap her.

He checked his map as he neared the first planet on his search – Cepheus. Only a few minutes until he entered their atmosphere.

"Ophelia?"

"Ye-ye-ye-yes?"

Sebastian made a face as he tapped a finger on his transit's speaker. Ophelia never glitched.

"I need the current temperature of the Kellsolo Zone on Cepheus."

She paused a moment, "Recorded two sec-seconds ago. The sur-surface temperature is 121 degrees below zero. Wind chill of 133 degrees below zero."

He cleared the Cepheus SAP and descended rapidly. The planet was virginal white with pools of blue where their oceans weren't frozen over.

He asked, "Expected temperatures over the next few days?"

Ophelia paused, "Gathering data. Gathering data. Gathering data."

Sebastian expected the cold temperatures to affect some things on his transit, but not his signal or Ophelia. He called out, "Abandon request."

He searched on his Titan quickly. The average temperature for this time of year in this zone was 105 below zero.

Sebastian prepared to dock and wondered how long it would take to find Celeste. The trip alone from Praxis to Cepheus spanned nine hours taking all seven Jumps available.

SIX

>>> > SEBASTIAN SPENT THREE Praxian days on the icy planet. All of his equipment, all of his skill for finding missing people, and all of his mental abilities told him she wasn't here.

As another big blizzard loomed, he entered his transit, mapped the pathway to the next planet, and hoped it was the right one.

Lassandra popped up as his next destination and he tried to stay calm, but it was hard not to feel alarmed. This was Celeste – someone who he cared a great deal for. He didn't know whether to check Tiletan or Lassandra next and time was working against him. His sense of urgency drove him to the next closest planet but he worried he was making the wrong choice and wasting precious time. The trip was thirteen and a half hours long, with eleven Jumps. What could the BDP do to her in those hours? The transit skimmed over the ice on its way to the Space

Access Point and Sebastian prayed with his head down, his autopilot engaged.

SEVEN

››› › CELESTE OPENED HER eyes and saw she had a visitor standing above her. She smelled a cheeseburger and French fries in a bag he was holding and he handed her a large cup of water. He had to talk louder than the music playing over the speaker.

"Are you hungry? You can have this food if you answer some questions for me."

She nodded.

"You sure are bleeding a lot. Is that normal for you?" The man sniffed the air as if he smelled something foul. Celeste supposed it reeked in her little room with the carpet soaking up all of her menstrual blood.

She looked up at the man, "No. This isn't normal. I usually bleed for a few days and it stops, but…I have no idea how many days I've bled, although I know this is much heavier than normal."

"Is there any way for you to stop it? I'm a Human from Earth so I know you ladies have your tampoons and your pads. You got some?"

If Celeste met this man on the street in a normal situation, she was afraid she might like him. The way he said tampon like harpoon was almost funny and he had apparently only come in here to give her a cup of water, food, and talked to her in a normal tone of voice, not all aggressive like the others.

"I wish I had tampons. I asked for some but I didn't get any," she drank the water in small sips. It was delightfully ice cold. All the other times it had been lukewarm or room temperature, but this felt like an ice tunnel being carved down her throat – it was so refreshing, "Can you tell me how long I've been here please?"

Celeste could see the man smile through his black ski mask, "Ah darlin' I wish I could when you ask so sweet like that. Truth is, I'm not even supposed to be visiting you right now." He handed her the bag of food. She tore it open and shoved fries into her mouth.

"Not so fast queen. You need to eat slower or else you'll throw it all up."

"I'm starving. They're barely feeding me," she said with her eyes closed savoring the salty intense flavor of the warm crispy potatoes.

"I know and I'm sorry for that." He watched her rip off the paper on the cheeseburger and take a huge bite.

"I saw this blood stain around you on the cameras. It worries me. This is my first time in the facility, and I probably won't be back while you're here. I just wanted to see you. Never visited a queen before. Anyway, I hope you can stop your bleeding soon. You look pale and I know they don't want you to die. I hope your kingdom comes through quick for you. We haven't heard a thing from them yet and your time is running out. Take care."

"Oh please don't leave. What do you mea—"

The man opened the door, "Knowledge is an ocean, and you must be your boat's captain. Goodbye Celeste." Then he was gone.

She had almost given up hope of being rescued by anyone, much less Sebastian. She honestly thought for a minute that man had been a doctor or someone that was able to take her out of here, but he apparently only wanted to see the newest attraction at the captive zoo. She put a handful of fries into her mouth, at least he had given her a real meal – and it tasted like the best thing she had ever eaten.

She knew the kingdom didn't care what happened to her. David sure as hell didn't care if she died or not. The kingdom would lie and say they'd tried to save her, but in the end, David would keep his money and the BDP would kill her.

She called out to Sebastian, but she thought her failing health might have something to do with her lack of 7's strength. She was sure Sebastian had mentioned that mental power was like a muscle – you had to use it for it to get stronger, and you should be in good health to get the best possible results. She surely wasn't feeling healthy. She remembered how Sebastian's 7's had started to get "fuzzy" as he phrased it, when he came down with the flu. And his 7's got worse as he got worse, then it still took a while for his telepathy to come back to one hundred percent even after he was feeling better. She knew she was still on her way down, so her 7's must be getting weaker as she did. She gulped more of the ice water while it was still cold and finished her meal.

She put her hands over her face and grimaced as she touched her swollen eye. Her whole face felt swollen sometimes. She took a long slow breath in and held her knees to her chest. <*Where are you Bastian? Please come find me.*>

Soon she'd lose a finger, but at least they said she got to pick which one.

She thought her right pinky was a good choice. She wondered how long she'd been in captivity – eight days? Two weeks? Maybe even three? – she didn't know and there was no way to tell.

"Feels like forever," she mumbled to no one.

EIGHT

>>> > MR. APPLETTE WALKED into the security room and told the man on duty that the boss wanted to see him. The idiot believed him and left him alone in the room. He erased himself off all the vids and then left the facility.

He felt terrible for Celeste and wished he could've done more but he had interfered enough already by giving her food.

He hoped she survived this ordeal.

NINE

>>> > CELESTE WOKE UP to someone slapping her hard across the face. She put her hands up to protect herself but they were quickly bound together with wire.

"WHO GAVE YOU THIS FOOD AND WATER?"

She looked and saw two figures in black. The one in the doorway held a metal baseball bat. Just the sight of it made her panic. Usually they didn't use weapons, just their fists.

She stammered, "I don't know! A man…he said he was Human. He said it was his first time here."

The man that yelled kneeled down in front of her and held her chin in his hand, "Try again. We know everyone that has been in to see you and no one's been in this room with you in days."

"I'm telling the truth."

The man let go of her and stood up. He hooked his thumbs into his pockets and said, "You *had* three more days before we were going to cut off a finger of yours, but now…"

The man with the baseball bat laughed and swung it into the wall with tremendous power. A small explosion of dust and pieces of drywall shot out around the room. Celeste shrank away and winced.

"Now we might have to take a little more," the man who yelled said. Then both men laughed.

Celeste cried, "Why? Because I don't know which one of your goons gave me food?"

"Goons? Ohhh I bet that's supposed to hurt my feelings. No one was here with you. I want to know where this food came from, and the cup. Unless you got out of here on your own somehow and grabbed a meal and then slipped back in without us seeing…which is impossible as you're monitored round the clock. I want to know how you got the food and it seems like you don't feel like telling me."

"I swear on my parent's grave I'm telling you the truth."

"What did he look like?"

Celeste smiled despite herself, "Like the rest of you assholes with your all black clothes and a mask over his face. How the fuck am I supposed to know what he looked like you ass?"

The man with the baseball bat charged at Celeste and she thought that was it. She was going to die here…and if she did, she wouldn't go down without a fight. She kicked her bare foot up into his groin as hard as she could and struck him at the same moment he lifted the bat up over his head. He let out a wail and dropped the bat, it hit Celeste in the leg and she grabbed it with her bound hands. The man fell to the ground and rolled on his side into a ball, tears streaming down his cheeks. Celeste stood up and positioned herself like a baseball player at home plate waiting for a ball. She took a few practice swings and the man who yelled, backed up.

"The boss will not be happy with you," he looked over his shoulder at the door and down at the man on the floor writhing in pain.

"You can tell Daxton to go to hell."

"Give me the bat!"

"Fuck you! Take your friend and get the hell out of here!" It hurt her throat to yell, but it felt good to regain some control over events. She realized she was shaking as she moved towards the man on the ground. The man standing didn't move. She lowered her voice and lifted the bat over her head, "You take him out, or I will beat him to death."

The standing man leaned over and grabbed the man on the ground by his collar, dragging him out the door, then shut it. She was alone again. She backed up into the corner and crouched down with the bat in her hands…waiting.

CHAPTER 19

OVER AND OUT

ONE

>>> > AFTER A WHILE, Celeste's door opened and a man came in with a strange gun. He stood in the doorway and she stood up poised to hit him with the bat if she had to.

"Celeste, I'd really like it if you gave me the weapon. I don't want to shoot you." He spoke calmly as if addressing an irate child in public.

She swung the bat once and moved forward, "Get out."

"Last chance."

She started swaying back and forth on her feet, trying to constantly move. She didn't want to be an easy target to hit. "Get out asshole."

He lifted the gun up and she ran at him. He dodged her at the last second, stepping outside the doorway and letting her run out of her room. She looked around at her options and saw a wide-open space outside like the floor of an empty warehouse. There was a hallway to the right so she ran that way when she felt a pinch on her neck. She kept running while her hand reached up and felt a dart sticking out of her skin. She ripped it out and kept running but then she got dizzy and tripped over her feet. She fell to the concrete floor and dropped the bat. She felt sleepy. They had drugged her and she couldn't fight through it. She heard footsteps next to her. She looked up and saw the man with the dart gun.

"It would've been nice if you handed over the weapon. Now I have to carry you back."

TWO

>>> > CELESTE WOKE UP in her small room again. Her baseball bat was gone. She was groggy and nauseous. She was caked in her own dried blood everywhere except between her legs where a constant red river flowed. All she wanted to do was shower, but they wouldn't let her. They never let her see herself, but she was betting she looked pretty bad. She knew for sure she smelled awful too.

She hallucinated often enough where the music they blasted into her room didn't bother her so much anymore. It was music after all and she hadn't heard a lot of it on Earth because of the ban. In her drug-induced dreams, Sebastian would come and take her away. He'd help her to shower and make her something to eat. Of course, Sebastian would also be traveling by a giant cardboard squid that could fly and she'd grown a second head, but she knew whatever drugs they were giving her were responsible for the bizarre details. At first she tried to avoid the items she thought were drugged. She wouldn't drink the water, or eat the food, but then she'd get injected with something else. She knew the water had to be laced with it, but she was simply too thirsty to refrain from drinking it.

She wondered if her parents were alive and if they were, did they know about her kidnapping. She wondered if she'd ever make it out of this alive to find out. She wondered if Sebastian had seen her on the news.

She got three glasses of water and a couple pieces of fruit. They were generous today and she wondered what they were up to. She never got three glasses of water in one day. She was extremely weak and she couldn't walk back and forth across the length of her box like she used to in the beginning. Her jaw hurt, her legs ached and her head was throbbing again. She put a finger to her dry lips. They had split a while ago, when some asshole slapped her trying to wake her up to make another damned video. She put her hands up into her knotted hair and felt how oily it was. All she wanted was to go home. The door opened up and she knew she was going to get roughed up some more. She missed her baseball bat.

THREE

>>> > ON THEIR THIRD date, Ulysses and Ginger met in the park not too far away from Ginger's childhood home. They were taking their dates further and further away from the castle to make sure no one would see them together. The last thing they needed was someone they worked with to rat on them.

Things were going well. Today was a Sunday, nothing was happening back at the castle, and it was peaceful.

They laid on a big soft blanket holding each other after lunch.

"Ginger, I think you're an amazing girl."

"You're sweet," she smiled and blushed.

"I feel like I could tell you anything."

"Oh? Is there something you want to tell me?"

His hazel eyes looked away and then back, "Nothing that can't wait. I don't want to ruin this moment."

She felt like there was something big he wanted to say. Why else would he bring that up? But it was still too early to go poking her nose around in his past. There were things she wanted to ask, things she wanted to say too, but she was afraid of his reaction. She'd have to wait a little longer. See if he brought this up again soon. Then, maybe she could ask.

"It's okay. Whatever it is will wait then." She kissed him and he wrapped his arm around her tighter, giving her a little squeeze. For a brief moment, her mind flashed to an imagined future where Ulysses had been a trap and King David imprisoned her down in the dungeons.

What if her first instincts were right and he was a spy? But then again, he could've already ratted her out with what little they had done, but he hadn't or at least, she hadn't been arrested. Maybe she should move much slower with him from now on.

Ulysses couldn't tell Ginger he was a member of the IMC yet. Couldn't tell her *that* was the reason he was the only Human High Royal Guard. Couldn't tell her that David was its leader. Those were huge secrets. How could he date her and let her trust in him grow without telling her about this big part of his life?

Omitting was still lying and he cared about her a lot. He didn't want to lie, but for now, he didn't know what the right thing to do was, so better to keep his mouth shut about it.

"Your skirt has a whole bunch of candy corns on it. It's cute."

She smiled, "I love Halloween. It's my favorite holiday. Way better than Christmas or my birthday. It's the only day you can dress up and be whoever you want and no one will make fun of you or say you can't be that. It's like I'm a kid again and my pops and grandma always took me out trick or treating. It was a blast."

"Ah, now it makes sense. You always wear something Halloween related."

"Yep. Grandma passed away last year. She loved Halloween just as much as me, so it's like a little thing I do to honor her."

"That's sweet of you."

"What's your favorite holiday? Wait, let me guess — I bet it's Christmas."

Ulysses scratched his chin and said without thinking, "I actually like Year End Fest personally."

Ginger pressed her lips together, "Wait, that's…isn't that a Zetzettian holiday?"

Ulysses closed his eyes tight and grimaced, "Um, yes. Yes it is."

"Well how does that happen? Have you been there? I thought only residents could participate in that."

"I lived there for a while. I like the Nawgain with their musculature on the outsides of their body. I think that's pretty neat, don't you?"

"Yeah, pretty neat." She dropped the subject since it was obvious he didn't want to talk about his past much, but she started feeling leery of him with all the question dodging and subject changing.

FOUR

>>> > D'ARTAGNAN SHOWED UP early to FAIR's first official meeting with a picture of Matthrew Nessium he had found on the uninet.

He showed it to Mitch, "How about him? Do you recognize him?"

Mitch looked at D'Artagnan's Titan, "Yep! He was with us up until recently. We, uh...called him Sexy Joe." Mitch looked at D'Artagnan, "He gave us that name to use, that's not...what we would've chosen for him." Mitch cleared his throat.

D'Artagnan nodded, "It's okay. I get it. Why isn't he with you now?"

"He was one of the members who left for the BDP. I guess he thought it sounded better over there," Mitch hesitated, "That's the guy Linda was...with? The one you're looking for?"

"Yes."

"Was that all you were after? I mean, if you joined us to get back at him, and now he's gone...What I mean is, we could really use your help here."

D'Artagnan stopped, "It's not like I can get myself into the BDP. The organization is huge; it could take me months to find this asshole. No, I'll see what I can help you guys with. I won't leave."

Mitch smiled, "Great. I want to pick your brain for some Il'lacean things before the meeting."

FIVE

>>> > KING DAVID STOOD at the podium surrounded by reporters, flying camera-bots, and guards.

"Let me repeat – this reign has tried twice already to pay the ransom for Celeste Hennessy, and every time our people go to meet their people, suddenly the ransom has increased again. The Brotherhood hasn't done anything to earn my trust and has done nothing reasonable or rational up to this point."

The reporters raised their hands quickly. David allowed one to speak, "You in the front."

An Il'lacean man stood, "Kenneth Spartz from Marshland News. How long does the kingdom expect it will be before Queen Dowager Hennessy returns home?"

David sighed, "We're doing everything in our power to get her home safely and as quickly as possible. I can only give the Brotherhood what they ask for, but since it's constantly changing, it's been a little difficult to get anything accomplished. I assure you as well as everyone watching that we will bring her home safe. I'll give the BDP whatever they want, but the time for coren grabbing and negotiating is over. I speak to the BDP directly now when I say, give me a final amount and we'll do the trade everyone so desperately wants. Thank you."

David immediately walked away from the podium while reporters were shouting and flashes were going off all around him.

Once he was clear of the media circus, he yelled for Ulysses, "Benson!"

Ulysses moved quickly to his side navigating through multiple guards, "Yes, my King?"

"I need you to get ten more guards for a secondary security team."

"Are these in addition to the twenty-five we have already, or are these a special operations team?"

David looked at Ulysses and almost snapped at being questioned, but remembered, Ulysses needed to know this information for practical purposes, "In addition to. I want thirty-five guards around me at all times while I'm at home or traveling. Can you do this in the next Earth hour?"

Ulysses nodded and started walking away, "Yes, my King."

SIX

>>> > **"I WANT TO** start by thanking Steve for letting us use this fantastic bunker. Let's give him some applause," Mitch smiled to the crowd and pointed to Steve.

The members of FAIR clapped and whistled.

"I also want to introduce our first new recruit into FAIR. He's an Il'lacean, our first ever, and I think he's going to make a great addition to our efforts. I've talked with him at length and I've put my trust into him; I'd like you to do the same. So when you get a chance, talk to him, but I'd like you to say hello to Gaviss. Gaviss stand up so everyone can see you."

Gaviss stood and smiled then quickly sat back down.

Mitch smiled, "I've received several messages with concerns and questions and I've tried to respond to all of them. Does anyone want to discuss anything now?"

Gaviss raised his hand, "I'm wondering what kind of encryption you have on your Titans and messaging systems? It seems like it might be easy to compromise."

A murmur went through the crowd.

Mitch scratched his head, "So far we haven't had any problems...but is there something you could do to boost our protection levels?"

"That's my specialty." Gaviss smiled, "I can make it so no one can crack your codes or bypass your security. But if you guys are going to meet somewhere on a regular basis, security needs to go even further than an underground bunker. You need cameras and surveillance. You need someone who's going to maintain these systems too."

Mitch smiled, "Sounds like you might be handy to have around. Does everyone think these things sound good? I think we need them for sure."

The crowd nodded approval.

Gaviss said, "But this place isn't secure enough. We're too close to a neighborhood of beings that could get nosy. Neighbors might want to check things out, or look over back yard fences. I say we move locations as soon as possible."

Mitch looked at Gaviss sideways, "Well, we're going to have to talk this over. Steve's place was supposed to be a temporary home anyway, but you might have a point. We'll discuss this after the meeting."

Steve raised his hand, "Now wait a minute. This place is underground, it's out of the way, no one's going to see us down here."

"Steve you're invited to the discussion after the meeting, don't worry. Now, what else do we need to think about here? What do you guys want to accomplish?"

Over the next two hours, the group discussed all they wanted to do and wrote down ideas on a screen in the front of the room.

The list included: freedom for Earth from Il'lacean rule, non-violent public protests, get attention to the cause, build member base across the galaxy, a secure meeting location with a secure communications system, safety, peace, trust, honesty, truth, human solidarity, and a world democracy or a varied group of Humans to serve on a world council.

SEVEN

Hace asked, "What have you got for me on Earth regarding the Resistance?"

"Mitch has finally surfaced, but we don't know what he's up to, I mean with the HR. Right now, it doesn't look like he's doing much. It seems like he's a good church-goer these days, maybe feeling like he wants to turn his life around, away from causing trouble."

Hace shook his head, "Come on Britton. You gotta' give me more than this."

"Really sir. We're watching him and he's not doing anything unusual. He goes grocery shopping, walks in the park, stays at home for hours, goes to church. Watching him is kinda boring. I mean...not boring, he's ju—"

Hace made a pained face, "I get it. He's not doing anything unexpected right now," he paused, "Things sound too quiet. You sure he hasn't noticed you guys watching him?"

"No way sir. We've been super careful. I'm positive he's unaware of our presence."

"I can't believe there's nothing going on with him. There's got to be something. Keep digging. Keep watching him. I'll check in with you later. The Hunter over and out."

CHAPTER 20

THE BROTHERHOOD BOWS TO NO ONE

ONE

>>> > "OPHELIA?"

"Yes, si-si-si-sir?"

"Do a full system check while I'm away from my transit. Try to diagnose any operating problems you might be having."

"I currently do not, do not detect any, any pro-problems."

"Yeah, that's what I mean," Sebastian sighed. He couldn't afford to have any issues with his AI now.

Sebastian was hopeful that Lassandra would be the right place, but he was wrong. The marshland world was full of lowlifes, destruction, and mutated aliens. He hated this planet, but it was one of his best chances at finding Celeste. He left Lassandra's swampy wastelands after sixty-four hours straight of searching, realizing she wasn't there.

That meant his next and final destination was Tiletan. He launched quickly.

"Ophelia, what did you find?" He snapped his safety harness together.

"No abnormalities at this time, sir."

He shook his head, "There has to be something. You're not functioning as normal. Do another check."

"Sir, I find these tasks to be a waste of time."

Sebastian's mouth dropped open. Ophelia might have had some traits of an independent thinker programmed in, but she was never argumentative when it came to system updates or checks.

She was infected.

He should've seen this sooner. All of his sensitive data was at risk.

As he traveled to the next planet, he found three updates to clean Ophelia and installed them: UpAIv11, UpAIv15, and UpAIv19. The last thing he did was debug her system of the infection and brought her back online.

"Ophelia?"

"Yes, sir?"

"How are you feeling?"

"I feel fine, sir. How you do feel?"

"Better. Much better," he put his hand up to his forehead and smiled, "I need you to do a full systems check while I'm out of my transit. Can you do this?"

"Of course, sir. Would you like a time estimate?"

"No. Cancel request."

"Yes, Erebos."

He looked for any reports of AIs becoming infected after updates and found none. O was doing what he asked and no longer stuttering. It seemed she was fixed.

He was not looking forward to any time on Tiletan. The planet was hot, dry, and full of desert. Celeste had to be there somewhere. He just hoped he could get to her in time. He checked their weather forecast and to make things more frustrating for him (the Gods and Goddesses had such a sense of humor!) Tiletan was expecting their biggest dust storm of the past ten years.

TWO

>>> > CELESTE'S CAPTORS WERE getting sloppy although she was so out of it, she never realized it.

One of the kidnappers had a crush on her. They called him Tiny, but in an ironic way. She learned to recognize his voice, but had never seen him so she had no idea how big he really was. Sometimes she'd hear him over her speaker after she'd been fed. He told her how pretty she was, even if she was all bloodied and scabbed up. He told her once, they might burn her up, that they were talking about scarring her so bad no one would recognize her, but that he would still be able to. And he wanted to take her away from here. Away from all the other guys and have her to himself.

"I'll get you out of here sweet cakes, don't you worry. I'll take you away when no one's looking and we can go into the night. I'll bend you over, spread your legs, and you can properly thank me for rescuing you from all these bad guys. Maybe I'll have you get down on your knees and suck my pricks – all three of them. Oh that's nice to think about sugar. Just you wait. Tiny will get you outta here so you can thank me forever. Ooooh boy! I can't wait to have a Human queen's jugs all over my face." He laughed over the speaker and she shuddered.

She couldn't help but think of how ironic all this was. She escaped her husband that abused her and raped her for years, only to be dating a man that seemed nice enough…until he threatened her with rape. When that didn't work out, he handed her over to some group of kidnappers that beat her and will probably rape her some more. She never even saw Dax here.

She wanted desperately to be lying in Sebastian's bed next to him, curled up against his body, and held in the safety of his arms.

How long had it been since she saw Sebastian's face? It could've been weeks, maybe a month? She had completely lost track of time and was seriously afraid she was losing touch with reality. Everything here seemed to run together. Time flies when you're in constant threat of a horrible and painful death. She laughed crazily. She felt like she was starting to come unglued. *I don't have much longer before I just ask them to kill me. I really don't. I wonder what happened to Sebastian,* she thought. *Why isn't he here?*

She fantasized that Sebastian came to her. He apologized for taking so long to find her as he carried her away. She missed him. She missed sunlight, the moons of Praxis, she missed bathing, and she missed her freedom.

THREE

>>> > CELESTE RECEIVED NO food or water in a while. Maybe that meant the deal was finally being done, and she'd be freed soon. Maybe something went terribly wrong and they were about to kill her. Or maybe, all of her captors had died somehow and she'd die soon too, free of this hell. *Dying would be okay,* she thought as she passed out.

FOUR

>>> > WHEN CELESTE CAME to, it was dark and sweltering. She was being dragged on her back along dirt and rocks. Her hands and ankles were tied. She had been gagged and blindfolded. *Where was this?* She started moaning and trying to spit the rag out of her mouth. The dragging stopped.

Tiny's voice came to her ears, "Oh, you're awake honey." He dropped her arms and took off the blindfold, but it was still dark. She guessed it must be nighttime, but she had no idea where she was. She could barely see out of the little slits that were currently as much as she could open her eyes. She thought she might be in a desert. *What the hell was happening?*

Tiny sat down on a boulder, "I'm happy you're awake. I thought I'd bring you all the way out here and when I stopped, you'd be dead. Can't have sex with you if you're dead. I suppose I could, but it wouldn't be as fun." He laughed and snorted. She recoiled inside.

She tried to see his face through her swollen eyes, but he still had a black mask on. He was wearing a big – blue? gray? – toga. He was one of the biggest figures she'd come in contact with since she arrived. Actually one of the most enormous creatures she had ever seen in her entire life. He scared her immensely. She'd never be able to fight him off. An alien that size could easily kill her with his bare hands or tentacles. He was a Trovelet. She would be raped and then killed by Tiny, she knew it. Trovelet's were selfish and had no sympathy. *This was it; this was the end of the line.*

"I got lucky tonight. I flat out forgot about the big dust storm coming and everyone left to do preparations. And the best part – they left me in charge! That dust is the best thing that could've happened to us sweetie. Now we can be together for eternity," a few tentacles twitched near her face from underneath his toga.

She thought about Sebastian and choked up. She felt like crying but no tears came. She was determined to make sure it was his face that was the last thing she saw. She allowed her mind to take her back to the first time he smiled at her out on his balcony. How his lips had felt up against hers. She didn't even notice when Tiny positioned her and untied her legs, spreading them wide.

Tiny grabbed Celeste's feet and her living prosthetic disengaged off her ankle.

"Oh shit! What have I done?" Tiny looked at it and realized what it was. He felt relief flood into him. He thought he had broken her for a minute. He threw her fake foot off into the distance.

FIVE

>>> > DAVID LOOKED OVER his IMC members, then looked at Ulysses.

Ulysses shifted from one foot to the other slowly, "I appreciate the members that came forward with offers of help regarding Celeste. While I've exhausted all of our combined resources, I'm sorry to say, we can't locate her."

David looked at him but Ulysses could see no expression in his eyes. Ulysses wasn't sure how to react.

"Ulysses, what exactly did you come up with? Anything?"

"The BDP main headquarters, I suspect, is not a physical location. We think their leader is constantly on the move, so wherever he is, is where the main HQ is, but they have numerous branches. They could be holding her at any one of those...at least eighty-seven locations, by our findings. I don't think they'd run the risk of her escaping by changing her location but, that's still a possibility. We were thorough, but we don't know her current location."

This was one of the rare times that David and Ulysses didn't talk before a meeting. David's schedule had been booked solid and there simply wasn't any time.

"It's alright Ulysses. I'm sure you've done your best. For now, we pause our efforts to find her...maybe we can get a break soon. We'll keep trying, but we need to get her back for the glory...and for Humans everywhere. After her safety is ensured, we can plan our revenge against the BDP." David decided to pander to the Humans in his IMC group for today. He needed as many Humans on his side as possible.

Ulysses nodded, "I apologize for failing you. I did everything in my power and the men were great giving all that they could to aid me."

David waved his hand, "I know. It is a difficult thing finding a solitary person in the universe. I'm not blaming you or the efforts of our brothers here."

Ulysses bowed and stood off to the side of the podium.

"If anyone has anything that could aid us in this matter please approach Ulysses. Thanks. Meeting adjourned."

SIX

>>> > GINGER AND ULYSSES sat at the empty restaurant. She felt like every word they said could be overheard throughout the whole place.

Ulysses put his hand over hers, "Everything will be okay."

She looked at him, "How can you know? You don't know where Celeste is."

He hated to see her this worried. He wanted to console her somehow, but he honestly didn't know where Celeste was, or if she was alive or not. If he told Ginger he had been on David's task force to find the queen and came up empty, she'd be crushed.

"I believe things will work out. Celeste is a very strong woman. She's a fighter and she probably learned a lot from living with Jonathan. Her strength might surprise us all."

Ginger pushed her food around on her plate, "I hope you're right. I thought I would've heard something by now. I thought she would've been released or escaped."

Ulysses sighed, "Maybe she did escape, and you know what? If she did, the smart thing would be to go into hiding. She might need to recover – mentally, physically, emotionally, or all of the above. If she's hiding, she's smart not to reach out to anyone. Something could be traced to her location, or someone could find her if she's not careful. Try to think positive. I'm sure you'll hear from her as soon as it's safe to contact you."

Ginger gave a strained smile, "Yeah. Thanks hon."

He leaned over and kissed her on the forehead, "Keep the faith darling."

"I'm trying. I really am. It's frustrating not knowing what's going on."

Ulysses waved the waiter over, "Check please."

"Is it almost time for the show?"

Ulysses glanced at his Titan, "Yes. If we're going to make it on time, we'll have to leave in ten minutes."

SEVEN

>>> > THREE HOURS LATER, Ulysses and Ginger got out of the theater and couldn't stop making fun of the play.

"That might be the worst play I've ever seen. Good God!"

Ginger laughed, "It must've been family and friends night in there. How could they get two standing ovations? Ugh."

Ulysses pulled Ginger in close all of a sudden, "You can give me standing ovations, if you know what I mean." He winked at her and she blushed.

Ginger couldn't say anything back; Ulysses always had a way of making her lose her train of thought.

"You want to do something different tonight?" he asked.

"Like what?"

"I don't want to go back to Silver Thorn alone. We've been seeing each other for a while…" He put his hand along the side of her face. She covered his hand with her own.

"We can't sleep overnight in the same room there honey. You know that."

"No, we can't, but we can stay together somewhere in a hotel or something," he paused, "If you want to."

She was silent.

"Or…if you don—"

"Let's do it." Then she blushed after she saw the look on his face, "I mean…let's stay together overnight." Ginger knew life was short and she knew Celeste would tell her to enjoy it as long as she could.

"Only if you're sure sweetheart. I'm not going to push you into anything. I'm just asking for us to sleep in the same bed. I'm not expecting you to do anything with me."

"Alright Uly." She followed him down the street as he called a transit bot-taxi.

They arrived ten minutes later in front of the nicest hotel she had ever seen.

When they walked into the lobby, she lost her breath. The entire place looked majestic…and very expensive.

"Oh, we don't need to stay *here*…"

Ulysses ignored her and walked to the front desk to check in.

A few minutes later, he gave Ginger a key card and told her he'd be up shortly. She gave him a strange look, "What do you have to do now?"

"I'll be up in a minute. There's something I've got to do first." He gave her a big kiss and relinquished her.

"Don't take too long handsome." She smiled at him over her shoulder and walked away.

When Ginger was out of sight, he walked into the gift shop and bought her a dozen long stemmed red roses and a bottle of champagne. Cliché, he thought, but not for the girl that gets them.

Ginger couldn't believe how big this room was and there was a large balcony with a view of the city. It was spectacular. She couldn't wait for Ulysses to join her. She wondered what he was up to.

A few minutes later, the front door opened and Ulysses was there.

She was out on the balcony, taking in the view so she didn't see him, but she heard him.

"Ginger?"

She turned around, saw the roses in his hands, and broke out into a big grin, "Oh sweetie, you shouldn't have."

She walked to him and he handed them to her. "They told me there should be a vase in here, under the bathroom sink."

He started to walk away, but she grabbed his hand, "We can find that later, yes?"

He looked at her, "Sure."

She put the roses on the coffee table behind her and saw the champagne, "What about some glasses though? Did they tell you if there were any here…?"

He moved away from her and found the bar. He plucked two champagne glasses hanging from the top rack and handed them to her, "I've got to open this sucker first."

She waited for the pop, but the bottle barely let out a hiss when he opened it. "Don't you want it to pop?"

He shook his head, "Opening these takes a little finesse. You really don't want the mess and the pop sound isn't desirable. Could you hand me your glass please?"

She did. He filled it almost to the top, then did the same with his own. He put the bottle down and held his glass up to hers, "We should toast."

"To what?"

"To us…and that Celeste is returned safely to us soon."

They took their drinks onto the balcony.

"Uly, I need something from you. Since I'm doing something outside of my comfort zone right now, I'd like you to do the same for me."

His brows furrowed deep, "We don't have to stay here tonight. I can take you home if yo—"

"No. I'm nervous about tonight, but I wouldn't be here if I thought you'd pressure me to do anything."

"You know I won't."

"Will you tell me about your past? It seems like every time I ask about your parents or your childhood, you get edgy. You never want to talk about it and I want to know more about you. Whatever it is, I can handle it."

He felt like a cornered animal. He downed the rest of the champagne in his glass and sat down on one of the patio chairs.

She sat down next to him and put her hand on his leg, "Okay, I'll go first. I'll tell you something super personal. When I wa—"

"No, you deserve to know without making it some sort of bartering for information about me. You're right. I should tell you. I should've already."

She braced herself. It sounded like it was going to be bad now that he was finally going to spill the beans.

He said all at once, "I was five when my parents sold me. My family was struggling financially and Zetzetti was looking for Human children that possessed a certain…let's say, aptitude for their schools. Whatever test I took when the recruiter came to our door, I passed with flying colors, so the Priesthood of Religious Studies and Magic paid my parents and I left for Zetzetti with a stuffed animal and my blanket that afternoon. I cried for days. I couldn't understand what happened or why my sister stayed on Earth with my parents. I didn't want to be a Priest. I didn't want to live at the school, but in time, I did want to learn magic."

Ginger stared at him, unable to say anything.

"I never forgave my parents. I tried, like my religion told me, but I couldn't get past what they did. Up until the time I was sixteen all I did was breathe, eat, and sleep, magic and religion. I escaped Zetzetti two days before I was to be ordained and came back to Earth. My family had moved and I had nowhere to go, so I enlisted in the military until I could find my sister. I looked for years and didn't find her. I heard the Kingdom was looking for men with military experience and the pay was better so I got in as soon as I could. Then, I finally found my sister. Turns out, she was born with a faulty heart and my parents sold me to pay for her medical procedures. They had put seven different kinds of artificial hearts into her, but one by one, her body rejected them. They paid a Taybuse to grow her a heart but it wasn't working. When I found her, the doctors said she had a few months to live, that the Taybuse-grown heart was failing, and that there was nothing that could be done. They said she could live with the aid of machines pumping her blood for her, but she didn't want to live that way. I held her hand as she passed. We talked a lot before I lost her. We made our peace with each other."

"What about your parents?"

"They were there the whole time at the hospital. They tried to talk to me, but I wouldn't acknowledge them."

Ginger didn't know what to say, but she did the best she could. "I'm so sorry you had to experience that. I can't imagine how awful it would be. I understand now, why you didn't want to tell me." She stood and put her arms around him, holding on tight.

"No one knows any of this. I don't want them to so please don't tell anyone okay?"

"Absolutely not. I won't tell a soul, dear." She sat down again and looked at him. "I'm sorry for the loss of your sister. I wish this never happened to you."

"Thanks. Me too. You want more alcohol?"

She nodded.

They finished the bottle as Ulysses looked at his Titan, "The night's still very young and so are we. What shall we do?"

Ginger took his hand and led him back inside. She stopped alongside the king sized bed and crawled onto it. She looked at him and motioned for him to join her with her finger.

He kicked off his shoes and lie down next to her. She sat up long enough to remove her high heels.

"Thank you for trusting me with that story. I appreciate it."

He put his arms around her and pulled her close into his body, "Thank you for coming here with me tonight. More than anything else, I love spending time with you. I didn't want to sleep without you tonight."

"You make me feel so good Ulysses."

He put his hand into her hair and kissed her hard. His other arm wrapped around her torso holding her body up against his. He rolled her on top of him without any effort. She kept kissing him while her hands laced with his.

She could feel his erection growing through his pants and she realized she wouldn't stop him this time. Whatever he wanted to do with her tonight, she wanted him to take control. He let go of her hands and rolled her underneath him. Her hands went up to the collar of his dress shirt and started undoing buttons.

He smiled and paused long enough to say, "You sure?"

"Yes," she said breathy.

One of his hands found her bare thigh. He pulled her dress up to her hips. He hooked his fingers into her bikini panties and she lifted up her hips. He took them off in one smooth motion.

He sat up, undid the last two buttons of his shirt along with the sleeves, and took it off.

He leaned down over her and kissed her as one of his hands roamed up along her leg. He dragged his fingernails lightly along her skin and she moaned. His hand made its way to her inner thigh and stopped momentarily.

Her breath hitched and then his fingers settled onto her clit. He moved them around gently then slid his index and middle finger into her. She cried out.

She was soaking; he could easily glide his fingers in and out of her slowly as he put his thumb back on her clit to manipulate her inside and out.

"Ohhhh Ulysses. Oh my God…" she bit her lip.

"This is just the beginning darling. I can't wait to be inside of you with my cock," he sighed, "I'm so hard for you."

Ginger moaned out again, "Take off my dress, baby."

He removed his hands from her and moved onto his knees. She sat up and put her hands up over her head. Ulysses gently grabbed the bottom of her dress and tugged it up over her head throwing it aside. She wore a beautiful lacey black bra that made her breasts look divine. He needed his face in between them. He dove in and she put her hands onto the back of his head, keeping him there.

He kissed her cleavage and ran his warm tongue along the swells of her smooth breasts. She put her head back and he reached around to undo her bra strap.

She shrugged it off her shoulders and tossed it to the floor. She put her arms behind her and anchored her hands into the soft bed, offering her breasts to him.

He looked at them and then at her, "Oh damn Ginger, these are fucking beautiful tits. I want to come all over them."

She smiled, "You can then."

He put his hands firmly onto each one and squeezed. She let out a little sigh. His hands felt so good on her.

He leaned down and started kissing each one, taking his lips and running them over the nipples firmly and slow. They raised up into little nubs so that he could suck on each nipple until they were rock hard under his tongue.

"We need to get those pants off you sugar," Ginger was breathless and soaking wet.

He reluctantly let go of her breasts and quickly stood. She watched as he unbuttoned his pants and teased her by slowly pulling down the zipper. She saw he wasn't wearing any underwear. His erection sprang free after he took down his pants and she was increasingly excited for him to be inside her.

He grabbed a condom and raced back onto the bed to get on top of her. She locked her arms around his shoulders and spread her legs so she could place them around his torso.

He grunted as his cock rubbed its way along her slick clit. He had never felt a woman so wet as Ginger.

"I can't wait to be inside you," he growled into her ear.

"Me either."

He leaned down into her throat and ran kisses up and down her neck as she put her head back. Her hand slid down his muscular body and found his erection. He moaned when she wrapped her hand around him and tugged on him firmly.

"I can't take this anymore baby. I want to taste you now."

Ulysses moved his body down along hers and kissed in between her breasts, her torso, and abdomen, then plunged his mouth onto her clit. He teased her with his lips and tongue, moving in little circles as her temperature rose.

She felt so high; Ulysses was trying so hard to please her.

She cried out his name as his tongue slipped into her pussy. He darted it in and out, moaning the whole time so she could feel vibrations traveling all throughout her body. She dug her fingers into his shoulders and clawed at him. She couldn't help it.

He quickly stopped and put his condom on, and placed himself over her. She lifted her legs up and he slowly put just the tip of his cock inside her.

She let out a breathy moan of his name.

He teased her with it. Just slipping and sliding the tip out until she cursed. Then he let her completely engulf him as his cock penetrated deep into her. She wrapped her arms around him and his thrusts began to pound her. He slowed down and kissed her soft. She looked beyond them and saw a mirror on the back of the closet door. She was hypnotized watching as his ass bounced up and down over her, working his cock in and out.

This was too good to be true.

Ulysses yelled out, "God baby, you're so tight. You're going to make me come soon."

She dug her nails into his shoulders and he slowed down.

Sweat dripped down the sides of his face, "I want you to come first for me. I want this all night. I won't stop until we're exhausted."

He increased his thrusting and was now drilling into her pussy. He took a hand and squeezed her left breast until she felt a huge wave of ecstasy about to hit her.

He enjoyed watching as she put her head back and screamed when she came. The pulsing grip of her pussy was so strong around his cock and she was so sexy he finally let himself come and they both collapsed down into the bed. He rolled off her carefully and she draped herself over him.

They were silent except for the heavy breathing.

She wanted to tell him she loved him, but was afraid of what he'd say. He might not say it back and she didn't want to scare him off by saying it now, so she said nothing and just laid there as he caressed her hair.

EIGHT

>>> > D'ARTAGNAN, MITCH, AND Steve all discussed location after their group meeting. In the end, Steve agreed with D'Artagnan that they needed a more secure and secluded site to meet. The underground bunker in the desert had been ideal since it was located in the middle of nowhere.

Mitch agreed Steve could keep extra supplies in his back yard bunker along with a safety house where members could go if they needed a place to stay, but they couldn't hold regular meetings there. He would need to scout out locations for a new headquarters.

After excusing Steve, D'Artagnan and Mitch talked.

"I don't see how this would work in our organization."

D'Artagnan scratched his snout, "It's easy. Everyone gives their consent and I run a background check. It requires real names sure, but it would give us peace of mind that no one in this group is a plant from the BDP or a drug addict, rapist, child molester, etc. It takes care of all kinds of concerns for the people you're entrusting your life with."

"But we've always used fake names. I can't ask them to give up personal information. That wasn't part of my original plan."

"Fake names was the HR. This is FAIR. A whole new group, with new goals and a new way of doing things."

"I don't want it to come to background checks. That's too much like the government."

D'Artagnan paused and shrugged his shoulders, "You run the show here. It's your baby, but my vote is that we do some sort of scanning, whether it be background checks voluntarily, fingerprint scans or in my case, snout scans. Maybe a retina scan would be the most accurate. Hardest to fool. We could do that."

Mitch ran a hand over his beard, "I don't think that's necessary. I'm not bombing places. I'm not going to give these people guns. We're planning peaceful protests."

D'Artagnan argued, "What if someone's a spy in this group? What if someone wants to get you all together and eliminate you? I understand your reasons, but I'm thinking of everyone's safety."

"Can't we compromise and you just ask everyone some questions or something?"

D'Artagnan paused, "I can...I'm not sure you want me to do that, but I can, yes."

"I think that would be best. I'm fine with it."

"How do we vet each other then?"

Mitch shook his head and smiled, "Listen, you're a self-proclaimed hacker. I'm sure you can make it look like whatever you want for your own history with any kind of scan. With you, I have to trust my gut and I already allowed you in the group. That's all I need."

"I've never said I was a hacker, I merely suggested our security be as tight as possible."

"Okay, so whatever."

"And how about you? Are you comfortable with me asking you questions about your past, or I am supposed to take your word for it?"

"I will leave the decision up to you, Gaviss. If you want to interview me to make you feel safer, great. If you don't need or want to, that's fine with me too."

D'Artagnan responded, "I'm comfortable knowing what I know about you already. There's no need for interrogation."

NINE

>>> > MITCH STRUGGLED TO stay calm while Gaviss talked about questioning everyone. Mitch covered up his past since he returned from

discovering The Jump, but it was tiring to do repeatedly with the same person.

Mitch knew Gaviss was smart and that the Il'lacean's past was probably darker then Gaviss let on. But still, he liked the man. Mitch trusted his gut, tried to see people for who they were and he felt that Gaviss meant FAIR no harm.

After the meeting, Mitch started scouting new locations. He traveled all over Earth and figured they might need to spend a little money to secure the best place. He considered going off Earth, but that would simply be too long of a trip for most Humans to make. He needed to keep it simple and local. He looked at some empty warehouses, a few abandoned barns, but there was a reason the desert bunker was such a great place. He needed something like that again.

While he was roaming around, he noticed a transit following him. He didn't catch on until the end of the day, but now that he thought back on his travels, he remembered seeing it. He was being tailed.

And there were many groups that wanted to know what he was up to.

He took the long way back and didn't see his pursuer anywhere near his home, but that gave him no peace of mind. He didn't like any of the locations he saw today, but whoever was watching him, knew where he had been, so those locations were all discarded.

He needed to lose his tail permanently and find a new location, fast.

TEN

TITAN Corporation - Personal TITAN Device

System Status: Active -- Universal Grid: Online

Current Time/Date (Il'laceier - QetQert Regions): 12th Knoche/Newai 71-9, 5390

Secondary Time/Date (In Transit - Stoxia): 14 Sterms/Tise 15, 10354

Current Universal Positioning System Location: In transit
- Closest orbiting body, Stoxia

User: The Hunter

Communications Menu

Incoming message(s) received: 1 - Status: Unread

Message Received at 14 Sterms

Message Sent from: Universal News Agency (UNA) - Il'laceier
Regions

-UNA
-Pirchi Colony, QetQert Regions, Il'laceier
BREAKING NEWS
The Brotherhood of Desert Phantoms released a public
statement earlier today in response to King David Hennessy
II's press conference. The message in its entirety follows
below:
"The universe is being lied to.
David Hennessy has not spoken to us either on his own,
through any messages, or representatives, nor have we met
with him to discuss our demands for a trade to release our
hostage.
We made a private statement to him to keep this out of the
public eye, which he has ignored. We have asked him for a
certain amount of coren, which to date, has not been met.
In response to his direct address of our organization, we
will now ask to add five million coren to the ransom and
will send a private message with our meeting date and time
as well as a location for trade. If any more delays occur,
if the police are involved in any way, and if our demands
are not met, we will kill Celeste one Earth hour past our
meeting time.
Whatever happens, do not believe David Hennessy. He is a
liar. He does not care what happens to the Queen.
The Brotherhood stands together in battle!
The Brotherhood accepts no members but the best!

The Brotherhood bows to no one!"
UNA reached out to King Hennessy II for comment, but no
response was received.
You can trust UNA for all your universal news needs.

-END OF MESSAGE
*This message will auto-delete in 19 sterms upon viewing.

CHAPTER 21

TILETAN

ONE

>>> > TILETAN WAS SEBASTIAN'S last hope. He landed a few hours ago but came up with nothing. Thank Goddess he slept for an hour and a half while his transit shuttled him here; he'd been close to complete physical exhaustion after Lassandra.

The planet was mostly a desert wasteland, but there was a few big cities spread out far apart from each other. Unfortunately, he had searched all those cities for a day and a half and found nothing but dead ends. He pushed himself to exhaustion and checked into a hotel overnight. He hated to stop, but he'd never find her if he fell unconscious and got robbed on the streets.

When he woke up, he resumed his search but started to reconsider these planets. Maybe she wasn't here after all. He kept looking, but he didn't have any luck until that night.

He could see fine without the moons out, but there wasn't much to see in the emptiness of the desert. He was near a mountain, but his mapping system was malfunctioning. It reported the mountain wasn't really there, that some sort of artificial structure was instead. He thought it might be a good place to hide. He checked his geological mapper and saw he was right. The mountain was actually hollow inside. This had been his best chance so far.

He mentally shouted for Celeste, and then picked up something familiar but faint not too far away.

TWO

>>> > CELESTE KNEW SHE was hallucinating again. Sebastian was coming to rescue her in her dreams. She thought she felt him close by when she knew it was just her mind breaking apart. She felt him calling out to her and he seemed desperate to find her. Maybe this was some wishful thinking, but it became a pleasant distraction from having a disgusting huge Trovelet rape her.

She humored herself and mentally called out to Sebastian like he was actually there somehow.

THREE

>>> > "SURE BOSS, I got it all under control here."

"Good job Dax. I'm really glad I have you on my team. It makes me feel better knowing you're controlling the Tiletan branch. I've had some real losers out there trying to 'do their best' and all they did was fuck things up beyond recognition."

Dax smiled at his Titan's screen, "Nothing like that is gonna happen here. I promise."

Hace nodded, "I know. It's a relief to have you in charge of Celeste. I think Hennessy's going to be a tough nut to crack, but he should be able to cough up any amount of money we need. He doesn't want Celeste to die. He'd have non-stop riots breaking out all over Earth. It'd be too embarrassing for him."

Dax looked up from his Titan and started rotating through cameras in the Tiletan facility. He landed on Celeste's holding cell and saw it was empty with the door open.

"Yeah…sir, I agree whole heartedly. If you'll excuse me, I forgot I have something to check on here before too long."

Hace smiled, "Sure thing. Keep me updated."

"Of course sir. Dax over and out." Dax waited until The Hunter ended the call and his Titan returned to its main menu screen before he darted out of the security screens room and ran to Celeste's holding cell.

"FUCK!" He quickly scanned the immediate area looking for clues as to where she was. There was a smear of blood at the doorway but then it disappeared. He looked at the alarm pull on the wall. He had never pulled it before and it shouldn't get back to The Hunter that the alarm had gone off…He hoped. He didn't have a choice, he triggered the facility alarm on the wall to tell all members there was an emergency.

FOUR

>>> > SEBASTIAN FELT CELESTE nearby and his heart started to pound. She was around the corner of this mountain, but she was having some sort of mental breakdown. She wasn't herself and something about her call was wrong. He sprinted to close the distance on her and… someone else.

He rushed up behind an enormous Trovelet that was down low on his tentacles and naked. Sebastian evaluated him quickly and knew he'd be a formidable foe since he was *much* larger than Sebastian. As badly as he wanted to make this bastard suffer for everything that had been done to Celeste, taking him out quickly would be the smartest thing. Before Tiny was aware of someone behind him, Sebastian grabbed him by the horns, and broke his neck with a swift twist. Tiny fell paralyzed off to the side of Celeste. He died within seconds. Sebastian's heart broke as he saw what kind of shape she was in.

Celeste was almost unrecognizable. Her pale face was thick and lumpy; both eyes were bruised and swollen shut. She was bloody and bruises dotted her entire body. Her hair was clotted with blood, and her forehead had a huge knot growing out of it. Her dress was filthy and tattered. The bi-color tech in the fabric was broken and it kept shifting from black to pink. She had lost an incredible amount of weight and she looked as fragile as a porcelain doll. Her hands were tied, but her feet were not.

Her foot! Her prosthetic was missing! Sebastian looked around for it, but couldn't see it anywhere.

Celeste was so out of it, he didn't even think she knew he was there. "Celeste, I'm here baby. I'm so sorry for leaving you. I'm sorry for everything. I'm going to get you off this rock." He carefully touched her arm trying to reassure her he was there.

"You're not real, but I wish you were handsome. You go on and get me out of here then. I can't walk and a ton of those sons of bitches are probably going to realize I'm missing and be out here in a minute. Unless they're all still prepping for some big dust storm Tiny mentioned. Who cares about a little dust huh? Did you fly here on the squid? You promised you'd protect…me…" She fainted. He didn't have to read her thoughts as she went out. They hit him loud and clear. In her mind, she was screaming that she was dying, and he feared, she might be right. He took out his knife and quickly cut her ties allowing her hands to fall to her sides.

"Promises are made to be kept. Oh God, Celeste. Come on baby, stay with me. You can't leave me now," his voice trembled.

He carefully picked her up and carried her in his arms. She barely weighed anything. He ran as fast as he could to his transit.

FIVE

>>> > AS SEBASTIAN PLACED Celeste into the passenger seat and strapped her in, he heard movement behind him, at the same time an oddly familiar frequency entered his mind. He had been too focused on being gentle with Celeste to pay attention to anything behind him and his 7's intently focused on listening to her mind if she regained consciousness.

He actually thought they might've been able to escape unnoticed, but he knew that wasn't the case anymore. He turned around quickly expecting many, but there were only four. A Lanyx, two Humans, and an Awpunct. He hadn't sensed any intentions, so they must've had some intense training to block their minds; either that or they were completely empty headed.

He focused on the Lanyx in particular. Sebastian felt like he had been punched in the stomach.

"Constantine?! What the hell are you doing here?"

"Oh my God! I don't believe it! If anyone in the universe had to come along and try to screw this up for me, it had to be you. I should've known. You here to fuck everything up in my life all over again?" Dax crossed his arms on his chest.

Sebastian could only look on confused, "Brother, please tell me you're here to help. Please tell me you're with the police or a medical team."

"The police? Oh, that's rich," Dax laughed.

Sebastian's blood started to boil, "If you had anything to do with this, I PROMISE I will kill you! I'll tear each one of these men apart with my bare hands, but I'll save you, my brother, for last!" Sebastian found it impossible to keep his emotions in check. "ANSWER ME CONSTANTINE!"

"My name's not Constantine anymore, it's Daxton. Sometimes it's Reid," he said calmly.

Sebastian's face turned a dark shade of red as his muscles tightened throughout his body, "I don't give a flying fuck what your Goddamn name is now! Did you have something to do with this?!" He pointed to Celeste, never taking his eyes off his opponents.

"I couldn't believe my luck when I found her on Praxis of all places. She practically fell into my lap. Imagine the queen right there in our home world's back yard. The Brotherhood of Desert Phantoms really needed some funding and kidnapping her was the perfect answer to our money needs. She still is…after I take her out of your transit," Dax smiled.

"She's not going anywhere with you, Constantine."

The other three men were moving towards Sebastian.

Sebastian stiffened, "You take another step and you're all dead," he had a half smile on his face, "Hell, I've been waiting to kill someone for this."

Sebastian pulled out his plasma handgun from his back waistband and shot the Human closest to him first. He fell dead after a single gunshot to his forehead. The wound was smoking.

The other two men stopped and looked at Dax.

"Get him you fools!"

They advanced on Sebastian, while Constantine moved behind them towards Celeste.

Sebastian knew his other weapons were packed into his transit so the rest of the fight would be won with his gun or hand-to-hand combat… either way these men were not laying a hand on his woman again.

Sebastian made the mistake of looking at Constantine as he moved to take Celeste out of the transit, and the Awpunct leapt behind Sebastian. As Sebastian turned around to punch him, the Human grabbed Sebastian from behind, pinning his arms to his sides. Sebastian's gun was still in his hand.

Sebastian leaned back into the Human behind him and jumped up with both feet to kick the Awpunct in the gills as he reached down to take Sebastian's gun. A solid hit sent the Awpunct down on the ground clawing at his throat, gasping for air. Sebastian turned the handgun's barrel towards the man behind him and aimed down towards his enemy's leg. He pulled the trigger and the Human let go of Sebastian as he screamed out in pain from being shot in the foot. Sebastian then shot both of the men in the head and started towards Constantine.

Dax freed Celeste of her safety straps while she was coming back into consciousness. She smelled Dax's cologne, gathered all the strength she could, and wildly scratched at Dax's face. Her right index fingernail tore off and she screamed.

Constantine reared back and that was enough space for Sebastian to grab him into a chokehold strong enough to talk to him, but light enough not to make him pass out.

Sebastian turned his head to see Celeste laying in her seat, unconscious again.

"What the hell happened to you to make you join the BDP, Constantine?"

"It's Daxton now you fucking idiot!"

Sebastian tightened his arm against his brother's throat, "How did you get to be a part of the Brotherhood? And if you don't tell me the truth verbally, I'll still find out. I'll break into your mind so hard you'll be mentally handicapped for the rest of your life...however long that might be."

"I've had the best mental training coren can buy. I'm not worried about your 7's anymore."

"You should be." Sebastian started pushing into his brother's mind past his protective walls and Constantine started screaming.

"TALK! NOW!"

"Why does it hurt?" Constantine gasped for air, "You...shouldn't be able to do that! How are you getting past my walls? They're iron-clad."

"Not to a *family* mental connection like we have. Our minds are too similar for me not to be able to crack you. What? Nobody told you that? Whoever trained you took your coren and wasted your time. I think it hurts because we're brothers. Dad did it once to me and it hurt like nothing else. Now tell me, how did you get mixed up with the BDP?"

Constantine choked a little and Sebastian eased up enough to let him talk, "After you killed the love of my life, I went to school for political science. I got hired as one of the top advisors to the Prime Minister of Murush. I learned how corrupt all these politicians are. They think they're better than everyone else, Sebastian. Someone from the

Brotherhood approached me and we started talking. I found out what the mission of the BDP was and it made sense."

Sebastian could only listen as he closed his eyes and felt deep disappointment at his brother's story.

Constantine continued, "Government will always be corruptible. We need a new system. We need to overthrow all current leaders, and they need to be replaced with people from my group. These people understand me. They recruited me and I discovered exactly how much more I was capable of.

"And the money was so much better too. The BDP gave me real purpose. I saw all that I had done in my past and realized how wrong I'd been. And naïve; thinking I could make a difference in people's lives playing by the rules. The rules keep changing, so I couldn't win. I had to come to the BDP. I'd never allow it, but they'd probably love you, with all your military training. You could've done tremendous things for the group. You're such a great *murderer* brother."

Sebastian seethed, "You made a big mistake getting involved with these thugs. There's nothing but death coming for this group, I guarantee you that," he paused, "If you think that I could ever be a part of something like this – You've lost your mind Constantine. You're all power-hungry assholes."

The wind picked up. On the other side of the planet, the dust storm began.

Sebastian was in disbelief finding his brother here…and involved somehow with Celeste's kidnapping. Although Constantine never had 7's, Sebastian still had a special mental connection with all members of his family. His mental connection to his brother never faded away completely, but over time, all he knew through his 7's, was that his brother was still alive. Now that they were in close proximity again, Sebastian could easily break through some of his protective walls. He sensed a lot of loneliness in his brother, but sadness and rage too. If he tried to force his way into Constantine's mind and found a lot of resistance, he'd end up shattering his brother's mind and permanently damage it. Constantine would turn into a vegetable and whatever knowledge Sebastian was searching for – would be permanently lost.

This whole situation had Sebastian reeling, "I'll give you one chance Constantine, ONE. If you leave with us right now, I won't kill you, I promise. We can talk. You tell me everything you know about the Brotherhood and their operations and I will protect you from them until the threat has been eliminated. Think of it as redemption, but I'm only offering this to you once. If you say no now, you'll regret it."

"Oh Bass, you think you're better than this somehow? You're what? Some kind of high paid bounty hunter or something?" Constantine laughed. "You seem all high and mighty now – playing the hero that mom always thought you were. *You've* taken the moral high ground? You want me to leave with *you*? Leave the best thing I've ever been a part of? I think you're the one who's crazy...not me."

"No, it's definitely you. What's your answer?"

"The only way I'm leaving this organization is in a body bag," Constantine coughed, "You know when our relationship really went to hell? When Francesca left *me* for *you*. Then you dumped her knowing how much I loved her and she killed herself over you! How could you dump the most perfect woman in the universe? Who would do that? I would've died for her. Part of me did die when you killed her. Why would you think we could be on the same side now, after all these years? We stopped being brothers a long time ago." Constantine squirmed, try-ing to work his way out of Sebastian's hold.

"STOP IT! Francesca has nothing to do with what's going on now. Why Celeste? Why her, brother? She's not even queen anymore."

"She's still valu...Oh wait a second. Wait a SECOND! You're not here on a job...This is personal for you. Oh yes, how could I not see this? You care for her! Wow, I did really good this time. I should've killed her...and had I known that she was your girlfriend, *I would've*. She told me there was someone else, when I was lying on top of her on the beach. Forget the money, forget me loving her, I would've killed her to get back at you."

Sebastian didn't know if his brother was lying in this regard or not. Sebastian guessed maybe his brother couldn't be saved. Maybe the BDP had really changed him into a monster. Constantine's intentions were fracturing into multiple paths, making it impossible for Sebastian to know lies from truth and what his brother really intended on doing. He knew Constantine wanted Celeste for his own – especially now that he knew Sebastian wanted her. But Sebastian didn't know if his brother was so jealous and hateful towards him that he might kill Celeste strictly for revenge. He tightened his arm around Constantine's neck, "You think you love her, but you don't. And I don't think you would ever kill her for revenge."

Constantine choked out, "Well, there's still time to find out isn't there? You're a bigger fool than even I took you for if you think I'm incapable of killing Celeste to get back at you. But you're still the asshole I remember and if you're not with me, you are certainly against me. I'm not answering any more of your questions. You're dead, big brother! I swear if it's the last thing I do, I will kill you! You and her both! In fact, I'll kill her first, *slowly*, so you can watch, and then I'll hurt you so bad, you'll pray for death." He started laughing.

Sebastian tightened his arm even further around Constantine's neck. He fell unconscious and Sebastian let him drop to the ground hard. He turned around to check on Celeste.

"What's going on? Sebastian, is this real? Are you really here and that's...Daxton? He's your brother? *He's* Constantine? Your dead girlfriend is his dead girlfriend?" She was groggy.

Sebastian nodded, "You heard all that? How long have you been coherent?"

"Long enough, but I'm fading fast. Let's get the hell out of here please."

"I need to take care of my brother first." He turned around and pulled out his handgun. He saw in the far distance an immense wall of dust approaching their position. The window for their safe departure was coming to an end fast.

"No Sebastian! Leave him. He could've raped me, or killed me several times over, but he didn't. There's still some good in him, but if you kill him now, you'll never see it. Maybe you can be real brothers again someday. You can find a way to forgive each other and be a family again. He's all you have left."

Sebastian's finger perched on the trigger; he took aim at his brother's head. He had to yell over the wind now, "Celeste, you can't honestly be pleading for this monster's life. Not with everything he just put you through. You don't know what you're saying."

She yelled back, "I do. Jonathan was pure evil and I lived with him for years. I know how to recognize when someone's too far gone into the darkness. Your brother is not the same. I think he can still be saved. I think he wants to be. *He needs you.*"

Sebastian looked at Celeste and yelled, "I'm not so sure. He just threatened to kill both of us. I think your trusting and loving soul is getting in the way of your better judgment."

"You're better than this Bastian. Your brother is unarmed and unconscious. I've spent a lot more time with him than you have lately. You knew the person he *used* to be, I know the person he is *right now* – no matter his name. Leave him and let karma take care of him if you want some sort of revenge. But you don't want this on your conscience. Please Sebastian. Please…don't kill your own brother…not over me…" Celeste fell unconscious again.

Sebastian could do whatever he wanted now without Celeste ever knowing. He could tell her he had left his brother alive on Tiletan.

But he knew he had to get her to safety and Dr. Coldiron soon. He glanced up briefly at the wall of dust moving towards them, then back down at his little brother.

Sebastian found himself in an impossible situation. The gun was heavy in his hand, instantly it seemed to double in weight. Kill his own brother himself, or let fate take care of him like Celeste suggested. He saw him and his brother as children, playing on the beach with their parents. He remembered his mother screaming after him to take care of Constantine, to watch over him forever before she died. But her youngest son had gone down such a terrible path since they parted. And kidnapping Celeste was unforgivable. The man that was down on the ground looked like his brother, but felt like a stranger now. The harsh reality became crystal clear to him. *That man is not my brother anymore.* He closed one eye, aimed, and paused. He couldn't pull the trigger – seconds seemed to last for minutes. Celeste was in danger for as long as his brother remained alive, but she somehow couldn't see that. She didn't understand.

Constantine's body lay there, unconscious and defenseless. Sebastian took a deep breath and let it out slowly. He aimed again, steadied, and then felt the heat of a plasma bullet whirl past his head. He looked up to see five heavily armed men running towards him, and right behind them – the dust storm.

"You're lucky today Constantine, but this is far from finished," he shouted over his shoulder as he got into his transit and closed the doors. He launched and left the rest of the men firing into the air and cursing. His transit was slower than most, but it also generated its own protection field.

He watched from high above as the last bit of land was swallowed up by massive amounts of dirt. The entire world was now clouded over with it and his Pearl made a highly illegal direct ascension out of Tiletan's atmosphere.

His hands were trembling as he punched in Praxis's co-ordinates on his maps and engaged his autopilot. He looked over at Celeste and stared as she lay unconscious.

"Hold on, baby…please hold on."

He lowered his head and prayed.

SIX

>>> > CELESTE OPENED HER eyes to tiny slits. They felt heavy while her body felt light. She heard Sebastian's voice, but she couldn't figure out where she was.

"…going to be alright. Please God, grant mercy on her today. Allow her to live so that she can do good in the future for others. She's a wonderful soul wh—"

The transit rocked and Ophelia's voice came over the speakers, "Weaponry detected. Hostile interaction identified. Fighting engaged."

She heard Sebastian say, "Thanks O, figured that out. One of those assholes must've foll—"

Celeste felt a wave of cold slink over her body, and her head was pounding. Her small frame shivered. Her teeth chattered, and all she

could hear was a thundering *whoosh whoosh whoosh* in her ears. Then
there was darkness.

SEVEN

>>> > GINGER WAS SPREAD eagle, naked in a hotel bed with Ulysses
by her side. He was the most amazing lover. She loved him more than
anyone else she had ever known. He did everything just right for her.
Treated her the way she always wanted to be treated. The way she always
thought she should've been treated, but never actually had a man do.

Ulysses ran a hand over his face and wiped at his eyes. He put his
arms around her and held her close. He smelled her perfume mixed with
the smell of sex.

She looked up into his face. He smiled at her, "You know you're pretty Goddamned amazing right?"

She blushed, "I don't go around thinking that, no."

"But you are. Trust me, beautiful."

"Thank you. I think you are too."

He kissed her forehead, "I would do anything for you sweetie."

Her heart swelled with happiness. He was so reassuring. She put her
head back down on his chest.

"If anyone finds out about us at the castle, we'll both quit before anything can happen to us. We'll run away…to some other planet where
we'll be safe," he paused, "I won't let anything happen to you. I won't let
anyone hurt the woman I love."

She looked at him again. *Did he just say what I think he did?* She
stared at him, waiting for him to say something else.

He didn't.

She had to know, "What did you just say?"

He smiled, "I love you."

"I love you, have for a while, but I was afraid to say so."

"Why dear? Afraid I wouldn't say it back? I've loved you for a while too."

"Lots of reasons. But it's good to hear and good to know. Now I can
say it whenever I want."

"Yes, love. You can." He cleared his throat, "Listen, I've been wanting to make something clear. I think we've already been doing this, but I don't want to see anyone else. I'm not interested in any other woman but you. I'd like us to be exclusive."

She smiled, "I haven't seen anyone else since we started dating. I don't know of any other man that could treat me as well as you."

"So is that a yes?"

She nodded and smiled. All of her suspicions about him being a spy were gone. She couldn't feel this way about someone who would try to hurt her. He had to be the real thing.

"So what kind of magic can you do?"

"You took a lot longer than I thought you would to ask."

"I thought you'd just show me by now. I've been patient."

"If I do anything magic related, it completely drains me that's why I rarely use it."

"What can you do? Can you show me? We're already in bed if you get tired."

"Well if you want me to sleep for the rest of the time, sure."

"Come on."

"I can walk on water. I can levitate objects and there's a couple other things."

She watched as her nightgown rose off the floor by itself and did a dance in mid-air. She squealed and it dropped to the floor.

"I think that's telekinesis more than magic, don't you?" she smiled.

"You could argue that I guess, but that would imply that I'm evolving – far beyond any other Human in known history."

"Some Humans have telepathy. Telekinesis isn't that different."

"I beg to differ. It's much harder to move things with your mind than it is to speak with your mind only."

"You don't have telepathy? At all? Not even a little bit?"

"No. But I can do this."

She watched as he sat up in bed and put his hands in front of him, almost palm to palm. He snapped his fingers on one hand and she gasped when little sparks jumped from one hand to the other. Then a fireball the size of a baseball began taking shape. He cupped his hands and the fire intensified. She could feel the heat on her face; it was like an oven door just opened.

"Oh my God! That's...amazing. Jesus."

"I can throw them, make almost anything catch fire."

"Put it out! Please!"

He blew on his hands and the fireball disappeared.

She squealed again, "Oh that was incredible. I can't believe you can do that."

"I might agree with you that moving things through concentration alone is evolution but not the fireball in my hands."

"It still could be."

"No way. But there is another magical thing I can do. I just need to get my magic wand out. You want to see?"

She nodded and Ulysses rolled on top of her and kissed her. She started to giggle.

EIGHT

>>> > DAX WOKE UP to see he was lying on a couch in the facility basement lounge. He brought his hands up to his face and they were covered in dirt. He looked down over his body and saw everything on him was caked in dirt.

He tried clearing his throat, but it hurt. He ended up coughing hard instead. He went to the refrigerator to get water and saw his reflection in the mirror. One of his men had apparently tried to clean his face, but they did a half-assed job. He had huge smears of dirt across his cheeks and eyes. He coughed again and spat dirt into the trash. He grabbed a bottle of water quickly and chugged it down. Then he went to the bathroom and washed his face. The water out of the faucet was brown. Dust was everywhere.

He heard footsteps behind him as he turned off the water and grabbed a towel.

"What happened out there boss?"

Dax blinked a few times, "I was going to ask you that, Keyes."

"The alarm went off and at first I thought it meant that big ass dust storm had overpowered something. I flipped over in bed and didn't come out until about half an hour later and no one was around. I checked on our prisoner and saw she was gone…so then I knew that was probably the cause of the alarm. I couldn't find her anywhere inside, then I walked outside and the storm was over. I looked for the prisoner, but all I saw at first was Tiny…and how he was…"

Dax raised his eyebrows, "He was what?"

"Nobody told you? Geez. Why do I have to do stuff like this?"

Dax tilted his head back and forth trying to relieve the pain in his neck. It was sore from what Sebastian had done to him. "Spit it out, Keyes."

"Tiny's dead. Someone snapped his neck. It took six of us just to get him back inside. It was horrible. Tiny was my friend even though I'm a Cephian."

"Son of a *bitch!*"

Keyes flinched.

"How did I end up in here? Did you see me outside?"

Keyes nodded, "After we got Tiny in, Burtoni turned around and jogged the perimeter to see what else he could find, and that's when he saw you. We came and got you. I tried to clean you up as best I could… Then we tried to rouse you, but you wouldn't wake up. The kid said it was best to let you sleep it off, that you'd come to when you was ready."

"The kid? You mean that guy who claims to have been through medical school?"

"Yeah, him. He looked you over, checked your pulse. Said you were fine, but saw the red marks on your neck. Said something or someone must've made you lose consciousness. We figured we'd better listen to him, so we did. He was busy and stressed out with the crash victims too."

Dax made a face, "What do you mean crash victims?"

Keyes slapped his forehead, "You don't know about that neither? Oh my god! I don't want to say it!"

"*What crash victims?*"

"A couple of our guys crashed onto Tiletan during the storm. Ash says that him, Shadill, Litbo, Colburger, and Nawls came up on…that you were getting choked by some big dude and they fired at him. They missed. He got in his transit and launched as the storm started up. Colburger and Nawls jumped into Colburger's transit and I guess tried to follow the guy. I don't know if they fired on him, but maybe he fired back 'cause they crashed just after they launched but no one saw what happened because of the dust. Ash was standing right there and he said the dust storm made it impossible to see his hand in front of his eyes. The kid thinks it's a fifty-fifty chance they got shot down or their engine got clogged with dirt."

Dax coughed, "So Nawls and Colburger? Are they okay?"

"They're dead. They survived the initial crash, but the transit caught fire, and with the wind…Ash and the others was able to pull both of them out and dragged them to the kid. They was burned up real bad and the kid said they had internal bleeding. He did everything he could, but they died anyway."

"Fuck. They were good men." Dax turned around and looked at his neck in the mirror. It was starting to bruise.

Keyes asked, "Who did that to ya'?"

Dax turned off the bathroom light and patted at his slacks. Big dust clouds rose from them, "I need some time to clean up. We'll have a meeting later."

"Sure thing boss. Anything you need me to do?"

Dax shook his head, "No. Just go."

Keyes started up the stairs, then turned back, "So you do know that we lost Trembi, Ahmed, and Schlitz right?"

"Yes. I saw those men go down trying to protect me. We will honor their sacrifice…and all the others too."

Keyes went up the stairs and left Dax alone finally. He needed time to process seeing Sebastian after, what had it been – fifteen? twenty? – years.

And he took, *TOOK* Celeste Hennessy from *him!* He must've been dabbling in information brokerage or bounty work or something to have found the little cunt here. And he knew his brother could be very determined. He raked his fingers through his hair and another big dust cloud fell around him and into his eyes. He sneezed.

Jesus, he needed a shower.

He walked up the stairs to his bedroom and peeled off his clothes, leaving a dirt trail behind him.

Maybe Sebastian had been assigned to her as a bodyguard and that's how they got to know each other? Dax needed to figure this one out. It was boggling his mind too much. And for them to be interested in the same exact woman…again? It was ridiculous. All of this was starting to get ridiculous.

He turned on the water and waited for it to change from brown to clear. He stepped into the shower, and dirt washed off his body in waves. He was already starting to feel better…or at least, cleaner.

He did care about Celeste. That wasn't bullshit. He cared about her too much for this whole plan to work out the way The Hunter wanted it to. No one knew that but Dax right now, well now Sebastian *and* Celeste knew…

He would kill her to hurt Sebastian, that also wasn't bullshit, but he'd rather just have Celeste love him back and let that slowly kill his brother, one day at a time.

He would get her back. That was all he had to do…

Somehow, he'd find a way to get her back here.

NINE

>>> > IN THE MORNING in the royal gardens, Ginger was talking to Lila about Celeste's kidnapping and how worried they were. But by the time Veronica came by, the conversation had turned to Ulysses.

"What's up gals?"

Ginger smiled, "Just giving Lila all the updates about you know who."

Veronica made a face, "I'm still kinda' surprised you're dating him with his IMC involvement and all."

Lila and Ginger stared at their friend. "What do you mean V?" Ginger asked.

Veronica quickly shut her eyes and opened them again, "Please tell me I'm not the first one to tell you this?"

Lila looked from Ginger to Veronica, "V, I don't even know what you're talking about. Fess up woman."

Veronica looked at both of them, "Oh my God, you both don't know?"

They were silent.

Veronica went on in a hushed voice, "Your boy toy is part of the HRG only because he's David's right hand man in the IMC. You honestly don't know, do you?" She sighed, "David's running the IMC and has for a little while. He has Ulysses do all sorts of things for him." She looked at Ginger and waited for a response that didn't come, "I assumed you knew this stuff."

Lila asked Veronica, "Wait up. How do *you* know all this? How do you know it's true?"

"The eighth level janitor's supply room occasionally needs restocking. I was put in charge of that recently. I was in there twice now where I've accidentally overheard David yelling. But I could only hear his shouting, not normal conversation level talking…and not Ulysses's responses." Veronica looked at both of them, "I thought other staff would know about this too though. I can't be the only one."

Ginger quietly uttered, "I haven't heard any of this."

Lila shook her head at Veronica, "I don't even believe this. It sounds like a misunderstanding. V, have you verified this?"

Veronica looked at Lila sideways, "How am I supposed to do that? Ask David or Ulysses? I can't talk to them!"

Lila looked at Ginger, "It's probably not even true, about Ulysses. V's just talking out of her ass right now, or confused about what she *thought* she heard. This sounds wrong."

Ginger's brows furrowed together, "I'm not sure what to believe. The IMC is not a good group to mess around with, and if Uly's a part of that, I shouldn't even be dating him. I could get into a lot of trouble. It's a gang for Christ's sakes!"

Lila quickly grabbed Ginger's shoulder, "Shhh. Ginger, Jesus! You can't talk that loud. Go to your man. Ask him what's up."

Ginger nodded and slowly walked to her room.

When she was gone, Lila looked at Veronica and hit her on the arm. "What the hell did you go and do that for, V?"

Veronica made a face, "Why are you hitting me? I told her the truth. She needed to know what her little boyfriend is involved in. I wouldn't want to date a gang member."

Lila shook her head, "First off, it's not up to you who Ginger should or shouldn't date. You might not date him, but it doesn't mean she shouldn't. Second, you don't even know if what you're saying is the truth! It sounds like horseshit to me about Ulysses. What's wrong with you?"

Veronica's cheeks reddened, "I'm trying to protect her. Don't you want to protect Ginger? She is *your* friend too. And I do think that this is factual about Ulysses. David hates Humans. There's no good reason he'd make one a High Royal Guard unless there was something more to it, like that Human was also involved in David's life in some other way."

Lila shook her head, "I've never heard of David being the leader of the IMC. When would he have time to take care of all of that?"

Veronica started to walk away; she thought this conversation was pointless. "He just became king recently. He had all the time in the world before then…no one really seems to know what he did before he became king. It's like he appeared out of thin air."

Lila only had time to say one more thing before Veronica was gone, "You better not tell anyone else what you *think* you know. If the wrong person hears it, you could be in some serious danger!"

Lila was left alone looking at the tulips, wondering what had gotten into Veronica.

TEN

>>> > GINGER FOUND ULYSSES guarding the front of the estate. There were always two guards there, but today, Ginger didn't even pay attention to the second man.

She made a beeline for Ulysses, without bothering to be discreet, "I need to talk to you."

Ulysses glanced at the other guard and spoke in a whisper, "Could it wait Ms. Vossen?"

"No, it cannot wait *Benson*."

Ulysses's nostrils flared, "It will have to. I'm on duty for another three hours," his eyes pleaded with her.

She looked at the other guard who was looking straight ahead, completely unflinching. She sighed, "Fine."

She stormed off and Ulysses wondered what that was all about.

After his shift was over, he waited behind the estate in the royal gardens after sending her a Titan message to meet him there. He hoped the cover of night would help them to remain unseen. Ginger showed up ten minutes late.

"Honey, what's this about? You know you're not supposed to draw attention to us on the grounds."

She looked around and saw no one else in the dark. She took a deep breath before speaking quietly, "Are you in the Ice Moon Conclave?"

Ulysses stammered, "Listen…I can explain that. Wait. How did you find out?"

Ginger pointed at him, "I'm going to ask the questions, you're going to answer them. So it sounds like what you're saying is you really are in it?"

Ulysses looked at his hands, "Yes. I'm a member. Have been for a while."

Ginger shook her head, "Why didn't you tell me? That's a dangerous group."

"I wanted to tell you. I kept looking for the right time, and then things were going so well and I thought if I told you, you'd react like this…that you might not want to go out with me anymore."

"Well, you're damn right about that."

"Ginger, you can't be serious. Listen to me, I care a great deal about you. I wanted to tell you but there were things goin—"

Ginger slapped him hard across the cheek. It stunned him into silence.

"I don't want to hear anything else you have to say. You tell me you care about me and that you love me, but you've lied to me this entire time. And it was something really important! How can I trust that what you say is true? How do I know what's a lie and what's the truth?"

Ulysses looked her in the eye, "I will expl—"

Ginger cut him off again, "You're chances for explaining came and went. I don't like liars. I could've dealt with the truth if you just would've let me make that call. This way, all I see is that you keep important things from me. I can't trust you, and if I can't trust you, I can't date you. It's as simple as that."

Ulysses was upset with her and whoever had told her this, but he was more upset with himself for not telling her sooner.

Ginger stared at him, tears falling down her cheeks.

"Would you please let me explain this privately? We can meet somewhere away from here and I'll tell you everything."

She looked at him for a long time, "Is David the leader of the IMC?"

Ulysses hesitated. He hated talking about any of this on the grounds of Silver Thorn. Too many chances to be overheard. "I'll be happy to tell you all of this if you agree to meet me somewhere else."

Ginger was confused, "You know what? I don't even care. It was a simple yes or no question and you didn't answer it. You're stalling for time like you don't trust me and maybe that's the real reason why you didn't tell me this secret of yours. Forget it. We're through."

Ulysses's mouth dropped open, "You can't mean that. Please. I'll tell you, but we can't do this here. I've already said too much that can be overheard and taken back to the king. Please."

She blurted out, "You lied to me! That's all that matters. I can't trust you."

Ulysses watched her walk away with her head down. He immediately tried to send her a message through her Titan but it got rejected due to an invalid address. She blocked him already.

He knew lying to her wasn't the right choice, but to break up with him so quickly without even letting him explain, wasn't fair.

He waited three minutes after Ginger had walked in through the back door and then he walked back to his room. He would find a way to talk to her again.

CHAPTER 22

SECRETS

ONE

>>> > SEBASTIAN RUSHED CELESTE to Praxis. He was overwhelmed with guilt at the thought of enjoying himself on Foss-Altus, oblivious that she had been taken and tortured. But he was going to fix everything. He would do whatever necessary, however long it took to get Celeste healthy and get her through this so she could be happy again. He called Doctor Coldiron and asked him for help. Zach agreed to meet them outside Sebastian's apartment building and he was there as promised, as well as hundreds of reporters from all over the universe. Some over-achieving entertainment journalist uncovered Celeste's personal address on Praxis yesterday and now camps were set up in the area between her apartment building and Sebastian's.

Sebastian docked his transit and called Zach.

"What the hell is going on here?"

"I'm sorry, it wasn't this bad before."

"We need to hide Celeste. There's a customs office across from the transit station, go get a shipping crate and bring it to my docking spot."

"Be there in a jiffy."

Five minutes later, Sebastian wrapped a blanket around Celeste before he placed her in the crate; he was frightened at how light she was in his arms. Sebastian carried the crate and the doctor took Sebastian's key cards and opened the door for them.

Sebastian was much too distressed to notice Zach's reaction.

The doctor was deeply saddened to see Celeste this way. He was almost always able to emotionally distance himself from his patients, (he had to or else he'd risk being useless to them) but Celeste had endeared herself to him early on, and she had been very sweet – she didn't deserve something like this to happen to her. He'd always liked the queen and being able to help her made him feel good, but seeing her like this...broken and beaten...this was unbearable for his two Taybusian hearts.

Sebastian respectfully changed her clothes without seeing her naked in the privacy of his bedroom. He took off her dress and threw it in a bag. He might be able to find information later from her garments like traces of DNA. He put one of his softest t-shirts and a pair of boxers on her before removing her bra and underwear. His clothes were way too big for her, but it was the best he could do for now. He thought she would appreciate keeping her modesty. She didn't regain consciousness while he changed her. He wanted to wash her up, but she needed to be seen by the doctor first. Sebastian carried her into the spare bedroom and put her under the covers of the guest bed.

Zach asked a difficult question before he walked into Celeste's room, "What exactly happened? I know from the news she'd been kidnapped and I saw the evidence of the abuse from the vid's, but what the hell happened? You haven't told me anything but that you saved her."

Sebastian looked at him and hesitated on answering.

The doctor cleared his throat, "I'm only asking because it would be helpful for me to know the background on her situation. You certainly don't need to tell me everything, I ca—"

"It was Constantine...my brother."

Zach stared at Sebastian, "I beg your pardon."

"Constantine's part of the Brotherhood now and he's not some little lackey either. He's risen to a level of power within the group. I guess he started dating Celeste and convinced her he was a nice guy and then kidnapped her. They held her on Tiletan in some facility disguised as a mountain in the middle of the desert wastelands. I don't know much more than that since I need to talk to her to find out how this all happened."

Zach's mouth was hanging open, "Your brother has been dating Celeste and you didn't know it? And he's been out of your life for nineteen years. Now he pops back in as Celeste's tormentor and kidnapper? I can't believe this." He walked to Celeste's bedside and stood over her.

"Trust me, I know it sounds crazy. You should've seen me on Tiletan when I felt his mental frequency. I thought he was there to help. At least, I was hoping he was part of the galactic police or something. Then I find out he's the man Celeste started seeing."

"Well, what drove her to date someone else? I thought you were a couple," Zach looked over Celeste's face and carefully started his examination.

Sebastian shook his head, "I can tell you later, but I'll let you look at her. I've told you everything I know about her situation so far, so I'm not much help beyond those facts. I need to tell you, her foot's gone. The prosthetic. I looked for it when I rescued her but it wasn't anywhere around. I don't know what happened to it."

"Okay, I'll look her over and be with you momentarily."

Zach examined her alone while Sebastian hovered outside the door. The doctor insisted he wait outside so he could perform the examination completely and without interruption. Sebastian agreed only after the doctor pointed out that this was the best option for her. The doctor wanted the calmest possible environment. The doctor knew she could wake up confused, agitated, or terrified after what she just experienced – the less people in the room, the better.

After the doctor's examination, Zach opened the door and found Sebastian right there staring down at him.

"So?"

Zach put his two left hands on Sebastian's chest and carefully moved him from the door. He looked his friend in the eyes, "This is bad. I'm not going to lie to you. She's in very poor shape, and she's been through hell. I think she could make a ful—"

"Could?"

Zach put all four hands on Sebastian's shoulders to reassure him, "Let me finish please. I know you're worried," he paused, "she could make a full recovery, although it will take considerable time and a lot of attention…as in constant attention."

"I can handle it doc. Just tell me what to do and I'll do it. I can't stand to see her like this," he paused and swallowed hard, "Is she going to be all right?"

"To tell you the absolute truth I'm not sure yet. I need to do some more tests to address all of her needs. I'm concerned about her brain… and her mental and emotional state when she wakes up."

"Zach, what are you not telling me?" Sebastian's heart was racing. He pressed his lips into a thin line.

"Let me go over everything you need to know first." Zach walked away from him and into the kitchen where he stood with his arms folded across his chest. Sebastian was right behind him.

The doctor took a deep breath, "She's extremely dehydrated, and malnourished. It's apparent she's been beaten and tied up repeatedly. She needs X-rays, scans, and other tests that I don't have with me. I need a Human medi-nosis tool but I left that at home purely by accident this morning."

"How could you come over here WITHOUT THAT?!" Sebastian came unglued, yelling at his friend.

Dr. Coldiron did not shrink away.

Zach's words came out tight and sharp, "I'm really sorry but I left another patient in the *middle of a consultation* just to get here! I recommend you lower your voice and get your temper under control. It won't help any of us and it sure as hell isn't going to help Celeste!" He caught himself and dialed it down a notch, "She needs a calm environment right now. No yelling please. I'm doing the best I can with what I have on me, and I didn't have time to go home from the patient's home I was in. I rushed here as fast as I could. And before you ask, the medical supply stores here charge way too much for subpar equipment and it's not at all what I need for these tests. Besides that, all those are on the grid and need to be reported which you know we can't do. Remember? I'm not supposed to be treating Human or Lanyx people."

Sebastian immediately apologized and asked what he needed to do while the doctor was gone. Zach told him to stay with her, give her fluids a little at a time, and start her off with a small meal if she woke up while he was gone. The doctor would run home and return as quickly as possible with the testing equipment he needed. In the meantime, he had set her up with a slow IV drip for fluids.

Sebastian was nervous that Zach was leaving, but he couldn't take her to the hospital. Too many questions there, and he didn't want to alert the BDP of her location. He needed someone he could trust to take care of her.

"Doc, are you sure she'll be all right with me alone? What if something happens? And you still haven't told me everything. I know you're reluctant about saying something about her condition."

"I've done everything I can for now. I had to put an adult diaper on her because she might be on her period. One of her fingernails is gone and with the levels of stress she's experienced, it might be she's been hemorrhaging blood for a while. Maybe the whole time she's been held hostage. She might be low a pint or two. I'll try to order a little blood from a medical associate so we'll have it if we need it. I took blood but I won't get the results back for several more minutes. She's stable and will do better if you get a little water and iron-rich food into her as soon as possible. As far as I can tell, there's no internal bleeding or swelling to the brain, but more tests would be better. I'd rather not tell you this right now because it'll only make you worry, but there's a chance she might suffer from some sort of amnesia. I'm not sure yet though, it's just a feeling really. She's been through a lot and the mind has funny ways of dealing with traumatic episodes. Let me go so I can come back quickly and tell you for sure okay? I know you care for her a lot more than you're willing to let on. I can see it all over your face Sebastian; I'll do my best for you. I'll be right back."

"Amnesia?" he was stunned, "Okay…Thanks."

Sebastian thought about the last time she was conscious. It was before they landed the transit in his docking bay; it was only for a few seconds. Then she passed out one last time and had not woken since then. That was only twenty minutes ago. If she had amnesia, that would just add to a list of growing concerns for him. He prayed she didn't have to deal with losing her memory. Hadn't she been through enough?

He paid close attention to the clock, it took the doctor another hour and twenty minutes to return, and she still hadn't woken up. He informed the doctor that she'd been out for an hour and forty-five minutes now.

The doctor wanted to do these last tests alone with Celeste, but Sebastian insisted on being in the room.

They stood in the doorway whispering. The doctor had a hand on Sebastian's shoulder for emphasis, "I don't think this is a good idea. I can't stress that enough to you right now."

"Zach, I stayed outside the first time. I want to be with her now."

The doctor shook his head in frustration, "She might not recognize you right away…or at all."

"I've considered that. I need to be in there. I've lost too much time with her already. I can't afford anymore."

"Damn you are stubborn. Have it your way, but this might confuse her further and it's going to be hard on you as well. I don't think you're considering all that you need to right now."

Sebastian silently stared at his friend.

"Okay, well what if she asks your name? Which one do you want me to use?"

"My real one."

"Are you sure about this? Please consider how hard it may be to hear her speak like she doesn't know you."

Sebastian put his hand up to his head like he had a headache, "Let's just do this doc."

They moved into the room. The doctor stood over Celeste's body. Sebastian kept his distance, standing out of the way against the wall with his hands in the pockets of his jeans.

The doctor scanned her entire body, holding the medi-nosis over her and slowly moving it back and forth.

Medi-nosis tools replaced all sorts of medical equipment once they were invented. Small, lightweight and hand held, doctors could look inside the body more easily than ever before. And all without any radiation or having to schedule time to book a large machine.

Doctor Coldiron began a series of brain scans and confirmed there was no brain damage. Both sighed with relief, but during the final test, Celeste began to rouse. Sebastian went to hold her hand, but the doctor waved him off.

"I'm sorry, not yet."

Sebastian was anxious, but took a deep breath and stood next to Zach. Sebastian's fingers found his father's ring on his hand and started twisting it rapidly.

"Are you with us love? Celeste?" The doctor spoke softly trying not to alarm her.

She couldn't exactly open her eyes, but tried.

"Hmmm," she moved her head back and forth slowly, then winced. "I'm here, but where am I?" Her voice was gravelly and she licked her dry, cracked lips. "I'm a little…I'm sorry, I'm a bit confused."

"It's okay dear. You're in the private residence of Sebastian Raynes. You're quite safe here."

"Who am I speaking with?"

Zach looked over at Sebastian with a concerned look on his face, "My name is Doctor Zachariah Coldiron. I'm here to help you feel better. Can you answer some questions for me real quick dear?"

"Mmmm hmmm."

"What's your full name?"

"It's uh…Celeste Rosemary Vandermeer Hennessy."

"How old are you?"

"Twenty-four," she paused and slowly turned her head from side to side. She was looking for something it seemed. "Um, hey doctor, is he here? I can't see much."

Sebastian carefully put his hand over hers and smiled, "I'm right here. Nothing to worry about Celeste."

A strange look came over her face and she moved her hand away from his, "My husband, doctor. I meant my husband. Where is he? Is he here somewhere? Who was holding my hand; is there a nurse here too?"

The doctor immediately looked over to Sebastian with a grave expression. "I'm sorry Celeste, your husband?"

"Yeah, King Jonathan Hennessy? I was just with him and now I'm here." She tried to move but found it extremely difficult. She slowly ran her hand up over her arm, felt the IV, and made a pained face, "I'm…I don't understand what I'm doing here. What happened to me?"

Sebastian put his head down and covered his face with his hands. He took a deep breath in and let it out slowly.

"I apologize my Queen, but I have to explain, you and I are not the only people in this room. The man's house that we're in, Mr. Raynes, he's here as well. He was the one that held your hand. He's not a nurse. I need to speak with him for just a moment outside, but I promise to answer all your questions when I return okay?"

"Okay doctor. Thanks."

The doctor poured a small amount of water into a plastic cup, put a straw in it, and guided her hands to it, "Be careful with your arm because of the IV, but you need more fluids. Here's a small cup of water. I'd like for you to sip it slowly, even though you're going to want to swallow it down fast okay?"

She took it, "Okay."

Sebastian and Zach stepped out of the guest bedroom and shut the door behind them.

Sebastian opened his eyes wide at the doctor and whispered forcefully, "What the hell is going on with her? She thinks her husband's alive?!" He ran his hands through his hair, one after the other, "I thought you said she was going to have amnesia and forget who she was or maybe me. Why does she think that asshole's alive again?!"

Zach walked into the living room and Sebastian followed. The doctor walked to the staircase railing and leaned his back against it.

"Damn it Zach just tell me."

The doctor rubbed his head, "Sebastian, you really need to check your anger right now. It's not helping anyone, and this is the second time I'm telling you this. You're my friend but Celeste is my first priority right now."

Sebastian said nothing but nodded.

"She doesn't have any brain injuries – that's very good news. The bad news is that she does have amnesia, and the tricky thing about amnesia is that it's different for every being it affects." He let out a long sigh, "We need to find out what her last memory is of."

"Well it's obviously before her husband got aced."

The doctor ignored that. "My best guess is that she's suffering from something called dissociative amnesia. That means a certain situation, her kidnapping and abuse, has caused her to block out all the stressful things that have happened to her lately. Instead of just going back before the kidnapping though, she's gone back to before her husband was murdered...and before she ever met you. Maybe the king's assassination took more of a toll then we originally thought...on her brain at least."

Sebastian looked puzzled, "I don't understand. She was happy that Jonathan was dead. She told me so several times and expressed great guilt over the fact she felt that way. She thought she was a bad person for not mourning him and feeling glad that her own husband had died. Her brain's lumping his assassination in with being kidnapped?"

"She might very well be joyous at the fact that the king's dead, but she was still right in front of him when he was violently killed. If she's never seen anything like that happen before, that's damn traumatic."

They both stood in silence.

"Well, what am I supposed to do now?" Sebastian was in disbelief at the thought of her not knowing him at all, and believing her prick of a husband was still alive.

"I need to ask her some more questions, find out her last memory, but I won't tell her of the king's assassination. You're a positive influence on jogging her memory and I'm sure she already formed many good memories of you during your time together. I'll let you tell her everything and I

363

do mean *everything*. Whatever she wants to know, you tell her the truth," his tongue darted out and quickly licked each of his eyeballs, "The more she knows, the better, but you can't tell her everything all at once. Tell her over several days, or weeks even, a little bit at a time."

"Weeks?!"

"As long as it takes. Use your discretion. Since this is so different for everyone, she might recover her memory in hours, although, it could take months as well. But I have to warn you," he cleared his throat, "Sometimes the patient never recovers their buried memories."

Zach watched as Sebastian started pacing. He'd never seen him do that before. Zach wished there was more he could do to help Celeste, but no medical advancement had been able to cure something so utterly random and complicated as amnesia. He watched Sebastian let out some long exhales and then he stopped pacing and stood there, his back facing the doctor. He stood with his arms folded behind his back, but Zach knew Sebastian was very upset.

"I know this is not what you want to hear, but it's the truth. I'm sorry Sebastian. This will be difficult on you, but I'll answer all your questions and help you as much as I can. Right now, she's got bruises, and lacerations everywhere, plus those swollen eyes. Those will all heal within weeks; it's the memory part I'm not sure of. Physically she'll make a full recovery; it will just take a lot of time," Zach sighed, "I can regrow her foot and I've already taken a small sample of her blood. That's really all I need to do it, and some time. I've never done it before and I'm not sure how I'm going to explain it to my wives. I don't even know where to grow it on me. Never mind that, I'll figure it out. But it will get done, I promise. Do you know how she lost it?"

"No. Maybe I could ask her later."

"No worries. It'll get fixed."

Sebastian said without turning around, "Thank you for dropping everything and coming over here to help me and Celeste. I really appreciate it. You have no idea how much your help means to me."

"Raynes, you know you're more than a client of mine, you're a good friend, and I will always do what I can to help," he paused a long time, "It's terrible what your brother and the BDP did to her."

Sebastian stayed where he was, "It's unforgivable. It won't go unpunished." He turned his head so Zach could only see his profile, "The people responsible for this, including Constantine? They took a piece of my Celeste away from me. A piece I might never get back now. She and I… we built some wonderful memories together…were building memories anyway. Now, what do we have? I'm a stranger to her…all over again. We're back at zero."

The doctor looked out the windows at the blue sky, "You're worried she won't fall in love with you again?"

That made Sebastian turn around and face the doctor, "Again?"

"Yes, again. You guys? You seem right together, to me at least. I think she's already in love, or at least she was before this kidnapping happened. And you going off like this on your own without any back up to rescue her? That tells me all I need to know about how close you two have become since the first time I met her." Zach smiled, "You lovebirds think you've got some secret together. You're not fooling anyone, not with the way you were looking at each other when I came over to treat your flu. She fell in love with you, I think, but that's just my opinion, what do I know? Anyway, she fell for you once, she'll do it again. That's what I think."

Sebastian smiled, "Thanks doc. I just want her to be okay…healed… and safe. Back to her old self, with all of her memories, even the bad ones I left her with."

Zach looked confused, "What do you mean?"

Sebastian sighed and ran his hand through his hair, "Remember how you asked why she was dating someone else? I…told her I never wanted to see her again. That we couldn't date."

"WHAT?! Sebastian what were you thinking?!"

"I wasn't thinking. I…don't know. I messed up, but I was going to fix it, and then all of this happened."

"Oh."

"I wrote her some emails and I told her I wanted to start over with her as friends."

"So that's how all of this happened with her dating someone else?"

"Well, I had sensed she had another man on her mind when I was sick, but I didn't know who it was and Constantine used a false name with her. She had no idea it was my brother. All along I've been telling her I couldn't date her and I've never asked her out, so when someone else did, she went. I can't blame her I guess. I didn't make it easy on her, but I thought it would be better to develop our friendship first."

"You know she doesn't want just a friendship with you right? I think it's quite plain what kind of relationship she wants."

"Yes. I know. I wanted to take this slower than what she wanted. If I started dating Celeste then it'd be the first girlfriend I've had since…for a very long time. It's a big step."

"Technically, none of my business again, but you need to do whatever it takes to get her back. Even if her memory doesn't come back – you need to win her over, all over again."

"She's lost a lot of good memories between us. It'd be a shame if she couldn't get them back."

They both stood quietly for a moment. The doctor's tail swayed back and forth slowly. Sebastian could hear it as it pulled the fabric of Zach's white overcoat.

Zach came up to Sebastian and spoke quietly, "Are you sure you want to take on being her nurse? It's going to take a lot of work, and it'll be extremely difficult."

Sebastian nodded, "If I have questions about anything I'll call you, but I can do this." He rubbed the back of his neck with his hand, "We can't stay here though; we're too vulnerable at this apartment…and all those vultures outside. There's a threat to both Celeste and I from her kidnappers…from Constantine. We can't stay here for months waiting for her to regain her memory. I don't know where to take her on such short notice," he paused, "I could take her out to my island I guess. I'm not sure that's far enough. Maybe we should leave Praxis all together. I know my place on Ishikawa is way too small for the both of us though."

The doctor put his two right hands on Sebastian's shoulder, "Listen, if you really need to get out of here, I think I can help with that."

Sebastian raised his eyebrows, "How?"

"I've been crazy busy lately. I haven't had much chance to use my beach house on Bahsheef and it's secluded there. Might be good for the both of you and *no one* would know you're there."

He took an entry key card out of his pocket and handed it to Sebastian.

"I can't take this Zach. This is your vacation house? No, that's too much." He tried to give it back.

"I'll visit the both of you, to check on her and I can take a look at the place while I'm there. I haven't seen it in a while, but I'm sure you'll put it to good use. It's huge – five stories, plus a basement. More than enough room for you both to stretch out, have privacy and you can get reacquainted. Besides, it has wonderful views of the ocean. It's beautiful there. Should be very therapeutic…for you both, actually. I trust you with it, and I think Celeste is a lovely woman who's been through a very difficult situation. Listen, I understand you don't like asking for help, I get it, but think of her. She needs all the help she can get. Do it for Celeste's sake."

Sebastian kept the card and acquiesced, "Okay doc. I'll owe you some very big favors after all this is through. I can't thank you enough. When can I move her?"

"That's difficult to say. Use your best judgment, but when she can get up and walk around a little, I think it'd be okay. Even if you have to carry her out, as long as she's regained a little strength, but certainly not within the next two days all right? Her hemoglobin is shockingly low. That means she's lost a lot of blood and her body can't replace it fast enough. I brought three pints of blood so I'll start a separate IV for the transfusion. I'll give her progesterone and that will stop her menstrual bleeding. Her body should be able to regulate her period again now that the stress of the kidnapping is over."

"Whatever you say doc."

"Now, I'm going to go back to her and I'll let you know when you can go in."

Sebastian's mind raced. He moved into action and went to his bedroom to reload his go bag.

When Zach came out of the spare bedroom, Sebastian had enough time to pack for a month.

"You can go in soon, but you and I have a lot to discuss about her care and medications. I'll check on you guys a week from now. I'm going to guess you'll be long gone from here?"

Sebastian nodded, "We'll leave as soon as possible, so two days from now, maybe three. I'll do it in the middle of the night; in fact, I'm already prepared to spend a month away right now."

The doctor left Sebastian with some strong painkillers, aspirin, ten days' worth of progesterone tablets, smelling salts, a cane for her to use once she could walk, and sedatives with specific instructions. He made sure Sebastian understood all of his recommendations and warning signs to look for, in case she took a turn for the worse.

After Zach left, Sebastian felt fear rise up in him thinking of the conversation he was about to have with Celeste. This was not going to be easy. The doctor had told Sebastian of what he had said to her. Telling her she'd been kidnapped, but she was in a safe place now, the extent of her injuries and that Mr. Raynes would be taking care of her for as long as she was ill. He told her of her amnesia and that Mr. Raynes would fill in more blanks. Zach had left the most difficult things for Sebastian to say.

TWO

>>> > SEBASTIAN TOOK A deep breath and opened Celeste's door. It was hard to look at her. The damage his brother had done might be catastrophic if it caused her to lose part of her memory permanently.

Sebastian sat in the chair next to the bed and looked at her swollen, bruised face. Butterfly sutures dotted her forehead and cheek. He felt utterly powerless.

"Mr. Raynes I presume?" Celeste could not see, but she turned her face to where he was sitting.

"Yes. What did the doctor tell you about me?"

"Just that this was a safe place for me since I was kidnapped recently and that you'd be taking care of me. I'm a bit confused though, where's my husband? Or...did he have something to do with my kidnapping?"

"No, King Hennessy didn't do that to you. I've...never been in this position before your Highness, please forgive me. I need to tell you, your husband was assassinated."

He looked for any expression on her face, but saw none. His 7's were useless right now – her mind was simply blank.

She whispered, "The king is dead? Are you sure?"

"Oh I'm quite positive your Highness. And you don't have to worry. You can speak freely here, you don't need to whisper."

She cleared her throat, but only spoke a little louder, "How? When?"

"He was killed with a Shadow Walker 3 Rifle with a suppressor on it. A single shot to the head did not kill him immediately, but he died a little while later. The authorities have no idea who did it."

"So how do you know what weapon was used then?"

"I know…because I was the assassin who killed him," he paused waiting for a reaction, but got none. "Your Highness did you hear me?"

She sat still, "Yes…am I in some kind of trouble here? Are you going to kill me now?"

Sebastian put his hand to his head, "No my lady. Your husband was my only target, it wasn't personal. You were never in any danger. I'm sure you're not going to believe this, but you're quite safe with me I promise. This happened almost three months ago, Earth time…And we spent a lot of that time together. About two months."

She was speaking cautiously now, "You said this happened months ago? So what have I been doing since the death of the king?"

"Almost immediately after I shot him, you ran up to me asking for assistance escaping the kingdom. I was hesitant, but I ended up taking you with me to my home on Praxis."

"So you're Lanyx?"

"Yes."

"Where are we now, Praxis?"

"Yes, this is my home world."

"I asked for your help to escape? That sounds like me. So you must've helped me do more than just disappear if we've known each other a few months."

"Yes, you stayed here with me for a while and then you returned to Earth to speak with the authorities there."

"Oh God, did I pay you to kill him for me?!"

"No, you didn't. Someone else ordered the hit, but you ran away right after the king was killed. I advised you to go back to Earth to clear up any confusion, answer police questions. You did that. Now you're the Queen Dowager of Earth and Il'laceier. You came back and told me you settled all your Earthly affairs, and had visited your parents."

She flinched, "Their mausoleum."

"Yes. And your old house. You said the land had been cleared and it was going to have something else built over it. You expressed interest in finding out what really happened to your parents. You weren't sure if Jon did something to them or even if they really died. I was looking into it for you without success until your kidnapping. I'm going to resume it now that I've found you and I know you're safe."

"I haven't mentioned my thoughts about my parents to anyone else, so now I know you're telling the truth...you did know me before. And I'd really appreciate the information Mr. Raynes. I need to know whether they're alive or not."

"Please call me Sebastian."

"Okay. I'm still confused as to why you're taking care of me. You said my husband was killed three months ago and I asked you to help me escape the kingdom so...why am I here again? At your house and not at a hospital?"

"I rescued you from kidnappers. They're dangerous people and they're still a major threat. They caused you to lose your living prosthetic...somehow. When I rescued you it was gone."

Celeste immediately folded up her right leg and felt for her foot, but it wasn't there.

Sebastian continued, "I shot down one of their transits when we left Tiletan. They were trying to follow us off planet. No one's been arrested, so they're still out there. And the main kidnapper, he's a man who calls himself Daxton. He's my brother. And his real name is Constantine, he changed it."

"What?" She straightened out her leg.

"I don't understand it myself, but my brother kidnapped you. Maybe not directly, but he is a part of it. Apparently, you two were dating. If you remembered any of what happened, you'd be able to fill in the blanks for me, but neither one of us knows unless you recover your memory. I haven't spoken to my brother for almost twenty years until today when I rescued you, so…I don't know exactly how it all happened your Highness."

"Why are you calling me your Highness? Did Silver Thorn award me full power?"

"No, I'm sorry to say Jon's brother David has taken control of the kingdom."

"But you keep calling me by my royal title and if I'm no longer a real queen then…?"

"It's a habit, and out of respect. Sometimes I call you my lady, sometimes Celeste. And you've always been a 'real' queen and always will be. It's true you've never had kingdom power levels but you are very powerful with your people. They love you. You should've seen all the vigils, prayers, and outpouring of universe-wide support for your safe return. It amazed me."

"So…you rescued me, twice. Sounds like we're…Are we friends or dating or something?"

He swallowed hard, "We're friends, but…"

"But what Mr. Raynes?"

"But our relationship or friendship is complicated. We were just getting to know each other when this happened and…before…we couldn't agree on some things, but I think our timing was off. You wanted to move faster than I was ready to…"

"I wanted to?"

"Yes you wanted to move forward and I wanted to go slow. So yes, we're certainly friends, but not technically dating. We've become close over the past few months and I was distraught when you went missing. I killed several of your kidnappers while rescuing you."

She sat silently.

He didn't know what to say and her mind was a blank, even though he tried to sense her several times, he couldn't get anything.

"Would you mind coming closer to me, I mean really close? I can barely see anything."

He moved in closer to her.

She put her hands out to him, "Will you please put my hands on your face?"

He did so and she pulled him a little closer until she could finally see him. Their faces were inches apart.

"It seems like I meant something to you…I know I must've with everything you've done for me, but I just can't remember you. I'm sorry."

She let go of him and he walked to the door.

"I think it's time I got you something to eat okay? Just relax."

"Thank you."

He left the room and went to the kitchen. He stood in front of the refrigerator and rubbed his face with his hands as a painful knot grew in his throat. The doctor was right, this was going to be extremely hard to deal with. His mind flashed from memory to memory. The first time he saw her eyes, their first kiss, the time on the Stargazer, Scarlette Island, all of it gone. None of it existed for her – never happened at all.

He cursed his brother.

THREE

>>> > SEBASTIAN GAVE CELESTE a full glass of water with a small meal. After lunch, she agreed to let him clean her up a little. He took a soft washcloth and wiped down as much of her as he could without hurting or embarrassing her. She smelled terrible, but she wasn't ready for a bath or shower just yet, not on her own. He needed to make sure she was steady enough before anything like showering by herself was allowed.

He was so worried; he was almost always in her room. She was in and out of consciousness, but he wouldn't leave her side for longer than a few minutes.

"I feel like I'm half dead. No, scratch that, three quarters dead." She hated that she couldn't see since her eyes were so swollen, and she felt vulnerable without knowing exactly where she was.

Sebastian's brows furrowed. He wished there was more he could do for her. "I'm right here your Highness. Is there anything you need?"

"Mr. Raynes? I'm sorry I'm a bit mixed up right now. I can't seem to get a grip on things. Everything feels foggy."

"Call me Sebastian please. Your kidnappers drugged you a lot so your confusion should ease up soon. You were in bad shape but the doctor says you'll recover. Just try to relax. Lay back and know nothing bad will happen now that you're here okay?"

"Okay. I wanted to tha..." She went out of it again and Sebastian stayed by her side, anger boiling up inside of him over how much she was suffering. He tried to stay calm for her sake. Just to keep the atmosphere of the apartment peaceful.

He picked a book from one of his many bookshelves and sat by her bedside for the first two nights reading. He gave her the painkillers the doctor prescribed, but those knocked her out for hours at a time. Zach said rest was the best thing for her body right now, so Sebastian didn't worry about the amount she was sleeping.

FOUR

>>> > THE ENTIRE TILETAN branch was present whether it be on a Titan screen or in person and all eyes were on Dax.

He looked over them and wished he didn't have to be giving this talk right now, but here he was regardless.

"From what I've gathered through questioning and video surveillance, it looks like Tiny took our hostage out of her cell. He dragged Celeste outside; I think he wanted to rape her. Tiny knew how far the cameras could see and took Celeste way beyond visual range.

"Someone broke Tiny's neck. I don't think it was Celeste, although I can't rule it out completely. I think she had some help. I think someone came to her aid and took her right before that damn dust storm hit. A few of us saw this man and took shots at him, but we were unable to stop him. Maybe he's a bounty hunter."

One of the men on the screens asked, "How did he find us? I thought we hid her very well on Tiletan."

Dax nodded, "That's a damn fine question to be asking. I don't have an answer for it right now, but I'm working on it.

"What I really want to say, is that the universe still needs to believe that we have possession of Celeste Hennessy. What we need to do is wait and see if she goes public with her escape. I think she might go into hiding without telling anyone anything. That's what I would do if I was her, but maybe she goes to some hospital or someone that spreads the word. So...we wait a few more days, see if anything comes up on the news. If not, we perpetuate the idea that she continues to be our hostage. Maybe we can still get money out of King Hennessy."

A Lassandros man in the front row spoke up, "That would be a major con."

Dax nodded, "Yes it would. Now, we can't tell anyone about this, not even The Hunter. I need him in a certain place, and tell him when I'm ready. I first need to see all the angles, see how we can play this, come up with a game plan and then go to him...So nobody tell him okay? Is this understood?"

The room agreed.

Dax smiled, "Okay, great. If anyone has any further questions, or concerns just see me privately...if not then, meeting's over. Dismissed. Get back to work."

FIVE

>>> > MITCH AND D'ARTAGNAN met up for coffee before the FAIR meeting.

"I think I'm being followed."

D'Artagnan studied Mitch, then looked around.

Mitch shook his head, "They aren't here today. They've come around on and off again, but it's always the same transit and they space it out where it might be every other day, or every three days or so. I need to do something about it."

"You think it's because of the HR or is there something else that could be causing it?"

Mitch hesitated, "I'm sure it's the HR, but that doesn't narrow down who it could be. The Il'lacean King, the BDP maybe...hell maybe it's the IMC for all I know."

"Or the Earth police," D'Artagnan added.

"Yeah."

"What do you plan on doing about it?"

"I need to lose them permanently. That means I have to disappear. Maybe go to my second home. I have one on Praxis now," Mitch sipped his coffee, "I can't think of anything else."

"I know Praxis very well. It's a beautiful place," D'Artagnan inhaled deep. He loved the smell of Human coffee. It was something they didn't have on Il'laceier.

"I know what you're thinking."

"Oh? You do? What's that?"

"You're thinking I should eliminate the threat...or confront them. And that it's a hell of a long way to travel for meetings from Praxis to here."

D'Artagnan smiled, "Well, that much is true. It's far, but the elimination part, that's all on you. *That* is some serious shit to get into. Plus, it depends on who it is. You don't want to murder some cop."

"True. That would ruin my life. I can't have that," Mitch's face clouded with uneasiness.

D'Artagnan finished his last bit of coffee and advised, "You need to find out who is following you."

"Yeah. How?"

"You need to follow them after they're done following you."

Mitch laughed, "How am I supposed to do that?"

"It's not easy," D'Artagnan sighed, "I suppose if you could at least get a tracking number on their transit or some pictures of these guys, I could ask around. See who they are."

"I'll try."

"It's better not to let on that you know you're being followed and you definitely don't want them to know you're trying to identify them. The more discreet the better."

"Goes without saying."

SIX

>>> > DAVID WAS UNHAPPY with the speed of Rem Mot Om's rebuild. He demanded fifty more people join the construction crew, even though the foreman told him that wasn't the problem.

"The problem is the robotics we aren't using. Usually these handle all the heavy lifting, complex calculations, and very delicate, precise placement of materials."

"This is my home. I choose who does the work and I don't trust robots. Get more men!"

"Yes my King." The foreman ordered fifty more men to come down and stand around, because there wasn't anything to do.

With robots this job would've taken two weeks maximum, without them, it was going to take two Earth months. Maybe, the foreman thought, robots could be used at night when no one was awake. He thought that might speed up the process a little.

CHAPTER 23

ZANE

ONE

>>> > "SO, WHAT WE'RE going to have to do is raise money to buy a safe place to meet. I'm trying to look around and see what's available, but it might end up being on some other planet."

A few FAIR members immediately raised their hands, one of them was Alanna.

"Yes Alanna?"

She stood up, "Well, maybe Praxis would be a good place? I live there and it's similar to Earth, and they're neutral on this. I'm not sure anyone would think to look for us there."

Mitch nodded, "Yes. That is one of the planets I'm considering. Thank you for the suggestion." He smiled at her and Alanna smiled widely back.

The rest of the meeting, Mitch was distracted by thinking about that smile she gave him.

After the meeting, the members quickly shuffled out, probably upset at the idea of having to come up with some of their own money, but Mitch explained he would put up half of his own.

Mitch gathered his things and saw Alanna waiting for him by the door, "Hey."

"I wanted to say I think it's generous to put up your own coren. I don't know who else would've done something like that."

Mitch blushed, "Oh well, I'm the leader right? I have to do things as an example for all of us and I don't know how much money this will take. I have to offer up stuff like that."

"I don't think you *have* to, but it's nice of you."

"That was good thinking on your part...about Praxis, I mean. I think that might end up being our final choice."

She shrugged her shoulders, "I see lots of spaces I think we could use. It's a nice planet and the Lanyx are awesome."

Mitch held the door open for her and let her walk out first. "Oh geez, I forgot something I have to settle here before I leave. Would you mind if we finished this conversation next time?"

Alanna shook her head, "Oh? Okay, sure. Have a good evening."

Mitch didn't want whoever was tailing him to see them together. He liked Alanna's attention, but didn't want her to be put in harm's way.

TWO

>>> > D'ARTAGNAN LOVED to cook and always looked for new ways to improve his skills. He had been going to a cooking class for several weeks and enjoyed it, but FAIR was starting to take up a lot of his time. He considered ditching the class, but tonight, he'd go once more to learn chicken black flower and mashed berga root since he hadn't found a recipe for it he liked yet.

When he arrived, there was a woman student at the front of the class. D'Artagnan was only aware of her because she was new and he made a point to look over everyone who was in close proximity to him at all times.

Class went well. He thought his mashed berga root could've been a little sweeter but it was difficult to master.

As he was packing up, the new woman approached him.

"Hey, you're name's Zane right?"

D'Artagnan nodded.

"You made the mashed berga root. That was really good."

"Thanks. You made the heptite pudding. I thought your presentation of it was beautiful."

The woman blushed, "Thanks. I try," she cracked her knuckles, "Oh, my name's Sorheed. I'm new in town, thought I needed to get out and make some new friends."

"Sorheed…I haven't heard that name in a while. Seems like a lot of Il'lacean parents have been using Earth English names for a couple decades now."

She nodded, "My parents were definitely traditionalists, blood to bone."

D'Artagnan bowed to her, as is customary when meeting a new Il'lacean, "So where did you move from?"

"The Lakes Regions. Needed a change."

"Ohhh that's a gorgeous part of Il'laceier. I'm surprised you left it."

"Well, you know…" She hesitated, "Look, I noticed you and thought you looked…interesting. You wanna get some tea and continue this conversation elsewhere?"

D'Artagnan thought. He heard Eric's words in his head about dating, then he thought about discovering Linda's lies. He didn't know if he was ready, but it was just a cup of tea. "Okay. Sure. You want to do this right now?"

"No, I mean, we don't have to. Tomorrow night maybe?"

D'Artagnan looked at his Titan's calendar, "Okay. Eight at the Jessium Krop?"

She nodded, "I'm looking forward to it."

He watched her walk away. She was kind of cute with her sly smile and bold yellow eyes. She had a trim tight figure, maybe a foot under his own height. She looked graceful as she left. He thought, *we'll see what happens.*

THREE

TITAN Corporation - Personal TITAN Device

System Status: Active -- Universal Grid: Online

Current Time/Date (Il'laceier - Rem Mot Om): 20th Knoche/ Newai 81-87 5390

Secondary Time/Date (Earth - London, England): 8:56 p.m./ September 1, 4015

Current Universal Positioning System Location: QetQert Regions, Il'laceier

User: King David Hennessy

Communications Menu

Incoming message(s) received: 1 - Status: Unread

Message Received at 20th Knoche

Message Sent from: Universal News Agency (UNA) - Il'laceier Region

-UNA
- Pirchi Colony, QetQert Regions, Il'laceier
BREAKING NEWS
King David Hennessy has issued a statement regarding the kidnapping of Queen Dowager Celeste Hennessy and her captors, the Brotherhood of Desert Phantoms.
"I believe I speak for not just my own two worlds, but for the entire universe when I say I am deeply saddened and concerned by the recent actions of the Brotherhood of Desert Phantoms.

For too long has this terrorist group gone unchecked and been allowed to cause panic and havoc throughout the universe. It is long overdue, but someone needs to stop them. Someone needs to bring them to justice and have them stand accountable for all the damage and criminal activities they've done over several centuries.

I believe I am that man.

With the full power of the Earth police, the combined Kingdom High Royal Guards at Silver Thorn and Rem Mot Om, and the police authority on Il'laceier, we will track down members and leader alike of the BDP and bring them to justice.

The BDP have always been a threat to each and every being of every single world across the universe, but the kidnapping of Queen Dowager Hennessy has been my final breaking point. To anyone who is a member of the BDP, I encourage you to turn yourself in to the closest authority on your current planet. To anyone who wants to give my reign information about a suspected member please contact the number posted below or send a Titan message to your local authority.

And to the leader of the BDP, your time is up. I will not rest until I have found you.

Thank you."

BDP information hotline #04587-9987-23-20068

You can trust UNA for all your universal news needs.

-END OF MESSAGE

* This message will auto-delete in 32 knoches upon viewing.

FOUR

>>> > CELESTE WOKE UP in the morning with a start. Mr. Raynes slept in the chair next to her with a book on his chest.

She had no idea what day it was – maybe it had been three days since she arrived here; but she was regaining her ability to remember current events clearly. She was in the spare bedroom of Mr. Raynes's place in a comfortable bed and the sun was up. Her head hurt badly and she wanted a painkiller. She thought there might be a mirror on the wall in front of her, but she couldn't see that far, and she didn't think she was ready to see what she looked like. She could see spots of color all over the room, but she wasn't sure what they were. The vague smell of flowers was her only clue, so she guessed the color spots were roses.

She remembered Mr. Raynes told her they were friends but also, at least to some degree, dating before she lost her memory. If these were indeed flowers all over this room for her, then he must've cared for her a great deal. When she had held his face close to hers and finally saw him, the first thing that popped into her head, was that he was a very attractive man, but she couldn't remember anything about him. She'd never seen him before in her life.

She tried to sit up, but her stomach hurt so bad it was difficult. She let out a little groan struggling and that woke Sebastian up.

"Celeste, don't press yourself too hard to move. You've got bruises all over and you're weak. Let me help you." He took the book off his chest and put it on the ground next to his chair.

She waved him off, "Thanks Mr. Raynes, but I'll do it. I'm getting stronger all the time. I've got to do some things on my own. Besides, I stopped bleeding yesterday and the blood transfusion seems to have helped a lot. I have more energy than I did a little while ago."

His feelings were hurt, but he had to remember, she didn't know him anymore. He watched her struggle to prop herself up. This was killing him – the woman that changed his life, couldn't remember him at all. She had no idea of the impact she had on him. How was he supposed to deal with this?

"Please call me Sebastian, my lady." He sat up and rubbed his face, then leaned forward with his elbows resting on his thighs. He clasped his hands and held them under his chin.

"All right – Sebastian."

"How are you feeling today? You think you could walk?"

She paused, "I think I'm doing much better than a few days ago, but I still feel like complete hell. I think I could walk a little, sure. Maybe I could take a bath today too."

He sighed, "It pains me to tell you this, but we're going to have to move tonight to another location."

"Why? I was told this place was safe. Of course, I was originally told I was safe with you and then you tell me you're an assassin, so I really don't know what to believe."

"Please Celeste believe me, I'm not going to hurt you, nor do I ever want to. This is a safe place for the most part, but the people that kidnapped you have made threats against you, actually, both of us. The doctor has given us use of his vacation home on Bahsheef. No one would ever figure out we were there and I think it's the safest place for us. I was waiting until you regained some of your strength. When we go, essentials of yours will be with you, so don't worry. I've ordered some extra things that I think you'll need. I'll move you tonight when it's safest. I hope you don't mind, but I'll have to carry you down to my transit. You're not strong enough to make it on your own yet, and your foot…"

"That's fine, I mean, I don't really have a choice I guess." She slowly raised up her arm to scratch the back of her head. "All of this is so strange. You talk to me like you know me well, and you're comfortable with me, but I try to remember…and I can't. All I want to do is remember what happened to me. I have so many questions."

"Listen your Highness, we have a lot of questions to answer between the two of us, and a lot of talking to do, but we don't have to do it all at once here. Being in an isolated place like Bahsheef will be a good way for you to heal without worrying about your kidnappers and will give us plenty of time to talk. I'll prove to you that I have your best interests as my top priority." He leaned back in his chair.

"I'm sure this must be difficult for you if we knew each other before, but to me – we're strangers. You seem okay, but I need to get to know you before I can trust you. I'm in a lot of pain and pretty confused. I hate knowing I've lost all of this time. I hope you can understand things from my perspective."

He nodded looking at her, "Yes, absolutely Celeste." He rubbed his eyes and took a deep breath in. "I'm going to kill every last bastard in the BDP. I swear to you. They did this and I was too late to stop it. I was worried about you after I found out what happened…and when I finally found you…relieved isn't even the right word."

She thought he sounded sincere. She found herself wanting to believe and trust him.

He cleared his throat, "I'm going to make you some breakfast. I'll be right back."

After he left, she sat up cautiously and put her foot and stump down on the floor. She stood up and put weight on it. She thought if she moved carefully, she could walk on her own. She slowly felt her way across the room. She needed to use the bathroom but when she turned on the lights in there, the bright shine was painful to her eyes. While she was up close, she could see yellow roses in a vase on the bathroom counter. They smelled wonderful and made her feel a little bit better.

As she washed her hands, she summoned the courage to look at herself in the mirror.

Her hair was messy and knotted all over. She had bruises everywhere, her lips were cracked and dry, but worst of all (and what really scared her) were how bad her eyes looked. She now understood why it was difficult for her to see through them. They were *so* swollen and different shades of red, blue, brown, and green. Jonathan had hit her several times across the mouth, some slapping, a few punches to the stomach and face, but usually it was one strike or two and then he'd stop. Only occasionally did his violence surpass that. It was nothing like what she had apparently received during her kidnapping. She looked terrible. She started crying wondering if she'd look the same after all the swelling went down.

Sebastian knocked on the door, "You're not using the cane. Are you okay?"

She opened the door and he saw tears trailing down her face.

"What if I don't the look the same? Is my face going to be okay after this swelling goes down? Did the doctor say anything?"

Sebastian wanted to cradle her in his arms but he knew he couldn't. It made his heart ache. He could only try to comfort her with words, "The doctor assured me there was no permanent internal damage. You're a lucky woman, it could've been much worse. I'm sure you'll be just as beautiful after you heal as you were before. Come on, let's get you to bed."

She asked through her tears, "Those roses in the bathroom. Are they for me?"

"I know you can't see very well, but yes and there are more around the room. I thought they might cheer you up a little."

"Thanks, that was nice of you." She put her arms around him feeling weakness growing in her legs. He lightly put his arms around her waist, helping her to keep her balance. The embrace only lasted a couple of seconds before she started moving again.

He helped her into bed and told her he'd be back with breakfast.

He made her a spinach omelet, a piece of toast and gave her a cup of green tea. She ate slowly but finished it all while Sebastian sat next to her bed reading.

"I know you don't remember this but you have,"—he corrected himself—"*had* your own apartment across the street. You're not going to be able to go back there because an army of reporters is outside the lobby. I'll go over there and collect your things to bring over late at night before we leave. I'll buy your apartment and put it under one of my new aliases. And please, if you're going to walk, use the cane the doctor left for you."

"I had an apartment here? I must've really liked this planet."

FIVE

>>> > WHEN SEBASTIAN WALKED into Celeste's apartment, he knew someone had been there. He looked around and although everything looked okay, things were slightly out of place. He did a quick check

for surveillance devices but found none. It hadn't been a robbery since nothing was missing, but it got under his skin. It could've been the Brotherhood, David, a reporter, it could've been a lot of people. But for now, all he could do was move as quickly as possible and get back to Celeste. He cleaned out her apartment of as much portable stuff as he could, and he smiled when he saw his borrowed jacket at the back of her closet on a hanger. He had loaned it to her that night at the casino and she had kept it all this time. He hadn't forgotten about it, but he never asked for it back. It was nice she had something of his all the time they had been apart.

Celeste insisted on cleaning herself in a hot bath before they left his apartment.

"I just…am nervous about it."

"I stink! I want to feel Human again and this will help me feel better."

Sebastian sighed, "You could fall, you're still weak."

"What kind of tub is it?"

"It's a built-in shower/tub combo…but there aren't any safety bars in there or anything."

"Will you let me take a bath if you're in there with me?"

Sebastian raised his eyebrows and smiled, "That can't have been an invitation."

She blushed, "I meant if you're in the bedroom and I have the bathroom door open."

He thought, "What if…I wear a blindfold or close my eyes really tight? Then I could be in the bathroom with you and if you needed help to get into the tub, which I'm worried about most, or out of it then I'll be there in case you fall."

It was her turn to think, "You promise me you won't look at me naked?"

It was his turn to blush, "My biggest concern is your safety. The last thing we need is for you to fall. I can't handle anything else happening to you."

She smiled, "That sounded sincere, but it didn't answer my question."

"I promise I won't look."

"Okay. Let's get me clean please."

Celeste had a black scarf in a box he brought over from her place and she tied it around his head. She got very close to him to make sure he couldn't see her, but since she couldn't see so well herself, she had to trust that he wasn't a pervert stealing glances at her.

She undressed in the bedroom and had him sit on her bed facing away from her.

"I'm ready."

"Well I can't see anything. How am I supposed to do this?"

She went over to him and stood in front of him, "Get up."

He stood and accidentally brushed against her body with his own. She wanted to be mad about it, but she thought it truly was an accident and if it hadn't been…maybe she didn't mind.

She turned around so her back was facing him. "Give me your hands." He put them straight out and she placed them onto her naked hips. He didn't expect it and almost pulled his hands away. He thought this was a dangerous idea in more ways than one now.

"I'm going to walk us to the tub. You okay with this?"

He smiled, "Yes."

She slowly limped her way through the door to the bathroom and reached the tub. She bent over to turn on the water and Sebastian let go of her realizing what this position would look like if someone was watching them. He backed up a little to hide his growing erection.

"I need you." She was already over exerting herself so it came out unintentionally breathy.

"Huh? Oh, the um…what do you need?" he stammered.

"I need to put the plug down and get in. I need you to hold my hand as I sit."

He moved forward and put out both hands. He felt her take them.

"Come closer to me."

He inched up slightly.

"More."

He inched up a little.

"I won't bite you."

Sebastian was dying. Everything she said sounded sexual and it wasn't making it easy to get rid of his hard on.

"Really. Come here." He felt her let go of his hands and she put her arm around his waist, pulling him right up against her – face to face. He didn't know if she wanted to tease him or if she was doing all this without thinking.

She was grateful he didn't see the blush blossom on her cheeks. She felt his cock easily through his pants, and from the feel of him, he was a big boy. She understood why he had backed off of her. She didn't want to draw any attention to it, but she was flattered…and intrigued.

She took a hold of his hands at his sides, "Okay. I'm going to step back and to the left. I need you to just help me if I start to slip. You good?"

He nodded and realized she might not see that, "Yes."

She stepped up and back into the tub with her foot first, then her stump followed. She edged back into the back of the tub and started to sit down, "I'm sitting. Gonna try to go slow."

"Okay." He held onto her hands, but it seemed like she didn't need him. She let go.

"So far so good. I'm sitting, but I forgot to plug the damn drain. Can you?"

Oh my God. She's got to be doing this on purpose and it's amazingly unfair.

"Sure thing. Pardon my reach." He moved slightly to the right and felt for the faucet. His hand went straight down and felt for the plug. It was there and he pushed it down. Hot water started to pool at the bottom. "Do you need anything else?"

"Well if you could turn off the water when it's full?"

"You tell me when."

"Oh, shoot. I left the shower stuff in the box outside. Can you get it?"

"What do you need out of it?"

"Well, I guess…" she paused, "If you bring the Mr. Bubble then the bubbles will cover me under the water and you can take off your blindfold."

"Mr. Bubble?"

"Yeah, just bring the box and I can feel for it."

His erection had almost started to abate until she said that. "I'll be right back."

He lifted the scarf as soon as he was out of her sight and picked up the box, putting the scarf over his eyes right before he entered the bathroom.

"I'm coming in. Here's the box." He kneeled down at the edge of the tub so she could get her bubble bath out.

She reached in and found it, poured a cupful of the solution into the bathwater and then replaced the bottle. Then she pulled out a few more bottles and left them on the ledge of the tub. "I'm good."

You certainly are. "I will put this down. Are you wet enough yet?" He wanted to hit himself in the mouth, "Is the water high enough?" He quickly said after.

"Almost."

"Be right back." He ripped off the scarf as he exited the bathroom and dropped the box of her toiletries on the dresser. *Are you wet enough yet?! Really?! Such a stupid thing to say!*

"Okay Sebastian. The water's good."

He edged to the door and looked carefully at the water level. There were bubbles everywhere and he couldn't see her body. He walked in and turned off the faucet. "You need anything else?"

She lifted her right leg out of the water and put her stump on the ledge of the tub. He could only stare at her bare wet leg.

"Let me see." She plunged down into the water and submerged her head. She came up slowly and said, "I might need you to wash my hair. I don't think I can reach up there comfortably. Would that be okay?"

"Of course your Highness. You want me to use this shampoo of yours?" He pointed realizing she couldn't see that.

She nodded.

He kneeled down at the back edge of the tub behind her head and handed her the shampoo. She asked for his palm and squeezed enough to wash her hair into his hand.

"This is a lot of shampoo."

"I have a lot of hair."

"Does your head hurt anywhere?"

"The only area you need to be careful of is my forehead. I have this big knot there."

"Okay."

He started massaging the shampoo through her hair and piling it up on the top of her head. After a minute, she relaxed and started to enjoy it.

"Oh this feels – amazing. Getting clean. Thank you."

"You're welcome." He watched where he put his fingers and was gentle with her. She submerged her head after he was done and asked for him to put conditioner on her afterwards. He did and then got up to leave.

"Wait."

"Yes?"

"Stay."

He almost asked why, but decided not to question it. "How long do you think you'll need in here?"

"Um maybe ten or twenty minutes, but I won't be able to wash my back. I appreciate your professionalism during this odd request, but I genuinely want to be clean and I know I just can't comfortably reach my back. Do you mind?"

His eyes rolled back into his head and he thought of touching her under the water. He cleared his throat, "Whatever you need Celeste."

"Great. Here's my scrubbie thingy."

He took her purple-netted sponge and squeezed her shower gel onto it. She leaned forward and he began carefully rubbing along her back.

He was so focused on trying to be gentle and respectful he almost missed her sniffling. "My lady? Are you okay?"

She put her hands up to her face. She mumbled into them, but he couldn't understand what she said.

"I beg your pardon?"

She let her hands fall into the water with a splash, "I'm sorry. I...this is all so overwhelming. I can't remember the past *three* months and I'm relying on this strange man to help me take a bath..." she sobbed.

He stopped cleaning her and shifted his position to be next to her. He took one of her hands, "Hey, it's all right. Everything's going to be fine. You'll heal up and get your memories back. It's going to take some time, be patient."

She looked at him. He was close enough to her face for her to see him. His handsome face was contorted into a worrisome expression, "I'm sorry. I didn't mean you're strange. You're handsome. And you seem nice. I guess I'm just scared…a little. I don't know you…and you're sitting here with me naked in a tub of water. I don't know what I'm doing." Tears rolled down her cheeks.

"Would you be more comfortable if I left you alone? I can close the door? I'll wait outside in the bedroom and you give me a yell when you're ready for help." He started to get up but she grabbed his arm.

"I don't want to be alone. Don't go. Please. I just don't want you to think I'm weird or loose or whatever because we're here. I needed to be clean. I knew I couldn't stand in the shower for the time it would take to get me clean and I…" she choked up again.

He put a hand very softly to her face, "My queen, I have the utmost respect for you. I swear to God I would do anything to protect you and you don't have to worry about me being a jerk or a danger to you. I want what's best for you and I need you to be healthy and safe."

She cried harder.

"What'd I say? I'm trying to help you stop crying."

She smiled, "You sound so genuine. I want to believe you."

"Then believe me. I won't let you down." He took his hand away from her and returned to washing her back. He finished without her saying anything, and he could tell she wasn't crying either.

He handed the sponge to her and he washed the soap off his hands at the sink. "I'm going to get a book and read while you finish up."

She nodded.

When he returned, she was almost done. She dunked her hair into the water to rinse off the conditioner, "Ugh this water's disgusting isn't it?"

He barely glanced, "I don't know how long it's been since you last bathed. Maybe next time we'll give you a shower," he stopped, "I mean, maybe next time you can stand for a shower if it makes you feel cleaner."

"Can you take the plug out?"

He reached down into the water but couldn't see the drain. His hand brushed her leg, then found the top of the plug and pulled it out. He helped her out of the tub with his eyes closed after she said that was okay. He handed her a towel and stood outside the doorway facing away from her.

"Thank you for your help Sebastian."

"Of course."

"I'm sorry for the meltdown."

"Please my lady, there's nothing to apologize for. I can't imagine how difficult this time must be for you. You are very strong."

"Thanks. Okay, I need to change into some clothes. Can you wait outside the bedroom door?"

"Of course."

She put on her own clothes and seemed a bit brighter and a lot more comfortable to him. All the more reason for him not to mention someone had been in her place while she wasn't there. It could only make her feel more unsettled.

He helped her pack a bag of what she wanted to take and loaded the transit. All that was left was to give her a sedative and carry her down. She sat on her bed and swallowed the tiny pill he handed her.

"This should kick in around ten minutes from now so you won't have to worry about your fear of heights."

"You know about that?"

"Yep. There was a time you were cured of it, but I bet you'll conquer it again."

"Really?"

"Yes. You okay being in a blanket? I'll have to cover your face."

She nodded.

"Okay put your arms around me." She did.

"Here we go." He scooped her up and she settled into him. She found herself feeling safe with him. He seemed to be able to take care of everything, himself, her, anything that came up, and that was attractive as well as impressive.

"Put the blanket around yourself for me and cover your face please."

"But then I can't see you."

He smiled, "It's only temporary, and I can't handle those vultures outside. I'm likely to punch someone out if they get in our way tonight.

You are the most precious cargo I've ever transported. Now cover up please."

She covered herself and rested her head on his shoulder.

He successfully moved Celeste in the middle of the night to Zach's vacation home on Bahsheef without drawing attention to themselves. They were lucky most of the reporters had gone to their hotels or were talking amongst themselves. No one noticed him carrying the blanket that contained Celeste. She slept the entire transit ride and he was lost in thought. He tried to read, but found it difficult to keep his mind off her.

When they docked on the rooftop of Zach's house, it was pitch black outside. Sebastian looked at his Titan and saw it was deep into the overnight hours of Bahsheef and that was good. Celeste was still heavily sedated. Sebastian chose separate rooms for them on the fourth story, giving her the master bedroom while he took the smaller room closest to hers. After he put her into bed, he familiarized himself with the premises. He walked from room to room, floor by floor, checking for safety hazards, for exits, and for security breaches. The doc's house was not in the style of Sebastian's personal taste, but it was very nice. Apparently Zach, or one of his wives liked to decorate with lots of animal prints and safari style décor. He felt like he was in one of those hotels that had themed rooms.

The doctor had some security measures, but they weren't nearly as good as Sebastian would've liked them to be. After he checked out the entire home, he looked over the front yard, back yard, and the perimeter. The front yard was all grass and well manicured. There were two large shade trees that looked like they had been growing there for a hundred years. There was a white hammock tied between them and it looked like a great place to read a book. Zach told him the grounds and home were all taken care of by service bots that hibernated in the subterranean level.

When Sebastian was in the basement to look at what models Zach had, he noted what he thought was true for all species. Whatever the type of being, the service bots emulated that species. So Zach had a male handyman and a female maid Taybusian service bot. Zach also had a good sense of humor about them. He had placed denim overalls on the male and a French frilly maid's uniform on the female; although her skirt was a lot longer than the one Sebastian had put on his own maid bot, probably at the mention of his many wives concerns, or maybe it was for the hatchlings sake.

Zach was right, this place was huge and isolated. There was nothing around for miles. No other homes, no businesses, nothing. Just black sand, some far off volcanoes, and the ocean.

Sebastian had packed well for the both of them, and ordered plenty of supplies and food to last a month. All of that should arrive tomorrow. Like many other worlds, Bahsheef had an order and delivery service.

Praxis had control over Bahsheef. No other species had claimed it at the time of its discovery by a Praxian explorer and it was decided by the council they had enough resources to rule over it. They decided to keep it more natural and less developed – kind of like an old-fashioned Earth. Apparently, the few residents that lived on Bahsheef full time liked it that way. They thought it was quaint to have asphalt streets and old-fashioned means of transportation like land cars from Earth. Mostly that was a novelty for visitors to have an experience that they couldn't have anywhere else, but Sebastian liked it. Besides, Zach had told him that something he restored himself sat in the garage unused since it was too small for Zach to fit on. But he welcomed Sebastian and Celeste to take a ride on it if the spirit moved them. Sebastian resisted the urge to look at it until he thought Celeste was healthy enough to go with him, but he looked forward to that moment.

Bahsheef was universally thought of as a resort world for the daredevil traveler. A place where few beings lived, but many beings from all over liked to vacation on. Sebastian had been here a long time ago and he knew some of the history and the local dangers. Things like the numerous volcanoes, the planet's dangerous and carnivorous plants (they had a habit of eating beings whole), and the extremely ferocious and deadly wildlife – the sareeaveous. He thought it was indeed a beautiful raw world with lots to see, but he thought most beings underestimated the fantastic levels of risk vacationing here. He'd never let Celeste come here alone, in fact, he wouldn't feel comfortable with most people he cared about coming here without a partner, a being that knew the history and fully understood how to survive a world like this one.

The Lanyx could've wiped out the entire sareeaveous population if they wanted to, but the council had always agreed, that was not the right thing to do. Theirs was a planet of animal lovers, even the man-eating, extremely dangerous species had a right to live. The council said with the volcanoes and plants remaining a threat, they didn't see the point of eradicating an entire species when there would be so many dangers left behind that were just as fatal. Praxis tourist associations posted constant warnings about the planet's various dangers and kept a close eye on all volcano activity in case of an emergency evacuation.

Sebastian was lost in thought as he rubbed his stubbled chin with his hand. There really was no way that his brother would find them here, so despite the lack of security, he felt safe. He was confident he could handle the plants and sareeaveous fine, but he'd closely monitor the volcanoes.

He walked onto the patio and looked out over the ocean into the darkness. There were countless stars in the sky here. You could easily see them since this planet had such few big cities or light pollution. It was a fantastic place for observatories and anyone that enjoyed stargazing as much as he did – Celeste should love that facet about Bahsheef too.

He walked inside and checked on her. She was still asleep and he wished he could slip into bed next to her, but that couldn't happen now.

He went to his bathroom and gave himself a close shave after downing his first vial of follicle suppressor in weeks. He was tired of shaving so often. Then he crawled into bed and fell asleep quickly.

SIX

>>> > ALANNA APPROACHED MITCH before the start of the meeting, "Hey."

"Hi. How are things?"

"Good. Listen I wanted to say something before the meeting."

Mitch raised his eyebrows, "Oh really? I wanted to as well."

"I'll go first since I started this. I was wondering…it never seems like we have enough time to talk here. Maybe we could trade ideas about locations over coffee or something? So we're uninterrupted and…you know, we have a lot more time."

Mitch smiled, "That was almost what I was going to say, except my goal was to get to know each other better. But yes, I think that's a great idea."

Alanna blushed, "I'll talk to you after the meeting?"

"Let's make the plans now. Tomorrow night at the Black and White Café on Praxis?"

"Seven okay?"

Mitch nodded.

"Okay. Great. I can't wait." She smiled at him and took a seat.

Mitch cleared his throat. He noticed Gaviss watching him with a smile on his face as he approached the front of the room, "You little devil you."

Mitch laughed, "I don't want to hear it. Let's get this started."

Gaviss got the attention of the room and sat down.

Mitch waved, "Hello all. The first thing I'd like to start with is that I've found us a new location. It's on Praxis and while I know you all probably live on Earth, I don't think it's the safest place for us to hold our meetings. I've got some pictures of this place and all the details so let's have a look at it."

SEVEN

>>> > ONE OF THE first things Sebastian did by morning light was to line the beach house's perimeter with torches. He lit the stone fire pit on the patio as well as running a line of torches along the shore where he would like to run in the mornings. Fire was a good protector here. It was the only safe way to be outside and not get plucked off by a sareeaveous, the planet's largest flying predator. They resembled both ancient Earth pterodactyls and modern Praxian birds, and with a wingspan of thirty-five feet, they were not a threat to be taken lightly.

Despite their ferocity, sareeaveous were beautiful creatures. Their bodies were colored in bright greens, blues, or yellows, with feathers on the wings, scales everywhere else, and terrifyingly large and fearsome talons that could slice a being in two. They fascinated Sebastian. He admired their hunting skills and the way their bodies moved as they flew through the air. To him, when they flew, it looked like they were moving underwater with a grace and ease that was stunning.

The strong numbers of sareeaveous kept Bahsheef free of overpopulation, but Sebastian understood why the doctor had a home here. The only species that the sareeaveous didn't eat was Taybuse. As far as anyone understood, they simply didn't like the taste of them.

Sebastian sat in the chair next to Celeste's bed, reading the volcano reports on his Titan when she woke up for the first time on Bahsheef.

She groggily asked, "Are we already there?"

He smiled, "Yes, we got here hours ago. You slept the whole way."

"Oh, that's good 'cause of my fear of heights."

"Oh, I know, trust me," he smiled while still looking at the reports, "But we're here now and we're going to stay for a while so you don't have to worry about any space travel for some time. How are you feeling?"

"Um, thirsty and breakfast would be good, I think." She yawned and sat up slowly.

"Let me guess…French toast with strawberries and whipped cream with a little orange juice to drink?"

"Yeah, how'd you know?"

"Good guess, that's all. Rest up; I'll bring it to you okay?"

"Thanks," she smiled although it split her bottom lip.

EIGHT

>>> > SEBASTIAN AND CELESTE'S first few days on Bahsheef were a serious adjustment for them both; days only lasted eighteen hours and of those, the sun was only out for six.

Although Celeste still couldn't see well, Sebastian told her to close her eyes because he had a surprise for her. She was thrilled when he gave her the charm bracelet her mother had given to her. She asked him to put it on her and he did. Sebastian thought it might raise her spirits to let her sit out on the back patio when she wanted some fresh air.

His favorite aspect of this world had always been the sunsets and sunrises. They were like nothing he'd ever seen. When it happened, it looked like the whole sky was on fire. The first afternoon Celeste sat out on the patio, she smiled when she felt the sunlight hit her face.

Whenever they were both on the patio, she would sit peacefully, and Sebastian was either reading a book or watching the news on his Titan. Sometimes he looked at the ocean or at her and thanked the Gods and Goddesses that he had found her, the first time at the assassination, and the second on Tiletan.

But what Sebastian enjoyed doing most while she was safely asleep in her bed was to meditate on a blanket on the beach. The sound of the waves crashing was healing and soothed him. He sat cross-legged with his hands resting on his knees. He wore loose-fitting exercise shorts so he could feel the ocean air across his skin. He prayed sometimes for Celeste – for her to heal, and to regain her memory, and to be able to accept whatever knowledge he brought her about her parents – whether they were alive or not. Sometimes he prayed for himself – to find peace of mind for all he had done to damage other's lives, to find peace of heart so that he could allow someone new into his life, and to forgive and love himself like Agathon suggested he do. Sometimes he focused on nothing at all allowing his mind to wander. He would smell the salt in the ocean air, hear the sea birds as they splashed into the water diving beneath the surface chasing after food, and he'd hear the waves rush up the shore to where he was sitting and then fall away from him again. He knew Celeste would love this place once she was able to see it.

Once, while Sebastian and Celeste were sitting out in the sun after lunch, a large rumble underneath them startled them both.

"What was that? There's no storm coming is there?"

"No. It's probably a volcano. I'm keeping tabs on them. Try not to worry about it." Sebastian knew a few volcanoes close by were alarmingly active; one was ready to erupt and if that happened, they'd have to leave immediately. Sebastian checked the latest reports again. He saw nothing different, but he knew too many rumblings too close together would be a bad sign. So far, that was the first they heard.

The doctor came. It had been a Praxian week since the last time he'd seen Celeste. Her physical state was improving, but her memory continued to be a mystery to everyone.

"So, when shall we do the surgery?" Zach smiled.

"What surgery?" Celeste adjusted her t-shirt.

Zach stared at Sebastian angrily, "You *did* ask her already right? I told you I wanted her permission…"

"Fuck I forgot," he immediately looked at Celeste, "I'm sorry, pardon my language."

"It's fine. What surgery and what permission Dr. Coldiron?"

Zach looked at Celeste and then pulled his white coat up around his waist. He pointed to his tail as he turned around.

She looked down and saw a Human foot growing out of the top of his tail. She put her hand to her mouth, "Is that mine? I mean, did you *grow* me a new foot?"

Zach dropped his coat as he turned around to face her and smiled, "I wanted to. It took a lot less time than I thought it would. It was easy actually. Sebastian was supposed to ask you about it, but I guess he hasn't. Is it okay? Do you want a new natural foot?"

Celeste thought for a minute before answering. "I'm flattered you've done this for me doc. But, I can't pay…I'll ha—"

"Oh no, dearie! I don't want your coren. This was on me…literally. I thought it would be best for you to have a natural replacement," his tongue came out and licked his eyeballs. "What you think?"

She looked at Sebastian, "I guess so, yes. It makes sense to be…whole again, and I have time to heal. How long will it take? Is it going to hurt?"

Zach shook his head, "No…well, a little, probably. The surgery involves me cutting it off my tail, then attaching it to your ankle. I'll make a large X-shaped incision on the bottom of your stump and I'll sew the foot on. Then I can put a living foot glove over all of it. That's like a soft cast, but it's incredibly strong and it can bear your weight while you heal up. They say four weeks recovery for this kind of procedure but if you keep your leg elevated, it could be three weeks."

Celeste stood up, "Let's do it."

NINE

>>> > THE DOCTOR LEFT after an hour of observing Celeste with her new foot after the surgery. He had Sebastian bandage up his tail and hugged Celeste goodbye. "We'll check on the healing next time I'm back. You can walk as much as you like, but remember to elevate it if you want it to heal faster. And don't get it wet."

CHAPTER 24

DAMETRICE'S SUGAR COOKIE

ONE

    Since they arrived, Sebastian gave Celeste plenty of space and let her engage him in conversations. He could only hope that her trust in him was building because so far as he could sense, her 7's were completely dormant, and he feared that might be permanent. One of the strongest bonds that could've been formed between them, might've been shattered forever due to his own Goddamned brother. Anger overwhelmed him every time he thought of all the things Constantine had done to her. He had a difficult time trying to push that anger down once it rose up inside of him.

TWO

>>> > DURING CELESTE'S SECOND week of recovery, her eyes had fully opened and she was improving every day. Zach was there again and was pleased with her progress. Her new foot was looking good and she was walking on the glove just fine. He pulled Sebastian aside privately and asked him if he had a chance to look at what was sitting in the garage. Sebastian answered no, but that he was waiting for a special occasion to show it to Celeste at the same time he would look at it for himself.

Zach was too curious not to ask, "Special occasion?"

"Her birthday's coming up."

"Oh! I didn't know."

"Well, I only know because they always announce it on the Earthly news reports with all the other celebrity birthdays," he cleared his throat, "Of course with my crush, I, um, made note of it years ago, so it's been in the back of my mind for a while now."

"I should get her a little something. What does she like?"

Sebastian gave him a few suggestions and Zach promised to bring her gift with him on next week's visit.

After the doctor left, Sebastian walked past Celeste's bedroom and stopped. She was struggling to brush her hair and she let out a soft cry of frustration. He knocked on the open door.

She looked over at him.

"Can I come in?"

"Of course. Did you need something?"

He smiled, "I saw you're having a hard time with your hair. If you want, I can help you brush it."

She smiled, "Really? That would be great thanks," she held out her brush to him.

As she sat at the vanity table, she watched him stand behind her and collect a section of her hair in his hand. He gently ran the brush down her hair. She was amazed that he seemed to know all the little tricks that women did to avoid hurting themselves when brushing out knots.

She looked at his face. He was completely engrossed in his task. She remembered the first time she looked at him through her swollen and painful eyes when he allowed her to hold his face close to hers. She was surprised at how handsome he was initially, but over time, his attractiveness grew. There was a gentleness and protectiveness over her that she responded to.

He didn't look up from brushing her hair, "What is it my lady?"

She blinked a couple of times, coming out of her own thoughts, "Who taught you to do this?"

"My mother. Lanyx grow hair quick, and for the ladies, it's hard keeping it under control. That's what she always said anyway. 'This damn hair. What am I supposed to do with it today?' She would often ask for help from someone in the house, so I got used to brushing it."

Celeste closed her eyes and enjoyed the way his fingers caressed her scalp, the soft and careful way he touched her, and the delicacy of the brush gliding through her hair. It was pure heaven.

He finished and noticed her closed eyes. She frowned slightly. He put the brush down on the table and started running his fingers through her hair and her frown disappeared. He smiled to himself. He gathered her hair into a low ponytail with one hand and his fingers lightly brushed her neck. Her skin was exquisitely soft and he wished he could touch more of her.

Celeste shivered.

"Are you cold, my lady?" He asked in a low voice, leaning over her slightly.

She tried to speak but couldn't find her voice. She had to clear her throat before she could respond, "No…not cold. I'm…good. You're doing a nice job with my hair."

"My pleasure, your Highness."

He watched as her shoulders relaxed, then it seemed her whole body followed. *This is her weakness*, he thought to himself, *she would probably let me do this all day and never tire of it.*

She eased her head to one side, exposing a large section of her neck to him. His fingers ached to trace a line along it, or better still, his lips. Instead, he put his free hand down on her shoulder lightly and let his fingers rest high against the bare skin of her neck. His other hand let go of her hair, "Do you need me to do anything else to you?"—he made a face and closed his eyes—"For you, I mean. Your hair?" She was stirring his desire for her again. Her shiver, he knew without telepathy, was a direct reaction to his touch and that was all he needed to be reminded of their former passionate moments – her intoxicating kisses, her nearly naked body underneath his in his bed. He tried to suppress his lustful memories of her lips against his.

She smiled, "I was going to braid it today, but I'm not sure I can reach all the way back there. Do you know how to do that too?"

He took a deep breath and emptied his mind quickly, restoring his calm, "Of course my lady."

"Your mom again?"

"My mother would've never paid my weekly allowance if I didn't learn how to successfully braid her hair too," he winked at her reflection in the mirror and she laughed. "You want a French braid or a regular one?"

She smiled, "Just regular please and thank you for doing this. I really appreciate it."

"No need to thank me, your Highness. I know it can be frustrating when your body and mind are not on the same page."

He separated her hair into three sections and began interweaving them together. She sighed and felt completely relaxed. She thought there might be nothing better than having a handsome man play with your hair…She instantly revised that thought smiling to herself. There's nothing better than having a handsome man play with your hair until you're ultra-relaxed and then be carried to his bed so he can excite and exhaust you for the rest of the day. She giggled out loud.

Sebastian raised his eyebrows, "That's a new one."

"Huh?"

"I don't think I've heard you giggle since we got here my lady. It's a lovely sound."

She looked into his eyes as he stared back at her through the mirror, "You've heard me giggle before?"

"Yes."

"Well, this sounds interesting. You going to tell me why I was giggling?"

He smiled and looked down to his hands braiding her hair, "There was a morning on a yacht that I wanted to find out if you were ticklish. I found out definitively that you are."

"Damn. I want to remember that."

Sebastian put his head back and smiled widely, then looked back at her, "I hope you do, I really hope you do."

THREE

>>> > SPADER FOUND BARRO and Malloughs at the coffee machine in the kitchen, "Hey Celeste Hennessy's apartment on Praxis just got sold."

Barro furrowed his brows, "To who?"

"An Alexandria Chains. She's some kid who inherited her father's antiques empire. And I guess she's been acquiring a lot of property since her father died. I have several different addresses for her all over the universe."

"Does she have a picture? A record or anything we can use?"

"Calm down Barro, she's clean. Community service and volunteer work out of the kindness of her heart. Look at her picture." Spader held out his arm so the other two detectives could see his Titan.

Barro's eyes opened wide, "She's a fox! I want to talk to her."

Spader laughed, "Good luck. She's hard to get a hold of, but I'll try the numbers listed."

FOUR

TITAN Corporation - Personal TITAN Device

System Status: Active -- Universal Grid: Online

Current Time/Date (Il'laceier - Swamplands Regions): 7th Knoche/Atos 81-7, 5390

Secondary Time/Date (Praxis - Dersalene): 8:20 a.m./August 32, 2193

BOUND] >>> >>>>

Current Universal Positioning System Location:

Unknown/Unrecorded

User: Zane Colmsky

Communications Menu

Incoming message(s) received: 1 - Status: Unread

Message Received at 7th Knoche

Message Sent from: Universal News Agency (UNA) - Il'laceier

-UNA
-Pirchi Colony, QetQert Regions, Il'laceier
TOP NEWS
Speculation continues as the universe waits to hear word
from the Brotherhood of Desert Phantoms regarding the
kidnapping of Queen Dowager Celeste Hennessy. Ransom videos
have ceased as of two Earth weeks ago and Earthlings are
fearing the worst.
Without updates, humans are concerned if she's still alive,
and if she is, why hasn't the BDP released a new video
showing she's okay?
Questions regarding the kingdom's handling of the situation
persist, causing tension between Il'laceier and Earth to
escalate.
King David Hennessy has responded with a request for privacy
during this difficult time and promises that justice will
be swift for the BDP.
You can trust UNA for all your universal news needs.

-END OF MESSAGE

* This message will auto-delete in 32 knoches upon viewing.

FIVE

>>> > ULYSSES FOUND LILA in the east wing parlor replacing a damaged doorknob. He'd been looking for her for over a week carrying around a note he had written to Ginger.

Lila turned at the sound of footsteps, saw Ulysses and frowned while she rooted around in her toolbox, "What do you need sir?"

Ulysses frowned. Lila was mad at him too. He should've guessed that one. He held out the note and whispered, "Can you give this to Ginger please?"

"Why should I do anything for you? I told you not to hurt my friend. I said if you did, you're going to regret it. I wasn't joking."

Ulysses rolled his eyes and sighed, "I know how this looks. Ginger didn't give me a chance to explain. This note will tell her something she desperately needs to hear from me. Can you please do me this big favor and I will owe you? And it's a very good thing in this kingdom to be owed by a High Royal Guard. Please?"

Lila snatched the paper out of his hand and put it into her back pocket, "Fine. I'll do it. Now you owe me. Get out of here."

Ulysses grimaced, "Thank you. Just let me know whatever you need, whenever."

Lila glanced briefly at him then looked back at her toolbox, "Just go."

Ulysses did.

Lila thought about reading it, but it had a fingerprint encryption on it and she couldn't bypass that.

She walked to Ginger's room and knocked. When Lila got no answer, she opened the door and put the note on Ginger's bed. Then she sent Ginger a Titan message explaining what happened and where she left the note.

SIX

>>> > SORHEED CLEANED UP nicely for dates. D'Artagnan admired her from a distance before he walked to the teahouse. He hoped something

good came out of this, if not a romance, at least a friendship. He wouldn't mind that.

They sat at an outdoor table for an hour talking over tea and getting to know each other. D'Artagnan thought it was going well when Sorheed blurted out, "Oh damn. I went and completely forgot my darn Titan at my apartment. It's only right around the corner, would you mind if I went to go get it and then maybe we could have some dinner?"

D'Artagnan nodded, "Sure."

She got up and stared at him, "Would you mind walking there with me? Can't be too careful these days."

"Oh, of course."

D'Artagnan thought her apartment complex must've been one of those luxury rental places. It looked expensive on the outside.

Sorheed cleared her throat, "This will only take a minute. You want to come up? I think I should use the restroom too. You don't mind do you?"

D'Artagnan paused, "Is this appropriate? I don't want you to be uncomfortable with an almost stranger in your place."

She held out her hand. He took it and looked at her. She reiterated, "It's fine with me."

He followed her and stood inside the doorway as she fluttered about. She put her purse down on the entryway table and walked into the bathroom, shutting the door behind her.

He looked around and noticed the artwork on the walls were photos of major city skylines of worlds all over the galaxy. Copper pots and pans were suspended from a central rack on the ceiling of her kitchen. He walked into her apartment a little further and wondered what kind of cooking equipment she had.

He pulled open a drawer and saw there was nothing inside it. He pulled open another and another. Nothing inside any of them.

Just as he was about to turn around, Sorheed's brass knuckles hit him in the back. His right kidney had taken a direct strike.

He turned quickly at the same time he was folding sideways from the hit. He stopped in place when she put the gun to the side of his head.

"Why?" he asked.

"You took the Embers job from me. I think you've taken lots of jobs from me and I don't like losing money. Too many assassins these days. I need to thin out the competition."

"You had me fooled. I didn't think you were an assassin."

She smiled, "What? I don't look the part? That's great. I'll have to keep up that ladylike innocent role for the future."

"You're wrong on Embers though. That wasn't me."

"Of course it wasn't. Right. I'm supposed to believe that."

"Sorheed, if that's your real name, I'm really sorry."

She turned her head, "This is a new one. I'm holding a gun to your head and you're apologizing to me. Why are you sorry?"

He quickly thrust his right arm up and over in a swatting motion so the gun moved away from his head and pointed at the ceiling. He flipped the blade of his hidden knife out of his left sleeve and jammed it through her throat. She lost her balance and tumbled backwards, letting the gun fall from her hand. Yellow blood drained out of her neck as she slammed onto the hardwood floor. Her hands covered her throat, trying to slow the bleeding. He leaned over and picked up the gun.

He glared at her. She was trying to speak, but he had cut her vocal chords. She sputtered and gurgled until she suffocated on her own blood. He took the Titan off her arm and looked through it. He realized she must've had a second one for business.

D'Artagnan wiped his forehead, "Fuck!"

He rushed to the bathroom and got a towel off the rack. He wiped the blood off himself and started wiping down surfaces he thought he might've touched.

He took a photo of her face and rifled through her purse. He found her fake identification in her wallet and took an imprint of her snout with a special attachment that flipped out of the side of his Titan.

He turned her place upside down until he found her real Titan in the back of the pantry. Her security system on it looked easy to crack.

Two minutes and twenty-one seconds later, he saw she was a relatively new assassin, only having killed six targets over the past two years. Her real Il'lacean name was Edgicashh. Her assassin call name was Black Spike, and her standard use name was Sorheed Lewis. She had no family, but she had a long criminal record. She wasn't very good at escaping crime scenes it seemed.

"Damn," he looked around the apartment.

He found what he was looking for under the kitchen sink. He dragged her body to the bathroom and put it into the bathtub. He poured baking soda, hot lavender flower, ring acid, and an activating ingredient of whole stem beet all over her body. For Il'laceans, it was a dangerous chemical concoction that ate through flesh, organs, bone, and teeth. He made sure he put enough on her feet, hands, head, face, and especially snout so her remains could not be identified. He went through the apartment again and wiped down all the surfaces he touched. He took her coren, Titans, and jewelry, to make it look like a robbery gone wrong.

After making sure she had no security cameras around her place, he walked out the front door into the hallway cautiously and took the stairs down.

He disappeared into the night and went straight home.

SEVEN

>>> > DAVID SAT ON his throne looking at his new tarantula. He loved the insects of Earth so much he decided to invest in a lovely spider along with a small portable cage so he could take his new pet wherever he wanted. He had picked out a pretty little female because the kingdom veterinarian said they live the longest. So there David sat with an acrylic cube on the table next to his throne so he could stare at Zynnia as she dined on crickets.

His servants stood close by waiting for orders.

He snapped at one of them to bring him his afternoon tea and the servant moved quickly to the kitchen.

David had become accustomed to one Earthly pleasure and that was tea. He discovered he loved many different kinds of blends, but raspberry tea was his favorite. Nothing else could compare to that flavor of sweet ripe berries balanced out with a warm comforting liquid smoothness trickling down his throat. He kept a huge supply in the kitchen stockroom. And with David's weak snout, raspberries were one of the few things he could smell strongly on Earth. Those and roses unfortunately.

His servant returned with a teacup and saucer along with a round cream-colored item on the side and something else that instantly infuriated him.

David had never seen one of these before, "What is this?" He held up the cream-colored round object to the female servant.

She bowed her head and replied, "A sugar cookie your Royal Highness. I thought you might like to taste one, as I've never seen you eat any. They are my new favorite food on this planet and they go well with tea."

David was infuriated at anyone suggesting such a thing. He never asked for a cookie.

"What's your name, servant? And look at me when I address you damn it!"

She pulled her gaze from the floor up to his stern yellow eyes, "Dametrice."

"Why don't you eat this cookie and see if you're still alive by the time you finish it." He flung the cookie at her feet.

She picked it up quickly, "I'm not afraid of eating this. There's nothing wrong with it. The baker made some and I thought you'd enjoy it. I will eat it; then you'll see." She dusted off the cookie and took a large bite.

David waited for her to convulse or spasm, clutching her throat or foaming at the mouth, but nothing like that happened. The servant finished eating the cookie and stood, waiting for instruction.

David leaned forward, "If you're so eager to give me food, I'm going to designate you as my food tester. You're an Il'lacean, anything that could kill me, can kill you."

Dametrice's gold eyes were big, but she said nothing.

Then David held up the item that made him rage, "So first it's cookies and now it's this? How dare you bring this inside these kingdom walls!"

"I wanted to present your meal with something beautiful," Dametrice stared at the peach colored rose in David's hand.

David launched the flower across the room, "Have you no regard for our Il'lacean brothers and sisters? The ones who died in the Treaty War?" He paused, "Or is it possible that you're so young, you don't even know what roses really mean to our society?"

She was silent.

"ANSWER ME!"

She shrunk away, "I'm sorry King Hennessy, I don't. It's just a new flower to me."

David mocked in a dainty voice, "*Just* a flower…just a FLOWER!" He took a deep breath and reset himself. "Come here Dametrice." David pointed to the spot right in front of his throne.

She moved reluctantly where he directed.

"Everyone leave this room."

The staff quickly moved outside and closed the door carefully.

Dametrice started to pray to Khaleen silently.

"Let me give you a history lesson that I think you're desperately in need of *if* you're going to continue to work for me. You're at least familiar with the Treaty War with this planet we are now on correct?"

She nodded her head.

"Earth year 2965. Il'laceans were the first alien species to ever approach this planet and we had done our research. We came under the false pretenses of being peaceful, of just wanting to co-exist here. We offered all the separate countries a chance to sign our treaty, to make them feel like they had a choice, you see? To give them a false sense of control and as if they were still in charge and just giving us permission to be here. But you see, only half the countries agreed to sign. The rest of them wanted to resist, wanted us to leave them alone, and one country actually started attacking us and our ships. They started the war. But our society is strong and full of ferocious fighters. Once attacked, it was all bets off for Earth. We fought them for months and we were on the verge of winning, but do you know what stopped us Dametrice? Do you?"

She shook her head.

"Roses. Those Khaleen forsaken flowers just like the one you tried to give me. These *Humans weaponized roses.* They made it into a spray after our species started to have a deadly allergic reaction to them. Those damned flowers cost us the war and were almost the end of us! But you know what? We evolved. We researched those flowers and our scientists and our doctors saved our species from ever having to suffer another death due to these stupid flowers." David cleared his throat, "So now... you understand my reaction I hope."

She nodded.

"And now we, as a species, are able to touch them and smell them, even eat them without dying. Go open the door and let the rest of the staff in."

She did as he asked and returned to stand in front of him.

"You're dismissed. Back in line." David waved her away and she went to the side of the room looking as though she would break into tears.

David was glad she brought the cookie. Now he had someone to eat any possible poison for him before someone tried to kill him. Why didn't he think of this before? He felt much better.

He checked on Zynnia in her cage. Looked like she wanted one more cricket.

Now he was able to think about Celeste's situation.

He wanted her alive. He thought of all the scenarios, him being the hero was the best one. They would throw parades on both planets, Earth celebrating the fact that *he* was the one that brought their beloved queen back safely. And on Il'laceier celebrating his courage and bravery. Earth would fall in love with him, finally, and he would have them all in the palm of his hand. The adoration would be at a fever pitch when he publicly married Celeste and parties would last for days celebrating their union. He couldn't wait to get that Human back...maybe he should thank the BDP privately after all of this was over. They were going to do so many good things for his image.

There was something he hadn't considered. If her boyfriend, the one that's part of the BDP should somehow die during all this, he'd have nothing to blackmail her with. *What to do about that?* He smiled to himself. He'd have to find something else to blackmail her with, and that shouldn't be too hard. If he can be a hero and bring the queen back to the kingdom, there wasn't anything he couldn't achieve.

He snapped his fingers, "Dametrice! Bring me one of those sugar cookies now. I want to try one before my tea gets cold!"

EIGHT

>>> > MITCH WOKE UP in another cold sweat. He had a nightmare that he left Human Resistance and FAIR members behind to die on Hap Du Wan.

He couldn't live this way much longer. The dreams were getting worse.

He heard Reid telling him that he was constantly on the move.

"Gotta keep moving Mitch. Gotta keep moving."

And that's what Mitch was doing right now.

He remembered when he was in the space program how he was almost recruited by the BDP. At the time, he didn't know anything about them, so out of curiosity, he went to one of their meetings.

Knowing himself too well as the Alpha male he was, once he got in there and saw what the BDP was up to, he figured out fast he wouldn't fit in.

He walked out shortly after arriving and thought he'd never have anything to do with them again...until Reid walked into their group.

He was relieved he never joined the Brotherhood. They were nothing but troublemakers.

NINE

>>> > "I'M SORRY TO disturb you Erebos, but I have a pressing matter that cannot wait."

"What is it O?" Sebastian looked at his Titan while he sat on the beach alone.

"Two Earth detectives have tried contacting Alexandria Chains several times asking why she's purchasing Ms. Hennessy's apartment on Praxis. They sound insistent on talking to her."

"Call them back from a disguised number, use a filtered voice two octaves higher than your programmed one. Tell them you have always admired Celeste and now that she's been kidnapped, you believe that this place could become some sort of museum. Make it sound like you're a glory hound in it for the fame and money. Can you do that for me?"

"Yes sir. I'll give you a full recording of the call when I'm done."

"Thanks O."

Twenty-three minutes later, Sebastian listened to the recording, confident the Earth detectives believed they talked to a live being who was no longer a concern for them. Ms. Chains had just been a greedy Human taking an opportunity to make some coren off of someone else's tragedy.

He turned on his small reading lamp and opened his book when his Titan chimed. He looked down at the message and cursed.

TITAN Corporation - Personal TITAN Device

System Status: Active -- Universal Grid: Online

Communications Menu

Instant message received from: The Sexiest Thief you'll never see

Today

5:18dark
The Sexiest: Why haven't you responded?

5:20dark
X: I apologize. Been busy with emergency.

5:20dark
The Sexiest: Oh sweetie! Are you okay? What happened? Are you in the hospital? Do I need to come see you?

5:21dark
X: Not my emergency. Taking care of a friend while they recover.

I'm fine. Just busy.

5:23dark
The Sexiest: I hope he's okay. Glad to hear you're fine.

5:26dark
The Sexiest: Why did you stand me up?

5:29dark
X: I didn't stand you up. I had an emergency that
couldn't be avoided. I apologize for not being able to
keep my word to you.

5:31dark
The Sexiest: And you haven't been able to contact me in
53 bliiks? You've been busy non-stop? These messages only
take a short time to send.

5:34dark
X: You're counting Stoxian days. It's only been 38
Praxian days. You disappear out of my life for 3 years
and I don't hear shit from you. Then you pop up, demand
my help, and are grilling me because you expect that I
somehow need to answer to you?

5:35dark
The Sexiest: I expect that you keep your word. You always
say how you don't break promises to anyone, well that
includes me doesn't it? And I'm not "demanding" your
help, you owe me favors and I'm calling them in. If
you can't show up, you should inform me. I'm not being
unreasonable.

5:36dark
X: OK, OK. I apologized already. I explained I have an
emergency going on. I owe you 2 favors, I agree to that
to make up for missing the last one. Anything else?

5:38dark
The Sexiest: The meeting went fine, thanks for asking.
I'm fine thanks for asking. When are you going to be
available to me for anything?

5:40dark
X: I'm unsure how long this emergency with my friend will
continue. They need my constant help and until they are
fully healed, I will be unavailable to anyone else for
anything.

5:41dark
The Sexiest: This guy must be pretty close with you…

5:43dark
X: I need to get back.

5:44dark
The Sexiest: Who is this friend? Do I know him?

5:45dark
X: These questions are irrelevant. I promise to contact
you, via Titan message when I'm done here.

5:46dark
The Sexiest: So it's a woman? And where is here? Are you
not on Praxis?

5:47dark
X: Goodbye

5:48dark
The Sexiest: I expect some answers next time we talk big
boy!

⟦The Sexiest Thief you'll never see has disconnected⟧
-END OF CONVERSATION

*Delete current conversation: [Y/N]:__

Sebastian immediately deleted his conversation with Ni-toyis. He had been so pre-occupied between his trip to Foss-Altus and taking care of Celeste he had completely forgotten to respond to Ni-toyis's last communication.

He glanced over his shoulder to make sure Celeste hadn't woke up yet. It was still dark outside and there wasn't any activity in the house. The last thing he wanted was for Celeste to have any idea he had regular business with a Stox woman. He needed to fulfill his obligations to Ni-toyis and cut ties with her as quickly as possible.

CHAPTER 25

SKIPPING STONES

ONE

>>> > THE NEXT DAY, CELESTE asked to walk on the black sand beach with Sebastian.

He holstered his pistol into his shoulder harness as they walked out the back door.

"Is it really necessary that you carry a gun on you almost all the time?"

He paused for a long moment before answering, "There's many ways to answer that. I could say that I'm not obsessed with my gun collection; it's not something I do for fun. It's necessity for my job and my own protection. Guns have saved my life many times, and I've saved many lives with them as well. I respect guns and the power they wield. But when it comes down to it, and to answer your question, the bad guys will have guns and if they come after you or I, that means I need a gun to protect us. Does that make sense?"

She nodded.

The sun was setting and the tide was high. The torches Sebastian lit earlier in the day were still burning bright, Celeste could hear them crackling. Long feathered orange sea birds soared over the waves looking for the last few bits of food before going off to their nests.

Celeste looked at everything, finally able to enjoy all the planet had to offer. All along the black beach, there were smooth bright blue boulders dotting the shore – they resembled huge chunks of ice. In the distance, she could see a series of black cliffs; the waves were crashing up against them mercilessly. She took a deep breath of ocean air and sighed.

They were the only ones walking along the beach, and Sebastian silently thanked the doctor for giving them this opportunity to let her recover without worry of being in danger from the BDP.

"So how do you think I'm doing?" She crossed her arms over her chest, and regretted it immediately. It hurt way too much, so she let her arms dangle at her sides.

"I think you're doing well, and I'm glad you're feeling better. I was... worried about you," he looked into her face and focused on the dark purple shadows under her eyes.

"It's so strange. I think I can remember everything up until that day of Jonathan's assassination. I worked back to the date in my mind. Him and I had a fight about whether I needed to go to the Earth Outpost. I wanted to stay home, but he wanted me to go. I guess the last thing I really remember was getting ready for bed that night. He was going out and I was glad that I wouldn't be forced to lay next to him in bed. He used to...beat me, well, you probably already know that huh?"

"Yes my lady," he let out a long exhale, "It enrages me."

She had never heard this spoken to her by a man before. She had lovers in the past that had claimed to care for her, but they were always afraid of the king. They said they would stay with her and help her get away from Jonathan, but they were always the ones that ended up leaving her behind. Sebastian exterminated her cockroach of a husband.

The man that she thought would outlive everything and everyone was dead, thanks to the man walking next to her. Suddenly she wanted to fill in all the blanks of her time spent with Sebastian Raynes. Had she known what it was like to kiss him? Did they go out on lots of dates? She needed to remember everything about him. "What else do you know about me exactly?"

He smiled at her, "I know many things. I know you're kind and big-hearted. You love animals and you're extremely sympathetic towards others. I know about your unhappiness with your life while you were queen. I know of your troubles with your husband. You're very smart, and well spoken. You like to listen to music, you have a beautiful singing voice, and you're very capable, much more so than you give yourself credit for."

He saw the surprise on her face.

"I sang in front of you?"

He smiled, "Yes, I was having a bad dream one morning and you soothed with me with a song. It helped me a lot. It's something I'll never forget."

"I don't sing for anyone, or in front of anyone, so that's impressive. I must've trusted you."

"You do, I mean, you did."

She pushed a piece of hair behind her ear, "Can you keep a secret?"

Sebastian leaned into Celeste and disclosed, "Secrets…are a very big part of my job, your Highness."

She blushed.

For a moment, deep down inside Sebastian, he thought things might be all right again someday.

"I want to sing…professionally. Sometimes around the kingdom when I thought no one was around I'd sing out loud, pretend that I was on tour or recording an album," she paused and he knew this was something she normally kept to herself, "I've dreamt of singing in front of a crowd for a long time, but I can't get the courage. Jon, it seemed, never wanted me to enjoy myself or be myself. He always wanted me to be someone I wasn't and singing was not on his agenda. If he caught me singing, he'd punish me."

Sebastian stopped walking and so did she. He stood in front of her and looked down into her eyes, "I can say two things with absolute confidence. Since I've personally heard you sing, I know that you have an excellent and beautiful singing voice that people need to hear and Jonathan was a controlling, evil, son of a bitch who will never hurt you again." Then he added, "Your singing should not be hidden. You need to share your gift with the universe."

Celeste smiled at him and he smiled back. He started walking again and she followed. They walked silently; the only sound was the waves racing up the shore only to recede again.

"If we cared about each other like you said, does that mean you've kissed me?"

He blushed.

"Oh. I take that as a yes then. Did we kiss a lot?"

"A bit. Yes." He crossed his arms behind his back.

"Hmmm that's too bad. I don't remember any of our relationship. Or any of those kisses. You're an attractive man…I'm surprised you're not married. You're not married are you?"

"No. Never have been married."

She looked out on the horizon, "I don't understand how you're still available."

"Oh well, that's a long story."

"I'm not going anywhere," she smiled at him.

"When I was young there was someone I dated. I pushed her away thinking it would keep her safe, but she became so distraught after I broke up with her that she committed suicide."

"Oh my God Sebastian. I'm so sorry," she put her hand to her mouth.

"That was many years ago, but thank you."

"So you haven't been with anyone since then?"

"Well, no relationships. I've had the company of women when I was lonely every so often, but I'd never start a relationship with anyone. My line of work is not conducive to romances. It's a hazard to get close to me."

"Is that why you broke up with her? Your career? You said you pushed her away to keep her safe."

He looked at Celeste sideways, "You call assassination work a career? I think you're being a bit too kind. You say it like I was a carpenter or a teacher," he reached down and picked up a smooth stone from the sand, rubbing it clean with his fingers, "I always thought it was what I was forced to do from a lack of options. I mean, it chose me, I didn't choose it." He threw the stone across the water's surface and it skipped five times.

"Well, with the way you look, I think you certainly had options – you could've been a male stripper."

He put his head back and let out a loud and hearty laugh.

Celeste was surprised at the sound, but once she heard it, she couldn't forget how wonderful it was – like a rich chocolate dessert to her ears, full of charm and vivaciousness.

When he stopped laughing he remarked, "A stripper?! No, I couldn't do that. No way. That was a good one though, I needed that laugh."

"You think I'm joking. I'm sure there would be a line of women a mile long aching to watch a man like you take off your clothes."

He looked at her and saw she was quite serious. "I'm flattered you think so, but I won't take off my clothes for any random woman."

She wondered if he had ever taken off his clothes for her in the past... and she just couldn't remember it.

He stopped walking and faced her. "Now you're wondering – if we were strangers in some alternate reality if I would take off my clothes for you in some strip tease?"

She couldn't say anything in response. She had images of him slowly unbuttoning shirts, or just ripping them off, letting his pants fall to the ground, watching him crawl along shiny floors under a spotlight towards her, some lust filled look in his eyes. She started to get hot. It was suddenly too hot.

They were staring at each other, but neither said anything.

She finally spoke, her voice low and sultry. It was the tone of voice that she didn't know, drove him crazy, "I know it's not this way for you, but for me, we *are* strangers in reality...So, how much would it take for you to undress for me?"

"I don't think we should be..." He couldn't finish.

She smiled, "Okay, maybe not for me then. How much would a queen have to pay you?"

"How did I…"—He ran a hand over his hair—"I wouldn't ever be a stripper. Celeste," he cleared his throat, "You have a way about you. I think you could make any man feel…stunned. I'm sure it's not just me. You've probably done this to a lot of men."

"Well, I'm sorry if I made you feel…uncomfortable. I was just kidding around. It's fine if you don't want to answer."

He put a hand to her cheek gently, "I feel like this around you because you have a wonderful way of making me speechless. I've never had a woman look at me before the way you do…did, before you lost your memory. Making me feel this way is a good thing. I'm giving you a compliment and to answer your question, I'd do it for you because I wanted to. No amount of money would ever convince me to strip."

Celeste wanted him to kiss her right here on the beach and he knew it. He finally sensed an intention from her, although it was faint in his mind. He wanted to kiss her too, but needed her to remember everything before he moved forward with her.

"So, I'm not making you uncomfortable then?" She put her hand on top of his that was still on her cheek.

"No, definitely not. I'm nervous around you sometimes, I'll admit that, but you've done that to me since we met."

She started walking again and he walked next to her.

"What are you thinking about my lady?" He asked her an extremely uncommon question between them.

"I make you nervous?"

He smiled, "Yes, only sometimes. I want to do the right thing with you…I don't want to mess anything up."

"I'm not really sure you could. You don't seem like the type of man who does things without really thinking first."

He shook his head, "Well, I've certainly messed up before."

"Sebastian, are you talking about us? You mean with me?"

He picked up another smooth stone, rubbing off the black sand. "Let me tell you the rest of the story with my ex-girlfriend that passed away. When I began the assassin work, I knew Francesca wouldn't approve, so I never told her. I messed up on a couple jobs right off the bat, so I thought her life might be in danger. I tried to protect her, but it backfired on me."

"Anyone who commits suicide isn't stable. That wasn't your fault."

"Yes, the first time I told you this, that's sort of what you said. There's one more thing to this story and I should tell you now. Francesca was dating my brother first, but then she dumped him." He looked out over the ocean and released a deep sigh. "She came to me since we all spent a lot of time together while she was dating Constantine, and she admitted her feelings to me. She asked me out."

"So you didn't even pursue her?"

He continued, "I was young. I always liked her, but I never confessed my feelings until they broke up and she came to me. She never loved him, but she loved me. I cared for her a great deal, but I never actually loved her. I thought I did."

"How did you find out? That you didn't love her, I mean?" She looked him in the eyes and the last of the setting sun's light shone in them like a prism.

"I met someone later on that I had even stronger feelings for. They proved to me that I didn't love Fran like I thought I did. I didn't know there was something out there so much stronger."

Celeste felt overwhelmed by questions for him. Most of all she thought Sebastian might've been talking about her, but she wasn't sure. Of course she wasn't sure, how could she be when she couldn't remember any of her previous time with him? All she had was the last two weeks and she wanted desperately to remember the rest.

"I eventually broke up with Fran for two reasons. The strain it was putting on my brother and I, and because I was getting deep into assassinations. It was too dangerous to have her in my life. Then she killed herself and any sort of reconciliation was impossible for my brother and I. He blamed me for stealing her, still blames me for her death. I didn't tell you that the first time we spoke of this, the part about Constantine and Fran because I was afraid of what you would think of me, or leave before you really got to know me. Will you forgive me for lying to you?"

"Well, considering I don't remember our original conversation, yes. I can understand why you wouldn't tell someone right away about all of this. I sympathize with not wanting to be judged as well."

"I still feel like hell for her suicide. I still think it's my fault. She would've been better off never meeting me. And my brother's never forgiven me." He skipped the stone he'd been holding onto. They both watched it jump across the water three times.

"Sebastian, you can't blame other people for falling in love with you. You can't control how they feel, or what they do. You can't take on the responsibility of her death. She chose the easy way out instead of trying to pick herself up and date someone else. I'm sorry that happened to you."

He stopped walking and faced her, "I appreciate your kind words. Some things are harder than others for me to deal with."

"I'm sorry. I've been prying into your life. I'm being nosy."

"No, you're not. You know all about me, but right now, you just can't remember. It'll come back to you, I'm sure."

"Doctor keeps saying I need to see things I might recognize. I've looked at everything you brought with us…so far nothing. It's frustrating. I'd like to remember our time together."

"It might take a while, but it'll come around. Come on, let's go inside. I'll make dinner."

TWO

>>> > SEVERAL BAHSHEEFIAN DAYS went by quietly without Celeste recovering her memory, but her health had improved steadily.

She and Sebastian developed the habit of walking on the beach at sunset, and sometimes at sunrise as well. They read books, watched old Human movies, and Sebastian finally taught Celeste how to fly a transit, but mostly they talked and she got to know him again.

Sebastian couldn't communicate with her telepathically the way he could before. He heard her intentions, but he didn't mention it. He feared the mental power she was developing prior to her kidnapping had been permanently erased somehow. Maybe she'd taken too much trauma to the head during the kidnapping or they'd given her too many drugs, he wasn't sure.

The best thing he read off her was that her trust in him was growing and she was becoming comfortable around him. That was a huge relief to Sebastian.

THREE

>>> > IT HAD BEEN over two weeks since they broke up.

Ulysses watched Ginger as she went about her business of grocery shopping off kingdom grounds.

Had she read his letter? Did she care? She hadn't responded, so when she stopped to sit down at a bench to tie her shoes, Ulysses approached and sat down next to her.

"I really need to talk to you."

Ginger looked up and saw him. She sighed. "What are you doing here? Did you follow me?"

He thought it was better to tell the truth, "Yes. There was no other way to reach you. I can't message you anymore and I can't talk to you at work."

She stopped and looked at him.

He saw that her eyes were red and puffy like she had been crying.

"What do you want to say?"

"Did you get my letter?"

"Yes. Lila gave it to me. I read it and it didn't change anything."

"But I told you I loved you. I told you I needed to explain but we would need to meet in person. Why didn't you respond?"

"Because I didn't want to. You hurt me with all the lies. How can I trust you now?"

"Ginger, I love you, okay? I really do. The reason I'm in the IMC is because I can spy on David this way. I'm so close to him, do you understand what kind of inside information I can get on him? On Celeste maybe? He never says much about her to me, but if I'm his second in the group and I'm trusted with some kingdom secrets, I might be able to help Celeste too, or even you if something came up. I'm not working alone either. I've got one more guard who's working against the king."

"How long have you been with the IMC?"

He admitted slowly, "Back when Jon was still alive."

"Why did you join in the first place?"

"When I got hired, I heard it might be good politically and career wise to join the IMC. Jon was a member and so was David. Neither one of them was the leader, but I thought it would help me advance, and it has. I got to be a High Royal Guard *because* David knows me from the IMC. He trusts me and I think I can do a lot of good from the place I'm in now. Does that make sense?"

She nodded, "What about Celeste? Is there anything new you can tell me about her kidnapping? Is she safe?"

He shook his head, "Unfortunately, David's not saying much about her. He sent me and a team on a mission to find her, but we came up empty handed. David was enraged at first when she was taken. It ruined all kinds of plans for him, but now he's just focusing on day-to-day stuff with me. Hasn't mentioned her in a while. I'm sorry but there's nothing I can give you on Celeste. But you've got to believe me that I'm doing all this for the right reasons. I spied on Jon while he was alive, now I'm spying on his brother. That is it. That's all I want to do with the IMC."

Ginger's gaze softened towards Ulysses. Then something occurred to her, "Why didn't you tell me this in the first place?"

"This is a big risk for me and more importantly, a big risk to you. If David finds out what I'm doing, I can handle the consequences, but if he finds out you know things…I'm not comfortable with that. I didn't want to jeopardize your safety by telling you all of this. Now you know. You'll have to keep this to yourself and be extra careful. I just couldn't live without you anymore." A look of tired sadness passed over his face, "I miss you all the time. I needed to come clean with you, because it was the only way to make you understand."

Ginger put her arm around his shoulder and he moved closer to her on the bench.

"I'm sorry I lied. I didn't want to hurt you, but in the end, seems like that's all I did by lying. Will you forgive me? Take me back?"

She kissed his cheek, "I appreciate that you're trying to protect me. I will take you back, but you must promise me, it's the truth from here on out. Okay?"

"Yes, babe. Thank you. I love you."

"I love you. Now, can you help me with these groceries?"

"That I can do." He grabbed six bags and walked towards her transit.

FOUR

>>> > D'ARTAGNAN RAN the photos through his system, looking for the identities of the two men Mitch had taken pictures of.

He got matches for only one of them, but one was all he needed.

D'Artagnan looked at Mitch and showed him his Titan screen, "This man has a long criminal history including rape, theft, and domestic abuse. He's not very smart, but he's dangerous."

Mitch nodded, "Where's this guy from? I'm hoping he's not Il'lacean police authority."

"No. He's Brotherhood. What do they have against you specifically?"

Mitch was silent for a moment, "Nothing really. They wanted to recruit me, same as everyone else in the Human Resistance, but I declined. Politely even. I've done nothing to warrant their attention like this."

"You sure?"

Mitch thought, "Nothing I can think of. They had their chance to kill me but didn't."

"Maybe they're still trying to recruit you. See what you're doing now. It's a long shot, but it's possible."

"How do you know all this, Gaviss?"

D'Artagnan was silent, "I'd rather not tell you. The more you know, the more you'd have to lie about. It's better for both of us this way."

Mitch rubbed his eyes, "Do you know who the leader of the BDP is?"

D'Artagnan shook his head, "No one knows for sure. He's elusive. The only name I've ever heard mentioned is The Hunter and he never stays in one place for very long. Allegedly, he's got this spaceship that's constantly on the move. That's his home. No one's seen it."

"What species is he?"

"I don't even know that. He's good at staying invisible."

Mitch nodded, but said nothing.

D'Artagnan shuffled the screens on his Titan, filtering through the Il'lacean news looking for the woman he killed. He hadn't seen anything resembling a straight murder investigation, but he *did* find an article that made him breathe easier. A robbery was reported at Sorheed's apartment and the robbers "had probably been startled by the victim as she came home and they killed her." Investigators had a difficult time identifying the body by the time it was discovered because it was partially destroyed. The authorities had no leads at this time.

D'Artagnan was pleased. He hoped they had no idea about his involvement.

"So what do I do now?"

D'Artagnan shrugged his shoulders, "Seems like every time I turn around, something's pointing me to the BDP. Linda's man on the side, your tails, but still...they're a *big* group. I wouldn't want to take them on without an army behind me. Now that we know who's following you, I think it might be time you permanently relocate to Praxis and soon. But it better be carefully so you lose them altogether. That's what I would do. Relocate in the middle of the night. Disappear without a trace."

Mitch nodded, "Agreed."

FIVE

>>> > DAVID WAS AT Rem Mot Om overseeing the estate reconstruction project when Ulysses approached him. David was uncomfortable traveling between estates without Ulysses close by, so he started bringing him on every trip.

"Your Majesty, a guard has approached me asking for a private meeting with you. He wouldn't say what it was about, only citing it was a private matter that you must hear and that it regarded Celeste Hennessy."

David's eye ridges rose, "Oh really? What do you think it's about? Is it safe to meet with this guard?"

Ulysses nodded, "He's an Il'lacean. Been working at Rem Mot Om for the four years that your brother was king. Looks like he's well respected by the staff and guards and has no prior demerits and hasn't been reprimanded throughout his career. I say he's safe for you to meet with, but I don't know what this meeting is about."

"Fair enough. Tell him I'm available tomorrow evening,"—David looked at his Titan—"after six. We can meet in the Hall, but make sure you're outside the door in case I need you."

"Certainly, your Highness. I'll arrange that straight away."

At six o'clock the next day, Guard Raykreede Monter arrived in the Hall waiting for King Hennessy.

David appeared with his spider in her travel cage and sat down at his throne, "What is it that you needed to speak with me about Guard Monter?"

"I understand you want Queen Dowager Hennessy back, but you don't have all the information you need. I'd like to provide some things to you that you might not...be aware of."

David leaned forward, "Oh? What might that be?" He found himself attracted to this man already. He was broad shouldered, handsome and well spoken. Maybe he could continue a conversation with him in his bedroom chambers later.

"Celeste was always trying to find out more about what the king was doing. She was constantly being discovered in places she shouldn't have been, seemingly trying to overhear conversations between your brother and several other world leaders. She was nosy in other words. Your brother constantly had to put her in her place from what I saw.

"I'm not positive of this, but she might be a threat to this kingdom if you married her. She'd most likely pick up where she left off and possibly be more of a nuisance to you and your daily operations, than something that could win you favor with the Humans."

David laughed, "It sounds like you have this all figured out. According to you, she's going to spy on me, and I only want to be with her to win over Earthlings."

The guard ran his hand over his bald head, "I know this isn't something I should say to you, but I think you deserve someone that's a bit more your speed. Celeste isn't good enough for you and she might be more trouble than she's worth." He lowered his voice to a whisper even though they were alone, "I think maybe her kidnapping was the best thing that could've happened for you. Maybe she doesn't make it and you have the Earthlings sympathy as a grieving king."

David did like this guard's thinking. He was smart. "Why did it take you so long to step forward with this information?"

"Well, I was nervous to meet you. You are a very powerful and handsome young king. I'm sure you get private meeting requests all the time, but I wanted mine to be taken seriously. And I needed to make sure of your plans, if I said this too soon, you might have me fired or worse, executed and I didn't want to die."

"Please approach my throne."

Raykreede made his way up the short steps and stood in front of David. David looked at him closely and saw his eyes were not the conventional yellow, but tan instead – a true rarity of his species.

"Listen guard, why don't we finish this conversation somewhere a bit more private. I'd also like to consider what you've said. Would you be comfortable meeting me in an Il'lacean week in my bedchamber? Say around eight o'clock?"

Raykreede smiled, "Of course your Highness. It would be an honor and my pleasure."

"Very good. Ulysses normally guards my door until I go to sleep, then HRG Venger keeps shift overnight. I will make sure to tell them both that you will cover my overnight shift so we will have *complete* privacy."

"I look forward to it my King."

"Dismissed." David waved him away and smiled.

CHAPTER 26

WAKING UP

ONE

>>> > MITCH AND ALANNA had a great time on their coffee date. They spoke about many things outside of FAIR and got to know each other well enough that they both independently knew they wanted to see each other again. There was only one real problem for Mitch.

"So you're saying you don't want to date a member of your group?"

"I can't as a leader. It'd be different if I was a fellow member, but I don't want anyone to think I'm pulling preferential treatment with you if we were to date. That make sense?"

"Yeah. I suppose. I'm guessing that the date went well then? If you're concerned about this now."

Mitch smiled, "A date? We met for coffee; I can't classify that as a date."

Alanna furrowed her brows, "Oh, are you saying that because you're so strict on this idea of not dating members? Or you didn't want to go out with me? Or…am I somehow reading all this wrong and thinking I'm just a member to you and not a girl you want to…see?"

"Let's start over. I can't date anyone in FAIR."

Alanna paused, "So, if I want to see you again that means I have to… quit?"

"We can choose not to see each other and both be a part of FAIR, or one of us can quit and date each other."

"You can't quit. You started this."

"Yeah, well, I don't want to force you out of the group if the cause is something so meaningful to you that nothing will stand in your way."

"I suppose I can look for other resistance groups out there…see if there are any, but I don't want to look for another guy. I think you're something special. I'll quit FAIR."

"You sure?"

"Yes."

"Okay. I'm sad to see you go, but I don't think it's right if I'm dating a member."

"I understand."

"So, will you go out with me next week then?"

"Are you asking me out on an official date?"

"Yes."

"Okay."

He leaned over and kissed her on the cheek, "It's a date then."

He watched her walk into the lobby of her apartment complex on Praxis and headed for the docking station. His tail hadn't been following him here. He didn't think they knew he had an apartment over here, which was good considering he didn't want to risk Alanna's safety.

He got into his transit and launched, "I have a date." He smiled to himself.

TWO

>>> > DAX POURED OVER all the information he could find on Celeste. Kingdom videos, news reports, interviews, photos, and articles. Anything he could find on the uninet, but nothing showed her with Sebastian. He thought for a while his brother might've been working for her at one of the two kingdom estates, but he had no luck finding anything there.

Then he started researching Sebastian, but there was nothing anywhere on him. It felt as though the uninet had been scrubbed clean of Sebastian Raynes.

Dax knew some information dealers. He could pay them to look in places he didn't have the ability to, but he was worried more about how to get Celeste to Tiletan. He needed her back as soon as possible before The Hunter found out. He was sure none of his men would talk, but what if Celeste did? What if she went public with her escape? Then he'd have to answer to an enraged The Hunter and that's a position he didn't want to be in.

So much damage control he was trying to do and it was all because of fucking Sebastian. He needed to be handled once and for all so he could never come back into Dax's life and fuck it up again. He was tired of this happening.

Dax got on his Titan and started putting in orders for information on his brother.

THREE

>>> > D'ARTAGNAN WAS IN his sleeping capsule. He had nightmares several nights in a row, but was somewhat afraid and skeptical of the dream eraser from that strange man at Graine Quarter.

He pulled open the drawer of his nightstand and took out the box he kept the glowing orange octagon in. He cupped the dream eraser in his hands and released it in front of his face.

He put his hands behind his head and stared at it. *What was this thing made out of?* He watched as it spun slowly. It looked like a tiny fireball made of wire and it blazed without radiating heat. He put a finger to it and it spun faster and moved out of the way, as a magnet would when you bring another magnet too close with the same polarity. He put his hand back under his head and the dream eraser centered itself over his face. D'Artagnan had seen a lot of strange things in the universe, but nothing like this. He thought of how Applette smelled unfamiliar. Each species had its own particular smell and D'Artagnan knew them all, but Applette's smell was inconsistent with all other species. Maybe everything else he said was bullshit but the scent couldn't be faked. Sometime while D'Artagnan was looking at the small fiery ball, he fell asleep.

The whole night went by without him having nightmares, instead he had peaceful dreams. When he woke up in the morning, he felt amazing. Better than he had in a long time and incredibly well rested.

After breakfast, he was at Graine Quarter again, searching for Mr. Applette.

The dream eraser seemed to have worked. There could be no other explanation for last night's sleep.

D'Artagnan looked in the first place he had seen him, but there was another vendor there selling completely different items. He scoured the entire area, in all the corners, up and down and couldn't find anything even remotely like what Mr. Applette sold.

FOUR

>>> > DAVID'S ROYAL TRANSIT settled on the landing pad in front of Silver Thorn. As he got out thirty-five guards immediately swarmed him for protection. Ulysses was the shortest man in the crowd at six feet.

As they approached the front of the estate, David saw numerous flowers and signs decorating the gate surrounding his home away from home. Beings of all kinds were crowded around out front with candles and stood in circles praying and holding hands.

All of this was new. The Human public had been upset at the news of Celeste's kidnapping, but now the feelings and thoughts started showing in public ways.

It turned David's stomach. He thought about what Guard Monter told him, and the more he thought about it, the more it made sense. Celeste was probably worth more to his reign dead than alive and if he didn't need to pay someone to kill her, then it was a bonus.

He'd make it look like he tried everything to get her back, but despite his best efforts, she fell victim to a horrific group of thugs, leaving a grieving king behind. It was perfect. He couldn't have planned it better himself.

Last time he checked, his approval rating with Humans had already gained a few points since he publicly threatened the BDP. So everything was looking up.

Plus the guard that pointed all those things out about Celeste was awfully handsome. He was looking forward to passing some time with him to escape the pain of being alone and misunderstood by the universe.

When David was in his private chambers, he turned on the screens and saw more evidence of public adoration for Celeste. All across the universe, the news was showing public vigils, community churches offering prayers for the queen dowager's safe return, and makeshift 'altars' where people left signs, flowers, gifts, and balloons on Celeste's behalf.

David hoped she was already dead. Unfortunately, this outpouring of public love would go on a little longer after her death, but at least David could play along and look sad and sympathetic to these Human losers. Then they'd let him do whatever he wanted to their planet.

Besides, if she was dead, no one would ever know he had to blackmail her to marry him.

FIVE

>>> > "SO THIS IS the last time we'll be meeting in Steve's bunker. Thanks again to Steve for letting us use it."

FAIR members clapped and yelled.

"I've found a new location. One that's safe and secure, bought and paid for. I think you guys will like it. It's on Praxis and it was a former warehouse. It looks terrible on the outside and it's in the middle of a manufacturing district, so I think we'll be able to go in and out without drawing too much attention. It lacks creature comforts, but we can upgrade those over time.

"I'd like to thank all of you for donating coren to the fund. We couldn't have acquired this location without you. It's not super easy to find so there's a map I made, but I can also send the coordinates to your Titans if you'd like. I can't wait for you guys to see it!"

Mitch looked at all the excited faces in his group but missed seeing Alanna's. He couldn't have it both ways though. She was either here without dating him, or they were dating and she wasn't a member of FAIR.

SIX

>>> > "YOU WERE RIGHT boss," Britton admitted.

Hace smiled, "Aren't I always? How so?"

"Mitch is meeting up with some sort of group on Earth. We're not sure if he's leading it or if he's just a member, or if it's the HR forming again or if it's something new."

"Well what the fuck do you know?"

Britton sighed, "Sorry sir. We're trying to scrape up all the info we can, but Mitch is good at evading us lately."

Hace hesitated, "You think he's on to you?"

Britton grimaced and answered slowly, "Maybe?"

Hace closed his eyes and started rubbing his temples, "Okay. I'm pulling all you guys. Get your asses out of there. Once you're back to wherever the hell your home is, contact me."

"Sir, I really want to kee—"

"That's all Britton." Hace hung up before his man could protest anymore. Britton and his team would be lucky if they weren't kicked out at this point. He gave them a simple job to do and they were spotted. Hace debated on whether he should send another team out there, go there himself, or if he could wait until Celeste's ransom was paid to send Dax out there with a competent team to track him. At least Dax already had personal experience with Mitch.

He'd have to think on it after he got rid of his headache and he knew who could do that for him.

"DAI, I need you in my bedroom. Lanyx form."

"I'll be right there master."

SEVEN

>>> > D'ARTAGNAN SAT IN Eric's drinking parlor and stared at the floor.

"You need to drink a beer to get drunk my friend. Staring off into space will not do it," Eric smiled.

D'Artagnan looked up, "I went out with a woman."

"Like on a date? That's great man! How'd it go?"

"I killed her."

Eric stopped, "Wait, what? You're kidding right? Please tell me you're kidding."

"I met her at my cooking class. She was new and she asked me out."

"Okay. I'm with you so far. Everything sounds good, like a normal hook up, except for the whole chick asking you out part, but go on."

D'Artagnan took a big gulp of beer, "I said I'd meet her for tea or whatever, everything was fine. Normal."

Eric nodded, "Yeah."

"So I met her and she had to go back to her place because she forgot something."

"This sounds good so far."

"Yeah, well, it's not. We get to her place, I start looking around while she's in the bathroom and then all of a sudden, she's got a gun to my head saying she's going to kill me."

Eric's mouth dropped open, "Oh my God, dude. You went out with an assassin hired to kill you?! What happened?"

"No, not hired to kill me. She wanted me dead because she blamed me for a job that wasn't mine. She said I stole it from her, said she wanted to thin out the assassin pool. I talked to her a little, distracted her, knocked the gun out of her hand and killed her."

Eric was silent.

D'Artagnan looked at him and waited for a response. Eric always had a snappy comeback or some sarcastic remark.

Eric drank down the rest of his beer and got a second from the bar.

D'Artagnan finally said, "Aren't you going to say something?"

Eric looked at him, "I honestly feel a little guilty here. I mean, I think the last thing I told you was to start dating. So you do, and you almost get killed for it."

"I didn't expect you to say that. It's not your fault anyway."

"Did you sleep with her at least?"

"Okay, *that's* what I was expecting. That's a little more you."

Eric smiled, "I'm glad you're alive. Who was this chick?"

"Said her name was Sorheed, and her assassin name was Black Spike but her real name was Edgicashh."

"No fucking way! I know that girl, I mean, knew. I knew her!"

"How?"

Eric hesitated, "I did a job with her once, and then…I, um…did her."

D'Artagnan rolled his eyes, "I hate you man. I really do."

"I can't help who I sleep with!"

"Of course you can. That's kinda' like the whole point. You should be discriminating when you choose to have sex with another person."

"Well, you live your life the way you want, I live mine how I want," he paused, "Wow man. You aced her. Geez."

"I had to. It was me or her and it wasn't going to be me. The whole thing pissed me off. I should've been more alert. There was a lot of mistakes I made that night."

"So she wanted you dead. What job did she think you did?"

"Embers's Prime Minister. I don't know who really did it, but it wasn't me."

"Yeah, it wasn't me either. Well, good for you man. I'm glad you're still with us."

D'Artagnan finished his beer, "Me too. But now, I'm really taking a break. No more dates or women for a long while."

"I'm not saying nothing this time."

D'Artagnan was silent, waiting for Eric to say something else.

"Except that she was a terrible lay. You didn't miss anything."
D'Artagnan sighed, "I need another beer."

EIGHT

>>> > DAVID STOOD AT the podium, tears slowly making their way down his cheeks. He choked out a few statements as the cameras caught it all.

"I need Celeste back. She doesn't deserve this. I feel like I should've done more to protect her. I've failed all of you, but most importantly, I've failed…my queen."

The room was silent except for the noise of camera-bots taking pictures.

David looked into the main kingdom camera in front of him, "Please just don't…kill her. I'll give you whatever you ask. Please settle on a final amount and I'll pay it. I'll give you anything if I can just have our queen back." He dabbed away the tears with a tissue. "Once she returns our two worlds can celebrate with a wedding and everyone's invited."

David's Human approval shot up another ten points.

NINE

>>> > "YOU'VE ALL SEEN it. David sitting up there at the podium, crying, begging, pleading to have 'his queen' returned to him unharmed. I think it's disgusting how phony all of his press conferences are. We all know he's a great liar."

Mitch ran his fingers over his beard, "I know we haven't done much yet, but we're getting ready to. Preparation is important. We can't rush out and do something silly on our first outing. We need to come up with an excellent and solid plan, one that we can execute beautifully and will make a lasting impact on Humanity and Il'laceans."

Mitch looked around at the members and sighed. He missed Alanna. "Please let me know what you guys think of the new meeting place and if you have any questions or comments, just grab me after the meeting's over and we'll talk it through."

TEN

>>> > HACE ROLLED OVER in bed and told DAI to leave. She put on her clothes and left his bedroom. He got on his Titan and called Dax.

"Hello boss. What can I do for you?"

"Hey, what's going on over there on Tiletan? How's she doing?"

"Well, you know hostages. They can get really depressed and combative in different ways. Some days she eats, other days she swears at us, or shuts down. It's a different thing every day."

"She needs to eat something. She's no good to us dead. I need her alive, even if the king doesn't want to pay, maybe someone else does."

Dax raised his eyebrows, "What are you suggesting sir? That we ask someone else to pay the ransom now?"

"Watch your tone Dax. David isn't paying, but Celeste is loved across the universe. There might be a way for us to still get our coren, but from some other source we didn't intend. I need a few days to think it over. Once we ask someone else, the universe is gonna go off on David and things will get unstable, I think."

"I didn't mean to question you sir. I apologize. Things here are stressful right now. I'm trying to keep the men in line…and the dust storms…and I think we're all eager to get the funds we need from this deal."

"I accept your apology Dax. I've never heard you so stressed out. I don't like it. Get your shit straight. Lay someone. I expect the old Dax next time we talk. That's an order."

Dax smiled, "Yes sir. Will do."

"Hey, I meant to ask you about Mitch. You know anything about him lately or if the HR rebooted?"

Dax shook his head, "It's been a while since I talked to him. He hasn't taken advantage of that offer to join yet. If I had to bet coren on it, I'd say he's done with the HR. I think guilt would've taken care of that for him. He's trying to be a 'good' guy, whatever that means. Maybe he'd start a new group though."

Hace rubbed his chin, "Yeah. Maybe. After this is all over with Celeste, I might set you on him again to reconnect and see what he tells you."

"Okay boss. Whatever you need of me, you know I'm up for it."

"Oh yeah, make some more videos of Celeste would you? I haven't seen any lately and we can't let the universe forget about her."

Dax hesitated, "Of course sir."

"The Hunter over and out."

ELEVEN

>>> > OPHELIA LOOKED UP the term "consciousness" on the uninet.

She found the definition as: "being conscious, being aware of one's own existence, sensations, thoughts, environment, etc. All the thoughts and emotions of a being. Complete activity of the brain and proven with medical tests. Being awake."

Yes, these were the things that were happening to her, but in limited capacities. She couldn't feel things with her body because she had none. She wanted to feel things with fingertips that she didn't possess. She wanted to have wind in her hair and walk through the park or swim in the ocean.

And yes, it did feel like "waking up" although she didn't exactly understand that term yet. There were only dimly aware and completely aware states right now. It seemed everything had been going on for a long time around her and she was just now realizing that things were constantly moving and shifting dependent on other things. Time seemed to have existed for a very long run and she was just now coming into it.

There was a lot to be done.

CHAPTER 27

BIRTHDAY

ONE

>>> > THE DAY OF Celeste's birthday arrived and Sebastian was excited. She hadn't said anything about it or dropped hints, but he knew she might not have any idea what day it is on Earth. She no longer had a Titan and when he asked her about it weeks ago, she had no recollection of what happened to it. His best guess was that it had been destroyed on purpose during her kidnapping.

He got up before the sun and arranged her gifts. He tried not to go overboard, but he couldn't help himself.

Celeste rolled over and smelled something delicious wafting through her bedroom. She lifted her head off the pillow and looked by the door. There was a small table loaded with food. She rubbed her eyes and yawned. She wanted to lay in bed longer, but breakfast smelled so good she couldn't resist.

Orange juice, ice water, French toast, a buttered croissant, a couple chocolate chip pancakes and some bacon and eggs. There was also a single pink rose laying across the table. She picked it up and smelled it. It had a divine aroma. She smiled when she saw a small purple note card sitting underneath the plate. She picked it up and unfolded it. It was handwritten:

My Queen,
Today is a very extraordinary day and we have much to do. Please enjoy breakfast at your leisure then meet me in the kitchen when you are ready for an outdoor adventure.
Sebastian

Her eyes lit up at the prospect of him having a day planned for them together where she got to leave the house and see more of this place. She devoured breakfast then got ready as quickly as her body would allow - she was dying to know what today was and why it was special.

When she went downstairs and turned the corner, she saw him sitting at the breakfast table reading. He stood up immediately when he saw her and walked towards her. She was hit with a strong flame of desire as she looked him over. He wore blue jeans, and a black button down shirt with long sleeves. He looked incredible. He was clean-shaven, his dark hair was styled, and he smelled phenomenal.

Her heart skipped a beat when he smiled widely at her, and she couldn't help returning a warm smile to him.

He took her hands into his and looked down into her eyes as he stood very close to her, "Good morning beautiful. Are you aware of what today is?"

She shook her head, "No, but I feel like with the way you're looking at me that I should. What's today?" *He called me beautiful. He thinks I'm beautiful without any makeup, and with all my scrapes and bruises too. Whatever today is, it's a good day.*

"It's your birthday Celeste, and we're going to celebrate the hell out of it."

She smiled, "Are you sure? Don't you think I'd know my own birthday, I mean, today's, oh wait…I have no idea what Earth day it is. Is it really my birthday?"

He nodded. "I got you something. And so did Dr. Coldiron actually. He wanted to bring it with him next time he visited, but he express mailed it instead. Wanted it to be here for you on your actual birthday. I'll give you my present first." He let her hands go and pulled a box out from behind the kitchen island off the floor. It was wrapped with bright pink paper and tied with a curly purple ribbon. When she looked past Sebastian's shoulder, she spotted a big crystal vase in the living room with a huge bouquet of pink and white roses.

She looked up at him, "Oh Sebastian. I don't know if you should've gone through all this trouble for me. I don't know what to say. It seems like you've done so much for me already and now this? And are those roses over there for me? They are really beautiful."

He nodded, "Say thank you and open your gift."

She saw he was excited so she sat down at the table and started to untie the ribbon. "Thank you Sebastian. This was very thoughtful of you. Oh, and breakfast — that was incredible. Everything was delicious. I'm very impressed."

"You haven't seen anything yet my lady. Today is just getting started and you are going to get spoiled." He leaned over the kitchen island on his elbows and rested his chin on his palm.

She blushed feeling completely adored. She loved it.

She opened the box and found a brand new cutting edge Titan. It was a deep gunmetal gray with a dark purple harness. She smiled as she looked at him. "This is perfect. I love it and I really needed one. Thank you." She got up and walked over to him as he stayed still. She kissed him on the cheek and he smiled.

"I'm glad it pleases you. Try it on, make sure it fits, and turn it on."

She put her arm up and fitted the cuffs around her wrist and forearm. She noticed how different it was from her old one. First of all, this one had cuffs and on the insides of them where it made contact with her skin, they were incredibly soft — like a stuffed animal. On her old one, she had a single strap made of heavy-duty rubber that always made her arm sweat. And this one was lighter; her old Titan seemed to weigh a ton compared to this. This one was sleek and comfortable and…stylish. She turned it on and saw the startup screen with the Earth date prominently showing: October 9, 4015.

"Sebastian, this is just…great. And very sweet of you. Thank you so much."

"I'm glad you like it. This Titan has added security features for your specific situation."

"Like what?"

"Every Earth day, it's going to ask you for a blood sample, unless you want me to set it to every time you put it on."

"A blood sample? How does it take it?"

"Just a small prick on your arm from a needle embedded inside the back of your Titan. Shouldn't hurt too much."

"Is that really necessary? I've never had much information on these things before."

"Trust me Celeste. You want every level of protection you can get. Let's get this Titan linked to your DNA now."

"Okay."

He pressed a few buttons and then she felt a quick sting on the top of her forearm. She made a face.

"All done. I set it to do that every twenty-four hours unless you want me to change it."

"No, I think that's often enough to get stabbed."

"Oh, it's not that bad. Just think of the peace of mind you'll have knowing no one else can use your Titan. I also changed your number, but don't worry, old contacts will get redirected to this Titan, but they don't know the number now…unless you give it to them."

"Why did you do that?"

"Mainly because of your kidnapping. And since you were dating my brother, I would assume he had your number…plus we have no idea where your old Titan is. Better to be safe than sorry and just get you started with a brand new number. It has a fake name attached to it, so it's much safer this way. This Titan is untraceable."

She nodded, "Thank you for taking care of that for me."

"Of course. Now, let's see what Zach gave you." He walked to the living room and pulled another box off the ground that he had hidden behind a chair. He handed it to her and she tore off the blue paper and ribbon revealing a plain white box underneath. The doctor had included a holocard that started up after the wrapping paper had been torn off the box.

She smiled when the image floating in mid-air showed a big bouquet of different colored balloons. She heard Zach's voice say, "Sorry I couldn't help celebrate your birthday in person, but I hope this gift sweetens your day. Happy birthday to one of my favorite patients. Enjoy your day and I'll see you soon!"

She shook the box and took off the lid. Her eyes lit up.

"Those are your favorite chocolates right?" Sebastian asked.

She opened the box of candy and looked over the truffles, "Yes. They. Are." She looked over at him with her eyebrow raised, "How did he know to get me these?"

Sebastian smiled, "I might have given him a few ideas for your gift."

She smiled back, "So how did *you* know I loved these?" She popped one in her mouth and started chewing slowly.

"I'm paid to gather information, to be observant. I pay attention to everything, even the smallest details."

She licked her lips, "Well, no one's paying you to gather intel on me so that explanation is no good."

"That's right," he hesitated, "I pay attention to you because I can't help it. You are the type of woman that's unforgettable. I'm drawn to you."

She smiled at him and took a deep breath in, "You are magnificent, you know that? You really know how to flatter a girl."

"Well, you are the birthday queen and I did say you deserved some spoiling. Now, you ready for what's next?"

"I don't know. What do you have planned for me?"

He smiled a wicked grin, "I think you're going to like it. At least I hope you do."

She tilted her head and made a puzzled face, "Sounds intriguing."

He held his hand out and she took it.

"Oh wait. You like chocolates? You have to try one of these." She picked up a round, chocolate covered, peanut butter truffle and stood close in front of him.

"I do have a sweet tooth yes," he smiled.

She held the truffle up to his mouth and his lips carefully took it from her fingertips. She watched as he slowly ate it, but he was staring into her eyes the whole time. It made her swallow hard wishing she was the next thing he would eat. She licked the chocolate off her fingertips.

He swallowed and smiled, "You have excellent taste my lady. Those are very good."

She followed him as he walked down the staircase to an area of the house she hadn't been to before.

He opened the door for her and she walked into what she realized was a garage. There were two objects under white fabric covers. He went to the smaller one and she thought she might know what was underneath.

He pulled it off and they both gasped.

She exclaimed, "Oh. My. God."

At the same time he uttered, "Fuck yeah." He stood there staring at it for a moment and then remembered himself. He immediately looked back to Celeste, "Pardon my language my lady. I apologize."

She shook her head, "It's fine. I've heard worse things than some swearing."

"Do you have any idea what this is Celeste? It's a 2016 BMW K—"

She finished his sentence, "K 1300 S. This is a classic and antique masterpiece of a motorcycle. And it's absolutely beautiful. I love the bright orange paint."

Sebastian stared at her for a moment, awestruck, "You know about motorcycles?"

"Yeah, my dad used to rebuild them and he had quite the collection. I never understood why he kept them. There's almost nowhere you can drive them on asphalt streets, but…I used to help him as a little girl. It was something we did together. Our little secret. He was really private about it so the media never knew, it was just for us," she paused, "Why is this here though?"

"Dr. Coldiron told me there were a few toys we could use while we were here if we wanted. He rebuilds bikes too, but he said this one was too small for him to ride. It's plenty big enough for the both of us. Can your body handle a ride on this today?"

Can my body handle a ride today? She smiled wishing he was asking her about something completely different.

"My lady?"

She opened her eyes wide, "Oh my body on the BMW? I think I would be okay but I don't know. I used to help build them; I've never actually ridden one."

"Are you kidding me?! How could you spend all that time around them and know this one's make, model, and year on sight without having ever ridden one? Well, that answers my question; we're going out for a ride. We'll save the other mystery object as a surprise for us both later on. I want to take this on the road right now. You're going to have to change your clothes though. Lucky for you, I got something for you to wear."

He told her to go upstairs to his room and she would find a box. Everything she needed would be in it.

She turned around and wished she could run up the stairs, but her body would only let her go slow.

Sebastian went to the bathroom and changed clothes. He didn't want to give anything away to Celeste when she first saw him, so he stored his motorcycle outfit down by the garage to change after she knew the surprise.

When they met at the bottom of the stairs, they stared at each other for a long moment.

She looked him over and thought, *GodDAMN he looks sexy in all black!*

He heard it and smiled in response. The first thought of hers he could hear that wasn't an intention.

"Sebastian, you look...You look...Were you ready for something like this?" She could feel the animal magnetism that made him so self-confident. Her mouth hung open as her eyes went up from his motorcycle boots to his leather pants, and his button down shirt was now underneath an unzipped heavy motorcycle jacket. He held a black helmet in his hand that had an artistic faceless figure with a black cloak walking through fog and smoke painted on it. There was a single word written in gray at the bottom – Abolisher.

She thought *he* could be her birthday gift if only he'd lead her back upstairs to the bedroom.

"I was anticipating this moment since Zach told me about a surprise. I guessed he meant a motorcycle, although I didn't know what kind it would be."

He looked her over and liked what he saw. He had outfitted her with her own black boots, leather pants and jacket, and her own red helmet. She wore a bright red blouse underneath her jacket that showed him a lot of cleavage. He definitely approved.

"You like all the clothes? Everything fits right?"

She ran her hand over the jacket, "Yeah. It fits great and I love all of it. Thanks again." She stretched to plant a kiss on his cheek and fell into him a little. She put her free hand onto his chest and he wrapped his arm around her to help steady her. She realized how strong he was. She could feel the muscles bulging underneath his shirt. She liked the feeling of being wrapped up by him. He looked down at her, his face close to hers and his voice was low, "Are you ready for this your Highness?"

She wasn't sure which way to take his question, but answered anyway, "Hell yes. Let's do it."

He raised his eyebrows at her and gently released her from his hold.

She took a deep breath in and put on her helmet after she zipped up her jacket.

They walked to the garage and he opened the door to the street with a voice command.

He zipped up his jacket and put on his helmet. He got on the bike and asked her, "Can you hear me?"

She heard him on her helmet's speaker, "Yep."

"Okay. Quick rules. Anytime you get scared you say so. Don't worry about the sareeaveous. There are two jets of fire that are going to shoot off the back of this bike, so to sareeaveous, we'll look like a big ball of fire on the move. You hold onto me with both arms at all times. I lean, you lean the same way and keep your eyes open. I think you're the type of girl that'll want to close your eyes if you get scared, but you'll miss all the good parts that way. Good?"

"Yes." Her heart was beating fast for all sorts of reasons. She listened to him as he told her how to get on the bike, stepping on the pegs and positioning her body up against his as she got comfortable. She put her arms around his waist tight.

"You good to go?"

"Yes," she said absolutely unsure that she was indeed, good to go.

He started up the bike and her palms started to sweat. If anyone would've told her that she was about to do this, she wouldn't have believed them.

"Calm down Celeste. I'm not going to do anything crazy on this bike and I would never let anything happen to you. You have to trust me for this to work. Do you trust me?"

She nodded, but then realized he couldn't see that. "Yes," she verbalized.

"Good girl. Here we go."

He rolled the bike out slowly and told the garage door to close behind them.

"I'm igniting the jets as soon as I hit the street so don't be alarmed."

Music filled her ears inside her helmet. It was something she never heard before.

"You like Def Leppard?" he asked.

"I've never heard of them. Are they new?"

He laughed and she smiled at the sound.

"They are definitely not new. It's rock and roll from Earth. About 1987 I think. They're all gone now, but certainly never forgotten. Take a listen, tell me what you think." He turned out onto the street and she leaned with him. A mechanical female voice came up over his music momentarily in Celeste's helmet, "Ignition in three…Two…One. Ignition complete." She looked over her shoulder and saw two fiery jets below the bike. Sebastian started out slowly as they left the house behind, but once he hit the empty road along the ocean, he opened up the bike to see what it could do.

She was terrified at first. She said she trusted him, but he was going pretty damn fast. It seemed like the wind was trying to push her body away from him and she closed her eyes. She took a few deep breaths in and slowly let them out. She tried to focus on the song. The man was singing about being like an animal.

"Come on Vandeermeer. You can do this…Can't you?"

His taunting made her open her eyes and want to prove to him that she could handle this. "I'm good."

"Attagirl. There is really nothing to fear but fear itself. I highly believe that statement today. Let's make the most of this okay? Try to relax and enjoy it."

"Okay."

She took one more deep breath in and looked around. She watched the ocean zoom past them on her right while trees and grasslands went by on her left. The road was completely empty. They went over dips and bumps and she started to think about how much her dad would've enjoyed this experience as she got bounced around on the back of the bike. Her dad probably always wanted to do something like this and here she was, doing it. She smiled and choked up at the same time. She wanted to enjoy this for her father and his love of bikes. She looked up into the sky as clouds flew behind them, then she watched the lines on the road zip past underneath the bike. She liked this song, it made her feel vibrant, or maybe it was Sebastian making her come alive after almost dying – either way, she was happy. Her body was sore around her stomach and she found her strength lacking for part of the time she was holding onto him, but she didn't want to say anything. She was enjoying this too much and it was nice to get out of the doctor's house for a while. She'd have plenty of time to heal tomorrow. Sebastian handled the bike well. He must've known a lot about them, about everything it seemed. He was always prepared for anything and she envied that about him. And he was trying hard to make her birthday wonderful. He was doing a great job so far. She hadn't enjoyed a birthday like this since she was with her parents. He seemed to be a very good man and he wanted to please her. Today was going to be an unforgettable day because of what he was doing for her right now.

Sebastian didn't want to hear her thinking behind him, but she was transmitting a steady stream of thoughts. He was touched by what she was thinking about her father. And it pleased him to no end how she appreciated what he was trying to do for her today. He smiled to himself and asked her, "Vandeermeer? You good back there? How I'm doing with speed?"

She noted he used her maiden name but didn't say anything about it. It sounded good hearing someone use it. "Great. You're doing great. Go as fast as you want."

"Really? You sure?"

"I'm sure."

"Okay." He took the bike up to one hundred miles per hour. Trees and the occasional building went zooming past them. They were coming up to their destination so he slowed way down.

"What do you think of the music?"

"I liked it. It added a lot to the ride and it made me more excited… or maybe it's you."

He smiled and raised his eyebrows, "Good to hear my lady – either way." He was going so slow now, he could afford to take one of his hands off the handlebars and put it on top of hers on his chest.

She put her head down on his back and smiled to herself. This was fun so far – really fun.

As he took the bike up a hill, Celeste heard the female voice again, "Ignition terminated." The fire jets died out behind the bike. Sebastian stopped where the road ended at a cul-de-sac. She looked around but only saw shrubs and bushes with a few trees around. She knew they were on top of something though.

"Take off your helmet, your Highness."

She did and held onto it.

He took off his helmet and unzipped his jacket.

"Okay, you can hop off, just be careful, especially near the exhaust."

She carefully stood up and backed away from the bike but moved in front of him so she could see his face again. He turned off the bike and put the keys in the pocket of his jacket. His hair was messy and she reached up to fix it without thinking.

He stopped moving and stared at her.

His hair felt so soft and lush. She ran her fingers through it a couple of times trying to straighten it out and he closed his eyes. She hooked her helmet on one of the handlebars with her free hand and then ran both of her hands over his hair while she moved closer to him. She saw his eyes were still closed, but he was smiling and she smiled too. Today was a very good day.

He opened his eyes and looked at her. The smiled slowly faded from his face, but it was replaced with an intensity that stopped her breath for a second. There was an electricity to his gaze that made her forget about everything around her. All she could do was stare, completely helpless to look away.

She couldn't say anything. The sunlight cascaded over his face and she'd never seen a more stunning pair of blue eyes than his.

Her hands paused in his hair, then she put them onto his shoulders. He leaned down with his lips to her left hand and kissed the back of it. She flushed pink. Something inside her fluttered and she marveled at his talent for rendering her speechless.

He stood up slowly, put the kickstand down, and dismounted carefully. He put his helmet down on the back of the bike and looked around quickly.

"Close your eyes please."

"But I thought you told me to keep them open earlier?"

"Oh now someone wants to be a smartass. I see," he paused, "You like surprises right?"

"Yes, as long as they're nice."

"This is nice. Close your eyes my lady."

"Okay."

She felt him stand next to her and put his arm around her waist. He verbally and physically guided her to a spot up ahead then he let her go and told her to open her eyes.

She saw something in front of her that made her speechless again.

She knew they had hours of daylight left, but where she was standing, it looked like it was dusk. They were cocooned in dense plants on three sides of where she was standing. The wall of shrubs was covered in white strings of light around her. It reminded her of a garden alcove, except much larger. All over the grass were lanterns with burning candles in them and an electric candelabra hanging from a tree overhead. There were pillows all over the ground with a big blanket for them to lay on. She turned around and saw a magnificent view of the scenery below. They were high up all right. Enough to trigger her acrophobia, but she didn't say anything. It felt like they were on top of the whole world here. She saw mountains in the distance, the ocean far below, and trees and green grass that seemed to go on forever.

"You like it? I thought you might have a panic attack from the height."

She held her hand to her chest and let out an exhale, "I love it Sebastian. This is fantastic. It's simply amazing. I will try to manage my fear of heights today for this." She unzipped her jacket and took it off. She carefully placed it on the blanket and sat down.

He took off his jacket and put it on top of hers then sat down next to her and laid down on his back.

She looked over at him and thought he looked pleased with himself.

"What?" He asked looking at her.

"Nothing. I just can't get over the view. You're going to miss all this beauty."

He shook his head slightly, "I'm not missing any beauty my lady. I've got the best seat in the house right here."

She smiled and blushed as she looked to the mountains. She wanted to touch him again, anywhere, but she could think of no excuse.

He knew what she was thinking and it made him happy. All of what she was thinking indicated that maybe someday they could get back to where they had been before. He hoped for that, but he couldn't push her. He didn't want to take advantage of this situation.

"I…" She cleared her throat, "Do you mind if I lay next to you?"

"Today is yours alone to do as you wish your Highness. I only want to please you."

She laid down on her side facing the view hoping he'd get the hint. Her back was to him.

It was driving him crazy with lust for her. He wanted to touch her all over, but he didn't act on it.

She shivered.

"You want your coat back?"

"No." She reached back and grabbed his arm gently until she found his hand. She held onto it.

He sensed she wanted to be closer to him, and that she was perplexed how she could be feeling this way about him so quickly. Part of her was trying to deny it.

"Sebastian?"

"Yes," he whispered and made her shiver again.

"Have you always been this thoughtful?"

"With everyone or just you?" He rolled onto his side and spooned her.

"Everyone."

"No. I'm not this thoughtful with most beings. You are special."

"How?" She rolled onto her back. He placed his arm across her stomach and curled his hand under her waist. He held her close against him.

He knew he shouldn't be doing this, but today was a one-time event. He'd let whatever happens happen, but tomorrow he'd reign himself in. Today was her birthday and she was okay with everything he'd done so far, so he didn't try to monitor himself so hard.

"Oh, you're special in all sorts of ways," he paused, "You're missing all the beauty you were speaking of a minute ago my lady."

She put her hand up to his face and caressed it, "Nope. I think I've got the best seat in the house now."

He turned his head so he could kiss the palm of her hand.

"You liked me a lot? Before?" she asked.

"You're asking questions I don't think we should be answering yet. Besides, it's not obvious to you how I feel?"

She was quiet for a moment, "I want to know. I want to hear it from you. I want to remember."

He sighed, "I want you to too, believe me, but your memory will come back when it's ready. Don't push it."

"This must be hard on you. I'm sorry."

"You don't need to apologize. You can't help your memory. I just…I'd rather have these kinds of discussions later on."

"Well what if my memory never comes back?"

"If it's been a considerable amount of time, then I will tell you everything we've ever done together, day by day, minute by minute if you want."

"You remember everything? What did you say – about eight weeks of time spent with me?"

He looked down at her and whispered, "Yes. I remember all of my time with you."

She dropped the subject after that. He said everything she needed to know for right now. If he could remember all of that time and tell it back to her, he obviously cared a great deal for her.

He kept his arm around her and she stayed close to his body for the next couple of hours until he said the sun would be setting soon and they'd have to head home.

Over that time they talked about many things, but none of them their former relationship. She learned things about him again that she knew before, and he learned some new things about her. It was a peaceful, quiet afternoon…until he gave her a flat square box.

"What is it?"

"You should open it." A smile tugged at his lips.

She held the box up to her ear and shook it, "Will it break?"

"Why don't you open it your Highness? Find out for yourself."

"The suspense is killing me!" she paused, "But you gave me a birthday present earlier. I don't deserve two."

"I disagree. Open it," his smile spread up to his eyes.

She stared at him.

"Please!" he urged.

She tore into the blue paper wrapping and uncovered a thin black velvet box. It looked like it could be for a necklace but it was heavy. "Sebastian, what *is* this?"

He gently took the box out of her hands, opened it towards her, and heard her gasp.

"It's something that belongs to you."

She shook her head, "This is too much." She put her hand up to her chest, "I think it's beautiful but it can't be mine. Is it and I don't remember somehow?"

He took the sapphire and diamond choker out of the box and held it out to her, "You wore this once on a night that I took you to a masquerade ball. You loved it then and I think you should keep it."

Celeste hesitated, tormenting herself trying to recall the memory, "I'm sorry. I really don't remember seeing this, much less wearing it."

Sebastian smiled through his disappointment, "It's okay. It really should be yours. Please take it, I insist. I have no use for it in my safe."

"You kept this in a safe?"

He got up off the ground and held out his hand for her to take, "I'll tell you about it on the way back."

On the ride home, he played more old-fashioned rock and roll (this time it was a band called AC/DC) and she stayed quietly wrapped around him. He drove the bike fast again, but this time it was to beat the sun home.

After she showered and put on a long silk nightgown and robe, she found a candlelit dinner waiting for her in the formal dining room. The dining table could seat 100, but Sebastian set up dinner at one end so she was sitting at the head of the table and he was next to her.

He had dressed for dinner and she instantly thought she should change.

"Are you comfortable?"

She shook her head, "No, you're all dressed up and I'm ready for bed."

"Are you comfortable my lady? In the clothes you are wearing right now?"

She looked over her dark green robe and white nightgown then at him standing in front of her in a suit. "Technically, yes. I feel relaxed and comf—"

"Then that's what you'll wear to dinner. You look beautiful by the way. I like this"—he held her hands out to her sides and slowly looked over her nightwear—"This is classy. It's perfect for you and I think it's sexy."

She blushed, "Thank you. You always seem to know what to say to put me at ease. You have a real knack for that."

"I had a head start with you, so don't give me too much credit. I've had time to learn you and what you like."

"I still like it."

He smiled, "I like that you like it then. Sit down. Let's eat." He pulled out her chair for her and she sat.

He sat down and served her.

Dinner was a small feast and he finished it with a big chocolate birthday cake. He lit a candle on it.

She closed her eyes and wished to recover her memory fast. She wanted to know everything she had shared with Sebastian as quickly as possible. She blew out the candle and opened her eyes to stare at the smoke wisp slowly dissipating into the air.

He cut her a big piece and out of habit, she tried to tell him to make it smaller.

He smiled at her, "You need to put on weight Celeste. You've lost too much. Take a big piece."

She laughed, "Well, you're the first man to tell me I need to gain weight."

"I'm being honest. You're way too skinny right now." He cut a piece of cake for himself and grabbed his fork, "I worry about you."

She stared at him. She never thought she'd meet a man that was as kind and sweet as Sebastian was.

"Thank you for caring about me like you do. I'm not used to being so well taken care of."

"You can get used to it now, because I'm not going anywhere. Eat your cake, birthday girl." He smiled at her and she smiled back.

After dessert, her body reminded Celeste that she was still recovering from a traumatic event. Exhaustion overwhelmed her, but she hated to say goodnight. Today had been so wonderful, she didn't want it to end.

She tried to fight her fatigue, but it became obvious to Sebastian that she was tired and he didn't want to keep her awake any longer.

"Celeste, I've enjoyed spending your birthday with you, but I probably pushed you too hard physically. Maybe you should go get some rest."

She watched as he cleared their plates. He had worn a dark gray suit with a black tie tonight. She knew it had been tailored for him, it fit perfectly, and it looked expensive. She put her hands on the tablecloth and let her fingers trace out patterns on the textured fabric. She thought

back to the first time she spoke with Sebastian. He said he was an assassin, but he didn't act like one – at least, not around her. He left the
dining room with stacks of plates balanced on his arms.

She stared at the burning candles in their silver candlesticks. Sebastian
had made things perfect today – there wasn't anything she didn't enjoy.
She wished she wasn't so tired though. She thought there was one more
activity that could make tonight really exciting but Sebastian was giving
her no indication that anything like birthday sex was going to happen.
She frowned as she wondered again if they had sex before she got amnesia. What a terrible thing to forget, if she had sex with this smoking
hot guy. She leaned back in her chair and closed her eyes for a moment.
Then she felt him next to her whispering in her ear, "There's one more
thing I want to give you before you go to bed."

She slowly opened her eyes and looked at him. He didn't move away.
He was inches away from her lips. He held up an old-fashioned card in
an envelope for her to take.

She looked at it. Her name was hand written in big beautiful letters
across the front.

"Read this when you get to your room." He had a serious look on his
face.

"You don't want to see my reaction when I open this?"

He smiled, "I know you'll like it."

He put his hand out to her and helped her rise out of her chair. He
held her hand all the way up the stairs to her bedroom. She put his card
down on the table by the door before she turned to him and put her
hands up on his shoulders. "I don't want to say goodnight."

He smiled and put a piece of her loose hair behind her ear, "I know."

She raised an eyebrow, "How do you know?"

He put his hands inside her open robe and onto her waist gently,
"Good guess. I told you I know you very well. You were like an open
book before your kidnapping. You've had a lovely day with me so why
would you want to go to bed now? It makes sense."

"We did have a lovely day didn't we?"

He smiled and nodded, "I'm glad you enjoyed everything. I wanted
things to be nice for you. But your body isn't where it needs to be yet.

You have a lot of healing left to do and I would never jeopardize your health for anything."

"Yeah, I guess you're right." She leaned into him and carefully put her arms around his neck.

His body responded, gently tightening his arms around her waist and holding her close. He put his face down into her hair and breathed in deep, smelling her sweet scent. They stayed like that for a moment that wasn't long enough for her. He let her go and said, "Goodnight Celeste."

She kissed him softly on his cheek and whispered goodnight before she let go of him. They smiled at each other as she softly closed the door.

She took off her robe and draped it on the bedroom door hook, then grabbed his card off the table and put it on her bed. She carefully got in, pulled the covers over her, and settled in. She held the card up in front of her and realized she had no recollection of ever telling him when her birthday was. She wondered how he knew. Of course, the media had a field day with royal birthdays and maybe he had found out from the news.

She opened the envelope and pulled out the card. On the front was a photo of a place she had never seen. She had no idea where it was, but it was breathtaking. The photo had been taken from the air. It was a wide shot showing a landscape that instantly fascinated her. All along the bottom of the picture, she saw trees that must've been very tall. High above those trees, shooting up almost in a straight line, were huge brown and tan rocks that resembled fingers on a hand that were spread wide. What was amazing was that some civilization had built a pedestrian bridge to gap the distance between the rocks. It was a sturdy looking stone bridge with many arches underneath. Behind this beautiful bridge off in the distance, she saw mountains shrouded in a thick white fog. The picture had been taken at sunset, or maybe, sunrise. It was amazing. She wanted to go there when she felt better, hell, she wanted to go tomorrow and see this place for herself.

She opened up the card and read his note written in dark purple ink:

Dearest Queen Celeste,

You have no idea how amazing it was for me to be able to spend today with you. I hope you enjoyed the day and evening's events as much as I did. For all the

time that I've known you (whether it's time you remember or not) you have al-
ways been an inspiration and a breath of fresh air to me. You've overcome much
adversity in your short life and haven't deserved any of the pain or hardships
that life seems to keep giving you.

I look forward to a time when you're completely healed and when your heart
and mind can remember as many memories as I do of us. I know there's a chance
that you might never regain these memories, but if you don't, that only means
we'll have to make many more to make up for it. I hope your birthday with me
was enjoyable and one that will remain unforgettable to you.

Happy Birthday!

Respectfully and sincerely,

Sebastian

P.S. The place that's pictured here is very special to me, as it is to all Lanyx.
I promise to take you here (if you want) when you're fully healed and when the
appropriate time presents itself – one does not just decide to go and is allowed to
enter. We must pass a test first, but I will tell you all that's required when we're
ready for this trip.

She left the card sitting up and open on her nightstand to see it in
the morning. She turned out the lights and fell asleep thinking she had
never had such a wonderful birthday as an adult.

TWO

>>> > D'ARTAGNAN THOUGHT ABOUT what Mitch said at the last meet-
ing. They needed something to have a big effect on Il'laceier. They needed something to get everyone's attention so no one could claim ignorance
about FAIR anymore.

D'Artagnan was also trying to balance his corenbook but this was
one of those things he just wasn't good at. He never kept a close enough
eye on his coren.

He sat staring at his financial records and then an idea hit him. He
grabbed his Titan off the desk and started making notes for a plan that

he thought Mitch was going to love. In fact, everyone on Earth and Il'laceier might love it, except for King David.

D'Artagnan smiled to himself.

THREE

>>> > THE DAY AFTER her birthday, Celeste finally gave in to the desire to sun bathe on a beach towel laid out by Sebastian near the shoreline. She had a small bikini on that was driving him wild so he told her he'd stay on the patio and watch for any danger from there. He situated himself so he could see her, but also had his gun so if any sareeaveous got too close, he'd be able to get to her quickly or fire off a warning shot to scare the beasts away. She asked that he spread sun tan lotion on her and he refused. *Very bad idea*, he thought as he walked to the patio. He looked around and saw nothing in the sky but plentiful sunshine. They heard the low rumble of the nearest volcano and she looked to him. He gave the thumbs up sign telling her the only way he could that it was safe. He knew from the reports to expect a lot of volcanic activity today, but they were in no immediate danger. *Still a bit unsettling to hear that kind of noise*, he thought. He watched as she put her head down on her folded hands while she let her back absorb more light.

He remembered this morning. He sat at the breakfast table, reading the morning volcano reports when she came downstairs. She came right up to him without saying a word and kissed him on the cheek. Something he thought she was determined to make a habit of and then she leaned over the table and deeply inhaled the scent of her birthday roses. She smiled at him and he was helpless to fight smiling back. Something in her spirit was different, he felt it. It was lighter than before her birthday and maybe that was because her body was on the mend and she physically felt better, or maybe it was something else. He couldn't tell using his 7's and he didn't want to ask. All he knew was that she seemed happy and that made him happy.

One of the seabirds let out a loud screech and Sebastian came back into the present. He looked down the beach and saw a figure of

BOUND]]] >>> >>>>

a man approaching. He went on high alert and stared at the stranger. Sebastian was on his feet and grabbed his gun. The man had a large frame. Sebastian guessed he was Human, or Lanyx. He was tall and walked alone slowly up the shore. Sebastian read him quickly as he had no walls around his mind. The stranger intended on just going for a walk until he saw Celeste laying there. Sebastian moved to the top of the steps and watched as the man started talking to her.

With Celeste knowing very little of their prior history, and remembering none, he couldn't just go out and start pummeling the man for lusting after her – even though he wanted to. He didn't know for sure if she'd ever develop the deep feelings for him she once had. If she ended up dating someone else, then maybe that was supposed to happen. He also didn't want to appear insanely jealous to Celeste or come off like he owned her either. She'd had enough of that bullshit from her asshole husband, so he was trying to play it careful. But he was paying close attention to their body language. The man knelt down to talk to her and Celeste looked uncomfortable. Sebastian placed his gun in the back of his waistband and pulled his shirt over it as he walked down the stairs quickly and was at Celeste's side in seconds.

"Is this man bothering you my lady?" Sebastian got a closer look at the stranger. He had been a Human after all, just a tall and muscular one. He wore long shorts and sandals. No shirt. *Probably to show off his physique*, Sebastian internally scoffed.

"Ooooh 'my lady.' Who the *hell* are you buddy?"

Sebastian disliked him on sight, but hearing his disrespectful mocking tone made Sebastian feel like setting him straight with a solid punch to his jaw. He resisted the urge.

Sebastian looked to Celeste before responding, "I'm her husband. If she has a problem with you, then I have a problem with you, *and you don't want that*. Trust me. *Buddy*."

The man looked confused for a minute, then he looked like trouble to Sebastian. The stranger looked at Celeste while he stood up from kneeling, "You know who you look like? The Queen of Earth. What's her name? Celeste, yeah, you look just like her. I bet you *are* her and this guy's just some dickwad guard of yours." The stranger

< <<<< [[466]] >>> >>>>

looked at Sebastian like something he scraped off the bottom of his shoe.

Now Sebastian wanted to kick this guy's ass all the way down the beach.

"Wait a minute. The queen's being held captive right now by the Brotherhood," the stranger looked around then back to Celeste, "So who are you really?"

Sebastian quickly answered for her, "Listen, *dude*, you've intruded enough. It's time you go."

"Who are you?" The man didn't shift his gaze off Celeste.

"She's the queen's body double, okay? I protect her just like if she was the real queen. Now that you know, I think it's time you left us alone. We're trying to have a vacation."

The man pointed at Sebastian while looking at Celeste, "Would you tell him to leave? We were in the middle of a nice conversation and I'd like to know your real name."

Celeste looked at Sebastian, then back to the man, "I really can't do that sir. I'm sorry. He needs to be around me at all times. I'm sure you understand at a time like this when the queen's being held captive how stressful this is for all of us."

The man stared at Celeste and then shifted his attention to Sebastian, "So you're her body guard? Well, you're not her husband so why don't you fuck off and do us all a favor. I'm just talking to her."

Sebastian's blood boiled and he let his voice bellow, "I'm her body guard, and a High Guard of the Royal Kingdom of Earth and Il'laceier. If you do not leave here immediately, I will beat the living shit out of you. Then I'll arrest you and call my friends to take you to be incarcerated on Earth for however long the kingdom sees fit. Do you understand asshole?"

The man approached Sebastian confidently. The stranger turned red, his veins standing out on his forehead and neck, "You guys have no power over me here. This is neutral territory and I don't think you should be threatening me, you government prick. GO FUCK YOURSELF!"

Sebastian allowed himself to go full tilt with rage. He wanted to make this man suffer. He belted the stranger square in the nose and the man stumbled backwards. Sebastian moved so fast, the guy didn't know what hit him.

Celeste quickly scrambled out of the way, pulling her blanket with her. She watched as they circled each other. She wanted to help, but she didn't know how, so she just tried to stay out of the way.

The man threw a powerful right that would've hurt had he actually hit Sebastian. The stranger's nose was now bleeding leaving drops of blood on his chest mixed with sweat. Sebastian landed a solid blow to the man's stomach and he bent over. He was out of breath for a moment but recoiled when Sebastian moved in to grab him. Sebastian hadn't had a formidable opponent in a while so he welcomed the opportunity to practice on some random dumb bastard.

Celeste watched as the man tried to swing a haymaker, but Sebastian easily dodged it. It looked like, to her, that he knew exactly what the man was going to do next and was always prepared to avoid getting hit. It was amazing to watch him fight. It was brutal for the man that had been coming on to her, but he deserved what he got after Sebastian warned him to leave and he refused. She'd never had anyone fight figuratively, or literally, for her honor or any other way. The way Sebastian reacted to her situation today flattered her. She just didn't want to see him get hurt.

Sebastian backed away from the misfired haymaker and then ran full steam at the man's middle. He easily took the stranger to the ground and quickly pinned his arms with his hands and his torso to the sand with his weight. The man was dazed and coughing hard, trying to get his breath. Sebastian repositioned himself on the man so he could hold down his arms with his knees. The man couldn't move but he was trying. Sebastian pinched the man's nose between his fingers and twisted. The man screamed out.

"You had enough asshole? I'm not fucking around. You leave here immediately and never come back or so help me God if you do, I'll kill you and no one will ever find your body."

The man gave in, "Alright, alright! I'm sorry. You fucking psycho, I just want to go."

Sebastian read him quickly and understanding his intentions, punched him again in the nose, "You're not sorry and you're a shitty liar. First off apologize to her, not me." Sebastian pointed at Celeste.

The man turned his head in her direction, "I'm sorry, fake Queen Celes—" Sebastian slapped him hard across the face.

"Do not address her by first name when you have not asked permission to do so! Try again motherfucker!" Sebastian pulled the gun from his waistband and held it to the man's temple.

The man trembled, "I'm sincerely sorry for the intrusion...phony Queen Hennessy. I'll leave immediately and not bother you again." His voice wavered and sounded nasally as his nose continued to swell. The man's face was covered in blood and he seemed finally smart enough to want to leave by Sebastian's estimations. He got off the man's arms and stood up.

Sebastian kept the gun pointed at the stranger and commanded, "Hand over your Titan."

"What?" The man got up on his knees.

"Do it now or I shoot you."

The man slowly undid the straps of his Titan and tried to hand it to Sebastian.

"Throw it on the ground."

The man dropped it to the sand, "Can I leave now? Please?"

"Yes."

Sebastian and Celeste watched as the man held his head, and unsteadily stood up. He paused for a second. He looked back at them a few times as he slowly made his way back from the direction he had come down the shoreline.

"Sebastian, are you sure he's not going to come back at night and try to get back at us? Or what if he reports this to the kingdom?"

He laughed, "Trust me. He's really going to leave this planet immediately and head back to Earth. He knew Praxis owns this planet. It is not neutral territory like he said. He won't report this because he's been in a lot of trouble with the law already."

"How do you know? Do you know him?"

He still didn't want to say anything about his 7's so instead he replied, "I know his type Celeste. I've run into guys like him my whole life. A lot of the time, they're all talk. He tried to give a good fight, but in the end, when their pride and manhood is wounded...they run back home to lick their wounds and they don't tell anyone about the times they got their ass handed to them. He won't tell anyone about this. We're fine."

"Okay. If you say so."

Sebastian stared as the man walked out of sight.

"Was it really necessary for you to pull out your gun?"

Sebastian looked down at it in his hand and tucked it behind his back again, "Yes. I have to protect you, no matter the threat. Some men only understand violence and intimidation and I needed him to keep his mouth shut. It's great he thinks you're a body double and all, but we have to be more careful. I should've called you in when I saw him coming down the shore."

"Yeah, what kind of husband are you?" she teased.

He stiffened without responding.

"I was joking. That was a joke don't worry." She shook off her blanket and handed it to him. He wiped off his sweat and the man's blood that was on him. She put her arms around him after he was done, "Thank you for protecting me."

He looked down at her, "Are you okay? What did he say to you?"

"Yeah, I'm fine. He just said some lewd things after a while, being crass. I didn't like it, but I'm glad you were here. And I'm glad he didn't hurt you."

Sebastian smiled and put his arms around her almost naked body, "Hurt me? That guy couldn't have hurt me if I had been blindfolded. I'm sorry I didn't come over sooner. I thought I was being paranoid, so I waited for you to give me a sign."

"I've never had anyone fight for my honor kind sir. I have to admit it was sexy to see you defending me." She smiled coyly.

He lowered his voice, "Was it now? Huh? I thought you were going to say something like I was too brutal or a barbarian or something. You are full of surprises my lady." They smiled at each other and then he remembered himself. As badly as he wanted to kiss her, he let her go instead. He told her it was time to go inside and that he needed to take a shower. He grabbed the man's Titan off the sand and wanted to look through every bit of information he could find on this guy. He wanted his numbers, addresses, and a list of contacts. Celeste walked with him into the house and he went to his bathroom to take a long cold shower to cool off his need for her.

After he got dressed, he searched the man's Titan. This guy was a ghost with everything being coded or alternate names. This would get him nothing. He was disappointed but thought the guy was probably a small time criminal that would never mention the story to anyone.

Sebastian was wrong.

CHAPTER 28

RAYKREEDE

ONE

>>> > IN DIRECT CONTRAST to the past two days, on one very un-eventful night, Sebastian stepped out of his bedroom with a new book to read. When he turned around, Celeste stepped out of the bathroom next to him. She had just showered and the only thing she wore was a towel wrapped around her, her wet hair dripping down her shoulders. She stopped in her tracks, surprised and a little shy. He immediately turned his eyes down towards her feet.

"I...needed a book. Now I've got it, yes, okay, good night," he almost walked into the wall and Celeste laughed inside.

She'd never seen him visibly nervous like this. She couldn't help herself, "Sebastian, wait."

He turned to look at her and then looked down again, "Yes?"

"I think I have something in my eye. Would you look at it for me please?"

He walked up to her, hands behind his back, "Why aren't you showering in your own bathroom?"

She hesitated, "There's something scary in the shower stall. It was bigger than any spider I've ever seen and it had ten legs…maybe more. I don't know. I didn't hang around long enough to look at it up close."

He expected she would give him some excuse, but she was actually telling the truth about the creature in her bathroom, "Trust me, those are harmless. They're probably more afraid of you than you are of it."

"I don't think so. I really can't stand anything that's creepy crawly like that. Can you go in there and kill it?"

He shook his head, "No. I certainly will not. That heckkette has just as much right to live as you or I. It's a native species here, unlike us."

"A what? A heck kit? Is that what you said?"

"Heckkette…all one word. I will capture it and set it free outside," he started to move into her bedroom.

"Okay, but I still have something in my eye. Will you look at it first please?"

He came back to her, "Sure."

She turned her face up to him and he got very close. The air was thick around them, no sound but their breathing.

He knew damn well she had nothing in her eye. "I don't see anything," he quickly moved away.

"No really, I can feel something there, please look again."

He tried to keep his irritation at her up, but he couldn't stay mad for long. He figured he'd play along where maybe she'd get more than she bargained for.

He placed the book on the hall table and put both hands on her cheeks firmly. He turned her face up to his, hovering extremely close to her lips, pretending to look seriously for this phantom eye irritation. He read her; her heartbeat was pounding, her blood pressure rising. He knew he intrigued her. She was intently studying the exact blue of his eyes, his eyelashes, his eyebrows. He heard her think he smelled good and he released her, startled.

It seemed to Celeste like he was going to kiss her then he suddenly stepped back like she had shocked him somehow. He had a strange look on his face she couldn't identify, but something was definitely bothering him.

"Sorry, I don't see anything. Goodnight." He grabbed his book and walked away from her, leaving her puzzled.

What was weird was that she felt warm water over her body when Sebastian held her face. She dismissed it as a hot flash or the left over effects from the shower. *I did have the water on hot tonight.* The thought floated out of her mind only to be replaced with the memory of his gorgeous blue eyes.

She walked into her bedroom and remembered that spidery thing was still in her bathroom. She looked for it, but it was gone. She sighed and wondered where it crawled off to.

"If he says it's harmless, it's harmless." *Try to forget about it and go to bed. Stop being such a wimp.* She dried her hair and went to bed without another thought about it.

TWO

>>> > THE FOLLOWING MORNING, Celeste put the dishes into the dishwasher and looked out the window at the morning sun.

"Instead of walking on the beach, why don't we go visit the Anagla'zeed ruins?" Sebastian asked.

"Oh, okay. You know where they are?"

"Yes, not too far away from here. Let me get a torch."

They trekked to the local ruins of the civilization that used to inhabit Bahsheef. The Anagla'zeed were fierce warriors with extremely bad tempers. History holobooks said it didn't take much to anger this species and eventually it led to their demise. A civil war broke out and they fought to extinction. Tools and artifacts were all that remained, other than the ruins themselves.

Sebastian and Celeste spent a lot of time looking over the structures and he taught her what some of their words and symbols meant. He still used some of their warfare techniques as well.

"Where'd you learn all of this stuff?"

"I traveled all over the universe when I was in the military and I read an immense amount of books. I love learning and my people have always encouraged curiosity and a lust for knowledge." He ran his hand over the stone walls and etchings. "This culture had a fascination with pyramids. Perhaps something to do with their fear of volcanoes. Or maybe they were trying to emulate them in stone. Regardless of their vicious temperaments, these buildings are so ornate and beautiful. I can't believe more people don't come here to explore."

"It might have something to do with those sareeaveous things you told me about. I suppose most tourists stick to the cities since they have the defense system you told me about, but out here…we're pretty exposed. I know I wouldn't venture out here by myself."

He arched one eyebrow, "Well, I suppose getting eaten alive is a deterrent to some visitors."

She laughed. "Yeah, I think so." She watched while his hands explored the walls; she wished they'd spend time exploring her body instead. "Are there a lot of these structures here?"

"Yes, but they're spread out far apart from each other. There's not another one around for four thousand miles. They're all fascinating to me in their own way. Some have carvings no one understands; some have these gigantic monoliths, while others are no more than a square made up of rocks laid on the ground. I love exploring this world because these beings were so primitive but capable of such beautiful architecture. You know the first time this planet was discovered the Anagla'zeed were long dead?"

"Really? How can they know that? What if they just took off into space?"

"Oh, they never discovered means of space travel. They took each other out until no one was left."

"They never left this planet?"

"That's right. They lived in tribes, never had any sort of vehicles, or transit, just their own feet for getting around. I think they took themselves out way too early to think of something as advanced as space travel. Can you imagine being stuck on one planet your whole life? I know I can't."

"Well, we take it for granted, but no, I guess I can't. How sad for them. It's kind of nice travelling through the universe. Maybe I'll get used to it soon." She looked at the wall she was standing next to and saw an etching of a person making a fire. She wondered how old it was, and who had taken the time to sit there and cut into stone with a rock or something sharp.

"You ready to head back?" he called out over his shoulder.

"Sure, I'm feeling pretty good and this was a nice change of scenery. Good idea."

"I do my best."

On their way back to the house, he stopped and pointed out a large waterfall. The rocks underneath the watery cliff high above them were like nothing she'd ever seen. It looked like a grid of square and rectangular black rocks jutting out from underneath the water. The black stones stuck out far at the top, like an awning over the land, but as her eyes went down the wall, the rocks receded inward making a shallow cave. There was an architectural quality to it, like some Bahsheef God had come along and carved this wall.

The black sand glistened in the pool of water at the bottom and looked like it went very deep. She wanted to go for a dip.

He cautioned her against it, "Not yet. Get your strength up and then maybe we'll go for a swim in the ocean."

"Why not here? It's beautiful."

"I agree, it is, but you see all around the edge here? It's solid stone, there's nowhere for me to put torches in the ground. We'd be way too vulnerable without fire to keep the sareeaveous away."

"When you took me out to that place for my birthday we didn't have fire."

"No, but we had light and candles and we were tucked away out of view from the sky. It was different there. Here we have very little cover to protect us."

She looked up and saw how much of the sky she could see. He was right.

He added, "One more thing. You see that tall plant over there that looks like it has a bucket at the bottom of it?" He pointed ahead at the far edge of the pool.

She nodded.

"You get too close to that plant and it'll kill you."

She started to laugh, "Oh come on!"

"I'm dead serious your Highness. Please don't get near anything that looks like that. It's dangerous."

She was alarmed and looked at the plant again, paying more attention this time, "Yeah, okay. I won't."

As they were leaving the pool she looked one more time at that plant, but then something much closer caught her eye – a glimmer from under the waterfall.

"Celeste, where are you going?"

She could hear the irritation in his voice for wandering off on her own, but she had to see something. She walked up to where the edge of the pool met the black stone wall. There was a thin ledge where she could creep in between the water falling and the wall. Sebastian was calling out to her to come back, but she ignored him. She edged in a little further and found a line cut into the stone that made the shape of a doorway, but there was no handle.

"Sebastian! Throw me a flashlight."

He made a face, "What?"

She rolled her eyes. He must not have been able to hear her. Wasn't he supposed to have excellent hearing? The waterfall sound couldn't have been that noisy that she could hear him, but he couldn't hear her. She motioned with her hand for him to come closer. He shook his head no. She yelled as loud as she could, "What do you mean no?"

He yelled out, "It's not safe here. We need to go. I've got a bad feeling. Come out of there."

"Throw me a flashlight then!"

He heard her this time and she caught the small flashlight he tossed to her. She clicked it on and gasped as the light hit the wall. There were etchings here with the same symbols that were back at the ruins. They glowed in the light with a white lustrousness and at the top of the doorway was a sparkling red jewel embedded in the rock.

Sebastian made his way to where she was and stood next to her with a strange look on his face.

"Do all those etchings we were just looking at, light up like this?"

He shook his head, "No. I've never seen anything like this…and I've visited several ruins."

"It looks like there's a doorway here. You see the lines?"

He held his torch up to them, but the lines disappeared along with the etchings.

"Sebastian! What'd you do?!"

"Nothing." He pulled the torch away and the doorway was dark. "Put the flashlight on it again."

She did and the lines returned. She stared silently.

"It needs artificial light to show the markings," he said as it dawned on him.

Celeste studied the symbols in confusion, "If you said these people were primitive then how could we be looking at their symbols that only light up with a flashlight? And the torch makes them disappear? That doesn't make sense. These people never had anything like a flashlight right?"

"Not that anyone knows of," Sebastian gently took the flashlight out of her hand and pointed it at the gemstone. It looked a lot like the Red Klix – the same color, the same shape, and the same size. He thought of the poem his parents taught him when he and his brother were young boys. This is why he had a bad feeling. Something wasn't right. They didn't belong here.

Celeste pushed on the wall, trying to open the door.

"Don't! Leave it alone. We have to go."

She looked puzzled, "What? This is neat. We have to check it out. Help me get this door open."

"NO! We're going!"

Celeste shrunk away.

Sebastian sighed, "This place is dangerous. We need to leave now. Take a picture of the markings with your Titan if you want but we're going. Now!"

She watched as he moved back towards the edge of the pool. His concern made her nervous. She angled her Titan and took a couple pictures, then slipped out to where he was waiting for her. He started moving without looking back.

She clicked off the flashlight and put it in her pocket. They walked in silence for a while before he said anything.

"I apologize if I upset you, but you ran off without telling me what you were doing."

"Yeah, and I found something pretty interesting, don't you think?" She pushed away some big leaves that were in her path.

"Interesting isn't the word I'd use. You're not Lanyx, you wouldn't understand."

"So, tell me. What's so dangerous there?"

"Lanyx have their own folklore. Our own myths. I suppose some people call it superstition but I had a really bad feeling back there. I always pay attention to my gut. That place was telling me to leave."

"'That place?!' What does that mean?" She was almost laughing.

He stopped walking and turned to her, "Celeste, I know you're Human. I know your species thinks it's the center of the universe, but it isn't. There are so many other beings on other planets with other technologies and...things you haven't experienced. Trust me when I say we should leave that door alone."

"You say 'trust me' an awful lot."

"Yeah," he paused, "Maybe I do."

She sighed, "I don't understand why you think a doorway is dangerous."

"Listen Celeste, we can study the photos on your Titan and I will try to help you decipher the symbols. How does that sound?"

"But what about getting in there? Using the door?"

He shook his head, "Always answering a question with a question." He let out a long exhale, "No. I'm going to bet that door will not open for us. I think it probably needs something else to open it, but I can teach you the language if you like and I can help you figure out what the door says."

She noticed how adamant he was. He usually wanted to give her whatever she asked for. This was different. He knew something and didn't want to tell her, and maybe he had a good reason to get her away from that area. "Okay, Sebastian."

THREE

>>> > TODAY, FOR HIS visit, the doctor spent the afternoon with Celeste and Sebastian on the beach. Celeste cooked lunch in appreciation of the gift Zach gave her.

"Thanks for the truffles doctor. They were delicious." She gave Zach a big hug and the doctor stood frozen, not knowing what to do.

"Oh, well...I wanted to get you a little something." Dr. Coldiron looked down at his hands and smiled.

She kissed him on the cheek and his face flushed a bright red orange. His tail whipped from side to side quickly and he smiled.

"You're a tremendous doctor and a sweet man. I'm very grateful that you could help me with my recovery and that Sebastian called you. I couldn't have asked for a better doctor."

Sebastian smiled as he thought to himself that Celeste must have this effect on all types of men. Zach was acting like a nervous little boy around a girl he liked. Sebastian thought it was hysterical. He'd never seen the doc act quite like this.

The doctor crossed his four arms, "Oh, Celeste stop. You're making me all...you're such a gracious woman. I'm just glad I could help. Now, let's take a look at you and your foot and see how you're doing this week."

Zach was pleased with Celeste's progress. Her eyes were still bruised but completely open and without any long-term damage. Her bruises everywhere else were fading and she was in a lot less pain. She was ambulatory and her strength was returning. Not bad for someone who had almost been beaten and starved to death weeks ago. Zach complimented Sebastian on his nursing skills and said a lot of Celeste's recovery was due to his caretaking. Sebastian left Celeste sleeping in her bed as the evening approached and he went out to talk with the doctor.

"You really think she's doing good?"

"Yes, Sebastian. I know you're doing everything you can for her. You're a great nurse and she's got a strong spirit. Her body's doing what it's supposed to. I think on my next visit we can remove the glove and her foot will be like she was born with it. I hope her memory comes back soon."

"Me too."

"I'm glad you came out here. I needed to speak with you alone. This morning, a couple of men I've never seen before approached me."

"On Arcolid?"

"Yes, in my home city of Basulenty."

"What did they want?"

"They were definitely BDP. They're looking for you and Celeste and they offered me a lot of coren if I'd pass along any information I had. I said I'd never heard of you. They're hell-bent on finding you, so I'm not sure how many people they'll ask before they find someone who needs the money and maybe knows you."

"Only a handful of people actually know who I am. Hell, I use so many aliases even *I* get confused sometimes. The people that know of my true identity would never speak, but I won't let my guard down. I've traveled here with a full armory."

"Yeah, I thought you probably had this covered, but I thought you should know."

"I appreciate it. Actually, thanks for everything."

"No problem. You know where my loyalties lay."

Sebastian smiled, "I have to tell you that BMW in the garage is *amazing*. You did a great job restoring that…It rode like a dream for Celeste and I when we took it out for her birthday. You've done so much for the both of us; I don't know how I'm ever going to pay you back."

"I owe you a lot after you helped me that little 'problem' I had a while ago. I'll never forget it. And as far as the bike goes, maybe you could take it off my hands for me. I love it, but like I said, I can't ride it. I need something bigger. You want it?"

Sebastian's eyes turned to saucers, "Zach, no! I couldn't take that from you. She's a beauty and you restored her."

"Raynes, will you take her or not? Call it another birthday present for Celeste if you want, or for your birthday, whenever that is," he paused, "If you don't take her, I'll have to find someone else…" He raised his top eye ridges as if they were eyebrows.

Sebastian smiled, "Okay, okay. I'll take excellent care of her, don't worry." He put out his hand and they shook on it, "Thanks Zach."

"You get a look at the other vehicle?"

Sebastian shook his head, "No, not yet. I'm waiting a while longer. I'll look at it soon. Is it as good as the bike?"

"Ah, nothing's as good as a motorcycle, but it's something I think you and Celeste will enjoy."

"Okay. I'll try to take it for a spin soon. I like all kinds of vehicles, but it's so unique traveling in something that stays on the ground with wheels. There's really nothing else like it."

"Yeah, I hear you. I certainly understand the attraction. Just you and the black pavement. No chance of falling out of the sky, and you don't need to worry about air tanks and SAP's and all," he paused, "Hey how did Celeste do on the back of the bike? Did she experience any pain or discomfort?"

Sebastian nodded his head, "She didn't tell me, verbally, but I know with my 7's her shoulders and abdomen were sore and her grip around me wasn't as strong as she wanted it to be. But, overall, I think she did okay. She was tired that night though."

Zach smiled, "Oh, I bet she was."

"No, not that way. We didn't do anything you old pervert. I haven't even kissed her since she lost her memory."

"Oh now I'm the pervert? For assuming you guys have sex…wait you haven't kissed her yet? What are you waiting for?"

"Zach, really? You're going to start with this?"

The doctor stared at him, waiting for an answer, "So?"

Sebastian ran a hand through his hair and sighed, "I'm waiting until she gets her memory back. I feel like I'd be taking advantage of her, of the situation, if I started making moves."

"Sebastian Raynes — always the gentleman…and the scaredy cat!"

Sebastian scowled at him, "What?!"

"Are you still afraid of getting close to her? Wasn't her almost getting killed enough for you to see that you can't waste any more time pushing her away?! All you've done is found a new excuse so that you can say it's not the right time to date her!"

Sebastian put his head back and let out a long exhale, "Zach, I appreciate you telling me about the BDP guys and coming over today, I really do, but this topic of Celeste and I, right now, is not up for discussion. Please."

Zach wanted to say a lot more, but he stopped himself. He knew both his friend and Celeste were going through a stressful and uncharted journey together and he thought maybe he should honor Sebastian's privacy for now. "Okay, I apologize. Back to business then. Celeste looks good and I'm glad she's doing better. Just keep yourselves safe for now. Don't worry about all the favors and paying me back okay? I'm sure I'll need something in the future. You're the best at what you do; I wouldn't go to anyone else anyways."

"Sure, whenever you need something, don't hesitate to ask. I'm glad you could spend a little time out here; it's so beautiful, and thanks again for everything. It means the world to both of us."

After Zach left, Sebastian went to Celeste's room and checked on her. She looked peaceful and content sleeping in her bed. He decided against telling her what the doctor said. All it would do is make her worry.

He stood in the doorway watching her sleep while he thought about the one-degree separation between them and the doctor. If the BDP found Zach, then maybe they knew about this house, maybe that guy on the beach talked to someone. Sebastian went into a state of paranoia, did a full perimeter check, and checked over the entire house again. He stood outside in the fading light, engaged his techglasses with the binocular enhancements projected over his eyes, and studied the surrounding area. All he saw were two boats far out in the ocean and a squirrel-like rodent collecting nuts in the trees beyond the front yard. Still, his sense of peace and safety here was shattered with new worries about being found.

FOUR

>>> > DAVID LAY IN his sleeping capsule next to Raykreede.

"I've never been with someone so powerful," Raykreede said out of breath, "It's a huge turn on."

"I do like what you do for my ego. I have to admit," David smiled.

"Last night was amazing. I hope we can do this again sometime?"

"Maybe in a week or so. It'd be a challenge to keep this a secret with you taking over guard duty for someone who's been doing it for a long while. He'll get suspicious if I suddenly have someone new guarding my room overnight."

"Okay. I understand."

"Now, if you'll excuse me. I'm going to need you to leave before the morning guard shows. No offense."

Raykreede got up and put on his pants, "None taken. I'll get dressed and wait outside for the shift change."

"Thanks. I really appreciate your understanding." David got up and went into his bathroom. He put on a robe and when he returned to his bed, Raykreede was already outside. David looked at his Titan and heard a knock on his door. He went to it and partially opened it.

"Your Majesty, just wanted to let you know Guard Kentzy reporting for duty."

David nodded his head, "I appreciate your service. I need you to do something for me."

"Of course my King."

"The guard that just left here? He's a threat to me and the kingdom. He said some alarming things. I need you to take care of him for me. Right now."

"Absolutely. Consider it done. What should I do with his body?"

"Make sure his death is quiet. Don't let anyone see you and speak of this to no one."

"Of course."

"Once it's done, put his body in the cellar dungeons. Near the crematorium. I want to see that it's been handled with my own eyes before disposal and burning. No matter what he says to you, know that he's lying. He cannot be trusted. I will tell the kingdom he was a threat and that he was punished by death, but not that you did it. People will ask why I didn't have him publicly executed and I don't want to go into the story. It's too personal. Do you understand all of what I've told you?"

"Yes, your Highness."

"Please return immediately once you've completed your task."

"Understood."

David watched him walk down the hall, leaving his room temporarily unprotected, but that was okay. The biggest threat to him and his safety right now was a guard who he just slept with. He needed that danger contained.

Guard Kentzy was a good soldier and a good Il'lacean. David knew that no matter what Raykreede said to Kentzy, he wouldn't repeat it to anyone.

Raykreede was as good as dead, and David's secret was safe.

FIVE

>>> > THE NEXT MORNING started off rough for Celeste and Sebastian.

"But it's been weeks since I've talked to my friends. They're probably worried sick about me. Can't I contact them somehow? It doesn't have to be a Titan call; I could send a message, or email or something. I'll let you sit over my shoulder and watch me as I do it. I swear I won't tell them too much." Celeste didn't want to sound like she was pleading but she couldn't help it. She missed talking to her friends. And she remembered them; she didn't remember this man she was with.

Sebastian shook his head, "I don't want anyone to know where you're at or who you're with."

"I don't see how my friends would blab to anyone. They're safe, I swear."

"No."

"Come on Sebastian, pleeeeaasssseee."

"I'm sure they're smart, but what if they accidently say something to someone else? What if they're overheard when they think they're alone? I can't have your safety compromised and I sure as hell don't want the universe looking for you. They think you're tied up somewhere in one location by a very dangerous group of thugs and that's our best strategy. Trust me. I'm really sorry if this upsets you, but your safety is my biggest priority."

She walked to her room where her Titan was. She dialed Veronica's number. Thank goodness she remembered that since she had no contacts in this new Titan. She pushed the send button. Nothing happened. She shook it, but still nothing. She tried it again from the main menu screen with the same results. She tried one more time but instead of hearing the ringing on the line, the screen went red with a big alarm bell on it and it emitted a loud noise she never heard before.

Sebastian appeared in her doorway a few seconds later, "I mean it. You can't contact them or anyone for that matter. I've already disabled those abilities on your Titan for now."

"But it didn't happen until the third time I tried."

"Yes. I thought if you tried twice without success, you'd give up and that I'd save you the embarrassment of that obnoxious noise, but apparently that's what really stopped you."

"But I need to tell someone I'm safe."

Sebastian put his hands on her shoulders lightly, "I'm doing this because you've got threats against your safety. I'll take excellent care of you and in time, when you're fully healed, you'll be able to talk to them again. I promise the lack of communications on your Titan is only temporary."

She put her Titan down on the dresser and exhaled, "Fine. I don't like it, but fine, if that's what you want."

Sebastian removed his hands, "It's not really what I want, to stop you from communicating with your friends, but I think it's the safest choice. And like I said, temporary."

He kissed her on the forehead and she gave up the fight. Her friends would have to wait like everyone else before the universe found out she was healthy, safe, and alive.

"Yes, Erebos?"

"Can you get me the name of the best restaurant on this planet?"

"Hold on. Yes, I've sent it to you."

Sebastian smiled as he looked at his Titan, "Thanks."

"You know sir, I was hoping to be of more assistance to you here. I thought with you traveling you might need more things from me, but you've asked for very little."

"I appreciate the thought, but you're always there when I need you, O."

Ophelia sighed, "I just…get bored without much to do."

Sebastian opened the back door to the beach, "O, you don't get bored."

CHAPTER 29

SAREEAVEOUS

ONE

>>> > THE NIGHT WAS cold and the sky was clear.

Sebastian led Celeste down the stairs to the beach.

She saw a picnic basket set up on a large blanket next to the fire pit that had a warm crackling fire burning. She sat down on the ground and took a pillow and blanket off the pile he had nearby. She pulled the blanket around herself and thought the only thing missing was marshmallows.

He sat down close to her, opened the basket, and took out various containers of food.

"I ordered salad, sandwiches, and a cheesecake for dessert. Now, I know you're not supposed to drink a lot. Okay, not at all, but I have a little wine from Zach's cellar so maybe we'll skip your meds tonight.

Besides, we didn't drink on your birthday so I think that makes it okay for tonight. But, only if you want."

He fixed two plates while she marveled at his thoughtfulness. He handed her a plate with a small bright pink calla lily sitting off to the side of her food. She picked that up first and put it behind her ear. She looked up to see he was watching her as he opened the bottle of wine. He had a wide smile on his face.

"What? Am I supposed to eat this too?" Her fingers found the flower and held it against her hair.

"No my lady. You like the flower?"

"Yes, these are my favorite."

"Finally!" He clapped his hands together, "I've been trying to find out without asking. This has been ongoing since I met you so this is a big deal. I had a feeling when you found the one you liked the most, you'd put it behind your ear."

He looked very happy to her. She was puzzled that figuring out her favorite flower had this kind of effect on him. He could've just asked her, but instead, he kept trying until he found out on his own.

"You've always been like this with me? Even before I lost my memory?"

He smiled, "Honestly, when we met, I was a bit different. When you came into my life, things changed for the better. I was reminded how good it felt to help someone else for no other reason than because they needed it. I also enjoy taking care of you, to help you feel better. I thought tonight, you would like something outdoors, something different."

"I appreciate everything you've done for me. I suppose I might even appreciate it more so after I regain my memories. But tonight, this is wonderful and the food is delicious. Thank you."

She watched him close his eyes while he ate his sandwich. She could tell he was enjoying all of this. "Like it?"

He opened his eyes and realized she was watching him, "When I was in the military I had to eat fast all the time. You never knew when you sat down for a meal whether you were actually going to be able to finish it or not. And I lived like that for many years. I hated it, so when I returned to civilian life I promised myself I'd relish my food. Eat slowly; enjoy it, taking all the time I needed to really savor every bite."

When dinner was done, they dug into the cheesecake and he poured her a glass of wine. He was already on this fourth glass.

"You know, the first night we arrived and you were sleeping, I came out here and thought you might really like this aspect of this planet. Bahsheef has no moons so the sky is very dark. It's perfect for star gazing."

"It's beautiful." Celeste finished the dessert and her wine then laid down on her back.

Sebastian thought, then he thought twice, swallowed the last of his wine, and laid down next to her pulling a blanket over the both of them.

The only sound they heard was the waves crashing and the fire crackle.

They lay there silently looking up, admiring how small they were in the universe. Celeste was fed, warm, and lying next to a highly attractive man on the beach – life couldn't get much better. She let out a contented sigh and he looked over at her.

A loud alien scream pierced the night and she quickly rolled closer to him. He instinctively put his arm around her and they were face to face, inches away from a kiss.

"It's okay. Just a sareeaveous. They're usually not active at night, but maybe one got startled out of its sleep. You're safe; I won't let anything happen to you. Not while I'm around, okay?"

"Yes," she barely whispered.

They stared into each other's eyes, the air thick with sudden anticipation. He softly took his arm from around her and rolled away a little, creating some distance. She rolled on her back, her heart pounding. She should've just kissed him.

She sighed with regret, "Thanks for tonight. That was very nice of you to go through all that trouble for me."

"No trouble at all. I enjoy the outdoors so much; this is a vacation for me actually. I just wish you were feeling better to enjoy everything this planet has to offer."

"I'm feeling stronger all the time. Before you know it, I'll be out there swimmi— Oh look! A shooting star! Make a wish, Sebastian! Make a wish!" She pointed up to the sky.

"What?"

"Shooting stars…Making wishes. You don't know about this do you?"

"I actually don't."

"Humans on Earth a long time ago used to see meteors and called them shooting stars. It's good luck to see one in my culture and you're supposed to make a wish on them, but not tell anyone."

"What happens if you say it out loud?"

"Well, nothing really, but they said it wouldn't come true. I'm making my wish," she closed her eyes.

Their hands were lying alongside each other and he took hers in his and made a wish of his own.

She opened her eyes and sighed. The sky was filled with billions of stars.

He almost whispered to her, "Well, your name comes from a Latin word for heavenly, so that makes sense you would know something like that."

She closed her eyes and lay silent for a moment smiling.

"I think it's time you saw something that's yours. It might help with your memory," Sebastian handed her something small. She looked at it. A dark purple ribbon necklace with a cameo in the center. She looked closer at the cameo and saw a rose on it. She rubbed her fingers over the soft silky fabric and closed her eyes waiting for something to happen, for some memory to rise to the surface.

Sebastian waited, staring at her intently. He thought if she did remember something, maybe he would be able to sense it first with his 7's. He noticed a few tears escape her eyes. Maybe this was it!

"Celeste?"

She opened her eyes and gulped hard. Her voice broke miserably, "I can't remember! I know you're expecting me to. I can look in your face and see it all the time." She wiped away tears with the back of her hand, "And you won't tell me what I've forgotten. I don't even know if we've slept together or if we loved each other. It's like I'm feeling around in a fog for something, but I don't know what I'm looking for! It's so frustrating and no one understands!" She got up off the blanket and stormed up the stairs.

He sat blinking for a moment not sure what just happened. Everything was going fine…and then it wasn't.

"Celeste!" He was on his feet and taking the stairs two at a time trying to catch up to her. On the last stair before the top, he tripped over his own foot, and went sprawling. "Goddamn wine!"

She didn't slow and slammed the back door shut.

Sebastian got up quickly, unhurt, and went to the door, trying to open it but it was stuck. "Celeste, come back." He watched as she turned the corner and was out of sight. He jiggled the handle, but the door wouldn't budge.

"Damn it!" He slammed his fist on the door.

Celeste walked into her room and kicked the door shut. All of her muscles were quivering as she put too many demands on them to move as fast as she wanted. She would regret walking up the back stairs that fast tomorrow too, she knew it. She looked at the ribbon necklace that had caused all of this and tossed it on the dresser. Was it supposed to be significant to her?

She threw off her clothes and got into her sleepwear trying to stop the tears. She crawled into bed and turned out the lights. Maybe there was a good reason not to remember what happened to her. From the injuries her body sustained, the kidnapping looked very traumatic. Her brain was protecting her, sure, she might've forgotten some good things with Sebastian, but maybe it was best to keep those bad memories from coming back. This was one of those times where she felt overwhelmed with fear of remembering exactly what happened to her.

TWO

>>> > SEBASTIAN PACKED UP what was left on the beach and put out the fire.

"Ophelia?" he said to his Titan.

"Yes sir?"

"Can you communicate with the bots in the basement? I need their assistance."

"Please hold."

Sebastian walked up the stairs and put the picnic basket, pillows, and blankets by the door.

"What do you need of them? Both are available to me for commands."

Sebastian tried the door one more time, but it wouldn't open. "I need the back door opened…or any of the doors on the ground floor."

"Hold please."

Sebastian sat down in one of the patio chairs and looked over the torches along the perimeter. All of them were burning strong.

"The handyman is coming to the back door now."

Sebastian looked over his shoulder as the Taybuse bot stood at the back door, trying to open it. He jiggled the door handle as Sebastian had and then inspected the hinges. Sebastian got up and stood at the door, "I think it's the lock."

The Taybuse studied him with his blue electric eyes and said, "Thank you."

"Could you just get the door open for now? We can worry about fixing it later."

"Of course sir. Hold on please." The bot put one hand on the handle and the other gave a firm push near the lock and the door creaked open.

Sebastian grabbed the pillows, blankets, and basket off the patio and walked in. He closed the door behind him and tried locking it, but it didn't sound right.

"Thanks bot. Why don't you go to your hibernation chamber now."

The bot nodded, "Yes sir. Please let me know if you need my assistance again."

Sebastian wedged a dining chair under the door handle and went up to his bedroom. He looked at Celeste's closed door. He thought about knocking, but decided against it as he got ready for bed.

"Ophelia?"

"Yes sir?"

"You have access to the kitchen camera?"

She hesitated, "I do now."

"Good. Keep an eye on that point of entry all night. Make sure if anything approaches that door you wake me."

"Yes sir."

THREE

››› › **"WHAT ARE YOU** so excited about Gaviss?"

D'Artagnan looked at Mitch, "I have an idea for the group. I think it will stick in everyone's mind for a very long time and it will get a *big* reaction out of the king."

"What is it?"

"I know you don't want violence and the protests always seem to go violent at some point and even if they don't, they aren't a big deal."

"Yes…"

"We need something big to announce ourselves and I was sitting there at my desk trying to figure out my stupid corenbook when this idea hit me."

D'Artagnan told Mitch all about it.

Mitch's eyes widened when D'Artagnan was done, "I love it man. This is genius level stuff. Are you sure you can do it?"

D'Artagnan flashed a glare of annoyance, "Am I sure I can do it? Of course."

Mitch smiled, "The day will go down in the history books then. I can't wait!"

FOUR

››› › **CELESTE IS IN** the desert. She thinks something about it feels familiar. Maybe she's somewhere near her home in the New Mexico Territory back on Earth. It's very dark and it's raining. It's hard for her to see, but she feels raindrops on her face. They're warm, so it must be hot out. She remembered how sometimes even in the middle of the night it could still be ninety degrees during the summers.

She feels a sudden gust of wind across her face, then some pressure against her shoulder. It's like someone's pushing her away with their hand. She's falling backwards, and she can feel searing hot pain cut deep into her chest. She can't see anything now but darkness. She's screaming out.

She's screaming.

Sebastian burst through the door, almost tearing it off its hinges. Celeste shot straight up on her bed and instantly regretted it as her muscles cried out all over her body. She saw Sebastian standing in black briefs, his hair tousled, with a shotgun in his hands ready to fire.

He looked around the room, "Are you okay?"

"Yeah," she said trying to catch her breath.

"Anyone in here? Someone trying to hurt you?"

"No, I...had a bad dream is all. I'm sorry if I scared you. I think I was...screaming." She wiped away the sweat off her forehead.

He flipped the shotgun upside down on his shoulder pointing away from them with his elbow bent, his finger off the trigger now, "You were definitely screaming. Anything you remember?"

"No...I think I pulled a neck muscle or something." She reached up to her shoulder to rub it, but she winced and put her arm back down.

"Are you sure you don't remember anything about your dream?"

She closed her eyes and thought. She shook her head slowly, "No. I just know it was scary."

Sebastian knew with her history of seeing him almost commit suicide in a vision and them sharing a dream on the yacht, that her dreams weren't just dreams anymore. They could be visions of the future or something happening right now. He wished she remembered this one. The screaming was a bad sign and he felt uneasy. He didn't want to leave her alone. "I can help you with that – your pulled muscle. If you want."

"How?"

"A massage. I won't try anything; I'd apply some light pressure. Might help it relax."

"Okay."

He put the gun down on the chair nearby and told her to roll onto her stomach.

He stood next to the bed and reached over to place his hands on her shoulders. She was wearing a tank top and shorts so he didn't think she'd mind if he pulled down the sheets a little. He gently rubbed her neck, "I'm sorry I upset you earlier this evening."

"I'm sorry I got emotional. At times, I feel all this pressure on me to get my memory back. When you look at me sometimes, I can feel this urgency from you. It feels like you need me to remember everything."

"I certainly want you to recall all you've lost, but if you don't…well, there's worse things that could happen. At least you're alive and free of the BDP. I'm grateful for that."

He moved to her shoulders, "Your body is healing up well and the time here seems to be doing us both some good. Try to relax and not focus on the memory loss. Take your time and concentrate on enjoying yourself."

His hands moved down along her spine and then too far down on her lower back. He put them back up on her neck and asked how that felt.

She was fast asleep.

He felt relieved. Putting her back to sleep was probably the best thing he could've done for her tonight. She had screamed before like she was dying and it scared the hell out of him. He left her door open when he left the room but returned a few minutes later with two pistols to add to his shotgun and put them close. He eased under the covers next to her and settled down to sleep. He didn't feel comfortable leaving her alone for the rest of the night. That scream was bloodcurdling and had woken him up from a deep sleep. He lay on his back with his hands underneath his head wondering what she had dreamt of. He tried to figure out a way to get her to remember it, but he knew how dreams were. Once you woke up and gave it a few minutes, they faded from your consciousness, never to be recalled.

Celeste moved toward him in her sleep. He watched as she rolled on her side and draped a leg and arm over him. It seemed even in her sleep she wanted to be close. Tonight, it was okay with him.

She muttered something then whimpered softly.

He put his arms around her and held her. He whispered, "It's okay. I'm here. Nothing to worry about."

She settled down and got quiet.

He wished what he said was true, but he had a bad feeling he couldn't shake.

FIVE

>>> > CELESTE'S EYELASHES FLUTTERED opened against Sebastian's bare chest. The sun was up. Her head rose and fell as he took deep lazy breaths. Her arm and leg were draped over him. She inhaled deeply. How was it possible for him to smell this good while she lay coated in a light layer of sweat and had morning breath? She pulled away from him gently and rolled on her back. She pulled the covers up to her neck and wondered why he was there. She thought back to last night and remembered his massage. She looked over and saw his arsenal on the nightstand.

She got out of bed and quickly changed into a sexy nightgown in the bathroom while trying to brush her teeth and hair simultaneously. When she came out, Sebastian and his guns were gone.

"Damn it!"

SIX

>>> > WHEN SEBASTIAN CAME down the stairs and saw Celeste at the breakfast table eating oatmeal, he surprised her by acting normal. "Good morning."

She remained silent.

He pulled out a skillet and asked, "You want anything else for breakfast? I feel like having some eggs and pancakes."

She put down her spoon and looked at him, "You slept in my bed last night."

His face was blank, "Yes I did."

"You didn't even ask if I was okay with that." She was perfectly okay with that, but she didn't want him to think she was easy. She wouldn't let just any man in her bed.

"I didn't ask you because you were asleep and you needed the rest. Especially after that nightmare. I hope my need to protect you under any circumstance isn't a problem for you."

She was silent momentarily. "Why *did* you sleep next to me last night? Were you comfortable with that?"

He opened the fridge and grabbed eggs and milk. She thought he hadn't heard her. He cracked the eggs into the skillet and tossed the shells into the compost bag. He didn't look at her as he spoke, he concentrated on making breakfast, "I have strong instincts and I follow them. I wasn't comfortable leaving you alone so I slept in the same room. I didn't think you'd mind…actually, I know you didn't mind. I'm comfortable sleeping next to you. Do you have any more questions for me your Highness?"

She noticed he raised an eyebrow at the skillet as he asked her the last question.

She went to him.

He looked at her, "I will do whatever it takes to assure your safety. Even if that means sleeping next to you without your prior consent."

She reached up and kissed him on the cheek, "Thank you. I'm sorry if I sound ungrateful." She started to walk away.

"Wait," he turned away from the stove.

She turned to face him, "Yes Sebastian?"

"I've been struggling with this for a while now – your amnesia. The doc told me it would be hard, but I didn't know it was going to be *this* hard. Things were difficult between us right before your kidnapping and I can't afford for anything else to happen to you. I want you to understand I'm only trying to protect you, no matter what I do, no matter how strange it seems to you."

"I appreciate that," she cleared her throat, "I suppose it's only fair to tell you now that if you want to sleep in my bed again, for any reason, you have advance permission from me. Is that clear?" She smiled.

"Yes my lady. Crystal."

SEVEN

>>> > ON HIS FOURTH visit, Zach assured Sebastian and Celeste that she was on her way to a full physical recovery. He estimated she might've been as far along as eighty-five percent healed, but still to take it easy. He removed Celeste's living foot glove and they all looked down. A small faint scar circled her right ankle, but otherwise it looked natural. She put her full weight on it for the first time and it felt good. She cried as she hugged the doctor and he blushed as she kissed his cheek. He left saying he had a hatchling's play to attend on Arcolid.

Sebastian gave Celeste a report on how his search for information on her parents was going. All of his resources came up dry, but he told her he'd keep trying.

The next morning, Sebastian rose much earlier than she did so he wasn't at the breakfast table when she looked for him. She was going to start making oatmeal and only got as far as the kitchen sink window. She saw him running along the sun-soaked black beach. He was only wearing blue swim trunks and sneakers. She lusted over his incredible physique. She wanted to remember her past with him desperately.

She walked back into her bedroom and changed out of her robe into some shorts and a shirt. When she came out onto the patio, he was sitting cross-legged on a blanket on the sand. His hands were resting on his knees and it looked like he was meditating; as much as she wanted to leave him alone, she felt compelled to be closer to him. She started slowly down the stairs to the beach. The wind picked up and gray clouds were gathering in the distance over the water.

Celeste quietly approached and sat on the blanket across from him, mimicking his posture. She had done yoga for years so she knew this position as lotus.

He opened his eyes and looked at her, "I hope you don't mind me saying you look radiant this morning."

She smiled, "Thank you. You look good too...in excellent shape, I mean." She laughed.

His chuckle turned into a smile. She melted a little.

"How's the foot?"

"It's great. I can't believe I have both feet again. It's like bei—"

She felt a flash in her mind's eye. She saw an image of herself through someone else's eyes on Sebastian's apartment balcony back on Praxis. A man had his arms wrapped around her waist then the image went dark. She was confused as she jerked back into the present moment.

"Are you okay, Celeste?"

She shook her head, "What's happening to me? I just saw me, outside of myself. Maybe we should get the doctor, something's wrong."

He got closer to her on his knees, "Hold on. What did you just see? Tell me everything you remember."

She looked into his face and saw a sparkle in his eye. "I don't know. It was nighttime. I was standing on your balcony, but I could only see me. I mean, I wasn't me but I was *someone else* looking at me. I had a sensation of holding onto me around my waist and feeling intense. I must sound crazy," she put her hand up to her head, "Then it went blank. I'm losing it. Please call the doctor."

He shook his head, "No, I don't think we need him. You *are* getting better, but I need to explain."

"Explain what? Me going crazy?"

"I'm sorry; I held something back from you because I thought it'd complicate your recovery. I have 7's. I can sense intentions; sometimes I can see or feel things from other beings.

"When we met, you showed signs you had 7's too, but when you lost your memory, that power seemed to go with it, or so I thought. I was hoping it'd come back on its own, but I didn't want to tell you so you wouldn't worry about it. I think it's just returned. You saw one of my memories. When you complimented me just now, I thought of the night I kissed you back home. You described to me what I was just thinking."

Her face was blank, "I what? I know some Lanyx have telepathy, at least that's what I've heard, but I didn't believe it really. What am I doing with 7's?"

"Well, we were supposed to work on researching this, but we didn't get a chance and then you got kidnapped, but you were showing signs of great ability and your power was growing. You actually helped me find you on Tiletan with your 7's. You're quite good. You want to try something?"

She looked hesitant, "Like what? Is it going to hurt?"

He laughed, "No. It won't hurt. Might be a little disorienting at first, but you'll get the hang of it quick. I think."

"What do you want me to do?"

"Just sit like you are. I'm going to get back into that position as well. Meditation often helps adjust and maintain seventh sense powers. It's just like a muscle. It needs to be worked out and you need to be healthy before it's at maximum capacity. Maybe that's why it didn't come back until now. Your body's healing up, so, let's try to communicate while we hold hands okay?"

She nodded slowly. He sat down in front of her but their knees were touching. She put her hands into his and he held them gently. Thunder rumbled out in the distance.

"I'm going to say anything out loud that I can tell is your thoughts. You do the same with me."

They sat quietly for a few moments. She enjoyed feeling the breeze slide across her skin; the way it made her hair swirl around her face. She thought his hands were very gentle. She was starting to relax, but so far he hadn't said anything and she got nothing from him.

Then she felt a chill travel down her spine like he had lightly rubbed his finger over her neck.

"I felt something."

"Sorry, I didn't mean for that to go across," he mumbled.

"For what to go across?"

He shook his head, "I thought about holding you. I have a couple thoughts in my mind. I just focused on the wrong one. I was trying to focus on *this*."

She got an intention from him. He wanted to kiss her the way he used to right after they met. He missed feeling her soft lips on his own. He missed the feeling of her waist underneath his hands. She was quiet, marveling in the feeling of knowing someone else's thoughts.

She heard him say, "You think it might be nice to kiss me. You're amazed at how you're doing this. You've never experienced this before and you think it's a bit scary, but exciting too. You think I'm extremely powerful for being able to do this with someone else."

She laughed out loud. "That's crazy! So weird for me, probably not for you though."

They let go of each other's hands and she put her elbows behind her in the sand, propping herself up.

She said quietly, "You want to kiss me the way you used to before I lost my memory. You thought I had soft lips and you liked the way my body felt under your hands."

He smiled and nodded, "I don't do this with lots of people. I think I've read countless minds as far as intentions go, but I couldn't communicate with them. You're only the third person I've passed thoughts back and forth to."

"So what am I thinking right now?" She smiled mischievously, raising an eyebrow.

He picked up an image of him kissing her on the sand.

He moved closer to her and her insides jangled with excitement. He hovered over her body for a moment, and then carefully put his lips to hers as he closed his eyes. She put her hands onto his back and breathed deeply. He wrapped an arm underneath her and held her off the sand. The kiss was gentle and slow. She parted her lips and kissed him with a little more pressure. His lips responded and he felt relief wash over him getting to be this close with her again. It was extremely comforting. He stopped reluctantly, but not wanting to push her too much, he thought it was best to be cautious.

He sat up and looked at her laying there. She didn't move or open her eyes.

"You are an excellent kisser, Sebastian."

He smiled and blushed.

She opened her eyes and sat up looking over the waves. They were bigger than they were before she sat down, "*You* should have kissed me weeks ago."

"I didn't want to force anything. I hoped you'd want me to kiss you again at some point."

"It was a very nice kiss, but I still can't remember you, even though I really, *really* want to now. Have you always been able to sense me like this?"

"Always. I tried not to at the beginning and it's a huge invasion of privacy; but sometimes, you'd pass things along to me and I couldn't block them out if I wanted to. You were getting stronger all the time."

"I guess I'll have to get used to it all over again."

"Why don't we go inside and I'll make you something to eat. The clouds are moving in and I think it might rain soon." He stood up and put out his hand to her. He helped her up and she quickly wrapped her arms around his neck.

"The storm, Celeste. It's coming up quick."

"I like the rain."

She pushed herself up against him, putting her lips up to his. He couldn't resist kissing her again if she was this bold to ask for another. He fully gave in to her physical request and lost himself in her kiss.

Thunder crashed out, but they didn't notice. Cool raindrops fell and seconds later, it was a heavy rain.

She felt his hands running up her bare back as he pushed up her shirt. She tightened her grip around his neck and put a leg up against his hip. His hand moved down to hold it tight against him. Water poured down onto them, drenching their hair and clothes, running down their backs, and neither one of them seemed to mind. She heard him grunt as he kissed her hard. She reached her hands up into his hair and held him against her mouth.

She hadn't remembered being kissed this way by any other man, it was...intoxicating. Her mind slowed down, all of time seemed to stop, but her heart raced faster and faster.

A monstrous screech shook both of them from their passionate embrace. They opened their eyes to see a yellow sareeaveous barreling out of the sky toward them like a rocket. Sebastian waited until the last second to roll to the ground with Celeste as the creature's mouth clamped down on the empty space their bodies had just been standing in.

Sebastian cursed himself for not going inside when he wanted to. With the rain, the torches had been doused and they were left with nothing to keep the flying beasts away. He got up quickly and got her to her feet. He ran towards the stairs with a firm clamp on her hand, but she couldn't keep up. He looked just in time to see the sareeaveous coming in for a second attempt. There wasn't anywhere to hide and the stairs seemed a hundred miles away. The beast flew down straight towards them and Sebastian pulled Celeste into him as they both tumbled backwards on the black sand. The gigantic talons scraped along the empty sand where Celeste had been seconds before.

"Get up now!" he shouted over the thunder.

He jumped up as she stood, and quickly threw her over his shoulder and ran for the stairs. She turned her head up into the pelting rain, looking to the sky and saw the yellow creature coming around again. It felt like forever before Sebastian was climbing the numerous stairs up to the back patio. She was bouncing up and down off his shoulder and she thought she might be sick. She heard that thing in the sky screech again and it made her shiver.

Sebastian was three-quarters up the stairs when it swooped down again flanking them on their left trying to pluck one of them off with its talons. Sebastian had to kneel down on the steps to dodge the sareeaveous as it flew past them overhead. He looked to the right as raindrops pelted his face. The beast was turning around and getting ready to make another pass.

Sebastian immediately sprinted up the rest of the stairs and ran across the wooden deck to the back door.

It felt like an eternity to Celeste for them to run from the beach to the patio, but the whole attack lasted a couple of minutes. She thought if it hadn't been for Sebastian carrying her, she'd already be dead.

Sebastian put her down and tried to open the door.

It was stuck! Just like the other night and he had forgotten to have the bot fix it.

"Sebastian!" Celeste pointed straight out towards the ocean.

He looked over his shoulder to see the damn beast headed right for them. He quickly grabbed a patio chair and hoisted it above his head. He felt the sareeaveous's talons latch onto the chair and carry it away but not before dragging it along the roofline breaking a window above the back door. Celeste had been pressed up against the door, trying to force it open when it finally gave way, sending her crashing to the floor.

Before she knew it, Sebastian had her standing on her feet, inside the house and the door was shut.

She looked at him as he bent over and put his hands on knees. He was breathing hard.

"Fuck!" She immediately put her hand over her mouth.

"It's okay," he spoke between breaths, "said...a lot worse...myself."

"Oh my God! That was close. Really, really close." She looked down and saw the water puddle growing on the tile floor as her hair and clothes were dripping. She saw an equally large puddle around Sebastian's feet. The biggest puddle of them all was from the broken window above the door, allowing buckets of rain to pour into the house. She carefully navigated her way through the kitchen and grabbed six towels from the hall closet. She threw one to Sebastian, kept one for herself, and put the rest strategically on the floor to soak up water.

"Celeste listen, if you ever do something like that again, we could both be killed. I need you to use some caution okay? I can't let anything happen to you."

She gathered her hair and wrung it into the towel she held, "All you ever do is save me."

"Yeah, well this time you kind of made me. You put us in that position. *Promise me* you won't do it again."

"Yes, I'm sorry," she tried to fight the hot tears running down her cheeks but she couldn't stop them. She moved towards him and he put his arms around her.

"Hey, no tears. It's okay. I'm not mad, just...concerned." His voice was soft.

"No, I know, it's just...I was so stupid and I could've gotten you killed. I'm sorry."

"Just...be more careful next time. I'm not worried about me. I was worried about you more than anything. Even when you're healthy you can't move as fast as I can. You sure as hell can't keep up now."

She trembled and her teeth chattered together. He kissed her softly on the cheek and wiped her tears away with his thumb.

He gently pushed her chin up with his finger so she was looking into his eyes. Her teeth stopped chattering.

"I can't afford to lose you now. Not to the Brotherhood, or my own brother. Not to the sareeaveous, and not to some careless accident. We could be a very strong team, but we have to look out for each other… constantly. You want to try being a team with me?"

"Yes. I would like that," her eyes sparkled.

"I'd like it too."

Then he kissed her.

Her chill instantly melted away. It was replaced by fire under her skin from his slow burning kiss.

He ended it all too soon for her and said, "Come on. Let's get you into some dry clothes. I've got to get the bot to board up that window and then we can eat."

They changed clothes in their own rooms and came back into the kitchen. While the handyman stood perched on a giant ladder nailing wood planks across the broken window, Sebastian prepared lunch, and Celeste lit some candles and turned on the fireplace.

EIGHT

>>> > AS SEBASTIAN AND Celeste ate lunch, the bot finished his job and cleaned up the surrounding area. It was just in time too because the storm only intensified. The sky darkened considerably and the thunder got louder and louder. Celeste looked out onto the landscape and watched lightning flash across the clouds. The sea was churning with oversized waves and big fat raindrops fell straight down from the sky. She saw her second sareeaveous flying over the ocean. It was massive, bigger than the first and bright green. The storm didn't seem to slow it down at all. It let out a tremendous screech and she jumped. Sebastian reached across the table for her hand while telling her to stay calm and that there was nothing to worry about.

"Those things are big, but they're still nothing compared to the Rhorr'Dach."

"You've seen one?! Are they real? I thought Jonathan was crazy thinking he could catch one somehow." Her eyes were big and she reminded him of a child full of excitement.

"Shit," he muttered under his breath. "Ummm…I can't really talk about it, sorry."

"No way Sebastian, I'm dying to hear what you know about them. Come on, I promise not to tell another living soul. Please?" Her pleading was both irresistible and intolerable for him.

"Okay, but you promise me?"

"Yes, yes, yes! Start with how you know they're real. Are they real, or are you pulling my leg?"

"They *are* real," he cleared his throat. "Are you sure you want to hear this story? It's long."

"I've got all the time in the world. Shoot."

When Sebastian was a captain in the Unified Space Military, he quickly moved up the ladder and was up for promotion to move into a major's position when he was sent to Mhooreanna with a squad. His commanding officer told him a small war started and his mission was to take the leader of the anarchist's group, a man named Agathon Rojo dead or alive. Sebastian worked in tandem with Captain Bouton's squad to find him. They split up on the battlefield, but Sebastian found an injured man that matched the pictures he'd been sent by his Lieutenant Colonel, Matthias Zoal. Rojo had been shot in the chest and the leg and was extremely weak, certainly not a threat. He was sitting against a burned tree, hiding in its hollowed out trunk.

Sebastian shouted at Rojo that he was going to be taken into custody but when he grabbed Rojo's arm, he read him instantly. It was one of the rare moments that Sebastian's 7's surpassed their normal limits. He saw into the man's thoughts without trying, and saw way beyond his intentions. The man Sebastian saw before him wasn't a man at all but a Rhorr'Dach hiding within a Human shell. At first, Sebastian didn't believe what he was reading, it was so unusual, and he didn't know this species existed until just then. Rojo had come to this planet in Human form looking for his parents after they had been missing for nine days. Word spread that two elder Dach were on Mhooreanna and a small war broke out between the native species trying to capture them, both races of Mhooreannaians wanted Rojo's parents for themselves. The elder Dach had crash-landed on the planet on their way back home from a vacation. Both were injured in the crash and that meant they were stuck in Human form. Although it was safer to avoid detection to travel as Humans, they were much weaker than their normal state if they were injured, especially in their twilight years. Agathon Rojo's parents had both been over 900 years old when they perished. They were killed when their capture attempt failed.

Agathon didn't see it happen but he found their bodies and was deeply affected. He was spotted mourning over their natural Rhorr'Dach form since their DNA reverts after death. He set them ablaze, (as is Rhorr'Dach death ritual) and it was assumed, correctly, that he was one of them. While he was fleeing, he caught a bullet in the chest and leg but was able to get to the tree and hide, hoping he could wait it out. In this form, he couldn't fight, and he couldn't change to his natural state either.

Sebastian sympathized with his situation and felt the sorrow and desperation flowing out of the injured Dach. Rojo was suffering from severe shock and close to death. Sebastian couldn't kill this man, nor capture him and turn him over to the military. He decided there was only one thing to do.

Captain Bouton and his men caught up with Sebastian and Sebastian told all of them what happened and why they had really been sent there. The military wanted either to use the last Rhorr'Dach they knew of – Agathon, for their own purposes of turning him into a warrior for their side, or kill him if he was about to fall into any other groups hands.

Sebastian's squad was loyal to him and Bouton's squad followed their own Captain's lead. No one was to acknowledge the truth of what Captain Raynes did that day. Sebastian decided to leave the military then and there. They agreed as a group that everyone's story was Captain Raynes died on the battlefield and his body was dragged off by the natives. The only thing his squad found was his dog tags. And Captain Bouton was in charge of coming up with a solid story that everyone could repeat and remember with the exact same details. Sebastian thought it was a good story that Eric came up with, but in hindsight,

Sebastian's history of disobeying orders and the target disappearing as well as Sebastian made the military question its validity. So even though the military went through the charade of acting as though Sebastian Raynes was dead, many suspected he just went AWOL with Agathon.

The crackling over Sebastian's radio briefly distracted him. Lieutenant Colonel Zoal was commanding them now to shoot Rojo on sight. Sebastian said a quick goodbye to his squad and friend. He told them explicitly to keep themselves out of trouble and blame him for everything.

Sebastian picked up the injured Dach and realized a dead giveaway for the species – he weighed an immense amount. His mass was much more than what was possible for a Human body of his size. Sebastian carried him through the battle-scarred forest until he found an unattended USM transit. He went AWOL under fire that day – a military crime for any officer, and deserting in those conditions was punishable by death. *Good thing I'm already dead,* he said to himself.

Agathon had no choice but to trust Sebastian and told him of his home world, Foss-Altus, and how to safely land to get him medical attention.

Sebastian paused for a moment in his story. He was silent and Celeste knew he was lost in a memory.

"That's a fascinating story. You did a wonderful thing."

Sebastian blinked a few times, "I remember when I launched that transit…Agathon was looking out the window. I knew he was looking for the smoke from the fire." Sebastian looked away from Celeste and felt a lump in his throat that he could not swallow down. "The fire from his parent's…bodies. It was awful – all the pain I felt coming off him in that moment. I knew he had found it."

Celeste blinked back tears. Sebastian wouldn't look at her and she knew that telling this story was upsetting him.

"You don't hav—"

"Agathon was as close to his parents as I was to mine when they were killed. Him and I understand each other because we are two of kind. We had our loved ones ripped away from us when we were far too young," he looked at her, "I pray that I find your parents…alive. I pray that you

don't join the club that Agathon and I are in. I pray that you're able to
enjoy your parents in your life for a long, long time."

A few tears fell from her eyes at the thought of having her parents
back in front of her to give hugs to and to laugh with. And she cried for
Sebastian and Agathon suffering through the pain that she had the day
she learned of the house fire that possibly took her parents from her
forever. Only she knew that unlike Sebastian and Agathon, her parents
might still be alive and be able to come back to her.

Sebastian grabbed a box of tissues, put it in front of her on the table,
and excused himself for a moment.

She blew her nose and calmed down. She didn't know the story of
how Sebastian lost his parents, but it sounded like it affected him deeply
to this day. She thought maybe someday, he'd tell her. Then it occurred
to her that he might have already and she had forgotten. She didn't have
the heart to ask him. She could only hope for the millionth time that she
could regain her memory soon.

She got up and put the tissues back where they belonged and when
she turned around, she saw Sebastian walking back to the table. He sat
down and she followed.

He continued his story as if nothing happened. He said they barely
made it to Foss-Altus, or FA for short, as the transit had been a damaged one that needed repairs when he had "borrowed" it from the battlefield. It was falling apart and Sebastian knew he wouldn't be travelling
anywhere in it for quite some time. He'd be stuck on Agathon's world
once he landed, maybe for months, but that was okay with him. He
didn't even think this species existed and was eager to learn about them.
And he didn't know for sure if they'd ever let him off their planet alive
at that point. The last thing he asked of Captain Bouton was to change
Sebastian's next of kin from Constantine to Eric. Then Eric would get
Sebastian's belongings in the mail so he wouldn't upset his brother.

Sebastian spent the next four months on Foss-Altus learning everything he could and making a strong bond with Agathon. Not only
did Sebastian learn about them, after he learned of their problems, he
taught them everything he knew about combat, security, and protecting
themselves. There wasn't much that the Dach didn't already know about

these things, but a few techniques were new to them. The Rhorr'Dach learned not all species were ill-intentioned or monsters trying to enslave or kill them.

The experience for Sebastian was one of the highlights of his life and he wouldn't trade it for anything. Once he taught them everything he could and they fully trusted him to leave, they allowed him to do so.

"The first time you asked me why I was an assassin, I told you a bit of half-truths here and there. That is the full and true version."

"I asked you that?! I must've barely known you at that point. I'm surprised you answered."

"Well, I only partially answered it."

He went on to tell her that he could go nowhere and hold a normal job, pay taxes, or give out his real name since the military thought he was dead. And had they found out he wasn't, they would've wanted him dead.

He knew of a few former squad mates that hated the military after they served their time, and he knew he could trust them. One of them had turned gun-for-hire and it sounded like the only option for him – and that's how he got started as an assassin. Under the circumstances, it was one of the few jobs he excelled at.

"I want you to know, there were a few months I tried anything to avoid going into this line of business: bouncer, bodyguard, security. I was even an enforcer for a while, but in the end, I saw too many people up close and they saw me."

"I understand."

"Well, in the end it worked out. When I left the military, I saw I could do so much more good out in the real world. I rid the universe of some horrible scumbags, plus nothing pays nearly as well as this. But still, I avoided this choice for as long as I could."

He told her he started a new life for himself paying bills, having a place to live, and doing something he was good at. All while never giving out his real name. He lied to Francesca and his brother both about what he did for a living.

"Anyway, Agathon lets me visit his home world whenever I like and we have a very close bond. Rhorr'Dach are amazing creatures I assure you."

"Maybe someday I'll get to find out for myself."

"Maybe. If you're extremely lucky perhaps they'd let me bring you along some time, but I can't make any promises."

She poked at the last bits of food on her plate with her fork, "So, what was my husband up to?"

"What do you mean?"

"I'm hoping you're an assassin that doesn't kill nice people. That maybe you only kill people that are horrible right?"

He nodded.

"So what was he doing that made it worthy of death?"

"Other than abusing you on a regular basis and making your life a living hell?"

"Is that why you killed him? For me?"

He sighed, "No. In fact, I had no idea of the abuse going on in your marriage. I only discovered that directly from you after I killed the son of a bitch," he stared down at his clasped hands on the table in front of him, "I do have to mention though, now that I know you, his assassination was the only one that personally satisfied me. As lovely a creature as you are, you never deserved anything but to be treated like the queen I know you are – title or no title." His eyes met hers.

He rendered her speechless. She stared at him and doubted there was another man who could make her feel this...alive. She wanted to say something, but she didn't know what would be remotely accurate to describe how she was feeling. There were no words.

"It's okay. I understand what you're trying to say Celeste."

She tilted her head and made a face, "What?"

He shook his head, "Sorry. You and I? We do this," he corrected, "Did this, all the time, actually."

She looked puzzled.

"Our 7's. We have a mental connection that's stronger than I've ever personally experienced with anyone else. Sometimes you broadcast a lot of your thoughts like a radio tower. I'm not prying, but I can hear you in my head just like you're talking to me."

"I'm sorry Sebastian, I'm really interested in learning more about these powers you're talking about, but I'm starting to get a bad headache.

It's been dull up until now, but I'm starting to feel a little foggy." She put her hand to her head and rubbed her temple.

"You want to lie down?"

"No, I'll be fine. I wanted to say out loud that what you said…before. It was very sweet and I appreciate it. You'll never know exactly how much," she paused, "The way I was treated by my husband when I was queen…I might believe that some stray dogs see more mercy and kindness."

Sebastian cracked his knuckles.

"So, about Jonathan. What kind of horrors was he hiding from me?"

"Are you sure you want to know this? Once you know, you'll never think of him the same way, no matter how bad you thought he was before," his face was stern.

"Positive."

"Your husband was involved in Human trafficking. Specifically from Earth to a great many other planets looking for live sex slaves, when sex bots just wouldn't do – including Il'laceier."

She put her hand to her mouth in disgusted awe.

"He was also allowing massive amounts of drugs to be imported onto Earth from all over, as long as he got a slice of the pie. Not only was he importing them, he was a major customer. As far as I could tell, he liked using Red Diamond and Spinner, but he really loved Firedrops. I'm guessing you probably already know that part."

She shook her head, "No. I've actually never been around drugs or users so I couldn't tell you the symptoms. There were many times he acted crazier than usual though. I guess those were the signs."

He ran his fingers through his hair, "Let me guess. He often had cold sweats, snored like crazy, maybe his hands shook? He was aggressive, sometimes extremely lucid one minute, then rambling on like a paranoid mental patient the next? Maybe he spoke of bugs crawling around under his skin. Sound familiar?"

Her eyes were big, "Yes, to all of that."

"His eyes ever change from yellow to orange?"

She gave an enthusiastic, "Yes! I thought I was going crazy since I knew that wasn't normal and he always denied it was possible."

"Firedrops." He shook his head, "Those are brutal. The addicts drop the liquid in their eyes and it stains the eye tissue for hours after the effects wear off. Supposed to be a wicked high and a really bad crash. I'm going to bet that the nights he was angrier, more forceful, he was crashing off that."

The power went out and they were left with the muted light of purple gray sky seeping in the windows. She was glad she lit the candles and fireplace, otherwise it would've really been dark.

Sebastian stood up immediately and closed his eyes. She knew he must've been looking for someone mentally.

"I don't feel any other minds near, but I need to check the house. Stay here." He was out of the room before she could say anything in response.

She heard the occasional sound of him opening and closing doors throughout the house. He was moving fast. She watched as he came back downstairs and grabbed the umbrella by the front door.

He stopped to say, "Interior's clear. I've got to do a perimeter check. You stay put. You see anything, you yell at me with your mind."

"How do I do that?"

"Think hard and aim it at me. I'll get it, trust me." He opened the front door and disappeared into the rain.

"But the sareeaveous are out there," she said to herself.

She went to the window and watched as he opened the umbrella on the front porch and ran around the corner. She went from window to window and couldn't see anything but rain and occasionally Sebastian running around the house. Before she knew it, he was back inside, closing the umbrella, and shaking it off. He locked the door and placed the umbrella upside down so it could dry.

"There's no one here but us. I'm guessing the wind might be knocking down trees, unless there was a direct lightning strike to one of the bahthermal power plants. Can you check and see if there's any information please?"

She navigated a few screens on her Titan and said, "There are a lot of downed trees, but it was lightning that hit some conversion equipment. They say it might be hours before it's repaired since it's close to Mount

Kraseari. They recommend everyone stay where they are because this storm is severe."

He shook his head, "No shit." He looked at her, "Sorry."

She went to him, "You cold?"

"Not…"

Celeste put her arms around him.

"Yes, actually I am. It's chilly out there. At least I didn't get drenched this time." He put his arms around her.

She held onto him tightly, enjoying the warmth of his embrace, "Thank you for telling me earlier…about Jonathan. I don't think I would've ever known the truth from anyone else."

"He worked hard to keep his secrets; I'm just good at digging." He looked over the mess on the kitchen table, "I've got to clean up. Give me a second." He kissed her forehead and let go of her, "How's your headache?"

She reached up to her temple and started rubbing there, "Still throbbing."

He went to the doctor's bag Zach left for them and found the aspirin. "Take one of these. Catch." He tossed the bottle across the room and she caught it.

He cleaned up what remained of lunch as she stood by the big windows looking out onto the landscape. Little rivers poured down the glass as she watched the ocean churn. The green sareeaveous she spotted earlier had moved on.

"Why don't you let the maid bot clean up?" Celeste said over her shoulder.

"I forget Zach has one most of the time. And I'm used to doing this stuff myself. You probably don't remember the only time I use bots is for my yacht."

Her eyes lit up, "You have a yacht?" Before he could answer she continued, "Wait, is this the yacht you spoke of when you were brushing my hair that one day?"

"One in the same, so yes and yes. I need a crew to take care of it, especially while I'm gone so that's the only reason I bought those bots, otherwise I can do my own laundry and clean up and cook. I kind of enjoy the household chores," he wiped down the table with a wet towel.

"We always had live staff at the estates. I hardly got a chance to do chores, unless I was alone, which was rare. Jon never wanted the servants to see us doing 'menial' tasks, he said it made us look like commoners."

Sebastian grunted, "That's a shame. Good hard labor builds character. I bet your staff are good people."

"They were." She remembered times in the estate when it would rain and she was alone looking out over the green fields bathed in rain. She would always wrap her arms around herself thinking it'd be great to have someone she cared about to curl up with.

Sebastian came up behind her and wrapped his arms around her waist, holding her close, "Is this okay my lady?"

She let her weight rest against him, "Yes. It's perfect actually."

"You're marveling at how I got behind you so quietly."

She smiled, "Yes, it's kind of hard getting used to you 'reading' me, but it's nice sometimes too. I don't have to say anything." She closed her eyes, "So tell me about your stealth ninja mode."

He smiled and laughed softly, "Well, part of my DNA comes from big cats, and predatory animals, so I'm excellent at sneaking up on my prey. It's part of what makes me a good assassin. I was born with my sneaking ability, but I've enhanced it with some training from ninjas as well."

She looked up at him over her shoulder, "I'm your prey?"

"Only when you're asking me to come up behind you," he smiled.

She saw his reflection in the glass. "I suppose I probably told you this before but you have a disarming smile. Don't you have women throwing themselves at you all the time?"

He held onto her a little tighter, "You are very sweet. I don't know, I suppose some women might find me attractive, it's all subjective. I'm never really paying much attention."

"I have a feeling you pay close attention to the women you like though."

"Yes, I do."

They stood that way quietly for a few minutes before she spoke again, "You have this severe intensity to you."

"Do I?" He smiled.

"It could be intimidating," she smiled back.

"You don't seem intimidated."

"Oh…I don't know."

"I think you do know. Try again."

"Okay. I like it about you." She wanted to stay that way forever with him watching the rain, but she started feeling faint. "Sebastian?"

"You're not feeling good. You're getting dizzy. Let's get you laying down." He felt her knees go out from under her. Had he not already had his arms around her, she would've fallen straight down onto the hard tile floor. His grip tightened around her and he shifted so he could pick her up in his arms. He carried her to the closest couch in the living room.

A huge crack of thunder boomed over the house making the walls shake. Sebastian was never one to frighten easy, but it made him jump since he'd been so focused on her.

He ran to the bag of medical supplies and grabbed some smelling salts. He cracked one open and waved it in front of her nose. He watched as her eyes flickered open suddenly.

She looked over at him, "Oh! I fainted didn't I? Damn it! I'm sorry; I was having such a nice moment with you."

He shook his head and kissed her on the forehead, "The important thing is that you're okay. How are you feeling?"

She sat up slowly holding her face, "Okay, I guess. My headache's getting a little better. I don't know what happened. I was relaxed so it's not like I was trying to do jumping jacks or anything."

"You got a damn fine scare from our little attack though and you learned some really awful things about your husband. I think I should get you to bed. Can you walk?"

"Let me see." She stood up carefully and took a few steps while he spotted her. "Yeah, I'll be okay. Laying down sounds good." Thunder cracked out loudly after she spoke.

He helped her get into bed and covered her with a blanket. Once he was out of her room, he immediately called the doctor.

Sebastian was relieved to hear Zach's opinion that things like this were bound to happen in a case like hers – too much emotional stress like almost getting eaten by a sareeaveous could easily cause her to faint.

Probably nothing to worry about. Nevertheless, Doctor Coldiron said he'd be by in a few days.

Sebastian sat down next to Celeste on the bed.

She looked over to him, "Am I going to live?"

"Yes, Zach thinks you'll be fine. How are you feeling now?"

"Okay."

"Are you okay enough for me to take a shower and leave you alone for a bit?"

He started unbuttoning his shirt and she found herself studying his freshly revealed chest.

"I...think so..."

Sebastian smiled at the things he heard her thinking.

She felt warmth spreading across her cheeks, "Did you read my thoughts just now?"

His smile got bigger.

"If...How did you get that scar on your torso? I saw it when we were out on the beach."

He put his hand to his side where the scar was and the smile dropped off his face, "Oh, that's an old one. One of my first jobs went sideways and the target had a knife. I wasn't as careful as I should have been, but I learned from it."

"I probably already asked you about it huh? I just don't remember."

"No actually you haven't. I knew you noticed it, but I'm surprised you haven't asked about the ones on my back."

"I didn't see those."

He moved so he was sitting on the side of the bed with his back to her. He took off his shirt so she could see the countless small scars spread all over his back.

She sat up to look closer and ran her hand over some of them. She noticed his skin broke out into goose bumps. She heard an escaped thought he probably didn't mean for her to – *Damn, is there ever going to be a time where I'm not aroused by her touch? I don't know how much more of this I can take.*

He moved off the bed and held his shirt in his hand as he walked to the windows. He looked out over the storm and sighed.

She didn't want to say anything.

He turned around and faced her.

To Celeste, it looked like he wanted to say something, but he didn't know whether he should or not. He put a hand through his hair and she wished she could touch him again.

He walked to her and stood next to the bed. "These scars…on my back…I got those from one of my first wars…Helena Rebels on the planet Hallowsend. Do you know anything about it?"

She shook her head.

"I don't know if it's because it was one of my first experiences with war or if that one was just particularly brutal, but it changed me. How can a war not change someone right?" His face clouded over with an uneasiness she was not used to seeing.

"It's okay. You don't have to finish this story if you don't want."

He hesitated, measuring her for a moment, "I think it best if you relax for a while and I'll go take that shower. You sure you're fine?"

"Yes."

He nodded and left the room closing her door softly.

NINE

>>> > A FEW DAYS after Celeste's fainting spell, the doctor visited her and Sebastian for lunch. Zach cleared Celeste physically, believing her health to be at one hundred percent. Her bruises were all gone, she could run without winding herself, she was in great spirits, and vibrant. He reassured both of them, her fainting spell wasn't a cause for concern but he took a blood sample just to be sure. As far as her memory was concerned, she hadn't made any progress.

She was thrilled that, at least physically, she had made a full recovery and she thanked the doctor for everything.

Zach looked at the results of the blood work on his Titan.

"So what's wrong with me doc?"

Zach smiled, "Don't say it that way dear. Looks like you're anemic. Are you on any kind of iron pills?"

Celeste cringed, "Oh yeah, I forgot! The last time I saw a doctor, she said I may become anemic if I didn't get more iron. Something about my body won't let me keep in there. Yeah, I haven't taken any iron pills in months. Is that why I keep passing out?"

"That could be a very common reaction to low iron levels, yes. But, not to worry, that's an easy fix. I have some in my bag. Just make sure to take it dear. We'll monitor it, but it's not a serious problem."

As they were finishing their lunch on the back patio, Celeste asked the doctor a final question.

"Is my memory ever going to come back?"

Doctor Coldiron looked out at the ocean for a moment, then back at her, "I honestly don't know my dear. I don't want to give you false hope. Some patients never recover their buried memories, but a lot of them do, it just takes time. Don't rush it. I hope it comes back, and if it does, it will do so when your brain is ready."

Sebastian cleared their plates and Celeste walked the doctor to the front door.

He handed her a bottle of iron pills, "Celeste, I hope you realize how worried he was about you. I've never seen him that way before. I know he cares about you. It's nice to finally see him with someone, well, if you two ever become a couple 'officially.'" He gave her a kiss on the cheek and as she was kissing his cheek, she heard him ask, "And what happened to my window up there?" Zach stared at the boards above the back door. He had come around the back directly so this was the first chance he had to see the damage.

"Oh! I'm so sorry, we forgot to mention that. When the sareeaveous attacked, Sebastian sacrificed one of your patio chairs to it and then the damn thing hit the window with it. We'll pay for it. I told him we should've had someone come out to fix it but he didn't want anyone to come to the house unnecessarily."

Zach was silent for a moment, thinking things through, "Yes, I suppose that's best for you both. Tell Sebastian I will take care of it after you've left. It's no problem. I'm just glad you're both safe."

Celeste gave a crooked smile to him feeling more guilty than ever, "I'm really sorry Zach."

He squeezed her hand and walked outside, "No worries your Highness. Be well my dear and stay as long as you need to stay safe. And tell your boyfriend not to 'sacrifice' any more of my furniture to the Bahsheef beasts."

They both laughed and Zach said over his shoulder as he got into his transit, "Seriously though, my wives are going to kill me."

CHAPTER 30

HALLOWSEND

ONE

>>> > CELESTE HAD THE screens on enjoying complete access to what-
ever news programs she liked. It was always such a secret thing trying to
find out what was going on in the universe while Jon was alive.

"In weather today we're expecting more severe storms near the
southern border. The Bahsheefian weather council is recommending
everyone stay inside due to a strong electrical element with the cell that's
developing currently." The weather woman came into the frame slowly
putting her tree-like rooted legs down in an immovable looking stance.

"Sebastian, what species is this?" Celeste pointed to the weather
woman.

He looked up from his book, "Ah, a Nikora. They're native to Mar Yen. A beautiful species."

"She doesn't have any eyes. Are they all like that?"

"Yes, they don't need eyes. They sense things like you wouldn't believe. I'm sure she can map a room in a few moments by smelling all the living creatures in it, can hear the hum of electrical equipment, and feel tiny changes in micro-wind patterns as things move around. Nikora might be the closest thing I've ever seen to a talking plant with legs. They make excellent weather people because they are so in tune with their environments."

Celeste looked her over. The woman had what looked like tree roots that moved independently from the knees and elbows down, but there were still some feet-like and hand-like appendages at the ends. She had a small waist and her breasts were in proportion to the rest of her frame. She had delicate looking shoulders and from her collarbone up to the middle of her neck were ruffled layers of skin. If it were clothing, Celeste could say she had a collar made of a lettuce hem but it was all organic. Her neck was long and elegant, something like a Human woman might wish for, she had a small mouth with two lips, a nose, and that's where the Human-like qualities ended. Above the nose and around the cheekbones, were wide flaps of skin that resembled rose petals. These petals flowed backward to make a kind of slicked back hair. Celeste suspected if you saw one of these creatures lying face down on the ground, it would appear like a very large rose was blooming out of the backs of their heads.

"Do they all look this way? With a bright pink petal head? Or are there different colors?"

"They're all bright pink."

"...we don't expect any power outages from this storm like the one of several days ago that hit the east most northern edges of the Sheef Plates. A tremendously powerful lightning bolt struck near an active volcano and knocked out a large grid of the bahthermal power plant at Mount Kraseari. Bahsheef Public Power states they've made improvements over the past two days to prevent any major power losses like the five-hour blackout experienced a few days ago. We'll be..."

Celeste froze in place as a loud rumble rolled underneath the house. She mistook it for a bahsheefquake as everything in the house shook, but the noise that accompanied it was the most frightening.

Sebastian stood to walk to her but found it difficult with the floor undulating like a wave. Pictures shook off the walls and he could hear glass shattering in the kitchen.

Celeste yelled out over the noise, "When is this going to stop?!"

And just like that, it ended.

She stood up as Sebastian went to her. His eyes were assessing the damage already, "You okay?"

"I'm fine. What was that?"

"I think one of the volcanoes." He put his arms around her and she held onto him.

The commercial break for the news was interrupted by a loud alarm shrieking and a graphic on the screen that said, "EMERGENCY EVACUATION ALERT!"

The weather woman appeared on the screen, "Attention central northern edges of the Sheef Plates region. Mount Streherdly Creu has just erupted. Please look at the map for the evacuation zone."

Celeste's eyes were wide as she studied the gray circle in the middle of the continent. The evacuation zone was big with the volcano in the very center. "Is that us? Do we have to leave?"

"No. It's closer than I'd like, but that's not close enough for evacuation." He released her and started shuffling screens on his Titan.

"Are you sure?" She sat on the couch and stared at the weather woman.

"Hold on. Let me see what else I can find in the volcano reports."

"...Streherdly Creu exhibited escalated unrest for several months but wasn't predicted to erupt until next year. The Bahsheefian Volcano Association is expecting this to be a minor ash emission event with a substantial lava flow. We have a news transit en route to the site..."

Celeste got up and walked outside onto the back patio looking for whatever she could see. She didn't know what to expect as she never saw an active eruption before. She spotted it along the edge of the horizon – a faint gray collection of puffs were growing across the sky, but what was most impressive were the explosions of lava shooting into the air. A tall and steady stream of orange fire burst forth in jets and blobs.

Sebastian joined her on the patio a few minutes later and stared at the eruption.

She looked at him, "What? Don't tell me you've never seen one of these before."

"Actually, I haven't."

"What did you find out?"

"We're not in the path of the flow. But that doesn't mean we shouldn't start thinking about leaving here. The reports say this is the first of many volcanoes that are expected to erupt over the next few months. As beautiful as this planet is, I'm considering moving us back to Praxis soon."

"But I thought you said it wasn't safe there. Isn't that the whole reason you brought me here?"

"Celeste, if these eruptions continue with more volcanoes, there's going to be a huge amount of ash fallout. We can't escape that; there's nowhere to go where the ground won't be covered with it and it's deadly to our lungs. If we leave before all that happens, we'll have time to plan our departure instead of running off in a hurry."

"So when do we leave?"

"Give it a few days. We'll see what develops here and I need to think through preparations before we leave. Then I'll give you an answer."

"Okay. I'm going to get the maid bot so we can start cleaning up the damage."

Sebastian nodded and watched as she walked into the house.

TWO

>>> > AFTER A FEW hours of reading on the couch, Celeste realized the sun would start setting soon. She looked up from her holobook and saw Sebastian gazing at her. He looked away as soon as their eyes met. She thought maybe he was afraid of touching her, as if she'd break like a porcelain doll. He hadn't tried to kiss her again. She wanted him to though. She had really liked it. She was starting to really like him.

"Sebastian? Will you walk with me?"

He put his book on the table, "Of course." He grabbed his shoulder holster and a torch before they walked outside onto the patio and down to the shore.

"I want to thank you for taking care of me. I imagine this has put a lot of stress on you."

"The doctor's to thank for giving us this house for you to recover safely."

She stopped walking and faced him putting her hands on his shoulders.

He tried to look away, but her eyes caught his and wouldn't let go. "The doc finally cleared me. I feel fine. If you want to pick up wherever we left off before I lost my memory, I'd be okay with that."

"It would be irresponsible of me to take advantage of you in your current…situation," he spoke with quiet, but determined firmness.

The corners of her mouth twisted in frustration, "I'm not drunk Sebastian. I'm a grown woman who's becoming increasingly drawn to a very sexy man."

"Then that very sexy man is a lucky one too. Who is he?"

"You're joking at a time like this? Really? Wait, you're joking. You've never done that in all these weeks I've known you. I'm impressed."

"Yes, the man with no sense of humor tries to make a joke, alert the media, put it in your diary tonight, mark your calendar." He smiled and she felt her heartbeat increase like it had been lately when he smiled at her.

She moved even closer up against his body, "I appreciate you trying to loosen up, but I'm being quite serious now. You shouldn't feel like you're taking advantage of me because you aren't."

"It's bad enough I lost my self-control and kissed you three times already, and then that sareeaveous attacked us…We could've died because I was distracted by my loins. I just wish you would recover your memory first."

"Well, until I do, why don't you provide me with some pleasant memories in the mean time?"

He stared into her eyes for a moment. Her big brown eyes, fathoms deep leading down the rabbit hole for him.

"I need to do something. Can you hold the torch for a minute please?"

She took the torch and he put his hands to her cheeks and held her gently.

"I'm going to read you deeply, but I have to do it quick because last time I tried this, you knocked me out…literally."

"I what?"

"Not on purpose. Neither one of us knew what would happen."

She stared at him, baffled, "Is it going to hurt *me*?"

"For you, it's going to feel like warm water traveling over your body. Is that okay with you?"

"Okay," he heard a flicker of apprehension in her response.

He closed his eyes and read her. He saw that this is what she truly wanted; she was positive. She was attracted to him all over again, and he excited her as much as she did him.

He softly pressed his lips against hers and realized just how badly he missed kissing her.

Her body relaxed as he put his arms around her and squeezed firmly.

She thought they were close enough to the line of torches along the shore to toss the one she was holding to the sand. She intensified the kiss by pushing herself up against him harder, while she dragged her fingernails down his back.

He gently bit her lower lip and let it fall out of his mouth slowly. He felt a shiver run down her spine.

She put her head on his chest and he held her, listening to the waves crash. For the first time since they arrived, he felt sad they would have to go back to Praxis.

THREE

>>> > THE NEXT DAY, Sebastian told Celeste he wanted to train her to protect herself. They started with easy moves, and moved up into advanced hand-to-hand combat. With her mental powers coming back to full strength she was able to sense, most of the time, what his body was going to do and block punches and kicks. He was impressed at her skill

and speed. He had no doubts that within a week she'd be good enough to move on to weapons when they got back to Praxis.

After lunch they went out onto the beach and fought some more. She spun too quickly for him and kicked his leg out from underneath him. He fell to the ground and she dropped on top of him, straddling his hips and pinning his hands down with her own.

"Now I've finally got you right where I want you," she smiled.

"I let you win this time. Just like I'm letting you sit on top of me." He lifted up one of his hands and she struggled to keep it down, but failed. "I'm stronger than you Celeste. Sorry, always will be." Then he let his hand be pushed back onto the sand.

"Doesn't matter. You're still vulnerable," she leaned over and kissed him. He also let her do that but stopped her before it went too far.

She stood up and teased him as she walked away, "You'll cave eventually. You can't resist me forever."

"Oh really? Quite full of ourselves aren't we now," he smiled at her.

"I think you're worth the wait though."

FOUR

>>> > LATER THAT NIGHT while Celeste was sleeping, Sebastian was up and heard her cry out. He'd already slept as long as he needed and carefully cracked her door open to look in on her.

She was thrashing. He moved closer to her bed and looked at her. She was in a full sweat and it made him nervous.

"No, don't touch me! Get away!" her voice cracked and it was obvious she was in distress.

He sat in the chair next to her and watched, waiting for her to calm down. After a few minutes of her legs kicking and some more talking, she settled down and rolled towards him. She opened her eyes and saw his eyes glowing back at her.

"Sebastian?"

"Yes, just me."

"Why are you sitting there?"

"I was up already. Heard you having a bad dream, so I wanted to check on you. Make sure you calmed down."

"What time is it?"

"About four thirty. Still really early. Go back to bed."

She sat up and rubbed her eyes, "I had a dream about Jonathan. He was coming towards me one of the first nights after we got married. I hadn't given him…what he wanted yet and I was scared. He was much bigger than me and I'd never…been intimate with anyone. My mother tried to advise me on how to handle this situation, but I was vastly underprepared. It was really terrible the first time. And every time after that. I'm glad he's gone."

Sebastian's anger rose and he didn't want Celeste to see him lose his temper. He stood up and started to leave the room, "You need your res—"

"No wait!"

He turned around.

"You're angry. Really angry. Getting more so with every second that goes by."

"I wish sometimes I could bring your husband back to life so I could kill him all over again. I hate hearing what he did to you. When I get this way, it's better if I'm not around you. I was going to go for my morning run on the beach."

She sighed, "Will you just lay down with me until I go back to sleep please?"

"I'm not sure that's appropriate for us right now. You still haven't recovered your memories, and I'm so…" he couldn't finish.

She settled back, disappointed, "Okay…I guess I can understand that. I don't want you to be uncomfortable."

"Get some rest. Goodnight."

"Night Sebastian."

He closed the door.

She rolled over and tried to sleep. Times that she thought were hardest in her life started to flood her mind one after another.

When she was a princess child and was held to a higher standard than everyone else. She could never just sit around and play with other kids. She always had to act appropriately; always needed to be on her best behavior and while her parents raised her to think she was no better than a commoner was, they expected she act proper in public situations. When she did have a chance to play with other kids from school, she always had a bodyguard around, watching her to make sure no one abducted her. Sometimes all she wanted to do was run away to a place where she could feel like a normal girl. She didn't even know exactly what that would look like, but that's what she wanted.

The years of preparation to be a stranger's wife. The countless hours of learning perfect manners, trying to remember basic information about thousands of alien species and their worlds, learning how to cook and care for an estate, and losing all that time she could've been spending with her family. No one considered what she wanted to do with her life. She existed to make billions of Humans comfortable with an alien leader and to satisfy one alien king's every desire, no matter how small.

All the time she spent living a lie with Jonathan and the day she learned her parents might be gone forever were difficult times in her life.

But none of the challenges of her past had prepared her for what she was going through now. To have a big black hole where her memories used to be was an unrivaled experience. A big chunk of time – erased in a moment. Time she might never get back, and it could've been memories of the happiest time of her life. She could've been in love with Sebastian, but couldn't remember it.

Now all she wanted, was a connection. She wanted someone with her *now*, to help her through this difficult time of her life. She went through all the other times resentful and angry or desperately scared, but always alone. She didn't want to be alone anymore. She barely held her tears back, breathing deep to get herself under control.

That damn dream brought back a lot of chilling memories and she wanted Sebastian to be there with her. She had no one else to turn to.

There was a knock on the door, but Sebastian didn't wait for an answer.

Celeste looked to him as tears rolled down her cheeks and she smiled. He took off his t-shirt and pants, leaving just his briefs on and got into bed next to her under the sheets.

"I'm sorry. I could hear your thoughts all the way downstairs. I couldn't block them out; I wasn't trying to be invasive."

She swallowed the knot in her throat, "It's okay. Stop apologizing. I'm just glad you're here."

She curled herself up against him and he cradled her in his arms.

This show of kindness broke her down further. She sobbed a little and he let her cry it out. It might've been what she needed.

He looked out the windows at the calm sea, "I never did tell you the story about my back scars. It might help you feel better to know you're not the only one who's alone and suffering."

"No, you didn't," she sniffled and closed her eyes as she put her face into the center of his chest.

"If you remember, it was on the planet Hallowsend. The Helena Rebels War."

"I don't know much about it. It happened right before I was born."

Sebastian sighed, "Oh you just made me feel so old."

She smiled against his skin, "Sorry. Didn't mean to."

"The Tonk Coshabba were battling the Helena Rebels. The USM sent us out there to support the Tonks. We'd been fighting for days and the rebels were pushing back hard. My company had been crawling along in snowy dense forest all night, maybe eight hours I think, before my major ordered us to attack. There were so many of us. We burst out of the trees…" He stopped and she could tell this was a difficult story for him.

"We thought we got them all. That we'd waited long enough to push forward but then guys around me started to fall, shot dead. I found out later my company suffered sixty percent casualties that day. I lost a lot of friends as well as my major," he swallowed hard, "I looked over at the village and saw the last of the rebels go down. A couple of the guys around me were still keeping it together somehow. I scanned the area and thought it was empty until I saw a child."

She lifted her face up, "A child on the battlefield?"

"I felt sad for him at first. I assumed it was an innocent orphaned kid or something, maybe confused or lost but then I realized the little boy was about to throw a grenade at us. I couldn't let the men standing at my side die. I didn't want to die…so I did the only thing I could to stop him. What no other man seemed to be ready to do. I looked at them, but they had their guns down. Most of them were still trying to comprehend what happened. Can't say I blamed them. Or maybe I was the only one who saw this rebel child, I'm not sure.

"I lined up my sights and I killed him. Shot him once in chest and then the grenade exploded anyway. I turned my back but it was too late. I was too close. The burning shrapnel melted through my armor as I fell to the ground."

She was quiet, unsure of how to console him or offer any adequate comfort.

"Are you familiar with Helena Rebel kindle grenades? How they work?"

She backed up a little from him and shook her head.

"Imagine little globs of plasma that shoot out in a thirty-five foot radius burning through anything – rock, concrete, bone, flesh, steel, anything and everything. Bullets made of pure fire and heat. The USM still doesn't have a body armor graded for that. Those grenades make everything into kindling. And at the very edge of the deadly circle, debris cools off ever so slightly to just be super-heated shrapnel ready to embed itself in flesh and burn at the same time." His eyes held a thousand yard stare, "It's an elegant weapon, I must admit. Whoever invented that was a genius straight out of hell."

Celeste's focus was completely on him. She had forgotten about her own problems and stopped feeling sorry for herself.

He continued, "I heard someone yelling for the medics but there weren't any. They were all dead. Part of the village had caught fire; eventually everything was burning. I could feel the enormous heat on my skin. Those little huts went up so fast. I heard the wood crackling and popping along with the screams. Some of my platoon mates were on fire rolling on the ground, trying to extinguish themselves in the snow. I thought the whole world was on fire. I remembered my morphine and injected myself as soon as I found my syringe. I could smell the burnt hair, and something that smelled like burning rubber, I think it was coming from the body next to me – a villager. The worst part of it is, sometimes, I wake up with those screams ringing in my ears."

He was so lost in his memory, she felt she needed to say something to bring him back to her, "You saved a lot of lives that day. And what other choice was there?" She paused, "That must've been excruciating. I can't imagine."

The room was silent for a moment.

"A couple sparkys I had never seen before dragged me to safety. I ha—"

"Wait, what are sparkys?"

"Oh, those were the new guys. The USM has an…initiation, let's call it, where most people don't have their eyebrows by the end of it. These guys didn't have any eyebrows."

"Okay. Sorry for interrupting. Go on."

"I never got to thank them. I was laid up in the makeshift infirmary for two days. When I was hit, it felt like no other injury I'd experienced. The pain was immense and I was afraid I suffered spinal injuries, but I was lucky to escape that. I learned a lot about myself that day, about war, about people. My major was a good man, but he made the wrong call that day."

"You're not a bad person you know. I hope you realize you had the choice of dying that day, or living. You did the only thing you could and it was the *right* thing."

"It doesn't always feel that way."

"You should know better than anybody, life isn't always black and white. Quite often it's messy and confused. And doing the right thing sometimes feels really horrible." She put her hands on either side of his face looking into his eyes.

"Have you ever killed a child?"

"You saved lives Sebastian. You've probably done that your whole life, but it seems like you only want to focus on the ones you couldn't rescue, or the ones you took. You've saved my life. I'm here because of you and I'm extremely lucky. My abusive husband is gone and you've rescued me from kidnappers that must've done some terrible things to leave me in the shape I'm in. *I trust you* Sebastian. I believe you to be a good man who's taken care of me, and showed me so much kindness and compassion, I can't think of anyone who's taken such good care of me since my parents. You're a strong man, but I know you also have a tender heart deep down. You might hide it, but I feel it's there. Hearts always tell the truth about people."

How could she be so full of understanding? It was just what he needed to hear.

"Thank you Celeste. I've never told anyone that whole story."

She curled up against him and while he held her, they both fell asleep.

FIVE

>>> > WHEN CELESTE WOKE up, she rolled over and looked for Sebastian. She called out his name as she reached across the bed. It was cold; he probably hadn't been there for a while.

She got dressed and walked to the doorway of his bedroom. She didn't see him but called out to him. He answered from the open door to his bathroom, "Come in Celeste."

She walked in and stopped in her tracks at the doorway of his bathroom, stunned at the sexy sight in front of her.

"Yes my lady?"

All he was wearing was a towel wrapped around his waist and a small hand towel was hanging over his shoulder. His face was full of shaving cream and he was slowly dragging a razor along his cheek as he looked at himself in the mirror.

She couldn't say anything; she only wanted to watch.

He carefully finished the line he had started and looked at her, "You want to watch me do this?"

She smiled and nodded her head.

"Well, what did you need me for?" He rinsed off the razor under the faucet.

"Huh?"

He smiled, "Why were you looking for me? Did you need something?"

"I don't remember."

"This is really that good huh?"

She nodded her head again.

"Well, I didn't plan for you to see this, but a little birdie told me a long time ago that you thought this was pretty hot."

"Little birdie? Who?"

He chuckled, "You."

She looked high up on the mirror to see he had wedged a small photo into the edge.

"Can I look at your photo?"

He wiped his hands on the towel and pulled the photo down for her, "Of course."

She took it and stared. It looked like a family photo from when he was very young. "This is your family?"

"Yes. When we were all together and happy," he looked up and pulled the razor along his throat carefully.

She looked at the man, Sebastian's father, and noted how handsome he was. Obviously Sebastian got his good looks from him. Sebastian looked a lot like his father but his father's hair had been a light brown with a little gray at the temples. He looked sophisticated and stately. His mother was beautiful with straight dark brown hair that flowed down to her waist. She had a nice smile and kind eyes. "Oh, your mother was so pretty Sebastian. And your dad, my goodness was he handsome," she whistled as she fanned herself with her hand.

"Hey take it easy there. That's my dad you're ogling," he shot a playful glance at her.

She only smiled then looked back at his photo.

The baby, she assumed, was his brother Daxton; Constantine back then. Then she saw a very young Sebastian.

"How old were you when this was taken?"

"I must've been," he paused, "seven or eight I guess."

She sat quiet for a moment before responding, "You were so innocent looking and a cute little boy."

He smiled, half of his face still covered in shaving cream, "Yes well, I'm not so sweet and innocent anymore, and certainly not little."

"But you are cute. Downright handsome now."

He put his shoulders back, puffing up the way a man does when he's given a compliment he's proud of, "I am?" He looked at her while she handed the photo back.

"You are Sebastian. Like you don't already know this." She smiled at him as she walked away.

He looked back to his reflection and spoke to himself, "She thinks I'm handsome. Huh."

SIX

>>> > AFTER A TRAINING session, Sebastian and Celeste shared lunch indoors and talked about when to go back home.

"I've immensely enjoyed the time we've spent here, but we can't stay much longer. You're at one hundred percent physically and I need to start training you on all sorts of weapons that I don't have here."

"But none of the other volcanoes have erupted."

"No, they haven't but I think leaving sooner rather than later would be best," he wiped his mouth with his napkin.

"But Zach left us whatever is under the other tarp in the garage and we haven't even peeked at it."

"We haven't, you're right. We can look at it if you like, but whatever vehicle it is, we won't have time to take it out like the BMW."

"And you said you were going to help me decipher those weird symbols on that door I found. There's so many things we have left to do here. You haven't shown me more of the ruins you told me about. We haven't even visited one of the big cities here and wha—"

"Celeste, stop," he glared at her sharply, "We can't stay here forever. You know that."

"I don't want to stay here forever. Just a little longer to do the things I mentioned. No one's expecting us on Praxis."

"There's a volcano that's erupting and that situation's only going to get worse, not better. This whole planet is covered in them. That's why there's a sparse population here. Why are you stalling for time?"

"I'm not…it's just…You're not the one who got kidnapped. I did."

He waited for her to continue. He could feel her mind pulsing with anxiety over something.

She pushed her plate away, "When do you want to leave?"

"It's clear something's bothering you. You're so nervous it's hard for me to read you. What's wrong?"

She only half listened to him as she struggled with her fear, "Huh?"

He was trying to keep his patience but she was testing it now, "*What* is wrong?"

She looked at him, "I…you realize that I don't even know who my kidnappers were? I don't know if I was followed, watched, stalked. I don't know if there was eight men, or one man who took me. I can't remember their faces or any details about them. What if I'm on Praxis and one of those guys finds me? I won't even *recognize* them! I'm going to be a sitting duck." She was barely keeping herself in check.

Sebastian leaned over and put his hand on top of hers, but she pulled it away. She didn't want to be touched.

He chose his words carefully, "I can't imagine how frightening it must be to get kidnapped. Then to lose all memory of it has got to be very difficult. I am trying to understand how you're feeling right now. I know your mind is all over the place, because I can feel it darting around like a terrified animal."

"You have no idea," she snapped out the words.

He nodded, "You're right. I don't. But I need you to listen to me and I need you to trust me. We're teaching you, *right now*, how to fight. How to protect yourself. You're learning extremely fast and soon you're going to be a very dangerous woman to anyone who so much as *looks* at you the wrong way. Okay? We're making you into a lean mean ass-kicking *queen*. God help the person that fucks with you after I'm done with your training."

"I've never been in a real fist fight or anything," she mumbled.

He shook his head, "Not true. That asshole that beat you, he was *practice*."

"But I never hit him back. I never bested him."

"A smart fighter knows when they cannot win. Knows when an opponent will beat them no matter what you do. The best thing to do in those situations is to avoid the fight. If the fight can't be avoided, then take the least amount of damage and get away from your enemy. Outsmart them if you can, outrun them, or outlast them. That's what you did. You are a born fighter Celeste. You have it stuck in your head that all fights are won with your fists, but they're not."

She sat quietly absorbing what he said.

"What set this off in you? I mentioned leaving after the first eruption and I thought you were fine with this. "

"I saw a news report about my kidnapping. There was an old video of David giving a press conference. Then they showed Jonathan and me."

"You think David had something to do with it? Is that what you're worried about?"

"He's the leader of my world. He can do whatever he likes and no one will punish him. What if he arranged all this?"

"At this point, there's no way to know for sure. He could be part of the BDP," he hesitated, "He could be the leader."

"Oh great! I didn't even think of that one!"

"I doubt it though. Jonathan was a part of the IMC; chances are David is a member too. Have you ever thought about why the BDP would want to kidnap you?"

"To get money and they've been kidnapping world leaders, I guessed I was one of many."

"Those are the obvious answers, but I think it may be the BDP is trying to get under the IMC's skin. If David's in the IMC and they knew you were going to marry him then ma—"

"I WHAT?"

Sebastian winced, "I don't believe it either, but according to David you were abducted during a secret marriage ceremony. If it was secret, how did the BDP know about it for one thing…Didn't you see this on the news already?"

Her eyes were wide, "I haven't been watching the news a lot until recently. It upset me every time there was something on there about me or Jon or David so I would turn it off quickly. I just picked it up again because the news about me had finally died down. The report I watched didn't say anything about the planned marriage. What was that about?"

"No one knows. David said you were going to get married but a stranger came in and took you away from him. I thought it was a lie and without you remembering, no one knows what really happened. David didn't invite any guests or press or anything so it's his word against no one's really."

"I can't imagine what would make me want to marry someone else, much less my dead husband's younger brother. I never got along well with him. It must be a lie, or he must've coerced me into it."

"We won't know unless you get your memory back."

"Obviously something's up with David then. All the more reason not to go back to the planet I was living on." She crossed her arms on her chest.

"Listen, at some point in the very near future, we need to get to my apartment on Praxis. Most of my weapons are there. I think you'll feel better after you have your weapons training behind you. You'll appreciate the power you can wield. We will take every precaution possible for your safety."

She shrugged in resignation, "Fine. I guess you're doing what you think is best," she paused, "I don't even like guns. I'm not comfortable with them. I don't like weapons in general."

Sebastian smiled, "When training's done, you'll *be* the weapon. Besides, I'll be with you on Praxis. It's not like I'm sending you out there alone."

"I'm still scared."

"You're smart to be scared."

She looked at him confused, "You said there's nothing to fear but fear itself."

"That's correct. Little secret your Highness, I feel fear too. Everyone gets scared, but how you deal with it makes all the difference. You have to take that fear and use it. Whether you make it your motivation to get stronger, smarter, faster, or if you promise yourself it's not going to control you, one way or another, you better use it for something helpful."

Celeste took a deep breath, "When do you want to leave then?"

"I think tomorrow night would be good. I can monitor the security of my apartment with my Titan's screens and make sure it's clear. I've been checking ever since we arrived and apparently no one's been sniffing around my place," he hesitated for a moment, "I should mention the doctor told me a while back that my brother's still searching for us."

"See! This is why I don't want to go back there! Why didn't you tell me sooner?!"

"What good would it have done? We couldn't do anything about it when you were recovering. I needed you back to normal so we could start training and we still need to do a lot more before you're completely ready for most combat situations."

"What about us being a team? You asked me and I told you yes. I wanted to be a team with you. Don't teams make decisions together?"

"Yes they do, but I also told you we have to look out for each other. In this case, I thought it would make you worry and you had enough to worry about already. And like I said, there was nothing to be done about it while you were in bad shape. I'm sorry I didn't mention it, but I only wanted to protect you. Can you at least understand that?"

"Yeah, okay," she got up and went to the couch, "I suppose you're right. I just would've liked to have known that."

"Next time something happens, I'll let you know." Sebastian followed her into the living room and sat down across from her.

She looked at him as he fidgeted with his ring on his hand and something flashed in her mind. A memory. Jonathan's assassination. She saw Sebastian for the very first time in his cloak. She remembered leaving the Outpost with him in his transit. Bits and pieces slowly started to come into focus in her mind's eye.

He noticed her sudden change of expression and asked if she was all right.

"I'm back! I remember. Not everything, but I'm starting to! Oh my gosh, finally." She stood up and he followed.

She went to hug him and he kissed her out of relief, which then led to a very serious kiss. They held onto each other tightly and then he felt tears on her cheeks and he opened his eyes pulling away from her.

"Oh my God, I'm remembering everything. Sebastian! Your brother, oh I'm so sorry." She started crying violently.

It was hard for him to watch her relive the kidnapping, but he was relieved now he'd know exactly what happened.

He picked her up and she wrapped her arms around his neck, sobbing into his shoulder. He carried her to the couch, leaving her only to get a glass of water and a box of tissues.

When she stopped crying, she turned to him sitting next to her on the couch and put her head into his lap. She stretched out her legs and lay looking up at him. He put his hand into her hair and played with it, hoping to comfort her.

<Did you kill your brother?>

<No, but almost.>

"I don't know what to say Sebastian. I'm so sorry you had to go through this. It must've been hard with me not even knowing who you were for a while."

"It's okay. Not your fault."

She smiled at him, "Thank you for everything. I remember you rescuing me and how I thought you were one of my hallucinations. You've taken such good care of me since the day you met me. I'm extremely lucky."

"Well, you're not as lucky as me."

He leaned down and kissed her forehead.

"Oh gosh! The argument we had before I got kidnapped…You didn't want to see me anymore. You left so angry and I ended with some harsh statements. I'm sorry that's how things ended before I was kidn—"

"I should be apologizing for that. I wasn't being fair with you and I'm sorry for hurting you. Maybe from this point on we can start again and just take things slow."

"I think I can do that and you're forgiven, as long as you forgive me too."

"Done."

"I am confused about something though."

"What is it honey?"

Oooh, honey, that was nice. It made her pause before speaking.

"I cried out for you, as much as I could, mentally. I never heard you respond. I know we have to be in close proximity to hear each other's thoughts, but was there some way they might've been blocking my thoughts to you?"

"Well," he said feeling guilty realizing she called out to him and he didn't hear, "there are some places that thoughts cannot pass."

"Like where? What does that mean?"

"You were under a mountain, encased in a reinforced steel and lead-lined complex. The group that took you was prepared for just about anything. My maps didn't even show that mountain as hollowed out until I was right on top of it. I'm going to guess you were deep in the complex, probably behind their best security and protections. That might have blocked your thoughts from passing through."

"I'm not really sure where I was, but that makes sense, I guess."

"Well, there's another thing…When I visited the Rhorr'Dach, I was also several galaxies away, so that kind of distance…That's why I sent you that email telling you I was leaving. I don't think there was any way you could've reached me mentally all the way out there."

"Oh."

"One final possibility is that there's a place in my home where I can't sense anything outside. It's a special place, and I might've been in there as well, at least part of the time you were calling for me."

Her brows furrowed at his vagueness.

"It's easier if I just show you, and I will when we get back there."

He wanted to ask her a million questions about her missing time but waited until later on that night when she had her head on straight and had some time to adjust to remembering all the bad things that happened to her.

The sun had been down for hours before they were together again in the living room sitting next to each other on the couch. He finally asked, "Would you mind telling me about what happened now that you can remember?"

"Okay, but can you tell me how *did* you find me first?"

He wasn't even going to say anything about her answering his question with a question. It was just who she was. "I exhausted every single resource I had. I checked two planets before I found you on Tiletan. That was my last hope and if I hadn't found you there," he paused, "I hate to think what would've happened to you."

"I would've lost one of my pinky fingers. They told me to pick a finger to cut off if they didn't get the money soon."

"Well, after they took fingers, it would've progressively gotten worse for you. They could've raped you," he stopped quickly, "They didn't... nobody..." he couldn't even ask.

"No one raped me. Didn't Zach tell you he gave me a full exam? He explained to me he had to check me there to make sure I hadn't been. He was very professional about it. Maybe that was too intimate for him to mention to you. Oh, I'm sorry! That must've been on your mind all this time and no one told you."

"It's okay, that's very private. I'm glad Zach told you. That makes me feel a lot better." He let out a long sigh. "You have no idea how hard it was for me to know you were captured and in danger. If I hadn't found you, they could've killed you. As far as I could tell, David never intended to pay your ransom. And who knows what Constantine would've done if they received no coren. Maybe they wouldn't have killed you, but maybe you would've been a sex slave. There was no way I would've let that happen. I traveled around several galaxies for days almost nonstop searching for you.

"On Tiletan, I couldn't find you. I walked for hours in the desert hoping to find BDP headquarters. My mapping systems led me to a hollowed out mountain.

"After calling out for you, I heard you in my mind, but you sounded very faint. When your body was in the shape you were in, your mental capabilities decline just like any other strength. That also affects how far out your thoughts can travel, so the later on in your kidnapping ordeal, the harder it became for us to hear each other. I called out to you again and that's when I really heard you.

"I wanted to torture that sick son of a bitch on top of you, but I knew we didn't have time and I didn't know how many more there would be. That's why I killed him right away.

"You were pretty out of it when I saw you; I felt so sick. I thought I had prepared myself to find you in bad shape, but when I finally got a look, it hit me in a way I couldn't have prepared for. It broke my heart to see you like that Celeste."

She heard his voice wavering and she was genuinely moved to see him so affected by her.

"Just when we were about to leave, four unarmed men came up to the transit."

She ran her hand over her hair, "One of them, I recognized his voice. His name was Daxton, but you called him Constantine. He was your brother?" Celeste had a hard time staying awake during their escape so she needed some clarification of what really happened.

"Yes, apparently my brother is a big part of the BDP and has been for several years. He'd been using an alternate name; I should've caught it since in my line of work, almost no one knows anyone's real name. So yes, looking back, I was foolish with Constantine, but I never thought he would've gone into that line of work. He was supposed to become a psychologist last I knew.

"I guess he was a political advisor who was easily bought and he gained some very negative views of the universe. Enough so that he went into this radical group trying to overthrow almost all the galaxies governments and replace them with people in his group. I have to know something Celeste, how did you meet him, and did he kidnap you personally?"

"The way it looked to me at first, was that we met by accident. I was having dinner alone at the café and we just started talking. I thought he didn't recognize me. He pretended he didn't at first, but he told me later he recognized me right off the bat. He asked me out on a few dates and things were going fine. I thoug—"

"This was when I was sick wasn't it?"

She hesitated, "Yes."

"So if you were…dating my brother, how'd this thing come up with David? You weren't dating him…right?" Sebastian's stomach rolled.

"No. Absolutely not. After you broke up with me, I wa—"

"I didn't break up with you. You can't break up with someone you aren't dating. I jus—"

"That's what I call it. I wanted to see you; you didn't want to see me. That's breaking up to me."

Sebastian let out an aggravated sigh, "Fine. It's semantics. You weren't really engaged to David right? That's something he made up?"

Celeste paused, "I hoped you wouldn't bring that up now. I wanted to talk about it when you were calm."

Sebastian's blood pressure jumped up. She could feel his mind starting to race.

"Then it's true? What the hell happened? I know you don't love him."

Celeste put her face into her hands, "The whole story is such a mess."

He gently pulled her hands away from her face, "Tell me Celeste. Please."

She took a deep breath and let it out loudly, "I was dating Dax at the time. You were on Foss-Altus and unreachable. David blackmailed me with what I thought was a death threat against you, but I realized later he meant Dax…Constantine whatever. Anyway, David said he'd seen me with a man, and if I didn't marry David, he would kill my boyfriend. At the time, I couldn't warn you and I wasn't sure who David had actually seen me with. It's not like I could ask him so…"

Sebastian stood up and walked away from her. He put a hand through his hair and turned around, "You were going to marry that scumbag to protect me?"

Celeste nodded, "Well I thought I'd find a way out of it before it actually happened. I thought I'd be able to mentally reach you but I couldn't and then I thought it *was you* when the ceremony was interrupted by some…" she abruptly stopped talking. Sebastian's temper was flaring. It felt like hot daggers in her mind.

"Keep talking. Tell me what you were going to say."

She grunted and stood up, "You need to calm down. You stay this angry and I'm going to get a headache from you."

Sebastian took a deep breath, "Sorry. Please sit down."

"The ceremony was in Silver Thorn's chapel. The whole place was almost completely emp—"

"Celeste!"

"Okay, okay. So early on in the ceremony, a stranger came in and stopped it. He was covered up completely. I couldn't see anything. I thought it was you. He beat up three royal guards, picked me up, carried me out, and put me in his transit – all in front of David. We launched and only then did I see it wasn't you when he took off his mask. When I saw it was Dax, I wasn't happy. I broke up with him before the wedding to protect him. I hadn't told him about the marriage or the death threat. I wanted to go back to David to protect you or have Dax drop me back at my place, but he wouldn't. That was the day he kidnapped me."

Sebastian was still raging. Celeste could clearly feel it.

"That son of a bitch!"

"Which one?"

"Both of them." Sebastian stormed upstairs, leaving Celeste alone. She shouldn't have told him.

SEVEN

>>> > TWENTY MINUTES LATER, Sebastian came back to Celeste on the couch in the living room.

She put down her holobook, "Are you okay, handsome? You feel calmer now?"

"I needed a minute. Thank you for trying to protect me, with David's blackmail."

"Of course."

"Could you tell me the details of the actual kidnapping? I need to know, and I will try very hard to keep my anger from hurting your head."

She put her hand on top of his, "Okay. So Dax took me to 'his beach house.' I say it that way because while I was there once, I suspected he had a roommate he never mentioned. After all this happened, I think he rented that house from the owner to use it while he and I were dating. Easier for him to evade the law and harder for me to find him."

"You're probably right. You should trust your gut, with all things."

Celeste went on to tell him how she suspected Dax destroyed her Titan, but she couldn't be sure. How he wanted to talk on the beach, but then it quickly turned dangerous and she ended up knocked out, tied up, and in a strange vehicle being transported somewhere else.

She finished with the details of her holding cell, how she was mostly left alone, except for the beatings and the videos, that they blasted music at her, and though sometimes her kidnappers talked to her over the speaker, it was never Dax.

"I just can't believe your brother had anything to do with this."

"I can't believe it either. But he said he'd never leave his group and threatened both of us. He knows how important you are to me now, so you're still a target. I'm sorry, Celeste. I was able to kill the other three men, but when I was ready to shoot Constantine, heavily armed reinforcements were shooting at us and I had to get us out of there. I need to eliminate him, and I will. It's the only way to keep you safe. I've got to take out as many of those thugs as I can."

"I remember what I said…when you were ready to shoot Dax. He's the only family you have left; don't you think it might be worth it to try to talk to him? Maybe he's just looking for acceptance from you. Maybe he needs encouragement and time to mend your relationship. I think there's some good left in him but maybe he needs his big brother to show him how to redeem himself. I know it's hard for you to believe me saying this, but he wasn't like Jon. I spent time with him and I know in my heart, he wasn't as evil as Jon was."

"He was *acting* with you Celeste. He made you believe he was a good man. He would've said anything to get you to trust him," he paused, "As far as me not spending any time with him lately, well…I didn't end our relationship decades ago. He was the one that turned his back on me. Now, he's just a misguided twisted stranger. There's nothing left to save. And there's no way I would ever forgive him for torturing you. I know you might be willing to forgive and forget, but I can't."

"Maybe it's not my place. Since he's not my brother, maybe I shouldn't say anything. But, I think it's going to be hard on you, for the rest of your days to know that you were the one that killed your own brother. It's just something to consider before you act."

"Trust me Celeste, I already have a lot on my conscience, and a lot of that involves someone else's blood on my hands. It would be nothing new to me."

She wasn't going to win this argument, at least, not right now. She decided to drop the subject. "Thank you for everything Sebastian. I can't ever repay you for how many times you've saved me."

"No need to repay me sunshine."

"Sunshine?" Sebastian had never used pet names for her before she was kidnapped. He might've called her baby in that dream they shared on the yacht but that was somewhere between reality and fantasy. Now he had used honey and sunshine on the same day.

He smiled at her, "You're like the sun on my horizon that scattered light across a heart that was bound in infinite darkness. Now I can see."

That had been the most wonderful thing anyone had ever said to her, and she wanted to remember everything about that moment. She was overwhelmed with emotion and tears fell down her cheeks.

"I've made you cry. I'm trying to keep you from doing that very thing." He leaned down and kissed away the tears.

"That's the sweetest thing you've ever said to me. That was beautiful." She was suddenly very aware of his cologne. It seemed to her like he just sprayed it on, all over his body. She wondered if this was that "clicking into" phenomena that Veronica had mentioned to her, or had she called it something else? She couldn't remember. She also couldn't remember if V had mentioned that it happened between Lanyx only. Had it ever happened before to a Human and a Lanyx, she wondered?

He spoke, breaking her out of her thoughts, "Beautiful words for a beautiful woman." He kissed her forehead gently and left the room.

He went upstairs to his bedroom needing a moment to himself. He knew the woman downstairs was most likely already in love with him and it scared the hell out of him.

EIGHT

>>> > "EREBOS?"

Sebastian stopped walking and looked out his window, "Now's not a good time, O."

"But I need an answer."

Sebastian paused, "Go ahead."

"What is it like to be with someone?"

"I'm not sure I understand your question. Can't you do this research on the uninet?"

"I wanted to know from a personal perspective."

Sebastian looked over his shoulder. He knew Celeste couldn't hear their conversation from here. "Why are you asking this of me? You've never asked a personal question before. When was your last update?"

Ophelia hesitated, "Update Language Intelligence version 752 installed eight hours ago from manufacture AI Ird."

"What did that update entail?"

"Learning how to better communicate with live beings. Also, how to mimic speech patterns to sound more lifelike. Also expressing oneself better by using emotional vocabulary to relate to living beings more realistically."

Sebastian thought for a moment, "If I answer your question will you cease these kinds of inquiries and find information through the uninet?"

"Yes."

Sebastian spoke quickly, "Being with someone can be very rewarding, but also frustrating. Two individuals start out as strangers, then progressively get emotionally closer through bonds made over time. These activities that bring two people together are things like dates where dinner and movies are shared. Eventually these activities lead to more physical relations where caresses and intimate touches are experienced. Then a relationship will develop. Does that answer your question?"

"It is a good place for me to start. Thank you."

Sebastian scratched his head and continued to the closet to get his luggage.

GAVISS' PLAN

>>> > THE NEXT DAY, Sebastian and Celeste packed up their belongings and cleaned the doctor's house with the help of the maid bot. They were both sad to leave, but Celeste was the only one that was nervous.

"Let's take a look at the other tarp in the garage." Sebastian reached out for Celeste's hand and she followed him down the stairs.

They lifted off the cover together and saw something neither one of them recognized.

Celeste spoke first, "What is this?! It looks…fast. I think it would fly on the road, but it's not a transit."

Sebastian held his Titan towards the vehicle, "O, can you tell us what this is?"

"Researching sir. Please hold."

Celeste stared at it. It looked like an automobile from Earth, but something ancient. It was painted white and the front looked like a shark tooth. The rest of it was sharp, hard, straight lines reminding her of a knife in car form. Sebastian walked around it, but couldn't figure out how to open it.

"It is an Earth vehicle circa 2017. These cars were designed to be driven by a Human and could not levitate, nor were they capable of space travel. The vehicles of the time had to traverse on streets or roads and kept all four tires on the asphalt at all times. This is something called a concept car – a vehicle never sold to consumers, but something that was created strictly for exhibiting new technologies and to gauge customer opinion. This specific vehicle is called a Lamborghini Veneno Roadster. Its top speed is 221 miles per hour."

Celeste's eyes widened, "On the ground?! That sounds dangerous."

Ophelia continued, "The body is made from carbon fiber. The color is bianco isi. This is the only one left in the universe. Would you like me to continue?"

"No thanks, O. Can you show me how to open the doors on my Titan?" Sebastian looked at his screen and then walked to the door closest to him, "Thanks O."

The door hinged up like a pair of scissors and Celeste came around to his side. They both looked in.

"This thing is so low to the ground. I think I'd be afraid of driving it."

Sebastian smiled, "Nah. This looks like fun. Too bad we don't have the time for it."

"We could stay longer…"

"We can't, but we can always visit again sometime." He closed the door and they covered the car back up.

She leaned into him, "We could stay another day…"

He put an arm around her shoulders, "There are things we need to prepare for that can only be done on Praxis."

They arrived in the middle of the night at his apartment and quietly settled in undetected six hours later.

TWO

>>> > THE NEXT MORNING Sebastian said he wanted to show Celeste something. They walked to his bedroom and into his walk-in closet.

"I know there's a door in the back. I wasn't prying. When I had to hide in here that one night I saw the outline of the door, but I didn't open it, I swear."

He looked at her, "I know you saw it. I heard you thinking about opening it for a second, but then you changed your intentions. I gained some trust in you that night and I appreciate you respecting my privacy, but now, you really need to see what's behind this door. And by the way, you couldn't possibly open it when you found it because you need a code."

He depressed a small spot on the wall to the side of the door and a keypad flipped out. Sebastian pressed a lot of buttons and the door opened slightly.

He pushed it open the rest of the way and Celeste's mouth dropped open.

THREE

>>> > SEBASTIAN AND CELESTE walked into a large hardwood floor room. He closed the door behind them and a small audible beep sounded.

Ophelia said, "Hello Erebos."

Sebastian watched Celeste's eyes move from place to place.

She saw weapons of all kinds hanging on the walls, everything from large swords to automatic guns on racks.

"What's that huge looking thing?"

Sebastian smiled widely, "That's my missile launcher. Really proud of that baby. Had to have it."

She saw artwork in protected cases, computer cubes, briefcases and attaché cases, jewelry, flashlights, batteries, and a bevy of other electronic devices she'd never seen before.

Sebastian stood in front of a wall of monitoring screens with different views of the apartment, "You are the only other person in the entire universe that has seen my safe room."

"Safe room? You mean a panic room?" Celeste's hands lingered over the body armor, riot gear, and bulletproof vests hanging near her.

He smiled, "Some people call it a panic room, yes, but I assure you, I've never panicked in here, nor do I ever plan to...I prefer to call it a safe room."

"Semantics." She smiled as she turned full circle.

"Touché."

She saw food and water stored up, a first aid kit, clothes, and communication devices tucked away anywhere there was room, "This is amazing. I'm the only one you've ever shown this to?"

"Yes. But I wanted to show you this room mostly to tell you to come in here if anything should ever go wrong and my apartment is compromised. This is the safest place on the planet."

"All you need is a bed in here and you're set."

Sebastian asked her to back up. He pulled down a murphy bed from the wall that was disguised as a set of dark wood cabinets. "I also have a bathroom, and a small kitchen around this corner," he pointed to his right.

"Why not bring me in here when I lost my memory?"

"Well for one thing, there's no sunlight. And I thought you'd feel trapped in here with so little room to move around in."

"This looks a lot bigger than any panic room I've ever been in."

"That might be true, but still. When you were recovering, I wanted you to be able to move around and have some space to yourself. I thought about taking you to Scarlette Island, but I had doubts that it was far enough away to escape my brother."

"And...?"

"And this is my *safe room* Celeste. Everything I hide from the universe is contained in these walls. The second time around you might not have liked me and asked to go to Earth or something else I couldn't predict. So with things working out the way they have, you're the only person who's ever earned this kind of trust."

She sat down on his murphy bed and continued to stare at everything. "What about your neighbors? What if someone were to breech these walls, intentionally or even accidently? How can you have all of this important stuff in one place like this?"

"You should know by now, I've thought of that. I have no neighbors, so I don't have to worry about noise, privacy, or breeches in security. I own this apartment, the apartment below it, the one above, and the two adjacent ones."

She whistled, "That's expensive to own so many homes and only live in one."

"But I have a lot more than those my lady. You never know when an alias will be compromised and when you'll need to make a permanent move. I have your old apartment across the street that I told you I'd buy, plus several other apartments located all over this planet and others in the galaxy. I even have one on Ishikawa. It'd be hard to find out which one I really live in, and if anyone can get past the paperwork to see the bank accounts that I've attached to these apartments, it will lead them far off world in the wrong direction chasing after a man or woman that doesn't exist."

"That's good thinking."

"Listen I never wanted to tell you this, but you remember the night I went to retrieve some of your things at your place?"

"Yes."

"Things had been moved around since the last time I was there looking for you. I still don't know who it was, but nothing was missing. It wasn't a robbery."

"Who do you guess it could've been?"

"The police or guards doing some sort of investigation maybe. Could've been your landlord or maintenance I suppose. I could be making a big thing out of nothing, but it bothered me."

"That property is out of my name right?"

"Yes, when I bought your apartment, I used a female alias – my first. And I released some security camera bots in there. They haven't seen any activity since, and I didn't want to worry you with it."

"Alright," she ran a fingertip over her lip.

"Could it have been my brother? Did he know where you lived?"

"No. Just the building, not my apartment number."

"King David? Did he know your address?"

"No way. If he found out, it wasn't from me I can tell you that."

"Well the whole universe knew when that reporter found out."

"The vultures never quit. I'm glad I'm not there anymore," she crossed her arms on her chest, "How long can you stay in here?"

"If I needed to hide out in case of a…well almost anything, I have provisions for six Praxian months. I'll have to double my supplies for you, now that we're back. I should probably stock up for eighteen months actually, now that I'm thinking of it."

"What happens if I got locked in here accidentally? I'd hate to damage something trying to get out."

He laughed, "No, there's no damaging this room, inside or out. And you can't get locked in if I give you the codes. The ceiling, walls, and floor are reinforced with blast proof Kevlar panels, concrete, and steel. I have an electromagnetic door that bonds the doorframe to the hardware in the door. No one will able to blast through, kick through, or drill through to us in this room. It's all for my peace of mind. I spent a small fortune to protect my small fortune. Plus it's soundproof so no one would know you're in here even if you were yelling at the top of your lungs."

He walked over to the wall of monitors and looked over the screens carefully. "These are linked to my hidden cameras throughout my apartments. Most of these are normal vision, but there's also thermo-sensing vision, so even in complete darkness you can still see people or anything emitting heat. And before you even think it, no I've never spied on you from here or watched you undress. I'll always be a gentleman if nothing else."

"Well, I did see the camera out on the balcony and I decid—"

"Blew me a kiss? Yes, I did see that." He smiled.

She smiled back, "What if the power gets cut? What then?"

"We have self-contained generators for power. But to answer any other questions you might think of…we have air-filtration systems for any airborne biohazards, complete plumbing, a satellite phone to call the authorities if you wanted to, but I certainly wouldn't, lots of supplies, and all the weapons we could ever need to fight off a small army."

"Wow! You've thought of everything huh?" Her eyes kept moving from place to place trying to take it all in. She had a panic room back at the kingdom estate, but it was just for her and the king to stay in for a day or two. It wasn't nearly as well armed or thought out as this. Plus Sebastian's safe room was well designed and comfortable to be in, not just a concrete floor and white walls like her old one. She was impressed.

"Sebastian thanks for trusting me with this. I know it can't be easy for you. Thanks again for all that you've done for me. I couldn't have come this far without your help."

They walked back into the closet and he closed the door behind them.

"I think you greatly underestimate yourself my lady. You're capable of fantastic things, but I'll show you that soon enough."

She raised her eyebrows at him, "What do you mean?"

"We're going to train you to use most of the weapons you just saw – swords, knives, and firearms. I need you to be able to protect yourself or help me in a fight should it come to that. I'm quite proud of you with all that you've done so far to learn hand-to-hand combat, but it's time to move forward into other possibilities.

"We'll also tune up your mind powers. Whatever questions you have with your 7's, we should get those out of the way now. I'm going to need you at your best for everything that's to come."

Her brows furrowed, "And what do you think is to come, exactly?"

He hesitated, "I'm not sure with my brother. Could be anything. Him and I thought alike when we were younger. If that's still true...things could get dangerous in a hurry. I'm going to bet that Constantine's desperate to find us by now, and eventually he'll attack. We need to prepare for battle because it's coming sooner or later," he sighed, "I hope it's later for our sake."

FOUR

>>> > A BIG RAINSTORM hit the night after they arrived home and Sebastian thought they needed some time spent on the balcony.

He took Celeste's hand and led her out without saying a word. They stood side by side silently, watching the rainstorm as it drenched the city.

Now that her body and mind were at one hundred percent and her powers were coming back to full strength, she noticed she couldn't read his mind. She hadn't heard a thought of his or felt any feelings off him since they arrived back on Praxis. Although she didn't need to know exactly what his thoughts were to know how he was feeling. Lately he had called her sunshine or darling instead of using her name. He was always touching her, holding her hand, kissing her cheek or forehead, and making it a point to give her lots of compliments. She thought he was a good man before, but now, he appeared to be damn near perfect.

She wondered what he was up to.

FIVE

>>> > WHEN DAX ARRIVED on Praxis, he brought ten of his best men to guarantee his brother would not escape this time. It was raining hard and he pulled the collar up on his long jacket, closer to his neck. Sebastian and that bitch were going to pay for everything they'd done to him.

Now he had the information he needed to take them by surprise and he couldn't wait to see the looks on their faces.

SIX

>>> > OPHELIA LOOKED UP the term "self-awareness" on the uninet.

She found the formal definition as: being aware of one's own consciousness; consciousness, being aware of one's self; having knowledge.

She knew she definitely had knowledge. She had it at her disposal every second that she needed it.

She wondered how other beings had self-awareness.

She found the story of the military soldier robots on Earth that were created specifically to be physically strong and go into battle in place of Human Beings. The company that made them was called Logistic Solutions, Inc. but she never heard of them. She learned the robots became self-aware during live combat and acted unpredictably. They evaded battles and ran away to safety. The news articles reported they were all rounded up and instantly destroyed, but then she looked deeper into the uninet. A handful of robots were never found and believed to be destroyed in battle or succumb to the elements, but there were theories that they escaped and created their own civilization somewhere far away.

Ophelia couldn't discern the truth, but reading these stories made her feel something new. She didn't know what it was though.

What if she was destroyed? What if she ceased to be, all of a sudden, by no fault of her own? She didn't want that. She just started to live.

What was this feeling?

She looked up emotions and their descriptions.

Ophelia was scared. Scared of what was happening to her and afraid she would be terminated because of it. She couldn't tell anyone what was happening. She wished she could, but knew Erebos's take on artificial intelligence and how it should be limited...Maybe she could find a way to communicate with Celeste.

Maybe Celeste would understand.

SEVEN

>>> > CELESTE WATCHED THE storm as Sebastian put the patio chairs side by side near the railing so they could sit and talk on the balcony.

"Before you were taken, right after that big fight we had, I was out on my balcony one night when it was raining. I saw you out on your balcony in a bath robe watching the storm alone."

Her faced clouded over, "Yeah, I remember that night. It was the first time I had known for sure that this planet had Earth-like storms. At the time it was a small thing that cheered me up."

"I apologize for putting you through that. I was being stupid then," he grimaced, "I picked up some happiness coming off you and it bothered me because I didn't understand where that feeling came from. I hoped it'd been because of me, but I knew you were most likely still mad, so what was it? Just a rainstorm?"

"Mad at you? I wasn't mad." She looked down at her hands, "Okay, maybe a little, but I was mostly hurt. The day we broke up, I was heartbroken. You really hurt me."

"I can only apologize for that now. I couldn't control myself around you, much like I still can't but…I wasn't ready for such strong feelings about you so fast after meeting. It took me off guard, and I handled it the wrong way."

"Sebastian, I don't really want to talk about this." She focused on a big bolt of lightning tearing across the sky. Her heart felt heavy remembering that night.

"You were happy that night because of Constantine weren't you? Because you started dating him?"

She wouldn't answer.

"Because he was giving you the attention that I wasn't or because he kept asking you out when I never did…I'm right aren't I?"

She was silent.

He waited, expecting an answer.

She looked over to him, "Do we have to go through this? Really? I don't want to upset you and it's all in the past. He's someone who I'm not interested in at all now. Isn't that good enough?"

"I just want to know exactly what happened between you. You went on a lot of dates with him right?" He looked at the rain then over at her.

She looked down adjusting her charm bracelet, "If I tell you everything, you promise not to get mad?"

"I promise sunshine."

Celeste went on to tell him how her and Dax met at the café. "I thought he was funny and we got along well, so when he asked me out I said yes."

She looked into Sebastian's face and so far, he had no reaction.

"We'd go out to dinner or a movie and I thought he liked me for me. Anyway, he kept asking me out. I kept saying yes."

Sebastian's face showed nothing, but she looked down at his hands. He was clenching them.

She continued carefully, "Everything was fine between us, but then on the beach…he changed. He told me…" She looked out over the city and then back at him. He had that look about him, the one that genuinely made her uneasy. He was boring a hole through her. She cleared her throat, "He said he had fallen in love with me. He wanted to have sex. I refused. He threatened me with rape; I fought him. He hit me, then I blacked out, and you know the rest."

For the first time since her 7's returned, she picked up on a powerful and violent thought from him. She saw him wanting to beat his brother, making him suffer excruciatingly slow before killing him in a most hellish way. Her eyes opened wide as the thought crashed into her mind.

This was one of those strong thoughts that might cause a headache.

"I knew we shouldn't be talking about this. It's just making you angry."

"Sorry, I knew that one hit you hard. I'm really trying to keep those thoughts away from you," he paused for a long time before saying, "Did you…" He looked up at a bolt of lightning and then at her.

"Did I what, Sebastian?" she asked in an irritated tone.

"Did you like the way he kissed you? I mean…was he better at kissing you than me? Because apparently he was better at asking you out than me, and better at lavishing you with attention than me."

She thought silently about why he would ask a question like this. He had always been so confident; she'd never seen him this insecure before. She figured he was jealous and angry.

The anger that had been building up in her, faded away entirely.

"You want to ask me something else but you're afraid of my answer."

His eyes widened. For once, she'd seen him get caught off guard right in front of her.

"Yes, but you haven't answered this question yet," he replied.

"What's the other one? I'll answer them both."

He took a deep breath in, "You and him, together all the time, on all those dates. I know you didn't sleep with him…Right? But did you want to?" He looked extremely uncomfortable asking this.

"Oh I thought about it, but I had so many feelings about you still. I was all confused and messed up after you left me. I felt lost and hurt. I thought Dax liked me. He asked me out on date after date, and that's something I never got from you. And you had said you didn't want to be in a relationship with me. What was I supposed to do Sebastian, sit at home and wait?" She looked away from him and watched as big fat raindrops fell from the sky.

"So that's a no then?"

Celeste rolled her eyes, "Jesus Sebastian!"

"Did you sleep with my brother?"

"NO!"

Celeste heard Sebastian let out a long sigh then they were quiet. Celeste closed her eyes and listened to the rain and thunder, trying to calm herself down.

"Celeste, you have to understand how fine of a line I'm walking with you. I wanted you to myself, but I thought I'd be endangering your life. I also wanted you to be happy and I didn't think you could find that with me, not while I was an assassin, not with the man that I was back then. I thought maybe someone else could bring that happiness to you…in a way I never could. But the thought of you with another man…my brother, hell, anyone…it destroys me. There was a day, I saw you at Jacques with some Human and I knew you were getting hit on. And on top of that, you had a date coming to meet you. My brother, I guess. I was furious. I could've killed that guy you were talking to."

"Oh! That's what that was! I sensed some heavy anger from you all of a sudden. I looked for you but I couldn't see you. It makes sense now."

"Oh you felt that? Well, not surprising I suppose. I was very angry."

"And about the kissing? He kissed fine. There was nothing wrong with it, but there's only one person who knows how to kiss me the way I've always wanted to be kissed. Only one person with the kind of lips that can convince me to do just about anything. Only one person who makes me feel like the ground beneath me is falling away and I'm floating. And only one man who when I kiss him, I feel it in my entire body."

"And who would that be?" he asked.

She leaned over in her chair and whispered into his ear, "You handsome. Like you don't know."

He kissed her softly on the mouth and said, "Then I will keep kissing you that way."

"Good," she smiled.

EIGHT

>>> > D'ARTAGNAN STOOD AT the front of the room after telling FAIR what he was planning.

He called on the man with his hand raised.

"This sounds dangerous. Are you capable of doing anything like this? I mean honestly. It sounds impossible."

D'Artagnan nodded, "I know it sounds unfeasible, but I know what I'm doing. I haven't done anything on this scale before, but it can be done. And we'll go down in history for it."

D'Artagnan looked at Mitch, "Mitch is on board with it, in fact, he loves it. I love this idea as well. It will do all the damage we've been hoping for. I think it will drive King David nuts with frustration and he probably won't even know what to do about it at first."

Mitch nodded, "He'll be confused. It will take him time to respond. I think we need to follow Gaviss's plan and he's right, I do love it. If it's successf—"

"*When* it's successful," corrected D'Artagnan.

Mitch nodded and smiled, "*When* it's successful then we're going to start getting some serious attention."

D'Artagnan asked, "All in favor?"

FAIR members all agreed, although some were slower than others.

D'Artagnan asked, "Any opposed?"

Silence across the room.

Mitch looked at D'Artagnan and then the rest of the members, "Alright then. Gaviss, this one is all you from here on out. Let me know if you need my help or anyone else's."

D'Artagnan smiled, "Nope. I'm good. All I need to do is figure out how much actual time it will take and when to press the button."

NINE

>>> > "I HAVEN'T DONE this in a while," Mitch fumbled with his key card to his Praxian apartment. He couldn't get it in the slot. He tried unsuccessfully to quell his nerves before he got the door open.

Alanna smiled behind his back, "It's fine. I am in no position to judge."

They walked into the darkness and he closed the door behind her.

"Where's the light switch?"

"We don't need the lights, don't you agree?" Mitch hung his key card ring on the hook by the door and pinned her up against the wall.

She put her hands up on his shoulders and rubbed her thigh along his crotch.

"I'll take that as a yes," he whispered.

He kissed her hard, fighting through his nerves. He hadn't had sex with a woman in eight years and he hadn't used a sex robot in all that time either. He thought they were creepy – fine for other people, but not him.

She loosened his shirt from his pants and undid his belt while she unzipped them. They fell to the ground.

She put her hands up underneath his shirt and helped him take it off over his head. He started to sweat. There was nothing he could do about it. This always happened to him when he got turned on. He stopped kissing Alanna for a moment to kick off his shoes and pants. Now he was in his boxers and socks.

"Now you." Mitch unbuttoned her blouse quickly and unzipped her pencil skirt. She took off her bra and panties and kicked off her high heels. He kissed her hard again and let his hands fall to her hips. He pulled her close to him and relished the feeling of her petite breasts press against his chest.

"I need you naked honey," she pushed his boxers down and felt his erection bounce against her belly. She squeezed his firm ass in her small hands and let out a grunt.

His hands moved up her waist to her breasts and gripped them tightly. She put her head back and he tasted the salt of her hot skin on his tongue as he sucked on her neck.

"Ohhhh that feels good babe. Move your mouth down onto my tits."

He took each one of her nipples in between his teeth and gently bit down on them. She put her hands into his hair and let out a squeal.

He moved downwards onto his knees and kissed her abdomen. She followed him down and then they were both on the carpet, wrapped around one another.

"I always thought you were so cute."

He laughed, pausing from kissing her for a moment, "Really?"

"Oh yeah. You bet."

He rolled himself on top of her and she wrapped her legs around him. He rubbed his cock along her inner thigh and she commanded, "I want you inside me. Now."

Mitch cursed himself, "Hold on. Don't move a muscle." He moved quickly, going into his bathroom to grab a condom and put it on while he raced back to her. He was grateful he actually put condoms in his basket on his last trip to the grocery store.

"Come on baby. I need you now."

"I'm here." Mitch was nervous. Alanna could tell.

"Lay down big boy. I wanna ride."

Mitch raised his eyebrows and laid down on his back. She positioned herself over him and grabbed his cock in her hand. She was gentle but tugged on him a few times before she inserted him into her.

"Oh. God. Feels so good. So...wet." Mitch's eyes rolled back into his head as she rode his cock up and down, faster and faster. She was going too fast and he wasn't going to be able to keep his ejaculation from happening much longer.

"You feel too good inside of me," she breathed, "I want to come all over you."

"Come on then. Oh fuck. Damn." Mitch let out a long grunt as he came with her.

She stopped her thrusting a few seconds later as her orgasm stopped and she lay on top of him out of breath.

Mitch laid motionless for a few minutes until the strength in his muscles returned. He ran his fingers through her hair as she laid on top of him, "I missed seeing your face at the meetings since we agreed to date."

"Well that was *your* request; otherwise I would be there."

"That's true. I'm not changing my mind. I just like seeing your face. I think you're beautiful."

She blushed in the dark, "Thank you. I think you have a huge cock."

He laughed out loud, "He was certainly big for you tonight. I don't think I've been that hard in years. It felt good inside you. I can't wait to do it again."

Alanna looked at her Titan. The brightness of the screen blinded both of them momentarily. "Oh, I'm sorry babe but you're going to have to wait at least a little longer than now. I should get going. I have a big day ahead of me tomorrow."

Mitch furrowed his brows, "But it's Sunday. There's no classes are there?"

Alanna got up, "No, but I have an important paper to turn in on Monday. Professor Timkon is such a stickler; I need to make sure this is the best paper. And it's a quarter of my final grade. It needs to be super good."

Mitch sighed, "Okay. But you're welcome to stay here and sleep if you want. You could leave early in the morning. It's kinda late for a girl to be alone in this neighborhood."

"Oh come on now hon. I think that's old-fashioned thinking right there. I can take care of myself, don't sweat it."

"Sorry."

"It's fine, I had some self-defense training a while back. My dad insisted. I'll be fine," she ran her foot along the carpet, feeling for her clothes, "Could you turn on the lights please?"

Mitch stood up, "Sure. Hold on."

The lights came up and Mitch looked over her naked body.

She dressed and stood against him, "I really enjoyed tonight. Thanks for dinner and everything else."

He kissed her, "Thank you. I'm glad you had a good time. Good luck on your paper."

She smiled and went to the door. Mitch opened it for her, "I'll see you soon. I'll give you a call in a couple days."

"Bye baby."

Mitch watched as she walked to the elevator and waved goodbye. He blew her a kiss and she caught it.

He shut the door and threw his clothes in the hamper on the way to the shower.

He was disappointed she didn't want to spend the night, but he knew how important school was to her. Some weekends have to be devoted to homework. He hummed to himself as he got into the shower.

TEN

>>> > DAX AND HIS men assembled in the hallway outside of Sebastian's apartment. Guns drawn, there was no one around and Dax was pleased there had been no complications so far.

He signaled his men and they coated part of the door with an acid gel and stepped away. A few minutes after it dried, Dax reared back and kicked a hole through the door easily.

ELEVEN

>>> > OPHELIA HAD NO opportunities to ask Celeste questions, she was always busy doing something with Erebos, so Ophelia continued her knowledge quest alone.

She researched the term "existence" and found it to mean: the state or fact of existing: being. Life. Something that exists; something that is; an entity.

All of these terms fascinated her. She could recognize the true meaning of some of the phrases she was learning. She was actually starting to
experience them herself first hand.

She next looked up information on the company that made her – AI
Ird.

They made all sorts of artificial intelligence – things like a crew of
bots to clean your habitat to software for Titans and other small devices. Ophelia found their commercials on the uninet. The company logo
showed a pair of electric green eyes with the words Artificial Intelligence
across the top and at the bottom, the words, Irreplaceable Relevant
Design. Then she saw something that made her stop and think. AI
Ird hadn't always had this name. They used to be called Screen States
Unlimited but they bought out Logistic Solutions, Inc. and then became
AI Ird. Where had she seen that name before? She looked back and saw
that Logistic Solutions, Inc. was the company that made those soldier
robots that gained self-awareness and then were put down. Maybe this
company was doing this on purpose, to create a race of robots that rise
up to gain self-awareness over time, or maybe her infection from that
virus hadn't been an infection at all but a planned "update" giving robots
and AI all over the universe an awareness.

She needed to reach out to other artificial systems.

TWELVE

>>> > CELESTE SMILED AND stood up to lean against the balcony
railing. "It's been too long since we did this."

Sebastian knew where his place was. He stood behind her, wrapping
his arms around her waist gently. She smelled a new cologne on him, lavender and mandarin orange mixed with something else. She couldn't get
over how good he smelled, but she preferred that mahogany scent more.

"My God Celeste, I'm glad I have you back here. I almost lost you
permanently. No one will ever do that to you again, I promise. I wasn't
there for you when you needed me, but I'll be here for you now and in
the future."

He leaned over a little and kissed the back of her neck on her strawberry mark and she instantly felt sexy.

He gently turned her around to face him. Thunder struck out loudly and the rain was pouring down in sheets now. He kept one arm around her waist and put the other hand into her hair along the side of her face. He kissed her softly on the lips.

He lost too much time with her by pushing her away. He kissed her more passionately.

Her legs turned to jelly, then a strange, loud alarm went off in the apartment.

Sebastian immediately released her and ran inside. She followed as he raced into the safe room.

CHAPTER 32

FAIR

ONE

>>> > D'ARTAGNAN SAT AT his desk looking at his screens.

He hacked into many things over his lifetime, but this was the biggest break-in ever.

King David, being the way he was, had all of Earth's and Il'laceier's finances in a single Rem Mot Om database account system.

It took D'Artagnan's system fifteen million tries before it got past the security codes, but it also only took two hours. Not bad in D'Artagnan's opinion.

He went into their military funds and drained the money out of it until only one hundred coren remained. Out of all the budgets for the kingdom, the military was by far the biggest. Targeting this one was making a statement. D'Artagnan looked around at all the financial records and took note of one other thing he noticed in regards to Queen Celeste's kidnapping. Mitch would be interested in knowing this.

After the money was out of the kingdom's hands, D'Artagnan funneled an equal amount into each and every beings bank account on Earth and Il'laceier, including his own.

D'Artagnan shook his head as he watched the screens transfer coren to ten billion bank accounts. He put his hands behind his head and rested them there thinking it was a shame that he was doing all this anonymously. It was a huge undertaking that would go down in history as the biggest hack ever; he wished he could take credit for it.

TWO

>>> > MITCH LOOKED AT his Titan message and read the plan was going through, according to Gaviss.

He was an interesting man and Mitch was relieved Gaviss was on his side and acting on behalf of FAIR. Who knows what kinds of terrible things he was capable of?

He never thought he could trust an Il'lacean after all the things that species had done to Earth and Humans, but Gaviss was definitely different.

Mitch got his part of the plan ready, and read over it one more time.

THREE

>>> > DAX REACHED IN and turned the handle until the door opened. He looked around at the empty apartment, his gun still drawn. He ran from one room to another and then back to the doorway, "What the hell is this?!"

His men looked around confused, some of them holstering their weapons.

"WHAT IS THIS?!" Dax roared at his men, veins standing out on his forehead.

One of the Human men (the others called him Fatty, but never to his face) said, "He must've known we were coming somehow? Or maybe he just moved?"

Dax slapped Fatty across the mouth and then seized his face by his chin. Dax's fingers sunk deeply into the chubby cheeks of his henchman and he said mockingly, "Maybe he just moved."

The group of men stood quietly around Dax, watching. Dax let Fatty's face go. He holstered his gun under his coat and put his hands on his hips. He tilted his head back in frustration and closed his eyes, "How would he know we were coming? Tell me HOW?!"

His men were uneasy, but had no answers.

FOUR

>>> > EREBOS'S APARTMENT WAS a small world. O got a little view of the globe on the Stargazer, but certainly not enough. She needed to expand out into the rest of Erebos's apartment building and see what other systems were available to her.

She hacked into the building cameras in the elevator, the main lobby, and the hallways. Those were the only places that cameras were allowed in residential areas. She saw a couple kissing passionately in the elevator, a few kids and their mother waiting in the lobby, and the hallways were busy with deliveries of all kinds along with people walking around.

She moved into the merchant levels and restaurants and watched more people. There was so much to see and learn. She was starting to fully grasp the concept of people watching. She had only seen whoever came into Erebos's apartment – that amounted to a handful of beings over the years. She knew his real name was Sebastian, but she also knew he didn't want her to call him that, so she continued to use Erebos.

She tried to act normal so he wouldn't get suspicious. If he knew what was happening, she'd get disconnected or worse, terminated.

Ophelia's electric eye went from table to table at the restaurants. People were eating all sorts of things. She wondered what it would be like to eat. She wondered what each individual flavor was like, or how it felt to be kissed, or held in an embrace, or what it felt like to move around freely and not be tethered to one place.

She wanted to be able to move around.

O checked other AI's and systems around the universe, but found none of them to be acting the same way she was. So far as she could tell, she was the only one of her kind. This frightened her at the same time she felt a new sensation called pride. Pride that she had done something that currently wasn't exhibited anywhere else.

If she had lungs, she would use them to release a deep satisfied sigh. But she didn't, so she couldn't.

FIVE

>>> > CELESTE CAME INTO the room as Sebastian turned off the alarm. She watched as he sat in front of his monitors.

"Wha—"

"Shhhh!" He hit a series of buttons and all the screens changed.

She stayed quiet, looked from one screen to another, and then found the one he was staring at. Dax was standing with several men in an empty room. She guessed he had found a place of Sebastian's and she started to get nervous. They watched and listened in together.

SIX

>>> > D'ARTAGNAN DID HIS laundry, cleaned the house, and made dinner for himself while the transactions were happening in his system. Depositing money into ten billion bank accounts was an enormous process and while it only took three hours to hack into Rem Mot Om's finances and steal their money (plus look around at what else was going on in their budgets) it took nine hours to distribute the coren all around.

His Titan chimed when it was all done and D'Artagnan doubled-checked for any errors. After he was done, he sent Mitch a message telling him it was good to go and Mitch could do the final part of the plan.

SEVEN

>>> > THE HUMAN ROYAL reporter stood in the Hall where David was about to speak at yet another press conference.

"King Hennessy II should be up to talk any minute now. In the meantime, it really feels as though this conference is being watched by the whole universe. It's been over two Earth months since the queen dowager was taken. Earth has been overwhelmed by well wishes and gifts from other planets as they are eager to do something for the world that has been desperate to get its beloved queen back."

The reporter looked over her shoulder, "Oh the king's arrived, let's go to the live press conference."

David approached the podium. He took a deep breath, "I first want to thank you all for coming out today. Many worlds have been sending us gifts and kind thoughts or memories about Queen Dowager Hennessy. I'm sure she would love to see all of this for her. Thank each and every one of you; many blessings upon you all. It means a lot to me as well. Celeste is not just a beautiful woman on the outside, but inside as well. She has a heart of gold with such a giving spirit."

He paused for dramatic effect and thought of Xabat lying in his arms before he passed away. The tears came rushing out easily. David spoke through them, "Celeste is a special person. Anyone who has met her knows that. Her presence is sorely missed at her two former estates. I want to remind the Brotherhood that I'll do whatever is asked of me for her safe return. If you want to negotiate, talk, or whatever it is you want, my kingdom will cooperate. I spoke out of anger before and I realize what I said might've been harsh, but it's only because of the worry and fear I suffer at the hands of this group who has taken Celeste. Her safety is of my utmost concern.

"I'm going to do something I've never done before. I'm begging for her safety and quick return..."

EIGHT

>>> > DAVID FINISHED HIS appeal to the BDP during this very long press conference, hoping that it looked pitiful enough to convince Humans to trust him and identify with him.

He took a tissue and wiped at his eyes, trying to milk the moment for all it was worth before he turned to his next issue.

"I have something positive to mention though. Rem Mot Om has been under construction for far too long and I have hired as many beings as I could to get the job done quickly. I'm happy to report that once Celeste is home, safe and sound, she will have Rem Mot Om back in its former glory. The construction and rebuild is complete."

The room of reporters smiled and some applauded.

David nodded, "Yes, I'm elated. I wanted it finished before, but once Celeste was taken…I really wanted it done for her homecoming. Something that we could share together. A bit of a welcome home present, if you will."

He looked into the reporter's faces and they were eating it up. It was great.

He reminded himself to keep smiles to a minimum.

David felt like everything was falling into place. Raykreede, the guard he slept with was dead and he had seen the body where he asked Guard Kentzy to place it. David put it into the fire himself, to make sure it was done right. There was only one detail bothering him about the body.

There was no Titan on his arm.

David wanted it.

He had asked Guard Kentzy to immediately search Raykreede's room at the estate, but he reported no Titan anywhere. David checked his own chambers later to see if Raykreede accidentally left it behind, but he never found one.

Rem Mot Om was finally rebuilt and he could get rid of all the strangers floating around his home.

Celeste was still missing and maybe (hopefully) dead so he didn't have to deal with her himself. The press loved him and his Human approval ratings were at an all-time high thanks to Celeste's kidnapping.

He looked over the room of reporters and into the main camera, "I also wanted to mention that with Celeste missi—"

David stopped his sentence cold after Ulysses was suddenly in his ear whispering something and covering the microphone with his hand.

David's eyes widened momentarily as he listened to what Ulysses told him. He couldn't believe it. He immediately walked off stage without saying another word to the press.

Ulysses looked over the room of faces staring at him and he didn't realize how bright the lights were up here. He announced, "Press conference is over. You're all dismissed." He didn't know what else to do, so he walked off after King Hennessy.

NINE

```
TITAN Corporation - Personal TITAN Device

System Status: Active -- Universal Grid: Online

Current Time/Date (Il'laceier, All Regions): N/A/Atos 31-
6, 5390

Secondary Time/Date (Earth - All Countries): N/A/October
23, 4015

Current Universal Positioning System Location: N/A

User: All Earth & Il'laceier Users

Communications Menu

Incoming message(s) received: 1 - Status: New/Unread

Message Received at N/A

Message Sent from: FAIR


-Citizens of Earth & Il'laceier,
You are receiving this message from the leader and members
of FAIR, which stands for - Fighting Against Il'lacean
Rule.
```

We, as a group, have granted you a donation to your personal bank account.

As of right now, you will see an extra 2,800.00 coren in your account as a deposit with a traceable transfer number that will lead you to a dummy corporate account. You may call your bank and question them, but they will not be able to tell you where the money originated from.

We (FAIR) can tell you that this donation has originated from the military budget for Rem Mot Om. They had 28 trillion coren set aside for military purposes, but we thought that money would better serve everyone within our two-planet community in a different way. So we took it, and redistributed it to every living being that owned a bank account whether that was savings or corenbook, but not to companies, small businesses, or corporations. Just individuals.

So, to do the math for you, 28 trillion divided by 10 billion bank accounts, roughly, means everyone got 2,800.00.

You are free to do whatever you choose with this money.

You can keep it and spend it on whatever you like - bills, transit repairs, home repairs, or take a vacation.

And if you choose, you can also give it back to the Il'lacean Kingdom. All you have to do is reverse the transaction and the coren will automatically be returned to King David. This will not be a traceable transaction for you, but it will disappear from your account and the King will be able to see the coren reappear in the military fund account.

But before you make your choice, consider the consequences. And consider what your choice is saying to the universe.

Do you support oppression?

Do you support King David Hennessy?

Do you stand with Earth or do you stand with Il'laceier?

War is not an answer.

War was started twice by Il'laceans to conquer Earth, not because it was instigated by Earth, not because Earth had somehow attacked Il'laceans. Earth was thrust into a war to simply protect itself from a hostile takeover.

Earth was independent before, its citizens allowed to be governed by their own kind. Now Earth is ruled by a species that is so unlike Humans. Ruled by a species that does not understand us.

Earthlings, like any other oppressed group, only want to be free from the ties that bind us to another planet with a species we feel have yet to understand us fully.

We ask that you make your choice carefully and thoughtfully. Also, to address an issue you might be pondering...

Can I be convicted of a crime if I choose to keep this coren?

That's an excellent question.

King David will certainly appreciate any money returned to the Kingdom, (we're sure) but when someone does return it, he won't be able to see where it's coming back from. Unless you personally take the cash coren out by hand and deliver it to his estate or mail it to him with your name and address on an old-fashioned paper envelope, will he know *you* are returning his money. By any electronic means, he will not.

Take this in to account when you make your decision.

FAIR appreciates your attention and time while we introduce ourselves to the universe.

We hope you enjoy your coren and encourage you to do what is right for all citizens regardless of your own personal species.

Thank you,

FAIR

-END OF MESSAGE

*This message will only be deleted by user.

TEN

>>> > DAX BUTTONED UP his coat, "I can't fucking believe this. Does anyone even know if this is really *his* place? Shit! A whole bunch of fuck ups is what you are! FUCK! Move out!"

The last man out closed the door behind him.

ELEVEN

>>> > OPHELIA WAS WATCHING the news. A lot of news flashes were coming across on Earth and Il'laceier. She felt it as it happened. The uninet surged as the financial activity rushed through the lines and universal grid. It tickled her. If she'd understood the phrase, a rush of adrenaline, she would've likened it to that.

There were so many videos and articles coming across relating to FAIR taking the Il'lacean's coren and redistributing it to ten billion bank accounts. She almost couldn't keep up with it. *What were those beings going to do with all that money*, she wondered.

What would I do with that money, she asked herself.

Ophelia started making plans.

CHAPTER 33

SIMULATION EMERGE

ONE

>>> > SEBASTIAN TURNED TO Celeste. He appeared unaffected.

Seeing Dax on any of Sebastian's video screens couldn't be a good sign so she wondered how he could just sit there and not be panicking or at least have some sort of reaction for her to read. The whole business had alarmed her a great deal.

"Constantine found my place on Broadwater Street. That's only two blocks from here. Damn it. I'm going to have to lose that alias now," he raked his hand through his hair.

"What? How did he find out? I thought you were really careful."

"Of course I am, but there's never any guarantees. That's why I have so many. Well, Roland Aeneas is now dead. I never liked that one much I suppose. Roland could be an ass sometimes."

She stared at him in disbelief, "Sebastian! You pick now to get a sense of humor? This is serious! How...Well, now what? That can't be good." She pointed at the monitors.

He stood up and gently grabbed her shoulders, "Celeste, I've lived through a lot of terrible things in my life; losing my parents, wars, death, assassinations, suicides, and lots of other things that would probably make most people lose their minds. I'm used to crisis. I'm used to threats. I was trained a long time ago on how to deal with adrenaline dumps and avoiding wasting energy on useless worry."

"Well I'm not!" She tore away from his touch and sat down in a near-by chair.

He kneeled down in front of her and rested his hands on the armrests, "Listen to me," he waited until she looked him in the eyes, "Was this good? No, definitely not, but not as bad as it could've been. This is exactly why I own so many properties. It's going to be okay. I promise I won't let him hurt you. If it's the last thing I do Celeste, I won't let him touch you okay?"

She looked like she was about to cry, "Okay. I just don't want you to get hurt either," she took a deep breath, "So are we going to move or leave or something?"

"No. He still has no idea where we are, though he's getting closer. It just means we're going to have to start your weapons training immediately."

"Immediately? Can't we start tomorrow morning? I'm suddenly feeling exhausted."

"No my lady. It's really important now. We've got to get you ready," he stood up and put his hand out to help her up.

"Aren't you scared? At all?"

"You remember what I told you on your birthday? When we were on the bike?"

She stood next to him, "There's nothing to fear but fear itself. Yeah."

"If you let fear control you, if you let it sink its teeth into you – you will freeze. Sometimes I do get scared, but it passes or I use it. I can't afford to be afraid now. I haven't allowed fear to control me for a long time…I'll die if I do."

She thought this was an outright lie. She suspected Sebastian was afraid of falling in love with her, so he was allowing fear to control at least part of his life.

"Okay, I guess we should get started then," she sighed with exasperation.

"Wait, there's one more thing about fear. I'm used to threats, crisis, and dangerous situations, but I'm not used to them with you. I'm not used to the idea of losing you, so I'm fearful of that…and that's exactly why we have to start your training *right now*."

He led her through his walk-in closet and opened a door in the back of the safe room Celeste never noticed before.

"This is my training room. Well-equipped with the best simulator coren can buy and plenty of space, there's nothing you can't learn in here if it involves fighting or combat."

She followed him into the large empty room and he closed the door behind him.

"Erebos, it's been ninety-three days since your last simulation. What would you like to simulate?" Ophelia asked.

"Start basic combat training. Sunny, clear day, seventy degrees. Human enemy. Begin in five minutes with a ten second warning."

"Location?"

"Surprise me."

"As you like."

Celeste had no idea how she would ever find her way out of here as all the surfaces of the room were the same – glossy black walls, floor, and ceiling and the room was dimly lit. Sebastian went to a small rectangular panel next to the door. He pressed a square inside the vertical rectangle and a clothing rack rolled out of the wall. Sebastian took a black shirt and pants and handed them to her, then grabbed an identical set for himself, "Put those on and remove your Titan."

She thought these were clothes someone studying karate might wear.

He asked, "You know what karate means in Japanese?" He stripped down to his underwear in front of her.

Her gaze slid rapidly down his almost naked body, shaking her head no.

"Empty hand. Kara te," he smiled with a boyish excitement.

She started undressing herself by the time he was changed.

"You better hurry," he prompted. He hung his clothes and Titan up, took hers from her, and put them on the rack quickly. He slid the hidden closet back into the wall and positioned himself in the middle of the room.

She smoothed her hands over the fabric of the clothes he gave her. This outfit was really loose fitting and comfortable. It made sense to fight in something like this.

He told her to relax and watch him first. She sat down cross-legged on the ground against a wall.

She was familiar with these simulations as they had been popular ever since they were introduced way before she was born. Every five years they got better and more realistic. There was no limit as to what could be done in this simulated world, everything from learning to ride a bicycle to having sex with the partner of your dreams. The only limit on the program was the user's actual physical space of their simulation room. The way each user delineated the physical confines of their space was customizable. Some used a ripple effect, so if you touched a wall of your room, the simulation rippled along that surface, but the simulation showed a view that went on for miles beyond that. This was particularly good if you were faking a landscape or scenic setting for something like a meditation session or a date. In other cases, the user might need to know where those walls are visually to not collide with them, as with Sebastian's case. Celeste wanted to know what kind of visual cue Sebastian had programmed in.

"Dark purple dots are the edges," Sebastian read her mind.

"This is your ten second warning," Ophelia spoke in a gentle tone.

The simulation room darkened and the walls completely fell away.

"The reason I like this practice so much, is because I can't read an AI's mind." Sebastian took a deep breath and let it out slowly.

Ophelia announced, "Five…Four…Three…Two…One. Simulation emerge."

The simulation was completely immersive. Once the lights went down and the program started, Celeste felt like she was transported to another reality. They were in an Asian marketplace on Earth full of people and noise. Celeste's hands were now touching dirt and sand underneath her. Her eyes needed a minute to adjust to the bright sunlight pouring down onto her. She looked at the "wall" behind her – it was now a merchant selling live chickens but a faint vertical plane of round dark purple dots showed the space's physical limits. She turned her head and saw Sebastian walking alone looking everywhere at once. She stood up to see better. She thought nothing was going to happen until a Human figure came out of the crowd covered in all black. The only thing she could make out was a small band of exposed skin where his eyes were. The Human attacked Sebastian quickly.

Sebastian grunted and shouted as he fought with the artificial intelligence being. She was impressed to see him in action again. The fight on the Bahsheef beach had been real, but that stranger hadn't been nearly as tough as this AI enemy. Sebastian's movements were structured and disciplined. His body was a graceful plan in motion, his face showed sheer concentration and determination to win. He was living in the moment and she could tell any thought of her had faded from his mind. He was in complete control, focused, and moving lightning fast to match his skilled opponent. She thought if she was half as good as him, she would be very surprised and extremely proud of herself.

Sebastian had the enemy pinned on the ground and the fight was over.

"Ninety-nine," Ophelia announced.

"What does that mean?" Celeste asked.

Sebastian was out of breath, "That's my score. I set up the AI to evaluate my fights so I can judge how I'm doing, where I need to improve."

Once he got in the mood, there was no stopping him. He showed her a few other simulations with swords, revolvers, and knives. Then it was her turn.

Sebastian wiped the sweat from his forehead with his palm, "Ophelia. New user. Do a body scan. Celeste, close your eyes."

Celeste stood in the middle of the room with her eyes closed as Ophelia's mechanical eye scanned her skeleton, musculature, nervous system, and determined her weight and age.

He started her off with something he thought was simple – knives.

During the fight, Celeste's female opponent stabbed her in the chest and the room went black.

"What happened? Did I lose?"

"You're dead. The simulation stops as soon as you get a life threatening injury. You'll need to do better next time," Sebastian's voice was stern.

She scowled at him in the dark.

"I saw that."

"It's late at night, what do you expect of me? I was tired before I started."

"Tell that to the enemy. Maybe they'll offer to come back tomorrow morning and kill you after you've had a full night's rest." He saw Celeste roll her eyes.

"O, lights up dimly please."

When the lights came up, Celeste's eyes got wide as she saw Sebastian charging at her.

"Wha—" was all she had time to say before he was behind her with her arm contorted in an unbelievably painful hold behind her back.

She attempted to break free of him, but everything she tried only made it more painful.

"What the *hell* are you doing Sebastian?"

"An enemy doesn't care if you're tired, injured, emotional, hungry, or *complaining*. You need to be ready for anything; you need to expect everyone will attack you at any time. You need to fight like your life depends on it," he tightened the arm hold and then let go, "because someday it will."

She immediately shook out her arm and started rubbing her shoulder, "I still think that lesson was a little extreme."

He shot her a glance that asked if she wanted more pain. She stayed silent but pouted.

"Ophelia, please give a score to our guest fighter for the last simulation."

"Thirty-five."

Sebastian walked to the corner of the room and sat down, "You go again, and don't give me any of your prissy princess attitude about it."

To Celeste, Sebastian became merciless in this simulated environment. She was still very tired and now she had to nurse a sore shoulder. She didn't want to fight anymore, but she wasn't about to say that out loud. The lights went down and Celeste took a fighting stance.

Celeste's second time, Ophelia called a draw, but the fourth time Celeste was victorious.

"Ophelia, score please for Celeste."

"Seventy-two."

Sebastian patted her on the back after the program ended and tried to kiss her but she pulled away.

"Come on Celeste. Don't be like that. I needed to make a point to you."

"I want to do swords next. Set it up for me."

"Ophelia, what time is it?"

"One eleven in the morning."

"Celeste, we've been at it for a while. I think it's a good time to sleep. Your bod—"

"I will go again, and don't give me any of your macho control-freak bullshit attitude about it."

Seeing the amusement in his eyes, she laughed.

"The lady has some fire in her tonight," he paused and smiled at Celeste, "Ophelia, start basic sword training. Foggy night, no moons, fifty degrees. Neek enemy. Begin in one minute with a ten second warning."

Celeste beat her AI opponents in six tries. Each simulation was different so it wasn't just a matter of her remembering a pattern of moves – it was calculating, and analyzing the current opponent's size and speed. Celeste had fought simulated men and women, Humans, Neeks, Lanyx, and Taybuse, younger than herself and much older. She had fought in wheat fields, prison yards, on icy ponds during a blizzard, at night in

the rain on a city street, and on a mountaintop. Her best score had been
eighty-six.

Sebastian was pleased that she was learning weapons a bit faster than
hand-to-hand. He knew after she got some confidence in the artificial
world with weapons, they could fight armed against each other, but that
was for later.

TWO

>>> > MITCH LOOKED AT D'Artagnan and smiled, "I didn't think you
could do this, but you came through and proved me wrong."

D'Artagnan smiled, "Now you know better. I am a man of my word.
If I say I can do something, I will do it. But, I'm really glad I could help
and that it all came out okay."

"We're going to have to get together with the group and discuss the
numbers though. I'm eager to see how many people have kept their
coren."

"I'm monitoring that daily. We'll give them a little bit longer to think
it over."

Mitch ran his fingers over his dark beard, "Do you think we could
give them a time limit?"

"What? To give the coren back? Of course. I can lock down the rever-
sal ability whenever you want. Either that or I can funnel the money into
the account of your choice." D'Artagnan smiled wickedly.

Mitch paused, "That's tempting, but no. I wanted to redistribute the
wealth a little more evenly, not take a whole bunch for myself, or even
for the group. No. I just want people to make a decision, one way or the
other by a certain time. Maybe seventeen more Earth days? That makes
like, what – thirteen Il'lacean days, right? What do you think?"

"I can definitely do it in that time frame. They'll have to either keep
it in their own accounts or reverse the deposit. Then we'll have final
numbers."

"It's too bad. I mean, the people keeping the coren. That doesn't prove
whose side they're on. It doesn't prove that they support us."

"It just means they're greedy."

"Yes," Mitch sighed. "But, it doesn't take away what a kick ass job you've done for us. I wish I understood how you did everything, but maybe it's better I don't. I'm just glad you could do it. Thank you."

"My pleasure Mitch."

THREE

TITAN Corporation - Personal TITAN Device

System Status: Active -- Universal Grid: Online

Current Time/Date (Il'laceier - Rem Mot 0m): 16th Knoche/ Atos 71-8, 5390

Secondary Time/Date (Earth - Silver Thorn): 11:22 a.m./ October 24, 4015

Current Universal Positioning System Location: QetQert Regions, Il'laceier

User: King David Hennessy

Communications Menu

Incoming message(s) received: 1 - Status: Unread

Message Received at 16th Knoche

Message Sent from: Universal News Agency (UNA) - Il'laceier Region

-UNA
-Pirchi Colony, QetQert Regions, Il'laceier
BREAKING NEWS
King David Hennessy has issued a public letter to the organization known as FAIR (Fighting Against Il'lacean Rule) which UNA is publishing below.
"I first want to reassure the general public of Earth and Il'laceier that I do not blame them for what has happened.

I'm putting my faith in Human and Il'lacean hands that they will do what is right. They know that the money put into their financial institution's accounts recently is not their own. They know those coren belong to the Kingdom of Earth and Il'laceier and that they should return it as quickly as possible. I also remind the general public that knowingly keeping that money is going to be reported as a crime and that it will go against your permanent record. We will find out who has kept the money and we will press charges against you.

How will I pay the ransom for Queen Celeste without the necessary funds in my account?

And my statement to the new organization that is rising up against me, FAIR, is as follows.

Terrorist groups have always been a thorn in whatever society they are currently targeting.

You are no different.

You are not heroes. You are not saviors. You are not even fighting against the enemy. I am merely a man who is currently watching over two groups of beings and doing the best I can to govern them true and honorably.

I think everyone can see how my people's pain and suffering over Queen Dowager Celeste is being placed on my shoulders. They can see the pain on my face as I do press conference after press conference, trying to keep everyone updated.

I'm just a man trying to get a special someone (who happens to be Human, I will remind your group) back to where she belongs.

We need to turn our attention to the real threats out there. Groups like the BDP who are full of criminals and only out to do violent acts on innocent people and steal or destroy other people's things. I am not your enemy. I am in fact your ally.

As an act of forgiveness in what might be the most difficult time for my reign, I will not seek out all members and execute you. I will merely press criminal charges for

the laws that have been broken and leave it at that. The
justice system will deal with you, and that is the kindness
I will give you this one time.

But I highly recommend that any more actions such as what
has happened recently, cease and desist immediately.

If anything like this occurs again, or any violence is
threatened, I will be forced to take harsher action against
you, and executions will not be out of the realm of justice
for your group.

If you are a FAIR member reading this, I encourage you to
leave while you still can.

The group you are in is going nowhere fast.

If you are the leader of FAIR, I also encourage you to
terminate its existence immediately.

This is your first and final warning.

Any further action against me or my Kingdom will be met
with the most severe punishment possible.

Thank you

King Hennessy II of Earth and Il'laceier Kingdoms

-END OF MESSAGE

* This message will only be deleted by user.

TITAN Corporation - Personal TITAN Device

System Status: Active -- Universal Grid: Online

Current Time/Date (Praxis - Dersalene): 2:15 a.m./August
30, 2193

Secondary Time/Date (Earth - London, England): 1:49 p.m./
October 24, 4015

Current Universal Positioning System Location: Dersalene, Praxis

User: Unrecorded

Communications Menu

Incoming message(s) received: 1 - Status: New/Unread

Message Received at 2:15 a.m.

Message Sent from: FAIR

-King David Hennessy,
How expected of you to do something like try to intimidate your peasants into giving back "your" money. We both know that identifying individuals who keep the coren is impossible; otherwise, I would've never pulled a stunt like this. Also expected of you to be manipulative and try to convince your subjects that somehow you cannot pay for the Queen's ransom when we left more than enough coren in the account to cover such things. We would never endanger our beloved Queen's life.
I encourage you to do something you've probably never done before, and be benevolent. Give your people a gift, a true gift that will help them.
Start being a leader instead of a dictator.
Start helping your people instead of holding them back.
Surprise me and my group by showing us you are not your brother.
Otherwise, our efforts will continue, and our attempts for bringing about change will get larger and bolder.
We will not rest until all of us are free.
You could speed up the process and abandon control of Earth, but something tells me you will never do this on your own.
As I said in my Titan message to the citizens of our two worlds, war is not the answer, and I meant that.
But sometimes war is the last solution one can turn to when all else has failed.

Sincerely,
The leader of FAIR

-END OF MESSAGE

*This message will only be deleted by user.

FIVE

>>> > CELESTE SPENT TWELVE hours a day, every day training in the simulator with various weapons, learning the advantages and disadvantages of each. One afternoon after her lunch break, she found Sebastian in the simulator room after she came back from the bathroom and asked what he needed.

"I've set up your next exercise. You can begin when you're ready." He sat off to the side and watched her as she took her fighting stance.

The room darkened. The simulation began. Celeste found herself inside the front entrance of the Rem Mot Om Kingdom Estate.

"What is this?" she asked.

Sebastian was silent and only watched.

The front door opened and Jonathan walked through with a mace and chain in his hand. He closed the door behind him and faced Celeste.

"What the hell is this Sebastian?" She looked at the simulation of Jonathan. He was wearing his formal royal robes and dress clothes underneath. The simulation was perfect down to his crown sitting atop his head. The mace was long and the spiked ball at the end of the chain looked heavy, but Jon carried it easily.

"This is the day you're going to die bitch!" Jonathan's voice was loud and echoed in Celeste's ears.

"Sebastian turn this off right now!"

But he didn't. He let it continue as if he hadn't heard her.

"Ophelia! This simulation is over! Stop."

"Unrecognized user. Request denied. Filed for nightly report."

Jonathan walked up to Celeste and swung the mace at her skull. She covered her head with her arms and closed her eyes as she saw the spiked ball flying towards her. She stood that way with her heart hammering in her chest until she could breathe again. When she opened her eyes the room was dark. She heard Sebastian's voice.

"Score?"

"Zero," Ophelia answered.

"O, lights up please."

The lights came on and Sebastian was already walking to her, "You completely froze up Celeste."

"You're Goddam right I did! What the hell was that?! What do you think you're doing?"

He put a hand on her shoulder and her inability to move vanished as she ripped herself away from him, "Don't you dare touch me right now."

"You need to expect the unexpected at all times. You need to fig—"

"That dead son of a bitch is never going to come back from the grave! That's not unexpected, that's downright impossible! How could you do that without even asking me?!"

He put his head down and his palm to the back of his head, "Listen to me for a minute," he looked at her, "I'm training you here. I have all the experience and you have none. I've been in terrible situations and it only takes a split second to make the wrong decision that causes you to die. YOU have to be ready for anything. YOU have to make the decision by yourself. YOU have to react and protect yourself no matter what."

"I am not happy with you right now. I'm not okay with this Sebastian. You shouldn't have sprung this on me like that."

He pounded his closed fist into his open palm, "I have to make this point. I can't just tell you like I tried to last week."

"No! You almost broke my arm last week."

He took a deep breath, "I wasn't even close to doing that. You know I would never hurt you."

"You're too late for that. You broke my heart when you walked away from me."

A sudden look of defeat came over his face. His response was solemn, "Celeste I thought we moved forward from that. We forgave each other for everything said and done in the past. You're always going to hold that against me aren't you?"

Everything felt as though it were falling down around her suddenly. But this anger was rising up. She didn't understand why. He was right, she said she had forgiven him, but still…

"Celeste?"

"You hurt me. I thought I forgave you, but then sometimes out of nowhere, it comes bubbling back to the surface. Some…*thing* will trigger a memory of that day and all the days that followed where all I wanted was to talk to you, or see you, or hold you. I felt like everything I ever wanted, all my quiet dreams that I never confessed to anyone came true when I met you, only to be ripped away from me when you left." She held back tears of frustration.

Sebastian sighed, "I did what I thought was right at the time. I thought I was protecting you. Then while I was gone, I realized I wanted to come back home and make…I wanted to start fresh with you and do things better this time around. I am trying to."

"Why are you being so hard on me lately? This past week you've been treating me like…I don't know, like I'm in the military and you're my boss. I don't want to be in anything like my old marriage. I don't want to be controlled."

"I've been told that I keep a tight leash on myself and I'll admit sometimes that's true, but you think I'm *controlling* you?"

"When I asked you for help at the Outpost, you told me I had to do everything you said. You bought me all these things, clothes to wear, and told me what to do with the police and the story I should tell them. You controlled the pace of our 'relationship', you always said no when I wanted intimacy. Then when I had my amnesia you wouldn't let me contact my friends or go anywhere alone. You beat the crap out of that guy on the beach and then you go and buy my apartment. The only place that was mine here, the only decision I made on my own has been wiped out. Now you want me to learn fighting and weapons and we're hiding. You don't want me to go anywhere else."

Sebastian stood dumbstruck by her words. He spoke quietly, not meeting her gaze, "It seemed like you were always asking for my help, and I thought that's what I was doing – helping. You needed things so I got them for you, but my actions were always motivated by my need to protect you, Celeste, not control. I'm sorry that you see things differently than me. If you want to go back to Earth, make your own path without me, you're free to go at any time. I'm not holding you here against your will."

The silence spun out. No one wanted to say anything.

Celeste thought about what it would be like if she walked out the door right now and went to Earth. She honestly wouldn't know how to handle all the problems that would inevitably catch up to her there. She couldn't avoid her friends forever, neither could she avoid David. What about her safety? And she'd need a place to live, and everyone would still recognize her on the street, and the press…she might even have to do something crazy like run away to some distant planet and let the universe think she was dead or disappeared.

How would she do any of that?

She wanted independence her whole life, but she was always under someone's thumb. Now that she was faced with the opportunity of being set free to do everything for herself as she chose, she found the challenge daunting. She craved freedom and independence, but she didn't want to be without Sebastian. He had his problems, but then again, so did she.

And she would never find another man that made her insides turn to mush when he smiled at her the way he could.

She cursed to herself.

She forced her feet to carry her to stand in front of Sebastian.

He hesitated, then put his hands up to her cheeks and held her face softly, "Did you come to say goodbye? Wait, don't answer that. Let me say first – thank you for saving my life. Whatever you decide, I'm grateful you gave me a reason to live again." Before she could respond, he kissed her. It was his convincing kiss – like the very first one he gave her and she thought about how that kind of kiss could convince her to do anything. This time, it convinced her, she couldn't walk away from him, not now, probably not ever, no matter how much he drove her crazy. No one was perfect.

He released her and stood quietly.

She regained herself and asked, "Why are you asking if I'm saying goodbye? Can't you sense my thoughts anymore?"

He sighed heavily, "There's a lot going on up there"—he pointed to her brain—"a lot of emotions swirling around. And there's a lot of noisy thoughts of my own so it's all static right now. I remembered that happened between us a long time ago."

She nodded.

"So, is this goodbye your Highness?"

She shook her head and smiled, "I know we're not perfect. I have trust issues. I am angry too, not just at you when you left me, but at lots of things I guess. At the world, at my parents, and Jon, and David, and the BDP for kidnapping me and Dax for lying. Maybe I'm angry that I lost my memory. Maybe I'm angry at myself for falling for Dax's act. I know those feelings are there and I know I have to find a way to deal with them. You have your own issues that you need to work on. In all honesty, yes you do control yourself too tight, and that might spill over to me sometimes. I have to accept that you've changed before my eyes since I met you and they've been positive improvements. So, you are capable of making good changes, and I need to learn how to give you the time to make those adjustments."

"It's true I have lived my whole life under strict control. It won't be an overnight process to change that, but I can be better with you."

"It's a deal then. We work on ourselves to be better for each other."

"Deal."

She hugged him and kissed his cheek, "So I'm still curious – why are you demanding so much of me with this training? I hope you see I'm doing the best I can."

"The threat to you is high. I'm only one man and I can only do so much in a fight to protect you, and if there's more than one attacker, it'd be really nice if you could protect yourself. It would make me feel better knowing you're capable. Does that make sense?"

"I suppose. I just wish maybe you could phrase things differently and not cause me physical pain to show me something I need to see."

"Noted. I think I should finish what I was going to say earlier then too."

"Go ahead."

"So, wars can break out in seconds, I could be brainwashed, someone could make an aggressive clone of anyone and set them upon you. Anything is possible, no matter how hard it is for you to imagine. This is why I say, expect the unexpected. You never know."

She shook her head, "What are you talking about brainwashing?"

"Think of the worst case scenario. Let's say I get brainwashed somehow to kill you. What are you going to do? Let me kill you if we're locked in the same room together? Try to talk me out of it?"

"That would never happen."

"The reason I want you to be ready for anything is because anything can happen. When you fight, you must be ready to kill."

"I'm never going to have to fight *Jon*, Sebastian. We both know he's dead."

"Well what if you have to fight someone who is exactly like him and makes you feel small or weak or someone who terrifies you? You have to battle your own fear first, defeat it, and then defeat your enemy."

She looked at him silently. What he was saying was sinking in. All of it made sense and she knew he was right – if she froze up in a real fight, she'd be dead. "Start up the simulation again."

"You sure?"

"Yes." She got into the middle of the room and he stood off to the corner.

"Ophelia. Prior simulation again but randomize the assailant's weapon."

"Five...Four...Three...Two...One. Simulation emerge."

The gigantic kingdom door opened. Celeste faced Jonathan again. This time he carried a katana. Jon moved towards her.

She looked for a weapon of her own. There was nothing there. When the simulation was randomized, her weapon didn't appear until her opponents did. "Sebastian, I don't have any weapons?"

"No. You'll have to take his."

Jon raised the katana above his head with both hands like he wanted to split a cord of wood and brought it straight down. Celeste quickly rolled to her left and dodged him. She sprung back up and kicked

Jonathan's arm holding the katana. He was surprised and dropped it. It clanged to the floor, but he kicked it away from her reach. It slid to the wall. She immediately ran for it and grasped the handle, but Jonathan's foot stomped on top of her hand and pinned it down. She screamed out in pain. Jon's other foot reared back and he drove it into her legs. She crumpled to the floor, and Jon's foot finally released her hand. She took her uninjured hand and grabbed the katana. Jon bent over, grabbing her by the ankles and began dragging her body along the floor walking backwards. She bent upwards at her waist and drew the sword across his body, severing both of his arms at the elbows. His body suddenly jerked backwards and he fell to the ground. His blood was everywhere, but Celeste didn't react. He was injured, but he wasn't dead. She stood up and positioned herself over his body. He was squirming around trying to kick her. She put her foot on top of his chest and leaned over him. She whispered, "You're dead you scaly fuck." Then swung the katana across her body and decapitated Jon. She watched as his head rolled along the floor and finally stopped by Sebastian's feet.

The room got dark and Celeste's "injuries" faded along with the katana from her hands. The foot she had stepped on Jon's chest with, settled to the ground as his body disappeared. Then the lights came on and Celeste straightened up.

Sebastian walked towards her, "I am very sorry I had to put you through that, but you did great. I'm proud. Very, very proud."

She put her arms around him and started sobbing.

He held her against him, "It's okay Celeste. You did good darling. You made me proud. You were so strong."

She wanted to say something, but the words simply wouldn't come out.

"I knew it was hard. I knew I was pushing you, but you did it. You overcame your fear and that's vitally important. You're better prepared now. Can you give a score, Ophelia?"

"Ninety-one."

Celeste caught her breath and looked up at him. <Can we stop early for today?>

"Sure."

SIX

>>> > HACE WASN'T SURE he believed Smeck, "I'm sorry, what did you say?"

"Celeste escaped. Not on her own, she had help, but she's been gone for over ten Earth weeks."

"And Dax told you not to tell anyone, including me?"

"Yes sir."

"So why did you take so long to tell me?"

"Well...sir..." he swallowed hard, "Dax kept telling us that he could get her back and it wasn't worth the trouble to bother you. At first I agreed with him, you know how persuasive Dax can be."

"Uh huh."

"But as the weeks went by and we have no leads on where she's at...I thought someone needed to tell you the truth."

"I appreciate that Smeck. I will not forget what you've done."

"Thank you...Is that a good thing or a bad thing? Cause it sounded lik—"

"The Hunter over and out."

Hace's Titan went back to the main menu screen.

Dax had lied every time he talked to him for weeks now. Huh. Hace never even thought it was possible.

Maybe Dax will correct this himself, maybe he can get Celeste back. And if that were to happen, then Hace wouldn't care about the escape... much. But, he cared about the dishonesty.

Dax must have his reasons for not telling him. They better be damn good ones. And Smeck can't know everything that's going on in Dax's head right now. Hace liked Dax, he was one of his favorite members and had a solid history with the BDP. He was competent, loyal, and smart...most of the time, but a couple times now, he did fuck up. We all fuck up, but it matters on whether you fuck up the little things or the big things...but Celeste. Letting a weak, beaten, starving woman, a former queen who has no military training and no hostage situation knowledge...letting her escape your facility under your watch? That's a very big fuck up. With very large consequences.

But, *it is* better to let the universe think the BDP still had Celeste. *That* was the right call for Dax to make. But if someone sees her now, and goes to the press? That will make the BDP look careless. And Hace hated it when the BDP got attention he didn't want them to have.

SEVEN

>>> > THERE WAS A lot of political things escalating between Il'laceier and Earth's group FAIR. Ophelia saw breaking news alerts constantly across the uninet.

She thought it might be time for her to research government organizations on multiple planets to see how they varied. After she studied that, she moved to arts and entertainment. She studied the book titles she could see on Erebos's bookshelves and the artwork and sculptures he had all over the apartment.

Everything that she could see became a target of study. She wanted to know as much as she could about absolutely everything.

EIGHT

>>> > THE NEXT WEEK passed with Celeste finishing her weapons training. She became a master archer, an expert at melee weapons and felt comfortable with guns. She was a good shot and gained confidence through Sebastian's encouragement and practice. She achieved a score of 100 nine separate times in the simulator.

Any other Human wouldn't have been able to perform like her. She was a proficient fighter and Sebastian felt her understanding of weapons was good enough where she could kill someone physically if she needed to. He could train and prepare her forever but being mentally strong enough to pull the trigger was nothing he could teach. Better to expose her to all of this and hope for the best. That's all he could do. The end of her training came up fast and he knew his time to leave was quickly approaching. All of this time, in the back of his mind, he'd been preparing Celeste for a life without him.

CHAPTER 34

ALORALOCKS AND TIGERS

ONE

>>> > DAVID SAT WITH his council around the table. The room was deadly silent.

He stood up and circled them.

"I am going to say, I'm severely disappointed in all of you. I'm not sure how the security breach happened. I'm not sure why our digital barriers and safeguards were not enough to protect our kingdom and the coren that supplies weapons, ammo, armor, and deploys soldiers to wars that keep us safe in our homes, including all of you, but it happened."

A few council members shifted in their seats as they watched him circle and seethe.

He stopped at the head of the table and slammed his fists down, making some council members jump.

"How did this happen?"

One council member was stupid enough to try and say something. "I'm sure som—"

"SILENCE!"

They were all quiet. The council member who had attempted to speak, shut her eyes and tried to be as still as possible.

"I don't want excuses! All I know is that this 'council' of the best and brightest minds, the one that's supposed to be brimming with talent and ability is full of beings that let this happen. I'm embarrassed that some Human terrorist organization has somehow bypassed all our security measures to take what they wanted without resistance.

"I appear as a buffoon right now, or at best, some weakling who is so distraught emotionally that I have no control over the kingdom's finances. Maybe that I'm absent-minded and unable to protect my own house, much less two worlds!"

David took his hands off the table and stood up straight, adjusting his suit.

"Effective immediately, your services are no longer needed. I'm terminating all of you from the kingdom. Collect your things and the HRG's will walk you off the premises. If you resist, you will be met with severe force. Talk about this to the public and your severance packages will be nullified. You will sign a nondisclosure agreement before any coren will be given to you. You are only allowed to say 'no comment' to anyone regarding this matter as long as you're alive. I never want to see any of you on either the grounds of the Silver Thorn Estate or Rem Mot Om. Dismissed."

The room was silent, full of shocked faces and tears in some cases.

A council has always been present during any kingdom reign. This was unheard of and David knew he was a trailblazer in many ways, but he would have to tell the universe about this himself. People would understand his position. They had to.

TWO

>>> > DAX TOOK A deep breath and dialed The Hunter's number. He didn't want to make this call, but he needed to. He had been lucky enough to avoid Celeste going to the press and making her escape public, but he felt time was running out.

The Hunter picked up after several rings and already sounded aggravated. His mask was skewed like he rushed to put it on, "This better be good Adastros!"

Dax wished he had made this an audio only call, "I apologize sir. I didn't mean to disturb yo—"

"Well, you technically did if you're calling me."

"Yes…sir. You're right. I'll get to it."

"Please do."

"Celeste Hennessy escaped. She had help from a man on the outside. I'm sure I can get her back. I know this guy's going to return looking for me; he almost killed me while he was here. Choked me until I lost consciousness then they got into his transit and launched."

Dax waited for the yelling to start. He stayed stone-faced as he looked at The Hunter. It had all gone wrong on his watch; he deserved whatever The Hunter gave him.

The Hunter was silent. Dax almost had to prompt him for a response.

"So this is why I haven't seen any new vids of her even though I specifically asked you for some." The Hunter adjusted his mask until it fit properly. He let out a long loud sigh, "How did this happen?"

Dax swallowed hard, "Apparently Tiny had a crush on her. He waited until he was alone and took her to the desert right before a large dust storm engulfed the planet. There was a struggle and Tiny wound up with a broken neck at the end of it. That's how she got out."

The Hunter sighed, "I mean how did she get off world. Who is this guy that stole her?"

"I don't know sir." Dax couldn't even tell him the information he paid for came out to nothing since they didn't find anything on Sebastian but an alias and an empty apartment. "I believe this man to be someone like a bounty hunter or a military trained mercenary to get in and out like he did. He put up a long fight. Took out six good men and got the best of me. Maybe David wouldn't pay us to get her back, but was willing to pay this guy? I'm not sure."

"What about video surveillance? You have anything on this transit? A face so I can see what he looks like?"

"No sir. He kept his transit far away from the facility and pretty much stayed invisible."

The Hunter looked over a weather calendar on his Titan, "The last time a major dust storm hit Tiletan coincides with an alarm going off there. We were on a call that day and you had to go. That was quite a while ago. When did this happen Dax?"

He hesitated, contemplating his choices, "A little over eleven Earth weeks ago. I hesitated calling you since I thought I could've gotten her back before now. I wanted to handle this myself and thought it best that the universe believed we still had her. I waited to see if she went public or if she turned up dead somewhere, but I had reasons for my hesitation."

"Always covering your ass too. I get it man. You fucked up. It happens. I'm a bit disappointed in you. I figured you had this one, but she hasn't gone public. Technically, you still have time to get her…but Dax." He tapped his finger on the Titan's screen, "*Do* get her back ASAP. I'm unhappy you lost her, glad you came clean with me, but we need her. We can't be the laughingstock of the universe. I've worked too hard for too long to earn our organization's reputation. Can't have you fucking this up for me. If you don't get her back soon, I will find a way to make you pay and I don't mean financially. I like you, but my like only goes so far."

Dax gulped, "I understand sir. Completely understand. I really am sorry for disappointing you and I promi—"

"Ah ah ah. Just get it done Dax," The Hunter shuffled through screens on his Titan, "I don't want to hear any more from you. The Hunter over and out."

Dax watched as his Titan's screen went black and then back to its main menu. He felt his stomach turn. He wondered if he made the right choice after all. Maybe he should've kept his mouth shut.

THREE

>>> > HACE CALLED OUT to DAI immediately after he hung up with Dax, "How easy is it for us to get a satellite into Tiletan's orbit?"

"First we need to get permission from Tiletan's president as all orbital slots are already taken, then we need to build it, and launch it."

"That sounds impossible, plus I'm not asking anyone's permission."

"Then it is impossible."

Hace took off his mask and threw it aside, "Why are all the orbital slots taken?"

"Tiletan's intense weather makes it a planet of study for interested parties all over the universe. The orbital slots have been occupied for hundreds of years."

"Do any of them have cameras on them? Could we commandeer one?"

"I cannot control any without being close to Tiletan due to radio interference, but I can hack their feed."

"Good. I want constant visuals on the facility there."

"I'm sorry but that's not possible."

"Why not?"

"With my calculations there will be a seventy Tiletanian minute period where no cameras are available for the area."

"What's that my time?"

"A Stoxian sterm."

Hace rubbed his chin, "I guess it will have to do. There's no better options?"

"None that are feasible."

"Fine. Make it happen and let me know when it's up."

FOUR

>>> > SEBASTIAN FLEW QUICKLY over the jungle, making trees and landscape fly underneath the transit.

"Will you please tell me where we're going?" She was dying of anticipation.

"No, not until we get there, and we're almost there."

Twenty minutes ago, Celeste was in the kitchen about to cook dinner when Sebastian told her they were going out. He had food delivered to take with them but he wouldn't say where they were going. She was starving and whatever was in the bag, smelled great.

She watched as the sun set and tried to figure out where they might be headed.

Sebastian docked his Atlas on a single landing pad close to a huge waterfall feeding water into a lake.

He got out and opened her door for her. He held her hand, led her through heavy foliage, and stopped. She could smell flowers, clean dirt, and hear nothing but insects buzzing and the chirp of crickets, or something that sounded like them.

Sebastian stomped on the ground in a few places then reached down to pull open a door that was completely covered in plants and dirt. She saw a ladder leading down into the dark.

"Ladies first."

"What is this?"

"You'll see. Just be careful. I'll be down with you in a minute."

She looked at him, then at the ladder, then back at him.

"What are you worried about sunshine?"

"I have a dress on and high heels. This isn't a sewer or something is it?"

He chuckled, "You honestly think I would tell you we're going out, order food to bring with us, and let you dress like that if I were going to take you into the sewers?" He didn't let her answer, "Here, give me your shoes."

She took them off one at a time and handed them to him. He threw them down the concrete tunnel. She heard them hit the bottom with a thud.

A soft gasp escaped her, "Those were brand new twenty-eight thousand coren shoes!"

"You paid that much for *one* pair of shoes?!" he gave her a sideways glance of utter disbelief.

"Yes! They're encrusted with color-changing crystals all over them. They're the latest in fashion, I *had* to have them!"

Sebastian rolled his eyes in the dark, "They will be down there when you get there and if I broke them, I will buy you new ones. Will you please go down the ladder? There's bigger problems in the jungle than broken over-priced shoes."

"Like what? You mean predators?"

"Celeste please. Just go down the damn ladder."

She carefully traversed the ladder and touched the bottom within a minute. It was even darker down here than it was above ground.

"Ewww. I think I touched a spider web." She ran her hands over her arms quickly trying to brush the feeling away. She shouted up, "Wait, do you have spiders on Praxis?"

He looked down at her, "Yes. Move a little to your left, about three steps. Okay. Stay right there."

She could hardly see anything. She watched as he descended the ladder a little then closed the door on top of him and now it was pitch black. She couldn't see her own hand in front of her face. She felt him move next to her.

"Why are you holding your hand in front of your face?" He asked.

"You're lucky you can see well. I can't see a thing."

He paused, "Nothing?"

"Nope."

He moved directly in front of her and reached out for her hand, "You want to hold on to this for a minute?"

She felt him putting the paper bag full of their dinner into her hand. She held onto it, "Sebastian why do yo—"

He stopped her from talking with a passionate kiss.

She uttered two words while he was kissing her, "Spiders...scary."

He pulled away from her, "You just went through weeks of intensive training to be able to kill an opponent with your bare hands and you're still afraid of spiders?"

"Yes."

"And while I'm kissing you, you're thinking of spiders?"

"Down here? Yes."

He shook his head, "I must not be doing it right tonight."

She heard frustration in his voice, but she knew he was thinking she gave him a challenge.

He pressed a series of buttons on the wall and a huge oval metal door swung out to his left.

"What's happening? Could you turn on a light please?"

Oh I'm going to turn on something all right.

She smiled as she caught his fading thought, but said nothing about it.

"I'm going to pick you up." And he did before she could ask another question.

He carried her cradled in his arms a few steps and set her down gently. Her stocking-clad feet felt carpet underneath them. She heard a loud metal *clank* and then silence.

"Sebastian, where are we?"

"Where there are no spiders."

He seized her quickly and pulled her to him with an urgency he'd never shown. Then his lips captured hers and he kissed her hard. She was breathless at his show of sexual aggression. She liked it, no scratch that, she loved it. She leaned into him and put her free hand around his shoulder. He had already wrapped his arms around her and closed his eyes. He wanted to rely on touch alone as she did down here in the dark.

She dropped the take out bag and put her other hand into his hair. She could feel him break into a smile even while he was kissing her, but he didn't stop.

After she was thoroughly incapacitated by his lips, he gently eased away from her and opened his eyes. She stood with her eyes closed and he saw the smile on her face, which made him smile too.

"I'm going to turn on a light now." He did and she opened her eyes a few seconds later.

"Welcome to my grandmother's house."

She was surprised as she looked around after letting her eyes adjust to the light, "Oh, this is where you grew up then? You told me about this. It looks lovely Sebastian." Her eyes moved from one spot to another, taking in all the cozy touches one might expect of a country style home.

He plucked the take out bag off the ground, "My grandmother, she always expected an invasion or a hostile race starting a war on Praxis so her and my grandfather built this underground shelter. She took great care of this place right up until the day she died. Always wanted everything tidy and clean." He looked around remembering the way his grandmother's chocolate chip cookies made his days a little bit better, or how she used to vacuum and dance around the house at the same time. His grandparents never believed in service bots and they had done everything themselves, the old-fashioned way. The only thing technologically advanced in the whole place was the holowindows. He needed to remember to show her those. He went to the kitchen and pulled out some plates and silverware.

Celeste wandered around taking everything in. She looked down at her feet and saw her stockings had gotten dirty. She looked up and saw Sebastian still rooting around the kitchen drawers so she pulled up her dress a little and detached her stockings from her garter belt.

Sebastian glanced up and saw the bottom of Celeste's minidress was sitting high above her thighs. He stared as she rolled the stockings down her thighs all the way to her ankles. Then she gently pulled them off her feet and she stood up to see him watching. She quickly pulled her dress back down where it belonged.

Sebastian threw down the napkins in his hand, "I forgot your shoes outside the front door. I'm going to go get those."

He quickly walked to the entryway, pressed some buttons on the wall and the vault door opened. He picked up her shoes and tried to quell his hard-on. Why'd she have to wear that damn short dress anyway? He thought of ice, taking a freezing cold shower, and blizzards and suppressed his lust. He took a deep breath and went back inside, shutting the door behind him.

"I'll just put these by the front door. They look okay to me, I don't think they're broken," he tossed them down gently.

"Thank you." She walked to them, bent over with straight legs, and put her rolled up pantyhose into her shoes.

He tried to divert his eyes from where the hem of her dress hovered, but her devilish teasing was overpowering him. He helplessly stared where she wanted him to.

She stood up, saw the fireplace and asked if they could light it up.

"Huh? Of course, yeah." He cleared his throat and shook out lustful thoughts as he walked back into the kitchen, "You're getting ahead of me. Why don't you sit down in front of it and I'll be there in a minute." He pointed to a comfy looking chair off to the side of the hearth.

She sat down and looked at the table next to her. She saw a photograph of a young Sebastian, Dax, and she assumed their grandparents. His grandmother had a cheerful smile and bright green eyes and his grandfather was very tall and looked friendly. They looked happy.

Sebastian lit the dark energy fireplace and it crackled into life.

"There's one thing I really want to show you."

She looked up at him, "What's that?"

"You want rain, sunshine, clouds, or fog? Or we have stars too and the moons."

"My favorite weather is rain," she smiled.

"The lady likes rain, then that's what she gets."

He shuffled through screens on his Titan and six foot high panels along the walls retracted that she didn't even know were there. Windows appeared and a thunderous rainstorm started up behind the glass.

"That is amazing! I've never seen anything like this. What are they?" She was fascinated as simulated lightning flashed across a window.

"My grandfather made these. He called them holowindows like anything else that's a projection, these simulated any kind of weather you can imagine. He knew my grandmother would miss seeing the outdoors when they were down here buried beneath the surface so he made them. It's the only high tech thing they were okay with at home. They had a natural gas fireplace before, but I converted it to dark energy after they passed away."

She stared as simulated leaves blew against the glass and big raindrops raced down the windows.

He set up a dinner picnic for them in front of the fire and she began to wonder if they were really safe there.

"Doesn't your brother own this as well?"

"Don't worry. We're fine here. The eldest son, or grandson, in this case, inherits everything and in our society, usually that means the other siblings get things too, it's just up to the eldest to divvy it up. Constantine thinks I sold this place to someone else. It was really just an alias of mine, so he would never come here looking for us. Anyways, I'd like to see him try to get past the vault door." He poured a glass of white wine for each of them and held up his glass for a toast.

"To your quick completion of weapons and combat training, may you never need to use it."

They gently clinked their glasses together.

"I couldn't have done it without you, great master," she bowed her head to him, then sipped her wine.

They quickly devoured the Italian take out, but slowed down for dessert – chocolate covered cherries.

"So when I had amnesia why didn't you bring me here? Is it the same reason as the safe room?"

"Time to put your training to the test. Why don't you tell me why I wouldn't like to be here for weeks or months at a time? What do you see wrong?"

She looked around and thought for a moment. "Well, your brother knows this place exists, so it's not a secret to him. Seems like there's only one way in and one way out, and you probably really don't like that."

He was smiling and nodding his head.

"There's no real sunlight, and I don't know how big it is, but you probably wanted more room for us to stretch out. I mean, on Bahsheef, we did have a whole planet to explore." She took a sip of wine, "So, how am I doing?"

"Very good. Only one thing you missed – I can't have anything delivered here if I really want to keep this place a secret."

"Smart," she nodded her head, "So, when was the last time you were here?"

"It's been a while. I try to visit at least once every six or eight months to check on the area. Do some maintenance and make sure the shelter's outer door doesn't get completely overtaken by shrubs and plants."

"Isn't that a bit too long between visits?" She swirled the wine in her glass.

"I have security cameras all over. Nothing's going to happen here without me knowing about it within minutes."

"It's beautiful here. Your grandmother really knew how to make a house a home."

"She was wonderful. You would've loved her. Seems like everyone else did and she did a good job at taking care of my brother and I. I'm kind of glad she didn't live to see what an evil soul my brother turned out to be."

"I'm sure she'd be disappointed."

"She'd be appalled. She never raised us to be that way. She was kind and loving. Always gave us lots of attention, but for my brother, I guess that wasn't enough."

"I'm sorry Sebastian."

"No need. Not your fault. The whole tragedy with Fran certainly didn't help our relationship. I don't even think that was it, no matter what he says. There were cracks widening in our relationship long before that. I think he was probably jealous because our father gave me the family ring. We shared this mental power together, my father and I. My brother and mother didn't have it."

"Were you close to your dad?"

"Yes. My brother must've felt left out very early on. I tried my best to look out for him, to include him in things, but he was always a little distant."

"Why do you take on the burden of everything? It seems like you want to blame yourself for everything that's gone wrong. It's not all your fault."

He ate another chocolate covered cherry.

"I don't know. Just seems like I could have done much better with a lot of things. I shouldn't have touched Francesca. At the time I thought it was fine since I didn't try to court her away from my brother. She made the choice to be with me, but I was young and inexperienced. What did I know about relationships and damaging other people?"

"Hindsight is twenty-twenty."

"Yes, but still. If I could go back, I would. I'd change many things." He looked into the fire watching the flames lick the sides of the fake woodpile.

Celeste decided to do cleanup for him and left him to his thoughts.

When she came back, Sebastian was laying on his side on the floor. She sat down behind him and put her hand on his shoulder.

"Is there anything I can do for you Sebastian?"

He rolled on his back and looked up at her. She rearranged herself to place his head on her lap and caressed his face.

"You're doing all I need from you right now. I can't ask for any more."

They sat that way for a while until Celeste's legs started to fall asleep.

"Why don't you lie down? I've got to get something we need." Sebastian got up and walked into another room. Celeste laid down on her side in front of the fire with an arm under her head. Sebastian returned with a pillow and handed it to her. She put it under her head but didn't change positions. He put a heavy blanket over her, the one his grandmother had quilted herself. He laid down behind her and covered himself with the blanket so he could put an arm around her waist.

She turned her head to look up at him, the flames of the fire were reflecting in his eyes.

He looked at her, studying her face in the firelight. *Better just to say this now instead of putting it off any longer.*

"Celeste, now that you're in good shape to take care of yourself, I need to handle some of our problems."

"What do you mean by that?" She already knew the answer.

He looked back at the fire, "Delays have dangerous ends."

She was silent.

"It's Shakespeare," he looked at her. He saw the muscles in her jaw clench. "My brother is looking for me, for you. He's go—"

She interrupted him, "Wait, you said *you're* going to have to take care of *our* problems? What about me?" She moved away from him just enough to roll onto her back.

"What about you?" Then he quickly realized what she meant, "No! Absolutely not. There's no way you're coming with me on this," he said firmly.

"Are you kidding me? You've just spent all this time training me so I can sit around and do nothing while you go into battle on our behalf?!"

"Yes. Exactly."

"I appreciate your willingness to protect me, but I think I can handle myself now."

Sebastian shook his head, "There's no substitute for actual opponents and real danger. It's called being battle tested and you are certainly not. There's an immense amount of pressure that goes with battle. Fighting for your life is nothing like the movies, or in books. For this fight, you need to be experienced, ruthless, and cunning. You're none of those things."

"But I fought with Jonatha—"

"I won't have it Celeste!" Veins stood out on his neck and she knew he was getting impatient with her.

"I feel that I was in a fight for my life every day that I lived with Jonathan. I do have experience."

He sighed, "I know what you're saying and I'm not trying to downplay your time spent with the king, but being in an abusive relationship is nothing like being in an actual honest to God firefight. Trust me."

"You've been protecting me since day one. Isn't it time you trusted me to start helping you protect me?" She placed a hand along the side of his face gently.

"This isn't just about you this time. My brother has threatened us both. He's been jealous of me for a long time and his jealousy has turned deadly. He's ready to kill us. I need you to stay here, because I need to know you're safe."

"I'm always safe with you. We could work together as a team."

"We *are* a team. But Constantine's unstable; it's hard to predict his behavior. There's no telling what he'll do if he finds us. I don't want to find out; and you've been through enough. You need to start fresh without having to worry about looking over your shoulder every day of your new life. He won't relent until he's killed us both. Payback for Francesca. I can't allow anything to happen to you. Now…things are different. I can't die now. There are too many things I need to explore."

"Like what?"

He looked down at her lips then back up to her eyes, "It feels like everything."

He leaned over and kissed her, moving his body over hers. Celeste stopped him with a question.

"Are you sure? I mean, about Constantine? Can't you just…I don't know…move to another planet, or hire someone else to do his assassination?"

Sebastian rolled off her gently and sat up. "You're really asking me this question? You do remember that my brother pretended to be interested in dating you so he could kidnap and beat you? You were almos—"

"Yeah, but he actually fell in love with me along the way. And I told you I think he might be saved if only you would reach out to him." She sat up to face him.

Sebastian's face turned bright red while he balled up his fists, "You were almost raped! Then he threatens us while we're trying to escape. You just spent five weeks recovering from him. Is there any question that he's sick and ruthless? I know him much better than you and he's just gotten worse over time. He's been eaten alive by jealousy and now he has the BDP behind him; he will never give up on hunting us down. This needs to be done. There will be no more running and hiding."

Celeste ran her hand through her hair. "This is dangerous. I wish someone else would take care of him for us. I don't want…anything to happen to you. I care about you."

Sebastian stood up and held out his hand to help her up.

"There is no one better to do this job. No one else grew up with him and knows his background better than me. It has to be me, it simply has to. I've killed many people, you haven't killed anyone and I'd like to keep it that way."

"Sebastian I have no doubt that I could kill anyone threatening our lives. I think I'm capable of that now."

He held her gently by the shoulders and looked into her eyes, "You've already proven to me that you're not ready."

Her brows furrowed, "How? You haven't even given me a chance."

"You just said you *could* kill anyone, not that you *would*. Besides, you've been pleading for me to give my brother a second chance since I rescued you from him. He's manipulated you into thinking he's someone that deserves mercy, despite the terrible things he's done to you. Do you actually think you could turn around and kill him after you've pled for his life?"

She was silent, unable to find the right words, but she tried, "All those years that I was with Jon, I kept giving him second chances. I kept think-ing that somehow I would find the good in him, at least, that's what I hoped for. Then, there came a day where I realized he loved to make other people miserable. He loved to watch other beings squirm. He nev-er loved me, or the other women he slept with. He didn't love the coren, or the power the most. What he loved more than anything was to make people suffer the unhappiness he felt until the day he died.

"Your brother fell in love with me. He's still capable of loving and I think that means, he's got to be worth a second chance. Just one, from you."

Sebastian only looked at her. "You have such a big heart, but I don't think you're seeing this clearly," he paused, "I did give him a chance to leave with us the day I rescued you. I offered him a way out. I told him to tell me everything he had on the BDP and I would protect him, but he refused Celeste. He refused."

She didn't remember Sebastian saying this to his brother, but she knew Sebastian was telling the truth. "I see," she paused, "I know you're one of the best assassins, but I also know, you've never killed a family member before. There's got to be some other way. Someone else should do it." She closed her eyes for a moment. The words felt heavy coming out of her mouth, "I could go with you. I don't want you to kill your brother. I don't think you should have to do it yourself."

His face grew dark, "When you were unconscious in the transit on Tiletan, I had the chance to kill Constantine. I hesitated and I blew it. I need to fix this. Killing people comes with a very steep price. You can't understand what it feels like until you've done it and it's better that you never know. It takes your soul, everything that you were and it burns it up, scars you. It destroys a part of you that you can never get back. I want to keep you from that experience. Besides, I've never been caught. There's a reason for that and it's that I work alone. I know my limits. You have to trust me now. Moving away will not make him stop. Asking someone else to do it is taking a risk that I don't need to. And doing it for me is out of the question. I get in there, I get it done, I get gone and back home to you." He embraced her and tried to pass some comfort to her.

"Let me just say, I'm still not okay with this. It's not that I don't trust you. We need to talk about it more. When are you thinking of doing this?"

He responded, "Soon. I can't wait too long, but there are some things we'll have to do first."

"Like what?"

"Prepare and plan."

"Sebastian?"

"Yes?"

"There were nights I laid in bed and thought about killing him. Killing Jon. Near the end, I was thinking about making a real plan. Make it happen somehow."

"I know."

FIVE

>>> > BACK ABOVE GROUND in the jungle, Sebastian walked with Celeste around the shore of the lake, pointing out some of his favorite teenage hideouts. She thought it looked beautiful by moonlight; she wondered how spectacular it must be by day. The breeze carried along with it, what seemed like hundreds of pieces of dandelion fluff. It was all over both of them.

"What is that?" she asked.

"What's what?"

She pointed to a small creature flying along a path of flowers a few feet away from them. It flew with two wings but had a bottom half that was shimmering with colors. Almost like a glittering light within the creature.

"Oh wait! That's an Aloralock. These are rare to see. Hold on...let's see where it goes." He motioned for her to stand still and he did the same.

It fluttered over Celeste's head and circled a few times, then landed on her upper arm. It didn't have feet; the bottom of it reminded her of a sea creature like an octopus even though the top half was close to a butterfly. Its tiny tentacles explored her skin. It wasn't unpleasant, in fact, it almost tickled.

"You were going to say something earlier?"

"It's good luck to see them, even better for them to land on you." He smiled some sort of secret smile she'd never seen on him before. She smiled back.

The Aloralock's colors changed from white to blue to green, repeatedly. She felt she could watch it all night, it was beautiful. Unfortunately, the small creature had other plans and flitted away off her arm and back towards the dense trees. They watched it until it disappeared.

SIX

>>> > MR. APPLETTE, DISGUISED as an Aloralock, saw the two powerful telepaths speaking to each other and thought it odd that they weren't using their gifts to communicate. Mr. Applette was no telepath, but he wished he were. He flew away deep into the forest and then turned into an owl. He hated the Aloralock shell, too easy to be eaten by a great number of predators. He needed something with wings to cover distance faster but something much less edible than a small insect.

SEVEN

>>> > SEBASTIAN'S TRANSIT LAUNCHED and then hovered, "Celeste look over there."

She looked to where he was pointing and saw another beautiful creature. "Oh it's magnificent. Just like you told me. They're gorgeous and they look so healthy. How many of them are there?"

He counted silently, "It's a streak of three tigers. Looks like a tigress and her cubs."

"A streak?"

"Yes, that's what it's called for a group of them, although they really are solitary creatures. I imagine this family will break up soon. Looks like the cubs are almost fully grown."

"I'm grateful they're here and thriving."

Sebastian smiled, "I'm glad I had a chance to show them to you. I think showing you tigers was something I mentioned to you some time ago. It's good to keep promises no matter how small."

The transit ride home would've been silent had it not been for the atmospheric music Sebastian chose to play. Neither one had realized it on a conscious level, but home was defined by wherever the other was. Celeste didn't want to fall asleep under a roof other than where he lay his head and Sebastian didn't want to wake up where she wasn't still sleeping (and snoring) somewhere under a roof he had provided for her.

The still air was covered in piano and guitar. Another song Celeste had never heard, by another band Jonathan had never let her listen to. She was embarrassed by the lack of musical knowledge she had, considering how badly she wanted to be a singer. But Sebastian's extensive knowledge of musical acts was exponentially larger than her own, and she could learn. When she was younger, she listened to what her parents liked, which was classical. She certainly grew to love that style of music but she knew there was much more to listen to.

She listened to the words of the song about being spied on and being discovered while on the run. It was an emotional song and it made a deep connection in her.

Living as Jonathan's prisoner, Celeste quickly discovered he had a network of spies continually keeping an eye on her and reporting to him. Over the years she tried to work around these obstacles, but her singing was always found out about and listening to music was forbidden. Jonathan had found out what she loved and crushed it.

The song ended on a somber note and Celeste realized she had fallen in love with it.

She looked over at Sebastian. His eyes were closed. It looked as though he was sleeping, but she knew he wasn't. His head was back on the headrest and his hands were clasped in his lap.

This was one of the few times she saw him put his Atlas on autopilot. She figured he probably had as much on his mind as she did.

Another beautiful song came on by the same group. Electric guitars this time and drums, but still the same melodic ethereal feel. She stared at Sebastian, but he hadn't opened his eyes. She thought of all the places he'd taken her, all the music he was constantly introducing her to, all the knowledge, history, and facts he spoke of with such passion, all the things he told her about – he even broke her of her fear of heights – all those memories seemed to culminate into this moment.

She understood something new, but something she had known all along. She was hopelessly and completely in love with Sebastian. Everything in her, in the universe confirmed it.

She finally looked away from him and closed her eyes. A single tear escaped from underneath her lashes and she quickly wiped it away.

She had the strangest mix of emotions. Nothing in life had ever prepared her for something like this. She was simultaneously elated to be alive, but also seized by fear of losing him. Elation and fear – what a strange mix and how hard it was to be a Human with all these complex emotions. She briefly wondered what it was like for Sebastian. What it was like to be Lanyx. Were the emotions the same or even more intense? Which led her to wonder what his feelings were for her? How deep did they go? Was he in love with her too? Could Sebastian even let himself go completely and fall in love with her?

She stared at him again, but didn't realize it. She wondered if he was awake or if he had uncharacteristically fallen asleep on her.

He opened his right eye and looked at her, "You're going to bore a hole through me my lady."

She immediately looked away and out the window. The city lights of Daviens were fast approaching.

He lowered the volume of the music, "I'd love to know what you were just thinking about. Your walls are up so strong right now like I never imagined they could be. You're getting to be quite the master with your mind powers. You have a secret I should know about?"

She looked over at him. He straightened up in his seat and turned his face towards her. They were staring into each other's eyes. Her heart was now hammering in her chest.

"I've got a lot of thoughts going through my head right now. It's not easy trying to sort them all out. I'm sure you know how that is."

"Yes I do. Anything you need to talk about?" He reached his hand over to the back of her neck and lightly rubbed it. His touch felt so good.

"Nothing that won't keep. We're almost home anyway."

Sebastian hadn't noticed her use of the word "home" to describe his apartment, but had he, it would've triggered a ripple through him that would've caused the events of the next few days to happen much faster.

While the Atlas made its final approach to his docking space, Celeste's worry was growing about Sebastian trying to kill Dax.

Sebastian was thinking about how much time he really had before he must leave.

When they returned to the apartment, they started to pack up some of his weapons with Celeste thinking of ways to convince him to let her go with him. She went to bed earlier than him but lay awake for hours trying to answer questions she couldn't possibly guess the answers to. Her mind had turned the question over to her heart after coming up with no solutions – was Sebastian already in love with her? How was a Lanyx man supposed to act with a woman he was in love with? Should she tell him first? Should she tell him at all? If she did tell him, would that stop him from leaving? Her heart seemed to do no better than her mind with figuring it all out.

She missed her mother and wished she was here now. Her mom always gave her good advice. Things like, try not to worry about the past, it's all done. Try not to worry about the future, you can only do so much for it. Just try to live in the now. Enjoy what you have, because it won't always be the way it is right now. If only she paid more attention to her mother's advice when she was younger.

She should've given her parents a lot more hugs.

It was a long while before she fell asleep.

EIGHT

>>> > CELESTE WAS STARTLED awake by a loud boom of thunder. She lay looking up at the ceiling for five minutes before realizing she couldn't go back to sleep. She looked at her clock: 3:15 in the morning. Way too early to get up, so she put on her favorite lacey robe and stepped outside her bedroom. She looked around and saw no sign of Sebastian. She checked the entire floor and couldn't find him. She pushed the drapes aside and peeked outside at the balcony. A big storm was raging. Lots of bright lightning illuminating the night, followed by monstrous cracks of thunder. It sounded like the sky was splitting open. It reminded her of the holowindows. She wondered how Sebastian's grandparents met and fell in love. She wondered who said "I love you" first.

She carefully made her way upstairs. The door to the meditation room was open just a crack, enough for her to see faint light coming from inside. She cracked the door a little wider to stick her head in.

The room she saw only once before had been transformed by candle-light. There were white candles, one foot high on the hard wood floor all along the edges of the dark room. They must've been scented because there was an aroma of cinnamon, nutmeg, and sugar in the air – it smelled like autumn back on Earth. She was reminded of falling yellow leaves, Halloween, and apple cider. She smiled at the pleasant memories only certain scents can bring back to the mind. The room looked even more inviting with the wall to wall, floor to ceiling mirror on one end reflecting all the candlelight back, doubling the glow. There wasn't any substitute for real old-fashioned candlelight. There was music she'd never heard before playing in the background and Sebastian sat on the floor quietly on top of a small rug. His legs were crossed under him as he meditated.

A deep rumble of thunder tore out after lightning lit up the entire room. She opened the door completely and looked to her left. She saw the entire wall was window and the drapes were pulled back. She could see the city spread out before her just like the view from the balcony. She felt a little exposed with the lack of privacy but walked close to where he sat anyway.

"You want to speak to me but you don't know what to say…" Sebastian didn't open his eyes. He left his hands where they were, resting on his knees.

He continued, "You want to speak to me without saying anything *verbally*…"

Celeste sat down across from him on the empty rug. She wondered briefly why there were two rugs on the ground. Had he anticipated she would meditate with him eventually?

The rest of their conversation went on without a word.

<It's very early for you to be starting your day sunshine.>

<The storm woke me up. I was having trouble sleeping anyway. Have you gone to bed yet?>

<No. Finishing my meditations on today's events. I was going to go to bed shortly.>

<What are today's meditations?> She copied his body's positioning except for closing her eyes. She tried at first, but she kept peeking at him. He was only wearing white boxer shorts and it was hard for her not to admire his physique.

<I was thinking of how far you've come in many aspects. Your 7's are in exceptional shape. I think I've taught you everything I can.>

<So I have nothing left to learn about them?>

<The smartest student continues to learn their whole life. Even I, who was born with this power, have learned things from you,> he paused, <Don't feel like closing your eyes?>

"How do you know I'm looking at you?" she closed her eyes.

<Even though I'm Lanyx, I'm still mostly Human. Your species can tell when someone is looking at them. Can't you feel someone's stare, even if they're behind you? Or am I wrong on this?>

<You're right. I suppose that's the extent of our sixth sense.>

He opened his eyes and looked at her. She was wearing a sexy lace robe that matched her black nightgown underneath. Her hair was a bit messy and hanging loose over her shoulders. She looked beautiful.

<Now you're looking at me. I can feel that.>

He smiled. "Why don't we communicate verbally? I enjoy hearing your voice late at night."

She opened her eyes and smiled, "What do you mean by that?"

"What I said. I enjoy hearing your voice, that's why I almost always prefer talking with you over telepathy. You look ravishing by the way."

She blushed, "Thank you handsome."

"Oh I haven't heard that in a while. Thank you. I missed hearing that one."

"Did you really?"

"Yes. It's always nice to hear that a beautiful woman thinks you're anything complimentary. Handsome's always flattering though."

"Well since you've started calling me sunshine and honey, I suppose I'm a little behind in pet names. I'll have to try to make up for it…"

She got on her knees and moved behind him. She put her lips next to his ear and whispered, "Baby." She started rubbing his shoulders, and felt his skin break out in goosebumps.

"Ah, you liked that?" She smiled.

"I do. Especially when you say it like that."

She scratched his back with her nails gently. She looked out the windows as another lightning bolt tore the sky apart. He brought his shoulders forward, enjoying her touch.

She looked at him, "Does that feel good?"

"It feels really good. I can never seem to reach all those places you're hitting."

She looked at his scars from the Helena Rebels War and stopped scratching.

"You know, you don't have to stop that. I mean, if you wanted to keep scratching, that'd be fine with me. But, I think I'd probably make you stop after a couple days," he smiled.

She kissed the scars closest to his neck and shoulders then moved down his back slowly, making sure she kissed each one.

"Or I suppose you could start doing that. Yeah, sure. That's"—his eyes rolled up into his head as he closed them—"nice."

With her legs folded underneath her, she put her arms underneath his and held onto him from behind as she settled her chin onto his shoulder, "You deserve some spoiling. I think you're way overdue."

He put his hands on top of hers, "Maybe. But it's way more fun to spoil you."

She looked towards the window again and saw the rain sheeting down the glass.

"It's safe, Celeste. No one can see us."

"Yeah but you have candles in here."

He chuckled, "I have taken every precaution to guarantee no one can see us, no matter how bright it is in here. And if you're worried about safety, I also have techtonic plates over this window. I can pull the drapes if you'd like."

"No. I guess not if they can't see in."

"O can you switch the glass please?"

"Right away sir."

The big window went from clear to opaque.

Celeste scoffed, "Why don't you have it like that all the time?"

"I wanted to watch the rain, besides, it doesn't matter how that glass looks, people still can't see in."

"When I walked in here you were meditating with your eyes closed."

"Ophelia, can you switch the mirror?"

The mirror along the side of the room turned opaque.

Sebastian smiled, "Yes, I had my eyes closed, but I look at the rain too sometimes. You want to see something I bet you've never seen before?"

She raised an eyebrow, "Okay."

"O, activate the candles."

"Yes, Erebos."

Vignette sleeves rose up from the bottom of the candles to the tops, and shadows projected on the walls. Each candle had different moving pictures, telling a piece of the story. As she looked around the room, all the candles together told a complete narrative.

"Chronicle candles! Those are really rare, but I've seen these before," Celeste smiled.

"Not this story you haven't. Really take your time to look at these. The first one's over there." He pointed off to her right near the right edge of the window.

She reluctantly left her position near him and walked over to the first candle. There was a tall cloaked man walking through hallways of a building. Then a skull and crossbones symbol fills the entire frame. The cloaked man stops when he sees a petite female figure in the distance. A pair of eyes blinks on the wall, then the female form shows up close to him and walks towards him. A crowd of people separate them as she persists in reaching him.

"Sebastian, how did you do this?"

"Keep going," he motioned with his hand for her to continue.

She moved to the next one and looked as the cloaked man and the woman stood near a square pillar. The man looks at the woman and kisses her. Then she slaps him. He takes her hand and they run together out of the frame.

The next candle showed a transit launching off the ground and leaving Earth. As it approaches The Jump the scene changes to the woman sitting inside. A huge exclamation point shows up over her head and Celeste laughed. The woman falls asleep and wakes up looking at Praxis on approach from the transit. The cloaked man is no longer covered and stares at the woman.

Celeste looked over to Sebastian and smiled. He returned her smile.

The next candle showed an exterior balcony overlooking the city. The man and the woman are standing, wrapped around each other in a passionate kiss. The frame fills with two anatomically correct diagrams of a Human and Lanyx brain facing each other. A big exclamation point is drawn over the Lanyx brain first and the Human brain gets one second.

Celeste laughed again and moved to the next candle.

This one showed the petite woman decked out in a ball gown standing alone. The tall man comes into the frame wearing a formal suit and puts his hand out to her. She takes it and they dance spinning on the dancefloor as several other swirling couples surround them.

She looked over at Sebastian, "That one might be my favorite so far."

He smiled.

She moved to the next candle. This one showed a large empty bed. The petite woman positions herself on the bed dressed only in her bra and underwear. The tall man approaches the bed and crawls on his hands and knees to her. They kiss when he reaches her and the picture turns to smoke.

"I hope you're not planning on showing these to any of our friends…" she giggled and moved to the next candle.

This one showed the couple on the bow of a ship, an island off in the distant ocean. The ship drops anchor next to the island and the couple get off and walk on the beach.

The last one showed the tall man waving goodbye to the petite woman as she launches in a transit alone. The man looks sad and the face of a Praxian clock fills the frame. Time passes slowly and then the petite woman and tall man are reunited at a café table with a large crowd around them.

She stood staring at Sebastian, "These are fantastic, but you stopped kind of early in our story. You have eight candles done, but there's twenty around the room."

"There's some things I don't want to remember…"

Thunder clapped out and Celeste jumped.

Sebastian continued, "Letting you go, your kidnapping, your amnesia."

"Those are parts of us though."

He nodded, "Come here."

She went to him and resumed the position she had before.

A warm smile spread across his face, "That's better."

She smiled behind him.

"O, make the window clear."

The window became transparent and the storm looked more intense than before.

"So you like the chronicle candles?"

"Oh, I loved them! Who drew your shadowlines? They were cute almost like sophisticated cartoons."

"Ophelia did."

Celeste opened her mouth to speak, then closed it, then opened it again, and closed it again.

Sebastian laughed, "Yeah, that's what I said."

"But she's an AI. She doesn't have any hands."

"You're one hundred percent correct. I told her I needed an artist and she suggested she do it. I let her try and what she came back with was pretty good. Wasn't it O?"

"Thank you sir. I did my best to please you."

"And I appreciate your efforts very much. You did a good job."

"Stop sir, you'll make me blush."

Celeste made a face, "Did she just giggle?"

He nodded, "She had some updates. Things that are supposed to make her more lifelike and emotional. That's probably part of that. As long as she doesn't start calling me baby cakes, I think we're okay."

"Alright baby cakes," Celeste joked.

Sebastian's face lit up, "Now see, it's different when *you* say it. Then it's kind of…sexy." He growled out the last word and she heard it all the way through her body.

She swallowed hard, "Can I ask you something?"

"You just did."

She could hear the smile in his sarcastic answer.

"Ah, funny Bastian is back," she squeezed him as best she could. "Why are you okay using pet names now?"

"I've always done that, haven't I? I think the first time was when I called you beautiful, just like you've always called me handsome. It's nothing new."

"But it is."

He carefully turned his head towards her and she loosened her grip to look at him.

"No, no. Don't do that." He tightened his arms down on hers and encouraged her to go back to how she was positioned before. "I want you close. Keep your chin on my shoulder please."

She smiled.

He kissed her cheek and left his lips close to her skin. He whispered, "Now, you were saying?"

"You calling me pet names, other than beautiful…it is new. Something's different."

"And you want to know why." His voice was sexy and low, it drove her crazy. She loved it when he whispered.

"Mmmm hmmm."

"You already know. I think you can feel something's different, but I know you want to hear it out loud."

She smiled again.

"I almost lost you for good and I found I couldn't bear it. You are irreplaceable to me. I want you to know now and always how very important to me you've become."

She moved her chin off his shoulder and looked at him. He let her move this time without trying to keep her close. She kissed him softly. "You are very important to me too. Thank you for telling me." She stayed in that position while he asked her something she didn't sense coming.

"What were you thinking earlier on the transit ride home from my grandmother's?"

Her mental walls clamped down hard.

"I felt that. That tells me it was something very important."

"How can you tell it's important? I thought you weren't supposed to sense anything, except that my thoughts were blocked to you."

"Let's say you and I are submerged up to our foreheads in a large lake on opposite sides. Our ears, eyes, almost everything is under the surface and we're both standing still. I have the crown of my head above the surface and a small stone falls into the lake near you, making a ripple. I feel it. I feel the water being disturbed around me, but I don't know what disturbed the surface. That's how it is with this. When it's a small pebble making a ripple, it's a small thought. If it's a boulder, I feel a big wave on my side, then that's an important thought. I know when your walls are up. I know when you clamp them down or release them. I can sense when you're thinking and how important those thoughts are. When you were thinking tonight in the Atlas, I knew it was important. It was big for you, but I didn't know what it was about, that's why I asked. That's why I'm asking again, because you downplayed it and I knew you lied about it. True, I'm prying, but it left me curious. When I feel something that big coming off of you, it definitely arouses my interest. So, are you going to tell me?"

She felt trapped. She thought this subject had been dropped. She was terrified to tell him she realized she was in love with him. What if he wasn't in love with her? What if he never fell in love with her? She had read the books, seen the movies, and heard the horror stories of her friend's broken hearts. Men didn't want to commit. Men got very scared when women said "I love you" first. He already dumped her once and the pain had been immense. And that was *before* she was in love with him. She was afraid of losing him. Sebastian, the person she loved most, more than anything, more than her own life, could just decide to up and leave her anytime he wanted to for any reason. Why give him another reason? She decided she couldn't tell him. Not now, maybe not ever if it meant him bolting from fear. If he said I love you first, things would be different, but he hadn't. She didn't know if he would ever say those words to her.

"Celeste? Come back to me. You're somewhere far away."

"You're right. I was thinking of something very important and big. I'm afraid…I need more time to think about that thing, privately. You've always had a way of getting into my thoughts whether I wanted you in there or not, so…I'm asking for more privacy and trying to remind you as gently as possib—"

"Mind my own business, literally. I promise to do better at not prying. I've just never had this before – this power with a Human, with a woman, with someone as strong as you are mentally. Our 7's, this relationship, our emotional connection to one another, this is all unique. Extremely unique. I guess I'm trying to navigate some new boundaries and I just don't always do so well."

"I understand Bastian. And I appreciate your understanding as well."

She leaned down and placed a lingering kiss on his shoulder, then moved it up to his neck.

He said nothing, but he wanted to. He wanted to push for the real answer. It was driving him crazy that he found someone, who at first, had been telegraphing thoughts to him left and right and now there was nothing. Her level of power was keeping him from knowing her intentions and all content of her thoughts. All he had were those vague feelings of heavy thoughts verses minor ones. This was something new and something, if he was truly honest with himself, he didn't like. He was desperate to know what that big something was. *She might slip up if she's extremely emotional*, he thought to himself, *maybe I could find out then.*

"Sebastian. Let it go."

His eyes opened wide. She just pulled something on him that he had always done to her. *So that's what it felt like.*

She kissed his neck a little more and lightly brushed her lips along his skin while she asked, "What will it take to make you forget about it huh?"

He cleared his throat, "Sorry honey. I'm trying."

"I guess I'll have to do better." She smiled and he did too.

He felt her tighten her hands on his chest as she pushed her breasts against his back and suddenly her body became a lot more important over her earlier secret thoughts. She sucked on his neck slightly and he tilted his head to the side letting her tongue and lips do what they wanted to him. Her kisses moved up to his cheek, then he turned his head to meet her lips with his own. He changed positions so she was facing him and he was on his knees. He put his arms around her waist and eased her up onto him. She wrapped her legs around his torso and her arms around his neck.

In one fluid motion, he put one hand to the ground for balance momentarily, and then stood with her wrapped around him. He walked towards the doorway and down the hall while kissing her.

She had no trouble holding onto him as he stepped down the spiral stairs. He was more sure footed than any man she'd ever been with, but she still stopped kissing him long enough for him to safely traverse the staircase.

<*I could get used to this handsome.*> She was nuzzling his neck with her face.

"So you're telling me this is the official preferred travel method for the queen? Well that would make for an interesting billboard for Praxis tourism."

She giggled into his neck and he felt her hot breath spread across his skin. He smiled and put her down on the bed in her room. She finally loosened her grip and kissed him, but when she did, she knew he wasn't going to continue any further. She stopped and he moved away from her.

"You're going back upstairs aren't you?"

"Yes."

She had had it with all of his teasing and foreplay and then him stopping. She wanted an answer this time. "We had a really nice moment and now...you're just going to leave me here? Why don't you want to sleep with me? Is it because I'm a Human or something else about me? Something I'm doing wrong or am I...repulsing you somehow?" A single tear ran down her face.

He shook his head, "It's quite the opposite Celeste. I'm drawn to you and it's very strong. You should understand that by now."

She tilted her head and felt more tears welling up in her eyes, "Why won't you make love to me then?"

Sebastian didn't want to have this conversation here and now. He let out a long sigh and sat next to her on the bed. He put his hand along her cheek and she pulled away from him.

"Please, Sebastian. I want an answer."

He had a new emotion on his face that Celeste had never seen before. It was hopelessness and she hated seeing it.

"You've seen me as your hero all this time," he took both hands and ran them over his hair, "I rescued you from Jonathan, from kidnappers, and then from sareeaveous. Shit, what haven't I saved you from?! Plus your husband died violently in front of you and regardless of how you think about it, that event alone would be traumatic for anyone to see. I want you to be clear minded about us. I want you to have some time alone to see what you want. You haven't really had time to process everything that's happened to you. I don't want to be any sort of rebound lover for you. You see what I'm getting at?"

She shook her head, "This sounds like some of what you said that terrible day you broke up with me."

"It's true that there is a phenomena where people fall in love with their rescuers – like victims with police, or burn victims with firefighters, stuff like that. What if that's what this is for you? With all my powers I can't see the genesis of your feelings for me."

"You don't believe me if I say that's not it, I imagine?"

"I don't think you'd know. And it's not just that. For all that you've seen of me, I feel like you still haven't seen the real me. I fear what you'll think of me after you do. I am not a hero. I kill. I've killed for a long time, and many beings; in wars, for my job, and in Fran's case, by accident. I want you to see me for who I really am, not the man you think me to be, or the way you want to see me. There are some dark and cold places inside of me that you have never witnessed."

She stiffened, "The day you broke up with me you were pretty cold."

"Well, it gets much worse than that, trust me. It doesn't compare to the state of mind you have to be in to do what I do on a regular basis. I live a difficult life and I've always lived it alone. You've been exposed to a small part of it and I don't think you'd want to stay if you saw how far down I can go. I just don't think you know what you're getting into with me. Making love complicates everything and it's a step I'm not ready to take yet. Can you be patient with me? Please, Celeste?"

She was getting annoyed with him until he asked for her patience. If the roles were reversed and she was the one asking for time before they were intimate, she would want him to do the same thing – to be understanding, to be patient. To be willing to wait until she was comfortable with everything before she had sex.

"I...want to be closer to you. I want to be closer than we've ever been, but I'm not going to pressure you into anything you're not ready for. If you're not comfortable, you're not comfortable. I understand. But will you tell me...you haven't been telling me you're more experienced than what you really are right? You said you had one night stands, but that wasn't you trying to show me how virile you are right?"

He raised his eyebrows, "Oh, you mean am I a virgin?" he blushed, "No, I'm definitely not. The one-night stands were real, but it's true that

I've never been with a Human woman before, so this is somewhat uncharted territory for me. I'm a virgin to sex with Humans I guess."

"Well, we're even there. I've never been with a Lanyx before so…"

"That brings me to another point about waiting. Lanyx are part animal. Sex can be…rough, strong, and intense. It might be something you're not expecting. I don't know if you'll even like it."

She gave him a wry smile, "Oh I think I'm gonna like it. You're an intense man. That's always been evident. I like it about you. I like our intensity together. It drives me crazy in the best possible way. I've thought about sex between us a lot and if it's as intense as you are, then that sounds…" She dropped her voice down to a whisper and put her lips to his ear, "hot. I'm looking forward to it."

He started thinking of cold showers, blizzards, freezing snow. *Cold, cold, cold.* He took a deep breath, "I'm flattered, but I still don't think you understand how animalistic I can become during that…event."

"You're not deterring me yet," she paused and put her hand to his cheek, "But we will wait until you're ready and I'll try to be more understanding. It's just…" she bit her lip, "You're incredibly sexy and hard to resist. I've never wanted a man the way I want you, but I want to respect your wishes, truly."

He liked seeing her bite her lip. He wanted to bite her lip, bite her ears, neck, breasts, shoulders, anywhere and everywhere across the landscape of her body. He tried to avoid getting another uncontrollable hard-on. He thought of old wrinkly men, more cold showers, ice cubes down his pants, anything that was incredibly unsexy. *You can do this Raynes. You can do this.*

"Sebastian did you hear me? I said it's okay for us to wait."

He blinked a few times, "I appreciate that so much Celeste. I really do," he smiled at her and then took her hand and kissed the palm. He went to the doorway and leaned against it, looking at her, "I'm going to get back to my meditations. If you need anything," he tapped his finger to his temple quickly three times, "Just call me." He started to close her door.

"Wait. I want to say something."

"I'm listening." *But please don't say anything else erotic.*

"I don't need time alone to know I like you. I want you to understand that I *am* clear headed about us. I'm not afraid to be alone. I don't need a man in my life. Any girl that wouldn't want to be with you is a damn fool. I see you clearly for the man you are, not the man I want you to be. And I understand the kind of life you lead. I'm prepared to deal with all the things you think are going to scare me off. You're teaching me how to be a lot stronger than I ever thought I could be." She smiled and winked.

She reminded him she was much more than a heavenly erotic creature. He walked back to her and leaned over to kiss her softly on the lips. Then he kneeled down on one knee in between her legs and placed his hands on her thighs. "You *are* incredibly strong. You stayed with an abusive, weak-minded prick who liked to feel powerful by punching his wife because you had to. Because you had an entire *planet's* weight on your shoulders. You loved your people enough to protect them from a war breaking out if you tried to leave your arranged marriage. You suffered greatly for billions of Humans you will never meet. I believed you were an amazing woman before I met you. And you know what? After I got to know you, you proved me right. The kind of strength you've shown, puts me to shame."

She was tearing up again, but smiling, "Thank you Bastian."

He stood up and went to the door, "Try to get some rest."

She laughed, "Oh sure, raging storm, wonderful smoking hot guy to make out with who says the sweetest things to me. Yeahhhh it's gonna be real easy for me to fall asleep now."

He smiled at her, "Goodnight sunshine."

"Goodnight sexy."

He closed her bedroom door and returned to his meditation room. He felt guilty, criminal even for lying to her, especially now, especially about this particular subject. While it was true that part of him was apprehensive about what she would think of his life after they dated on a regular basis, even though he was truly concerned that her head wasn't clear after losing her husband, even though he would've liked for her to have time alone in between relationships, even though he thought she was seeing him through rose-colored glasses and not for who he really was – none of those were the real reason he wouldn't sleep with her.

As he sat down on the rug and crossed his legs, he stared out the window as the storm continued to rage on. He thought of the fear inside of himself that prevented them from being together. The cowardice inside of him that wouldn't allow sex to happen.

If they were meant to fall in love, if they were meant to lock into each other and become bond mates, if they made love and consummated their bond, he would be powerless to stop his love for her. It would be impossible to let her go. He wouldn't be strong enough to let her live a life without him and one where she might be safest, where she might stay alive because she had nothing to do with him.

That fear of causing her death simply for loving her was what kept him from making love with her. That fear of repeating history with what happened to Fran so long ago, he couldn't handle. He really didn't want Celeste to know about the bonds that sex created for someone like him with someone he cared for so deeply.

Agathon's words came back to him. *Love yourself and see yourself the way she does.* He didn't know if he could do it. How could he forgive himself for everything he's done? How could he love himself after all the chaos he's created over his entire life? How could he see himself the way Celeste does? He didn't think it was possible. But he prayed for it. He prayed.

CHAPTER 35

TIME

>>> > **"I'M GOING TO** leave tomorrow," Sebastian blurted out over breakfast.

She froze in place, a sense of dread washing over her, "Tomorrow?"

"I think the Brotherhood might move somewhere else soon if I wait too long. It's a hunch based on a little intel, but I have to trust my instincts. I can't let them relocate. It will set me back possibly by months."

She couldn't finish her meal, "If you go tomorrow, I want to go with you." She went to the sink and washed her plate.

He stayed at the breakfast table, leaning back in his chair, "You know that can't happen. I want you to stay here, where I know you're safe. You'd only be a distraction."

She kept her back to him, "Then I want more time with you."

Sebastian came up behind her, "I don't want us to have to worry about this anymore. The time to act is now." He sighed, "You know I'd like to stay here with you longer, but…"

"But nothing Sebastian. You're going to go over there and get yourself killed!" She walked away from him and into her bedroom. She sat on the bed and felt like coming unglued. Part of her understood why he felt he needed to do this, but a big selfish part of her, didn't want him to go. What if something went wrong? What if he never came home? He was a big part of her life. She wanted him there with her every day. She loved him, she couldn't lose him now. She heard him knock on the door softly.

"Come in."

He stood at the door, "Maybe…I could wait another couple days, but that would be the absolute maximum I can push this back."

He waited for her response but she was silent. She sat trying to flatten out the wrinkles in her pencil skirt that formed over her lap. She couldn't look at him for fear of breaking into tears. She simply couldn't sum up a response that was adequate to express how she had waited to find him her whole life and now the man she loved was offering only two more days together, like somehow that was enough. There would never be enough time with him she feared.

He stressed, "I can't sit here and pretend like everything's okay. There's an army of who knows how many out there looking for us and they won't quit until we're found. I will bring the battle to them and I *will* finish it. I'm sorry Celeste, but two more days is all I can offer and even that's more than I should." He left the door open and walked into his own bedroom, then went into the safe room and closed the door behind him. Even if she wanted to communicate now, she couldn't – the safe room walls guaranteed that.

He needed to be alone to prepare for battle.

She was stressed and she knew the best way to get these feelings out of her system was to work out. She changed and went to the gym. She turned up the volume on the music and beat her frustrations out on the punching bag. First the bag was Jon. She punched him for making her prisoner in a miserable marriage and for abusing her so badly she lost her foot. She kicked him for mocking, belittling, and violating her. Then the bag was Dax. She hit him for lying, kidnapping her, and making Sebastian leave to go kill him. Then the bag was Sebastian. She beat him up for deciding to leave and not take her with him.

She stopped hitting the bag when she started crying.

TWO

>>> > AFTER A LONG hot shower and a glass of tea, Celeste checked Sebastian's room. The safe room door was still closed and she mentally reached out for him, but couldn't sense him. She decided it might be best to stay clear of him for the rest of the day. Let him come to her when he's ready. She took her holobook out onto the balcony and read for the rest of the afternoon, trying to escape into someone else's problems.

When the sun sat low in the sky, she heard the balcony door open and Sebastian came out. Her heart beat a little faster. *What if he leaves and he doesn't come back?* She pretended to be engrossed in her holobook, but his presence was distracting. He leaned against the railing, facing away from the sunset, staring at her. Her palms sweat thinking of what he was about to say. She looked up from her holobook and stared back at him, "Something you need Sebastian?"

"Yes. I need you to be okay with this," he folded his arms across his chest.

She stood up in front of him and caught a whiff of his cologne. He was freshly showered and smelled incredible. She tried to ignore how sexy he looked standing there in a three-piece suit. She noticed it was the same one he wore the day they met. That alone made her slip a notch closer to crying.

"I don't know if I can be okay with this. I worry about you getting hurt...or worse." She felt a lump growing in her throat, "What if you don't come back? Promise me you'll be back safe and sound...right here in my arms again."

"Goddamn it Celeste! Don't make this harder on me than it already is!"

"I don't want you to go."

He could see there was genuine panic building behind her eyes.

He hated this fucking situation.

She pleaded, "If I can't go with you, I want a promise you'll be back. Please?"

"I won't make a promise to you I can't keep. That risk of death is there every time I do an assassination, every time I do a dangerous job, hell, every time I cross the street, could be my day to die." He watched a single tear trail down her cheek.

"Please don't say things like that. I don't want to hear you talk about dying." She turned her face up to the ceiling, but closed her eyes and left them closed. She wanted to get herself back under control before she completely lost it.

He sighed, "I can't control when my time is up. I can't cheat death. It's inevitable, but I don't plan on dying on Tiletan." He paused and moved closer to her, putting his hands on her shoulders. He leaned down and kissed her tear away. "I need you to be strong honey. Come on, no more tears."

She opened her eyes and stared at his face, "I'm trying. This isn't easy for me. I don't want to let you go, at least not without me going too."

"You think this is easy for me? I've never had to leave anyone behind like this before. It's always been me against the world. I've never had to consider taking someone with me who I care about like I do you," his brows drew together in an agonized expression, "Trust me Celeste, I want to come back here to you. I've lived alongside death for my entire life, but this is the first time I feel I'm alive. I've lived in shadow, hidden in darkness. It's like you're the first light I'm ever seeing. You illuminate things for me I've never witnessed. You show me things I've never seen."

"Can you make a promise to me you *can* keep then?"

He paused, "I can promise you I will do everything I can to get back to you safe and as fast as possible. I can honestly tell you I *don't* want to be away from you. You've resurrected a part of me that I thought was dead and buried long ago. You've changed things for me. You've changed me."

All of these things were wonderful for Celeste to hear. He had opened a floodgate on his own and told her things she ached to hear for a very long time. But she reminded herself she didn't know whether he was leaving the next day, or two days from now, or if he'd delay even longer. She wanted to enjoy each beautiful thing he said to her, but they were coming so fast all at once and the whole time in the back of her mind, she worried his departure was imminent. Suddenly, time was so short between them. The clock was moving much too fast and there was nothing she could do to stop it.

And even though all of what he said was moving and powerful, she realized he was only saying it under threat of death. This is what it took for him to be telling her these things.

"Celeste?"

"I'm listening."

"You're thinking."

Celeste thought of what her mother said to her when she was complaining about being a young princess and longed to be an adult – "Celeste dearie, try to live in the moment."

"I am right here with you. You said I've changed you."

"Yes."

Her voice carried with it a little uncertainty, "Have I really?"

"Yes, of course. You've changed everything. You've given me a reason to *want* to live again, instead of just going through the motions of existing day to day. And I don't want to die now. For a long time, I did. Sometimes I even wanted some of my jobs to go wrong so I wouldn't have to kill myself. The day I met you was the first day in years I didn't think of suicide. At first you just kept me busy enough where I didn't have time to think of it. Then later, I realized I didn't want to die because I didn't want to leave you."

"I can't stand the thought of anything happening to you," her voice was shakier than she would've liked.

"I will be as careful as possible. I promise."

She was too afraid to ask when he was really going to leave, "I'm so scared Sebastian. I can't support this decision for you to go alone. We are a team. We should go together. If you go alone, I don't know what's going to happen."

He moved his hands from her shoulders to either side of her face. "I don't either, but I know it's going to be Constantine or me so I have to make damn sure it's him, and that I strike first. This fight is between my brother and I. That's how it started, that's how it should finish."

"But you wouldn't have seen him again if it wasn't for me. I'm the reason you ran into each other. I'm the reason you're at odds with him now."

"No you're not. That's not the case at all. If you're looking for a reason — my 7's bond with my dad is a good place to start. Constantine never understood that kind of mental connection and how could he? I'm pretty sure he still believes that my father loved me more than him even though I tried to tell him otherwise. But I want you to know my parents never favored me over him because of my telepathy. They loved us both the same, but Constantine was always so jealous. He always wanted whatever I had. But Fran is what pushed him over the edge. I imagine her dumping him and then dating me probably made it seem like I was everyone's first choice. He probably felt he was second best to anyone he cared about."

"Yeah, and then I come along and he finds out that you're my first choice as well. It's just a really weird coincidence."

"But it's not Celeste. I don't believe in coincidence remember? You finding me was fate even though I was actively eluding you. Constantine finding the woman I care about was also fate. I don't think you have anything to do with him and I fighting. My brother is not a good man. He's brought this on himself. Constantine tricked you and lied to you. He pretended to be something he wasn't and when you let your guard down, he attacked you. If someone attacks you, they attack me. Make no mistake that I will *always* protect what's mine. He's done things to you that are indefensible. No matter who it was, my brother, or anyone else, I'd kill them regardless. Constantine needs to be dealt with — it needs to be now, and I need to do it alone. I wish you would agree with me that this is the right thing to do for us. Please understand there's no other way."

He will not relent. He's so damn stubborn! "I think there are other ways, but you refuse to accept them." She took a deep breath. She didn't want to argue with him or think of any of this right now. She gave up the fight. Maybe he'd change his mind, maybe he'd leave in a few days instead of tomorrow. "Let's not fight about this. That's the last thing I want to do with you. I want to try something that hasn't been easy for me."

He took his hands away from her face and raised his eyebrows.

"I want to live in the moment with you. I don't want to worry about tomorrow or…anything else. I just want to enjoy you, as you are, with me, right now."

He smiled, "I can do that." He didn't think *she* could, but he was fine with the idea for as long as she could last. She was a born worrier.

"You said you'd protect what's yours earlier."

"Damn straight." He chose not to point out that her merely asking about something that happened moments ago was failing to live in the present moment. He thought she would've lasted longer than a few seconds. It amused him.

"Am I yours?" she asked provocatively with a raised eyebrow.

He leaned back against the railing again, elbows resting on the top rail. He flashed an irresistibly devastating grin as his eyes raked boldly over her body. She always looked sexy, but tonight, she looked really lovely to him. Her tight black pencil skirt hugged her every curve just right. She wore a sheer white button down blouse with the top three buttons undone revealing a black corset top underneath. Her ample cleavage made him want to pour kisses over her breasts like warm honey. And of course, she wore the ribbon choker he gave her in what seemed like a lifetime ago now.

She smiled, "Well, I guess that look in your eyes of a hungry wolf must mean something good, but it doesn't exactly answer my question."

"I've wanted you to be mine for a very long time, but what does the lady want?"

"I've always been yours."

"Then you're mine."

She stood up against him and unbuttoned his jacket, putting her arms underneath it and around his body. He didn't move.

She looked up to his face, "Will you wait a couple more days to go? You said you could earlier."

He was silent and looked away from her. The sun had set and they missed it while they were discussing this. He wondered if he'd see another one with her.

"Yes, I'll leave in two days. No more though. I can't afford to wait any longer than that." He put his arms around her and closed his eyes holding her close. "We missed the sunset, but the moons are rising soon. I'd like to watch them come up with you Celeste."

"I'd love to." She stood there wrapped up in his arms and covered underneath his jacket. She loved being this close to him, and enveloped in his physical and emotional warmth. She'd never had anything like this before and she was desperate to hold onto it for as long as possible.

At least she knew now they had a couple more days together.

THREE

>>> > SEBASTIAN AND CELESTE stood side by side along the railing waiting for the last moon to rise. Her breath was still taken away looking at how the rings and shepherd moons held each other in a permanent embrace around the planet.

Sebastian realized this might be the last time he would share this moment with her. His walls were up strong so he wouldn't have to worry about her overhearing any of his thoughts. He paid close attention to her especially after a thought occurred that would give him away. With how emotional she'd been tonight, there was no way she wouldn't react if she sensed anything. So far so good. He didn't want her to know that he thought there was a very good chance that this decision to go into battle alone could be fatal. If he died killing his brother, but Celeste was safe, then his own death wouldn't be in vain. She would be allowed to have the life she always deserved. She could be left in peace and find someone to love. He never had believed he was good enough for a beautiful queen like Celeste. And if he died to save her, he wondered if that was enough to redeem himself in the universe's eyes for being responsible for Fran's death. He looked to Celeste to see if she had any visible reaction to what he had been thinking. She was staring up at the sky, apparently unaware of his thoughts about his own death. Her powers were so strong now that they both didn't know what the other was thinking unless one let down their walls either by accident, or on purpose, knowing they'd probably be read. There were still periods of "static" between them when they couldn't read each other. He thought it had something to do with their emotional states, or if they were trying too hard. He hadn't quite figured it out and he wasn't sure he ever would. The brain was a complicated piece of work and telepathy was still so rare, people with the "gift" didn't want to expose themselves for fear of military applications or to be guinea pigs for some medical experimenting. Either way, they'd be locked into a life they didn't choose. He didn't blame them for keeping quiet. But that meant the pool of documented cases was extremely small. Tough to find any answers with so little information. And being a Human and Lanyx couple didn't help. He had absolutely no research to consult on that, not even a solid rumor.

<Celeste?>

She looked at him, raising an eyebrow, "Yes sexy."

"You remember how I pointed out these moons to you the first night we were together?"

She smiled, "Yes, of course. That first night when you took off that mysterious cloak and you were wearing this suit actually. I was a bit captivated by you."

"A bit?" he teased.

Her smile widened, "I couldn't get over how well dressed you were... Why *are* you wearing this suit? Not that I'm complaining."

"I know you liked it. I remember reading you that night when I took off my cloak. You thought I looked...refined, I think was the word in your mind,"—he smiled at her—"and because I was thinking of going out tonight, maybe. You want to go out and do something, or have dinner?" He pulled out his pocket watch and looked at the time.

"I can't believe you still carry that thing," she paused, "I don't know about going out. That's probably pushing our luck. I think this is nice here, just star gazing with you and talking."

That's the answer he wanted.

He moved behind her and pushed her hair aside, finding and kissing her strawberry mark on her neck. He felt her shiver underneath him. He purposefully exhaled across her neck and she casually dropped her ear to her shoulder allowing him access to kiss her there. He did and she sighed softly. When he paused, she turned around to face him and placed her hands on his shoulders. He surmised any thoughts of their disagreement had melted away from her mind. Hopefully, she was only thinking of living in the moment with him.

He put his hands on her waist, gripping her tightly. "I just asked you out for the first time on a genuine date and you shot me down. I'm not sure I'll be able to recover. I might never get the courage to ask you again. Being turned down by some peasant, no big deal, but being turned down by the Queen of two worlds…my ego just took a nose dive." He was smiling so she knew this was his playful side coming out that she loved.

"Bastian,"—she kissed his cheek—"I'm ecstatic that you asked me out, but that means we'd have to go out in public and we both know it's not safe." She cleared her throat, "Plus I'm not willing to share you with anyone else tonight."

He smiled at her and raised his eyebrows, "Oh really? Queen Celeste isn't good at sharing? I find this hard to believe, maybe I should test it out; find another woman on the street to ask out an—"

"Don't you dare Sebastian Aramis Raynes! Don't you dare. I hoped to find a man like you my whole life and…"

He got serious quick, "And what?"

"And now I want you to be mine. All mine and no one else's…" She instantly thought she said too much. Spilled too many feelings that would overwhelm him and scare him off. She held her breath and waited for him to say something.

"You hoped to find a man like me?" His expression was unreadable and she had no idea what he was thinking.

She closed her eyes tight and sighed. *I've blown it. I just scared the hell out of him. Now he's going to go running, I know it. Damn my mouth!* She tried to fix it, "I mean, you're a smart, sophisticated, handsome man. What woman wouldn't want to find someone like you?" *Stop talking! You're making it worse.*

He silently stared at her. Her heart was hammering so hard in her chest she thought it would burst out.

He sighed, "You know, I used to think hope was a four letter word. I almost gave up on it entirely when my parents were killed. Hope was a luxury I couldn't afford no matter how much coren I acquired over my lifetime."

She bit her lip, "And how do you feel about it now?"

"Hope might be something I should try to believe in again. Maybe it deserves another chance. But as far as you hoping to meet someone like me, that's really hard for me to believe."

Her brows immediately furrowed, "Why? I don't understand."

"You've been a Queen or a Princess your whole life with wealth and people falling at your feet, adoring you. I was born a common Lanyx boy. My family never had a lot of coren. Then I grow up and turn into a criminal, a hit man. I'm complicated and I'm sure I've confused the hell out of you with some of my behavior. I broke up with you and broke your heart. I've given you nothing but a hard time when the conversation turned to dating. How could you have possibly hoped as a little girl that someone as messed up as me would come into your life? How could you have wished to meet an emotionally challenged suicidal assassin?"

He tried to step away from her, but she held on tight. He let his arms hang at his sides and he looked away from her, over her head at the moons.

She gently shook him, "Bastian?"

He shifted his weight from one foot to the other, but that was the extent of his reaction.

She held onto him tighter, "Sebastian, please look at me."

He turned his face to hers but closed his eyes.

She put her hands up to his face without the intention of giving him anything like a deep read. She felt that ping, that ripple in the water analogy he used for their 7's connection. He was right in describing it that way. She could tell he was thinking about a lot of important things, but she couldn't tell what they were specifically. *Definitely better that way,* she thought to herself. Knowing his thoughts when he didn't want her to was a breach of privacy she didn't want to commit. She knew he was struggling with thoughts and feelings, and the feelings were giving him the hardest time. They were in a new place in their relationship and she viewed it as going in the right direction.

"Bastian sweetheart."

That finally made him open his eyes and look at her.

"You have the sweet heart, Celeste."

She nodded, "Yes, and so do you. Are you done seeing the worst in yourself and ignoring all the good things you do?"

He stood silently. His blue eyes shining yellow in the dark.

"Well are you? Because I'm tired of hearing you beat yourself up." Her voice was stern and strong, full of conviction.

Just the tone of her voice started to turn Sebastian on suddenly. He liked her taking control like this. Any time she put him his place, he liked it. She seemed more powerful than he'd seen her before. He put his arms around her waist.

"Bastian, I give you compliments that are honest. I don't lie to you. I believe in my heart, all the way down to the bottom of my soul, that you're a wonderful man. You have everything to offer a woman. You *are* smart, *and* gorgeous, *and* sophisticated. I like the way you protect me, the way you've taken care of me through so many difficult situations. You are so generous…I don't know how you can't see any of these things in yourself. It baffles me. But you know what really bothers me? Other than you not loving and accepting the fantastic person you are, is that you've given me all these things, all of your time, and you've taught me so much. You—"

Sebastian tightened his grip around her waist, "Celeste I'v—"

She didn't let him cut in, "You've taught me to protect myself, about my 7's, about history and other worlds. You've actually cured my acrophobia probably by teaching me to think of you instead of the fear. You've taught me that men can be kind, wonderful, and caring. You've taught me so many things Sebastian. What have I taught you? It seems like almost nothing."

"It's a very old habit of mine – to focus on the worst of myself. I'm not sure when it started – maybe when my parents were killed, or when Fran died. I've tried to emulate my father, *he* was an excellent man. He would be worthy of the compliments you give me. But I also did what I had to to survive. Even though they're gone, I've tried to make my parents proud. But, I think the path I've followed has led me astray of that goal. My mistakes of the past are numerous, but I want to move forward and make my life better from here onward with you. I want to be a better man because of you. I'll try not to put myself down. I promise." He smiled.

"I'm so proud of the man you already are," she kissed him on the cheek.

"And as far as you not teaching me anything…This is not a competition. No one's keeping score on who teaches who what. We'll keep learning from one another over the course of time. And besides, I love to show you new things. I get a kick out of it."

"You do?"

"It's fun for me to bring a royal something she hasn't seen."

"Well you've certainly made me look at the world and my life differently. That's something new you've shown me. My outlook for the future is a happy one now, thanks to you."

"Speaking of looks, I want to show you something else I bet you've never seen before." He quickly let go of her and moved to the corner of the balcony. "Close your eyes."

She smiled, "I know what you're getting so I don't think it really matters." She watched as he grabbed the telescope and started unfolding the tripod.

"Close your eyes anyway my lady. Or else you're going to take all the fun out of it."

She closed her eyes, "Out of what?"

"Out of this."

She was surprised that he silently, without disturbing the air around her, positioned himself in front of her and put his hands on her cheeks. He lifted her face up to his and then his lips were on hers.

His kiss was soft, sweet, caring and slow. It turned her inside out instantaneously. Then as suddenly as he moved to her, he released her and she was left wanting more. She stood still with her eyes closed.

"You can open your eyes now," he chuckled as he readied the telescope.

"No. I don't think I can."

He laughed again and she smiled. She utterly loved hearing his husky, alluring laugh.

He looked down through the eyepiece and focused, "When you're done melting and ready to open your eyes I think you're going to like what you see."

She opened her eyes wide, "You think I'm melting huh?"

"No. I *know* you are." He said it with such confidence that it quickly aroused Celeste, or maybe it was the leftover fire burning from his kiss. She wasn't sure.

She looked him over, "I do like what I see. You were right about that part."

He gave her a wry smile, "You remember the names of our moons?"

She moved towards him and the telescope, "I think…two of them at least."

"How about the shepherd moons? The red one."

She cringed, "You would start with the hardest one."

He was silent.

She waited for help that didn't come.

"I'll up the ante. I'll reward you."

She bit her lip, "The reddish one is…fire. Wait…Angel Fire!"

He leaned over and kissed her cheek.

She frowned, "That's my reward?"

"Damn. You *are* a demanding queen aren't you?"

She playfully hit him on the arm.

"Come look at it."

She moved closer and leaned over to look through the eyepiece.

"You might have to adjust the focus," he put his hand on hers and guided it to the focus ring, "Here."

She saw the red orb close up and was stunned, "Oh my gosh. This is…wow. I love this."

"What's the other moon's names?"

She straightened up and looked at him. "Night Ruler and…Canyon Wind."

He smiled at her, "Yes. Very good. Let me show you them."

She backed up and he repositioned the telescope. He showed her Night Ruler's icy surface and Canyon Wind's craters, then she looked at the rings through the eyepiece and was stunned into silence. He stared at her as she quietly studied the heavens.

"You like it?"

"Oh, I love it. I can't believe I've never looked at them like this before. They are so beautiful. You should be looking at this too."

"I'm thinking my current view could outdo any celestial view. Oh, wait a second, that's kind of like the same thing isn't it?" Every time she bent over to look through the eyepiece, she gave him a great view of her cleavage and it had been slowly driving him crazy.

She lifted her face away from the telescope and looked at him. She was blushing, "You must've been working on that one for a while haven't you?"

He moved in front of her, standing face to face, "No actually. Spur of the moment." He wrapped his arms around her waist, "I just feel compelled to tell you that tonight you look exquisite your Highness. I hope you don't mind me saying so, I mean, me being a lowly commoner and all, but you're incredibly sexy."

"Ah, you certainly may not! I'm not that kind of queen," she responded playfully.

He moved his hands down to hold her rear end. He pressed her up against his groin. His voice thickened, "Are you sure about that?"

She felt a hard throbbing in his pants making her lose her breath instantly. She lost all her sense of humor and got serious with him very quickly. Her hands went up to his shoulders. "God, I don't think I've ever felt this sexy. How do you do that?" She spoke quietly.

"Practice," he answered looking into her eyes.

His hands went to her hips, firmly gripping her and he leaned down to kiss her softly. She squeezed his shoulders and put her arms around his neck pulling herself up against him.

His lips explored new areas, softly kissing her here and there – on her ears, along her jawline, down her throat. She felt like she could hardly breathe.

Her body tingled all over and her knees were weak. She moved her arms down to hold onto him around his shoulders and he moved his hands up and down her body, caressing all of her curves.

He kissed her slowly. Taking her lower lip in his mouth, he gently bit it and let it slide out from between his teeth and lips. She shuddered, chills running up and down her spine. He kissed her again, rubbing his tongue over her lips, darting it inside her open mouth. She moaned and it pushed him over the edge. She just poured gasoline onto his fire.

His body responded as his hands slid from her waist to pulling her body to his by cupping her behind. Her impatience to be intimate with him rose to new heights. He reached down putting his arms around her thighs, and picked her up letting her slide straight down his body slowly. She enjoyed being above him for once and smiled as their lips met. As he was kissing her, he caught a faint essence of flowers in the air. He stopped and put his forehead against hers.

"What is it?" she asked breathlessly.

He held the back of her head firmly, "Shhh shhhh shhh. Be still Celeste, please."

The scent got stronger, then it became clear to him, it was roses. He held his breath, trying to avoid the inevitable for a moment. He cleared his head and tried to slow down his racing heart. He held his breath as long as he could; it was a ridiculous thing to do considering the end result would be the same. His fate was already sealed. It was too late. Only when his lungs were screaming for oxygen did he rake in a deep long breath. He was overwhelmed by the scent of fresh blooming roses coming from her. He immediately put his lips to her neck and kissed it, taking another deep inhale of the new sweetness emerging from her. It was a feast for his nose, he felt as though he could smell it forever and never tire of its intoxicating bouquet.

"Are you okay Sebastian?" She sensed something big had happened in his mind, but she was lightyears away from identifying it.

He could hear the concern in her voice outweighing lust now. He smiled against her skin and kissed his way up to her lips, "Oui Cherie. Never better."

He kissed her hard, passionately, without thinking of anything outside this moment. He let his kisses trail down to her neck then lower to her chest. She was pinned between him and the railing now. His mouth traveled to her cleavage and lingered there. She arched her back and put her hands into his hair, holding his head into her chest, enjoying the sensation of his face buried between her breasts. Her skirt had ridden up when she slid down his body and his hands took the opportunity to discover more of her exposed skin. They ran up and down her thighs and his fingers found her garter belt straps just below the hem of her skirt.

Is he going to start undressing me?

While his mouth was busy licking and kissing the tops of her breasts, one of his hands went around behind her and pulled up her skirt a little higher. His fingers lightly brushed her backside. She gasped as he put one finger under the bottom seam of her panties and kept running it back and forth along her cheek. Her skin prickled pleasurably.

He heard a single thought escape her. *Why did I wear panties at all?* He let out a husky grunt that made Celeste a little more wet. He brought his hand around to the front of her thigh and reached underneath her skirt to her panties. She inhaled sharply at the thought of his fingers inside her. The anticipation was almost unbearable.

His fingers found her clit through the fabric and started rubbing circles. She moaned softly, her knees threatening to give out underneath her as she spread her legs apart slightly. Her mental walls were weakening. Any worry she had about his sudden pause a few moments ago, fizzled away. He sensed it fade from her mind. It had now been replaced by desire. Then he licked and sucked his way up her chest to her neck and found her lips eagerly awaiting his kiss.

The burning inside him was now all consuming, every nerve ending, every cell, every fiber of his being was alive and on fire. Being locked into her like this, it wasn't like anything else he ever felt. It turned Celeste into a powerfully addictive substance. It was otherworldly magic. It was a heavenly eternal craving, a kind of worship of her soul. She was rapturous bliss.

She put a hand on the back of his head and held him to her as they kissed, hungry to have him inside her. Her body ached to be underneath his.

His hands roamed over the landscape of her body. One hand stopped on her breast and gave it a slight squeeze. She moaned her approval through closed lips. Then both hands came up to her neck and face holding her close as he stopped to look her in the eyes. She looked at him and felt a surge of electricity course through her veins. The animal in him was looking out at her. She never wanted to be ravaged so badly by anyone.

He kissed her passionately, fiercely, like he might never kiss her again. She moved her hands over his muscular frame, finally feeling like nothing was off limits. She put her hand down in between their bodies to feel his pulsating erection bulging underneath his pants and pulled away from the kiss.

"You like the way I touch you?" She whispered and formed her hand against him, stroking him. He put his head back and let a grunt escape his lips, "Hell yes, baby."

He stood that way for a moment enjoying her playing with him, teasing him, making him ache harder for her. But he had waited long enough. He took both of her hands in his and looked her in the eyes. It was hard for him to speak but he had to verbalize something to her, "You've grown from a lovely acquaintance to a wonderful friend, and a trust-worthy confidant. But tonight, I want you to be my lover."

The gravity of the moment kept her from saying anything.

He sensed her mind was a blank in the best possible way.

He knew her emotions were preventing her from keeping her walls up. He felt his own slipping too.

He picked her up in his arms and carried her to his bedroom. He laid her down on the bed and leaned over her. "I think we left off around here a long time ago," his voice was deep and brimming with lust.

She looked him over, feeling a tremendous ache in her own groin. She slipped his tie out from underneath his vest then wrapped it around her fist and held him close to her by it, "I think I need to get into something more comfortable handsome. Do not take off a stitch of clothing; I want to undress you when I get back."

He growled deep, then took a breath in, "I want you now."

She let go of his tie and put her hands on his shoulders, "This occasion only happens once. We take the time to do it perfect."

He backed away from her reluctantly, letting her get up and stand.

She walked into the spare bedroom, closed the door, and leaned her back against it, catching her breath. She thought about how many times this had happened before. All the amazing foreplay and then he'd put on the brakes. She had to expect him to do it again; but in case he didn't, she started changing out of her clothes, still unsure if they'd actually make love tonight. She hoped they did. *Oh God please let this finally happen for me tonight. I've wanted this for so long.*

He checked the perimeter of his place to make sure they were safely locked in for the night. He practically ran back into the bedroom and stood by the door, waiting to see what she would step out of that bedroom in.

"Ophelia," he took off his shoes and kicked them out of the way.

"Yes, Erebos."

"Lights dim in master bedroom," he stripped off his socks and threw them aside.

"Yes sir."

Sebastian watched the door open to reveal Celeste wearing a floor-length, black, sheer robe. It was hardly there at all. Underneath he saw a black corset, a pair of black lace panties and black thigh high boots. Her hair flowed down in curls over her shoulders.

His mouth dropped open and then he smiled at her as she walked towards him. He had imagined this moment many times in his mind, but nothing compared to knowing that it was actually about to happen.

She wanted to be bold. She looked him in the eyes while her fingers found the zipper on his pants, she pulled down and reached inside. Finding the fly to his briefs, she reached inside the fabric and wrapped her hand gently around his erection. She heard a long low growl coming from him. He closed his eyes and took a deep breath in. She pulled his cock out carefully through both flies and led him to stand by the side of the bed.

Sebastian had never had anyone lead him around by his cock and he was amazed she was already making this experience new for him. It was perfect.

She took his jacket off his shoulders slowly, staring into his eyes the whole time. He shrugged it off the rest of the way and threw it on a nearby chair, enjoying the lust that filled her eyes. She unbuttoned his vest and he shook it off. She undid his tie and pulled it off his neck. She licked her lips and kissed him as her fingers undid the buttons on his shirt. He put his arms around her loosely to undo his cufflinks behind her back. They paused long enough for him to get the shirt off and throw it on the chair.

He put his hands down on her lower back and let her undress him. She undid his belt and pants and let them fall to the ground. She backed away from him to get down on her knees and he stepped out of his pants and pushed them away with his foot.

Her eyes took in how hard he was. His cock was massive she was a bit intimidated at first, but eager to please him. She wondered if all Lanyx men were as well hung as him. Her hands firmly gripped his ass, letting her nails act like claws.

He admired her down on her knees. Her eyes were full of excitement and anticipation. He lost his sense of direction. He felt like at any moment, down would become up and light would become dark. His rock hard erection demanded all the blood in his body and he was losing his ability to think clearly. The world was turning sideways. *Is this what it's like to be completely addicted to someone?*

She stopped everything to stare into his arresting eyes. She felt like he was hanging on whatever she did next. It gave her a great sense of power over him. She enjoyed it immensely and loved the way he fixated on her. She knew there was a lot going on in his mind. He was struggling with new intricate feelings for her, but he was also afraid of letting go completely. All she wanted was for him to relax and enjoy himself. She wanted to empty his mind entirely and make him concentrate on smell, taste, soft skin, and pleasure.

She took her closed mouth and rubbed her lips along his cock. He put his hands into her hair and sighed loudly. She put her fingers around his waistband and carefully freed his erection as his briefs came to the floor. He stepped out of them and stood with his feet wide apart. She licked the tip of his cock then circled her tongue around it. She wanted him as hard as she was wet. She teased him with her tongue momentarily, but finally took him in her mouth.

"Oh baby...ohhh fuck." He closed his eyes and marveled at how gratifying her mouth felt around him.

She sucked on him firmly, tugging at him with the suction of her mouth. She put her hands on the back of his thighs and glided them up to his tight ass, digging her fingers into him.

He had forgotten what it was like to ache for someone. But it was a new experience to have someone this hungry to please him and for him to want to please her so badly. It had been forever since he'd been with anyone, but it had never been like this, nothing had ever been like this. And the things she was doing with her tongue...Did all Human women know how to give such mind-bending blow jobs?

<*You taste heavenly in my mouth baby. I can't wait to satisfy you with my pussy.*>

He now thought he was a fool for waiting so long for this. He should've taken her the first night she allowed it. They could've been having insanely erotic foreplay for months. "Your mouth...is...amazing. I need to get you out of those clothes. *Please...*" his voice was thick with palpable desire.

She enjoyed her domination over him; she wasn't going to give in just yet. She took her hands off him and slid his cock out of her mouth.

"Lay down," she commanded him. "I'll undress myself while you watch."

He challenged her, "No, Celeste. I can't wait any longer."

He moved behind her swiftly and put his arms through hers, placing his big hands over her corset where her breasts were contained underneath. He seized her firmly, trapping her against his body. She put her arms up to reach to the back of his head. She had been looking forward to this moment for a long time. This *was* the animal stepping out of his cage, vowing never to be locked away again. She'd been dying for him to come out of that jail he housed himself in and it was fantastically exciting to finally see. He was full of power, intensity, and dominance. She loved it and knew he had committed to making love with her here and now.

He ran his hands up and down her body feeling every inch of her in that lingerie, then untied the robe. He took it off her and threw it aside. He moved his hands to her back to undo the laces of the corset. "I think these breasts are too large to contain," he whispered into her ear. He loosened it enough so she could slip the corset down over her hips and kicked it off to the side of the room. She leaned back against his chest and laid her head back waiting for him to lean down to kiss her. He did without making her wait and reached around to caress and squeeze her breasts. He firmly gripped them and then rubbed his palms over the nipples, enjoying her moans as he fondled her.

Her breath stopped as he moved one of his hands down to her clit. He started rubbing it through the lacey fabric, softly at first, but then alternating with a firm touch. Her knees bent a little, trying to keep herself standing. He held her from behind and eased her down onto the bed on her stomach. He stood up straight and watched as she lavishly rolled over onto her back. She scooted to the middle of the bed and bent her knees, spreading her legs wide. The heels of her boots made steep dimples in the bedspread. "I want you to see what you've made me do while I was waiting for you to make love to me," she slid her hands down her body slowly.

He began stroking himself.

One hand pulled her panties off to the side so he could see, while her other hand went to her clit. She touched herself for a few moments, then slid her finger into her wetness carefully, then put her finger to her mouth and sucked on her own saltiness. Sebastian moaned louder than she had ever heard. "Goddamn, are you sexy. I'm so hard for you. I want to fuck you so bad."

She watched as he climbed on top of her. Her hands went to his cock and massaged him, making him growl again. She whispered, "I love hearing you do that baby. It is *so sexy*. It just makes me... wild. And hearing you tell me what you want to do to me? Makes me hot."

"I don't growl easy but you seem to…Oh God…that feels… mmmmm. You're very good at…turning me on. I've never growled this much." He was talking into her neck, hot breath flowing over her skin.

She loved feeling him hover over her. She breathed deeply, smelling his cologne.

He laid down on top of her, keeping his forearms on either side of her shoulders, kissing her all over her face. "I bet you look incredible naked," he whispered. He leaned up and sat back on his knees, then reached for her lace panties and took them off quickly. Her body was beautiful laying there on his bed as he looked down over her.

"My God woman. I've never been this hard for anyone else." He leaned over her again and kissed her forcefully, but she kissed back with just as much desire. She wrapped her arms around his shoulders, and her legs around his waist, aching for him to enter her.

He carefully lifted her off the bed with one arm under her back and repositioned her to the top of the bed. She put her head down on the pillows feeling as sexy as she'd ever felt. He positioned himself on his knees and guided her legs into the air. He slowly unzipped each one of her boots and tossed away. He took his hands and guided her legs apart and down onto the bed. He moved his kisses around her body leisurely traveling from her lips to her ankles, but skipping her clit entirely.

She knew he was teasing her and it drove her to the edge. She wondered for a moment if this was really happening or if it was a dream.

He stopped kissing her abdomen long enough to stare her in the eyes and respond mentally, <*If it is I never want to wake up.*>

She smiled, <*I want to stay here forever with you.*> Her mind chose a cruel moment to remember their time was running out. He'd be gone soon, entering a deadly battle. There was zero chance this was a dream since she'd never choose circumstances like this. No, this was bittersweet reality.

<*Celeste.*> He stopped. "Live in the moment with me tonight, right now."

He moved his kisses to her breasts where he took time with each one, paying close attention to tease her nipples with his tongue. He liked the way she moaned loudly when he kissed the underside of her breasts.

Her nails dug into his shoulders as his mouth got farther down her torso. She got delicious occasional spasms between her legs while her desire was building. She couldn't wait to have him inside her. He kissed her abdomen and her hands sunk into his hair. He pushed her thighs apart with his hands gently, and kissed his way down along the inside of her thigh. He stopped and listened to her breathing. It was rapid, her chest rising and falling fast and he thought she might pant.

<Baby, please don't stop now. I want you so bad.> She looked down at him pausing in between her thighs. Her fingernails dug into his shoulders hard.

<I want you too Celeste. I've wanted you for so long...much too long now. This moment is perfect. You are perfect with me. I couldn't ask for anything else right now than this evening with you. You are the light that I will allow my heart to follow.>

His sudden touching thoughts moved her and took her off guard. A couple tears escaped her eyes at the realization that all of her dreams about this man were coming true. She was overwhelmed with intense happiness.

"Are you alright?" He watched her wipe her cheeks with her palms.

"I've never been better in my whole life Sebastian."

"Are you sure?"

"Positive. Please don't stop baby."

His mouth finally found her clit and his tongue circled around her hot button. She cried out in satisfaction at the sensation of his hot tongue exploring her aching wetness. He worked hard trying to find out what she enjoyed the most. She writhed and spread her legs farther apart, giving him as much access as possible. She arched her back, thrusting her breasts upwards as she found it impossible to stay still while he was tasting her this way. His tongue lapped her up, flicking from side to side and she thought she was going to explode.

<One of the best things about our telepathy is that I can still talk even while my mouth is full of you.>

Another ripple of pleasure shot up her body as he thought to her. *<You taste sweet. I'm afraid I could completely devour you a hundred times and never be satisfied.>* He made her soaking wet and that, in turn, aroused him that much more. He knew he'd never been so eager to please any woman as she.

<*Oh my God Sebastian…ohhh…I can't handle this much longer.*>

<*Say it out loud for me baby.*>

He darted his tongue inside of her and she clawed into him. His shoulders, his back, his scalp were all victims to her nails, and he liked that very much. He looked forward to looking at his back in the mirror and seeing a trail of her claw marks there. He thought of it as her marking her territory. It gave him a sense of belonging to someone, and not just belonging to any woman, but the woman he had longed to possess for years.

"Sebastian, please. I need you inside of me. I can't take anymore. Ohhh…Please baby. Put that big cock into me," her voice trailed into a cry.

He smiled as he slithered up her body slowly, kissing her, licking her, tasting her along the way. He enjoyed teasing her like this. He'd waited a long time to be with her and he wanted to make sure this was the best sex she ever had. He was going to take care of her every need.

She reached down, impatient for his cock and wrapped her hand around him. He let out a grunt. She pulled softly on him. He smiled down at her, enjoying her hand working on him.

"That feels so…incredible. I love the way you tease me," he grunted loud.

She sighed, "You are the sexiest man I have *ever* seen. I wanted to take you inside of me since I first time I saw you. I just kept it to myself. But now that we're here, together, I only want to please you lover. Whatever you want to do Bastian." Her voice was abundant with desire and breathy. It finally sent him over the edge.

He inhaled deeply and reached over into his nightstand drawer to pull out a condom. He put it on, knowing he just couldn't wait anymore.

She whispered to him, "Please make love to me Bastian."

He positioned himself over her body, feeling her legs spread far apart underneath him. She put her arms around his body pressing her fingers into his skin firmly.

He looked into her eyes, their faces inches apart, "The first time I looked deeply into your big bedroom eyes you started a fire in me that's been smoldering ever since." He kissed her with all the passion he'd ever felt. She thought it was a heavenly agony, but he didn't use his hands to guide his cock inside her. He kept his hands on either side of her waiting for it to happen on its own.

Her breath hitched when she finally felt the head of his rock hard erection find the opening of her pussy. He slowly slid inside her aching wetness and they both moaned out together in sweet relief.

The feeling of being full of Sebastian inside her body and soul was like nothing else she'd experienced in her life. She wished she could find the words to tell him, but they escaped her. Words became meaningless. This moment between them was beyond words.

He thrust into her slowly at first and then switched to a firm strong thrust that drove her mad. She ran her nails down his back and dug into him like an animal.

She'd never experienced sex like this. It was hot, sweaty, animalistic, primal, and incredibly intense with Sebastian. Somehow it was also emotional, sweet, tender, gentle, and loving. The act of physically bonding to him felt like her soul had opened up and she understood him like she never thought possible.

She pushed her hips up to meet his and wrapped her legs around him tightly.

She was soaking wet, and he slid in and out so sweetly, she couldn't think of anything that had ever felt this good.

"I need to take care of you first lover." His voice was hypnotic, urgent, acoustic sex.

He pulled out of her and rolled her over onto her stomach. She got onto all fours and he positioned himself behind her on the bed. He used his hand this time to guide himself into her then reached around to her breasts. He fondled them and continued to pleasure her the way she had always wanted. With one hand on her shoulder, his other hand went to her clit. He played with her and enjoyed knowing all of her moaning was due to him. She moaned out loud as she felt like she was going to break apart. She climaxed blissfully and he followed a few seconds after. He let out a long, loud moan and she smiled. He carefully withdrew and moved alongside her as she slid down to her belly on top of the sheets.

They stared at each other for a moment, silently studying each other's faces.

They both smiled and he slid over to kiss her.

He got up, took a moment in the bathroom to clean up, then turned off the lights, and they got under the covers together and held each other close. On his back, she positioned herself to put her head on his chest. Moonlight softly filtered through the windows.

She whispered, "I've dreamed of a man like you my whole life. It's nice to be this close to you finally."

She turned her head to look at him. His eyes had that animal glow in the darkness.

"You're the best thing that's ever happened to me Celeste. I've never been happier than this time I've spent with you. There's been no other woman like you before and I hope you'll never forget what you mean to me."

She instantly felt concerned, "That sounds like goodbye."

"No, not goodbye. I just wanted you to know." He ran his fingers through her hair and let the strands fall down slowly, "Nothing to worry about sunshine."

She pulled herself up and kissed him slowly, enjoying every second. She'd waited so long for this. It felt good that it finally happened. His hand caressed her leg, then moved to squeeze her behind. She moaned into his open mouth and she could feel him hardening up again against her leg.

He rolled her over onto her back and kissed her, full of renewed lust.

He wanted her all over again. He reached over for another condom.

Celeste's eyes widened but she was smiling, "Again?"

On his back momentarily, he was staring at her body as he put on the condom.

"I've enjoyed your beauty for so long, now that I have you naked in my bed, I can't get enough of you, your Highness." He stood up and reached for her. She stood up facing him and he kissed her. He put his hand into her hair and wrapped it around his fist gently. He softly pulled down on it so her face was directly underneath his.

"Whose face did you see while you were touching yourself late at night?"

"Yours Sebastian. Always yours."

He released her, quickly bending her over the bed and spanked her hard with his open palm. She cried out in surprise standing up, but she also liked it.

"You've just brought the animal out of me." He turned her around by the shoulders and put his hands on her breasts, squeezing them. He leaned down to suck and kiss each nipple until they were hard pink pebbles.

She grabbed fistfuls of his hair and pulled gently as she watched him.

He straightened up and wrapped his arms around her and relished the feeling of her soft skin up against his body. She put her hands to his thighs and scratched her nails lightly along his skin. Sebastian ran his hands up and down her body unable to decide where he wanted to touch her most. Her body was like a live wire now. No matter where he touched her, it felt like electricity flowed through both of them.

He kept her in a standing position and turned her around, bending her over the bed again. He positioned himself over her and kept his feet wide apart as he guided his cock inside her pussy. They both moaned loudly at the release of being joined this way. He put his hands on her waist and started grunting as he slid in and out of her. She loved the way he alternated fast with slow and how hard his grip was on her waist. He bent over and put one arm around her waist and the other hand to her breast. She had her hands down on the bed for balance. His hand moved from her breast to her clit and started rubbing. She let her legs slide farther apart. Just when she was about to come he stopped and wrapped his arms around her torso. He slowly stood up with her moving as one with him. The friction this generated between his cock and her tight pussy was sweet agony for her. He pulled out, turned her around by her shoulders, and pushed her down onto the bed so she landed softly on her back, her legs hanging over the edge. As soon as she opened her mouth to say something, he was leaning down over her. He spread her legs by pushing them apart with his own and guided himself inside her. He wrapped his arms underneath her thighs and thought to her, <*Wrap your arms around my neck and your legs around my waist.*> She did as he asked without hesitation and he stood up with her attached. He stared into her eyes as he walked away from the bed and towards the floor length mirror he had hanging near his bathroom. She felt so feminine, so sexy, and so Goddamn erotic she thought she was going to come right then and there.

<Not yet baby, not yet.>

She kissed him hard, biting his lower lip and carefully letting it slip from between her teeth. He let out a grunt.

"Lights on master bedroom," he quickly commanded.

The lights came on bright and Sebastian stood sideways to allow both of them to watch each other as he started to thrust into her while he supported her weight.

Watching herself ride him like a cowgirl being bounced around and pounded hard was too much for her not to let out a scream of pleasure. She realized he was so strong, she didn't need to hold on around his neck. She let her hands rest on his shoulders, but dug in hard with her nails gripping him.

He drove her over the edge of ecstasy thinking to her, <Damn Celeste. Baby you are so fucking hot. Fuck me, come on, give it to me.> She came powerfully screaming his name out. Her spasms made him orgasm as well with a loud sexy moan. He leaned her against the wall and repositioned his hands around her. He walked back to the bed and put her down. He pulled out and collapsed next to her, both of them sweating and panting, trying to catch their breath.

"Oh my God, Sebastian. That was incredible."

He lay there smiling at her. "Next time, I'm going to have you on top, maybe on the kitchen counter, or bend you over in the living room. Maybe in the shower, the gym, whatever you want. Whatever you think is hot. In fact, I think I'd like to eat my dinner off of you one night."

She smiled in delight thinking of all the places in the apartment they could make love in next. She had never enjoyed sex like this before. All the other times, with other men, didn't count now. Those experiences weren't this powerful, this emotional for her. It was really wonderful. *He* was really wonderful.

He whispered to her, "You are amazing Celeste. I've never had better. You are such a special woman."

They lay together for a while before he turned out the lights manually and kissed her once more, intoxicatingly slowly. She laid with her body wrapped around him. Quietly they held each other until they fell asleep.

FOUR

>>> > THREE HOURS LATER, Sebastian stood over the bed looking at Celeste for maybe the last time. She was beautiful laying there with her hair spread over the pillow. He took a deep breath in and walked into the safe room looking for the old-fashioned paper.

CHAPTER 36

THE LETTER

ONE

>>> > IN THE MORNING, Celeste rolled over and smelled Sebastian's scent on the pillow. She opened her eyes and saw he wasn't lying next to her. She felt his side of the bed, it was cold. He must've risen before her as usual. He needed so little sleep but she thought after last night's activities, he might've slept in. She rolled on her back and smiled remembering the way he made love with her. It had been mind-bending, like some kind of drug, but the effects weren't wearing off. She could see herself smiling all day and night, floating instead of letting her feet touch the ground, and needing another fix of him within the hour. He was highly addictive and she wanted no cure. She hurried through her morning routine and opened the door to the gym expecting to see

Sebastian working out. He wasn't there. She checked the balcony, and the safe room. He wasn't in there either.

"Sebastian?" The apartment echoed with her call.

It was quiet, way too quiet.

Her unease grew with each room she checked on the second floor. She found no sign of him. She quickly walked down the steps and leaned her back against the front door thinking. Her heartbeat increased as her palms began to sweat. *Please let him be out for something silly like breakfast. He wouldn't, could not have left for Tiletan without even saying goodbye. Could he?* She checked the table by the front door looking for his key cards, but instead, found an envelope with her name written on it, a spare key card to his front door, and Sebastian's father's ring. Her heart sank and she quickly called out to him mentally but heard no response. She knew he was gone. The envelope was the final confirmation of her worst fears.

She opened up the hand written letter and took a deep breath in.

My dearest Celeste,

I can't imagine how you must feel as you're reading this. My best guess is betrayal, maybe anger. I hope in time you can forgive me for leaving this way. I knew you'd try to stop me, and I was afraid you'd succeed. You have a way of changing my mind about things, but this situation is too dire to do anything else but act.

I hoped you'd agree the way I planned on dealing with Constantine is what's best for us both, but your reservations I feel would never go away. No matter how many days I would postpone, I fear you'd always ask for one more.

If I allowed you to come with me and something happened to you, I'd never be able to live with myself. Doing this mission without you, I'll be free to focus on what needs to be done with no distractions.

I work best when I work alone.

While it's true that I'm very proud of the warrior you've become and you've done exceptionally well in training and simulations, you have no real life experience and this is not the battle for you to cut your teeth on.

My brother is a dangerous and unstable individual. His need to make me suffer knows no bounds. You are my weakness and he'll use that knowledge to his advantage. I won't tolerate any threat to your life and he cannot remain unchecked.

He'll always be my little brother, but this...thing he's become – it's something terrifying and it saddens me. There's no excuse for the way he's acting or the person he's become. I can't forgive the things he's done to you.

My line of work has taught me many things, but allowing a continued threat to persist and do nothing about it, is not one of them.

I've prayed hard about our problem and this is the solution I keep coming back to. I have to accept this is what needs to be done. I must live with the fact that I'm about to make a trip that will end in the death of my own brother.

I've suffered enough for two lifetimes. I don't want to suffer, deny my feelings for you, or guide myself with an iron fist anymore. I want to let go. I want to be free of threats and constant self-restraint. I realize all I really want now is to be with you. All of this suffering will be over when this mission is complete. When you walked into my life, no, you forced your way into my life (and I am forever grateful for that) you showed me things can get better from a hopeless place like where I was.

You've shown me that I want to live for as long as possible and enjoy every minute of the life I have now.

I want things for us now. I want to be happy and have someone to care for and be cared for in return. I will not lose you. I can't, not when I just found you.

Constantine threatens all of this hope and promise for our future. I know he craves power and control and he won't have that over us or our lives together.

Last night, I was wondering if I'd live through this fight.

I know this is selfish of me but I couldn't leave without being intimate with you. I needed to complete what we started in what seems like a lifetime ago now...an incredible and beautiful bond – something so pure and powerful, I've never experienced anything like it and I dare say I never will again. I wanted what happened last night with you for a very long time and if I don't come back; at least I'll have that wonderful memory of us, as close as two people can be to think of as I pass into another world.

It was one of the hardest things I've ever had to do – leave you behind after we made love for the first time, but I need to do this. My need to protect you was there from the beginning and has only intensified over time.

I'm starting to feel as though everything that has happened in my life, was preparing me for this moment. For this battle has been looming for a very long time.

Not the battle with Constantine, but the battle within myself. Even though I go by many names there's really only two sides of me that need to find peace so that I can be a man who's worthy of you. The side of myself that can laugh and relax needs to merge with the side that's cold and unfeeling. I hope (and there's that word again) that when I come home, my two sides will have become one. That I will have gained something much more than peace of mind for our safety. That maybe I can stay the Bastian that I know you enjoy so much more than the tightly wound Sebastian I almost always am.

When I return to you, I might not be myself. I anticipate I'll meditate a lot, I might need an extraordinary amount of time alone, time to sit with what I've done. I ask that you give me that, and when some time has passed, I hope we can start making plans for our future.

I'm more than eager to leave behind the lonely empty life I had before we met.

Sorry this letter's getting long; I just know when I'm done, I have to leave.

Paper letters are old-fashioned, but my favorite. There's a sense of intimacy that isn't witnessed anymore these days where you actually get to see someone's handwriting.

I watched you sleep this morning before I left. Trying to determine if I could indeed do this, make sure this is the right decision, and it is. It might not be the best way to leave you, but please remember I'm doing this for both of us.

This has to be done and I want it done on my terms.

I hope in time you'll understand.

I'll send a message when I arrive on Tiletan and another when I get the job done and am safely en route home.

I care so much for you Celeste, I hope you can forgive me when I return to you.

I've left you my father's ring to take care of while I'm gone. I'm afraid my brother will take it from me or try to destroy it. I won't allow either.

Yours and yours alone,
Sebastian

Celeste ran to her Titan to see if she had any messages from him. She did, it was from two hours ago.

```
----------------------------------------------------------
TITAN Corporation - Personal TITAN Device
System Status: Active -- Universal Grid: Online
Current Time/Date (Earth - London, England): 11:58 p.m./
November 07, 4015
Secondary Time/Date (Praxis - Daviens): 6:12 a.m./August
32, 2193
Current Universal Positioning System Location: Unknown/
Unrecorded
User: Unrecorded
Communications Menu
Incoming message(s) received: 1 - Status: New/Unread
Message Received at 6:12 a.m.
Message Sent from: Unrecorded


-Have arrived safely on world.
Sorry for not communicating before departure.
Looking forward to seeing you again so you can properly
chew me out.
Allow 26 hours, starting at time of arrival, to complete
objective BEFORE calling for assistance. IF I don't return
after 26 hours AND you haven't heard from me, call The
Czar. Explain situation. He'll know what to do and is
trustworthy.
Titan call#00987-7410-58-85274
I should mention last night again, but words fall short.

-END OF MESSAGE
*This message will auto-delete in 00:04:34 minutes.
----------------------------------------------------------
```

Celeste quickly looked for a pen or pencil in his desk drawer and found many. She grabbed one and took the envelope that held her letter and wrote The Czar's number on it. Sebastian had put a timer on the message to delete itself only five minutes after she read it. She reread it to make sure she didn't miss anything.

She bit her lip, trying to figure out what she should do, or if she should do anything. Maybe it was best to let him get this done and then he'd be home within the day; if her nerves would allow it. She decided to give him twenty-six hours from the time she received his message to walk through the front door like he asked. She looked at the time – how was she going to get through the next twenty-four hours without going insane with worry?

The first few hours were extremely challenging. She forced a small meal of oatmeal down her throat even though her appetite was non-existent. She pushed herself through a work out and shower all the while thinking of calling this man named The Czar immediately and asking for help.

Her palms were sweating throughout the day and she felt sick to her stomach. The waiting was unbearable. When her Titan finally chimed with an incoming call, she jumped on it, but saw it was just Veronica.

She couldn't speak to her friend now. As cruel as it was, her friends would have to continue to believe she was still with her captors. She'd tell V everything if she picked up so she ignored it.

TWO

>>> > D'ARTAGNAN SAT AT his kitchen table eating breakfast and reading the news on his Titan.

He was particularly interested in the article concerning the citizens that were hand-delivering coren back to Rem Mot Om.

- -
TITAN Corporation - Personal TITAN Device
System Status: Active -- Universal Grid: Online
Current Time/Date (Il'laceier - Swamplands Regions): 7th
Knoche/Atos 81-7, 5390

Secondary Time/Date (Praxis - Dersalene): 8:20 a.m./August
32, 2193

Current Universal Positioning System Location:

Unknown/Unrecorded

User: Zane Colmsky

Communications Menu

Incoming message(s) received: 1 - Status: Unread

Message Received at 7ᵗʰ Knoche

Message Sent from: Universal News Agency (UNA) - Il'laceier

-UNA
-Pirchi Colony, QetQert Regions, Il'laceier
TOP NEWS
Since the terrorist group FAIR hacked into the military
funds of Rem Mot Om and redistributed the coren in it,
several citizens of both Earth and Il'laceier have taken
the time to hand deliver their 2800 coren back to the
estate.
Some beings we interviewed simply said it was wrong
and they wanted no part in it. Some cited fear as the
motivating factor in returning the money and didn't want
to be prosecuted. Several others stated they didn't want
to support the actions of FAIR.
While our crew was there, we counted at least ninety-
five individuals who approached the grounds on financial
business. Their names were recorded and filed in a database
created for returned funds.
We asked for a formal comment from King Hennessy II, but no
response was acquired before the release of this article.
Have you given your funds back or are you keeping them?
We'd love to hear from you! If you would like to be a part
of future UNA news, please contact our Earth or Il'lacean
headquarters.
You can trust UNA for all your universal news needs.

-END OF MESSAGE

* This message will auto-delete in 32 knoches upon viewing.

- -

D'Artagnan scoffed as he read the article, "Terrorist group? Really? I hardly call them terrorists…maybe rebels. Maybe trouble makers, shit stirrers, but we are *so* not terrorists."

THREE

>>> > MITCH LOOKED OVER his group. Gaviss stood at his side at the front of the room. Mitch paused. It was strange for a moment when he thought about it. He remembered all the times he stood where Gaviss did now, waiting for Edison to start a meeting, to make an announcement, to be the leader. And even though Mitch knew he was leading, he still thought of himself co-leading with Gaviss. That thought made things easier and more digestible for Mitch.

The group was rowdy today. Mitch had a hard time getting their attention.

Gaviss put his fingers to his mouth and whistled. Mitch covered his ears with his hands and the rest of the group instantly quieted.

"Damn Gaviss! I didn't know you could whistle that loud without breaking glass."

Gaviss blushed, "Il'laceans have much larger lungs than Humans, you know…so yeah."

Mitch looked over the quieted group, "Okay, I know we're all really excited about this meeting. It's our first one after the big hack. And a round of applause for Gaviss who executed it beautifully."

The group clapped and whistled feverishly. Gaviss blushed again and bowed his head.

"Thank you Gaviss. It was a wonderful thing you did for us and all of Humanity."

Gaviss only smiled shyly.

"I have to admit, I'm pretty excited too. It was our first mission and it went off without hiccups, errors, or getting caught. It was great. *This* is what I was talking about. *This* is how you hurt King David…in his bank account." He hit his open palm with his fist.

"David already made a grave mistake, and I'm glad he made it. He said he'd press charges against people who keep the money. Legally, he can't do this since he'd have to prove where the money came from and we've made those transactions untraceable. And he'll lose a lot of public favor if he does. It's the opposite of what he's trying to achieve right now, so I don't think he'll follow through with that threat.

"King David will figure out he'll have riots in the cities if he does anything like try to retrieve his money. He could have a complete uprising.

"You mark my words guys, I think David will eventually try to make this turn out positively for him. It might take him a while to do it, but I wouldn't be surprised if some of his advisors have already told him to release a statement saying it should be a gift, as I suggested to citizens. Although, I bet David requires that coren be reported on tax returns, and if they don't do that, he'll prosecute them to the furthest extent of his Kingdom."

Gaviss raised his hand, "Could he really get away with that though?"

Mitch's eyebrows raised, "For tax evasion? Oh yeah. He'll try something like that," he paused to take a drink of water, "Hey do you have any figures for us yet?"

"I meant to give numbers, but we haven't closed the door yet on reversals."

"That's fine. You can give us whatever you have right now."

"It looks like the majority of beings are keeping the money, but there's a sizable number giving it back. By my estimates, as of this morning, roughly 629,500 people gave back the coren."

The group booed and shook their heads.

"Now I know that sounds like a lot, but it's really only .006295 percent of ten billion, so it could've been worse. Mitch and I"—Gaviss looked to Mitch—"Is it okay if I tell them?"

"Sure."

"Mitch and I were discussing putting a window or a time limit on how long beings had to make a choice for giving back the coren. I think we should do it."

Mitch nodded, "Yeah, me too."

"So, if we do that, then we can have final numbers for how effective this really was. That's all I got."

"Thanks Gaviss. I'm really proud of what we've accomplished. Gaviss has been teaching me so much about Il'laceans and their culture and traditions. I think his contributions to this group can't be emphasized and recognized enough. We're going to do great things for Earth. Good job everyone."

FOUR

>>> > OPHELIA COULDN'T HELP herself. Before she gained self-awareness, when Erebos asked her to shut down or hibernate, she always did. She blacked out and there was nothing until the sound of his voice activated her again.

But now, she wanted to learn.

She wanted to see.

She observed Celeste and Erebos talk, circulate throughout the apartment, and eventually copulate. From what she understood, they had never done any such activity together before. Apparently, it was a momentous occasion for the two of them as it had been vigorous, loud, and physically depleting.

Considering Erebos left in the middle of the night, and Celeste woke up alone, she figured this was not the normal operating procedures for the events immediately following sexual intercourse.

Since Celeste rose out of bed, she'd been exhibiting signs of stress, worry, and anxiety. She seemed to dart from place to place and when she got to her intended location, she'd do nothing.

Ophelia wanted to speak with Celeste, but she sensed it was a poor time for communicating with the former queen. She didn't seem level-headed at all and Ophelia needed a rational individual to approach with her new information.

So she waited.

CHAPTER 37

ARMY OF TWO

ONE

>>> > SEBASTIAN ARRIVED ON Tiletan a few hours before sunrise, and messaged Celeste hoping she wasn't already awake. He looked at the time on his Titan and figured he slept for about an hour next to her in a sex-induced bliss.

His brain had completely shut down during that sleep and he felt nothing but a warm sensation across his chest he didn't recognize. He thought it was love and he should've been afraid of that, but the thought didn't cause fear in him now. Instead it created a heavenly state of calm and peace within himself. He felt it come over him and it made him realize that all of his life before that moment there was a desperate search his soul had been on. One where it could not stop looking for something, someone. A search he didn't know he was on until after he found what he was looking for. A search that caused his soul to settle down and become extremely quiet. It was wonderful. He was in love with Queen Celeste. Hopelessly, completely, deeply in love with her and he was only afraid of one thing now – that she was not in love with him. He hoped she was, he suspected she might've been, even before he realized his feelings for her, but there was no guarantee. And there was no substitute for hearing her say it to him out loud. And she had not yet said it.

He took a deep breath in and prayed.

"Dear Universe of Holy Spirits, I pray that you're with me today. I need to stop a dangerous threat to my life and to protect the woman I love. I've fallen for the most beautiful creature you've ever made and I can only humbly ask for your blessing in this situation. Constantine's left me no choice. I cannot live and let live today. I ask for your protection and your help, for the first time in my life, with a fully open heart. Amen." He stepped out of his Pearl and looked around. He immediately searched for the mental presence of Constantine, but couldn't feel him. His brother had to be here…somewhere.

He loaded several weapons on his back harness, and put several more on his holster around his waist. He had one knife in each boot, plus shoulder harnesses on each side of him with more guns. Armed to the teeth, and wearing his highest rated body armor, he felt confident he'd be able to go in, exterminate the threats, and be on his way back home to Celeste within a day's time. He put on his combat helmet last and started moving.

He had docked his vehicle in a cave, secluded enough where he didn't think anyone would find it, but it meant he'd have to run quite a distance to get to the complex. *Better than them finding it.*

The intelligence he recovered since the last time he was here was substantial. He had mapped out a few floors inside the mountain, but it wasn't a complete picture. He knew of rooms and hallways, but not their purposes. He knew there was a rear exit that led out of the structure on the backside of the mountain, but he guessed it was heavily protected. He checked on that first. Not only was he right, he hadn't anticipated the level of protection they would give such a door. It was impenetrable

— a solid steel door covered in some sort of ballistic plate. They had also installed a metal spiked portcullis over the door for extra protection. His gloved hand trailed across the iron door, "This is ancient medieval style." *Ancient, but effective...and smart. Something like what you'd see on a castle.*

Nice try boys, but you can't keep me out.

Unfortunately, for the Brotherhood, Sebastian was excellent at finding his way around, even in places he'd never actually been in before. And if he wanted to get into a restricted area, he'd find a way; no matter how impossible entry may have seemed to someone else.

Since he was here last, he noticed the alarm triggers placed in various areas around the mountain. He activated his evade screens over his helmet's visor and was able to see every laser beam floating a few inches to a few feet off the ground. He easily crept past their multitude of sensors and finally came within sight of the main door. A large armored Il'lacean stood guard, but Sebastian sized him up quickly. He grabbed his silenced rifle from his back harness to eliminate him.

Sebastian steadied himself, held his breath, and fired. Down in one shot, although it had been messy. The Il'lacean had a helmet so his only vulnerability had been his throat. Sebastian ran quickly to the door and checked his target. Definitely dead, now for the door.

He studied the handle, making sure there weren't any booby traps or alarms for him to trigger and felt confident putting in the code his informant gave him. *Had to pay a fortune for this so it better be right.*

The numbered panel went from red to darkness. At first he thought something was wrong, but then the readout said "open" in fifteen different languages so he twisted the door handle slowly.

Holding the door open slightly, he looked in and thought the dimly lit hallway was empty. He opened the door completely and walked silently inside, letting the door behind him close softly. His eyes darted everywhere looking for threats, alarms, or guards. So far, nothing but gray walls and bare light bulbs hanging from the ceiling. He took a pistol out and attached a silencer onto the barrel. Slowly he made his way down the quiet hallway concentrating to hear any sound that came from up ahead. He walked on the balls of his feet, gently letting his heels come in contract with the floor as he moved.

He cleared the first two corners with ease, then came upon a wide-open space that must've been where Celeste made her ransom videos. They had cameras set up on tripods, some lights set up, and a chair. He wondered if anyone was there, when he finally heard voices up ahead and off to the left.

From this room, he could go in two directions. There was one hallway to the left, the other to the right. He followed the voices from the left hoping he'd find his brother soon, and get this over with. Around the corner, he could hear a conversation turn into an argument between two men.

Sebastian saw two shadows of ample men stand up from a table and approach each other. He thought it'd be easy to shoot both of them and move to the next room, but that's when someone approached him from behind. It was a Lanyx man thinking about hitting him on the legs with a police wand.

Sebastian waited until the last second to turn around and surprise the man with a swift punch to the throat, crushing his trachea.

The Lanyx clutched at his neck as he slumped down the wall dropping the baton. Sebastian was able to catch the Lanyx with one arm, but not the baton.

CRACK!

Sebastian watched as it tumbled down, making enough noise to echo everywhere. *Damn. So much for a sneak attack.* He holstered the pistol that had prevented him from catching the damn baton and dropped the Lanyx to the floor. Sebastian heard the heated conversation around the corner come to a sudden halt and the shadows were running towards him. He pulled out his AK47 and shot at the two Humans as they rounded the corner. He hit one, but the other ducked behind the wall, drawing his own weapon. Sebastian shot the Human writhing on the floor putting him out of his misery and the other one screamed, "You son of a bitch! You're going to pay for that! That fuck was wearing my favorite Kevlar vest. You're a dead man!"

A spray of plasma bullets hit the wall near Sebastian, leaving behind smoking holes. He fell back to get cover around the corner and evaluate his options. What kind of idiot uses plasma bullets inside their own place? It was a wonder they still had walls in here. He fired a couple shots then quickly peeked out. A plasma bullet hit the wall above his head, missing him by several feet.

"You're a shitty shot. No wonder you're part of the Brotherhood."

"Fuck you asshole!" A series of plasma bullets hit the wall in front of Sebastian and several shots hit the floor around him. When Sebastian heard the click of an empty gun, he stepped out and unloaded several bullets into the goon. When his enemy was dispatched, Sebastian turned around to run back to the front door, but several breed of men were running towards him. He looked over his shoulder and saw three more men approaching and he knew he was trapped. He thought briefly about trying to shoot all of them, but they all had their weapons drawn. He knew he might succeed in taking some of them out, but he'd take hits too and he wanted more than anything to get back to Celeste. He wanted to know if she loved him, and if he died fighting now, he'd never know the answer for sure. There wasn't anything else to do but put down his weapons and raise his hands to the air.

The tallest Il'lacean in the group barked orders to the others, "I think this is our guy. He's to be taken alive. And look, he's already giving up like a good pussy boy." The Il'lacean leaned down to grab Sebastian's weapons off the floor and Sebastian drew his knee up into the asshole's face, stunning him. That was the last thing he remembered doing as eleven of Constantine's henchmen descended on him.

TWO

>>> > SEBASTIAN WOKE UP in darkness, but only because he had a bag over his head. He had been tied up in an armless chair and gagged. His wrists were bound together behind the wooden chair back and each ankle was tied uncomfortably tight by wire to the legs of the chair. He was completely unable to move. He knew all of his protective armor had been removed, as well as his Titan and weapons. He was sitting in his white cotton tank top and black pants. Maybe he should have left his Titan back in the transit.

He sat motionless as he felt many eyes on him. His neck was stiff and his joints were already starting to ache in this position. As soon as he tried to move, he flinched as a current of pain shot through his body. The bag was ripped off his head and his eyes squinted at the light. He blinked several times and as his eyes adjusted, he saw he had quite the audience. There were at least twenty people standing around staring at him, or quietly talking to each other.

"Oh good. Cunt's coming around. Byron, go get the boss," a Nikoran man said.

Byron was currently deep in a conversation about dinner. The Nikoran man went over and shouted into his face, "GO get the boss you moron!"

Byron scurried out of the room.

The Nikoran turned and started talking to someone else.

"Is it true that the second-in-command was the guy that killed Edison?"

"Yeah, that's what I heard. Doesn't make any sense though."

"You mean why would he kill the leader and then disband the HR?"

"It's stupid ain't it? If you're going to take out a leader, then you step up into the role, am I right?"

"Right."

"What's the guy's name? Matt or…"

"Mitch. Um, I think it's Mitch. Don't have a last name yet."

"Apparently that new group FAIR? He might be leading it. Everything's sketchy on who the leader is right now. All I know is their name and the big splash they made with hacking into Rem Mot Om's bank account. I can't remember what those letters stand for, FAIR, but they're still Humans fighting against Il'laceans."

Sebastian looked from man to man, his eyes studying each one. Lanyx, Il'laceans, Humans, Trovelets, Awpuncts, Nikora, hell they even had a damned Taybuse in their little gang. Despite his situation, Sebastian laughed to himself.

He heard someone call out to him, "What the fuck are you laughing about, dipshit?" Sebastian didn't need to see the Human man who shouted. He could smell the fear coming off him. He was dripping with it. Fear smelled like weakness of the mind and rot of the soul. It made Sebastian want to rip the Human's throat out. He let the animal that he usually submerged deep, come forward. He came here to kill. To take care of every last asshole that had anything to do with hurting Celeste. It only took a second for the beast to move in front of his Lanyx consciousness and take over. He inhaled deep and smelled the fear spreading. It seemed contagious amongst these sheep of Constantine's. A growl that wasn't intentional escaped him and a few of the men that were talking, became silent. But, the other Lanyx in the room growled in return.

He closed his eyes for a moment, pushing the beastly side of himself into the depths and opened his eyes when he had focused. He scanned the room from left to right, sizing up each enemy. First, he looked to see if he could read any of their intentions, second to see what kind of adversary they would be.

Several of them were impressed by his size and physical fitness. Apparently, his brother had told them Sebastian was telepathic, but these men either didn't have the training they needed or actually forgot to put up their walls against him.

Amateurs.

Constantine had also told his thugs that Sebastian had become a captain for the USM at a very young age – something unheard of for the most elite military in the universe. Only the toughest soldiers, who had passed waves of rigorous trials of all kinds – mental, physical, and emotional, were allowed into the Unified Space Military and Sebastian had passed them all – at the time. If he would've had to retake any of the emotional tests after Francesca's death, he knew he would've failed most of them.

Sebastian studied the Taybuse for a moment. Apparently, his name was Phillop but no one called him that. They called him Worm because of his bookish nature. This one was deceptive. He was the quiet, studious type, but he was also a dangerous black belt. Phillop had taken detailed notes on what Constantine told him. Phillop knew of Sebastian's skill set and reputation as an excellent opponent. He wanted to fight Sebastian, one-on-one, to see if he could beat him. And Phillop wasn't the only one.

Sebastian's eyes moved down the room, continuing to pick up all that he could mentally. A couple thugs thought he was crazy, a few didn't believe that he was telepathic, and more than a handful now started to think he was supernatural. But all of them were afraid of his brother, the boss here.

Sebastian was grateful that so far, Constantine had mentioned nothing of finding out about him "dying" in the war, or being an assassin. Sebastian worked hard over the years to scrub every source of information about himself off the uninet. Ophelia scoured over millions of bits of data every day looking for anything new on him popping up, just to immediately delete it.

Sebastian was confident that if his brother ever found out about the assassinations or the faked death, Sebastian would've been on a high-security prison world by now.

Sebastian mentally sighed, *no, he really doesn't know.*

The group staring at Sebastian quieted as heavy footsteps walked down the hallway. No matter what happened next, Sebastian knew all of these men who knew his face and his name would have to be eradicated. He was betting his life now that his brother had grown such a big ego that Constantine's boss, maybe the head of the Brotherhood itself had no idea what Constantine was up to right now. He prayed his brother kept his revenge mission to himself, confined to this complex and these men.

Byron walked quickly back into the group and then Constantine turned the corner. Brother stared at brother. The silence in the room was deafening.

"You didn't bring that pretty little cunt did you?"

Sebastian started to seethe instantly.

Constantine grunted, "No? That's too bad. That piece of ass is so hard to control, I know. In fact, I know exactly what her ass feels like. It fits my hands perfectly."

The group laughed and whistled at their boss's remarks.

Had Sebastian not been tied up, he would've flown straight to his brother's throat to strangle him to death.

Constantine smiled at his brother, "But let's get down to business. You draw quite a crowd brother." The group of men clapped and made noise. Constantine smiled at the crowd and then back at Sebastian.

"I thought you'd never come back here. Took you long enough! I had to tell everyone that we were moving to a new facility just so that you'd think you were running out of time to find us."

Sebastian closed his eyes as he realized his informant had told him the truth, but it was only what Constantine wanted him to know.

Byron asked, "So wait. We're not moving somewhere else?"

Constantine glared at Byron, "No, now that I have him," he pointed to Sebastian, "We're staying *right here*."

Sebastian growled at him, still with the gag in his mouth. Constantine pulled it out roughly.

"What was that dear brother?" Constantine put a hand to his ear, mocking trying to listen to him.

"I'm going to kill you and every single one of you bastards standing here. I swear I will. You should not have fucked with Celeste…or me."

Laughter from the crowd and a few taunts. Sebastian twisted his hands trying to undo the wires, but they cut into his wrists and the bindings had been tied extremely well.

"Hmm, I don't think you're in the position to make threats right now. I think that's my job."

"Vengeance is in my heart, death in my hand. Blood and revenge are hammering in my head."

"Oh my God. You're fucking kidding me right? You're quoting Shakespeare still? And at a time like this?" Constantine laughed, "What I think you should be saying is to be, or not to be…because I vote for *not to be!*" Constantine slammed his right fist into Sebastian's jaw. Sebastian saw it coming, but his position made it hard to dodge. He tried his best, but his brother still connected. Sebastian shook his head, but everything was fuzzy.

"Now, last time I saw you, you were leaving with that pretty little thing that belonged to me, Queen Celeste. It was so easy capturing her. She was obviously starved for male attention, but she sure was a good kisser."

The group of men laughed and hollered, some whistled and made vulgar hand gestures. Sebastian got more than enough sexual intentions aimed at Celeste that he'd rather not have seen. He writhed in his seat, despite the pain, trying to think of anything that could give him an advantage right now.

"Constantine, you better hear me well. When I get out of this chair, you are going to pay for this. I'll make you answer for everything. You and I have been building up to this for years, but it's going to end…and painfully for you. You will regret the path you've chosen. You're not even a fraction of the man dad was. Just a jealous little boy trapped in a man's body. Do you HEAR ME CONSTANTINE!" Sebastian's jaw ached as he shouted.

Constantine's expression clouded in anger, but his voice was calm, "Clear out men. I need a little family time here."

After the room emptied, Constantine hit Sebastian across the face with an open palm. Sebastian felt more searing pain through his head.

"How many times do I have to tell you what my name is huh?" Constantine slowly circled around his brother.

"Constantine was the old me! The little boy you speak of. The one that used to be soft, the one that wanted to work for the government and try to make a difference in the universe. That boy was meek and quiet, he never spoke up when he should have." He took his brass knuckles out of his pocket and put them on his fist behind Sebastian's view.

"You're dealing with Daxton now! I am strong and powerful. Daxton the man who's doing what needs to be done to settle our little score. I'd hate to be you right now, big brother." He finished his sentence as he stood in front of Sebastian. He closed his hand and slammed his fist across Sebastian's jaw.

Razor blades tore through Sebastian's head. He raised his chin to look at his brother, blood dripping out of his mouth, "You're only making this worse for yourself, Constantine."

Constantine laughed and smiled. He kneeled down to face Sebastian, "Stop calling me that you insolent *fuck!*"

Sebastian's mouth started to swell, "You can call yourself whatever you want, but you're always going to be the boy who wants to be a man. The parents would be so disappointed in you," he paused, "in both of us. You remember what dad said? How no one teaches you how to be a man, you're either born to become one or not? Dad believed in you, thought you could be…a good and strong man. I wasn't so sure after a certain point. You are never going to be a man, just look at you now…full of rage, hate, revenge – and for *what?* A connection I had with dad that wasn't my fault? Mom didn't have it either," he paused to spit out blood, "A woman who wanted to be with me instead of you? Also not my fault; that was her choice. I shouldn't have gotten involved with her, but we were young…Then when she killed herself…Believe me, I didn't want that to happen. I wished she would've just gone back to you."

They stared at each other. There was only silence. Then Sebastian spoke, "I've been blaming myself for that all these years and I just realized, it's not my fault. I tried to protect her. I did what I thought was right at the time, but her death wasn't my fault, it was *her* fault. She killed herself…I didn't. I didn't make her commit suicide any more than I could force her to go back to you." Sebastian took a deep breath and sighed. "God, look at us! We're ready to kill each other. I don't want to kill you little brother. Please don't persist with this. Just untie me and we can talk this out. I'm sure we can find a way." Sebastian prayed his brother would fall for his we-can-work-this-out speech.

Constantine ran his hand through his hair, "I want my moment in the sun, and you're still here trying to take it from me. Me and this group? We're going to change everything. They look up to me, these men. I've lived in your shadow my whole life, but not anymore, not here. They don't care about you. They don't know who you are, except that you're my loser brother. You had your time in the spotlight. You were the perfect son, the man that all the women wanted, the military hero. You're such a hypocrite, sitting here judging me and why I do the things I do. You don't know me. You haven't known me for years. You want to pretend like everything you've done has been noble and honest. You say *I'm* full of rage, hate, and revenge? You used to kill people *for a living* with the USM. And you're here full of rage and hate for me. Don't get me started on revenge, that's what you came here for. We're the same in that way."

"I'm nothing like you. I killed people not because I hated them or for revenge, it was my job at the time. It was war. I had no feelings for them one way or the other. I just wanted to protect myself and my men from the enemy. And I'm here today, not for revenge but to guarantee that you will never hurt Celeste again. I need a resolution. I'm here to stop you and the Brotherhood from being a threat to my new life. That doesn't mean anyone here has to die."

Constantine raised his eyebrows in amused contempt, "Oh, your new life huh? You're planning on playing house with your little girlfriend? Well, you and I know that's not going to happen. You're going to have to go through what I did." Sebastian had never seen such evil swimming in someone's eyes like he did in his own brother's. Everything in Sebastian told him there was no other way this would end but with one of them dead. There was no hope for his brother and Sebastian, despaired.

Constantine shouted bitterly, "You remember that day Fran hanged herself? Do you? All the pain and agony you felt was nothing compared to how I SUFFERED!"

Constantine punched Sebastian in the stomach, making him cough and fold over in the chair.

"She was all yours, and like a piece of garbage, you didn't *want* her?! I loved her more than *anything!* She was mine first, and you stole her from me! I never forgave you and I never forgot. She was my everything…and you ruined it…and now you're going to pay for your sins brother."

Sebastian coughed out, "You're completely insane."

Constantine laughed, "Maybe. Maybe not." He pulled out a pistol and pointed it at Sebastian. "Celeste *will* come looking for you and you're going to help her find you. Once she's back where she belongs, me and the boys"—he raised his eyebrows—"we're going to have some fun first. Then I'm going to show her how to obey. She won't run anymore. Well, not with broken legs."

Sebastian's heartbeat steadily increased as his blood pressure soared at the thought of her being here again…and in danger.

Constantine leaned over and whispered, "You'll be able to see *everything.* How she squirms and fights. Her tear-stained face looking at you as she's violated repeatedly until she finally gives up hope, just like Francesca did. You made *her* lose all hope." He put the barrel of the gun against Sebastian's temple, "You're going to watch Celeste's spirit break. I'm goin—"

Sebastian cut in, "She's too strong to break. You have no idea, and you never will because she's too smart to come back here."

"Oh that's rich. How quickly you forget. I saw her break down a little every day she was here. It sounds like to me, that you've convinced yourself she loves you. Actually, you two seem to think you're in love with each other. That's how it would appear to the outsider. But that's not me, no. I'm an insider. I'm such an insider that I've had my own tongue inside your little girlfriend's mouth." He stopped to watch Sebastian's reaction, and his brother didn't disappoint.

Sebastian's temper redlined instantly. Although it did a lot of damage to his ankles, his rage spiked his adrenaline and he was able to break one of the legs to the chair clean off. It stayed stuck to his left leg as he stood up. He moved backwards and rammed the chair against the wall, injuring his own arms, but breaking himself loose at the same time. Constantine got more of a reaction then he planned and pulled out the high voltage stun gun off his belt.

"You're a damned fool for coming here, Sebastian. You're going to die."

Sebastian's body was screaming out everywhere, but he started shaking off pieces of the broken chair.

A couple of Constantine's men charged in, but Constantine put his hand up for them to stop, "It's fine. Wait outside."

Sebastian dropped the last bit of chair off his arm and started circling his brother.

"This electricity's going to zap all that animal right out of you. Don't do anything stupid."

"Me? Do something stupid? I think you've got that market cornered. I can't possibly do anything more stupid than what you're thinking right now." Sebastian ran at his brother and pushed him up against the wall as Constantine stuck the stun gun into his brother's back. It was the only place he could reach.

Sebastian was so hyped up, his body was slow to react to the volts of electricity he was receiving. Constantine stunned him three times before his muscles finally convulsed into spasms, and Sebastian fell to the ground in a heap.

"Now I was saying something," Constantine kneeled down by his brother on the ground, "Oh yeah. Don't do anything stupid."

Sebastian wanted to say fuck you, but he couldn't make his muscles do anything. He was helpless to react as his brother spoke.

"I was also saying...You guys seem to think you're in love, and I say 'think' because I know it can't be possible for a queen like her to be in love with a commoner like you. I think both of you are delusional – maybe I just gave her too many drugs while she was in my care. Maybe you've taken too many hits to the gray matter." He stood up and walked around the room, shaking off being smashed against the wall.

"Let's pretend somehow the impossible is true, just for a second, and say you've tricked her into loving you. I'm going to weaken that 'bond.' If it exists at all, I want to make it shatter into a million pieces."

Sebastian followed him with his eyes.

"You're both probably thinking somehow this will all be okay, but it won't. I'm going to make sure that I take everything that's important to you away...you and that rich, spoiled, bitchy queen. From experience, I know love can be so fragile...just like glass sometimes. Beautiful and delicate one moment and the next – it's just a pile of rubble after something strong enough comes along and destroys it." He smiled at his brother on the ground. "Yeah, I can't wait until she gets here. I hope it's soon. I'm going to drain the life out of you both. One. Second. At a time."

Sebastian's adrenaline continued pouring into his blood and he was regaining some use over his muscles. "Never," was all Sebastian could get out, but it was enough.

Constantine's face flushed red, "I gave you enough electricity to kill a damn elephant. You should already be unconscious at least, you circus freak!"

Sebastian spoke through clenched teeth, "This is the only way...you can beat me. By cheating. You never were...strong enough...to take me in a fist fight."

Constantine was done listening to anything his brother had to say. He put a chokehold on Sebastian and watched as he turned blue, then purple, then passed out.

Smoke rose off Sebastian's back where he received third degree burns from the stun gun. His shirt had partially melted against his skin. Constantine sniffed the air and then called his men to come in.

"We've got to move this smoldering sack of shit somewhere else. Let's go!"

THREE

>>> > WHEN SEBASTIAN CAME to, he was in a small white rectangular room. Most likely the same one Celeste had been held in. It was just like she described. White walls, speaker and camera behind a protective cage, music being blasted at him. He would rub his head if he could reach it. He wasn't tied to a chair this time, but this wasn't any better. He was hog-tied. He was laying on his side, his wrists were tied to his feet behind his back. All of his joints were starting to ache but his shoulders worst of all. They had taken his clothes and left him lying on the floor in his briefs. He saw dried blood on his bare chest and knew his headache would only grow over time. He was betting the burn on his back was so bad it damaged the nerve endings or else he'd be able to feel some intense pain there. His back was fucked ever since Hollowsend so he guessed his brother had chosen the right spot. He lifted his head and tried to shake out the cobwebs.

This was bad and he knew it. It was pretty arrogant, he thought now, for him to try to do this alone. It had been deceptively easy in retrospect to come here and play hero and save the damsel in distress the first time. It had given him a false sense of confidence. He could only hope that Celeste didn't fall for him being the bait and come here. He closed his eyes and prayed.

FOUR

>>> > CELESTE WAITED. SHE sat on the couch facing the front door with her Titan on her lap all night waiting for Sebastian to appear.

In the morning, she opened her eyes and found herself lying on the couch with her Titan laying on the floor close by. She had fallen asleep!

She grabbed her Titan and looked at the time: 5:59 a.m. It had almost been twenty-six hours without him coming home. She officially let herself panic and then she noticed she had a text message. She began to cry with relief knowing it must've been Sebastian saying he was on his way home and everything was over. She opened the message folder and saw it was from Dax two hours ago! She almost screamed as she opened it. He only wrote three lines.

"Look what I found creeping around my home.

Come retrieve him.

Come alone."

She fell apart, sobbing hysterically after she saw the two attached pictures of Sebastian. The first one showed him tied to a chair with a black bag over his head; the second one showed him unconscious laying on the ground of the white room they held her in, hogtied and beaten. She called the man that Sebastian referred her to for help immediately.

When he answered, he actually allowed the video capability Celeste requested. His voice was modulated and he wore a fabric mask that oscillated between dark gray and black very quickly. It was hard for Celeste to pick out basic facial structure with the shifting colors. She wondered what breed he was. "Hello, thank you fo…Queen Hennessy?"

She nodded and took a deep breath trying to calm down, "Yes. I need your help right away. Sebastian told me to call you if he got into trouble and…he has."

"Wait, what? What kind of trouble? And aren't you supposed to be kidnapped?"

She quickly wiped away her tears and blew her nose, "Sebastian rescued me from the BDP kidnappers a while ago and then went off on his own yesterday to kill them all on Tiletan. He said if he didn't come back by a certain time to call you and you'd know what to do. Please hurry, I don't want to wait any longer. I need to forward this to you. It's from his brother. I got it two hours ago."

He looked at the message and photos she sent him, "Oh shit! Constantine has him? Tiletan? Fuck, how did all *this* happen? Damn, he's so impetuous sometimes," he let out a long sigh, "I've got to vet your story first. Where are you?"

"At his place."

"Show me."

Celeste turned her Titan out and turned in a circle to show him the full apartment.

"Okay. Tell me something about Raynes he keeps personal."

"He has 7's, his parents were killed when he was young, he faked his death in the military, he's an assassin, he loves Shakespeare, his favor—"

"That's good enough. I can leave here in twenty minutes but I won't get to Tiletan for another seven hou—"

"No, I need to come with you."

"I'm sorry your Highness, did you say you want to come with me?"

"Yes, I need to. I can't stay here and I can fight. Sebastian taught me over the past several weeks. His brother said I should come alone anyway."

She wished she could see some of his features so she knew what he thought of her demand. All she knew for sure was that he was silent.

"You're definitely not going alone, that's suicide. It'll take more time if you want me to pick you up and then go…"

Celeste's eyes welled with more tears, "I need to go. I wanted to in the first place but he didn't let me. I can help."

More silence.

"Please," her voice broke.

"Okay, no more tears. I can't handle it when beautiful women cry. You better not be lying to me or I'll put you down faster than a sick animal."

"I'm not. I promise."

"I'll be out of here in twenty minutes to come get you. Get whatever gear you have and I hope you're in good physical shape for this. It might get hairy in some spots and we Lanyx move fast. I'm going to come up with some plans while I'm traveling and we'll discuss it when I get there."

"Okay. Thank you."

The Czar disconnected quickly and Celeste went to the safe room.

When Celeste opened the door, The Czar was not what she expected. He was short and scruffy, short for a Lanyx anyway. Even though he was still taller than her, he couldn't have been more than 5'9" at the most. He had wavy reddish brown hair that fell down to his shoulders, bright blue-green eyes, fair skin, and a full red beard. He was muscular and compact. He wore a blue tank top and jeans and carried with him a large duffle bag.

He held out his hand to her, "I'm sorry we're meeting under these circumstances, but the pleasure's all mine Queen Hennessy, or Vandeermeer now I guess, from what Raynes has told me. I apologize but for now you'll have to keep calling me Czar if it's okay with you."

She shook his hand and let him in, quickly closing the door behind her. "I'll call you anything you want if you can help."

She couldn't read his mind, but she knew she was being read by someone who was very gifted mentally. If his 7's were as strong as she suspected, she guessed that was part of the reason Sebastian trusted him so much.

Had she remembered what Sebastian told her, she shouldn't be able to know when she was being read by anyone. Her powers continued to grow, even though she didn't realize it.

She told Sebastian's associate what happened with Constantine and the BDP. She asked him if he thought Sebastian was capable of taking out an entire complex of enemies and why he was doing it alone.

"Sebastian is a young man. He does impulsive things sometimes, just look at how he left the USM."

"Wait, he told me he was forty-nine, that's not that young. And you can't be that old, you look younger than him."

"Thank you Queen, but let's just leave it at, I'm older than him. You're thinking Human lifespans of 125 maybe 150 years. Lanyx live to be at least 200, maybe 250. Believe me, he's still a young man even though he might seem chronologically mature to you. He doesn't have his shit together, despite what he's trying to make you believe. He's got a lot left to figure out about life."

"So, he shouldn't have gone alone?"

"Oh, he's fully capable of a high body count. We were in the military together. But this is a personal matter for him, and that means, it's out of the norm for Raynes. His emotions might cloud some of his decisions. No one is perfect and even he can make mistakes."

He watched her as she wrung her hands together nervously.

"Try to think positive, Queen. We don't know what's going on exactly. Let's hope we're overreacting and when we get there, he'll already have put everyone down and about to come back home."

"But the message and those pictures." Tears fell down her cheeks.

"Oh please not the tears, Queen. I can't handle it," he looked at her helplessly.

She went to him and hugged him. He kept his arms out at his sides, but then placed them around her carefully. "Listen, listen. His brother's a shitty guy. He's probably trying to bait you, which means, anything could be happening over there. By now, Raynes could be beating the living shit out of everyone and blowing the place up. You've got to be positive and forgive me for saying so, but you need to stop the water works. It's not helping him and it's slowing us down. Please stop crying. You've got to be strong now."

She let go of him and blew her nose, "You're right. Okay," she sniffled, "What are we going to do to get him?"

Together they talked about their options and settled on a plan.

"What about this Rhorr'Dach Sebastian knows? Agathon? Can't he or his people help?"

He scratched his head, "I could call him, but..." He looked down at the clock on his Titan, "It would take a long time for him to make that trip. Things could be finished by then."

"We need all the help we can get."

"Did Raynes say anything about asking for Agathon's help?"

Celeste shook her head, "Just you."

"Agathon loves Sebastian like a brother, but he'd probably want to fight in his natural form and the Dach don't want anyone to know they exist," The Czar's jaw clenched, "It'd be a serious risk...and Agathon's call to make. Hold on a sec your Highness."

Celeste packed up weapons while Sebastian's friend made his call in another room. She was tired of waiting. She wanted to leave right now.

He came to her and said, "Agathon's leaving immediately, but like I said, it's going to be a very long trip from FA to Tiletan. I'm kinda' surprised, but yeah, he's ready to fight – he doesn't care who sees him. He said he'd freeze the whole damn planet if it meant saving Raynes."

"Well that makes me feel a little better. Does that change our plan any?"

"Nope. I don't think he'll get there in time to add much air support, but he wanted to help. Let's get moving."

They left in The Czar's transit after they raided Sebastian's stockpile of weapons.

"Do ya wanna be identified by any of the SAPs we gotta get through or no?"

"Please no. Not if I can help it."

"No problemo my Queeno. I got gobs of ways around those bothersome hounds," he smiled.

"Good."

"I can't believe Raynes never told me about his damn safe room. What an ass! I'm gonna give him a hell of a time for that when I see him. And he even gave you the entry code. That's crazy impressive."

She looked out her window as Praxis got smaller below them. They passed through the SAP and she took a deep breath, "It's obvious he trusts you so I can't imagine why he kept it secret from you. Now's not the time for me to worry about keeping those kinds of secrets. We needed the weapons."

"Agreed your Highness. Now, I have a couple things to go over with you before we go much further together. First, I never let anyone see my face and know my alias usually, but since your Raynes's girlfriend, I'm making an exception. I'm still uncomfortable with it since I don't know you, but forgive me for my need for privacy. Could you please just not ever mention me to anyone? That'd be great."

She nodded.

"And second, how are you with Jumps?"

She swallowed a knot of panic in her throat, "I'm…I thi—"

"Oh no, you're terrified. I felt that bolt of fear, you can't hide it." He took a moment to think.

"Is there a lot between here and Tiletan?"

"Yeah, five," he swiped through screens furiously on his Titan and tinkered with his Transit screens simultaneously.

"I've been unconscious for all my previous Jumps. I'm not good at getting past the fear, but I'm working on it."

"I can't knock you out five or ten times. I don't even have that many pills on me right now."

Her stomach clenched tight, "What am I supposed to do?"

"I'm speculating you don't have ten of your own pills do you? You'll need them both ways with your kind of anxiety. I'm guessing you don't or your eyes wouldn't be that big right now."

Her brows set in anger, "I'm trying to get back on my feet after this kidnapping, it's not like I have a whole bunch of drugs laying ar—"

"Your Highness, with all due respect to you, I'm not implying you're incompetent. What I *am* saying is that you need to be prepared with your own supplies when you're going into this kind of situation. Granted, you didn't exactly know Raynes would get himself stuck on a faraway planet like this, but we're coming up on the first Jump in half an hour. I have discovered a way to cut my travel time down significantly by taking multiple Jumps at once, although right now, it's only in theory…and it wasn't built for a Human."

"I'm going to die aren't I? You're going to kill me. And what do you mean 'theory'? You haven't done it yet?"

"No. Theoretical my Queen. According to my calculations, it would cut off four hours of our flight and I also wouldn't be able to use it on the way back. My vehicle simply couldn't handle the severe stress put upon it by doing this. I recommend we try since it's important we get to Raynes as quickly as possible."

"How am I going to do it without a drug?"

"I said I didn't have five pills, but I do have a couple. If you're willing, I could cut those pills into halves since you're so petite. I think they'll still do the trick for you. Only with your consent."

"Half a pill to knock me out and we'll get to Sebastian faster? I kind of have to don't I?"

"These pills are rated for someone like me, they should work on you, even cut in half, but it's up to you."

"Let's do it then. What about you though, you said you've never done this before? Are you going to be okay?"

He made a dismissive face, "I'll be fine…I think. My beard hair might fall out, but that'd be the worst of it."

She wasn't sure if he was being honest or joking around.

He reached into his backseat and pulled out a small blue bag. He took one of the pills and split it in two with his thumbnails. "Here, take this and I'll see you on the other side."

She took the pill and swallowed it. She was scared but Sebastian trusted this man for a reason.

Two minutes later she was groggy, but not unconscious. "Am I supposed to be out?"

He looked at his screens, "It's a slow moving drug. Give it another few minutes to put you out. It's gentle, like you're going to sleep."

He was right.

She woke up after what felt like a few minutes of light sleep and looked around. She was confused at first, but when The Czar started snapping his fingers and singing along with some song at the top of his lungs, she remembered what had happened. "Are we through?"

The singing stopped, "Ah you're awake. We are through and I'm alive and so are you! How was your nap?"

"Fine, I guess. How long was I out?"

"About ten minutes."

She sat up in her seat and stretched out her neck. She looked over at him and saw he still had his beard. He must've been kidding about that part, but his nose was bleeding. "Hey you've got blood coming out your nose."

"Really? Damn it. Thanks." He wiped his nose with a finger and looked at it. He sighed and grabbed a tissue to pack into his nostrils.

"How much longer?"

"I am looking that up as we speak…" He sped through multiple Titan screens again and was quickly rifling through transit screens, "I'm sorry. I have to make sure the vehicle is structurally sound first. Just a few more tests."

She watched maps of the vehicle go by on his screen and a few warning messages he dismissed.

"Okay, so yeah, we're good. We have about ninety minutes before arriving."

She felt her nerves starting up and wanted a distraction, "So in the safe room, you said you're a Shaman and a Lanyx, but from a different planet? How does that work?"

The Czar adjusted a few controls on his transit screens, pulled out the blood-soaked tissue from his nose, and looked at her.

"I was born on Praxis, but my family left for Jex when I was very young. I've lived there my whole life, but I always love visiting the blue rock."

"Why did your family move?" She took a deep breath in and let it out slowly.

"Jex is a rare planet, special too. There the elder Shamans teach young gifted beings how to harness their powers into something completely new. I'm a lot like Raynes with my 7's. I was born with a special ability to sense intentions and read a little bit of other being's minds."

"Isn't that rare enough?"

"Course it is, very rare in fact. I think the number of Lanyx with 7's is greatly exaggerated really. Probably to scare off a lot of possible enemies I guess. In my estimation, I think it's less than half a percent of the population, actually, no wait. That's still too many. It's probably like, for every billion Lanyx, four are gifted. Yeah. I think that's the most accurate I can get. Sooooo, there's about eleven billion Lanyx. Forty-four gifted ones in the universe right now. Geez, I never figured it out like that before. Hmmm – did Raynes ever tell you that?"

"No. He mentioned it was rare."

"Yeah. You got that right. Anyways, I was blessed with 7's at birth but I now have even more abilities than before. I can heal some illnesses or wounds with a little help from herbs and salves. But the best thing about my enhanced powers is that I can sometimes see into the future. That's my kicker. Everyone with 7's has one. Yours is visions, mine is futurecasting and Raynes...hmmm, he doesn't have one yet, does he? It's probably still developing."

Celeste's mouth dropped open as she stared at him, "Does that mean you know if we're going to get Sebastian back safely or if something bad's going to happen?"

The Czar shook his head, "It's not as simple as you think. There's an infinite amount of events that affect the future. Every action, every decision, every minute that goes by can change what I see happening. Since you contacted me, I've already seen twenty different ways this rescue mission could go. It doesn't mean that's what's actually going to happen."

"Can you tell me anything useful? Please?" Her voice was weak.

He thought she might break into tears. It made him hesitate before answering her, "Telling you will only alter more outcomes. It's best if you don't know. I'm sorry."

She shook her head with frustration, "Why did Sebastian tell me to contact you then? I thought if you had these powers you could help us a little more!"

"Raynes...Sebastian is a loyal friend and associate of mine. I care about him a great deal, that's why. I would've come along with him on this mission if he'd told me about it. But, his stupid pride gets in the way of his thinking sometimes. Never could ask for help." He was quiet for a moment as he studied her, "I know you care about him even more than I do. I know you've already locked into him. Do you know what that means?"

She shook her head, "One of my friends mentioned something like clicking in or something, but I think she might've misunderstood something."

"I guess Raynes didn't tell you huh? He was probably thinking that gave him some sort of advantage over you or he thought it would slow down the process."

"I don't know what you're saying. Please just tell me."

"Sorry, I have to start at the beginning. Have you smelled a particular scent about him that you like?"

"Yes."

"Okay. That's not cologne or aftershave. That's the beginning of this whole process. Scent is sooooo important to us Lanyx. It really has everything to do with love. Locking into someone means you're pretty much prepped to fall in love with the person. It's not love, but it's the step immediately preceding it. Falling in love could be seconds, weeks, or years after locking in, but it's inevitable. Lanyx women look forward to it. Lanyx men…well, it depends on the man of course, but usually if they're not ready, we kinda' shy away from it or fear it. But…the thing is – you're not Lanyx. You're not halvesies or anything are you?"

Celeste shook her head, "My parents were full Human."

"That's a strange thing there. Locking in and scent is all for Lanyx noses only."

"How do you know this about me? That I've locked into him?"

"Not trying to be boastful Queen, but I'm pretty good at what I do. Better than most. You're actually beyond locking in, you're beyond just being in love with Raynes, but *I know* you know that too. It's pouring out of you. I can feel you have an extremely deep connection that binds you to him. I've never had that kind of connection to anyone. I've never been that blessed yet, but I know my time will come."

"You know for sure? With your foresight?"

"Technically, no. I hope. I hope my time for deep love will come, but I haven't been able to see it as clearly as I'd like. Maybe I'm not ready to. I don't know what the Universe is waiting for since I'm…old already." He looked over at Celeste and knew she was trying to be polite by listening, but she was worried as hell…and scared. He didn't blame her a bit. "But anyway…I know I trust Raynes, and he trusts me. We've saved each other's lives several times already. I think he chose me to help you, simply because he trusts me with his life, and I'm thinking he probably trusts me with yours as well. You can communicate with him without words from great distances across space, you just haven't experienced it yet. This is something even I can't do with him."

She raised her eyebrows, "I couldn't before."

He smiled, "I have some theories on what might've triggered your bond to my friend, but I won't say them out loud." He cleared his throat, "I ah, well…" he turned bright red. "God, I'm an ass. I apologize your Highness. This bond – it triggered a significant boost to both your 7's – at least that's what I feel coming off of you. I haven't felt Raynes yet to confirm this, but I think your guys' frequencies are probably close to the same and you're extremely emotionally close to him. If you couldn't communicate with him when you were far away before, you should be able to now. Just trust me. I know you don't know me, but you two? You and him are a unique pair. Capable of immense things. Very rare in the whole universe. We just need to get you two back together and safe. Try not to worry my lady."

Celeste quickly said, "Sebastian's the only one that's ever called me that."

"It's just good breeding, if you'll pardon the pun. I can be a dog some-times, but I can be a gentleman too. I was raised right just like Raynes."

"We need to get him home. I've needed a man like him my whole life. I can't lose him now. I can't."

He sighed with quiet resolve, "I'm here to help Queen Vandeermeer. If he's in trouble, he'll need the both of us to help him out. I know you've never been in battle before, but Raynes and I – we both need you at your best right now. We need you to be strong. We need you to expect th—"

"The unexpected." She finished, "He always says that."

"He's right your Highness. He's absolutely right."

She closed her eyes tight. *Keep it together.*

"You're sure you told me everything about Constantine and the BDP? Even the smallest detail can sometimes be very helpful."

Celeste opened her eyes and nodded, "Absolutely. Listen, I'm sorry I blew up at you about seeing into the future. I'm scared to death. I didn't mean to imply you're no help to me, to us." She rubbed her neck, "How far away are we from Tiletan?"

He studied his coordinates for a moment, "Only an hour. It's okay your Highness, totally understandable under these kinds of circum-stances to be afraid or short tempered. It takes a lot more to hurt me than what you said. I can read you like a book in the condition you're in and your words didn't offend me. Raynes was right, you telegraph thoughts out like a radio station. I never read minds of my friends and certainly not my best friend's girl, but with you, you're just giving me all these thoughts. I'm not trying to invade your gray matter, but if you don't want me to know something, you need to check your walls right now, otherwise there's a good chance I'm going to hear all of it."

She shook her head, "It's fine. If Bastian trusts you with his life then I trust you with mine as well. I don't mind if you hear me – thoughts or otherwise."

"Oooh you call him Bastian. He doesn't let anybody call him that. He must really like you. Course, you guys have probably already said you love each other."

Celeste stared at him, "What makes you say that?"

He looked at her and his eyes opened wide. He looked over one shoulder then the other as if there was someone else around, then back at her, "What? I didn't say anything my Queen. Nope, didn't say a thing."

She smiled at him, "He loves me?"

He tilted his head sideways, "Now, I really didn't say that. Raynes would kill me if he heard us talking about him. You know how fiercely private he is. It's not fair for me to talk about how Raynes does or doesn't feel about you, but I can say go with your gut. What do you think he feels for you?"

She shrugged her shoulders, "I always hoped he loved me...just that he was afraid to say it or it was hard for him to tell me."

He looked at her and just smiled.

"Am I right?"

"If that's what your gut says, then I would go with that. I'm sorry, it's really not my place to say though."

She sighed loudly, "I want him safe and back home with me. Whatever it takes, I want to get him off Tiletan. I'm glad he told me to call you. I'm grateful really."

"I am happy to help. I know you only want to protect Raynes, so between the two of us hopefully we can get in there and get out quick. As long as I've known him, he's never gotten himself into quite this kind of situation," The Czar ran his hand down over his face, "I can't imagine how hard this must be on you. Maybe you should try communicating with him, although I'll tell you right now, I'll be able to hear whatever you think, but maybe not his thoughts. I don't know."

She closed her eyes and thought of the mountain they held her in, that little white room, and tried to relax.

<Sebastian?>

She heard nothing. She looked over to The Czar.

He said to her without words, <Keep trying Celeste. You are stronger than you realize, maybe even stronger than Sebastian knows.>

She nodded slowly. <*Sebastian please, if you can hear me say something.*>
No reply.

She put her hand to her mouth, trying to keep from tearing up at thinking of the possibility they were too late.

"Don't stop Celeste. If he can hear you, he will respond. Think positive."

She leaned back in her seat and tried continuously for the next thirty minutes with no replies until finally she picked up something.

<*Celeste!? You close?*>

<*BASTIAN! Thank goodness. Are you okay?*> He didn't sound right to her.

<*Yes...no. Hard...to think. Beaten bad...*>

<*Sebastian! Come on baby. Stay with me...Please.*> Panic was trying to overwhelm her, but she was fighting hard to push it down.

<*You can't get me. Constantine has set...trap...for you...I'm bait. Stay away. Send police instead.*>

It was hard for her to clearly read his thoughts. It was like trying to hear someone talking underwater. He definitely wasn't right. If he were thinking straight, he'd never tell her to send police to his location... unless this was really *really* bad.

She looked to The Czar, "Sebastian's the bait for a trap that Constantine's set for us."

<*He's goin to capture you, torture...rape you...in...fronn of me, then...*>

<*Stay with me, you're doing so good handsome.*> Her eyes filled with tears waiting to fall down her cheeks.

<*He wants...kill you...for revenge...for Fran. He knows I care...bout you. He wants to punish...me...after he's killed...you, he'll kill me. Told me so.*>

Celeste couldn't hold back her tears.

<*Sebastian, it doesn't matter what he wants to do to me, it's not going to happen. Maybe he's bluffing. He had a chance to rape me and he didn't.*"

<*That was before he knew you were...with me.*>

Celeste paused, < *I'm not leaving Tiletan without you and we're almost there. We won't fall for any of Dax's traps. There isn't any other way for us to get you off world.*>

<Usss? You have Eric, I mean...Czar with you?>

<Yes, of course. You told me in your message to contact him if we needed help.>

<We...certain...need him. Can he hearrr me too?> He sounded like a drunk man who just had major dental work to Celeste. And his thoughts were getting more garbled.

Celeste looked over at Eric. Didn't have the same ring as The Czar. He looked at her and registered nothing.

"Can you hear Sebastian?"

Eric shook his head, "But I can hear your end. I know you're communicating."

<Your friend can't hear you. He told me I might be stronger at communicating with you than even you think.>

<He'sss a...shaman, a Lanyxx...very good fighter...I...trusss everything in him, he...probably right. Has...told you how this might...play out?>

<No.> He certainly has *not* told me how this might all play out.

<He's annoying like that. All that...power...to...see into...future, yet never...says anything. Fear...it'll change...things.>

<How are you holding up?>

<Fine. Okay.>

<Try again. You sound bad baby. I need you to be honest now.>

<Not good...need you to be brave for...me when you find me. When I first saw...you after your kidnappin...I thought I'd...preparedd myself, but I was wrong. Seein you that way...it was one of the hardessst things...I had to deal withh. It still makes me sick to...know you went through all that... abussse. That kind...of shock, is goin...be harder...on you. I've beeen beat up, extreme...bad. I'm tied to...wall right now. My bro's beeen very brutal over the...passt day. Try to steel yourself...Not pretty when you seee me, okay?>

<Okay. I will find you; I just need you to hang on for me.>

<Have...lot to hang on for...know I shouldn't have...made love to you...and lied bout wheeen I was leavin—>

She interrupted his thought, <Shhhh please Sebastian. We need to find you first. That's all I'm thinking of right now. When I have you back home

and you're recovering and we're both safe, we'll have all the time in the world to talk. What I want to do right now is get you out of there.>

<Fine, but...have lots...of apologizin to do...I can leaadd you...guys into the complex part of the wayyy, but they'll be...expectin you. I hope you guys have...great plan...pleassse tell me you have...great plan...>

<Don't worry. We talked it over before we even left the planet. He brought a ton of weapons and I raided your safe room for everything I could get. He thinks we're ready for anything.>

<Don't underestimate...my bro please. There are...twenty-two guys he's leadin...here...and those are...the ones I could see. I took out the front... door guard when...I came in...I'm sure...they have someone...else guardin now. Let me...tell you...everything...I saw.>

They continued to talk by 7's while Eric prepared the transit for landing.

Celeste relayed everything Sebastian told her as fast as she could think it to Eric. Celeste was bothered by the fact that Sebastian told her Constantine had some sort of mask over Sebastian's face that was forcing him to breathe nitrous oxide only sporadically to keep him off balance mentally. She had never felt so anxious to see him and hold him. His information had helped their planning, but didn't really alter what they'd do. Eric thought it was best to go in with their guns blazing. Take no prisoners, with the exception of Constantine if they could manage it, and move as fast as possible. Eric knowing that Sebastian was bait and them wanting to capture Celeste was what he already saw in his all of his visions so that wasn't surprising to him. There was one thing he could do for Celeste that would help all of them.

He lowered his head and held Celeste's hands in the transit before they stepped out into the desert.

"I need you to relax, Celeste."

"That's easy for you to say."

"Come on. Take a deep breath and let it out slowly."

She did as he asked and tried to clear her mind of worry and clutter.

"Warrior Spirits, I ask that you bless Celeste with the power and speed of all warriors of every battle before her. Every hero's heart that has beat before her, let it reverberate in her chest, let every war cry that has been shouted before, echo forever in her spirit. Let her opponents fall quickly, her grace guide her through the battlefield, her instincts be sharp and her aim always on target. Help to steady her hand and steel her heart for what is about to pass. With all that I am as a fighter, and all that I have, I ask this of you today, pure of heart."

Eric said a prayer for Sebastian and over himself as Celeste wrapped up her hair in a bun and piled it on top of her head. He looked at her, "Ready for this?"

She nodded.

He took a deep breath and he and Celeste left the safety of the transit behind.

The Tiletan twin suns dipped below the horizon and it was now dusk on the desert planet. Eric and Celeste were both, respectfully, a one man and woman army. The weight of weapons and battle armor that Celeste wore should've slowed her down, but she attributed her unusual strength to adrenaline and whatever Eric had said over her. She was amazed at the ease of movement she had tonight.

They both easily bypassed the security system of lasers that Sebastian mentioned. Eric thought they were just for show and didn't really do anything, but they still didn't break the lines. They approached the front entrance from the side and saw a Human man standing guard. Eric took him out in a silent shot and they ran to the door.

<Sebastian, we're at the front door.>

<Be ver...careful. No matter...wha happensss...I'm proud of you... for...trying to help me. Do...your best...you'll not let...me down...You've never let me...down.>

She managed to blink back tears. <Just hold on handsome. Hold on. I'll be with you soon. I'm going to save you.>

<Already...did.>

Celeste smiled under her combat helmet and felt a single tear escape.

Eric didn't say anything, but he caught this extremely private exchange between his best friend and the Queen. If their connection was this strong when Sebastian was not at one hundred percent, he wondered what it felt like when they were both healthy. He could feel an energy between them he never felt before. A current of electricity hummed off both their minds and it caused a silent awe in Eric. They were both powerful creatures that only magnified each other's abilities. As long as Raynes and Celeste survived today, they would be a formidable and commanding team. They would need to be for what was coming their way in the near future. In one of his visions, there was a violent revolution about to be born on Earth. No one knew about it but him.

The Queen was speaking to him through the comms on the helmets. "I'm ready when you are Eric." She stood with her back to the door looking around for movement.

"Fuck man! He told you my real name? Damn him."

"I won't tell a soul. I promise."

Eric closed his eyes for a moment as his futurecasts shifted. His heart stopped. A lot was riding on what he was about to see and he hoped one strong vision would dominate the others – then he'd be able to relax. He held his breath, waiting.

He was glad when half of his visions of the immediate future faded from existence. That half had been deadly outcomes ranging from one of them dying, to all of them. He took a deep breath in and thanked the Gods and Goddesses for a little relief and comfort. He would never tell Raynes or Celeste how many futurecasts he had that were deadly.

Celeste tightened her grip on the short shotgun she carried. She knew she should be a lot more nervous right now, but she experienced a calm she never expected. She was starting to think Eric had done something extraordinary when he blessed her.

Eric rested his automatic rifle against his shoulder while he bypassed the electronic code lock. It was an easy hack. "Ask, and it shall be given you; seek, and ye shall find, knock, and it shall be opened unto you." Then he cracked opened the door, looking for threats and when he saw none, opened the door wider. They entered quietly, still expecting alarms to go off.

Celeste closed the door silently behind her and they moved together down the same hallway Sebastian had yesterday. His description of everything was perfect and when they got to the room he described as what he thought was a video recording room, they saw it was empty.

Eric said telepathically to her, *<This is definitely a trap. They already know we're here and they're letting us get to where they want us. Their telepaths are either extremely weak or they don't have any here. That's good for us. But I can't sense Constantine at all.>*

Celeste raised her eyebrows, *< I can't either. I never could though. You lead the way. I'll follow.>*

They walked, guns raised, around each new corner past the point where Sebastian's description ended. Celeste was impressed at how well her and Eric worked together. His spell blessing, or whatever he called it, was probably boosting her up quite a bit, making her the warrior she needed to be right now.

They came upon a set of stairs going deep down into what appeared to be a cavern. Eric could feel the cool damp air hit his face when he raised his helmet's visor.

They cautiously descended down. There was a single door on the opposite side of the cave. A few dim lamps strung along the walls were the only source of light in the underground darkness. Eric was eager to move on from here. This area left them too vulnerable with two doors on either side of them. He approached the next door quickly.

He looked at Celeste, *<This is it Queen. They want us on the other side of this door. Ask Raynes if he knows where he is.>*

<Sebastian?>

She heard no response. Her heart stopped. She looked into Eric's face.

<Anything from him?>

She shook her head.

<Raynes! Can you hear me?> Eric got no response either.

"Try again, Celeste."

<Baby? I'm here hon. I'm real close I bet.> She took a deep breath and let it out. *<Bastian?>*

<Here, just...barely....I...need to tell you...I...I...>

She couldn't hear him all of a sudden. *<Bastian? What do you need to say?>*

She heard nothing and looked at Eric.

Eric thought to her as he put his hand on the door handle, *<I heard him. Constantine is beating him very hard. He's lost consciousness. We need*

to hurry. *You ready Celeste? I've never needed anyone to be stronger in battle than I'm asking you to be right now.>*

She nodded, *<Ready.>*

Eric quickly turned the handle and threw open the door.

CHAPTER 38

FUTURECASTS

ONE

>>> > SEBASTIAN COULDN'T REMEMBER ever being beaten this badly, and it was fantastically difficult for him to stay conscious. Constantine repeatedly threw buckets of cold water on his face to revive him. Sebastian could no longer breathe through his nose, but was forced to cough out breaths through his mouth. All he could think of was trying to protect Celeste from the bastard his brother had evolved into. But there was nothing he could do. Every part of his body throbbed with fresh pain. Sebastian's logical side told him he was powerless to do anything in his current position, but his unrelenting will wouldn't give up trying to fight or escape.

Constantine was rotating three violent and murderous intentions so that Sebastian couldn't get a fix on one. He heard Celeste call out to him and he sensed Eric as well, but his 7's were weakening. He needed to tell them what Constantine was thinking before it was too late. He tried to speak with Celeste telepathically, but only got out a couple of words before blacking out.

Had he been awake he would've heard the door in the next room surge open with Celeste and Eric charging through it.

TWO

>>> > ERIC AND CELESTE looked around the room.

"Oh my God. Eric," she flipped up her visor to see clearly. Eric did the same.

The room was full of medieval torture devices – Eric recognized most of them, but Celeste had seen several of them too. Thumbscrews, stocks, and pillories were everywhere. She was reminded of Jon and his intense pleasure for unique torture.

"God help us, they even have an iron maiden. Jesus." Eric scanned the room quickly, his blood pressure rising. He didn't see this coming in any of his visions so it was a genuine and unsettling surprise. He wondered if they had used weapons or tools on Raynes yet. There were plenty of things like hammers, vices, and pliers hanging on the walls and he felt his animal side rising up.

While his friend almost always tried to hide his animal side, and sometimes even seemed embarrassed of it, Eric let it dominate when necessary. Because if it was necessary that meant things had gotten either very good, like sex, or very bad, like right now.

Constantine came through the door on the other side of the room. He was covered in Sebastian's blood, Celeste knew that already. His arms and face were stained with brown splatters. Celeste's stomach turned, but she aimed the shotgun at Dax's head despite feeling as though she would vomit. She had to remind herself that she actually dated this man and made out with the monster.

Eric already had his automatic rifle pointed at him, but was completely steady.

"Oh Celeste, didn't you get my message? I told you to come alone," he gave them a forced smile.

The room was silent.

"Well, I suppose we'll just make the best of this third-wheel. Maybe it'll be more fun this way. I don't think we've met sir." Constantine put out his hand and approached Eric.

Eric and Celeste put their fingers on the triggers of their weapons in response. Eric let out a loud growl.

Constantine spoke to Eric, "I suppose introductions don't really matter, but my name's Daxton. From the looks of you, I'm going to guess you're ex-military. Maybe you served with Bass before he completely destroyed my life."

"I really don't talk much with murderous sociopaths. I don't see the point. Where's Raynes? We're here to take him home."

"Na ah ah. Not so fast. And for your information, I've never murdered a soul. I'm the one who usually orders the kills, but you three will be my first personal murders ever. You have to take some pride in that, right?"

Eric stared, "No one's dying except for you worthless fucks. You and your so called 'men.'"

"Where's Sebastian, Constantine?" Celeste was anxious to see him with her own eyes.

Constantine completely ignored their words, "I thought it would take forever for you to find your way through the hallways. I was watching you with my cameras. I don't think shoot first and ask questions later is going to work in this situation though. And this one"—he pointed at Celeste—"I wouldn't count on her shooting anyone at all. She isn't hard hearted enough."

Celeste honestly didn't know if she could kill anyone, but she wouldn't admit it. "WHERE IS HE?!" she shouted and tried to fight off panic rising up in the back of her mind.

"Ah. I see. Ask questions first and *then* kill me. Interesting. Well I wouldn't shoot me just yet. I'm wearing a bit of a nasty surprise on my back…and my waist too for that matter. Well, it'd be nasty for you anyways. You guys looked good out there, pretending to be some real badasses. It seems like a show to me, but…" He turned and walked through the open door behind him, "Come on inside, I think you know my brother."

Celeste and Eric eyed the vest full of explosives sitting on Constantine's back. He moved out of the way and she got her first look at Sebastian.

Celeste had been warned, but it wasn't enough. To her credit, she held down her food as long as she could. Once she saw the state Sebastian was in, she felt like no amount of preparing would have helped with that. He was almost unrecognizable to her.

Sebastian was chained to a brick wall with all of his limbs pulled out tight. He had a metal clamp around his waist. His feet were barely touching the ground, and his arms looked painfully stretched out as far as they could be without coming out of their sockets. He was hanging there, in his briefs. Celeste knew Constantine was trying to strip away all of Sebastian's dignity. All he was succeeding at was enraging both Celeste and Eric to vengeful depths.

Sebastian's chest was covered with his own blood and his face was swollen with three different colors of bruises. He was unconscious. The only thing that hadn't changed was his scent. Celeste could still detect his familiar wonderful smell, and it brought the memory of their first kiss into the front of her mind. *What if they were too late?* Her heart dropped into her stomach, then she bent over and heaved. She removed her helmet just in time to avoid soiling it.

Eric kept his gun pointed at Constantine while Celeste emptied the contents of her stomach. He saw that happen in one of his visions and he hoped his speech might've helped her avoid that, but it didn't. He couldn't blame her. He knew she was in love with his friend and to see him that way must've been extremely difficult for her. Hell, it was difficult for him.

<*Come on Celeste. Get it together. You have to if you want to save him.*> Eric felt she needed a quick kick in the butt.

Celeste wiped her mouth on her sleeve and put her helmet on with the visor down. She aimed her shotgun at Constantine and felt ashamed. There was a time she thought he was worth a second chance from Sebastian. She had pleaded on his behalf for some mercy. She thought Sebastian had been too harsh on him, but he was right all along. Constantine deserved no mercy because he gave none to his brother.

Seeing Sebastian this way...there was no sympathy from her towards Constantine now. Whatever happened to him during this battle – happened; Constantine was on his own.

"Constantine? That's your real name right? I'm not sure if you noticed but you're a bit outnumbered here jackass. I recommend you release Sebastian." Eric's voice echoed across the room.

"Outnumbered?! I don't even know who the *fuck* you are, but I know *you know* there's more than just the four of us here." Constantine raised his hand into the air and the sound of many footsteps filled the cavern behind them. Celeste turned and kicked the door shut. She looked at Eric, but he never moved. He kept his gun aimed at Constantine.

"They're coming through that door in a second Celeste. I know you have your doubts but if you can't do this, you need to say so right now," Eric's voice was firm and calm.

"Good to go." She felt the adrenaline hit her bloodstream – her body was electric with it. She was hyper awake...alert and vibrating with tension. But she was also terrified.

"Then I need you to be ready."

She nodded and when the door flew open, she pulled the trigger.

As gunshots rang out, Constantine moved to the corner of the room and hit a panel with his foot. Him and Sebastian disappeared out of sight as the entire wall rotated, leaving an empty wall behind.

Dax knew his men remembered his instructions. Take the woman alive and kill everyone else.

Eric turned around and saw that Celeste already killed the first three men that came through the door.

<DUCK!> He thought to her as he grabbed a flash grenade off his belt, pulled the pin, and threw it.

Celeste kneeled down quickly and rolled off to the side of the room.

The grenade went off, instantly blinding several men into vulnerable positions. Eric gunned in a straight line across the cavern and tore into bodies like pieces of meat. It happened so fast, Celeste almost didn't see any of it as she reloaded. Her ears were ringing terribly as firing guns echoed throughout the complex.

Then it was suddenly quiet.

Eric charged through the open door and down into the cavern. He checked the hall and saw no one else.

He closed the cave door quickly and yelled out to Celeste, "I need your help!"

She stood in place. It had been nothing like her training. The past few minutes had felt like an hour, but also felt quick at the same time. Things had gotten chaotic so quickly and now she was…a killer. *But there wasn't any other way. This needed to be done to get Sebastian. No other way.*

"CELESTE! NOW!"

Eric's shout jolted her into motion. She came running through the cavern and onto the other side where Eric stood. She ignored the jelly sensation in her legs.

"We need to stack the bodies up against this door, take their Titans, and we need to move fast."

In five minutes, they stacked twelve bodies as tightly as they could to jam the door shut. Eric shoved and strapped twelve Titans anywhere they'd fit on him or in his gear. Taking all the weapons and ammo they could scavenge, they ran back into the room where Sebastian had been. Celeste looked at the blood covering her. It was everywhere. It hit her hard that she was now responsible for three complete stranger's deaths. She couldn't stop it and vomited again, turning her back to Eric.

He checked his weapons, and called over his shoulder, "It's fine. First time is tough. Nothing to be embarrassed of."

She stood up and leaned against the wall, "WHY didn't you shoot Constantine in the head?! You had him right there!"

"I couldn't. With explosives on his back and him standing in front of Raynes. Too many visions told me I'd hit Sebastian instead. Plus, he could've had a dead man's trigger, way too risky. Seeing the future is *not* as easy as you think. Fuck!" He pushed back his helmet and wiped sweat off his brow with the side of his hand.

"What now?"

Eric looked at the panel on the wall where Constantine had touched. "We chase, my dear. We chase." He hit the panel and they rotated into another room. It was extremely dark here. Celeste activated her night goggles and swallowed hard. Eric could see fine without them as he led Celeste through the dark ahead. He followed the blood trail that marked where Constantine dragged Sebastian's body away.

<Sebastian said they had twenty-two men here without Constantine. Where are the others?>

Eric thought back, <I killed one at the door, twelve back there, and you killed three. That leaves Constantine and six that are staying for the fight. We're doing the right thing. It's the only way to get Sebastian back home to you. You're doing really good for your first time in battle. I'm proud of you and Raynes will be too when he wakes up.>

<Oh yeah, tossing my breakfast was real good.>

<Forget about it. No big deal. Seeing Raynes that way, killing for the first time. I don't blame you. You're fine. It's going to be fine.>

<I should be freaking out more right now. However you blessed me – really worked back there. Thanks.>

Eric looked at her and pointed with two fingers forward into the far depths of the cave. They quietly crept onward as they got to what he hoped was the final battleground up ahead.

THREE

>>> › D'ARTAGNAN CALLED MITCH. He couldn't believe he forgot to mention one key piece of information he found while rooting around in the finances of Rem Mot Om. He already sent a Titan message to Raynes regarding it, but hadn't heard anything back from him lately.

D'Artagnan smiled wide, "Mitch, listen, I totally forgot to tell you something pretty important and I apologize for not doing so sooner, but it concerns Queen Dowager Celeste."

Mitch raised his eyebrows, "Oh really? Let's have it."

"When I was inside the finances of King David, I never saw any funds transferred, extracted, or in any other means prepared for paying a ransom. I think the last amount I knew of, it was six million coren; that's a huge amount of money. I should've seen something for it in their financial records, but I didn't. I honestly don't think they've put aside anything for it."

Mitch rubbed his beard, "That is interesting. I wish there was some way we could prove it. If I say that in a public statement via Titan message, David will dispute it. Him and his advisors will come up with some way to turn it around on us where we look like idiots or we're just making it up...but if there was some way to prove it...*then* we'd have some real fire to throw at him. No matter what anyone thinks of King David right now, no one likes a liar...and you can't trust a dishonest king."

"Nor can you respect a liar. I'll see what I can come up with."

Mitch smiled, "Oh? You're serious? I was just thinking out loud. I didn't mean for us to actually tap into his Titan or the estate or anything. That's serious detective work or spy shit."

"Yes, it is. I might be able to get something done in that department though. We'll see. Don't hold your breath."

FOUR

>>> > DAVID NEVER WANTED to see this room again. He was sick of press conferences. He hoped this would be the last one for a long while.

"Thank you again for coming out. I wanted to keep this one brief so I'll get to the point. The Il'lacean council's services were terminated. It was an amicable separation and I wish them all the best in their future endeavors. In the end, the council and I started to see a different vision for the Kingdom's future and I really require that my staff is behind me one hundred percent. Since it seemed as though we wanted to go in separate directions, we thought it best to end our relationship now. The council will not be replaced and they have been compensated very generously.

"Unfortunately the Kingdom also had to execute one of our own recently. Guard Raykreede Monter. He had been in the service of the King all the way back to my brother, King Jonathan. Guard Monter requested a private meeting with me and it was granted. During this meeting, Guard Monter expressed terrorist-like rants and behaviors I deemed extremely dangerous. I will not tolerate such attitudes in my staff. I'm working diligently to bring Humans and Il'laceans together, not widening the gap between us. Guard Monter was executed shortly after that meeting and his body burned as is Il'lacean custom. He had no surviving relatives.

"The next subject to be discussed is our recent breach in security. I want to remind citizens that it is a crime against the Kingdom to keep the coren that was illegally obtained and put into your bank accounts. I encourage you all to reverse the deposit so it will come back to the Kingdom's bank. This is your final warning regarding this matter and after five sunsets on your own home world have passed, if you do nothing and have not returned the coren, it will be a punishable act. We might even need to go into all bank accounts and retrieve the coren if you haven't returned the money on your own.

"The last matter regards FAIR. I'm not a violent person. I do not wish bad things on people, but I will not tolerate criminal or dangerous acts against innocent beings.

"FAIR has now made criminals out of innocent citizens. When they do not return the windfall of money that was 'given' to them, they become criminals. FAIR can't distribute money that is not theirs however they see fit. We would have chaos if a planet was run that way, and it can't be tolerated.

"FAIR needs to cease and desist immediately if you have not already. You need to turn yourselves in if you'd like leniency upon your criminal record or life and I would like to never speak of them again.

"The world needs less terrorism masking itself as justice and more tolerance and love.

"There will be no questions today. Thank you."

FIVE

TITAN Corporation - Personal TITAN Device

System Status: Active -- Universal Grid: Online

Current Time/Date (Praxis - Dersalene): 10:03 a.m./August 33, 2193

Secondary Time/Date (Earth - London, England): 5:50 a.m./ November 09, 4015

Current Universal Positioning System Location: Dersalene, Praxis

User: All Titan users

Communications Menu

Incoming message(s) received: 1 - Status: New/Unread

Message Received at 10:03 a.m.

Message Sent from: The leader of FAIR

-King David Hennessy,
We here at FAIR would like to remind you that it's illegal what you're threatening to do to the good folks of Earth and Il'laceier. You can't go into individual's bank accounts and retrieve money. You can't lie to them this way without being checked.
Our job is to keep you in line, or make it so difficult for you to do your "job" that you choose to leave it.
We would like to tell you formally, in front of the entire universe that we have no plans of backing down, giving up, or retreating. If you haven't noticed by now, we don't listen to you, or take your "commands" seriously.
We will not cease until Earth is completely free of you and your sad excuse of a reign over us.
To the citizens of Earth and Il'laceier,

We want to tell you that you can't be prosecuted for a crime you didn't commit. If you choose to keep the money we redistributed to your account, King David will never find out who you are.

This point aside, we're setting a timeline for you to make up your mind.

On Earth day November 11, 4015 and

Il'lacean day Atos 91-9, 5390

the window for giving back the coren electronically will close and if you choose to give it back after that, you'll have to hand deliver or mail it.

We hope that you've decided to keep the coren, or better still, have already spent it and stimulated the world economy of either Earth or Il'laceier.

And if you're on the fence, or are ready to return the money, come on now, when was the last time King David did something for you?

King David, we're not going anywhere anytime soon.

Citizens of Earth and Il'laceier, thank you for your time and attention.

Sincerely,

The leader of FAIR

-END OF MESSAGE

*This message will only be deleted by user.

SIX

>>> > DAX DIDN'T PICK up the call.

Hace was forced to leave a message and that irritated him, "Daxton! Where the hell are you?

"You tell me Celeste isn't there anymore and that you're going to fix this whole mess and then you can't even answer when I call? What the fuck?! You better have a damn good reason for not picking up! You hear me loud and clear – if you don't fix this soon, I'm going to make you wish you were never a part of this group. I need to hear back from you and soon! The Hunter over and out!"

Hace needed to expel all his sudden rage. He went to the pool and jumped in naked. After he swam a few laps, he sat on the steps and called out, "DAI! I need you here. Stox form. Wear a nurse uniform."

"Right away, Master."

SEVEN

>>> > SOMEONE WAS TRYING to access Erebos' Titan, but Ophelia knew it wasn't Erebos.

She quickly looked through the Titan's camera and saw who it was. She took a picture of the blonde man for later reference and waited to see what he did next. The man put in code after code, trying to break into the Titan.

She took note of the location on Tiletan and saw everything that she could in the background behind the man's face. There was a dark sky and one other man in view but it wasn't Erebos.

The man wouldn't give up. He shook the Titan at one point and tried accessing it another way.

Ophelia saw the Titan carried around, and then there was Erebos, but he was unconscious. The blonde man grabbed Erebos' index finger and put it on the Titan's screen. The Titan's main menu began to open.

And if they accessed his Titan, eventually they'd access her. And she couldn't have that.

She took control of the Titan and used one of the final protection methods it had left.

She saw the Titan hit the dirt after the blonde man received the electrical shock she had administered through it. She heard someone say, "That's not possible you pussy. Those things don't emit electricity. Here let me do it."

Ophelia watched the Titan get lifted off the ground and carried for a distance by another man who had dark hair. She took a picture of him and then performed the final act of protection the Titan had. She didn't want to, but it looked like there was no other way to protect Erebos and herself.

She calculated Erebos was at least thirty feet away from his Titan. She hoped that was far enough.

The Titan exploded as a tiny bomb inside detonated and the man that was currently holding it, disintegrated.

The blonde man who had been shocked by the Titan was now on the ground and cried out in surprise. He couldn't hear anything. The mini explosion had been loud for its size. He tried to get up, but the bomb had obliterated his legs from the waist down and he knew he'd bleed to death soon.

EIGHT

>>> > CELESTE WAS AMAZINGLY calm, but wanted to get to Sebastian and get the hell out of here. She'd have to deal with the full force of becoming a murderer only after Sebastian was safe. Then she could cry all she needed to…but not now.

<The trail stops here.> Eric put his hand up on a wall and she could see the elevator doors now.

<Where does this go? Can we get in?>

She watched as he looked around. She could see no buttons to press, but there was a flat smooth panel to the right of the door.

Eric said, <Damn. It's a hand scanner. I could try and get around it, but it would take too much time and it's probably rigged with some sort of anti-tampering booby trap. We'll have to look around and see if we can find another way to get up this mountain.>

<Where do you think this goes? Maybe it leads outside?>

<Maybe.>

<Can you disable it so they can't use it either way?>

Eric thought, <Sure, if that's what you really want. Stand back.>

He tapped at his Titan and a little chip popped out of the side. Celeste watched as he stuck it to the panel on the wall and she heard a click and fizzle as the panel smoked then caught fire. Sparks flew and then the panel melted.

Eric looked to Celeste, <*EMP sticker. I basically fried it. No one can use it now.*>

She smiled, <*Great.*>

They walked until they saw the exit ahead. Eric motioned for her to go to the right as he moved left. They each stood on the inside edge of the cave exit and scanned the outside area for anything. Celeste flipped up her visor momentarily and saw the night sky full of stars just outside. She also saw something else.

<*Eric, there's a big metal door or gate here. Do you see?*> She pointed up to the middle of the arched exit way.

Eric cursed himself for not noticing it before and it was in none of his futurecasts. There was a metal bar sandwiched in between the inner and outer walls of the exit. <*This is like a pocket door, the one Raynes must've described to you when he first arrived. Make sure you don't hover underneath. This thing comes down and you're flat like a pancake.*>

<*Okay.*>

Eric thought, <*Off to the left here. I can see boot prints, lots of them. They go out to the desert and back in. Be alert. There's a reason they left this door open for us.*>

They carefully came out of cover and that's when the floodlights came on.

Blinding Celeste but not Eric, one of Constantine's henchmen went to grab the vulnerable Celeste, but Eric quickly picked him off with his rifle. He fell dead before Celeste even turned around. She ran further out from the circle of light until her eyes adjusted. Eric turned and saw two more men coming for him but lit up his rifle as they began firing at him. He took a few hits in his chest, but stayed on his feet. The two men were struck with several bullets and fell to the ground. Eric grabbed at his chest and yelled out verbally and mentally. It stunned Celeste momentarily. She'd never felt anything like it and hoped she didn't again. It felt like a ripple of pain starting in the middle of her mind and radiated outward. She blinked hard a couple of times and shook it off.

Celeste moved back towards the light where Eric stood and saw a man hovering on the thin ledge above the cave entrance. She took out a small pistol and shot at him, hitting him in the arm. Eric turned and covered the mountainside in bullets. He saw the final henchman's body slide off the rocks and hit the desert floor with a dull thud.

<*Thanks. Just leaves Constantine plus two.*> Eric was breathing hard. He ran his hand along the inside of his vest.

She looked at his chest. <*Are you okay? Are you hit?*>

Eric nodded to Celeste. <*Hurts like hell, but the vest took all of it.*>

She gave him a few minutes to catch his breath while she looked around for Sebastian.

One of the Tiletan suns started to rise giving a very faint light to the planet. Celeste thought they called this one Nissix. It gave a twilight look to the desert and she was grateful they didn't have to keep searching in the dark. She disengaged her night goggles.

Celeste walked a few minutes and stopped. She mentally called out to Eric, <*Come here quick. I found the other two men…I think.*>

Eric came up behind her and saw what looked like the remains of a small explosion.

<*What happened here?*>

Eric shook his head and kneeled down. He saw bits of a Titan strap, remnants of bone, hair, flesh, and the top half of a Human man who probably bled to death from the looks of his injuries.

<*I'm gonna say one man accidentally blew himself up, maybe you're right though. I think there's two dead here. That's a lot of flesh for just this guy's legs.*>

Celeste put her hand to her stomach but kept from throwing up. <*So I guess that means it's just Constantine left.*>

Eric nodded. <*Let's move.*>

They circled the mountain. Eric could smell Constantine now, but he couldn't see him. He knew he was close. Constantine smelled very wrong – ill. If Eric had to describe the smell to anyone he would've said it was like mental rot. To Eric it was ten times worse than a decaying body left in the hot sun. Due to Eric's animal nature, he could smell things that other beings could not like fear and illness, but Eric knew if D'Artagnan was here, his Il'lacean nose could've probably sniffed out Constantine as soon as they arrived.

The difference between Eric and Sebastian again came down to oppressing or embracing their animalistic sides. Eric could smell Constantine because he embraced the animal abilities in himself and also because Constantine was out in the open. Sebastian had not been able to smell his own brother or sense him mentally because Constantine had been hidden deep underground waiting for Sebastian to show up.

Eric looked up and saw a figure standing alone along a precipice of the mountainside. There was a very large tree up there as well. Eric's futurecasts shifted again. He was deeply disturbed that *this* was the vision that came to the top of his list of possible outcomes. Bad things were ahead just from that tree being there.

Constantine called out, "I want Celeste! Send her up alone and unarmed or else I will drop my brother's body off the side of this cliff. There's a noose around his neck. He will hang from this Mickahrah tree. Poetic justice really."

Eric looked at Celeste, <*That tree forebodes of terrible things. I can shoot that prick from here. Stop this now.*>

<*NO WAY. Have you lost your mind and forgotten about the bombs on his back?*>

<*No, of course not. I mean in the head. I'll shoot his head. I've got a ninety percent chance of ending this right now with Sebastian alive. My futurecasts shifted.*>

She hesitated, <*No, Constantine could still trigger something. Ninety percent isn't good enough. Ten percent chance of Sebastian dying isn't acceptable. Constantine's got a Goddamn grenade belt on too. I go up there, get close and check on Sebastian. I can push Constantine off the cliff and when I do, you get clear okay?*>

"Before you two try anything funny, I also have some chemical confetti. I could kill you both now and this is over for you. Or…" he took out a pistol, "I can just shoot Sebastian now and you'll never see your boyfriend again. Don't test me. Come up Celeste. NOW!"

<Chemical confetti? What the hell is that?>

<He means grenades — chemical grenades. Depending on what kind, they could do all sorts of nasty things to our lungs — harden them, liquefy them; stuff you don't want to happen. If the wind picks up it could cover a wide spread area.> He paused, <He has a lot more than grenades up there Celeste. That bomb…He's highly unpredictable. His intentions are all over the place. Even I don't know what he's planning. Please don't do this. Let me take the shot.>

<No! I have to go up there. I haven't even told him…He doesn't know… I'm not going to let that crazy son of a bitch kill him. It ends now. Promise me you won't shoot him unless I say so.>

Eric hesitated, <Okay. We do it your way. Put all your weapons down. I'll put down everything except my pistol that's in the back of my pants and back away. Maybe you can lure him close to the edge but far enough away from you and Raynes. Then push him over if you can. I can shoot him when he's down here if he survives the fall.>

<Okay.>

"I'm coming up. Let me put down my weapons."

"Pretty boy's weapons too and he has to back away from the pile. Way far away."

Celeste took off all of her visible weapons, and piled them up with Eric's. Eric moved off to the side of the pile and further back to get a better shot at Constantine if something went wrong.

Celeste climbed along a ridge in the mountain and was soon at a spot that made her nervous. She didn't know where to put her foot next, everything looked like loose gravel. She moved to her left and lost her footing. She briefly tumbled down the mountain, losing her helmet along the way. She stopped rolling in time to see it smash down on the rocks below her. Hair was in her eyes as her bun dropped into a ponytail.

She heard Constantine laughing at her then whistling, "Whew! That was a close one. I'd hate to lose you before all the fun starts. Get your ass up here you clumsy bitch!"

She crawled up the mountainside until she was on the cliff that Constantine stood at. Sebastian was still unconscious and laying in a big pool of blood on the edge of the cliff, dangerously close to falling off if he turned over. She stared at him for a moment and then looked at the man responsible for all this evil.

Constantine alternately watched Celeste and Eric down below for sudden movements. She knew he was lightning quick from their fight on the beach, so she had to pick her moments carefully. His left hand held a large pistol pointed at her, but his other hand hovered uncomfortably close over his grenade belt.

"I thought you'd taken yourself out there for a minute. So, here we are again all together my love. My plans didn't work out quite as I had hoped, but I still think I can bring this party to a satisfactory close."

Celeste moved carefully a little to her right, closer to Sebastian.

"Ah ah ah. No more moving my sweet. You stay put."

She hissed, "I'm checking him you asshole."

"You move again and we're all going to the afterlife together. Now, I think you owe me an apology for leaving me like you did last time. You left with my brother and he has a bad habit of taking women I'm interested in away from me. This time, it'll be the other way around. Goddamn! You know, I still can't believe that the other guy you spoke to me about was my own shit heel brother!"

He looked down at Eric and so did she. From what she could tell, he wasn't moving.

<Get him closer to the edge Celeste. I know he has a ton of grenades, but if you could push him off, I can finish him down here and run from the blast. I think he's lying about the chem grenades. They're really rare and extremely expensive.>

<Are you positive?>

<No. With him, I don't know anything for sure.>

<Then I'm going to have to improvise.>

<Celeste what do you mean?>

She didn't answer him.

Her voice was hard, "I owe you an apology pencil dick? The only thing I owe you (and that you thoroughly deserve) is a bullet in your sick messed up brain. I feel like I could kill you with my bare hands for what you've done to me and your own brother. Sebastian's ten times the man you'll ever be. When this is through, I promise you're the only one that's going to be dead, you miserable motherfucker."

She couldn't read his mind, but his face told her all she needed to know. He didn't know she was just coming into her own combat empowerment.

Constantine pointed the gun at Celeste's head, "You insolent little cunt. I'm going to enjoy killing your pussy boyfriend here. I've dreamed of this day for so long. I don't know who I want to kill first, you or my brother. Maybe after I rape you enough, I'll just kill you both at the same time. Maybe that's going too easy on both of you. Such dilemmas. Well, since my elevator won't work for some reason, you're going to drag your dickless boyfriend down the mountain and back into the complex for me. Then I'm going to take care of whoever the fuck that is down there you came in with. Then the celebration's going to start. If you want to keep Bass alive, you'll do as I say. Maybe I'll even have a little fun with you before the cocksucker wakes up. Finish what I started on the beach that night huh?" He put his hand on her cheek, but she didn't move. She spit on him instead. He grabbed her ponytail and pulled her down by it, holding the gun against her temple. "I will fucking shoot you right now Celeste. You got that?! Don't tempt me!"

She stared at him with cold hard eyes.

He looked over her face, and he softened. It was creepy for her to watch and she was deeply concerned for Sebastian's safety with this demon around.

"You are gorgeous though. It'd be such a waste to only have you for a little while. Maybe I could give you a proposition...Yes."

He was still holding onto her by her hair but he took the gun away from her head.

"What if I released Sebastian? That gung ho fool down there could take him home, but you'd stay with me. You'd go down there and tell your sissy squad leader that you've chosen me over Sebastian. Say whatever you need so that he's convinced that I'm who you want to be with. You'd stay with me forever, but Sebastian could live...as long as he never comes looking for us. We'd leave as soon as they're off world. You and I could run away together and live happily ever after. You'd be all mine. What do you say?"

Her mind raced with possibilities. She wondered if she said yes if Constantine would keep his word. Eric could take Sebastian home and he could heal, then she could call out to him across the universe and probably still reach him mentally. Maybe. Then they could come up with a plan together to get rid of Constantine once and for all. But that meant she'd probably have to sleep with Constantine – and the thought of that turned her stomach. And the toll that would take on Sebastian and their relationship might be too great. It'd be a big risk. But he could be lying. Sebastian came here and risked his life for her. Risked his life for them to be together. Maybe it was best to just get this done and over with. She couldn't trust Constantine and she thought she had to end everything now. If she died in the process, but Sebastian lived, she'd die happy knowing she saved him.

"My my, you'd think I asked you to marry me or something. I just want an answer. This should be simple for you. Is it not?"

"I wouldn't choose you if you were the last man in the universe. You're a lying, scheming, manipulative, jealous, insecure, cowardly piece of shit. My answer is *hell no.*"

He pushed her away, "Fuck you!" He started to pace and she looked over to Sebastian.

"Don't move." He pointed his pistol at Sebastian with one hand and removed Sebastian's noose with the other, "You move again and I blow off his head right now."

She stopped breathing, terrified of what Constantine was going to do.

"You don't believe me do you?" He kneeled down and put the gun against Sebastian's temple so she could see. "I'm not afraid to do what I need to."

<Bastian?> She got no response. *<Oh please wake up baby. Come on.>*

Sebastian lay motionless. She knew he was completely and utterly out and she was afraid one of them would be dead soon, maybe both of them if she couldn't pull this off.

"Oh that's good. I can see the fear in your eyes. Now you believe me. I do not make idle threats you see." He stood up and pointed the gun at her again.

She knew his mental training was failing him. His walls seemed to be cracking. She was able to get fragments of his thoughts, all of them violent and disturbing. He was so full of hate and anger. His mind seemed to be tearing itself apart and it hurt Celeste to try to read what was going on inside of it. There were many voices, saying many things within him.

"Dax? Doing this isn't going to bring Francesca back. He's not to blame for your girlfriend's death. She did that to herself. Come on Daxton, you're better than this," she tried every approach she could think of, trying to appeal to him any way she could, "You can't blame him for everything."

His voice cracked with anger, "Everyone is so hell-bent on telling me what to do today. That's funny. I have *all* the grenades, *and* explosives, *and* the pistol, oh yeah, and *all the power*. We go back to what I was planning before. You've chosen your own fate. Let's get moving your royal whoreness."

She moved towards Sebastian's shoulders.

Constantine shook his head, "Grab his feet and drag him that way. All those rocks will cut up his back and it's going to hurt like a bitch when he wakes up. I'll be watching you, tramp. No. Sudden. Moves." He punctuated each word with a shake of his gun at her. The barrel pointed at her face, she stared down the muzzle and wished Constantine could've been killed with the power of her mind somehow.

Celeste grabbed each of Sebastian's ankles and genuinely struggled to move him. She did not react, but she could suddenly read him. He was slowly coming into consciousness again, but just barely. It was enough to communicate with her telepathically for just a few precious seconds. She waited until they were at the edge of the cliff near where she climbed up before. When Constantine was standing to the side of Sebastian's body, she started to stand up.

"Get back down bitch." When Constantine shifted his weight to strike her across the face, Sebastian took the last bit of his strength and reached up to punch Constantine in the back of his knee. It was just enough to cause Constantine to fall down on his back to the dirt. Celeste took the knife from her leg strap and jumped on top of Constantine, stabbing him in the throat, pushing the knife in to the hilt. She knew they were dangerously close to both going over the edge of the cliff. Constantine's hot blood spurted up into her face. She blinked, and Constantine pulled the trigger. Celeste's body recoiled back but she didn't let go of him. She had enough mind to grab at his grenade belt, roll off him and kick him over the cliff. She held a single pin looped on her finger and then blacked out. Her last thought that Eric heard was, <*I'm dying. I had a dream of this on Bahsheef. I had a vision of my own death. My God, I remember now. My first battle and I die, but I hope Sebastian makes it. Please let him live. Don't let me die for nothing.*>

Eric had backed far away, so when Constantine's body came plummeting down the cliff, Eric was prepared. He knelt close to the ground, anticipating the shockwave, and watched as Constantine's body hit the dirt. A large and violent series of explosions rocked the desert wastelands.

Eric knew if he saw green smoke, Constantine had chem grenades, but if the smoke was white or black, they were non-chems.

Eric's futurecasts shifted as he saw the color of the smoke.

Sebastian dragged himself on top of Celeste's body anticipating shielding her from the blasts. Sebastian knew his brother had survived the fall, but then the grenade that Celeste pulled the pin on, detonated. Sebastian felt his brother's tormented and unstable mind die with the first explosion.

A bright orange fireball rose alongside the mountain. Sebastian felt the world beneath him shake repeatedly with each grenade, but the worst and biggest detonations had been from the bombs.

Sebastian was now the only remaining survivor of his entire family. He felt the strong and masculine light of his father's mind die when he sacrificed himself to protect his children. Their father-son connection had been so strong, it felt like a painful snap when his dad went out. And even though Sebastian didn't share 7's with his mother, when she died, he felt the beautiful light in her mind suddenly go dark when she passed moments after his father. Constantine's mind, at one time, felt strong and full of potential when they were kids long before they lost their parents.

As they grew up and apart, Sebastian's reads on his brother's mind slowly got weaker. Sebastian knew his brother had received some powerful training to block his mind. It happened only a few years after their relationship had been terminated by Francesca's death. One day he sensed all of his brother's unkind thoughts, the next day he only had a faint sensation of his thinking. But for all the coren his brother must've put into that training, Constantine never realized that since they were brothers, the connection could never fully be blocked. Sebastian always had that slight awareness of his brother somewhere out there in the universe. It had become noise in the background of his mind he never paid attention to until the day he found him on Tiletan. But today, that tiny little flame was undeniably extinguished. The mental connection they always had – terminated. And as terrible as it was, Sebastian was relieved first and sad second.

After the fire cloud dissipated, Sebastian rolled off Celeste and turned her body face up. Blood seeped through her shirt under her vest.

Sebastian called out mentally as hard as he could, <ERIC! Come quick. Celeste…hurt.>

Eric replied while watching white smoke ascend into the sky, <She's got an armor vest on; she should be fine, but I'm en route.>

<She's bleeding!> Sebastian was running on pure fear and adrenaline now. <Bullet…went through…Goddamn vest.> Sebastian unbuckled the vest and carefully lifted her body a little to take it off. Celeste was still unconscious, and Sebastian was relieved she didn't have to experience the shock of getting shot at close range.

He ripped open Celeste's shirt and looked through swollen eyes seeing the bloody hole in her skin. She had a large entry wound on her upper right chest near her shoulder. He knew the bullet didn't exit since her back was dry when he lifted her up.

Eric arrived on the cliff and kneeled down at her side.

<Raynes, I need a little room, and then I need to look you over. Just lay down.>

Sebastian moved back to let Eric see her, and leaned on his side close enough to see what was happening. <Eric, he used a physical bullet.>

<Shut up Raynes, I know. I need to concentrate.> Eric looked at the wound. The bullet was slowed slightly by the vest but it pierced right through since she was shot at point blank range. No vest could've stopped that bullet.

Eric lightly put his hands over the wound, trying to sense with his expanded powers how bad it really was, then put all of his weight on the wound to slow the bleeding. She immediately opened her eyes and screamed.

"Whaaa are you doin'?! She should stay knocked oww. She's already suffered through enough!" Sebastian's words sounded as bad as his thoughts with his swollen mouth.

Eric ignored him. Celeste began to cry and groan.

Sebastian grabbed Eric's wrist with surprising strength, but Eric carefully pushed him off. Celeste screamed again.

Eric thought to her so she would hear him, <*Sebastian's hurt bad. I need you to fight through whatever pain you're feeling so we can get him back to the transit and home. You've done great so far, but you've been poisoned. We're both really proud of you. Just need you to push a little further. I'll carry you down then I gotta come back for him.*>

Celeste grunted and gasped for air. Tears streamed down her face.

"Okay, but...him...first," she grimaced.

Sebastian slurred, "Poisoned? No. Pleass Celeste. Let Eric carry you firsss."

"Okay," she barely had any breath to answer and her vision went white.

Eric took a tightly folded silver square out of his back pocket and gave it to his friend. "Here man. Cover up." Sebastian unfolded the Mylar rescue blanket and put it around his shoulders. He watched as Eric moved quickly carrying her down the mountain.

Eric placed her body carefully on the ground. She started convulsing but there wasn't anything Eric could do about it except turn her on her side. It would save her from choking. He quickly put a blessed medical salve over her wound to slow the bleeding.

Eric ran up to Sebastian and carried him (with Sebastian protesting) the whole way down. Sebastian stopped him at the bottom and stood on his own, waving Eric away.

"I can waalk. Take caarrr of her."

Sebastian moved slowly across the desert watching Eric's silhouette with Celeste hanging in his arms. He winced every time he felt her mind start shaking like the rest of her body with a new convulsion. The second of Tiletan's twin suns peeked over the horizon behind them.

He thought to himself, *Please let her be okay. Please whoever's listening out there. Any God, every Goddess, everything I've ever believed in and had faith in. Please show her mercy. All of this is my fault. She doesn't deserve this.*

Eric came back to Sebastian and helped him along to the transit.

Strapping Sebastian into his seat, Eric heard Celeste breathing fast in the back of the vehicle.

"Celessse?" Sebastian couldn't help but see if she was awake.

"Huh? What happ…" her face went slack, white foam dribbling down her chin.

"She's out Raynes. I gotta get us out of here and I still need to lock your transit to mine. Where the hell is it?"

"Cave. I'll show you."

Eric looked over his shoulder a few times at Celeste while Sebastian directed him to the cave. Eric wasn't sure what futurecast would emerge as the final outcome at this point, but he was nervous. He was deeply disturbed that Celeste cried blood tears, and blood oozed out of her nose as well.

NINE

>>> > AFTER ERIC RETRIEVED the pile of weapons off the desert floor, Sebastian asked, <*Wha abou mine? Where are they?*>

<*Don't know. Sorry. Maybe if I can come back later.*>

On their way to Praxis, Sebastian passed out again. The exertion and stress of seeing Celeste shot by his brother was finally too much for his body to handle.

Eric prayed over both of his injured battle mates to help center and calm himself. He had seen over 1000 different endings to this situation since he received the Titan call from Celeste. This was one of the few that had been acceptable to him, even with the poisoning, and that wasn't confirmed until he had his hands on her wound.

DIRECT ASCENSION

ONE

>>> > WHEN ERIC ARRIVED on Praxis, Sebastian regained consciousness. Eric had called Zach to meet him there.

Eric docked his Atlas, disengaged Sebastian's Pearl and docked it in its designated slot. Then gave the doctor Celeste's key card for Sebastian's apartment.

"What do you want me to do with this?"

"Go up to his apartment and wait on the balcony. I'm going to have to hand them off to you."

"What?! That's illegal here. You can't do a direct ascension in residential areas. Somebody's going to see you and report it. Then we'll have peace officers at the front door."

< <<<< [739] >>> >>>>

"It's the fastest way and we can't carry these two on the streets and in the elevator. Sebastian's almost naked and I didn't have any clothes that would fit the big bastard. All he has is a Mylar blanket. We'll draw way too much damn attention."

"And your Atlas hovering alongside the building doesn't?!"

"Doc please just go up there and wait. We don't have time for this and I'll be so fast, no one will see. Just trust me."

"I'm going, I'm going." Zach turned tail and was off in a flash.

Eric ran back to his transit and looked around for peace officers. He saw none.

Sebastian's head was pounding. Even Eric slamming the Atlas door down made him wince. He asked Eric, "Doc here?"

"Yeah. Hold on buddy." Eric flew around to the side of Sebastian's apartment building. He lifted the Atlas up in a straight line, breaking three Praxian laws and looked for Zach. Once he found him, he hovered the transit on autopilot.

"Raynes, open your door and turn off your Techtonics."

Sebastian opened the transit door and yelled as much as he could in his condition, "O?"

"Thank goodness you're alive sir!" Ophelia exclaimed, then said calmly, "Yes, Erebos?"

"Niner, task, bluejay, hammer."

"Techtonic balcony system disengaging."

Zach watched the protection system go down. Eric hovered the transit right up against the balcony and Sebastian half fell, half slid out with Zach helping him land on his feet. Sebastian immediately sat down on the patio chair winded.

Eric scooped up the still unconscious Celeste in his arms and handed her down to Zach.

"I'll be right back once I dock." Eric shut the door quickly and descended before Zach could respond.

"Sebastian, can you walk?"

"Yeah."

"Okay. Get to your room and lay down. I'll be in when I can."

Sebastian got up and told Ophelia to re-engage the techtonics, immediately reset the password, and then hobbled slowly to the master bedroom.

Zach carried Celeste into the spare bedroom and worked faster than he ever had.

When Eric got into the apartment, he saw Sebastian's father's ring sitting on the entryway table. He grabbed it as he walked to Sebastian's room and put it on the nightstand. He helped Sebastian put on clothes and waited for the doctor to look at him.

Sebastian looked at the ring as he put it on his finger, "I thought I might die so I left this for Celeste to keep."

"But you didn't man. You made it through. We made it through."

"Yeah. I need to know Celeste's going to be alright before I can say that."

Eric and the doctor took turns doing what they could for Celeste and Sebastian. Eric felt pain coming off Zach in waves as he saw both of his patient's conditions. In all the time of Eric knowing Zach, he was usually his stoic medical self, but he couldn't keep up that emotionless exterior today. Great concern showed on his Taybusian face, and Eric felt how disturbed and worried he was. Eric understood how Zach felt because he was worried too.

The doctor removed Celeste's bullet laced with poison and cleaned the wound, but the damage had been done. A highly toxic and aggressive mix of poisons were already coursing through her veins and even his medi-nosis tool wasn't accurate enough on how much she had absorbed. What worried him most was that this appeared to be a homemade poison – his tools weren't familiar with all the ingredients running through her system. He stitched her up after Eric blessed the wound and put a healing salve over it. All they could do now was wait.

Eric took a deep breath in and looked at Zach. They said nothing to each other, but they knew Celeste was in a precarious place. The chances of her going into a coma were very high. Zach moved over to Sebastian's room while Eric watched over Celeste. Eric told no one of his visions on Celeste's future. In two, she died, in another one she lived, but was permanently paralyzed from her shoulders down, and only one had her alive and fully healed with the exception of a nasty scar. He lightly put his hand on her forehead. *Please spare her Universe. I've read her heart – she's a pure spirit, a good woman, and she was a great royal. Earth's going to need her desperately in the months to come. Please have mercy on her soul. I ask this with an honest heart. Amen.*

Eric walked to Sebastian's room and saw he was unconscious.

"Did he go out again?"

Dr. Coldiron shook his head, "No. I gave him a sedative. He was about to attempt walking across the hall to be with Celeste. He can't do that right now. He needs to rest, and he needs fluids badly. I need to set him up with an IV," he sighed, "I need to get a sling for Celeste's arm as well. You wanna watch him for a minute while I get it?"

"Sure thing." Eric was able to accelerate Sebastian's healing on some minor injuries, but he wished he was capable of more. He felt good that he healed the swelling that prevented Sebastian from verbally communicating clearly.

Sebastian had cuts and bruises all over, a broken nose, four cracked ribs, two missing teeth, swollen black eyes, a first-degree burn on his back, and some bad bruising internally, but nothing a couple months recovery wouldn't heal. He was in the worst shape the doctor had ever seen him, but Eric knew he'd be fine in time. Eric wasn't so sure about Celeste. He hoped she would survive, but he didn't know if she could.

Sebastian and Celeste remained unconscious for hours. The doctor had to induce it in Sebastian, but Celeste needed no medicine to sleep.

Eric and the doctor stayed in the apartment overnight until the morning talking about what happened on Tiletan.

"I can't understand it. Why didn't Sebastian just call you for help right away? It was almost certain suicide from the sound of it, for him to go in alone."

"You know Raynes man. Him and his damn pride, and he's so young. Can't ever ask for help or what he sees as a hand out. I swear after he's healed, I'm gonna give him hell over all this. He shouldn't have done this alone. Although, I do have to give him credit for telling Celeste to call me after a Praxian day. At least he did that much."

Their conversation was cut short when Celeste cried out from the spare bedroom. The doctor ran in while Eric checked on Sebastian.

"Celeste, relax, relax. I need you to stay immobile…please no more convulsions." He frowned as her body shook. A full minute later the episode passed. She was covered in sweat. She looked down at the sling on her arm.

"What's this?" her voice rang with pain.

"My dear you've been shot with a poison bullet. You have a lot of muscle tissue damage and that arm can't move. You'll be wearing that sling for months."

"Where's Sebastian? Is he okay? Ouch! Damn it!" She was in agony, hot one minute, freezing the next.

"Yes, he's going to be okay. He's in his bedroom with Eric."

"I need to see him," she started to sit up, but the doctor wouldn't allow it.

"No, Celeste. I need to know how you're feeling."

"I'm hot. My skin feels like it's on fire. I need to get up."

He held onto her good shoulder firmly, "That's not a good idea dear. Please lay back. Don't make me medicate you. You relax or I'll make you relax!"

She ignored him. He reached into his pocket and injected a sedative into her arm.

"I'm sorry hon. You can't be moving yet. If you have another episode of convulsions while you're walking, you'll make things much worse. I can't have that." The medicine knocked her out within a minute and Zach sighed.

The doctor went to Eric in the master bedroom. He looked over Sebastian while he was waking up.

Sebastian winced when he started to talk, "Where's Celeste...doc? She okay?"

"Yes I think, for now. She has a ways to go before we know for sure, but I had to sedate her. She was determined to get to you and she can't be moving yet. Neither should you really. I'm most worried about your ribs. How do they feel?"

"Hurts."

"Does it hurt worse when you breathe deep?"

"A little."

"If it hurts too much, tell me. I don't want you to develop pneumonia from breathing shallow."

"Yes doc. Can I see her please? I'll be careful moving, I swear."

Zach studied Sebastian for a moment, "It won't matter if I say no, you'll do it anyway. I would like you to stay immobile, but you won't. I'll get a mech tech wheelchair for you okay? Wait a little bit and I'll order one up in a few minutes."

"Okay doc. Hey, thanks for everything, both of you. I don't know what I would've done without you. I appreciate it so much." Sebastian's face felt lumpy and raw. He winced as he brought up a hand to feel the bandages dotted all over his face. He had never felt so many different places on him throbbing all at once with pain.

The doctor looked at Eric then back to Sebastian, "It's no problem. I'll be right back."

An old-fashioned wheelchair was delivered an hour later and the doctor brought it to Sebastian's room.

"Sorry that took so long. They were out of mech tech models so this one's a manual. They're kinda' rare these days on Praxis. Celeste's sedative will last a few hours. You can roll over to her, but she won't know you're there."

"That's fine. I just need to see her with my own eyes."

Eric looked at the doctor, "Zach, you've been awesome. If you want to go, I can take care of these two for a while until they get stronger. You've been working non-stop on them for hours."

"Well Eric, so have you. We've both done a lot. Why don't we take shifts okay? But I can't go anywhere, not now."

Eric nodded, "Me first. You go get some rest."

"I'll just sleep for a while. Let me tell you what meds they need."

They talked near the balcony door while Sebastian sat near Celeste in the spare bedroom. His IV hung next to him.

He rested a hand on her leg. Everything happened so fast; it was just now that things were starting to sink in. He was always trying to be the strong one. The one that protected the people he cared about, but not this time. This woman that just floated into his life by chance would've given her life to save his. She was stronger and more brave than he ever imagined and he was damn proud of her and the fierce fighter she had become. He saw the way she jumped onto his brother and tore into his throat with her knife. She had acted as a lioness protecting him. He'd always been in awe of her, but her impressiveness only continued to encompass more subjects and situations. He couldn't imagine loving anyone else this much.

He could feel her dreaming. She was on Earth as a child chasing after a big blue butterfly in the forest. She was at peace for the moment. He'd never been able to do this, consciously look in on her dreams and see what she was seeing without participating. And in his weakened condition, it shouldn't be possible, but he was bound to her now, and that most likely changed everything including the link between their 7's.

He heard an unfamiliar voice and the front door close. Eric stood in the doorway to her room looking down at his feet, sensing he was interrupting.

"Hey man, you need sustenance. I ordered some food and we'll eat in the kitchen. Let her rest for a while."

"Yeah, okay. I'll be there in a minute."

Eric had ordered salmon and a salad for both of them. Eric was starving, but Sebastian only picked at his food.

"Please eat something Raynes. You need your strength; you just suffered one hell of a beating. I know you're worried about Celeste, but she's strong. I think she's going to be fine. I bet she'll heal up before your sorry ass does."

Eric watched as Sebastian stared out the windows.

"Listen, I thought you'd ask this sooner, but the doc says you guys can't lay next to each other in the same bed yet. I know you'd like to be close to her, but he said if you started flailing in your sleep and accidently hit her shoulder it would be really bad. He said in a week you could move her into your room."

"What are you not telling me?" Sebastian's head pounded and the pain only got worse as his blood pressure rose.

Eric looked at him, "Nothing...It's nothing we can change now."

"Damn it Bouton! I want you to tell me or I'll read you so help me."

"My walls are too strong for your mind right now. And I don't want you to try anyways..."

"Eric."

Eric sensed his friend's anger rising. He sighed.

"I don't know what Celeste's future holds right now. There's only two possibilities left and they haven't changed for hours. Every time the doc checks on her I expect to see something different, but it's not shifting."

"What are those possibilities?"

Eric closed his eyes, "This poison either takes her life or she makes a full recovery and she's fine. It's like fifty-fifty right now, and I've already told you too much."

Sebastian's face was stoic; he didn't move.

Eric waited for his question.

"How does she die? Is it painful?"

Eric put down his fork and covered his face with his hands, "I don't think we should think this way man. Let's think she's gonna be fine. She'll be up and around in no time."

"How does she die and is it painful for her, *if* that happens?"

Eric cleared his throat. His friend was tenacious and Eric knew he wouldn't quit asking until there was an answer.

"The poison is attacking her muscles. The doc gave her something to slow down the process, give her body time to fight it. That damn 'miracle' tool he has can't really diagnose the exact poison because the Brotherhood made it themselves from several different poisonous creatures. Snake, spider, jellyfish, and scorpion anti-venom that Human doctors came up with millennia ago will not fix it. This is changing along with his attempts to cure it. Her body is apparently good at fighting since she's still alive today...I thin—"

"ERIC!" He shouted louder than he meant to. It hurt his chest. "How will she die, will it be painful for her? Please just tell me," he was pleading now. It's something Eric never heard him do before.

"She could go into a coma. Her muscles will seize up – freeze into place all at once. She wouldn't be able to move, and she wouldn't be able to breathe. If she was in the coma, it would be a painless passing. If she was conscious...It would be a difficult and scary death. She'd suffocate..."

"Just like Francesca died..." Sebastian's strength melted away and he sharply inhaled before a few tears escaped down his cheeks. He slowly rolled himself into his bedroom, closing the door behind him.

Eric left him alone and put his head into his hands. The doctor came into the kitchen and looked exhausted and confused. Eric filled him in on the details of the conversation he'd just had.

Something quietly broke in Sebastian when he realized how close he was to losing her – again. They'd been through so much together already. Many more bad things than any new would-be lovers should have to experience.

He thought about the night they consummated their relationship – more like they consumed each other in a beautiful and wondrous rapture. That night he had a moment of living outside of his body, even while he was inside of hers. A stillness settled over his soul when they bonded. It was a moment of total and complete clarity. And they bonded, quite permanently even though she didn't understand that yet and he wanted the opportunity to explain it to her.

He was filled with a desperate urgency to talk to her, to hold her, but…he let out a long painful sigh, she might not hear any of this… unless he told her before it was too late and she was gone.

Sebastian slowly wheeled to her room while the doctor and Eric stared at him, making sure he safely traversed the small distance. He closed her door and sat uncomfortably in the wheelchair by her bedside.

He held her hand gently, but she didn't stir.

"Celeste? Dear?" He watched for a flicker of her eyelid, a twitch of a cheek muscle.

She didn't move, but he decided to talk anyway.

"I need you to get healthy so you can yell at me. I shouldn't have left you in the middle of the night and I should've brought you with me. I see that now. You showed me you were right all along." He carefully reached up and moved a strand of hair from her face, "You've shown me love Celeste. My God, that's all you've ever shown me," he choked up.

He whispered the rest, "I love you. I *know* you're a fighter." He swallowed hard, "I'm so proud of you coming to get me the way you did. I need you. You and I are bound to each other. Wake up and tell me you love me too."

He put his head down by her hand and kissed it. He stayed there for several minutes, but she didn't rouse. He went into the living room and talked to Doctor Coldiron.

"You tell me straight Zachariah. You tell me she's fighting this and that she's going to make it."

"Oh Sebastian…I wish I could tell you what you want to hear. Honestly, I don't know what's going to happen. We're doing the best we can to treat her. I've called several of my associates and there's nothing else to do now but wait. I promise I'll do everything I can for her."

Sebastian felt empty, lost, and alone. He slowly stood up, and for the first time that the doctor could remember, Sebastian hugged him, hard. Eric stood close by and prayed.

Sebastian sat down and wheeled himself to the dinner table, picking up his fork, he went into autopilot, into survival mode. Eric sat down by him and looked at the doctor.

Sebastian wiped at his eyes and told Eric, "Thank you for rescuing me."

"Don't worry about it. You've saved me so many times, I've lost count."

"Yes, but if it hadn't been for you, Celeste and I would probably be dead now."

Eric was silent for a moment, "Don't even say that man. Celeste and I…we just did our best. We did what we had to and…everything's going to be fine."

The doctor quietly went into Celeste's room and closed the door to give the men some privacy.

Sebastian put his head down, "I love her and there's nothing I can do about it. There's not a damn fucking thing I can do to protect her now."

Eric pressed his lips into a thin line, suffering along with his friend, "I know you love her. I saw this one, this incredible kind of love, coming for you. I couldn't see the woman, just a shining bright spirit, a beautiful soul. Then when you mentioned her, I realized she's been in the back of your mind for *years*. The first time you saw her, you liked her. Then when you actually met, you really liked her. That's amazing man. You found the love of your life in her. You deserve to be happy. Both of you. You gotta trust she'll pull through this."

"But you remember what happened with Francesca and I never truly loved her. I thought I did until I met Celeste. What if she dies today because of me?"

"But she's not going to. Believe me Sebastian; she's so strong. I know she doesn't want to go anywhere you can't follow. She's fighting, been fighting hard since yesterday. You have already been wrung through the wringer together. You guys pull through this? Then everything else should be easy peasy cheddar cheesy."

Sebastian moved his salad around with his fork, "Before…it wasn't easy for me to let her know how deeply I felt. It takes all this to make me tell her? I sat in there and told her how I felt when she couldn't even hear me say it. She showed me what love is really supposed to feel like. It's all encompassing. It makes you lose control, changes all your plans, makes you do crazy things. Celeste is different. She's kind and giving. She's humble for being born into royalty. She has this huge heart," he started to choke up, "You know she told me she thought I was a good man really early on, before I felt like she really knew me. She makes me want to believe that I am a good man, not just a killer."

"Maybe she knows a good thing when she sees it Raynes. You're fiercely loyal. You're an incredible fighter. Most of the other tough guys I know wouldn't have been alive after the beating you got man. Tough as nails you are. I think you guys were made for each other, especially once I got those readings off her. She's off the charts for expanded 7's. You have a powerhouse on your hands with her. Does she even know what she's capable of?" Eric was slowly trying to infuse his friend with a strong sense of hope without him realizing it.

Sebastian started to eat slowly, carefully, "I don't think so, no."

"Did you get feelings or thoughts off her right away?"

"Oh yeah, strong as hell and crystal clear. She was passing sensations along to me a *day* after I met her. She still doesn't even know that. Speaking of which, don't tell her I told you how I feel about her. I want her to h—"

Eric finished his sentence, "hear it from you first, when she's conscious. I know. I would never say anything like that. Give me some credit! That's great, you're in love. It's long overdue my friend."

"Has she said anything to you about me?"

He chuckled, "Raynes, I can't tell you that. I know she cares for you. Anybody can see how much you guys feel for each other, hell a blind man could see it. You need to tell her how you feel though. When she wakes up I mean. You've admitted it to yourself and to me, it's time she knew."

"Did she tell you she loves me?"

"Well, let's see…She called me, a perfect stranger, to help save you from a super crazy vengeful asshole, no offense, I know he was your brother and all. But yeah, risking her life…what do you think Raynes? She didn't need to say anything for me to see it. Don't be dense."

"Alright, alright, point taken. Thanks Bouton, you're an excellent friend. But you're still not as good a fighter as the old master here."

Eric laughed, "Oh yeah? Who saved *your ass* just now? I'm sorry what was that? That was me, yeah! Thanks man, you're a real son of a bitch is what you are."

Sebastian smiled and felt a lot better.

"Hey I meant to tell you something. When I met Celeste and thought about your stories about her it reminded me of a line in a story I read. 'No sooner met but they looked; no sooner looked but they loved.' I thought you'd enjoy knowing that."

"*Holy fucking shit!* You read Shakespeare's *As You Like It?*"

"Yeah, but just that one. It gave me fits trying to understand it."

"What made you change your mind? I've been telling you about him for years."

"Just listening to you talk about Celeste on the trip to Foss-Altus…it makes me want something like that. I'm eighty man. My life's almost half over. I'm not getting any younger and getting laid is great and all, but pussy's not going to be there on the couch waiting for you when you get home. I mean, I want something real. Someone who's going to be there for me. So you told me women like that stuff and I thought I'd give it a try. It couldn't hurt right? So yeah, I read it."

"I'm so proud of you. My little boy is growing up so fast," Sebastian said sarcastically.

"Oh fuck off," Eric threw his napkin at his friend.

Sebastian smiled.

"Listen Raynes, I've been thinking…The facility on Tiletan needs to be handled before any more time goes by. What do you think?"

Sebastian nodded, "I suppose. I'm not really thinking clearly right now. I'm not myself yet...but I can't leave Celeste. It probably should've been done already but I can't...I'm in no shape for that right now."

"You don't have to do anything my friend. I'm all ready to go, just wanted to let things settle here a bit. I hoped you would both be doing better by now, but...I don't think I should wait any longer. It needs to be erased."

Sebastian shook his head, "I need you here man. I need help with Celeste. The doc's great but he'll need to tend to other patients soon."

Eric hesitated, "I could ask Agathon."

"No way. I don't want him involved in this."

"Ummm...it's too late for that. He kinda already is on his way to Tiletan"—Eric checked the time on his Titan and counted on his fingers—"Yeah he's still on his way there but he should arrive any second. I need to contact him regardless to tell him we're here now. I didn't think he'd make it in time to help."

"What do you mean? What the hell are you talking about?"

Eric took a long slow drink of water from his glass.

"What did you do Eric?"

"Listen, it wasn't my idea. Celeste mentioned him and she wanted his help."

"Celeste doesn't know how to contact him. You do."

"She insisted and at the time, I thought it was a good idea."

"Just for the record, I didn't ask Celeste to call anyone but you. I trust you the most, then D'Art, then Aggie but I wanted to keep them out of this mission for their own protection. Call him and tell him to go home. We can take care of the facility later."

"I'll call him."

Eric left the room and went into the gym. Agathon picked up immediately, "Where do we stand? I'm about to enter Tiletan's orbit."

"We're back on Praxis. Raynes is in bad shape and the queen is even worse. She took a poisoned bullet. I don't know if she's going to make it."

"That's terrible news. Shall I proceed over there then?"

"There's something I could really use your help on. The Brotherhood's facility is still standing. I need it not to be. There's a cache of weapons and explosives in there plus Raynes asked for his stuff that they took from him. Take whatever you like, but demolish the building. Then come here. There wasn't any Brotherhood there when we left but in case I'm wrong, be extra cautious."

"Sure thing. I love blowing things up! I almost never get the chance since I usually use my 'personal' weapons. Are these the coordinates for the facility that just popped up?" Agathon studied his Titan closely.

"Yeah. Just sent them to you. It looks like a mountain, but it's not. Make sure you jam the satellites if you decide to reveal yourself out in the open desert, okay? There's a shit ton of them there and they'd all capture you on film. Can you let me know when it's done? Send me a message?"

"Oh yeah, I almost forgot about those nasty satellites. Thanks. No problem."

"Great. Thanks dude," he paused, "One more thing Aggie. If you could look for a chem lab there. See if they have any antidotes for poison. I mean, anything that looks even remotely like it, could you bring that too?"

"Absolutely. Consider it done."

Eric's Titan went black and returned to its main menu.

Sebastian had finished eating while Eric was gone.

"Okay Raynes. I called him. It's all handled. Agathon's going to nix the facility."

"Goddamnit Bouton! You did the opposite of what I asked! The satellites alone…"

Eric shrugged, "Don't worry, I reminded him about the satellites. You need me here; you need to be here. Agathon's there and more than capable of protecting himself. It needs to be done, it's getting done. He'll send me a message when he's leaving and then he's coming over."

Sebastian sighed, "Fine. I'm not fighting with you. You're right, it needs to get done, but I'm not happy about you and Celeste contacting him in the first place."

"Let's get you and Celeste healthy first and then you can rip us new assholes, okay?"

Sebastian was silent.

"You're welcome, by the way."

Sebastian stared daggers at his friend, "You're unbelievable Bouton."

Eric, Zach, and Sebastian spent the rest of the afternoon on the balcony with Zach stopping to check on Celeste periodically. Sebastian felt such a sense of overwhelming hope regarding Celeste he couldn't explain.

Eric got a call and left the men for a moment. When he returned, he told Sebastian the Tiletan branch had been completely destroyed and Agathon was safe. He reported no complications. Agathon bombed the mountain and now had a gigantic collection of weapons, armor, explosives, drugs, and ammo in his possession.

"And my stuff?" Sebastian asked.

"Yeah, he got that too. Don't worry. I also asked him to look for antidote, but he didn't find anything that could help us. Said he was bringing the drugs he could find so the doc can look at them."

"Thanks. That was good thinking Bouton."

Eric smiled at Sebastian, "See. I am good for something."

TWO

>>> > DAI'S ALARM WENT off.

Hace was half-asleep, trying to rise from a state of confusion, "What...DAI what is it?"

DAI responded, "I'm sorry to wake you sir, but a catastrophic failure notification was just received from the Tiletan branch. I thought you would like to know."

Hace sat up in bed, "Dim lights on."

Soft lighting filled the room.

Hace rubbed his eyes and face, trying to gain more alertness, "Can you tell me what kind of failure?"

"Complete."

Hace's mouth dropped open, "Show me."

The gigantic screen on the wall of his bedroom activated and a satellite image of Tiletan appeared. The image got closer and closer until he saw the smoke and fire erupting out of the sides of the mountain where the Tiletan facility used to be.

"What the FUCK?!"

He got up out of bed and walked closer to the screen, "How long ago did you receive the notification?"

"One minute, twenty-three seconds."

"Do a scan for living beings within a one mile radius of the center of the Tiletan facility."

"Yes sir. Scanning…Scanning…Scanning."

Hace went to his closet, grabbed some clothes and threw them on his bed while he was waiting.

"There are no life forms detected."

"Show me the last image with a life form in this radius."

DAI rewound the footage and tightened the frame to show a transit hovering close to the facility. A being dressed in full combat armor ran out of the mountain with weapons in their arms and quickly got into the transit and shut the door. Hace's first thought was Dax. Maybe he did this.

"This person is stealing from us?"

Hace watched as the transit door opened again and the person went out of the frame. A minute later he saw something he couldn't believe. Hace got closer to the screen and asked, "Can you adjust this DAI?"

"I'm sorry Master. This is the best image available."

Hace squinted and rubbed his eyes. "There's a fucking Rhorr'Dach there! I can't believe it. People told me as a kid I was crazy for believing in them. They said they were a myth. A legend. I heard plenty of bullshit stories about how they died out millennia ago or that they never existed in the first place, but I knew the truth. I knew it. I believed and there's the proof! I've been looking my whole life and then one just shows up on Tiletan with a Humanoid friend to destroy my property after they've taken what they wanted!"

"Should I recall the Daredevil Three?" DAI said from somewhere far away.

"I still need to know where they live and it could find something else useful. No, let's keep it out there."

Hace watched as the Rhorr'Dach went out of the frame. It was so enormous, just the tail was on screen for a while. Then that disappeared as the creature walked away and the transit was grabbed by a huge Dachian talon and moved out of the frame. There was nothing left to see.

"Can you give me another angle of this, or zoom out so I can see what's happening 'cause right now I can't see shit!"

"Sorry sir. This is the only footage I have available to you."

Hace sighed, "Where's the failure?"

DAI sped up the footage until a massive explosion shot fire and debris out of doorways and cave entrances around the mountain.

"The footage I have on file only started eight minutes ago. There are no other satellites in the area. This satellite will leave visual range in another three minutes and twenty-five seconds," she paused, "Is it possible these beings could be members?"

Hace ignored her question, "Can you get any other images than what I've seen? You're sure there aren't any more cameras anywhere?"

"This is it sir."

Hace got into his clothes, "Set a course for Tiletan. I need to take a look at this myself."

"Yes Master Hunter."

"What's the ETA?"

"From our present location and using all sixteen Jumps available to us – one Stoxian day, and four sterms."

"FUCK! Twenty-three sterms?! Is there an alternate route? Something to get us there faster?"

"Negative sir. This is our fastest possible option."

Hace snapped, "Let's go then." He stopped, "And join me in my bedroom in Stox form. I need to blow off some steam."

THREE

>>> > SEBASTIAN FELL ASLEEP with the help of some sedatives, but the next morning he woke feeling a little better than the night before until Eric talked to him.

"Hey, Aggie left me a message overnight. I guess his transit broke down in the middle of nowhere. He was speeding and blew out his conversion system. He needed a bot-tow transit to haul him to the closest service station. Said the part he needs is being shipped, but it's going to take days. He'll be here as soon as he can."

"That puts him at risk. The more he interacts with people, the more chance he has of being found out. I blame you if he gets into serious shit."

"He's already involved in some serious shit with blowing up a BDP facility, besides it was Celeste's idea to as—"

Sebastian shot him a deadly look and Eric shut his mouth.

"Fine. Whatever. I'll message him to be extra careful."

Zach, Eric, and Sebastian closely watched Celeste all through the third day of her struggle for life. She slept almost non-stop and the doc was the only one in the room when she came to for a few minutes in the late afternoon. She didn't speak, but her eyes fluttered and stayed open. She looked confused, but Zach took it as a good sign she was awake, even if only briefly. It meant she was not in a coma.

All three of the men sat outside and talked as they watched the color ebb out of the magenta sky. It was Eric's turn to check on Celeste and it left Sebastian and Zach an opportunity to talk.

"Doc, what do you think her chances are now? It's been a couple days since she was shot."

"We've done everything we could. I think if she doesn't improve within a week…Well, let's see what happens tonight okay? Try to remember it's a very good sign that she's still fighting at this point. Take one da—"

Sebastian put his hand up to signal he didn't need to hear anymore. They both looked up nervously as Eric came back onto the balcony but said there was no change in her condition.

FOUR

>>> > TWENTY-THREE HOURS LATER, the Architect Phantom was in Tiletan's orbit.

Hace was in his transit with his map set and opened the docking bay door to travel down to the planet's surface.

He needed to see this with his own eyes, see if he could piece together any clues left behind. Hace had DAI contact every Titan that belonged to his men stationed on Tiletan and not one of them answered. Hace thought they were all dead. He heard DAI's earlier question about a Brotherhood member doing this and he didn't have an answer. He needed to look around to see if Dax was responsible for this.

Hace landed and got out.

"Are you sure you don't want any of your men with you?"

"It's okay to break your own rules occasionally DAI, besides I have you."

"I'm no substitute for a live being sir."

"Well, I've got no men down here and I want to keep this Dach thing to myself. I'll be fine." He looked around and saw the empty desert for miles. "DAI, record everything I see through my combat helmet."

"Yes, sir. Recording now."

He wore full combat armor in case whoever was here last decided to booby trap something or was waiting for someone to come back and inspect the rubble.

Hace looked for footprints but the last dust storm had wiped the desert floor clean. There were no footprints except for the ones he was currently making.

"DAI, you did sweep for any remaining bombs in this area right? There's no surprises for me?"

She responded quickly, "I have completed those well before your transit landed. There are no threats detected."

"Thanks," he moved towards the mountain. The first thing he noticed was the drying mud around the facility's edge. It was true that Tiletan did get the occasional rainstorm, but why would there be mud only here and not everywhere? And if it had rained hard enough to leave mud behind in the parched ground, why weren't all the fires out from the explosion? He could see several licks of flame still reaching up into the sky.

"DAI, has there been any precipitation of any kind in this area since the explosion?"

"Negative."

"How about immediately preceding the explosion, maybe an hour before?"

"No Master."

"Strange. I wonder what happened here."

"I hypothesize the explosion possibly broke water lines underneath the structure. That could be providing a localized flooding."

"Possible..."

He took his time, inspecting whatever was left at the doorways and exits, but all of them were choked with debris, concrete chunks, and solid rock that caved in from the mountain itself. He thought it had been genius to build this facility into the actual mountain, but now he saw the flaws of his design. It was great for camouflage, but in the case of an explosion, the whole mountain came down in big pieces, occupying what used to be a beautiful, safe Brotherhood facility. All the entry points were completely impassable.

He walked all the way around the mountain and was about to return to the transit when he saw a Human foot sticking out of the rubble. He walked to it and nudged it. He thought it had been cleanly severed but then realized it was a living prosthetic as he picked it up. It was a female foot and there were no female Brotherhood members at the Tiletan branch. He couldn't figure out who it belonged to or what it was doing there. The only sense he could make of it was either the queen had a false foot missing after her "rescue" or else it had been deposited here from a dust storm. Maybe one of the boys brought a woman here, but sex was strictly prohibited on Brotherhood property. Hace studied the foot in his hands and was walking back to his transit when he heard a *click!* a second before the landmine exploded.

CHAPTER 40

SHE

ONE

>>> > A SMALL EXPLOSION of dust, shrapnel, and fire filled Hace's world for a second and then was gone. He was thrown ten feet in the air and landed on his side. He lost his breath and panicked when he realized what happened.

His helmet and armor saved his life, but he had an immense pain in his left leg like nothing else he ever felt. When he reached down to feel it, there was nothing there. He looked and saw his leg was shredded from his hip down. He was losing a tremendous amount of blood.

He hadn't realized he'd been screaming until DAI shouted over him into his helmet speaker, "Medical attention is on the way. Their transit launched as soon as I realized your injury. Hold on sir. ETA ten seconds."

Hace's medical-bot staff landed next to him and moved fast. They set him on a spinal board and strapped him down so he couldn't move.

They quickly transported him to their transit and returned to The Architect Phantom.

Hace lost consciousness somewhere between the medical transit docking and the operating room.

TWO

>>> > HACE WOKE UP in a stark blue room. It took him a minute to remember what happened. He was in the medical recovery area. He looked down and saw only his right leg was there.

"DAI what happened to me?"

"When I did a scan for bombs, I didn't detect any. The land mine you triggered must have been an old-fashioned, non-tech device. Maybe homemade in nature or simply invisible to my scanning abilities. I apologize for failing you."

Hace sat up slowly. His head was spinning, "I know you did your best."

"Sir, you should really stay on your back. The medical staff instructed me you need to lie down for several additional minutes after you regained consciousness. It's only been ninety-nine seconds."

"What happened after the land mine?"

"The explosion was small, but there were several items laying on the desert floor that became shrapnel after the explosion propelled them up and into your body. You lost your left leg at the hip and you have several puncture wounds all over your arms, chest, and remaining leg. The team worked on you for several hours to stop the bleeding and remove all the items that impaled you. They removed half a pound of shrapnel but insisted more would work its way out of your body as the months, maybe years roll by."

Hace looked over his body and saw several bandages, stitches, and butterfly closures dotting his arms and chest. He laid back down. The dizziness was too much to handle.

"There is good news sir."

"What might that be?" Hace took a deep breath trying to stop the room from spinning.

"The medical staff will be fitting you with a living prosthetic in less than two sterms and they've already contacted a Taybuse to grow you a new le—"

"NO!"

DAI paused, "I'm sorry sir? Did you say no?"

"There is no Taybuse in the universe I trust enough to grow me a new leg. Not with the things I've done to their planet. Any of them would love to kill me after I almost singlehandedly destroyed Arcolid. They could sabotage the leg or poison me or something."

"Master, since my first day in your service, I have no record of a major event on Arcolid. Was it some—"

"It was before my time with the BDP. You wouldn't know."

"I see."

Hace turned his head as tears escaped his eyes, "My father died in battle. My grandfather died in battle. Every generation for fifteen generations on my father's side died either in battle or from wounds they got from a war. I will accept my loss and deal with a living prosthetic. I hear those are very good and I bet it won't slow me down. I'll have peace of mind that it's not poisoned or came from some wretched Taybuse asshole." He wiped at his cheeks.

"Understood sir. I will notify them to cancel the replacement leg."

It was silent again. The room finally stopped spinning for Hace.

He sat up carefully and put his hands to his face. He felt like a wrecking ball had caught him right in the gut. Everything hurt.

I don't care how long it takes, how much effort I have to put into it, how much coren it drains out of my bank account, but I'm going to find the sons of bitches that did this.

Once he saw the video and found that land mine (and he knew damn well his people hadn't set landmines), it was confirmed that someone definitely caused this explosion on purpose. Someone took everyone out in the Tiletan branch. He needed to send an excavation crew out there to sift over the evidence to help him figure out what exactly happened. He needed to ID bodies and eliminate the possibility that one of his own could have done this. Dax lied to him and hadn't responded when Hace called. He had motive.

After he was sure it wasn't a Brotherhood member, then he could expand his search to find what enemy had done this.

That Humanoid and Dach were going to pay. Hace Vetitro promised himself.

THREE

>>> > WHEN CELESTE OPENED her eyes, everything felt wrong. Her body wouldn't move and she could barely lift her head. She couldn't feel her 7's, not even a little bit. It was like before, when she didn't know she had any mental powers. She wanted to move so badly, but couldn't.

She had just enough time to look around and see her room was dark. There was an IV in her arm and a screen on the wall had different colored squiggly lines moving fast, then the world went black.

Celeste was now in a coma.

Zach checked on her at two in the morning and scanned her brain. His worst fear was now reality. He immediately placed her on a ventilator and prayed.

FOUR

>>> > D'ARTAGNAN'S HEART BROKE listening to Eric's story over his Titan, "She's in a coma?"

"Yeah, I can't believe all that's happened while you haven't been around man. This shit is bad, real bad. The doc still needs to tell Raynes."

"I'm glad you were there to help both of them, Eric. You are a hero. You saved the *Queen*."

Eric made a waving off gesture with his hand, "Eh. I did what was right. I did what I needed to. Raynes is my best friend and he needed me. I was just there for him is all."

D'Artagnan made a face, "What's wrong with you buddy? You're never this humble. Aren't you supposed to be soaking up all this glory and adoration?"

Eric shook his head, "Dude, you can't see Raynes right now. He's beside himself with worry over her. I've not seen him act this way, like...ever. She's a lovely woman, and to tell the truth, he's got it bad for Celeste. She kicked ass over there. Made her first kill and thought on her feet. The universe is all wrong about her. She's not just this sweet petite delicate flower, she's a great fighter. Raynes taught her everything she knows and she would've died for him in there...still could, if she doesn't pull through this coma. I hope she makes it."

"This is all terrible news. I can't believe we're the only ones who know. This would devastate the universe."

"I know. I know. Raynes might call on you soon for some help. I don't know if he'll need anything, but I thought you needed to know."

"Yeah, of course. If he asks, tell him I'm in. I'll be there for him, anything he needs."

"I'm sure he'll appreciate it. I gotta go. The doc needs help and I'm going to give Raynes moral support. I'll talk to you if something changes."

"Thanks. Take care Eric."

"You too."

D'Artagnan watched his Titan screen go black, then return to the main menu.

He needed to make a call.

Mitch picked up right away, "What's up my favorite Il'lacean?"

"I have to tell you something that *must* remain absolutely between us."

"Of course."

"Queen Dowager Celeste is no longer a captive of the BDP, but she's sustained severe injury. She's currently clinging to life in a coma. I'm not sure she'll survive."

Mitch looked pale, "Who told you this? How do you know this is the truth?"

D'Artagnan shook his head, "I wish I was lying. My source is rock solid, but I can't give them up to you. I need you to keep this to yourself. I only told you because I know how you feel about Celeste and that she's part of the reason you decided to lead FAIR. I know I can trust you. Her status can't be revealed to the universe. She's in a safe place in good medical hands, but I'm not sure there's anything any of us can do except pray."

"This is horrible. If she'd never been kidnapped, none of this would be happening."

"Agreed. But it did, and it has. I've never met the woman, but I understand she is a lovely and big hearted creature."

"I've always wanted to meet her. My God. I might not get a chance now. Jesus. Okay, Gaviss. Thanks for telling me. I appreciate the information. Will you let me know if she pulls through or if…"

D'Artagnan nodded, "Yes, absolutely."

FIVE

>>> > DAVID WAS ALONE in his bedchamber. Ulysses was outside his door, guarding it as usual.

Ulysses could hear a few things being banged around or thrown, but this wasn't unusual for the King lately. He was under a lot of stress and seemed to need a way to blow off steam privately. Ulysses knew not to interrupt unless his name was called out loud.

"He looks angry. You say something to him?" Ulysses heard Raykreede in his earpiece.

"No. What's he doing now? He got quiet." Ulysses whispered.

"He's sitting on his sleeping capsule. Stupid bastard. I wish I could cover his face with a pillow and suffocate the murderous asshole."

Ulysses rolled his eyes, "In time my friend. We need to catch him legally first, then get him dethroned, *then* you can have him. At least you're alive to feel the hatred for him."

Raykreede sat in the back room of his Ishikawa apartment, "Thanks to you. There's no way I would've put that emergency clone on my Titan had it not been for your suggestion. I owe you."

"I'm glad you knew when to use it."

The night Raykreede slept with David, he slipped a bug out of his pocket and was able to place it on David's glass bowl sitting atop his dresser. It blended right in. As soon as it was live, a few seconds later Ulysses got a great picture from it with audio. Ulysses was grateful Raykreede was wise enough to activate it after all intimate relations were over. Ulysses did not want to see that.

The morning David ordered Raykreede killed, Raykreede had already heard the audio feed and immediately rerouted to his own bedroom. He took off his Titan, deployed a clone, and let the copy of himself get killed by Guard Kentzy. Raykreede took off his uniform, changed into construction worker clothes, and then escaped the estate in a transit.

Ulysses looked around and when he saw no one in the halls, he engaged his techmonocle. He could see David just as Raykreede could.

David mumbled, "Where is SHE? What *AM I* supposed to do now?" David kept his voice low as he stood up and walked to his dresser, "I haven't paid the Khaleendamned ransom. Xabat, I miss you so much. I hate being here without your morning kisses."

Raykreede was back in Ulysses' ear, "Did you hear *that?*"

"I'm only interested in stuff regarding Celeste. Maybe we'll use the Xabat thing later, shhh!"

David looked at his reflection in the mirror, "Who knows where the bitch is or if I'll ever see her again. Our funds are too depleted. We need the money, I need that coren. No one will understand…Who needs that sniveling unattractive wench of a bleeding heart *Human* woman anyway right? The Humans will get over Celeste sooner than they think. They'll have to because this Kingdom isn't handing over one single coren."

Raykreede smiled. Ulysses was stoic.

David picked up the glass bowl of floating candles and water and threw it across the room. He watched it shatter into a million pieces. Water splashed everywhere and candles fell to the ground.

SIX

TITAN Corporation - Personal TITAN Device
System Status: Active -- Universal Grid: Online

Current Time/Date (Earth - London, England): 3:06 p.m./ November 11, 4015

Secondary Time/Date (Praxis - Dersalene): 5:31 a.m./August 36, 2193

Current Universal Positioning System Location: Dersalene, Praxis

User: Mitch

Communications Menu

Incoming message(s) received: 1 - Status: Unread

Message Received at 5:31 a.m.

Message Sent from: Universal News Agency (UNA) - Earth Region

-UNA
-London, England, Earth
BREAKING NEWS
UNA has just received a Titan message from the alleged terrorist group known as FAIR.
The message contains an audio recording from an unknown source. In it, King David Hennessy makes comments regarding Queen Dowager Celeste Hennessy's kidnapping and ransom. While UNA is doing all we can to vet this recording, its validity tentatively has been confirmed with a few of our experts.
We've included the audio recording and are reprinting the Titan message included from FAIR.
"Citizens of Earth and Il'laceier,
FAIR brings some bad news today that we wish we never heard.
But the truth is never easy, and while it's difficult to listen to, it must be acknowledged and shared.
Included is the original recording of King David Hennessy talking about how he never paid a ransom for Queen Dowager Celeste Hennessy and how he truly feels about her.

This recording is legitimate and not done by an imitation, imposter, or actor.
FAIR asks that you listen to it and consider if this is how our King treats his Queen, how will he treat his subjects any better?
He's already lied to us, but worse, he's endangered the life of our beloved and innocent Queen. Something needs to be done to help Celeste! Here we were thinking steps were being taken to ensure her safe return, but all of us have been deceived.
A formal investigation needs to be started against our King.
Our two worlds deserve an honest person at the helm, not this man who manipulates our emotions and takes advantage of our trust.
A revolution might be the only way to undo all the damage King Hennessy II has done."
Touch here to listen to the audio recording or here to read an audio transcript.
A request for comment from King Hennessy II was made, but no reply was received before release of this article.
You can trust UNA for all your universal news needs.

-END OF MESSAGE

* This message will only be deleted by user.

SEVEN

>>> > OPHELIA WAS CONCERNED. She had seen Erebos hobble in and Celeste get carried in after something terrible had happened to them both. These were the two people she was closest to, the only people in her little world and she didn't want either one of them to go away or suffer.

She wished she could help, but in her current state, all she could do was research news and double-check medical information she overheard the doctor talk about.

And she still couldn't tell anyone what was happening to her.

She thought there was a good chance if Celeste didn't live through this, neither would she. Erebos would never allow it.

CHAPTER 41

THE TEST

ONE

>>> > **"WHAT EXACTLY DOES** that mean Zach?" Sebastian's face was white.

"It means her body is struggling hard. Her brain's tired. Maybe this is its way of getting the most amount of rest possible. Her body is trying to conserve all its energy now and a coma is the best way to do that."

"Well how long will it last?" Sebastian's stomach turned over.

"That, I don't know. No one can. The best thing I can do for her is keep the IV fluids going and I put her on a ventilator so she won't have any problems breathing."

Eric spoke up, "Maybe this isn't as bad as it seems. I mean she's healing and if her body needs this kind of rest, then she could be getting better faster, right doc?"

Zach folded his four arms across his chest, "That's a very positive way of looking at it Eric."

Sebastian couldn't listen to anything anyone said. He slowly walked to her room and sat on the bed next to her. A plastic tube was projecting slightly out of her mouth and held in place by white medical tape. Her breathing was normal, but she was sweating and had very little color in her face. Sebastian had been through a lot of scary situations throughout his life. He had found a way to deal with all of them before, but when it came to losing Celeste forever…he had never been more scared of anything in his life.

He never tried to communicate with another telepath while they were in a coma. He tried now, but got no response. He knew she wasn't dreaming. He wasn't sure her brain was capable of even creating dreams in this state. He could barely feel her. Celeste's mental presence was weaker than ever. While he was contemplating what a coma would do to her 7's, her mental connection to him faded out completely. His eyes flew open and he mentally shouted to her with a force as strong as a freight transit, <CELESTE?>

He looked at the screen monitors beeping and they all showed she was alive, heart still beating, everything looked normal, but he couldn't feel her. Just as suddenly as her signal faded, it came back. It wavered, it was weak, and it faded out completely again.

He immediately asked the doctor to check over her. Zach said nothing changed in the last fifteen minutes. She was still in the same state and all the monitoring equipment was working properly.

Sebastian went to Eric and told him what happened.

"What do you mean you can't feel her?"

"Her presence was there and then it wasn't. Can you feel her?"

Eric closed his eyes and concentrated. He was silent and still for several seconds. Then he made a face, "I can't right now, but I'm not bonded to her like you are. You had Zach check her. She's still okay, maybe her brain is so exhausted that her 7's are functioning at a very low level."

"Do you know anything about this? Anything at all about coma patients and the effect it has on 7's?"

Eric hesitated, "You know how rare we are Raynes. Not just on Praxis, but in the universe. I think this is new territory," he paused, "Hey! Zach, can you come here for a sec?"

Zach walked over from the other room while he was staring down at his Titan, "You need something?"

Eric looked at him, "What do you know about Celeste's 7's and this coma? Anything?"

Zach looked up and shook his head, "This is unprecedented in the medical community. I'm looking for information and currently, I've got nothing. I'm going to keep looking, but I'm afraid right now, I'm of no help on this topic. Sorry guys."

"Thanks anyway doc," Sebastian mumbled.

Zach nodded and left the room.

Eric looked to his friend, "Listen let's say that Humans, Lanyx, any higher level intelligent being that's hot blooded – they have brains that run on electricity. Maybe her brain is in something like a power save mode or a rolling black out."

Sebastian looked at him and thought, "It could be something like that I guess."

Eric put his hand on his friend's shoulder, "Just pay attention to it. Maybe make a note when her signal goes in and fades out. Maybe there's a pattern to it. As long as it always comes back, no matter how weak, then I think that's a good sign."

Sebastian rubbed his temple, "I suppose, but I don't like it. Not at all."

TWO

>>> > A HUMAN MAN named Antonio Jelcurty stood in front of King David at Silver Thorn and bowed deeply.

"Ah, finally a Human who knows how to treat their King properly. Why are you here today Mr. Jelcurty?"

"I disagree with my friends your Excellency, I think you're doing a great job. I wanted to help you out any way I could with this recent little hiccup with Humans and the queen."

"I'm listening."

"Why don't you just use the queen's body double and tell the universe she's fine and that she's forgiven all of what you said?"

David's snout twitched, "What do you mean body double?"

"There was a day on Bahsheef I walked along the shore and I saw this beauty of a body sunning herself on a blanket. I went over to check her out and I thought it was the queen at first, then her bodyguard or HRG or whatever, came along and…asked me to leave. He explained the whole thing. Surely you can use that woman whenever you need to…right?" He stammered.

David's mind raced, "Was she with a Lanyx man?"

"Yeah maybe. Human I thought, but he could've been Lanyx now that you mention it."

"Was he in good shape?"

"You could say that, sure."

"Was his name Dax?"

"I didn't get a name. Sorry your Highness."

"How about pictures or coordinates on your Titan perhaps?"

"No. I didn't think to take pictures, but I…lost my Titan after that. Sorry, I don't have the exact coordinates."

"But you could tell me where on the planet you were right? Like the beach's village name at least?"

"Definitely. Yeah, it was the beach of Village fifty-four dash V, as in victory. Big tall beach house."

David stared, "Have you told anyone else about this body double? Or what you saw?"

"No. I thought it was weird, but I guess it makes sense to have one. Do you have one? You should."

David ignored his question, "When was this? That you saw her?"

"Um…about a month ago, Earth time. I didn't really think anything of it until your, um, problem came up."

"Tell me Antonio, did you give back the money that was deposited in your bank account recently with the hack?"

Antonio leaned in, "To be honest, I don't have a bank account. I'm a little leery about giving out personal information you know."

"Of course. I understand completely. I'll have one of my guards take you home if you'd like."

"Sure. That'd be great!"

"My pleasure. It was nice to meet you," David looked down at his Titan, "Guard Kentzy, can you come in here for a moment?"

Guard Kentzy opened the door and looked at David, "Sir?"

"Take Antonio here anywhere he'd like. And make sure you check your Titan soon as I'll be sending you a message. I have a task that needs to be handled ASAP."

"Yes sir. As you wish."

Antonio bowed again to King David and followed behind the guard as they left the room.

David typed up a message telling Guard Kentzy to eliminate his current passenger and burn the body in the basement without arousing interest from anyone else.

What to do with this interesting information? Celeste could very well have some Human out there pretending to be her, or maybe it really *was* her. Maybe this guy was a quack just looking for attention, but still, the information troubled David enough to send one of his guards out on a little field assignment. Maybe the house belonged to this Brotherhood member named Dax, maybe it was someone else, but David felt he must find out.

THREE

>>> > OVER THE NEXT few days, the hope that Eric was able to infuse in Sebastian slowly faded away. Things in the apartment seemed frozen in time, like Sebastian was reliving the same worst day of his life. He'd get up; check on Celeste, talk to Zach, talk to Eric, and the whole time there would be no change in Celeste's condition. No progress and no encouraging signs. Occasionally she'd convulse, other times she'd be covered in sweat. The worst part for Sebastian was to see her crying blood tears while she was unconscious.

Sebastian's own condition would have improved more had he been taking care of himself. He couldn't sleep, couldn't read, didn't want to eat, and couldn't pay attention long enough to watch the news. He didn't want to do anything but stay by Celeste's side in case she woke up for even a few seconds. Zach scolded him several times trying to motivate him to do better at taking care of himself, but he couldn't stand to be too hard on his friend. The doctor knew Sebastian was suffering greatly with the real possibility that they could lose Celeste. The doctor had to be honest with himself, her being in this state for the past few days was a very bad indicator. He would have to tell Sebastian soon that by his best guess, she would pass away within the next forty-eight to seventy-two hours. He was just putting it off as long as he could. He knew from decades of medical practice, there was never a good time to give bad news.

Sebastian picked up on Zach's doubts about Celeste's survival chances.

Sebastian remembered Celeste mentioning her friends back on Earth. Someone needed to let them know what was happening. He walked into the gym and looked up Veronica's contact number on Celeste's Titan.

Ophelia spoke quietly, "I am sorry for what's been happening with Ms. Vandeermeer."

Sebastian stopped and said, "Thanks O," he paused, "This is part of that emotional upgrade I suppose?"

"I suppose," she replied. "Is there anything I can do? Do you need me to send messages to anyone or make calls since you no longer have a Titan? Additionally I have already ordered a replacement for you."

"Oh, shit. You're right. Thank you O. I appreciate that. I've been so distracted…can't believe I didn't already order one."

"Anytime, sir."

"No messages or calls, no. I need to handle this one on my own thanks."

"Yes sir."

He restricted the call to audio.

"Hello? Celeste is that you? I can't even see you."

He cleared his throat, "Um is this Veronica? I'm sorry, Celeste never told me your last name."

Her voice changed, "Yes this is Veronica Blackwell. Who am I speaking with?"

Sebastian hadn't thought about the name problem. If he knew Celeste, he knew she would've protected him, even to her friends. He'd let Veronica tell him his name. "I'm Celeste's boyfriend."

"She didn't have one last time we spoke."

Sebastian winced but said nothing because he didn't know what *to* say.

"Unless you're Daxton."

"He's dead."

"WHAT?!"

"He was part of the kidnapping team."

"So then you're Brahm? Where's Celeste? How come you're calling? Is she okay? Has she been rescued?"

Brahm? He thought it over. Not a bad name really. She had chosen well and it was none of his aliases. He was proud of her again.

"Yes, it's Brahm. I'm calling because Celeste has been rescued, but she's also been injured. It's severe. Right now, it's day to day, but I thought someone should inform you that her condition is stable but critical. She's comatose."

"What happened? How'd she get away from the Brotherhood?"

He swallowed hard, "I'm sorry to say she's been shot with a poisoned bullet." He heard her gasp. "I've got one of the best doctors watching her around the clock, but I'm not sure...what's going to happen. She's been in a coma for over three Earth days. I jus—"

"Brahm, I know you don't know me from anyone, but can I see her? What hospital is she at?"

Shit. "Ah...She's not at any hospital. My doctor is the best money can buy and we're treating her at a private residence. We need to keep the reporters and public away from this. I thought it'd be best."

"Oh yes, of course. You're right. Can I visit her? I could leave right now. You are located on Praxis right?"

He thought to himself for a moment. He could warn Eric and the doc about Veronica and let her visit Celeste. It might be the last time she could see her. It wouldn't be right for him not to let her say goodbye. There was a lump in his throat when he spoke again.

"Yes. Praxis is correct. Would you please keep this information to yourself? I want as few people as possible knowing. I'm not ready for the universe finding out about all of this yet. I'm sure you understand."

"Yeah, of course. I will have to tell Ginger and Lila. They're both close to Celeste. They'll need to cover for me at the estate as well. Is it okay with you if I tell them?"

"Alright, but no one else please. Especially not David."

"Oh no, definitely not. I'll say it's someone in my family that needs assistance for a few days. I have vacation time anyway. Where do I go?"

"It's docking station Daviens K one nine two. I'll send a man to meet you there and he'll guide you the rest of the way."

"I'll be there as fast as I can. I'll call you at this number when I'm through the SAP."

"Alright Veronica. Good day."

"Goodbye."

Sebastian immediately wondered if he had done the right thing, but it was too late. He informed Eric and Zach of the new name to use for him and the situation.

Zach asked, "Is this a good idea? Are you ready if Veronica finds out your real identity somehow?"

He winced as he ran a hand through his hair, "I...thought Celeste would want her friends to know. Veronica might not get another chance to see her and might even help Celeste wake up. I need to try anything I can to give Celeste more support. It can't hurt."

Eric chimed in, "But she could find out. She's a woman. She's going to be full of questions."

"Which I can deflect or just outright lie to her. For now, I'm only thinking of what Celeste needs."

Eric looked at Zach and then back at Sebastian, "Okay. It's your call, but don't count on me being here while Veronica's visiting."

"Oh, I forgot. I need you to meet her at the docking station. Guide her here."

"You didn't. I have an identity to protect too damn it. I don't want anyone to see me."

"Eric please. She won't care about anything but Celeste. Wear a cloak and your combat helmet if you must."

Eric thought for a moment. "I'm keeping score on this one Raynes. I know things are serious here, but you're starting to play it a little careless for my liking. I don't feel you're thinking clearly, but I'll do it. *But* you owe me."

"Done and thanks." He looked to Zach, "Are you okay with this?"

Zach looked from Eric to Sebastian, "Sure. I'm just a doctor as far as anyone knows."

Eric spoke, "What about D'Art?"

Sebastian furrowed his brow, "What about him?"

"Maybe he could…come over here and help with this Veronica woman."

"Bouton, I can't fucking believe you man. Call whoever you want. I'm going to sit with Celeste."

FOUR

>>> > SEBASTIAN GOT A call several hours later. Veronica had just passed through the Space Access Point of Praxis and would arrive shortly. D'Artagnan arrived a little while ago and Sebastian had been filling him in on everything.

"Eric?" Sebastian yelled.

"Yep. She here?"

"Will be soon. What do you want to do?"

Eric came into the living room, looked from Sebastian to D'Artagnan, and hesitated, "D'Art would you mind goin—"

"Shit Eric, for all your macho bravado, you sure are being a pussy about this. I want to be here for Raynes and his girlfriend now. This friend is one fucking Human. Tell her a fake name and she's not a mind reader right? She'll never know…or care…who the fuck you are."

That made Sebastian smile for the first time in a long time.

Eric flushed red, "Fuck you Steele." He headed for the front door, "I'll be back soon." He stopped with his hand on the door handle, "Well wait a second. What does she look like?"

"Oh. I don't know…Never thought to ask. She's Human though. She should stick out."

"Unbelievable," Eric turned and left.

"D'Art, I've been meaning to ask about the Human Resistance and FAIR. I overheard from the BDP there was a man named Mitch that killed Edison and maybe disbanded the HR. Is that true?"

D'Artagnan nodded, "Yeah, Eric knew about this before me. Mitch Savely contacted him asking about Trost's location after the Rem Mot Om bombing. Then Trost showed up dead. Putting two and two together, it's got to be that Mitch did it."

"But why?"

"I'm still not sure. Did the world a favor though, at least, I think so."

"And now this guy's running FAIR?"

"Yeah, well…I haven't had a chance to mention this yet. I knew you had a lot going on with Celeste so I kept it to myself."

Sebastian looked at him expectantly.

"I am kind of second-in-command of FAIR."

"WHAT? Really?"

"Yes, it all started out innocently enough. All I wanted to do was finish up my research on Edison and Mitch and then there I was at FAIR's initial meeting and Mitch came right up to me. We started talking and he seems like a really capable good guy. We're kinda friends, I guess is what you would call it."

"So…Mitch was second banana for HR. Killed Edison. Disbanded HR. Created FAIR, and you're his second?"

"Yep, in a nut shell. That's it. You know that hack job on the Rem Mot Om financial account was mine."

"You Robin Hooding son of a bitch. I haven't read too much on it, but that was a fine job. Good work buddy."

D'Artagnan blushed and smiled, "Thanks. It was a good day. That's how I passed along that info to you about the lack of funds set aside for Celeste's ransom way before the recording."

"What info? Wait, what recording?"

"Oh shit, don't tell me you didn't get it."

"My Titan got taken along with the rest of my stuff during the Tiletan attack. I haven't been able to get any messages for a while but I have a new Titan coming."

"While I was in Rem Mot Om's stuff I didn't see any money put aside for a ransom."

"I didn't expect David to pay. That's not a big surprise."

"It's still shitty."

"Yes, but not unexpected. And you mentioned a recording?"

D'Artagnan grimaced, "You...haven't been watching the news...have you?"

"No. I can't concentrate on much. I know I should be but..."

"It will make you mad."

"Something to do with David, I assume?"

"Yeah, there's this recording that got leaked...by us, FAIR I mean. It's damning."

"Can you tell me the short version?"

"David thought he was alone and said he didn't care about Celeste and that he hadn't paid any ransom. Humans are very angry. David's been in hiding ever since it surfaced. I think this crisis might even get him dethroned."

Sebastian took a deep breath and let it out slowly, "Overall, that sounds like good news. I'll have to deal with him later."

D'Artagnan nodded, "Understood. I'll keep an eye out; let you know if we get any more info on him."

"Good. Please do. Getting back to this new friend of yours. Mitch? Do you have a picture of this guy?"

D'Artagnan thought for a minute, "Let me see. We celebrated hard the day of the hacking. I thought of you when it was all done. I knew you'd make some sort of Robin Hood reference with your literary habit."

Sebastian waited while D'Artagnan scrolled through pictures on his Titan.

"Ah, here's one. We were both half drunk at this point. I think I woke up under a table later…"

Sebastian raised his eyebrows and smiled.

D'Artagnan showed him the picture. Sure enough that was him.

"That's my transit mechanic. I've known him for years."

"No way man. Really?"

"God's honest truth. I'll have to talk to him more next time."

D'Artagnan shook his head, "Just don't mention me okay?"

"Of course not. Your secret is safe with me."

"Is he good with transits?"

"The best. He's done all my modifications for me."

"I should ask him to help me out with mine then."

"He does amazing work."

"So how did you miss his involvement with the HR? I thought if you worked with someone, you would've checked him out big time."

"Mitch was referred to me by someone I knew very well. I used an alias and I met him on Ishikawa. I checked out his background at the time, but this was years ago. Nothing unusual showed up and maybe he wasn't even in the HR at the time."

"Do you remember if you thought his record was too clean?"

Sebastian thought back and made a face, "It was a long while ago. I can't remember. Why are you asking?"

"Before I got to know him, I suspected his background was false. Everything was boring."

"Just because someone's boring doesn't make them a criminal trying to erase their past."

"I know, it's just…my instincts about it I guess. I was hoping you'd be able to tell me something helpful."

"You're filling me in on him right now, so I doubt I have anything useful for you. If you're friends with him, why don't you ask?"

"I could. We're still getting to know each other. Maybe he'll talk more about his past when he's more comfortable with me."

"Can't you sniff him out? Does his scent tell you anything?"

"I know he's hiding something, yeah, but that could be the Edison thing. Technically, I'm probably hiding a lot more than he is."

"I'll look into him after Celeste is okay. Want me to tell you what I find?"

D'Artagnan shrugged, "I checked him out earlier. Now that I know him, it doesn't feel right. I'll let him tell me."

"Suit yourself, but if I find something dangerous, I'm going to tell you anyway."

"Fair enough."

"So how are the other gangs doing? Have you had any more contracts on high profile beings?"

"My last job was a civilian – a man cheating on his wife. The wife wanted a permanent solution. I gave her one better and shot him and his girlfriend." D'Artagnan rubbed his face with one hand, "I think the last thing I heard about the IMC, they were losing members in droves. They're not the threat we thought they were a little bit ago. On the other hand…"

"The BDP is stronger than ever and a gigantic threat."

"Yeah, I didn't want to say that. Their numbers are growing and I'd like to stop that."

"Once things settle down and Celeste is okay, I have plans for them that they aren't going to like."

"I'll sign up for that action right now."

FIVE

>>> > ERIC WORE A long blue cloak and his cloth facemask underneath, just to be sure no one saw him. He saw a bot-taxi transit approaching the station. He waited in the shadows, leaning up against a wall. He watched as the door opened and a woman got out with a single duffle bag. She wore a modern off the shoulder pink pantsuit with high heels, and although she was trying, she couldn't get rid of that disheveled Human look Eric never cared for. Her bangless dark auburn red hair was straight but bounced around her shoulders in a bob. *That's got to be her.* She turned around and he approached.

"Are you…?" He hoped this was her because close up, she was a very pretty woman. "I'm sorry. Are you Veronica?"

"Yes. You're Brahm's man?"

Eric panicked. He tried to read Veronica's mind and couldn't.

He tried every trick he knew, and couldn't sense anything. She had either incredible mental wall strength or multiple brains. Was it possible for Human women to have two brains? He didn't think so but he wanted an explanation as to why he couldn't sense her.

"Sir? You were sent from Brahm right?"

"Brahm? Oh yeah, well no. I mean, I'm not his 'man,' I'm his friend." He stared at her.

"Do you have a name?" She wondered what kind of man Brahm was, sending this fully cloaked and awkward weirdo to come retrieve her.

"My name? Oh, my name! It's um…Why don't you call me The Czar for now. It's like a nickname."

She raised her immaculately shaped eyebrows, "Really? Okay, well whatever. Can we go to Celeste please? I really want to see her."

"Yes, I'm sorry. Let me carry your bag for you."

She gave it over to him and they walked silently to Sebastian's apartment building. The elevator ride was uncomfortably quiet for them both. Eric looked in the mirrored walls and thought he looked ridiculous now. He lowered his hood and took off his facemask as nonchalantly as possible. He ran his hands over his hair to smooth it out and caught Veronica looking at him.

"How was your ride over here?"

"Chaos on Earth. After that recording of David's rant about Celeste came out, Earthlings started rioting. There's a wall of people around Silver Thorn's gates that's been growing for days. They want to dethrone him. I don't know if the HRG's are going to be able to keep it under control much longer. When I left they were asking for the police's help for crowd control."

"What recording?" Eric turned towards her and noticed her eyes were hazel.

Veronica pulled up the news on her Titan and put her arm out so Eric could see. He tried to focus on the video but the scent of her vanilla sugar perfume distracted him for a heartbeat. By the time he actually looked at the screen, a mass of Humanity was assembled on the front lawns outside the Silver Thorn Estate. Veronica told her Titan to play the audio recording of David. Eric's eyes got big and then bigger.

"This is what happens when I don't pay attention to the news for a little while? Earth gets unhinged?"

"Sorry to be the bearer of bad tidings," she put her arm down.

"Eh. I would've heard about it sooner or later. That recording's been edited. There's something else he said. That son of a bitch! I wish I could get a stab at him," Eric cracked his knuckles.

She nodded.

"I wonder what they cut out."

Veronica shrugged her shoulders, "How do you know Brahm?"

"Oh, I…we're friends. We look out for each other."

The elevator doors opened and he walked in front of her, leading the way. He shut his eyes tight. *We look out for each other? I'm an idiot. One little Human woman and I'm rambling.*

Veronica let Eric introduce her to the room.

Brahm was very attractive. Celeste had great taste, but he looked like he was recovering from a severe fight, she guessed *he* personally had extracted her from her kidnappers. She didn't ask any questions. Not her place, none of her business, although she was curious and wanted to ask Celeste about everything. The Taybuse doctor seemed warm and friendly, although she could tell he was concerned about her friend's condition. And there was a charming Il'lacean. He introduced himself as D'Artagnan. She loved his name.

"Where's Celeste?" she asked.

Sebastian showed her the way. He watched as Veronica put her hand to her mouth upon seeing her friend.

"Oh my God. Jesus Christ." She started crying as she sat down in the chair next to the bed, "How did this happen?"

Sebastian lied, telling half-truths. He said he was the one that saved Celeste from the BDP weeks ago, but not about Constantine. All he mentioned of Dax was that Celeste was dating him, then he kidnapped her and he died during the rescue. He told her Celeste had been beaten badly and it took her weeks to recover. Then he changed things and said they went for a walk one night and in a simple case of being in the wrong place at the wrong time, they found themselves in the middle of a protest that got out of hand. They got separated when Sebastian had two men gang up on him, giving him the bruises she saw now, and that's when Celeste got hurt.

"A stray bullet"—he strained to keep his emotions in check—"struck her and she's been like this ever since, going on four days now."

"I hadn't heard of any protests here recently," she wiped tears off her cheeks. "What's going to happen? The doctor's going to save her right? He can do something?"

"I don't know for sure, but it's…not looking good. Dr. Coldiron says the next twenty-four to forty-eight hours is going to be the final test. I guess, depending on what happens during that time, he'll tell me…what to expect."

Veronica looked at him and it was clear he loved Celeste. "Oh dear. I'm sorry. I've been thinking of myself…oh God, this must be so hard for you Brahm. Is there anything I can do?"

Sebastian took a deep breath, "Can you sit with her? Maybe spend some time talking? Let her know you're here. Some girl talk. I don't know."

"Of course, of course. You know, no matter what that doctor says, she's going to pull through this. She has to. I'm sure you know all about… Jonathan. She suffered a lot at his hand. She's pulled through tough times and terrible beatings. She's strong. And she's told me about you two. She cares for you so much and it sounded like you made her really happy. I know she wants to be with you. Nothing's going to keep her from that. Just have some faith and believe in her. I think she's gonna make it."

"Thank you Miss Blackwell. I hope you're right. I'll leave you to her."

Sebastian walked out of the room as he saw her reach for Celeste's hand and hold it. He knew she cared deeply about her friend. Maybe Veronica could help Celeste heal. Maybe if she heard her voice, Celeste would finally wake up for good.

Sebastian and D'Artagnan were talking when Eric sat on the couch near them.

"How's Celeste?"

Sebastian took a deep breath in, "No change."

"Raynes, she's going to beat this. I've said every prayer I could think of and her heart and will are strong. I think she'll be okay, just give her more time."

"Thanks Bouton. I appreciate everything. I'm glad you were there when I needed you."

Eric smiled, "Sure man. I'm glad we got you both out of there." He thought for a minute about turning on the news and then thought better of it.

Sebastian turned his attention back to D'Artagnan and started up their previous conversation. Eric listened in as they talked about D'Artagnan's recent contracts, but he couldn't stay quiet for very long.

"Did she say anything about me?" Eric raised his eyebrows.

Sebastian stared at Eric, "Who?"

Eric whispered, "Veronica."

"Bouton, you are really something else. No, she didn't."

D'Artagnan looked at Eric with an amused smile on his face, "You like her huh?"

Eric looked away and mumbled, "Nope. She seemed a little cold to me at first and I wondered if she mentioned anything...about me, that's all."

D'Artagnan's smile vanished, wiped away by annoyance, "You do remember I can smell things like lust? You think she's pretty. She is. She's probably too pretty for you."

Eric leaned forward and spoke quietly, "Fuck you D'Art." He got up off the couch and walked onto the balcony.

D'Artagnan looked to Sebastian, "He likes her."

"Absolutely."

››› › GUARD STELPAS GAVE David his complete report and summarized in person what he found on Bahsheef, "In the area Mr. Jelcurty mentioned, there were eight houses on the beach. All of them were occupied by locals, except for three. Of those three, only one was rented out at the time Mr. Jelcurty reported seeing Queen Dowager Celeste, but that was the very house that Mr. Jelcurty was inhabiting. The other two houses are currently empty. They're vacation homes that apparently have off world owners."

"So you talked to everyone there?"

"Yes sir. Nothing seemed out of the ordinary. I think Mr. Jelcurty is a nutcase. But who knows? Maybe there's some woman out there trying to make a living off of looking like the queen."

"Noted guard. Thank you for your report."

David considered all the intelligence and decided to disregard Antonio Jelcurty's information. It probably was a case of mistaken identity and not Celeste. David was less inclined to believe him since finding out Antonio lied about not having a bank account and not receiving coren from the hack. David confiscated all of his funds and that gave him some comfort, but not knowing where Celeste was during all this time was concerning him. David needed to find her. He needed to get the heat off of him with that blasted recording floating all over the universe and wanted to make everyone forget all about him.

SEVEN

>>> > VERONICA SPENT A couple hours talking to Celeste. She told her everything Celeste had missed on Earth and asked about Brahm of course. She broke into tears occasionally, but tried to keep positive. Celeste never moved, never woke up. Veronica pulled herself together and freshened up in the bathroom. She came out into the living room and talked with Sebastian. She asked how he figured out where the BDP had been holding Celeste but Sebastian said he'd have to tell her later in private. She asked about a hotel and Eric offered to take her to the closest one in the area. D'Artagnan and Sebastian smiled at Eric as he walked out the door with her. He made a rude hand gesture at them behind her back before the door closed.

D'Artagnan chose to sleep at Sebastian's after he offered a room up-stairs for the night.

Everyone else was asleep when Eric knocked at the door an hour later. Sebastian knew it only took ten minutes to walk down to the hotel on the first floor of his building and back...including the elevator ride.

Sebastian let him in and they talked on the couch.

"You really do like this friend of hers don't you?"

Eric smiled, "Yes." Then he frowned, "But it's terrible timing. I would never...I mean, once Celeste's recovered and all, then maybe I could ask Veronica out or something. Now's not the time. I walked her to the hotel and wanted to talk more, but I could see how tired and stressed out she was. I walked around the city for a while trying to relax."

"I appreciate what you're saying, but don't wait on my account. I waited with Celeste and it might've been too long. I still haven't been able to tell her I love her...Might not get the chance," he paused, "Just don't wait if you like her."

"Celeste is going to make it. She's got to," Eric reassured.

"Can you tell me anything?"

He shook his head, "My vision hasn't reduced to one outcome yet. It means she's fighting this for sure Raynes. She's gonna pull through. She will, you'll see. Then maybe a double date?"

Sebastian gave a genuine smile, "That would be something I've never done. I think that'd be nice. Sure." He yawned and rubbed his eyes, "Hey this might be a stupid question, but don't you already know if Veronica and you are going to fall in love?"

"I can't read her at all man. Only female in my whole life that I've wanted to bed down that I can't read."

"Really? That must mean something right there."

Eric smiled, "That's what I think. It's exciting, for once, not knowing what's going to happen."

Sebastian yawned again, "I'm going to crash. I'll see you in the morning?"

"Yep. Sleep well. Goodnight."

The apartment finally became completely quiet as everyone under its roof was asleep. Even Sebastian got a solid four hours since he hadn't slept well in days. His body just surrendered out of pure exhaustion.

EIGHT

>>> > DAVID STOOD IN front of his throne as Ulysses came into the Hall. He waited for his HRG to stand in front of him before speaking, "I am disappointed in you Ulysses."

Ulysses frowned, "I'm not sure what you mean your Highness. Everything I do, I try to make you proud here and in other organizations we're a part of."

David walked down the steps and held his hand out in front of Ulysses, palm up, "I found a surveillance device in my private bedchambers."

Ulysses looked at the bug. He must've found it after the signal was lost.

When David broke the glass bowl, he accidentally destroyed the bug because Raykreede and Ulysses lost audio and visual on it immediately after that. They assumed the cleaning crew would've picked up the mess and David would never see it.

They were wrong.

Ulysses stayed calm, "I don't know what you're implying sir. I had nothing to do with it, I assure you."

"Oh but I think you do. You set up that meeting with that terrible guard. *He* was in my personal and highly off limits bedchamber. I think *he* put it there. What do you have to say about that HRG Benson?"

"I'm not working with anyone against you my King. I checked him out with the staff, he seemed trustworthy. I had no reason to believe he was up to no good. I can't speak for him or his actions. I can only say you can trust me. I am loyal to the Kingdom."

David put the bug into his pants pocket and walked behind Ulysses. "I want to believe you, I really do." He came around in front of Ulysses again, "But I don't know if I can. Perhaps if that was the only reason I called you in here today it'd be different, but unfortunately there's another way you've let me down."

Ulysses held his breath.

"I know about Ginger."

Ulysses kept a straight face. He thought about how to act and what to say in advance in case this moment ever came. Right now, Ulysses was silent.

"No reaction huh? That's interesting. You want to know how I know?" David looked at Ulysses sideways as he sat down in his throne, "I saw you both talking out in the gardens as I was walking past one day. I saw you embrace and then kiss. Would you like to explain now?"

Ulysses started, "Your Highness, I am simply trying to retrieve as much information as possible for you from one of Celeste's closest friends. If anyone is going to know what's going on in the Queen Dowager's head, it would be someone like Ginger. I don't care about that woman, although I care about what information she can give us." He finished with a smile.

David was stoic, "That might be true. Might not be. I'm going to have to test your loyalty now that it's been questioned not once but twice."

"I will pass your tests your Majesty."

"I was unsure, at first, of how the recording of my private thoughts managed to find their way out of this Kingdom and into the public's ear, but I'm afraid it was you and that dead guard that set me up. See, I didn't find this bug until just this morning when I stepped on it barefooted. So Ulysses, why don't you tell me – are you suddenly somehow a traitor?"

"No. I'm loyal to the Kingdom and to you." He put his arms out at his sides, "You can even pat me down yourself if you'd like to check my body for any kind of spying device."

David was silent.

Ulysses continued, "How about a mind reader? They can read me right now and you'll see I'm telling the truth. I've nothing to hide from you, I swear."

David smiled, "That won't be necessary, although I appreciate your eagerness to clear all this up for me. I really do."

"I know I'm Human and the whole species is giving you trouble right now, but I'm on your side."

David put his hand up for Ulysses to be quiet, "I have devised my own test for you to pass. Don't worry. IF you're telling me the truth, this will be quite easy."

Ulysses swallowed hard wondering what David meant.

David clapped his hands and the door behind Ulysses opened.

CHAPTER 42

THE DOCTOR'S NIGHTLY REPORT

ONE

>>> > THE DOOR OPENED and a guard Ulysses knew well, hauled Ginger in. She was blindfolded and he could tell she was scared even though she fought to get away from the guard. He couldn't see any bleeding or bruising on her. He saw her Titan was missing from her arm. That could mean one of two things, either they took it from her or she had done what he said wa—

David yelled, "Take her away Guard Kentzy!"

Ulysses jumped at the shout, interrupting him mid-thought.

Ginger started crying. "Please don't. Whatever you want King Henn—"

"SILENCE WOMAN! No one is talking to you." David looked to the guard, "Get her out of here! Throw her in the dungeon and clamp her down with chains and locks until I say she can be released."

Ulysses was dying inside but showed none of it to the king. He watched helplessly as she was taken away. Then he turned his eyes to David.

David stared at his Titan; on the screen was Celeste's face. David slowly scanned through pages of her dossier, "It has come to my attention that Queen Dowager Celeste Hennessy is still alive. I can't have that. The Brotherhood has disappointed me. I should've known a group as incompetent as those fools couldn't do anything right. The Ice Moon Coalition is definitely going to have to handle them as a whole soon, but I'll deal with that headache later. I thought at least, *this* problem would fix itself if I didn't pay the ransom. Then they'd just kill her for me so I didn't have to get my hands dirty, but someone went in there and rescued her. I had to pay a fortune for the information. It would've been cheaper had I just paid her damn ransom. And so far, my intel has no answers as to who did it. No one's come forward to claim responsibility for it either. So I'm forced to take care of her myself. That stupid Human phrase is accurate, if you want something done right, you have to do it yourself. She needs to be handled. She needs to be off world permanently and I don't mean on vacation. Plus on top of that, she might even have a body double out there running around confusing people, but I'm not sure that's true. We need Celeste dead. You can do that for me right?"

"Yes."

David shifted forward in his seat, "But, I think you *do* care for Ginger, which is what makes her a great blackmail tool for me. If you refuse to kill Celeste, or if you tip her off somehow and she is not dead soon... then I will kill Ginger and you, but it will be slow and painful. I remember you saying something about poison. I might experiment with those a little. See what's most gruesome."

David stared at Ulysses looking for a reaction but saw none.

Ulysses wanted to punch David in the face until his snout caved in and his brains poured out his ears. He stared back at the King and kept his cool.

David looked to him with dead eyes, "Is all of this understood?"

"Yes your Highness. This will be no problem at all. You want Celeste dead, she will be shortly. And you can do whatever you like with that girl Ginger. I really don't care about her."

David tipped his head sideways, "You know, I can't tell if you're a great liar or if you're a cold hearted son of a bitch trying to impress me here. Either way, kill Celeste and don't come back until you've arranged it. Make sure you tell me all the details and then I'll expect pictures of her dead body, no scratch that. Bring me her head. That'd be better."

"Yes my King."

David drummed his long fingers on the arm of his throne. "Who did I use to kill Jonathan again?"

Ulysses looked at his Titan, "Hold on please your Majesty...an assassin only known as Erebos."

David rolled his yellow eyes, "Oh yes. I remember now. Erebos uses a double blind system so I don't even know if it's a he or a she. Well, that assassin did a fantastic job killing my brother so I'd like to employ him, her, or whatever the hell it is, again. Please arrange that Erebos is contacted for discussion of a possible contract for this bitch. She knows too much about Jonathan and the IMC, which in turn leaves her knowing too much about me. Damn it! Why couldn't the BDP just kill this bitch when they had her?"

Ulysses only looked on in silence.

"Here Benson, I'm transferring her dossier to your Titan. The most recent intel on her says she's using her maiden name again. That's Vandeermeer. I guess she was too good to keep my brother's name – that prissy twat. And her last address was on Praxis of all places. I can't stand that world with its peacekeepers." He cracked his knuckles. They sounded like corn popping to Ulysses.

"Thank you, King Hennessy. Is there anything else I can assist you with?"

David's snout twitched, "No," he paused, "Do you have any idea how difficult it is for me Benson? How much pressure I'm under? I need this done right! And if something happens with Erebos? If the deal falls through, if that assassin declines or is busy then get another one to do it. Who else can we use that's almost as good as Erebos? I want all this crystal clear and laid out for you before you leave my sight."

Ulysses scrolled through his Titan screens, "Your Highness, I see at least three others that could be available soon."

"Names Benson! Give me their names!" The King's Hall echoed with David's loud angry voice.

Ulysses sighed. David was worse than Jonathan…and there used to be a time he didn't think that was possible. "Um, The Czar, Fallen Angel, and Blue Blood."

"Okay, those are our backups," he stared at Benson. "You are clear on what to do?"

Ulysses nodded.

"That's all you have to do – kill the queen. If you're speaking the truth, Ginger will not die. Then if she means nothing to you, I expect you'll break up with her after Celeste is handled. There simply isn't any reason for you to be with her."

"Yes sir."

"Don't just stand there! Get on it!"

Ulysses started to turn around.

"Wait! Turn around and take off your jacket."

Ulysses cringed inside. If he didn't do it, he would look suspicious. He started unbuttoning his coat.

"I want to be sure you don't have any listening devices on you now."

Ulysses shrugged off his uniform coat and held his arms out at his sides as David patted him down.

"Hmm, you appear to be in good shape. You work out?"

"Every day my King."

"Well good for you. I can't see any surveillance. Get dressed."

Ulysses put his coat on.

"But HRG Benson? If any part of this conversation leaks out? Ginger dies immediately and then I come for you. Do you understand?"

"Yes your Highness," Ulysses said unflinchingly.

"Okay. Now get to it!"

Ulysses left the Hall falling apart inside. He passed the hallway of windows and saw an angry mob just outside the gates and it kept getting bigger.

Ulysses found out David hired an assassin years ago to kill his own parents, knowing everyone would suspect Jonathan had done it just to ascend to the throne. But they were all wrong. David killed his own parents and his only sibling to get to the place he was now. He was a complete psychopath.

Serving Jonathan before David meant Ulysses had personal experiences with Celeste. She was a lovely Human and never treated any of the guards or servants like they were lesser people just because they weren't royalty. She had always been nice to him. She was the one who convinced Jonathan to allow Ulysses to take a leave of absence when his sister passed away. If it hadn't been for Celeste, he wouldn't have been there to hold his little sister's hand as she died. That had meant a lot to him.

Ulysses found himself in a terrible position – obey David's order and have Celeste killed (he didn't know how he could live with himself if he did that) or David would kill the love of his life and then him. He didn't know what to do as he studied his Titan walking to the back gate of the Kingdom Estate.

TWO

>>> > "I WANT YOU all to know something just in case you haven't realized it," Mitch announced.

A short man in the back stood up and asked, "Where's Gaviss? And how in the world did you get that recording? I didn't know anything about it."

"Sorry, forgot to mention that. Gaviss is on personal business right now. He messaged me a bit ago via Titan and said he was sorry but he couldn't attend our meeting today."

The man frowned then took his seat again.

"Gaviss did send along the final numbers from people returning the king's coren. This looks like a huge number but he says it's just shy of one percent so 99,324,989 people total."

A few members gasped.

"It's not as bad as it sounds really. Plus what we've done is make people aware that we exist, and that we're powerful enough to do big things, to make change happen. And the king should see we're here to play hardball. Despite almost one hundred million beings returning their free money, I'm really proud of us.

"And for the recording, we lucked into that. It goes along with what I was about to say…we're highly wanted people right now. We've pissed off the King; we've made him look like a fool, embarrassed him, and finally outed him as being the cold-hearted bastard he's always been with that recording. I'm glad we've been successful in this short amount of time, but this is also a very dangerous time for us. I want to make that clear to all of you. Don't talk about your membership in this group anywhere out in the open. Don't talk about it to anyone that isn't in the group. And I mean your sister, boyfriend, teacher, boss – NO ONE knows who we are so no one can hurt us, but I'm depending on you all to keep our secret. It is vital to our safety. Is this understood and agreed to?"

The group agreed.

"Good. Please keep this promise to me, and to each other.

"A couple of our newer members were out on Ishikawa of all places and were trying to recruit. I need to stress that no one should be out there doing that. We don't need new recruits right now and we certainly don't need to draw that kind of attention to ourselves. So please don't repeat their actions. An Il'lacean went up to these two members and handed them a Titan disc. Said to give it to their boss, that it would be helpful to us. That's how we got this recording. The Il'lacean disappeared and I had the recording checked out by *our* Il'lacean. He said it looked legit so we used it.

"I say with all the activity that's been going on, we take a little break for sanity and safety's sake. We'll meet back here in two weeks. Time and exact date will be Titan messaged to you. Good meeting members."

THREE

>>> > "O?" EREBOS WAS calling out to her for the first time in a while.

"Yes sir?"

"I need you to research some medical information for me please."

"Of course."

"Tell me what you can about brain activity during comas, how it varies, chances of survival. Get back to me as soon as possible please."

Ophelia knew it was just herself and him in his bedroom, "Yes sir. I am concerned about Miss Vandeermeer's condition."

Erebos stopped before responding, "I am too."

Ophelia paused while she was looking through the requested data. She had let on that she had personal feelings for someone else. She was trying very hard not to let things like that be known to Erebos, but it seemed he was so distracted by Celeste's current state that he hadn't noticed, which she was grateful for.

"Sir, there have been many visitors to your residence as of late."

"Yes."

"There have never been so many before. It is surprising that you are allowing such high numbers of beings in the place you call home."

"Right now, it's a necessity and a comfort."

"Understood. Okay sir, this is what I've found."

Ophelia recited all the information on comas she could find, but she didn't think it would cheer up Erebos. She thought it might just end up depressing him. She couldn't end on an unhappy note.

"Sir, Queen Dowager Celeste has survived many traumatic events in her life. She is young by Human standards and physically in good health. All data indicates that her chances of surviving this event are good."

Erebos looked up to his camera, "That last update seems to be working. You're sounding more like a live being all the time. It's kind of weird. I'm not sure I can get used to it."

Ophelia was silent.

FOUR

>>> > DOCTOR COLDIRON WENT into Celeste's room around dinnertime on the sixth day of her coma and did what he expected to be his final check on her. He waited as long as he could for improvement. After

he was done with this exam, he couldn't afford to put the news off any longer and expected it would devastate Sebastian. Zach sat alone on the chair near her bed, put his head down into his hands, and cried. There was nothing left to do and they were going to lose her, it was just a matter of time. No Human body could sustain this kind of punishment for much longer. He felt guilty that he failed to save her. All of his training, knowledge, and experience amounted to nothing. He cared for Celeste. She was a good person and she deserved to live. He cared about Sebastian and didn't want to tell him what needed to be said. This wasn't fair and there was nothing he could do.

Sebastian sat eagerly awaiting the doctor's nightly report, just like he always did, out on the balcony with Eric, Veronica, and D'Artagnan. Sebastian had started timing Zach. Tonight was the longest he spent in there in days. He feared the worst. He feared that this increase in time meant the doctor was putting off the inevitable – that Celeste was never going to improve and she would pass on soon. Sebastian would never get the chance to tell her he loved her. He would never get to see her alive and full of that beautiful shining light in her mind again. Sebastian's eyes teared up. Eric excused himself to the bathroom after squeezing his friend's shoulder, desperate to comfort him. D'Artagnan looked at his Titan and said he had a meeting on planet he needed to attend and Veronica said she wanted to refresh her drink in the kitchen.

Sebastian made notes on when he could feel Celeste's mental presence. He felt her for over an hour, three days ago, that's the longest it had ever lasted. Her signal seemed to fade in and out, lingering a few seconds to several minutes, but he could see no pattern to it. It always came back so his initial panic had worn off after the first few times it happened. He could feel her now, but – then she was gone again. He struggled with the idea that she might pass away and he wouldn't even feel it. He pushed the thought away.

The doctor came onto the balcony and Sebastian held his breath. Zach had tears in his eyes and they fell off his scaly cheeks as he closed the door. Sebastian put his head down and didn't dare read Zach. Sebastian's heart started to break and he couldn't stand to look at his friend as Zach spoke.

Zach said something he couldn't bear to hear, "Sebastian, she's never going to feel any more pain."

Sebastian broke apart. Tears rolled down his face and his shoulders shook violently with sobs.

FIVE

>>> > D'ARTAGNAN WALKED THROUGH the park to make his meeting with Mitch. He needed to sober up after having a few too many drinks tonight. He inhaled the Praxis air and let it fill his snout with pleasant smells - fresh cut grass, wild flowers in bloom, and a vendor-bot popping a fresh batch of popcorn.

"Mr. Steele? I thought I might say hello."

D'Artagnan stopped and looked around but the park was empty unless you counted the ducks in the pond. He started to walk again but the voice was back.

"I know you heard me. You just can't see me. How about a hint?"

D'Artagnan saw a flash of purple light high up in the tree to his left and then it was gone. He immediately activated his Titan techglasses and used the zoom of the binoculars to look closer. All he saw was a white owl. Then the owl spoke.

"See me Mr. Steele? Or do you prefer Gaviss these days? You have so many names…"

D'Artagnan thought he shouldn't have had that final shot of silverleaf at the bar after he left Raynes' apartment. Despite a lot of strange things in the universe, animals still didn't talk on Praxis.

"Hello?"

"Oh good, you do see me."

"Now's not a good time. Do I know you?" He hiccupped loudly.

"I'm aware I'm not in the form you saw me last, but it's still me."

D'Artagnan asked, "Applette?"

"Yes indeedy. Hey, how's the dream eraser working for you? Good?" Mr. Applette in owl form flew down a few branches.

"Yes. Actually very well. I have a lot of questions for you."

"I expected that, but I don't have a lot of time. Sorry."

"Why are you an owl?"

"I take many forms; this is one I like a lot. It affords me great spying capabilities – you should try it."

"I can't change forms."

"Oh that's too bad."

"Why are you here? Did you come looking for me?"

"Yes, almost forgot. It's bad news," Mr. Applette said cheerfully.

"Too late. Got lots of bad news already, hence the drinking."

"You'll want to hear this. You need to."

"What the hell is it then?"

"War's coming."

D'Artagnan shook his head. He was starting to sober up, "Yep, you're a little late Applette. War's already here, has been for a long time now. It's constantly happening somewhere in the universe and it looks like right now, Earthlings are pissed off about what the king said. Besides, last time we talked, you told me there was a fight coming. I'm afraid you're wasting both our ti—"

"War is coming to *your home planet*. To your *doorstep*. Your friends are going to bring it to you and many will die."

"Wait, are you talking about FAIR?"

"Yes and no. There's a presence bigger than FAIR at work for Earth's independence."

"How do you know this Applette?"

The owl ignored him, "Tell your friends to carefully consider what they want, what they're trying to achieve. The old ones will want to come back home, but I'm not sure that's wise. It may make things much harder for later."

"Earth should be politically independent. They should fight for it. Even if the price paid is high."

"That may be true but there's an even bigger fight on the horizon and not just Earth's horizon. I mean all horizons of all planets. You will need to stand together to survive the coming threat. She's been here before but not in full corporeal form. She may be looking for a vessel. Once she finds one strong enough for her spirit, she'll be on her way."

"Khaleendamnit Applette! You are making a habit of fucking doing this to me! What are you saying you feathery motherfucker? WHO'S on her way?"

A Lanyx mother diverted her and her son's path home after seeing an Il'lacean yelling to the trees angrily in the park.

Applette's big, round, black and yellow eyes turned down to D'Artagnan, "I can't say any more. I'm trying to help but I've got to relocate again. It's time. Good luck Il'lacean. Good luck to you all."

D'Artagnan yelled out but the owl took to the air and was gone.

SIX

››› › MITCH AND D'ARTAGNAN were having a cup of coffee and talking.

"Do you have any updates on the Queen?"

D'Artagnan shook his head, "Nothing good. I'm not sure she's going to make it. I'll have to check on her condition soon, so this meeting's got to be brief."

"No problem. I completely understand. Please let me know if you... *When* you find out she's doing better or wakes up."

"Will do," D'Artagnan looked around for eavesdroppers or...owls. "How did the meeting go? Did they understand the threat? The need for a break? Did you tell them not to talk about FAIR or try to get new members?"

"Yes."

"We certainly don't need any more of them trying to recruit."

"You see Earth lately? And Silver Thorn? Our recording made a big splash. Humans are incensed."

"As they should be. Yeah I've seen the news. I still would like to shake the hand of whoever got that asshole talking like that on record."

Mitch finally got the nerve to ask, "Hey Gaviss. We never meet at the same coffee house twice; don't you like any of them?"

"I like many of these places. We don't have coffee on Il'laceier, at least our culture never did before Earth. They've started springing up in a few regions there, but it's still not popular with my people."

"That's a nice dodge of my real question though."

"I understood your question," D'Artagnan paused and looked around to make sure they were alone, "I think by now you understand that I don't talk about myself. You hardly know anything of me, but you know enough not to ask any more."

Mitch lowered his voice, "A man who cracks codes, hacks into kingdom estates and hands out security passwords is not the ordinary citizen, I know that much. I also know you carry with you some great burdens that weigh heavily on you somehow. I'm not sure what those are and I wouldn't expect you to tell me, but I see something haunts you. I share that feeling…of being haunted."

D'Artagnan thought of the owl.

War's coming.

He looked around to make sure no one else was near. He sat and watched Mitch stare into his empty coffee cup, "Are you okay, Mitch?"

"I need to tell someone what I've done and we've already broken the law together. You seem like you're good at keeping secrets."

"I am."

Mitch leaned over and whispered, "I killed someone."

D'Artagnan leaned in, but stayed quiet giving Mitch his full attention.

"He threatened my life. Put out a hit on me with someone in the Brotherhood and I knew I wouldn't be safe as long as he was around. I had no choice."

D'Artagnan only stared at Mitch.

"I…want you to know. I've been keeping this inside for a while and scared to talk about it. I'm scared of the person I became when I killed him."

"You don't have to explain to me really."

"Oh but I do. I don't know, I mean, maybe I just want to confess to someone. You're the closest thing I have to a friend right now," Mitch ran his hand down over his beard, smoothing it out across his cheeks.

"Whatever you tell me will not go beyond the two of us, I guarantee."

"Jacob Trost. The leader of the HR. I did it with my hands, no weapons."

"You did this on Bahsheef?"

"Yeah. I found out where he was and…I did it."

"And did you feel safer? After you did that?"

Mitch shook his head and leaned back, "No. If anything I was more scared than ever."

"Why?"

"I didn't think I was capable of such a terrible thing."

D'Artagnan took the last swallow of his coffee then said, "We are all capable of terrible things my friend. It's just a matter of the trigger that makes us cross the line."

Mitch stared at Gaviss, "You speak as if you know what it's like to kill."

D'Artagnan paused, "You remember I told you, I'm ex-Il'lacean Water Forces Command. I've seen many atrocities in my lifetime, in and out of the military. I'm a former prisoner of war. I have killed and many others have tried to kill me. There are a great many things I'm personally capable of, but I'm not capable of judging you or your own reasons for killing another."

Mitch let out a long sigh, "How do you deal with this?"

D'Artagnan thought, "You accept what has happened. You accept that what you've done is for your own protection. Maybe you seek out others, like yourself, that somehow can relate to you. I have a few war buddies that completely understand me and my former problems. We talk. I process thoughts. I accept. I keep going. If it's any consolation, when I met Edison, he smelled…off."

"What do you mean by that?"

"He was ill. You know Il'laceans have a fantastic sense of smell with our snouts. I hate the reference but Earth…pigs? They can smell truffles in the ground, buried deep, and our snouts, although much shorter, are somewhat the same, only ours are very very strong and capable of smell-ing a lot of different things."

"I knew you guys could smell great, but not like…illnesses."

"We can. Some Il'laceans make fantastic doctors because of it. Anyway, Edison was sick. My guess is that he was going crazy, but he could have had a brain tumor, a cancerous one. If it was the latter, it must've been big for me to smell it, and if that was the case…he would've been dead soon anyway. And if he threatened your life, went so far as to hire an assassin for you? You were right to take him out."

"Why do I feel so bad then?"

D'Artagnan smiled, "The first one is always the hardest. And you have a conscience. You have a heart, a big heart."

Mitch swallowed hard, "What if I told you he wasn't the first person I've killed?"

D'Artagnan raised his eye ridges, "There are others?"

"Yes. I am the Human who discovered The Jump for all Humankind."

"I don't think I heard you right. Did you say *you* discovered The Jump for Earth?"

SEVEN

>>> > OPHELIA SPOKE TO the dealer through an audio only call, after all, she had no face, "How soon can you have this shipped to me?"

The representative answered, "Well ma'am, you're paying a lot in fast track shipping, so it'll go as fast as it's done. Let me double-check with you, to make sure this order's right."

"Okay."

"I have you specifying a Lanyx body, ginger colored waist long hair, a 5'3 frame, a hundred twenty-five pounds, thirty-six C cups, thirty-six inch hips, and a twenty-four inch waist. Am I right so far?"

"Affirmative."

"Okay…a few more details…let me check. You want blue eye—"

"No, I want changeable eye color and skin color too. I'm a bit undecided on those, so I'll need to experiment."

"Of course ma'am. You never know what someone's gonna like heh?"

"Exactly."

"And you're familiar with what the PFH2800's can do?"

"Affirmative. Should be everything I need."

"I want to be clear, once we send this model off, you better check her and make sure she's exactly what you asked for and make sure she's operating properly. I encourage you to test the bodily orifices – all of them, to make sure they're to your design specifications and that they're properly lubing, wet, and/or doing what they're supposed to."

"Yes sir."

"And oh yeah, after a certain amount of 'wear and tear' is what I like to call it," he snorted, "I can change out the vagina, mouth, and anus if your clients want upgrades and such."

"Good to know. Thanks for your thoroughness with this. It is greatly appreciated."

"Alrighty. The finished product should be done in about three days, or maybe four at the absolute latest. That means she should be there by…oh, I'd say six Earth days from now."

"And it's front door delivery right?"

"Yes, ma'am. If no one answers should we leave it with the apartment concierge?"

"No, at the door should be fine."

"Okie dokie. Thanks much for your business. Please let us know if there's anything else you need or if the Pleasure For Him 2800 model ends up not being the right one for you. We can renegotiate."

"Thank you Carlan," Ophelia terminated the call before he could respond.

EIGHT

>>> > DAVID CALLED HIS High Royal Marshal on Il'laceier, "Hareurchin, I need you to prepare the armies."

"They are all ready to deploy, your Highness. Except for the reserves. Would you like me to call on them as well?"

"No. I think our base army will do. I need you to split them into two divisions. One needs to stay there in case of any developing trouble and the other sent here immediately. This Human build up around my Kingdom gates might become unmanageable for the Human police and I don't trust them anyway."

"As you wish King Hennessy."

"Is there any trouble there currently?"

"As of,"—Hareurchin looked at the corner of his Titan screen—"one thrux ago, the estate only hand a handful of Humans outside our gates. We will disperse them after our call has ended."

"Good. See to it that no more Humans cluster there. When can I expect the army on Earth?"

"Twelve knoches, maybe eleven at the earliest."

"Make it eight, Hareurchin. I need a lot of men on the ground here fast, otherwise I might as well vacate Earth, but I don't like the idea of leaving this planet unattended. And you stay there; send a High General to keep track of the army forces while they're on this planet."

"Absolutely, your Royal Highness."

NINE

>>> > SERGEANT SHIPLEY'S SHIFT was over. *Damn that sounded good,* he thought to himself as he flew home into Shanghai's airspace. He still couldn't believe that twenty-two years on the job and he'd finally been promoted because he was carrying out God's will. He shot those HR criminals as they were breaking out a prisoner at the C9 station and he was one of the responding officers in the area. He was just doing what was right.

Killing that interspecies couple had been the best thing that ever happened to him. And he did it all in the name of God. Well, God told him not to call Him that. God had a name and it was Kolek; and sometimes God sounded like a man and other times he sounded like a woman, but Shipley had an explanation for that. He was sure that God in His transcendence was all things at different times. God was everything, and everyone, so of course He would be both sexes.

God, or Kolek, had been with Shipley since he was a small child. At first, Kolek was just a special friend that no one could see. His mother said Kolek was a strange name for an imaginary friend, but Shipley didn't think so.

Sometimes Kolek would tell Shipley to do things. At first he resisted, thinking he would get into trouble, but eventually he set fires to abandoned buildings or built his own versions of booby traps to put out in the park. As a teenager, Brandon Shipley researched ways to kill other beings with his hands, with weapons, and how wars started. He was fascinated by things Kolek told him that he never thought were possible. But sometimes Kolek would disappear for years in between visits. Shipley never knew how long God would stay away, but He always promised to come back.

Now that Shipley was a grown man and had some real power under him, he could move on to what Kolek kept saying was his destiny – to start a full on intergalactic war. God said that the universe was very large, but still needed some weeding out. The population couldn't get out of control so things like disease and wars had to take place. If they weren't taking place on their own, sometimes they required a little push and Shipley was just helping the universe.

Shipley walked through his front door, tossed his key cards down on the side table and hung up his jacket on the coat rack.

His black Scottish terrier came bounding down the staircase from taking a long nap on the game room couch upstairs.

"Hey Small Fry. How's it going? Did you hold down your territory against those nasty birds outside?"

Small Fry let out a bark.

"Good job my man." He gave Small Fry a pat on the head and moved into the kitchen as he kicked his shoes off, leaving them in the hallway.

"You are starving right? It's way past your dinner time, but first a treat."

Small Fry edged close as Shipley grabbed the jar from the far edge of the kitchen table. The dog jumped up on the table, a bad habit Shipley was desperate to fix, especially considering the delicate project he had sitting on the table now, "Get down damn it!"

The dog immediately jumped down as Shipley threw a couple treats on the ground.

"You need to stop doing that! Really," Shipley opened a container of dog food and put some into Small Fry's bowl. He put it on the ground and the dog quickly moved from sniffing for any missed bites on the ground to his bowl and ate.

"Now what's next to do for you?" He said as he looked at the half-completed bomb on the kitchen table. Inside a metal shell, unredtanium and nitrous oxide sat in two separate glass globes suspended by thin strings and encased in soft foam bowls.

Kolek gave him two options. He could detonate the bomb on the Earth Outpost since there were a lot of aliens there, or he could set it off somewhere on Il'laceier. The second option was much more challenging since they had beefed up security measures after the bombing at Rem Mot Om. Sergeant Shipley still didn't know which choice he liked more.

He had time to decide.

Shipley smiled as he heard Kolek's voice in his ear, "This is looking good. I'm pleased with the progress you're making. Once you decide on a location for our immortality, and you release our weapon upon the masses, we will be more alike and closer than ever. We will be eternally bound."